Sol Li

GW00786630

book one of The Frontier Trilogy

JAMES COLLINS

SOL LIMITIS

Copyright © James Collins 2016

Acknowledgements

To Sally, as always, and to my family: Thanks for being the wonderful people you are.

And to the readers: Thanks for investing in this. I hope you enjoy it and, even if you don't, I'd appreciate it if you could take a few minutes to leave a review.

And please check in at my website, www.jamesdcollins.co.uk, for ongoing bonus chapters, character backstories, and additional short adventures, as well as news about the sequel, Book II in The Frontier Trilogy.

PROLOGUE

The girl ran.

Her bare feet pounded the grass and the frozen rushes whipped at her knees. The icy milk of moonlight had soaked into the air and settled itself like snow on the tussocky landscape around her.

She dropped to her knees beneath the dark of a winter-raw quercus tree. Her feet burned with the cold: a sawing, swelling agony. Breath flailed from her heaving lungs like torn clouds. She could hear the swollen thump of her heart in her chest.

Eyes moist and round with fear, the girl looked back the way she had come.

The Wall was a towering grey presence over her left shoulder, unfurling itself into the thick night; the peeling and cracked whitewash shone dully through the surrounding darkness. The vicus itself was a bleak smudge of dirty yellow lights.

...*mater, please*....

There was no sign of him. Of *it*.

The Horned One.

She rubbed her toes with ice-bitten fingers. The air seemed to gnaw hungrily at every inch of bare flesh. The weave of her linen shift was so loose she could feel the cold slicing into her like a hundred separate cuts. Her legs were numb and her feet throbbed angrily.

Mater had been crying. She had been crying a lot, lately, but today more than ever.

Maria, she had said, clutching the girl's head into the warm tears on her breast, *I love you. You must understand.*

Mater had smelled tickly to her nose. She was always making castrensis, a thick mustardy bread. The soldiers liked it, and paid mater well. Sometimes they forgot to take it with them, but they always paid.

You must understand.

Tonight had been like any other, apart from the tears. She had nibbled through some bread and beans, flavoured with muria. Mater had swaddled her in furs next to the crackling fire. The pop and hiss of the flames devouring the damp wood had sent her to sleep.

But the voices had woken her.

Mater's and another: thick and deep. Memories of pater rose like steam from the fire: his voice resonant and low, like the rumble of water on rock at Silvanus' Glade; the rich smell of sweat and wine from his mouth, his armpits; the glorious rasp of his dark beard on her cheek.

Distant memories, sunk deep into her bones. Pater had been gone for many winters.

The door of their hut had opened, and the icy air whipped furiously through the room, rousing her. The fire was dead, and only the moonlight spoke, draping itself across the broad shoulders of the figure above her. She saw a torn face, and smelt sour, spicy fumes from its breath. She saw the horns, the tight angry curls spinning out from its head.

The Horned One.

Mater, please...!

Mater, her face a ragged sweep of tears and pain, was standing in the corner, half collapsed on the table. Her eyes were red and thick and shiny, like bloodhoney, and her jaws were clenched around a sheaf of her own dark hair. Her head shook and her breast heaved as though some vile beast raged inside her.

Mater, please...

Maria had stretched out a hand towards her mother, pale fingers almost translucent in the moonlight. Mater would come, she knew, scoop her into her bosom and smooth her hair, whisper sad whishts into her ears, telling her how it was all a fear-dream.

But mater just turned and sank deeper into the shadows.

And Maria had fled.

She darted beneath the legs of the Horned One and through the open door, a trail of twisted oaths chasing her out. The blast of the frozen air struck her like a slap to the face, her breath retreating back into her lungs.

And now she had stopped running. Maria bunched herself into a thick incurve of the quercus and squeezed her jaws shut to stop the sound of her teeth clattering in the still air. She could feel her muscles squirming and juddering beneath her goosefleshed skin

The ghostly wail of an owl slid across the sky above her, just as the first soft flake of snow landed. She watched it melt, shimmering, on her bare wrist.

Maybe she would see pater after all, sooner than she dared hope. And one day, mater too. So she could talk to her, and ask her. So she could hold out her arms, and this time mater would scoop her up and take her into the warmth of her chest, feel the soft murmur of her heart in her ear.

Mater, please.

You must understand.

Seven summers she had seen and she thought she could understand most things: hunger and pain and death and fear and absence. Surviving in the vicus had taught her the strange agonies of life before she was ready to comprehend them.

The vicus's lamps glittered in the distance like sweet fiery needlepricks in the darkness. Further across were the more sporadic flickers of light from the garrison at Aesica itself. There were no lanterns there so the sentries could preserve their night vision. Maria wondered whether they could see her now. Her uncle Maximus was a soldier; her father had been, and her older brother too, though he had died a long time ago. She shivered violently, small tight rapid tremors under her flesh. Maybe if she could get to the garrison, she could shout and –

Maria thought she could hear the creature's breath on the wind, feel the heat of its angry respiration in the still air.

Run, Maria. You must run.

The voice was crisp and clear in her head; a man's voice. She didn't know who it was but she obeyed it instinctively, as though it were pater himself.

Her slender toes were tight and stiff, bursting with the agony of the cold. She worked them a few times, wept through the exquisite pain, and got to her feet. A few flicks of urine spattered against her legs, the warmth hypnotically pleasant. She turned her back on the sweet lights of her home, and ran. She didn't know where she was going, but maybe the voice would guide her. Her feet and legs were burning; she could feel the glorious heat of her blood thumping through her limbs, setting her flesh alight with each angry pump.

The world ahead was dark and solemn, the night sky leaning heavily against the winding hills. To her right, distant but massive, the brooding blade-like sweep of the Wall.

She had always feared the Wall.

The anger and danger of the dirty weeping greywhite stone had been beaten into her from a young age. She kept her distance from it, her and the other children, lest it swallow them up and spit them into the bleak and bleeding misery of the Otherside.

She instinctively angled her path away from it, and was conscious of the ground sloping downwards. The night seemed darker than ever. She realised her eyes were squeezed shut, and forced herself to open them. Her tears were beginning to freeze in her lids.

A white explosion of agony shrieked into her left knee and she felt the impact of the hard earth against her face.

She gasped hard and looked up, expecting to see the tight angry horns of her pursuer spiralling into infinity above her. But all she saw were the keen young wounds of the stars overhead: ursa and draco growling down at her through the feathery snowflakes fluttering onto her face.

Maria sat up and rubbed at her knee: the pain bucked and swelled like a trapped hare. Her mouth felt warm and sweet and she could taste the thick liquor of blood on her tongue. She wiped it from her lips and looked to see what had tripped her, her eyes dabbing through the murk of the night. A gust of wind sent fresh shivers through her skin.

It was the wheel of a cart. She could see the ghostly froth of the faraway stars through the spokes.

The cart was turned on its side, the rough wood splintered against the ground. She fought off the thick waves of pain that pulsed through her knee and limped round to the other side of the cart. Thick bags of grain were tumbled across the grass, huge mounds of them split and spilled and frozen in place. She carried on walking round to the front where she saw the horse. Dun-coloured by the look of it, it was sunk into the ground, with two of its legs angled rigidly into the air. Its neck was twisted into an unnatural contortion. The slats of its ribs jutted out, and the beast's belly was sunken and deflated. Its eyes were missing. She could see a spit of moonlight glisten off the frozen pink foam around its mouth.

A few paces downslope from the creature was the crumpled shape of what had probably been its rider. Maria stopped, shaking wildly in the night air. She felt the brief warmth of tears, before they froze bitterly against her cheeks.

She was so, so cold. She was hungry.

But most of all she was scared.

Maria backed away from the corpse and into the lee of the upturned waggon. She bunched herself up into a corner, then tried to drag a bag of grain towards her to use for warmth, but it was too heavy and frozen stiff to the ground. The girl let the tears stream from her eyes, and looked up to beseech ursa and draco, but they were covered with the thick wool of dark clouds.

The snowflakes drifted softly to the ground. Maria could hear the creak of the cart-base at her back as the wind swept across the scrub and hurled itself at the frozen planks. She whimpered for her pater, for the steady deep voice of guidance and safety. She needed advice, and comfort.

Her fingers and feet burned. Her legs ached dully. She spat blood onto her shift. Mater would be cross. Her eyelids felt so heavy and dense. She was so tired.

The pristine snow piled up outside, the wide and unknowable night pressing against its soft covering.

When Maria opened her eyes, she smiled at the creature in front of her. She had dreamt of warmth and bed, the smell of a fire in the room and the sweet chime of her mother's singing voice in the air. Her smile bled from her soft cheeks as the Horned One grabbed her wrist in a large rough paw, and she thought of her pater and howled for him, a wail that made her lungs burn and set the stars overhead shivering in their black sockets.

***

The scream shattered the brittle night.

But Silvius couldn't be sure it was real. He was awake again; the cold pinch of the air on his cheeks was proof enough of that.

Had he been asleep?

He squeezed his redraw nose between his fingers and shook his head from side to side. His dented iron helmet was on a crenel of the wall in front of him. It was too bulky and heavy to wear up here for long periods. Instead he'd bound his head with thick strips of leather to keep the cold out, like many of the other soldiers. They also muffled his hearing.

He used his frozen fingers to wrestle the leather up over his left ear. His digits felt the size of cucumeres.

Fuck this weather, he thought, and fuck this sentry duty.

The air was quiet again but for the occasional sough of wind through the crenellations.

He looked out over the ramparts of the Wall and into the sweeping nothingness to the north. The land was girt with fresh snow, the moonlight reflecting off it to create a soft humming light which seemed to pulse up into the sky. There was no foliage in sight; even the endless swathes of Erica shrubs had been meticulously uprooted and burnt back since the very year the Wall had been built. The sentries needed a clear view of the land, and they had to ensure that no scrub remained for the enemy to hide behind. So the land in front and below Silvius was a pale ocean, frozen mid-swell, rising up to bite the bitter black of the winter sky before sinking down again to froth against the base of the Wall.

How much longer did he have to be out here?

He craned his neck and looked up at the sky, the soft snow falling tenderly onto his rufescent nose. The clouds were solid up above, smothering the stars so he couldn't gauge the hour. The snow was affecting the light too: he couldn't say how far off daylight was. Somewhere close by an owl twooted. Thrice.

A bad omen.

The stink of the Wall drifted up to him. The brutal stone was dusted with snow, and the moonlight struck sparks from the ice gleaming from its pitted surface. The stench was like wet dog, noted Silvius. He hadn't grown up with it, had never been birthed and bred in the shadow of the murus, never inhaled the suffocating spores of its presence like most of the other soldiers had. Posted up from Eboracum, he and his brother had marvelled at the huge construction before feeling its dragging burden on their careers. It stank like a dying brach.

He would never forget his first tour of Aesica's perimeter. The strained faces of his commilitiones, the clouds seeming to press down on his shoulders, the sky so much smaller than he was used to, the landscape more.... cramped.

All along the horizon it spread: the Wall's rank grey whitewash, peeled and stained with excrement and urine. Occasional black scabs of dried blood marked tired battles. Here and there was the brittle scratch of some fresh graffito: *cinaede Questi*; *merdas edate*; *pedicabo Roma*. More, in some indecipherable language; crude images. Occasionally there was the blurred mush of fresh limewash where some particularly offensive or treasonous message had been erased.

Silvius exhaled into the air; the night was cold enough to split flesh. The grain of his coarse-wool cloak was nagging at the base of his neck, but the soldier dragged it closer round him anyway. The air was like bare steel against him; hard and dangerous. Even the lice seemed less active. Although, even thinking about them made him itch. He thrust a hand into the warmth of his breeches and scratched heavily at his crotch. He could feel one fluttering between his fingers. He pulled it out and lifted it up to his eyes, scrunching it between thumbnail and forefinger.

By fuck, it was the size of an apple pip. If only Gaius were here to see it, he lamented. It was twice as big as the runt he pulled off his balls last week.

He examined the louse a minute longer before flicking it off into the night.

Silvius rummaged around inside the folds of his cloak and plucked the bottle of mulsum from his belt, where it was tucked snug against his tunic. He removed the stopper and took a nip. The spike of sweet honey exploded onto his tongue before the wine shimmered down into his belly.

Thank Cernunnos for mulsum.

He looked at the pregnant air around him as he drank. Winter was starting to descend, crushingly heavy, and Silvius knew how hard it would be to survive a bad one. Especially after another dire harvest.

He stoppered his bottle and tucked it back into his tunic, then waved his fingers around, and held them in front of his bloodshot eyes, looking for any signs of blackness. He'd heard of nigrum, the terrible disease that had spread through the barracks last winter. He'd seen with his own eyes as Gaius's toes had turned black as carbo fresh from the western mines. They'd blistered and fallen off and Gaius had died a week later; some said by his own hand, others by his wife's.

And Meridiadocus, with his eyes frozen shut and his six black fingers. He'd never forget the smell after they put him by the fire and the skin had split and oozed. He hadn't been able to hold a spear properly since then.

Maybe he should visit him again, thought Silvius, guiltily. He hadn't –

He could hear iron-studded footsteps along the battlements, steady and solid.

Silvius cleared his throat, dragged his aching body upright and felt at his belt for his spatha. The long sword was hanging from the left side of his waist, its comforting weight dragging him down towards the cool stone of the walkway.

He hefted up the spiculum from where he had left it leaning in the crook of the crenel by the buttress of the milecastle, and stood alert and attentive, his tired red-rimmed eyes scanning the soft folds of snowy landscape in front of him. He waited for the footsteps to approach, and snuck in a quick rub of his nose between thumb and forefinger.

"Ave, Pedes."

Silvius snapped around to face his superior, the spiculum nestled upright in the crook of his arm, his eyes fixed on a point one foot above the head of the garrison's commanding officer.

"Ave, Praefectus."

"At ease, son."

Aulus Ambrosius Germanus Apullius, Praefectus of the garrison at Aesica, spoke. He had a rich, deep voice, cracked through years of howling a desperate barritus on countless battlefields; a throat bruised from shouting commands on dusty parade grounds.

"This is no night for formalities," said the Praefectus. "The gods are abroad." He held out a large fist and snatched at a drift of snowflakes, then showed his empty hand to the soldier. "You see?"

Silvius looked at the man in front of him, his strong mouth crooked in a bitter smile.

"Yes, sir."

Apullius sniffed the air and wrinkled his face.

"Have you been drinking, pedes?"

Silvius swallowed hard, his eyes dropping to his feet in uncertainty.

"Of course you have," smiled the Praefectus. "A godspit night like this. Some foul rat-piss, no doubt, if the stench can reach me here. Acetum?"

"Mulsum, sir."

Apullius raised an eyebrow. "Peasant shit," he sneered. "Have some real vinum."

The Praefectus took a goatskin from his waist and threw it at the sentry. Silvius tilted it to his lips and squeezed out a chain of liquid. It was ice cold, sweet and peppery. Beautiful. He handed it back.

14

"Thankyou, sir."

A thread of laughter drifted up from the glowing greyness beyond the Wall. The snarl and bark of banter.

It was the ground patrol, thought Silvius; they would be floating into range at the base of the Wall some thirty feet below. He cursed inwardly. If the Praefectus hadn't been there, he could have leaned over, shared some drink and chat. If it had been Germanus or Commodus, they would have some dried meat for him. Maybe some beer from the Arcanae, the roving spies, to the north.

"Anything to report, pedes?"

Silvius briefly thought about mentioning the scream. But whichever way he framed it, he realised he didn't come off well.

"Nothing, sir."

Apullius walked across the rampart and leant on a crenel, staring out north into the glowing ghostworld beyond. Coarse snowflakes, clumsy parings from the bloated clouds, fell down onto his hands. His breath shimmered silver in the sky.

"You need to be careful at night, alone. There are ghosts enough in a man's head to spill out onto the stones." The Praefectus turned round to face the sentry. His cheeks were flushed red, his heavy features chisel-sharp, as if rimed with hoarfrost. "A man may hear or see things that are not there. Mere reflections," he tapped his leather-strapped head, "on the inside of his skull. Do you understand, pedes?"

"I think so, sir."

Apullius moved closer to the sentry until their faces were a foot apart. He stared hard at the sentry.

"The gods are abroad, tonight, pedes, Cernunnos is out. Out there. Out *here*. Have you seen him?" Silvius did not have chance to open his mouth before the Praefectus continued. "I have seen him. Many, many times. As the days get more desperate, I see him more often. Working to help."

"That is good, sir."

"Good?" he replied. "Yes, bonum indeed. See how the snow doesn't want to touch the ground?" He gestured at the eddies and swirls which chased each other from side to side in the strong wind. "A bleak omen. But with Cernunnos here, watching over us, there is always hope for tomorrow. What is your name, Pedes?"

The sentry snapped to attention. "Tertius Aurelius Silvius, sir."

"Silvius," said the Praefectus, his voice suddenly cracked and weary. "You are relieved. Get some sleep. Drink some more cheap piss. Do whatever you need to on a night like this."

"Yes, sir."

The Praefectus turned away from him and walked over to the battlements. He stood staring out to the north, the thickening snow lashing his squinted eyes. Silvius squeezed his numb nose between thumb and forefinger, blinked twice, then walked off towards the wooden steps leading down to the ground. If he hurried, he could get to the bathhouse and warm up before making some serious money at dice. He wanted to make good yesterday's losses before hora prima.

"Silvius."

He turned round. The figure of the camp commander, hunched at the battlements, was draped in snow.

"You had a brother, is that right?"

"I had many, Sir, but—"

"I don't want your fucking family history, Pedes. A brother who served here."

"Caepio, sir. He was killed fighting brigands."

"That's right. I remember him. He was shit." The Praefectus continued staring into the night. The wind thrashed against his craggy face, snatching the words from his heavy lips. Silvius had to strain to make out what he was saying. "I saw him struck, his face cleft in two by a blunt peasant axe. He grunted for hours before dying; too ruined to even weep like a bitch. You're better than that, Silvius. Don't be shit, like your brother. Be good enough to do us proud. Make a difference."

"S-Sir."

"Go."

Apullius could hear the rasp of the sentry's nail-studded boots on the wooden steps. With any luck the foreign fuck would slip and strew his brains onto the virgin snow. Most of the recent intake was mere pabulum. Too many refused to understand the local gods, couldn't show the right amount of respect. The respect that they were due. Instead they grovelled and licked at whatever new foreign deities were dragged in by the merchants and traders and sutlers: Mithras, Heliogabalus, the crucified Christus. But especially Mithras.

It was only Cernunnos that was going to help them out here, in the half-life of this frozen wilderness. They had always been adrift, rudderless in the raging shitstorms of this fractured Britannia. But Apullius could feel things coming to a head.

From beyond the fort came another scream, thin in the night and more distant than the last.

Less lungs, less heat.

Cernunnos would help them. He had to.

CHAPTER 1

The rain-pitted, soot-stained walls of the city of Eboracum glowered on the horizon. Visible from miles distant, they seemed to chew up the surrounding countryside, shouldering off the winter dusk which settled on the crowns of the nearby hills. The city gave off a dirty orange glow of its own, and the roar of life from its bowels could be heard across the valley.

The dark-skinned soldier had arrived, daubed with the dust and sweat of travel, and presented himself at the south gate.

He had been asked his name, which he gave as Atellus, and his rank, beneficiarius imperatoris, but would say nothing else. He wore a sunbleached turquoise scarf, wrapped around his neck. A guard of honour led him from the south gate all the way through the city to the vast principia at its heart, where he was entrusted to the care of an elderly tribune of the sixth Legion.

Atellus was informed that the praetor was expecting him, and led into a cavernous antechamber. He was offered a seat, which he took in silence.

The grey-haired, pot-bellied tribune muttered apologies as he asked for the soldier's sword. The beneficiarius loosened his belt from which the sheathed spatha hung ponderously and held it out to the tribune. The man awkwardly gathered the belt, scabbard and sword in his pale, flabby arms and bowed out through a small side-door.

Atellus tried to make himself at ease in the plush chair, but it somehow seemed too small to be comfortable. It had probably been crafted that way to put visiting dignitaries at a disadvantage; to discomfit them, agitate their thoughts, tire their muscles. He twisted for a few minutes, then got to his feet, deciding it would be easier to stand.

He looked around him: sleek columns topped by Corinthian capitals rushed up from the ground to meet the vaulted ceiling some fifty feet above his head, painted with obscenely bright foliate designs. The floor was paved with coloured marble slabs worn smooth by decades of footfall. In the centre of the room was an intricate mosaic depicting what looked like a frenzied Bacchanal. Atellus noted that the workmanship was not far shy of the imperial residence in Treves; the craftsmen were probably trained in one of the Danubian schools, and most likely imported specifically for the job.

He walked over to the mosaic. Close-up it was dark and faded; the colours had lost their brilliance and tesserae were missing. There was obviously no-one local with the skill to maintain it. Or there was neither money nor inclination to pay for such skill.

The antechamber was the height of opulence compared to the city he had just passed through. The outward-facing walls of Eboracum, although structurally sound, were scarred and graffiti-slashed. Before he had even got through to the militarised zone, he had walked hundreds of paces through the civilian shantytown which swelled and surged against the masonry.

Layers of rough hide bivouacs, leather tents, and timber shacks – some round, some rectangular – pressed against each other. Any square foot not occupied by a dwelling was instead used as a workspace. Scrawny hares were being butchered next to a makeshift granary. Half naked women, mottled blue with cold, grinned gummily at him as he passed. Men carved arrow shafts out of mountains of damp lumber, their movements jerky and desperate. Swollen-bellied children sat gloomily against each other, and flicked their eyes hungrily towards him as he passed. The ground was churned up filth, frozen hard into ankle-twisting shapes. A stench hovered in the cold air: a lung-burning mix of shit and disease, mingled with the acidic pinch of stale urine.

A girl child lay trembling in the road, her eyes unseeing. A man with a huge bundle of sticks on his shoulder staggered past her, vomited noisily, then continued.

The makeshift town was one of thousands across the empire; desperate communities huddling together, grafting themselves to the city to benefit from the protection it offered from casual raids and wandering bands of brigands.

It couldn't, Atellus noted, protect them from planned attacks from organised enemies. He saw the newness of the dwellings, and the abundance of charcoal and scorch-marks on the ground. It reminded him of how Chnodomar's forces had treated the extra-mural settlements at Argentoratum: barbarians ankle deep in limbs and burnt flesh, child and parent alike raped, tortured, mutilated, killed. The ruined city walls bled for a month.

There were not Alamanni enough in the world for the Legions to kill as recompense for those atrocities.

How long before the same happened here?

As he approached the south gate of Eboracum, he was met by soldiers from the sixth Legion. They had seemed professional enough, if lacking in etiquette and regulation uniform. A couple of them had come out to protect him from the squawks and moans of the beggars by the roadside. The soldiers waved their spiculae and the broken rags of people rattled away like chickens into the mess of tents and shacks. The men of the sixth had walked him in through the wicket gate then escorted him through the inner city.

The periphery of habitation within the walls was not much different from the slums outside. The inhabitants were largely thin and dirty, bowed down under the

21

weight of hunger and hardship. They didn't meet his eye as he had walked along the via principalis but just scuttled out of his way.

Those shops which existed were sporadic and ephemeral: wooden shacks leaning at drunken angles into the road, sutlers' wares spilling from the backs of yawning waggons. Some buildings had collapsed and not been renovated, nor the debris cleared. Instead, fallen masonry was often used as the backs or sides of rude dwellings where families huddled and naked children grinned and pissed carelessly inside torn tents of stretched goatskin.

Atellus had looked along some of the sidestreets: open sewers trickling glumly through the trampled dirt. Piles of broken paving flags lay randomly outside buildings.

"Bin ere afore, sur?" asked one of the soldiers escorting him. He was a wart-faced man in his thirties, with pale sandy hair and an unkempt beard stained with the juice of his last meal.

"Many years ago," said Atellus. He loosened the linen scarf from his throat, and rubbed the slender band of pale flesh beneath.

The man nodded. "Probly ant changed much. Yawant food, wine orun bitches, go north. Still be a few good places up tharray. If yis got money, anyweys. Na go west of the principalis after dusk."

They carried on walking in silence.

Some buildings were standing proud, daubed in fresh whitewash – brothels, inns, baths. Probably ones funded through the army, either directly or indirectly. There were also whole streets of incredibly elaborate, ornate villas: huge edifices towering upwards, festooned with painted frescoes and fierce eruptions of wax flowers. Seemingly the elite maintained a Roman way of life, even if the rest of the city's romanitas was being washed away by the interminable rains of conflict.

Closer to the forum in the centre, the buildings became larger, closer together. Some were stone-built, others timber, most were a mixture of both. Many had stone foundations with consecutive stories added in timber, often in varying styles. Whole arcades of shops stretched out in all directions, tradesmen howling out for attention and thick knots of colourfully dressed people thronging around them.

There were the occasional burnt-out remains of buildings and the paved colonnades and roads were often buckled, cracked or broken. Atellus noticed groups of people warming themselves around fires built at the intersections of roads, on patches of rubbly wasteland or in the shells of vacant buildings. Once or twice he saw people lying in the street; whether dead or drunk he couldn't tell, but his escort didn't even notice them.

Men were shimmying up buildings and wooden columns with torches to light the huge iron-strapped lanterns dangling some twenty paces off the ground. Dusk had arrived and the streets were being lit up. The rumble of the city seemed to swell in response: a scream in the distance; a shriek of laughter up close; a tavern-keep bawling out the virtues of his beer over those of Barbus's two doors down. A man shuffled down the street and spat noisily onto Atellus's boots.

Atellus shook away the memories of his entrance to Eboracum and turned away from the mosaic in front of him; he had been engrossed in the intricate loops and whorls of the Bacchanal depiction, and lost track of time. The clack of approaching footsteps echoed through the corridor outside and the door of the antechamber opened.

"Titus Faenius Magnus Atellus?"

Atellus turned in the direction of the reedy voice. He was facing a tall, thin man with a pinched face and short stubbly black hair. He was dressed elaborately and read from a parchment held close up to his nose. He didn't look at Atellus, but instead fixed his half-lidded eyes on the document in his hands.

"Yes," said Atellus.

"Follow me."

The beneficiarius followed the man out of the quiet antechamber. They walked down a long, low-ceilinged corridor with chambers opening out on both sides. These rooms seemed to be full of clerks interspersed with the occasional soldier standing awkwardly and looking uncomfortable.

There was a deep and satisfied fug of conversation echoing from the stonework. Dull, weighty tapestries hung from the walls. They walked out into a large square room with a high ceiling. Two broad staircases flanked a central portico of dressed stone. A statue of Justitia peered down from an alcove above the doorway. Several tired and wealthy-looking men were waiting, and two very elegantly-dressed women, anxiously smoothing their exquisitely-decorated stolae, wrinkling their brows with impatience. They looked at him as he passed, curiosity sparking from their eyes.

Atellus's guide led him up the far staircase and through a central doorway at the top. He was now in a small, plainly decorated room. There was a cushioned wooden bench along one wall, and a thick oak door opposite. A short table painted with an image of Mercury squatted parallel to the bench. To one side of the door, sitting on a fluted marble column, was a lifelike painted bust of the emperor Valentinian.

His guide turned to him. "Your papers," he demanded, extending a thin hand.

This was the fourth time he had had to produce them since he had entered the principia. Atellus pulled the creased and torn scroll from his dirty tunic and handed it over. The attendant studied it in detail, holding it an uncia from his long nose. After what felt like a considerable time, he returned it dismissively.

"Take a seat," he said, flatly, ending with a belated, "*Sir*. Someone will be with you very shortly."

He turned round to leave, but Atellus stopped him.

"I would appreciate a drink," he said. "Something to clear the dust of the road from my throat."

The attendant gave a curt nod, then disappeared through the door in front of him. Atellus walked over to the cushioned bench and sat down. He could make out the thin murmur of conversation leaking through the door from the chamber beyond. After a few seconds had passed, the door opened softly and a female servant appeared with a tall mug of chilled wine on a tray, and a small bowl of figs. She set it down on the oval table in front of Atellus, then shuffled away in silence.

Atellus looked at the beads of condensation dappling the sleek bronze sides of the jug. He licked his lips and poured himself a goblet-full. He took a sip of the wine. It was heavily watered, but refreshing. Before he had finished the drink, the door in front of him opened inwards and a tall lean man stepped out.

"Titus Faenius Magnus Atellus?"

Atellus stood up. The man addressing him was angular and coiled, his movements betraying a suppressed animation. His eyes quickly accounted for Atellus, then scanned the rest of the chamber.

A personal bodyguard, perhaps, thought Atellus. Something of the man's stance and air of expectancy indicated such.

25

"The most serene and wise Clodius Bassianus," spoke the guard in a deep, monotonous voice, "Governor of Britannia Secunda, is ready to grant you an audience."

Atellus walked through the door. It was a square room, small but immaculately presented. A narrow scooped walkway draped with a rich turquoise Sassanid carpet led to a large polished oaken table in the middle of the room. Behind the table sat the governor of one quarter of the diocese of Britannia, his head down and his quill scratching away at a parchment in front of him. Servants were dotted around the room, upright against the walls or angled into corners, their eyes fixed unseeingly straight ahead, as much furniture as the desk or armaria. The ceiling was high, and painted with a deep green and brown foliate design. A large window to the right opened on to a narrow curved balcony flanked by bronze torch-bearing pillars. The last molten spray of the drowning sun was visible beyond.

The colours were angry this far north, Atellus remembered.

The lean man who admitted him to the room walked across and stood exactly one pace behind and to the side of the praetor. Atellus strode along the carpeted walkway. He stood a pace in front of the desk and watched the old man scribble away, head down. Atellus placed his forearm diagonally across his chest and inclined his head slightly. After a few seconds, the scribbling stopped.

"Ave, Titus Faenius Magnus Atellus," said the old man, gazing up at him.

The governor looked older and more tired than last time Atellus had seen him. His eyes were a damp sky-blue, his jowls pale and vellum thin. Delicate purple veins pulsed lightly across his wide forehead. The scant hair left on his scalp was thin and white and downy, waxed back tight against the dome of his skull.

"Ave, Flavius Clodius Bassianus Brocchus." Atellus inclined his head respectfully to the praetor of Britannia Secunda before relaxing and moving forward to clasp forearms across the wide table. The old man smiled, showing the large square white teeth which had no doubt given him his name.

"Nasty business," murmured the praetor, shaking his old head pendulously. Atellus couldn't tell whether he was referring to the reason he was here, or something else entirely. "Please, take a seat."

Atellus sat down and clenched the arms of his short-legged chair. They were broad and had proud finials carved in the shape of snarling lions. Brocchus sat down and laced his fingers across his baggy paunch. "Nasty business," he repeated. "How long has it been, Atellus?"

"Since I was last here?" he queried, but the old man just looked soggily across the table at him. He was certainly not as sharp as he had been last time; maybe that was to be expected. "Seven years."

"Seven years," repeated Brocchus, his chin sinking down to his chest. "Seven years." He nodded slowly to himself and looked up again. "Lupicinus did well, back then. Those were such very *dire* times, and he did well. You *all* did well. But...." He shook his head sadly, and splayed his gaunt fingers out in front of his eyes, palms towards Atellus. "It feels, sometimes, like trying to hold back the ocean with my fingers."

"It is not just Britannia that suffers," said Atellus.

Brocchus looked at him for a while. Atellus couldn't tell whether he was pondering this, or whether his mind was many leagues distant.

"No," replied the praetor, at last. "I daresay we are not alone in our tribulations."

There was silence. One of the servants cleared their throat quietly. Brocchus looked irritated.

27

"So, beneficiarius imperatoris," said the praetor. "We are honoured to receive you in our humble province. You act for the very emperor himself. We are *indeed* honoured by an emissary of the Worshipful Valentinian. Although, of course, the circumstances are somewhat...distasteful." The older man smacked his lips. "I had no concept, my dear Atellus, that you and the emperor were quite so *tight*."

Atellus shifted in his seat. "We fought together under Julian. Valentinian and I campaigned against the Alamanni, and in the East, against the Persians. We were promoted together. War creates powerful bonds amongst men."

"And, alas, enmities, sometimes."

"Indeed."

You would have no idea, thought Atellus. Your sagging arse is cleaved to that curule while your province burns around you. And has been for the last ten years, at least.

"And," continued Brocchus, "the emperor obviously has friends on the Wall for news to reach him of such a... *parochial* issue. Disappearing children, indeed." The old man snorted: a crumbling, bestial sound.

Atellus remained silent.

"Friends, indeed," continued Brocchus. "Lupicinus's men who settled up there, perhaps?"

"Perhaps."

"Well, the emperor has his reasons, and his motives, and it is not for the likes of me to query them." The praetor rested his elbows on the desk, and laid his chin atop his steepled fingers. "This is a nasty business, and I hope that you are able to find some clarity and resolution in it. Provide some succour to the emperor and inform him that maybe, in future, such matters could be dealt with internally?

"I *sincerely* hope," he continued, after clearing his throat, "that you can return to Valentinian with the news that Britannia Secunda is more than capable of looking to her own resources when dealing with matters of a criminal nature. Saying that, I have no doubt you will get all the help and support you need from our men, and I obviously extend the same offer myself."

"Thank you, praetor," Atellus inclined his head slightly.

Brocchus waved his thanks away. "However, I have more pressing issues to deal with myself." The old man rifled through the parchments on his desk. "When I heard of your approach, I sent word to Fullofaudes. I don't recall who held the post of dux Britanniorum when last you were here?"

"Proclus."

"Ah, yes," nodded Brocchus. "Tiresome man. Long dead. Well, Fullofaudes is now responsible for all the limitanei on the Wall. I requested his counsel on this issue. We received an emissary, yesterday I believe it was." Brocchus sifted through the parchments on his cluttered desk and produced a small curled tube of parchment which he unrolled and scanned, his lips moving silently. "Fullofaudes says that the matter is one for civil administrators, not the military."

Brocchus shook his head, dropped the parchment to his desk and rubbed his eyes with the thumb and forefinger of his left hand.

"The children," continued Brocchus, "you see, were from the vicus. The military are washing their hands of it. Can't say I blame them: their hands are full as it is. Times are not yet so desperate that we need charge whelps with defending our borders." He gave Atellus an anaemic grin. "So, I have transferred administration of this matter to my ab epistulis. Crispus is more than capable of helping you resolve this issue as quickly and discreetly as possible."

"Mettius Marius Crispus?" said Atellus, slowly.

"The one and same," answered Brocchus. "You know him, I presume?"

"I do." Atellus shifted in his seat. The name sent an ache running up from the base of his spine. He shifted in his seat, tugged gently at his scarf. "We were at Argentoratum together."

"Oh," said Brocchus, one fine white eyebrow raised. "I didn't realise he had a military background."

"He doesn't," said Atellus, trying to keep the bile from his voice. "He was with Julian's clerical staff. And he helped Lupicinus with the logistics of getting our men up to the Wall."

"Ah," smiled Brocchus. "I did indeed find him in Londinium, stagnating in the employ of that buffoon, Constantius." He removed his elbows from the desk and settled back in his curule. "Well, his office is just through there." He flung a hand in the direction of a large double-door over his left shoulder.

Atellus nodded.

"He is on business in the city at the moment," said Brocchus, "but I have sent for him. He won't be long. Perhaps your visit will cheer him up – I understand his wife is ill at the moment. Feel free to wait inside; he has a most interesting library."

Atellus rose from the chair.

"One more thing, beneficiarius," said the governor, not looking up from his papers. "If you please? Find the children if you can. Punish whoever is responsible, of course." He raised his gaze and Atellus could see a deep fury burning within the tranquil blue eyes. "But most of all, find me that snivelling wretch who bleated to the emperor; find me our informant."

CHAPTER 2

"All I need is a name."

She had stopped screaming now, and regarded her interrogator through treacly eyes glazed with pain.

Her tormentor sighed, wearily. He shook his head, his fringe of curls jangling in front of his dark brown eyes.

"I am not enjoying this." He spoke low, almost to himself. "No, no, no."

The small basement room of the villa was clean and square. A basic, functional room. The floor was covered with rough woollen sacking, and the fine cavity walls were panelled with a thick layer of pressed corkwood, imported at great cost from Lusitania. The ceiling was crisscrossed by thick oak beams.

The naked woman hanging by the wrists from one of the beams in the centre of the room was in her thirties, though the torments of the last day and a half had aged her considerably. If she wore fine clothes and was able to hobble into society once more, she would have struggled to pass for a fifty-year-old scullion. Her once beautiful green eyes leaked tears filmed with blood. The sacking beneath her dangling heels was stained dark with effluvium: sweat, urine and blood.

The man who paced around her, eyes to the ground, watching his steps so as to avoid soiling his artisan-stitched leather boots, was maybe a decade older. His creased face and the carefully oiled curls of his hair spoke of fine living. His fingers were thin and manicured and danced with jewellery; his palms were soft and pale and lightly stained with purple ink from etching calligraphic missives on scented parchment. The man's teeth were even and complete, unstained. His tunic was of a fine cotton, embellished with strips of silk woven into the fabric. A small child's gold ring, inscribed with a swollen phallus, hung on a slender chain from his neck.

"You know, cara...." He stopped abruptly, and raised his delicate head to gaze upon the woman's navel. "You know, um, Quintus and, and Dexter, do you? You know them?"

He stroked his large eyelids with a dextrous finger before continuing.

"Of course you do," he said. "My two best men. Strong! Courageous!" He rolled his tongue over the words, caressing the consonants, luxuriating in the sound of his voice in the small room. He had always possessed a gift for rhetoric; it was one of the reasons he had acquired the position he was in.

"First into conflict and ever the last to leave, Quintus and Dexter. Indeed! But of course you know them, Aurelia, of course you must have noticed the way they looked at you."

Here, he gave the woman a quick, disapproving look before shaking his head. "Strong and courageous, indeed! But animals." His voice dropped to a husky whisper as he dropped his eyes and shook his head heavily. "Wild beasts, feral hounds, wolves, Aurelia! Barbarians, indeed." He dropped his voice to a whisper; conspiratorial, appalled. "Their parents were Saxons, I think."

He approached the woman and caressed one of her breasts lightly, almost tenderly with the backs of his fingers.

"Ravenous," he continued, softly. "Ravenous for flesh, they are. Aurelia, I have heard the stories they tell. Oh, cara, such tales!" He laughed, withdrew his hand from her skin and wiped it absently on his tunic.

"Do I need to let them in here, Aurelia? Do I?" He stood below her, the cascades of her dark hair speckled with white almost brushing his cheek. "Just a name, mellita, and it will be over."

The woman's jaw worked, her mouth cracked. A dry tongue parted the flesh of her lips as she spoke, her words thick and slurred.

"Kill me."

She whispered from the depths of her chapped and bleeding soul, and turned her clouded gaze on the man beneath her.

He sighed with vexation then turned away from the woman, as if pondering. With a spasm of controlled rage, he spun round, launching his bejewelled fist into a backhanded blow which sent two of the woman's teeth clicking off the corkwood at the far side of the room. Bloody spittle spattered across her cheek.

"Death for you, delicia," he spat, mockingly, "will be a long, long way off."

He rearranged his fringe of curls and walked towards a small door at the far end of the room. He opened it and passed through into a narrow corridor. Hunkered down, squatting on their haunches were two dark, scabbed and angry men. Their faces twitched up eagerly at the sound of his approach.

"You have until I finish merenda," he said. "Do not kill her, or I will kill you. Slowly."

The two men got up, their faces etched with sick grins, and walked towards the room. The interrogator started off down the corridor, before clicking his fingers and turning round to face his bodyguards again just as they were about to disappear into the chamber. "Oh, and make sure she can still *talk*."

"Dominus," grunted the man named Dexter, nodding a tight affirmation. Quintus was already inside, eager to begin. Their master turned round and continued down the corridor and up the stone steps that led to his study.

He paused on the steps a moment, cocking his ear to catch any screams before the door clicked shut; but there were none and he continued walking with a mild disappointment.

The interrogator went on up to his personal study. There was a messenger waiting there for him; he listened to the communication, then dismissed him with a flick of his fingers. He sat at his writing desk and picked daintily at roast snipe seasoned with fennel, served with a hard, sour goat's cheese.

Their current cook was nowhere near as good as the last one, but at least he seemed honest. Too lumpen, too unimaginative to consider pilfering, most likely. So far, at least; all chattel seemed to reach a point when their boredom and complacency peaked along with their desire for garnishing their wage. But he was ready for them. Always.

He swallowed the last crumb of cheese, and sucked away at the thigh bone of the bird before clattering the bronze bowl against the serving tray. A servant – he was damned if he could tell which one, even if he had cared – appeared from the shadows and cleared away the remnants of the meal. A second servant came with a heated damp cloth, scented with lemon, and a full goblet of warm spiced wine mixed with water, three parts to one. The interrogator dabbed at his thin lips and wiped his fingers, then sat back in his chair and sipped at the drink.

A clepsydra sat heavily on a carved mahogany pedestal in the corner, just by the balcony doors. The soft, almost imperceptible, trickle of water was the only sound in the room. It had been a welcome gift from the previous governor of Flavia Caesariensis before he had been torn apart in the riots. A pleasant enough work of engineering, though it didn't tell him anything he couldn't see from the quality of the light through the window. It was approaching decima. He had given those animals long enough.

He slurped down the last of his wine, and tossed the goblet to the long-haired servant with the large breasts, then walked across to the steps which led down to his basement. He drifted down them nonchalantly, and sauntered along the thin, undecorated corridor towards his special chamber.

He opened the door; there was still no screaming. The air was thick and stank of sweat and sex. He could almost taste the metallic tang of fresh blood in the air.

Quintus and Dexter were naked and glistening with sweat, reclining by the walls. The woman was a broken heap, bluepale and quivering on the floor. Her left breast was a mass of angry fresh bruises, her body covered with bite-marks. Crusted scabs mottled her flesh and trails of blood leaked down her thighs and backs of her legs.

"Leave," he said, quietly.

The two men got to their feet groggily, spent and weary. They padded out, yellowbrown teeth bared in smiles directed at the woman. Quintus blew her a kiss and winked. Dexter coughed out a laugh and punched him on the arm. They shut the door behind them.

The interrogator knelt down beside the woman's face. Her eyes were open, but unfocused. He leant in to put his mouth close to her ear, brushing her dark hair aside. It was claggy with sweat.

"They have so much more, cara, so much more to show you. The days will become as years with your pain. Just a simple name. Tell me who he is, tell me who the letters are from and it can all be over."

He pulled away from the woman, and waited for her to speak.

36

He barely had chance to begin curling a twist of hair around his finger before his wife had given him the name he wanted. After he had finished with her, he rinsed his face, oiled his curls and set out for the principia.

CHAPTER 3

Atellus stared at the back of the heavy door, and willed himself to stay awake. He was sitting in the cushioned chair opposite the ab epistulis's desk. A servant had arrived to tell him that the ab epistulis himself would be with him shortly, but that had felt like half a day ago.

He had been posted as a beneficiarius before, and had borne dealings with others when he had been on campaign. Whilst they were meant to be treated exactly as if they were the person whose authority they represented, the reality was different. Very different: lip-service was paid to the position, but practically speaking he was still just a scruffy grunt with a piece of parchment in his pocket. People tiptoed around the authority of the beneficiarius whilst doing their utmost to denigrate him.

He had probably been the same himself, he thought, in fairness. Although theoretically his every word and action resonated with the entire potens of the emperor, the reality was a lot different. No grovelling or scraping, no dignitaries rushing to shower him with gifts. Instead, everyone did their utmost to respectfully keep him at arm's length, until his power was revoked, he left their sight, or died in duty. Whichever was sooner.

The door leading back out into the praetor's office was covered with soft green leather, studded with bronze nail-heads. The room itself was hot and muggy. He looked around him, then got to his feet to walk around and keep himself alert.

The chamber was quite large, surrounded on all sides with armaria, stretching from the tiled floor to the ceiling some ten paces above his head. Thousands of wood- and leather-bound volumes peered down at him. The effect was quite dizzying. Crispus's small desk sat opposite him, pressed back against the wall, just in front of a small fire which flickered lazily. Beside the fire was a naked man seated on a wooden stool, playing doleful notes on a large lyre. His shaved body glistened lightly with perspiration. Instead of eyes, he had coarse folds of toughened, stitched flesh.

Atellus walked over to take a closer look at the armaria; there must have been thousands of volumes within, from Ovid, Polybius and Plutarch to Eusebius, Apollonius and Flaccus. As well as the books crammed tightly onto the shelves, there were fold-out racks containing furled lengths of parchment. Some were brown with age, while others looked pale and fresh. Ranged along one side of the wall, in front of some of the armaria, were tall cabinets, each the height of a man, with numerous hinged doors, labelled alphabetically. He tried to open them, but they were locked.

Atellus sat down in the chair opposite the small square desk, and closed his eyes. He let the soft music from the lyre drift into his thoughts. He was tired from intense travel and lack of sleep. Images of his wife and daughter appeared in his head, as they always did in times of weakness. He felt better for having them there; it was almost as if they were here with him. The sound of the door being opened and shut interrupted his daydream and he looked round.

The governor's ab epistulis had entered the room and was walking across the woven rug overlaying the tiled floor. Atellus groggily got to his feet whilst Crispus walked lithely around his desk to embrace the beneficiarius.

"Titus Faenius Magnus Atellus!" said the man. "So *excellent* to see you."

Atellus grimaced inwardly, but forced his lips into a diplomatic smile.

"Ave, Crispus."

If the ab epistulis was offended by the immediate use of his familiar name, he gave no indication. He was tall and well-dressed with a bowl of immaculately curled hair and a slightly effeminate air. There was something almost reptilian about his smile, and his dark brown eyes seemed as impenetrable as the night sky. They were stresstight at the corners and burned with an almost feverish intensity.

"Come," he said, "sit with me." He led Atellus to a double curule beneath one of the interminable stacks of books. "Out there with that old fart Brocchus you must be formal, but we are old allies. What would you like to drink?"

Before Atellus could answer, Crispus shouted for a servant. One seemed to melt out of the wall. "Wine."

The servant scurried off. The music from the naked lyrist changed timbre slightly, to a minor key. Fast showers of notes cascaded from the strings, pattering into the deep rug like rainfall. Crispus noticed Atellus looking.

"That is my musician. Quite one of the best lyrists in the empire, I am reliably informed." The servant returned with a huge jug of iced wine and two large goblets, then departed, melting back into the surroundings. "It," he sneered, jerking his head in the direction of the musician, "was a gift from Jovian. I believe it had been a diplomatic hostage from the Chamavi, or other such animals."

Crispus poured a full cup of wine and handed the goblet to Atellus who nodded his thanks.

"A beast raised in opulence," continued Crispus, pouring a cup for himself. "Trained by the finest musicians of the emperor's court. Then when the Chamavi rebelled, its eyes were put out and its tongue severed. It makes a very excellent pet." He took a delicate sip of the chilled wine. "But how was your journey? You came direct from Treves?"

Atellus took a deep draught of his wine, swallowing it thirstily.

40

"Yes," he said after clearing his throat. "The journey was hard; I made good time."

"Did you have trouble with the pirates?" asked Crispus. "I am told that one cannot expect to cross the oceanus britannicus without some form of...adventure."

"We chartered a fast ship," replied Atellus. "We saw pirates but they could not match our pace."

"Very wise, very wise," said Crispus nodding sagely. "We lose trade to such attacks daily. Not to mention resources, of course, men and vessels are almost as hard to replace as wine and spices." He laughed then took another peck at his wine before resettling it on the silver tray. "I hear Nectaridus does his best to defend our coasts, but there is only so much one can do. A man is but small, and the oceans vast." He stretched his delicate fingers out in front of him in illustration. Atellus saw they were lightly stained with purple ink.

"Not that travel by land is much easier," Crispus continued. "I have the latest accounts here, somewhere." He flourished a hand in the direction of his desk. "More bad harvests and countless ransacked grain supplies. The north is suffering, Atellus. Yes, suffering badly at the moment. If it is not Rome's enemies doing the pillaging, then it is her own citizens. The people fear that the brigands are living more comfortably than the taxpayers; the people fear that there are more bands of robbers, looters and deserters than there are soldiers."

"The people are right," said Atellus, quietly, "from what I have seen and heard."

Crispus looked at him for a second before answering. "They are," he nodded. "But we can't let them *know* that, of course." He laughed, a high rich sound. "No, no, that wouldn't help at all." He picked up his goblet, taking another small sip of his wine, then set it down on the tray. "How is Valentinian?"

41

"I don't really have much discourse with the emperor," said Atellus.

Crispus clapped his bejewelled hands together and laughed. "But you are the beneficiarius imperatoris, Atellus! You are at this very moment the second man in the empire – your words and deeds are those of the emperor himself! Are you telling me that our worthy emperor would confer such responsibility and esteem upon someone he barely knew?"

Atellus emptied his wine and placed it on the tray. He ached from head to foot. His vision was bleary and his loose clothes felt like sheets of lorica hamata. He was bone weary from the travel, and the heat and smoke of the room were squeezing at his chest. The wine hadn't helped. He was in no mood to be interviewed and mocked by the oleaginous streak of piss sitting next to him.

"But seriously, Atellus," continued the ab epistulis, "I was glad to hear of your rise. Rumours of your execution had made it as far as Londinium, whilst I was there."

"Good news travels fast," Atellus grunted.

Crispus laughed again, a neat and prickly sound. "Of course not. No. Anyway, I can see you are tired. Shall we discuss the matter at hand?"

Atellus nodded. Crispus shouted for more wine, and meat.

"Down to business," he said, placing a delicate hand on Atellus's knee. The beneficiarius looked down at it as if it were a venomous spider.

"Brocchus would never admit to it," said Crispus, "but he is furious, simply seething, about this whole business. Mainly, about the fact that it has reached the emperor's ear and makes our worthy governor look incompetent. If he ever finds out who was in contact with Valentinian, that person's life would not be worth one nummus."

"I can imagine."

"Well, when I first read that the emperor was going to send someone to investigate, I requested you."

Atellus felt a slap of adrenaline shake his heart into action. His weariness sloughed off him like sweat under a strigil. He found himself on his feet before he was able to control his muscles.

"You asked for me?" he asked. "Why?"

"Peace, Atellus, peace." Crispus beckoned for him to sit down. "Please?"

Atellus sank back into the curule. He felt the tingling still in his limbs. The whole treacherous journey, the worthless commission and the return to this wasted, crippled bunion on the empire's arse was all down to the man next to him. He had been wrenched away from his family home, and spun into this joke of a commission. He felt his fists clenching spasmodically. It took an effort to stop.

"I asked for you," continued Crispus, twisting an oily curl of hair around his middle finger, "because I knew you were at Treves. I knew the emperor trusted you, and I knew that *I* could trust *you.*"

There was that grin again, stretched taut below the carbo-black eyes.

"I knew you had been here before," Crispus continued, "when you crushed those northern bastards with Lupicinus. You know the North. You know the Wall. You know the people. And I thought, in light of what had happened, it may have done you good to be away from your family home."

Atellus felt a stinging bright light in his head and before he was aware of his movement he was on the floor on top of Crispus, his iron fingers clutching the other man's sleek neck, the secretary's elegant curls strewn across the carpeted tiles.

"Who let an animal like you speak about my family?" spat Atellus. He could feel saliva dripping from the side of his mouth. Crispus' face was a dark red. A crackling noise was coming from within his throat. The lyrist strummed something atonal, charged with tension, before resolving into a triumphant dominant chord.

Atellus could feel the blood pounding against the scar tissue round his throat; it felt like it should burst through the flesh and shower them both with gore.

He forced himself to loosen his grip around the other man's windpipe.

The furious red of Crispus's face became an angry pink. A cough erupted from between his fat purple lips.

"Ben...ben...bene...fici...arius, please, *pax!*"

Atellus loosened his grip. His fingers had left white indents in Crispus' flesh. He got to his feet and scrubbed a hand across his face. His fingers ached. The ab epistulis rubbed at his throat and coughed and hacked onto the floor. His chest swelled and collapsed violently as he dragged air into his lungs.

"Do not talk of my family," hissed Atellus, quietly. "Ever."

He sat down on the cushioned bench and reached out for the jug of wine. There was a plate of sliced cooked meats and some hard cheese. The servants must have entered and placed it there even as he was squeezing the life out of their master, then departed just as silently.

Fidelity and loyalty, fidelitas et pietas, thought Atellus. Some men commanded it. Others demanded it. Few truly deserved it.

Atellus drank directly from the jug. The sliver was cold and smooth on his lips. When he lowered the vessel, Crispus was sitting opposite him, slightly hunched and shaking, his usually immaculate curls a truculent mess on his scalp.

44

"I meant no insult, beneficiarius," he croaked, his voice tremulous. "News travels. I thought only to help." His voice was hoarse, his eyes bloodshot.

Atellus felt good.

"And...and of course," continued Crispus, keen to change the subject, "you have experience of similar duties in other provinces. I remembered hearing of your work in...in...um...Noricum and Pannonia." Crispus poured himself some wine with a shaking hand. He drank it, slightly less delicately than before. Swallowing seemed to be painful for him. Atellus smiled darkly.

"As far as we can ascertain," said the secretary, as his breathing steadied and the redness faded from his face, "there have been twelve children murdered since last winter."

"How do you know they've been murdered?" asked Atellus.

"I... *presume*."

"Bodies have been found?"

Crispus shook his head. "No."

"So twelve children have disappeared," corrected Atellus. "All from towns along the Wall?"

"No, beneficiarius," said Crispus, still tenderly stroking his throat. The pale flesh was overcast with livid bruises. "Twelve chits have gone from the same vicus."

"All twelve from Aesica?"

"Yes," he nodded. "There may be more, of course, unreported. You know how they live in those areas." Crispus shook his head and reached out for a cube of cheese. He crumbled it between thumb and forefinger and placed some fragments on his tongue. "Like vermin. Uncivilised."

"Who is your contact?"

"Officially, I am in correspondence with Aulus Ambrosius Germanus Apullius, praefectus of the garrison at Aesica. A rough man, but good. He has been conducting, um, preliminary investigations, shall we say? He has not managed to produce anything of merit, thus far." He chewed pensively at the cheese in his mouth. "Being a senior officer on one of the most active frontiers in the empire does not leave much spare time for anything else. And the military are doing all they can to shift the onus onto the administrators, though the nearest ones are at Petriana."

"Witnesses?"

"Not that we know of."

"The family; parents: questioned?"

"I don't believe so," said Crispus. "Beneficiarius, this is all virgin territory to us. We are at constant war; if not the barbarians without the Wall, then with the brigands and usurpers and mercenaries within. Twelve whelps are not a large concern for us. Certainly not for Brocchus, not for Fullofaudes. Not even for Apullius. Such children and more are probably killed each day on the frontiers. If it were the enemy, no-one would take note.

"Now, may I speak frankly?" He leaned closer in towards Atellus; the easterner could smell the lavender and alumen on the other man's body. "The only reason you're here – the only reason anyone gives a cunt's fart about this at all – is because some barely literate imbecile with a... *connection*," – Crispus spat the word with contempt – "somehow managed to get a message to the emperor and cause all this fuss. *Twelve children*. Now, they may have been twelve glowing sparks who

46

would one day burst forth to become blazing beacons of romanitas. But living amongst the scum of those garrison towns, it is more likely they would have been sold as food by their own parents, or have grown up to become brigands and clap-ridden whores."

A silence stretched out between the two men. Crispus's large eyes dabbed at the beneficiarius's travel-worn features.

"But I *am* here," said Atellus, at last, through gritted teeth. He raised his gaze to stare hard into Crispus's eyes. "And I act for the emperor."

Crispus held up his splayed fingers. "Of course, beneficiarius, of course. And you must discharge your duty to the best of your abilities. But I am just putting the facts on the table. The runts? No-one cares about them. You would be lucky if you could find evidence of a single tear shed over them. But I – or we, Brocchus and I – have a more pressing concern. The disappearance of our agent in rebus."

"You sent an agent to the vicus?" said Atellus.

Crispus got to his feet and stroked his throat absentmindedly. He walked in a neat circle in front of his desk, his head bent down, eyes scouring the carpet beneath him. Music from the naked lyrist tinkled softly in the background.

"Not exactly," he said, as he walked. "We have had an agent on the Wall for a good while. It is a prudent location. If we need intelligence about low morale, deserters, even possible usurpation, the chances are we will get it from the Wall. It is the ragged tassel of the empire, the very limit of Roman control, of civilisation. It is just within nail-grasp of the outstretched fingers of the emperor. It is all too easy for rebellion and insurrection to take hold there. We need an agent in the area, to tap into the hardest-working limitanei in the empire. That would only be prudent."

Atellus nodded. He reached for the jug and poured himself more wine. Having his fingers embedded in the man's thrapple had enervated him; he no longer felt quite so groggy. He hated Crispus, and not even the memory of penetrating the man's wife was enough to slake his disgust. If anything, it exacerbated it.

He wondered where she was; he would be able to find out, if he really wanted to.

"When I first heard that Valentinian was interested in Aesica," continued Crispus, "I at once directed our agent to the garrison. Only Apullius was aware he was there. He sent me despatches every month. At that point only ten whelps had disappeared. So I have contemporary accounts from him of circumstances surrounding the other two. Not much to base an investigation on, but enough to pique one's curiosity. You are welcome to read them."

Crispus suddenly stopped in his tracks and stood upright. Atellus could almost see his ears twitching beneath his curls. The ab epistulis picked up the empty wine jug from the platter and walked over to the fireplace. He grasped the handle of the jug and swung it heavily into the face of the blind musician. There was a sickening groan that seemed to come from deep within the lyrist's chest and he tumbled off his stool, hitting his head against the stones of the hearth.

"By the gods!" spat Crispus, trembling with fury. "When did I give you permission to stop playing? You...you...fucking *animal!*"

He threw the jagged remnants of the jug down at the groaning musician, then walked back to the rug in front of his desk and resumed his circular pacing.

Atellus could hear the laboured breathing of the injured man from across the room.

After a while, the musician dragged himself to his knees and onto the stool. The fire was pulsing orange behind him. A smear of blood ran from his nostril. He gathered his lyre and began to tune it.

Violence always goes downhill, thought Atellus. It might as well have been he who had beaten the cripple. His own weakness was responsible for the hurt of others, yet again.

"Excuse me," said Crispus, shaking his head as he paced. "I try and maintain discipline amongst my beasts, where possible. Let things slide and before you know it there is a dagger blade between your ribs. A military man like yourself can understand, I am sure." He threw a look at Atellus, who returned it blankly.

Crispus cleared his throat softly and continued. The background was filled with the patter of notes from the lyrist once more. "As I was saying...," said Crispus, "you are most welcome to the agent's reports. His despatches cover the period of two of the disappearances. Then – nothing." He stopped walking, and turned to face Atellus. "I haven't heard from him since. He appears to have vanished, too. Chits disappearing from a frontier town? Pfft." He snapped his fingers. "An agent in rebus, on the other hand? That is a very different, and much more troubling, prospect.

"And that, beneficiarius," he concluded, "is why I requested *you*. The best."

"I am flattered," sneered Atellus.

"Yes, yes, I know you're not happy to be back in Britannia. But this could all be over, very, very soon for you. For everyone. We are all working towards the same thing: a quick, tidy resolution."

Atellus rose. A burst of wine to his head made the room lurch slightly. "If there is nothing else," he said. "I will seek my quarters for the evening."

"Of course," replied Crispus. "You must be weary from your travels. Here."

The ab epistulis walked across to one of the locked cabinets ranged against the far wall and inserted a small key from a bunch attached to his belt beneath his tunic. The door eased open smoothly and a stack of drawers slid out. Crispus rummaged through and produced a sheaf of carefully folded papers. He pushed the drawers shut and locked the door before walking over and handing the papers to Atellus.

"The correspondence from the agent in rebus," he said. "Read through them when you are more...refreshed. I have arranged for an escort to Aesica for you. You will leave tomorrow at prima." He smiled, his square white teeth visible behind his full lips. "I hope that won't be inconvenient? Brocchus desires to speak to you before you leave."

The beneficiarius took the papers.

"And, Atellus, remember: we are both on the same side here."

Atellus stared at the wiry clerk with an open contempt. "We both fight for Rome," he nodded tersely, "and for the emperor. But you? You, I tolerate."

Crispus's smile collapsed, his dark eyes sparking with suppressed emotion. "I am sorry you feel that way. I sincerely hope you won't allow our...history...to get in the way of a successful outcome in Aesica." He strode across the room and opened the door for the beneficiarius. "By the way, my wife sends her regards."

Atellus felt an icy wave ripple through his body, and he almost missed his step.

"And you can return mine," he said, his voice firm and steady. "I hear she is unwell."

"That is true," replied Crispus mournfully. "She was an imperial guest at Treves this summer. You may have noticed her? I fear she may have been exposed to one of those damnable Gallic pestilences that surface in the hot weather."

"I trust she will recover soon."

"Oh, of course." Crispus nodded, and opened up a smile that shone like a glinting sickle. "I have had my best people working on her."

CHAPTER 4

"Beer."

Atellus watched the tavernkeep limp away. He was a short, pale man with a bald head. Half his face was mottled with firescars, the flesh puckered and twisted. He wore a brown leather cap angled across his scalp. Probably an ex-soldier; he'd set up a business here in the city, and made a tolerable living doing it. Not that it looked any less risky than serving as a limitanei, judging from the clientele.

Atellus was sat at a short spare table in the corner of the tavern. The building itself was like a barn: a single hall-like room with a tall ceiling and sparse fixtures. A large fire burned against the far wall with bits of broken furniture stacked up next to it. Every time the door swung open, a rabble of icy wind roused the flames and sent a chill through the room.

In the far corner was a tall bench behind which the tavernkeep and his woman prepared drink after drink: adulterated vinum, mulsum, acetum, Celtic beer. In a grimy adeps-smeared kitchen a servant prepared cheap meals of roasted rat, bird meat and hard cheese with stale rye-bread. Half-naked women carried drinks and vittles to tables of howling patrons: knots of leering, vomiting, crying, tired, fighting men. A clattery fug of noise throbbed against the four walls, like the sounds of a distant battle. Even the smell of sweat and blood rose from the straw-covered floor. Micturants loosed themselves where they sat; others slept face down in the steaming pools. Men and whores danced on tabletops, and came crumpling down amidst spilled wine, curses and laughs. Whores serviced men against the walls or under the tables. Debased coins – clipped and snag-edged – swapped hands. There was the endless rasp of blades being drawn, in threat or fooling.

A girl brought Atellus his beer in a blunt wooden tankard. It was leaking slowly through the bottom. He thanked her, and pressed a follis into her palm.

"You ain arter fun tonight, captin?"

It was the second time she'd asked. Atellus shook his head, and took a swallow of his beer. Was it his seventh drink? His ninth? He couldn't remember. The girl walked away in favour of more amenable punters. The beer was sweet and effervescent. He belched and put the tankard down.

The table opposite him – sailors, by their complexion and clothes – started bellowing a loud song in cracked and sodden voices: something about a Numidian whore. The door opened and sent spits of graupel flapping into the room. The light of the fire shot wild ragged shadows across the walls. A stout man slammed the door shut behind him, and unwrapped himself from his cloak.

Atellus had chosen this tavern by the river as it was only a short walk from his quarters. The governor had offered him the use of the principia's accommodation, and even extended the use of his own villa in the north side of the city, but Atellus had politely declined. He knew it was an error of etiquette, but he was past caring. He was not on a diplomatic mission. He felt more comfortable in the riverside dives than in the sterile restrictions of governmental quarters. Maybe it was his eastern upbringing.

He'd walked past the Isurium, the truculent tide swollen with meltwater from the hills. It flowed against the banks, the foam a dirty brown. The occasional corpse bobbed on the wavelets, its bloated waxy flesh like globs of pale snow. Purlmen leant from their skiffs and yanked the bodies in and stripped the ragged flesh bare, looking for coin or tidy leather.

Tangled twists of limbs marked piles of bodies gathered by the wharves, ready to be burnt. Bilious-looking men with drapes of cloth over their faces sat and shivered and watched the carious bones, waiting for the order to burn.

There was sickness in the town, a plague, and men and women died in unmourned heaps. Longshoremen hauled barrels and amphorae from low-slung river ships. Other larger vessels disgorged soulless strings of bleak-eyed peons, frost-bitten refugees from the burned and battlecracked villages to the north.

Atellus had walked past the wharves and felt out the warmth and laughter of the hard taverns.

He took another slug of his beer as a lazy fight rolled past in front of him. Benches screeched, men grunted in pain and excitement. A head hit the side of his table, hard, sending a shiver through Atellus's arms. A well-dressed man, an official maybe, hunting for women, squeezed himself into the wall and clenched his wine cup to his chest.

With each sip of his beer Atellus could feel the old anger rising up from his crotch, swelling into his belly with a beautiful malignant warmth. His worst enemy and best friend, the anger was almost sexual in its physicality. He could imagine his wife's eyes, dark and soft, and the creamy innocence of his daughter, Petronia: he'd left them in Treves. And they were hurting. He was hurting. There had been whores and imperial bitches and equestrian wives but they would not be the same as Julia Faenia. She could tickle the underside of his soul with a word, send his mumbling heart to sleep with a glance.

Atellus tugged at the linen scarf round his throat, loosened it a little. The wound was over three years old, but the tissue felt as tender as babyflesh. The white puckered cicatrix stood out against his dark eastern skin. Sometimes he woke up in those small sick hours before dawn, skin slick with sweat, teeth clenched against a raging scream. He always dreamed of falling, falling hard, and his chest was crushed tight against his heart, his throat squeezed shut, the trapped air a scalding fire in his lungs, his eyes bulging with pressure and pain.

It took a few cups of wine before he could find sleep again.

Atellus finished the last of his beer and held his cup aloft. The girl from before scurried over with a jug. He slapped the cup back onto the table and she refilled it for him. A glaze of sweat stood out on her brow. The beer foamed up and over the rim, onto the tabletop leaving a sticky rime against the wood. She was about to leave when he caught her wrist, and twisted it hard at an angle bringing her to her knees by the bench. The jug slipped from her fingers and cracked onto the ground, belching thick fizzing liquid into the straw. She let out a hiss of pain and squirmed angrily in his grasp, but she did not shout out. These girls were used to such treatment, and worse, and the anticipation of coin was enough to tighten the slackest jaw.

Atellus studied the girl's hard blue eyes, the nicks of flesh around her brow, the furrows beside her mouth. She was young, maybe sixteen with pale skin and hair the colour of winter mud.

"Do you know pain?" he asked, softly.

She looked at him uncomprehendingly. The rumble of conversation around the room surged and retreated like the chunter of thunder through a cloudbank. Accents and languages from all across the empire: the brittle flakes of Noricum, the distended vowels of the Bithynian, even the clipped eloquence of the native Roman.

"Here," he said, and placed his other hand delicately on her chest. His fingers could feel the flutter of her heart through the skin. "Loss. Fear. My comilitiones. Do you know them?"

His voice was a tense whisper, a stiletto jabbing beneath the broad strokes of the noise around them.

55

She nodded briefly. "Sir," she said. "Let us go, please. The drink! Tontus will beat me."

"I am the fucking emperor, I *act* for the emperor," he said, calmly. "No one beats you but me, if I so decree." He laughed coldly at the thought.

A few of the topers had stopped singing and were nudging each other, looking towards him.

"How much?"

She told him her price.

"Rooms?" he asked.

She nodded slowly. With a flex of his shoulder, he brought her close to him, furling her into his chest. He pressed a coin into her hand and released the grip on her wrist. She wavered like a loosed sparrow, then gathered to scoop up the spent jug of beer. She beckoned him to follow and led him out through the damp heat and stench of the bar and through the kitchen. She placed the jug on a shelf and took him through a door that led outside. The cold air drenched them, wet snow and half-hail flicking their cheeks. She took him into a small shack with a sawdust floor and a goosedown sack for a bed.

He fucked her angrily, twisting, driving into her. Bruising her, biting. She wept but didn't tell him to stop.

Afterwards he gave her a solidus, enough to keep her away from men for a year, if she so wanted. She lowered her eyes and prostrated herself before him. He watched Julia Faenia looking at him, from a corner of his head. She didn't judge, just considered, studied. There was always sadness in her eyes but never reproof. Sometimes Petronia stood, looped under her mother's arm, her plumsoft face half turned away.

Atellus walked to the river-front, the beer fizzing in his belly and his head. Lanterns clanked and winked from shipmasts. A burning pyre of corpses crackled lazily to his right. The smell of charred pigmeat hung in the air. Beneath it was the scent of fish and salt.

He leaned back against the crumbling murum of an old villa. The building had been ripped in half, the rooms visible in a tumbled cross-section. The interior was charred and daubed with soot. There was a damp, stale, singed smell; cold and frozen by time, the carbon had seeped into the very stones themselves. He could feel tears budding through his eyes, warm against the cold night. The flailing wind sent gusts of wet snow snapping into his ears.

Submerged in his own thoughts, he barely noticed the well-dressed man from the bar leaving and staggering unsteadily down the street. A few calls from the stevedores and whistles from the ragwrapped whores passed the man, but he paid no attention. Atellus noticed the movement in his peripheral vision, as a group of four shades seeped out of an alley to his right and padded towards the drunk.

There was no talk. The first punch, an ugly swing, caught the drunk on the side of his head and sent him down to the shit-spattered street. A kick by one of the others connected with his nose; a scrunch, then a high shriek of pain. The cargo lumpers had fallen silent, suddenly busy at their work, and the whores had melted away into the night.

"*Stop.*" It took Atellus a while to realise the hoarse shout had left his own throat.

The attackers tensed and scanned around them warily. One was on his knees, patting his way through the victim's breeches. Atellus walked out from his vantage point and moved towards the muggers, slowly, deliberately, firmly. He knew he was too drunk to be of much use, but part of him – a large part – wanted to lose.

"Plus cibum," grumbled the tallest of the men. A coarse cloak hung down his back. His head and half of his face were strapped with cloth. A dark leather eye-patch cleaved to the side of his skull. The empty socket which it was supposed to conceal gaped out at Atellus.

"Go now," said Atellus, his voice clear and ringing in the cold air. The pyre burned brightly behind the group, sending tall shadows stretching out to the riverside, like searching fingers. "Go, and return whatever goods you have taken."

"What business is this of yours, nigger?" rasped one of the men. He was shorter than the others and did not stop rifling through the wounded man's pockets even as he spoke. His accent was reedy and Gaulish. "Fuck off back east and bare your arse to the Persian boys."

The others laughed. One spat noisily. The drunk groaned and tried to raise his head off the ground. Patch aimed a kick at his crotch and he sank back to the ground with a grunt.

Atellus watched coolly as two of the men started towards him. Time seemed to slow. He could smell the hairs of the corpses burning by the wharfside. He heard the rasp of a dagger being drawn from a belt; the barking of a dog four streets away; the river-tide slapping against the wooden hull of a pinnace. He felt the cool snowslush on the ground through the thin leather soles of his boots.

The beneficiarius rolled his neck, then clasped his hands together and sent a quick prayer to, the unconquered sun. He was here even though he couldn't be seen; he was everywhere.

Sol would be strong in the morning, just as Atellus would.

He could feel the power running through him. He sniffed in a lungful of the night air, the cold making the inside of his nose sting. It felt good. He almost felt sober again.

As Atellus did before any battle, he envisaged his wife and daughter by his side, and imagined pushing them to safety behind him. He was the only thing between his familia and death, or worse. He had seen enough battle and pillage to know that death was often the greatest mercy afforded to the conquered.

Atellus drew his spatha and felt comfort at the weight of it in his hand. He would not sheathe it again unless it had shed blood: others' or his own.

"Nice sword, catamitus," shouted the Gaul. "I'll use it to take your black balls off. Make a nice pouch out of them."

More laughter.

"I'll need it to carry all this cunt's gold!" he finished.

The two were within ten paces of him now. To his right was a small rodenty-looking man with a dark shifty face and long hair swept back with a leather thong. At his left was a tall man, long and thin like a stretched stake, a palus, with the wooden hilt of a peasant sword smothered in his gripe and a sneer dripping from his pale chops.

Atellus looked, and emptied his mind. His brain unconsciously calculated size, distance, speed, ground conditions, momentum. The Gaul was saying something again but he did not hear it.

Atellus moved without any tells, hurling himself to the left of Palus and bringing his spatha down one handed in a vertical slice which took off the man's kneecap. The blade was sharp, the resistance minimal.

Atellus was on his feet and facing the Rat whilst Palus was still in shock. The tall man collapsed to the ground and began screaming: a high, feminine wail. More dogs barked in response, until there was a cacophony. Voices shouted curses through the night. Palus screeched and wept wordlessly. The Rat was looking uneasily at his fallen mate.

Atellus felt rather than saw Patch coming round to his side to try and outflank him. The Gaul was getting to his feet and drawing a stout, half-rusted gladius. The short blade shone dully in the light of the pyres.

The Rat made a lunge and Atellus took the weight of the dagger on the edge of his sword. He rolled the blade off easily with a curl of his wrist, then danced round to deal the Rat a bone-splitting strike on the back of the head with the flat of his spatha. The small man collapsed onto the ground and lay there shaking.

Atellus watched as his assailant vomited weakly; it stank of mulsum and pinguedo.

Palus sucked in ragged breaths of air and renewed his screams, his voice cracked and hoarse.

Two down, two left.

Atellus knew something was wrong even before he felt himself falling.

He'd forgotten about the drunk; he'd backed up and caught his heel under the prone man's splayed leg, and felt the jolt as his arse hit the wet ground. The impact knocked the wind from his lungs.

There was a mutter of glee above him as Patch dived in to capitalise. Atellus wildly swung his arm in defence and felt the hard cudgel-blow shudder along his bone: the pain rang through him, hot and raw, and sent jagged waves sawing through to his stomach. He'd taken the weight of the blow on the cusp of his ulna.

60

Atellus grunted through the pain and held his spatha up to parry the next strike aimed squarely at his head. He deflected it, weakly, then managed to bring his blade down to block the next at his stomach.

The beneficiarius slithered backwards in the slush, desperately fending off the flailing attacks in front of him. The Gaul came up behind Patch, gladius clenched in his wiry fist, but he had no room to strike whilst his comrade was pounding away at Atellus.

The beneficiarius's sword arm was burning with the effort of the defence; he knew he couldn't withstand it much longer. It was a matter of time before Patch tired and the Gaul stepped in to finish him off with the blade. Patch, looking in the flame-flicked night like the maddened Cyclops of legend, was bearing down on him, his grim socket glowing red in the pre-dawn light, his huge face twisted with rage and exertion. His breath flared out like steam with each exhalation as he drove the cudgel down towards Atellus again and again and again.

Desperate, Atellus kicked out with his right leg and felt his boot connect with his attacker's shin. Patch emitted a grunt, but kept swinging, varying his stroke so it took Atellus all his mental strength to predict the angle of the next attack. He kicked again, wildly, then a third time, a fourth, a fifth. Atellus sensed a pause in the giant's flurry of blows and instinctively rolled to one side, the slush soaking through his tunic, the icy water splashing unfelt against his skin. He scrabbled to his knees and knew he was too late. He intuitively ducked his head but the cudgel smashed into the side of his neck.

Atellus's world exploded in a shower of pain and light. He saw the ground race up to meet his face and felt the mud splash up into his nostrils. There was a shrill whine in his ears, white agony pressing against the backs of his eyes.

He was dimly aware of another blow, on his shoulder blade, and he felt his skin split with the contact. He grunted as the breath was forced from his lungs.

A guttural shout from above; Atellus tensed himself for the anticipated blow to the back of the head. There was no fear or anger – just a strange seeping relief.

Nothing.

Atellus turned himself round, spitting thick, hot phlegm onto the sludge of the roadway. Patch was turned away from him; he was looking towards the drunk they had attacked, who was now on his feet and holding a fine ornate stilletto knife to the Gaul's throat.

The drunk's face was streaked with blood, one eye swollen shut. His clothes were ripped and muddied, his hair dishevelled. But the stout fist clutching the blade was unwavering.

"Move and he dies," panted the knife-wielder. His accent was thickened by his swollen mouth, but it sounded educated, cultured. He spoke the Latin of Treves and Rome.

Palus, hands clutching his severed patella, rolled and moaned in the background as the snow thickened the air around the four men.

Patch stood slightly stooped, his chest heaving, the cudgel still clenched in his fist. His attention was fixed on the dagger at his mate's neck, the point pressed tight into the crook of the Gaul's jaw.

Atellus got to his feet slowly. His neck throbbed and burned, his head felt cracked in a thousand places. In an unsteady, ragged movement he swung up behind Patch and kicked down vigorously at the back of the man's knee. He went down to the ground with a gasp. Atellus flung the hilt of his spatha hard into Patch's temple and felt the crude, solemn weight of the contact. The man dropped as if his bones had turned to water.

Atellus walked over to the Gaul and looked at him. He was sweating profusely, despite the cold. His narrow eyes were red-rimmed and tense, but there was a calmness and acceptance inside them. His face was tilted up, away from the point of the dagger pricking his skin; he couldn't talk without drawing blood. Atellus hefted his sword with a grin and saw the man's eyes bulb with a pulse of fear. He faked a slice at the man's neck pulling it at the last second, then kicking him hard in the crotch. The Gaul sank to his knees with a whine. The dagger-wielder took a small hopping run-up and kicked the Gaul in the side of his jaw, sending him crumbling down on top of Patch. Thin belts of snow started gathering in the crankles of their cloaks.

Atellus walked across and wiped the blade of his spatha carefully on the Gaul's coarsewool cloak. He re-sheathed it, offering a quick silent prayer to Sol, then walked over to the other man. The knife-wielder stretched his hempthick lips into a bloody grin.

"I owe you my life, amicus."

Atellus reached over and the two men gripped wrists solemnly. "Then we are already even," he replied. "Titus Faenius Magnus Atellus."

"Quintus Maximus Peltrasius".

"Well met."

"For me, certainly," replied Peltrasius. "Thank you for your help."

The man's words were slurred, and his faced was streaked with blood and muck, but his one good eye twinkled with an infectious jollity. The first blush of dawn was stippling the rudders of the dark clouds overhead. Somewhere distant in the city a bell was knelling through the crisp air.

"You are welcome," said Atellus. He turned to leave and spoke over his shoulder, the weariness settling on him like a heavy cloak. "Fair travel."

"Et tu, amicus."

Peltrasius went over to the Gaul and rummaged through the trusses of his clothes. The Rat grunted and squirmed in the background.

Atellus looked up to the slugblack bunches of snowcloud overhead. Faenia and Petronia were safe, he thought. Again. He clutched his throbbing neck and walked away towards his lodgings. He was to meet Brocchus at prima. Judging from the light, the most he could hope for was three hours' sleep.

CHAPTER 5

The youth woke up as the first slender finger of sunlight prodded his eyelids. He rose naked, skin pebbly with cold, and kissed the white cheek of the girl lying beneath him, her blonde hair enswathing the pillow and woollen coverlet. She stirred at the touch of his warm lips but did not wake.

The youth shrugged himself into his clothes, his breath misting in front of him. The servants had not yet stirred to stoke the furnaces of the hypocaust three stories below. He heaved aside the thick curtain and opened the door leading on to the balcony. A gust of icy wind squeezed through the opening and the sleeping girl roused with a shiver.

"Calidus?" Her voice was timid and confused.

"I'm here, cara. Shhh." He pushed the door to and dragged a finger across his lips. There was the faintest smudge of golden stubble across his jaw, soft still on his young face.

"It's cold," she whispered. "Are you leaving already?"

He walked across and knelt by the bronze bedframe. He took her small hand in his and spoke low into the curlicue of her ear.

"I must leave now, Marina. I meet my uncle shortly." He squeezed her hand. Her flesh was cold and tight across her small bones. The daylight stretched across the room and burned bronze against her face.

"You were not going to say goodbye...."

"You looked so peaceful," he replied. "And I must hurry."

65

"You will be back soon?" Her brow was furrowed.

"Before the fresh moon, carissima. My word."

He kissed the tip of his forefinger and pressed it to her bosom, then rose and walked back to the balcony door. She said something but her soft voice was lost behind the curtain as he squeezed his way outside, shutting the door softly behind him.

Outside, the stone was slick with ice, a sheer glaze across the masonry. The air was sharp and tight, bitingly cold. A spray of gold light from the bursting sun set sparks dancing across the underside of the fat grey clouds. The rooftops of Eboracum jostled and strained beneath him, the light licking the tile and thatch of a heaving feverish city. Far out, beyond the city walls, stretching up from the horizon like supplicant hands, were twists of dark smoke. They stretched up to merge with the grim clouds, these scabs of ransacked villages and burnt-out farms. The country was hungry and angry and sick.

Calidus turned away and faced the wall of the villa, then leaped up and grabbed hold of the window lintel. An angry scrub of bird's nest was level with his eyes. He pulled himself up onto the roof then ran lightly in a semi-crouch across the tiles to where it butted onto a lower scarp. He leapt onto this, and carried on along the length until the next, dropping a storey with each consecutive building. The roofs changed from tile to timber until he finally thudded onto the compacted mud of the city street.

Calidus dusted strands of sedge from his tunic and cloak, and walked through the stirring streets: past the drunk and the dead curled deep into themselves; past the spent firepits and braziers on the corners, still shimmering with heat.

Here in the Acula, Calidus noted as he walked through the chill morning, things had changed over the past five years. Originally a wealthy suburb of

Eboracum, the area had been an early victim of the last big plague. Wealthy houses died, the population dwindled, and the businesses that relied on them failed. Rents became cheaper, criminals moved in to deal with the black trade from the docks in the Rodam. Slums developed in once grand houses – entire families of refugees coughing and shivering in a single room of previously opulent townhouses – and respectable families, those that still had a solidus to their name, moved out.

Except Marina's family of course. Their wealth was tied up in the river trade, their magnificent villa the envy of even those who used to live in the brick-built estates along the via principalis, and the hill above the principia itself, mons Pinorum. Her father was too old to move now, too set in his ways, and her brothers were abroad making names for themselves serving in the comitatenses. Maybe in another five years the area would become respectable again. But Calidus doubted it: such things seemed to move in one direction only.

The city woke around him. The broad streets yawned into the pale grey light of winter, and people floated along wrapped tight in whatever material they could scrounge, squinting bitterly into the cold air. Some moved with purpose and determination, shifting goods, carrying messages, looting the dead and dying. Others drifted pale-eyed and breathless, hunched and desperate, wafting from gutter to gutter like bobbing corpses on the Isurium: refugees, paupers, beggars; men and women whose wits had been shook from them by toil and pain and hopelessness.

Crispus moved through the throngs, paying them no heed, the streets becoming finer, the buildings less ramshackle, shops and workyards spilling noise and sparks from the terraces. People were already queuing outside the low-rent bathhouse abutting the crumbling south Wall: for many it was the only way they could get warm; especially if they had no money for brothels, taverns or gamehouses. Eventually he hit the via principalis, the statue of Constantine smeared with crude graffiti and black with flies; it stank of piss and faeces. The stones of the base were all but robbed and Constantine's right arm, once raised in splendour and triumph towards the clouds now seemed to point accusatorily towards the ruins of the domus palatini which crested the mons Pinorum. Overhead the sun sent rippling tassels of violent gold across the pockmarked clouds.

Calidus knew he was going to be late.

***

"Have you seen my nephew?" asked Brocchus irritably. He swept into the office of his ab epistulis. Crispus was sitting placidly behind his desk, scratching away at a long roll of vellum. His finger-tips were black with ink. Lying snoring, stretched across a cushioned bench beneath one of the bookcases was his dark-faced bodyguard, Dexter.

"No, sir," said Crispus, calmly without looking up from his work. "Not yet. I'm sure he will not be long."

Brocchus grunted at his secretary. "Not good enough. The rascal always pushes my patience too far."

"And yet you always forgive him," murmured Crispus.

Brocchus seemed to think for a moment. "My brother was a good man."

Crispus nodded. "He was, indeed. One of the best. If only some of his maiesta had rubbed off on young Calidus." He lifted a wad of sponge and used it to blot the ink from the vellum. He dabbed delicately at the smudges. "I'm sure this time on the Wall will do him good."

"We can hope, indeed."

Brocchus looked at the recumbent figure of his ab epistulis's man at arms.

"What's that doing here, Crispus?" he said. "Very untidy. Does it not have a sack it can crawl into?"

Crispus looked over at Dexter whilst he pulled another parchment from the pile at his desk, and wet the nib of the quill in his full lips. They were stained a dark blue.

"Dexter," he said, quietly but firmly.

The man coughed out a snore he was choking on, then turned round and continued.

"Dexter." Crispus raised his voice. The bodyguard grunted and his eyes flicked open. He sat up on the triclinium and blinked his eyes a few times. He got his bearing and snapped to attention.

"Dominus."

Crispus looked at him, then jerked his head towards the door. "Fuck off."

"Dominus." He saluted with a furry forearm across his chest, then left, striding across the deep carpet and through the door leading out to the corridor.

The praetor grunted in approval, then walked out back into his own large office.

That damned joke of a beneficiarius would be here soon, Brocchus knew. Then there was the morning of petitions, the tour of the new temporary barracks in the Borras, the first hearing of the investigation into the grain shortages, a deputation from the vicarius to entertain and letters by the milia to read and write.

And that was all before lunch.

The days were so very long now. And yet never long enough for anything meaningful: the plague, the bandits, the famine, the insurrection in the east, the pirate problem. He could barely scratch the surface of any of them.

There came a rap at the door.

"Enter," said Brocchus.

His bodyguard Gargilianus moved across to the door, opened it and admitted the governor's nephew.

"Sorry I'm late, patruus, I was—"

Brocchus held up a flat palm.

"Silence, Clodius Bassianus," he said tersely. "I don't care, and we don't have time."

Calidus inclined his head towards Brocchus. The governor looked at his nephew: the lad was red-faced and out of breath. He had probably been round at the Cammurius girl's house again. A once mighty family crippled by misfortune and corruption. The house's days were numbered; they would be lucky if their wealth allowed them to see another summer. The daughter would be fortunate to avoid a future working the taverns by the docks. She was not a good match for a Bassianus. This excursion to the Wall could be useful in more ways than he first thought.

"Are you ready to depart?" he asked, raising his chin slightly so that he peered down his tapered nose at his nephew.

"My horse is saddled" said Calidus, meeting his uncle's gaze. "My belongings are packed and in the stable. I am ready."

"Good." The governor beckoned his nephew over to him, then led him across to the triclinium in the corner of the room. It looked out across a narrow balcony, beyond which were the grounds of the principia. Skeletal trees, winterbare, ranged across tough close-cropped grass. Behind, the walls of the principia and the stacked blocks of the city's rooftops stretched beyond sight in overlapping layers. Uncle and nephew sat down next to each other.

"Are you nervous?" asked the praetor.

Calidus laughed. "No, patruus. Excited. Eager."

"Indeed."

There was a rap at the door. Brocchus motioned for Gargilianus to attend. The large man, with his thick red beard a raging fire around his chops, went out, and shortly returned.

"The beneficiarius imperatoris, Dominus."

"Tell him I will see him shortly."

The bodyguard nodded and went back out to the antechamber. Within a few seconds he was back in the room, standing rigidly in front of the door; the veteran's soft, half-lidded eyes gave no hint of the quickness and violence within. He had been with Brocchus for twelve years, an ex-centurion, and a fearsome warrior. The son of an old friend from Noviomagus, Brocchus had protected the man from an investigation into the murder of a circitor from the sixth Legion at the retreat from Durocortorum. Although the circitor would not be missed by the men under his command, he nevertheless came from an influential family who were desperate to nail flesh to wood over the affair. Gargilianus had not forgotten the gravity of the debt, and he was repaying it well. He was a man of honour.

Not like Quintus and Dexter, those two hounds that sniffed around the crumbs of his ab epistulis.

"Life on the Wall," said Brocchus, "is not as it is here." He looked out over the shoulder of the triclinium and towards his city. A smudge of black smoke on the wind drifted past the windows. The plague pyres had started burning again. So early. At times he fancied he could feel the city's laboured breathing beneath his toes, could smell it like a diseased limb.

"I have been to the Wall countless times," he continued. "I have to. It is part of my job." He looked back at his nephew. "I would not go there by choice."

Brocchus pulled out a sheaf of vellum from a fold of coloured cloth within his tunic. He handed it to Calidus.

"This is your letter of introduction. Do not lose it. You are to present it to the praefectus at Aesica, Aulus Ambrosius Germanus Apullius. Apullius will provide you lodging for a while until he can arrange for a detachment to escort you to Petriana."

Calidus reached out and took the missive.

"Once there," said Brocchus, "you will be placed on the staff of the dux Britanniorum, Fullofaudes. He is a good man, strong and hard as the Wall itself. You will learn much from him – by looking; by listening."

"Yes, patruus."

"Bu most of all," said Brocchus firmly, "by *obeying*."

Calidus nodded and lowered his eyes,

"Discipline," said the praetor, "is everything. I have been lax with you. But on the all, you will learn. Punctuality, too."

72

Calidus dropped his head slightly, his cheeks reddening. "Yes, patruus."

"You will be accompanied to the Wall by Atellus, the beneficiarius imperatoris. Atellus is a worthy man. An Easterner."

Calidus nodded.

"But, Clodius Bassianus," continued the praetor, his eyes narrowing, "he is not one of us. He works to his own agenda; not even the emperor has full control over him. He comes from good stock, but disgraced." He lowered his voice and spoke as if to himself. "It may have been better for us all if rumours of his death had not just been rumours."

"But...patruus," said Calidus. "Beneficiarius imperatoris? I did not realise such a position existed."

"These are strange times for us all, Calidus," sighed Brocchus. "And just because something *has* never existed does not mean that it *will* never exist. If Valentinian deems a problem of sufficient import to send a beneficiarius, then we must presume there is some good purpose behind it. Even if the reason the beneficiarius is sent, and the reason he *says* he has been sent are not necessarily the same."

Calidus was silent for a moment. "And do you think," he said to his uncle after a while, "the problem is of sufficient import?"

"If it is, my dear privignus," said the old man, smiling, "then I am finished. He is here to investigate some issues we have been having in the North."

"The children?"

"Yes," said Brocchus, raising a single hoary eyebrow. "Have I mentioned it already? I am getting old, truly."

"Maybe, patruus," said Calidus, looking at the floor. "Perhaps I overheard you talking with Crispus...."

"Perhaps," said Brocchus nodding pensively. Or perhaps he should not underestimate the skills and intrigues of his own blood. The boy's father had always been keen to acquire and use information. Perhaps when this pup grew up, he would be able to put his talents as a sneak and eavesdropper to more useful purposes.

"Ostensibly," he continued, "Atellus is here to find out what is happening to the youngsters. He may well have other duties with which Valentinian has charged him. Find out what you can. Cultivate some loquacity, Calidus. It has got you into trouble in the past, now let it do us both some good." The older man laughed. "He is a closed man by nature, is Atellus, but a friendly ear may encourage him to divulge more."

"I will do my best, patruus."

"Good lad. It may also be the case that he tells you the name of whoever brought this sordid little matter to the emperor's attention. A name. Probably a soldier, or an ex-soldier."

"A name?"

"A name, nephew. That nomine, I would gladly give half of Eboracum for."

The youth inclined his head slightly. "I will do my best."

Brocchus clasped a hand around his nephew's neck and pulled him closer. He placed a kiss on the youth's crown.

"Do your father proud, Lucius Clodius Bassianus Calidus."

The boy looked up and met his uncle's eyes. His gaze was hard and unflinching. "I will, patruus."

Brocchus looked at him and nodded. The older man rose slowly from the triclinium, feeling his knees snap like knots of wood on a fire. His joints ached now, even at the simplest motions. The cold made him throb from his heels to his head, even if it was warm inside.

"Come," said the praetor. "Let us introduce you to our thrusting beneficiarius." He nodded to Gargilianus, who snapped to attention and opened the door.

"Beneficiarius imperatoris," announced the bearded man in a voice like a dying bull. "Titus Faenius Magnus Atellus."

The easterner walked into the room and squinted against the bright sunlight blazing through the balcony windows. His face was sallow and scratched, his eyes ringed with dark flesh, and he carried his neck at a slight angle, wincing with each footstep. He sketched the bones of a bow from the waist and placed his forearm across his chest.

"Ave, Praetor."

"Did you fall out of bed, beneficiarius?" said Brocchus, his mouth a tight line. "I understand those quarters by the river can be very cramped and uncomfortable."

The beneficiarius had a keen mind, Brocchus knew; the dig at his refusal to accept the hospitality would not be lost on him.

"The quarters were acceptable," replied Atellus. "The lawlessness of the citizens I found more disagreeable."

Brocchus grinned inwardly; the slight was repaid with interest.

"Atellus," said the praetor, "this is my nephew, Lucius Clodius Bassianus Calidus."

The beneficiarius looked at the boy, his obsidian eyes calculating and expressionless. He moved forward and they shook forearms.

"An honour," said Atellus.

Calidus smiled and inclined his head. "The honour is mine, beneficiarius. I look forward to augmenting our acquaintance in the days ahead."

Light sparked deep within the dark eyes, and Atellus turned to face Brocchus with the unspoken question.

"Calidus will be accompanying you to Aesica," said Brocchus. "He is to train under Fullofaudes and receive instruction in military leadership. You are a strong soldier, and a man of honour, Atellus. I would entrust my nephew to your guardianship, until you part company at Aesica."

"I will guard him with my life, praetor," said Atellus, tightly.

"Of course you will," replied Brocchus with a skewed smile that failed to touch his eyes.

"You knew Gaius Clodius Bassianus Paterculus, of course?" said Brocchus, addressing Atellus but nodding towards his nephew. "My brother?"

Atellus nodded and turned to face Calidus again. "I fought alongside your father at Vercovicium," he said. "He was a brave man: valiant, ferocious. He died nobly, not paces from where I fought. He was surrounded by mounds of slain Votadini."

Calidus nodded and inclined his head to the ground.

"Perhaps you two can catch up on the long miles north?" Brocchus nodded sternly. "There will be ample time for conversation. Are you ready to depart, beneficiarius?"

Atellus was still looking intently at Calidus, and the youth had raised his head to return the gaze. "I am, praetor. My belongings are at the gate. I require only a fresh horse, and the readiness of your escort."

"Excellent," said Brocchus. He walked past Atellus, and clapped him weakly on the shoulder. His blue eyes were keen, and their wetness diminished slightly. "You will forgive an old man if he does not see you out of the gates? The cold chews up my old bones on these winter mornings. Good luck with your investigations, beneficiarius, and I hope they are fruitful. I plead only that you keep me informed."

Atellus nodded his thanks, then turned and walked out of the office. Calidus, his eyes redrimmed with unfallen tears, stared at his back as he departed.

CHAPTER 6

They slipped from the city with the morning mist, thirteen riders punching holes through the cold and the crowds alike. Illumined by the chill light of the sun, they eased through into the greyness and snow and ice of the countryside.

Atellus rode silent at the back, his wounds throbbing in the cold, his dark hair heavy with thoughts and dew. Brocchus had provided him with an escort of eight legionaries from the Sixth: gristly, dour, well-armed men who rode their horses well and seemed immune to the weather. They were strung out along the pitted stone of the road, like knots along a string. Calidus rode upfront with the Decanus of the contubernium, Valerius Brossicus.

The other addition to their party had been a surprise to Atellus – Quintus Maximus Peltrasius, the man whose life and wealth he had saved the night before beside the frozen wharf. The heavyset man sat beclouded in his own thoughts, his face cut and swollen, and apart from a cursory nod at the outset, they hadn't communicated.

Atellus adjusted himself in his saddle; its leather was worn shiny and it twinkled in the morning sunlight. The fit was tighter than he was used to, and uncomfortable.

He'd checked over his wounds earlier that morning, using a goldleaf-backed glass the innkeeper had loaned to him. He had stared into a face that was scratched and puffy. The flesh around his scapula had been opened up and bled heavily through the night. It had scabbed over by the morning and was fringed by a nimbus of brilliant purple and orange, like a northern sunrise. His forearm was bruised too, though a darker colour, and it ached incessantly in the cold air. He thought maybe the bone was cracked. He'd tried hefting his sword this morning and found his movement was not restricted; a little slower perhaps. But moving it seemed to help the injury. His neck ached and rippled with pain when he moved it too much. He spent most of his ride looking to the ground, watching the endless bleak miles roll past beneath his boots.

Not that there was much to look out on anyway: the landscape was bleak and cold. Except for the occasional sweep of pale gold from the sun fingering its way through cracks in the clouds, everything was a sombre, dark grey. Even the fresh snow was curded a grim sackcloth colour beneath the sulking clouds.

Brossicus, set a hard pace once they had got used to their mounts. The beasts were hardy geldings, but undernourished and skittish, Atellus noted, like much of the Britannic stock.

The riders passed snowswept ruins of old villages; cracked timber and brick, fireblackened and deserted. Fresh tendrils of smoke could be seen shimmering across the horizon, shifting like distant rain on unfelt breezes. Besides the hooves of their mounts, the only sounds were the occasional caws of birds wheeling overhead and sudden crumps of snowfall from nearby copses.

An emaciated deer flashed across the road; one of the legionaries took aim with a sling and the beast staggered as if kicked in the rump, then flitted on fast, kicking up sprays of snow in its wake. The legionaries laughed. Some cursed in their native tongue.

They rode on.

Atellus saw bodies by the roadside. Some half covered with fresh crumbs of graupel, others tossed and dragged by animals into crazed and cursed positions imitating life. No arms, no eyes, no genitals.

"Refugees," one of the legionaries said to Atellus, when he saw him looking. His voice was thick and pebbly. The soldier spat onto the road and said no more.

Atellus wrapped his thick riding cloak around him, and shut his eyes against the angry wind. He remembered this north-country from years before, but he never dreamed he'd be back in the cold and the misery; back among the beaten people and their corrupt leaders desperately clinging onto their bastardised concept of romanitas while the peons starved and revolted and deserted and died around their ankles. Nothing changed. The country was hostile: to itself, to Rome, to everyone. And doomed. The whole empire was doomed, to some extent, though this far away the rot was quick to take hold. If the citizens had an ideal, a concept of civilisation to hold onto, then they might have been able to stave off the decay. But all they knew of Rome was misery, inequity and corruption.

"It seems," said a voice to his side, "I may get a chance to repay my debt after all."

Atellus stirred from his thoughts, and raised his head, painfully, into the spitting snow. The landscape was unchanged. They were riding through the heels of yet another burned village. His nose picked up the odour of damp, charred wood. There were no dead in sight this time.

Peltrasius had ridden up beside him and was looking across at him. His thick fingers were covered in rings and they stroked the mane of his horse absent-mindedly, like twisting burrowing creatures. Perhaps he was trying to warm himself.

"It is already repaid," said Atellus.

"Not so!" laughed Peltrasius. "My act was one of self-preservation. My own wellbeing was inextricably intertwined with yours last night. I did what I did for myself, more than for you, my friend, ashamed though I am to admit it."

Atellus shrugged. "You owe me nothing. Why are you here?"

"Why, the pure enjoyment of it, of course!" said Peltrasius, grinning. "What could be more bracing then a lovely morning ride in the depths of winter?" His good eye glinted.

"Indeed," replied Atellus drily. "All we need now is a party of storm-mad, starved brigands to parley with, and my day will be complete."

"Of course!" The large man laughed again. "My sentiments exactly."

Peltrasius rubbed his nose and Atellus looked over at him. His face was red and covered with cuts. His bad eye was still swollen shut, and frost tinged its edges. His clothes were fine and rich: fur-lined cloak and velvet tunic, bright red with ornate blue plavi and orbiculi. He wore a rimless Pannonian cap which was layered with wolf pelt. His thick golden hair blew across his chops in the wind. He kept plucking strands from his mouth as he spoke.

"I am here," said Peltrasius, "because the governor of Eboracum, in his wisdom, has decided that I should utilise my not inconsiderable expertise in some rather mundane enquiries upon the Wall."

"What kind of enquiries?" said Atellus.

"Trade," said Peltrasius, shouting into the wind. "I am a merchant."

"I would never have guessed," said Atellus drily and Peltrasius grinned into the snow. "But why would Brocchus send a merchant to the Wall?"

"Well," coughed Peltrasius, clearing his throat. "I began in iron. Importing the raw materials for weaponry from Gaul to Maxima Caesariensis. I began low. It was serendipitous really, that my trade coincided with the revolt to the North. You may have heard of it, though I can tell you do not hail from these islands?"

"I fought in it," said Atellus flatly.

"Really?"

Atellus nodded. "Under Lupicinus."

"Then," laughed Peltrasius, "perhaps one of my own weapons found its way into your hands. Perhaps even saved your life, eh?" He chuckled softly to himself.

"Perhaps."

Peltrasius stopped his laughter abruptly. "The fighting was tough, I heard. Lupicinus lost many man."

Atellus nodded. "One man lost is too many."

"Of course, of course," said Peltrasius, shaking his large swollen head. "I began with weapons materials," he continued. "And that took off, thanks to the filth in the north, and so I was able to invest in more prestigious materials. So I imported gold and jewels from Cappadocia and Mauretania. Sapphire, lapis lazuli, tiger's eyes. The finest stones for the wealthiest soldiers. I made weapons for officers; military and bureaucratic. The margins are a lot higher on those."

The merchant's good eye glowed and he tilted his face up to the milky froth of cloud overhead, floating lazily beneath the pale morning sun.

"And then," he continued, lowering his eye to Atellus, "I decided that the market for weaponry was too fickle. And importing materials was too risky, especially with the proliferation of pirates, and land-brigands. I was losing too much in transporting supplies here. So I localised. And dealt in grain."

"There is always need for that," nodded Atellus.

"Of course," the merchant concurred, shaking his head vehemently. "And I did very well out of it, for a few years. Then the blight hit. Bad crops, bad brigands. Bad corruption. I lost half of my capital in paying off the officials, even as the people were starving. I appealed to the governor. He listened to me. Perhaps too well.

"And so here I am," he concluded, somewhat wearily.

"He is sending you to the Wall?" asked Atellus. "As punishment?"

The merchant laughed, a hearty rich sound, full of meat and thick ruby wine. "No, no, I hope not, no! No, he wants me to find out why there is such a dearth of grain up here. How much is getting to the people who need it, how much is lost in raids, how much is paid in kickbacks to the officials and so on. He wants a full report."

"Good fortune," said Atellus, grimacing. "I imagine you will not have a favourable reception up there, asking such questions."

"I have my ways," said Peltrasius, pressing a thick finger against his bruised nose. He leaned over the side of his mount and blew a wodge of bloody snot into the snow.

"Why send you rather than his own staff?" asked Atellus.

"I think we both know the answer to that," said Peltrasius, righting himself in his saddle, his voice a stony rumble. "I am expendable. One way or another, our good governor Brocchus rids himself of me. But do not worry about Peltrasius, my friend. Not again, anyway," he smiled. "I always manage to endure. Perdurabo!"

He righted himself and looked across at Atellus. His gummed up, swollen eye made it look as if he was winking.

"Brossicus mentioned," continued the merchant, lowering his voice, "that you are a beneficiarius?"

Atellus nodded.

"Acting for whom, may I ask?"

"The emperor," said Atellus after a pause filled by the crunch of their beasts' hooves in the snow.

The merchant looked incredulously at him. "The emperor, no less." He gave a low whistle. "You must be on grave business for Valentinian to send you all this way."

Atellus ignored the implicit question and they rode in silence through the late morning. When the sun had reached its zenith − a slight watery pulse of warmth through the clouds above − Brossicus ordered a halt. The legionaries distributed food from wicker panniers lashed to the backs of the pack mules they led. They sat wrapped tight in their cloaks and gnawed at heels of tough bread, their fingers stinging in the cold, noses leaking into their beards. A chock of crumbly cheese was passed around, as was a stained goatskin of fiery mulsum. They ate in silence, the legionaries occasionally swatting conversation across to each other in their own language. A couple squatted down a few paces away from the road and shat into the snow. They crushed ice into their hands and began laving themselves clean before rejoining the group.

Atellus could see the slight figure of Calidus swaddled in his rich cloak on his own. The boy was looked over at him, but averted his gaze whenever Atellus met his eyes. The youth was a complication he did not need here; he'd be damned if he would go out of his way to babysit Brocchus's spoilt pup. He looked away from the boy and out at the landscape. The snow had stopped, but the air was even colder, brittle and sharp. The road was a stony outline in front of them, broad and cut deep into the earth. Snow bulged out of each fossus. He saw one waggon trundle past, the driver a crackfaced old peasant who looked at them with dark, suspicious eyes. His horse was grey with age; it shook in the cold, its chest heaving and expanding with effort. Steam shimmered from its nostrils.

The legionaries shouted over at the peasant and he stopped, sawing at the reins. They growled at him in Brythonic, and he answered them without lifting his eyes from the road in front of him. Two legionaries walked up to him, shaking the snow from their breeches. One of the soldiers laughed and slapped the man across the face; his broad nose bled bright in the white noonlight. The soldiers lifted some rags from the back of his waggon, and helped themselves to a pile of stinking furs on the back. They waved him on, and his woeful horse loped forward, straining at the waggon, panting into the cold air. The old man did not look back nor lift his sad eyes from the road. The soldiers laughed amongst themselves.

The land was wild and hilly around them: stunted bare trees groped out from beneath the snowfall, and sheer sodden crags reared from the greyness like city walls. A tree on the other side of the via dangled dead children from its branches, naked, bloated and blue. Their stomachs hung open, the ropes of intestines half snatched away by birds and climbing beasts.

"A warning," said Peltrasius, who had come to sit next to Atellus. "To the merchants. To the refugees." He leaned closer to Atellus and spoke into his ear; the man stank of sweat and dried blood. His breath was spicy with fresh mulsum. "They will not understand you here, Atellus. Wherefore you are here, they won't care. This is shit land, and the people are shit beasts. They care nowt for the emperor, nor for Rome." He jerked his chin at Atellus. Whereas his eyes usually twinkled with cheer, they were now hard as flint and as cold as the sky. "Even less for you. Things here are not as they are in the east. I know that much, and I am sure you do too. But you are not part of an army now. Be very careful, beneficiarius."

Brossicus shouted an order to continue, and the sounds of chuntering motion filled the crisp air. The merchant heaved himself to his knees, dusted the snow from his cloak, and walked towards his horse. Atellus finished chewing on a breadcrust and watched as one of the soldiers went over to the hanging tree and pissed into the snow. Steam fizzed into the air, and his contubernales barked and laughed.

They rode on hard along the road. They could smell warm smoke in the air and hear shouting, but they pressed on, each enwrapt in their own silence.

The party passed a checkpoint, but it was empty. Stone foundations and timber walls. Brossicus gave the order to halt, then dismounted and went inside. Even from his horse, Atellus could smell the inside: it reeked of shit and blood. The Decanus came out in silence and swung himself onto his mount and they rode on, deeper into the north. Calidus looked pale and scared; he said nothing but Atellus noted he rode a little closer to the others as they moved on.

Screams rose from somewhere across the empty land: shouts like the howls of ghosts rumbling upwards from the unseen horizon. They rode past a child, a boy of maybe five winters, naked and blue with cold, standing at the side of the road. His feet were black. The child looked at them through the large solemn orbs of his oldman eyes and watched dumbly as they rode past. No-one spoke. No-one looked back.

The earth turned dark and they passed through a somnolent grey netherworld, half asleep in their saddles, only the pinching cold keeping them from slumber. They climbed higher and higher up the steeply sloped road, until the wind beat at their cheeks and the undersides of the clouds seemed within their grasp. Atellus saw winks of flame rippling slowly across the far horizon. The lights seemed to blaze into the sky and chase each other across until the horizon burned behind them. After a while the flames disappeared, then repeated. Eventually they stopped.

Atellus rode up to Brossicus and asked him. The commander was short and wide, brown-faced with a thick beard that seemed to obscure all but his eyes and nose. His gaze was steady and keen and betrayed his experience on the limes, the militarised boundary of the empire.

"Signal fires," he said to Atellus, shouting against the savage wind. "From the legate at Eboracum to Fullofaudes in Petriana. A good way of communicating quickly, in either direction."

Atellus nodded. "What do they say?"

Brossicus thought for a while. "They say all is well in the north."

They slowly descended into a welcome calm, where they halted and made camp a mile from the roadside, tucked down against the leeside of a stone outcrop. The soldiers had a single large leather tent which they took from the pack-mule and erected without fuss. Inside they were dry and warm. A fire was made in the centre, which flickered and crackled through the night. The soldiers drew lots for watch, and Atellus lay down fully clothed beneath a fur the legionaries had taken from the waggoneer. Outside the men threw tesserae on wooden boards, shouted and drank. Others prayed to their gods – to Cernunnos, to Mithras, to Anextiomarus – to save them from the beasts of the night. Feral howls whipped into the air, carried far on the wind.

Atellus was woken by the sound of sobbing, hard tugged out gasps, but he could not tell from whence it came. He turned over and tried to sleep through the cold, but his dreams were of his wife and daughter and their absence inside him was more painful than the icy weather railing outside his tent and he wondered if the sobs he had heard were his own.

CHAPTER 7

Atellus woke early and went outside. The weather was dry and calm. He nodded to the legionaries on watch. The fire was a pit of hot red embers, but he could feel its warmth from paces back. There was the faint scratch of light on the skyline, a crimson gash through the bruised flesh of the clouds.

He took out his spatha, a gift from Julian years back. The fine blade of Damascus steel glowed blue through the darkness. Atellus trained through the cold, loosening the knots in his muscles, burning through the ache in his forearm, his back, the tight twisting agony in his cramped neck.

They set off through the dark and the spitting snow, riding towards the daylight pooling like spilt blood on the horizon.

Atellus rode silently through the frozen land, rags of snowflurry eddying across the horizon in front of his eyes. Towards noon, the clouds split, a mighty cleft in the wall of the sky, and a fine glowing blue poured forth, expanding until the day was lemonyellow light pulsing with a biting cold that gnawed through the leather of his gloves.

They rode past another abandoned checkpoint, and the blackened furrows of a burnt village. It could have been years gone, or only days. Snow settled pleasantly in crooks of old walls. The sleek bones of long-dead cattle speckled the near land.

Atellus felt uneasy, bobbing and dipping with the folds of the land; much as he had at sea, with the froth of pirate ships on the horizon and fresh vomit smeared across his lips. There was something insidious about the desolation and the remoteness. The land was too crumpled, all hills and cliffs and valleys; since they had descended from the plateau, it was rare to have a clear view of more than a hundred paces. Even the sky felt too close, a throbbing burden suspended ponderously above his head. In Constantinople, the sky was huge and high and wide, the heavens distant and untouchable. Which was the way Atellus liked it. Here he felt he could reach up and scratch at the soles of the gods' feet. And they could peer down, whisper into his ear; he could almost feel their breath on his cheek, keening in the cold.

Atellus rubbed his eyes. Calidus was riding up alongside him, looking at him. He had almost forgotten that the boy had been with them.

"Are you unwell?" asked Brocchus's nephew. His forehead was corrugated with concern. False or genuine, Atellus could not tell, but he shook his head, and spurred his horse into a trot that took him beyond the lad's gaze.

They lunched in a tight circle, arms wrapped around knees, blankets draped across shoulders. Their breath gathered and commingled like orgiastic spirits in front of their eyes. They ate mottled cheese and cold sciurus-meat that one of the soldiers had fetched with a sling in the morning.

In the early afternoon, wheeling carrion beyond the shoulder of a pristine white hill caught the attention of Brossicus. He sent three men galloping off to investigate. They caught up with them some time later, pale-faced and tight-lipped.

"Brigands?" asked Atellus as he rode up to Brossicus. The commander eyed him sideways and tugged thoughtfully at his thick beard. It was rimed with fine diamonds of ice, the bristles stiff and wiry. He nodded imperceptibly.

"Twenty to thirty, women and children. Heads hacked off and stacked in a cairn by the well. Huts burned through."

"Bleak times," said Atellus. Something was nagging at his mind; a half-formed thought ghosting around at the back of his skull. He couldn't grasp it.

"You don't know the half of it," said Brossicus, looking straight ahead. "*Sir.*"

89

"I've seen more than you think, commander," sighed Atellus. The wind whirred softly against his ears. His flesh was cold.

Peltrasius was the other side of Brossicus; he had ridden up silently. "I don't doubt you, beneficiarius," he said. "I wouldn't swap the harshest winter here for a month in your eastern deserts."

Atellus coughed out a laugh, and waved a gloved hand around him. "Really?"

Peltrasius smiled. "Warm climates disagree with me. At least the cold is honest."

Brossicus nodded. His eyes were perpetually scanning the landscape in tireless saccades, vision flitting from rock to gully to skyline. Occasionally his head would jerk in one direction as his peripheral vision caught some movement. He was either highly-strung, or an extremely good soldier.

"We northerners are born with the ice in our blood," said the Decanus. "As long as we have winters like this, it will never melt."

"I can tell you one thing, Commander," said Peltrasius, leaning closer to Brossicus. "This winter will be worse. Maybe next winter too. Maybe the next ten, or hundred. Those poor bastards back there?" He jerked his large head back in the direction they had come from. "Give it a month or so, but the brigands won't be making the mistake of leaving so much fresh meat behind them. Mark my words."

Brossicus looked at Peltrasius quietly, then cursed in Brythonic and spat onto the ground. "You are an animal, merchant, to say such things."

Peltrasius merely smiled and shrugged. "You will find, my dear Brossicus, that a week without meat or grain would make animals of all of us."

Atellus looked ahead at the thick snow stretching ahead of them. The wind whirred in his ears again.

Whirred.

A surge of heat in his belly, the thrill of adrenaline: Atellus stood up in his saddle and scanned the rest of the soldiers. They were sitting their saddles, shoulders slumped.

"*Shields!*" he yelled, his voice ringing through the air.

Peltrasius squirmed in his saddle to look at Atellus, but then the top corner of his head disappeared, from his eye socket to his scalp. He jerked backwards off his horse and onto the ground; his horse reared, terrified, and kicked at the air. The merchant's foot was caught twisted in the stirrup. Atellus saw Brossicus trying to grab the horse, but the beast bucked and whinnied and galloped away down the road, dragging the bouncing body of the merchant roughly behind it.

The air was filled with a tumult of shouting and the clatter of heavy shields torn from saddle straps. Loud cursing.

Atellus had no shield. He slipped sideways from his mount, rolling off the saddle, making himself as small as possible. He pushed himself into the flanks of his own horse, his cheek pressed tight against the neck, whispering soothing words into its leathery ear, letting it feel his hot breath on its eyes. It was trembling beneath him; he could sense the heat and hot musk rising into the air like vibrations. He looked around for Calidus and saw the boy wheeling his horse backwards and forwards, fear writ large across his smooth features. Atellus cursed and darted out, grabbing the horse's muzzle strap and dragging the beast over to where his own skipped nervously. He reached over and pulled Calidus down from his saddle; the boy fell untidily into his arms and Atellus pushed him down to the snow.

Brossicus was yelling orders for formation. Atellus could feel his body tensing, anticipating the impact of the next slingshot. He closed his eyes. Beneath the confusion around him, he could hear his mount breathing heavily, the panting of the boy beneath him and the distant hoofstrokes of the merchant's fleeing horse.

There was no sound of a wound-up sling; no whirring, no taut leather whipping through the air.

Atellus stepped away from his steed and looked around him. The soldiers were crouched behind their oval shields, half burrowed into the snow and mud. Calidus had got to his feet and was squeezed up against the broad, warm flank of his horse. Brossicus was bellowing orders to two of the legionaries. Atellus followed the commander's gaze: about a hundred paces away was a gnarled copse of frozen crackwood trees that would provide ideal cover for a slingsman. Icicles like slender daggers hung from the scabrous branches.

A couple of the soldiers advanced through the knee-deep snow towards the copse, hunched behind their shields, spathas drawn and held at their sides. Horsebreath and manbreath mingled in the still air. Atellus could feel the sheen of sweat on his beast's coat. He patted its muzzle. The dying sunlight twinkled red in the snow like a thousand shattered rubies.

The soldiers reached the copse and disappeared from sight. The remaining men fidgeted nervously and coughed. A couple laughed, the tension seeping away into the air. After what felt like a long time, the two legionaries could be seen running awkwardly through the deep snow, shields on their backs. They reported to Brossicus.

"Mount up," said the commander, "let's ride."

Atellus heaved himself back onto his saddle and trotted up beside Brossicus.

"Well?"

"No trace. Prints of two men, heading back through the snow. Pile of slingshots. Lead."

"On foot?"

Brossicus nodded tightly.

"Why don't we follow them?"

"It could be a trap," he replied. "Lead us into an ambush, or a pitfall. I've seen it happen. Shallow stakepits, overlaid with branches, covered by snow. Men crushed under the weight of their horses, driven deep onto the stakes." He shook his head wearily. "My orders are to get you to the Wall. Not to hunt brigands."

They tracked the prints of Peltrasius's horse for a mile. They could see where the merchant had been loosed from the stirrup, the snow crushed and smeared under the weight of his body, the hot red blood burning deep furrows into the ice. His body had been dragged off into the woods. Brossicus refused to send a man to follow it. The horse's tracks disappeared another mile further on, the prints veering away off the road and into the deeps of a winter forest.

They carried on riding, and no-one spoke.

The light was dipping to a dull violet when Atellus noticed Brocchus's nephew riding alongside him. The youth stared down at the bobbing head of his steed. He didn't smile.

"I saw his head cave in," said Calidus after a while. "He wouldn't have survived that. Would he?"

Atellus looked to the youth. His golden hair was matted and stained with travel, sweat and firesmoke. The soldiers shaved in the morning — a knifeblade scraped raw cross skin with meltsnow to soothe the burn — but Calidus boasted a grainy thatch of dark hair across his jaw. His eyes glinted less fiercely than when he had first seen him in Eboracum.

"Better for him if not," Atellus replied.

"I...I didn't know a sling...a slingshot could do that...," Calidus continued. "I mean, I know in war they are used. But I just thought of pebbles bouncing off leather. But...but the merchant..." He shook his head. "He was lifted out of his saddle. The...the *force*."

Atellus was silent for a while. "Slingsmen are to be feared. A good one can strike a man's eye with a pointed lead glans from a hundred paces. It can pierce armour. Smash through bone. You won't see them coming, unlike arrows. And they're mostly silent."

"You knew, though," replied Calidus, raising his eyes to meet Atellus's.

Atellus nodded. "I heard the funda being wound up. I shouldn't have. Maybe he was testing the weight; an amateur." He shrugged, feeling the tension in his shoulders. "A lucky shot."

"I didn't realise armies used slings as weapons anymore."

"Rome doesn't," said Atellus. "Too primitive. Barbaric. But the brigands, peons, farmers. The sling is their weapon. And they tend to be good at using it."

"Why the merchant?" asked the youth.

Atellus thought for a minute. Why the merchant? There was a possibility that the missile had been intended for the beneficiarius imperatoris: cast by one of

Brocchus's men even. Or maybe it had indeed been for Peltrasius, and someone didn't want him asking rude questions about grain. Brocchus, again? Or someone from the Wall, even.

He mulled it over and ruled out the governor. If Brocchus had wanted either of them dead, their honour guard could have done it in a blink, and their bodies never found.

"If it was a lucky shot," he replied, "then it could have been any one of us. Or none of us. Otherwise...the merchant probably looked the best out of us all, the richest. His clothes were opulent. They probably thought the guard was solely for him. A high-ranking official, maybe."

They made camp that night in a snow-dusted clearing, underneath the corpse of a huge tree, its sprawling roots clodded with frozen earth like a huge canopy above their heads. The men wrapped themselves in blankets and dived into the leather tent. Brossicus didn't allow them a fire, and they shivered and drank sweet mulsum huddled three to a blanket for warmth. Soft pale snow fell on the tents and animals shrieked through the clear night. Sleep was a long time coming for them all.

Atellus drew the second watch and stared into the burning cold of the night air as the milky coin of the moon gaped down at him. He flexed his fingers in his gloves and felt for his spatha and thought back to his parched deserts of the east with the sun a molten ball at his neck and the sweat beading and evaporating on his brow.

***

Calidus woke.

Although it didn't really feel like he had ever been asleep; merely mumbling and huffing warm air up into his nose and clenching his fingers in his armpits.

95

He looked around him; the two soldiers were gone, as was their heat. He thought back to the events of the night: he could tolerate the mumbled comments about his arse, and the cracked laughter snaking through the cold with the wisps of their breath. But when he'd felt someone's hand fumbling violently for his crotch, he'd bitten back a yelp of disgust, and peeled himself out from under the blankets. He had gone outside, grappling his way through weariness and the scratching ache of the cold air, and relieved the beneficiarius from his watch. When Calidus in his turn had been relieved and staggered back to his tent, the legionaries were snoring loudly, curled into tight bundles next to each other. He'd tentatively lain down and felt his eyelids falling shut.

Perhaps he had slept, he admitted. He had dreamt, at least. Marina had been with him, wrapped small and soft in his arms, her hair like warm silk against his throat. He was hurting; he couldn't tell why. He looked down, and his hands were black and rotting. He tried to scream, but his tongue was thick and swollen in his mouth, choking him. He looked to Marina for help, but instead it was the horned god of the north staring back at him, eyes a dark yellow and muzzle coated with fresh blood.

Then he'd woke, his fingers numb, the pre-dawn dark pressing deep against his mouth, and he had shivered and wept through the remaining night.

And now it was light, and the air was thick with the sounds of movement. He got up, dragging his cloak tight around his shoulders, and squeezed himself through the leather slit into the bright world outside. The sunlight was a glorious golden lake across the fresh snowfall. He squeezed his eyes shut and rubbed his temple to ease the pulse of pain and tiredness radiating out from the back of his neck.

A soldier hauled a rations-pack onto the back of his horse, and winked at Calidus, then barked out a laugh which peeled off into a lung-cracking cough. Calidus walked away to relieve himself behind a tree. He shivered violently as his piss sent steam hissing into the air.

"A-mornin, tyke."

Calidus looked around. One of the soldiers he'd shared with last night was next to him. A stringy, lean man, with pale freckly skin and angry red hairs across his arms and jaw. His eyes were a dirty green, like leaf mulch in a puddle, and he bore a crooked scar across his cheek which ended in a half-stump of a nose. He was looking at Calidus expectantly, his mouth twisted slightly in what he took for a smile. A few cracked tiles of teeth jutted out from behind the thick lips. Trentius, he thought his name was.

"Salve," said Calidus. He looked away and focused on his urine steaming into the snow. It turned the fresh white a bilious yellow. He was conscious of Trentius examining him, standing, looking. His skin itched, but he resisted the urge to scratch.

The soldier fumbled his cock from inside the heavy layers of his breeches, and pissed up alongside Calidus.

"Think you better'n us, eh, tyke."

Calidus heard the words tumbling around in his ears, trying to decide what the man's intent was. Was he dangerous or just sharing banter? Testing him out?

"No," said Calidus. He shook off and tucked his penis away.

"Ah but y'do."

Trentius turned round, his cock spraying warm piss onto Calidus, and grabbed at the youth's crotch with a large claw. Calidus gasped with pain; the grip was tight like straps of iron wire. Only a fold of cloth protected his balls from the soldier's talons. Trentius forced the boy down to his knees in the snow, piss spattering hotly off his tunic. The stream became a trickle, then died away into leaking drops.

"Thing is, tyke, you can be mine. Right now, if a could be arsed. Later, mebbe. Somewhere warmer, mebbe." He laughed. Calidus squirmed under his grip, but the grasp tightened and he moaned in pain. "There's others there, not as gentle as Trentius, ysee? Bitta fresh quim like yous all they dream about up on the Wall." Trentius laughed again. "By fuck, itll be weeks before ye can shit w'out cryin, tyke."

"Please," grunted Calidus. Tears were squirming from the corners of his eyes. He looked around but no-one was paying them any attention. "My...my uncle–"

"Governor fuckite can't do shit up there, tyke. He wonna be savin you from the animals up on the Wall." Trentius brought his face down to Calidus's mouth, and sniffed at him with his one nostril. Calidus squeezed his eyes shut. "I'd be a fuckin wet dream compared to them, tyke. A could look after you. Hm?"

Trentius lolled out his tongue and licked the side of Calidus's cheek, tasting his tears. He laughed. His grip on the youth's crotch softened, and turned into a rub, a grope.

"Up, soldier."

The voice came from above. Calidus opened his eyes; Atellus was standing over them, looking down.

"No time for fornication," said the Easterner. His tone was light, but his eyes were obsidian, shining through the pale morning sun.

Trentius cleared his throat. "Jus helpin youngsta twis feet. Sar." He rose and stretched out a hand to Calidus. The youth ignored it, and scrabbled backwards in the snow, getting untidily to his feet. Trentius sniffed and spat. He looked up at Atellus, tucked his damp cock into his trousers, and walked off towards the horses.

Calidus looked down. There were tears in his eyes; of fear, of relief. Shame. The wind blew cold against Trentius's slime on his cheek. He scrubbed it off with a cuff then walked past Atellus and made for his own horse.

They rode on, opening holes through the icy air around them, the steeds lolloping wearily across the rough, tussocky landscape. The once-bright sky now seemed dark and sombre, like a gauze drawn across the sun, filtering and choking the daylight.

Calidus kicked his horse into a canter and rode up alongside Atellus. He loitered in silence for a while.

"Thank you."

Atellus looked over at him, and nodded, but said nothing.

The road gradually became hardier, the surface metalled beneath the snow. Calidus could feel the difference through his horse's hooves. They passed mileposts thrusting through the snowfall like monstrous stone phalluses. He noticed the first few grave markers lining the flanks of the cursus. They were moving into romanitas, away from the untamed wilderness and into the embrace of civilisation. He breathed easier. The sun lilted and danced off low clouds once more.

"Where are you from?" asked Calidus, looking across to the dark-skinned man beside him.

"East."

"Greece?"

"Constantinople."

"A great city, they say."

Atellus remained silent, staring ahead.

"I have wanted to travel east," pressed Calidus. "I want to see the great cities of the empire."

"You will need to be quick," said Atellus softly.

"Why?"

The beneficiarius shook his head, but did not elaborate.

"Treves, and Rome," said Calidus. "Alexandria, if the waves left anything behind. Constantinople. Londinium, even. I have heard that it is a fine city."

"The cities of Britannia are choked," said Atellus. "Dirty, crumbling, infested, ridden with bandits and bodies. They weren't so, many years ago. But you have missed the best of this island. As have I."

"How did they used to be?" Calidus was disturbed at the thought. Eboracum was all he had known: its towers and stone houses stretching tall into the sky; the principia, causing peons and travellers to crane their necks up in awe; the massive encircling walls, and the bath-houses and brothels serving people from miles in all directions. He had grown up amongst the throb and bustle of the market in the crisp mornings, pinched his nose shut against the stench around the docks, and watched the dawn mist drifting up like shades from the filthy skin of the river Isurium.

"Vast and clean," said Atellus. "The wondrous cities. New houses and temples built each week. Food enough for all. Ever expanding. Now our oppida contract, and shiver under the weight of the poor. People used to be content, and happy. Maybe somewhere, they still are. But I haven't met them. Not in many years."

They rode in silence for a while. Up ahead the soldiers laughed and whistled and farted.

"Uncle says you used to be a soldier," said Calidus to break the silence. There was no response, so Calidus continued. "Where have you fought? In the East?"

"The East, the West. South and North. All over."

"You fought alongside the emperor?"

"Says your uncle?" smiled Atellus. "Let him sniff and scratch for his secrets himself, boy. Don't sneak and snipe for Brocchus. It is bad for the cambia."

They rode on whilst an easterly wind whipped in fresh spits of cold rain. It soaked their clothes and sent chills down their necks. They broke for lunch and spread out, the soldiers gathering around a felled tree, Atellus and Calidus sheltering in the lee of tumbled mass of stone at the base of a hillside. They ate hard bread in silence at first, until the beneficiarius broke it.

"I fought alongside the emperor," said Atellus, speaking over the soughing wind. "Under Julian. A great man. The empire wept when he died. Now he is all but forgotten." He shook his head sadly and chewed on his food. "He united the army, inspired loyalty, fealty, by his deeds and actions. He fought against taking the purple, clung to his role as Caesar, until the men thrust him onto their shoulders. Death or glory. The purple usually means both."

"My father told me stories of Julian" said Calidus, "when I was young. He was a mighty warrior, tall as a giant and with a flaming sword that melted through armour." He sketched an imaginary strike across his chest. He could almost feel the power in his hands. No-one could get near him with such a weapon.

Atellus laughed. "He was shorter than I, Julian, and his sword was Damascus steel, no different from mine. But he was a great warrior," he nodded, "a formidable fighter. And even better, a great leader. A tactician."

Brossicus rose and stirred the men to move again. All were tired and sore and cold. Atellus rose, and Calidus got wearily to his feet. The world lurched in front of him, and a swell of dizziness passed over him.

"What is your name, again?" asked Atellus.

"Calidus."

"Are you hungry, still?"

"Very."

Atellus produced a shrivelled apple from underneath his tunic. It was bruised. He threw it to Calidus, who snatched it from the air with his left hand, and tore into it hungrily. The apple was dry, but juice ran down his chin.

"Scaeva, I will call you."

Calidus swallowed, then looked away. "Don't say that."

"It is true, though."

Calidus remained silent. All the taunts and beatings from his youth surfaced like pestilent bubbles. The sinistra, the laeva. The left-handed freak, the evil omen.

"Mater beat me for it," said the boy. "My brothers too."

"Not hard enough, it would seem."

Calidus looked at the beneficiarius. Was there a trace of a smile? He was squinting into the sleet. They started walking over to their horses.

"I bear my sword and stylus in my right hand. What more must I do?" He took another bite of the apple. It caved soggily into his mouth. He chewed the pulp and swallowed. "Mater said I was their doom, their burden. A bad omen."

"Where are they now?"

"Dead. All dead." Calidus chewed thoughtfully. It had been a long time since he had missed any of them. Mater raped and murdered by soldiers paid for by the Martinus family, his uncle's adversary to the praetorship. Two brothers dead, young, from sleeping sickness, and another from drowning, swimming in the Isurius. Another brother dead at war, and a fifth, the firstborn, in the riots following Paulus Catena's investigations.

"Then she was right, Scaeva," said Atellus. "You were a bad omen."

Calidus finished his apple by crunching through the core. He looked across at the beneficiarius, and spat a few pips onto the snow.

***

They mounted and set off as the high watery sun bleached the landscape around them. The metalled road became firmer and wider. They stopped at a checkpoint along the cursus publicus and Brossicus dismounted and hailed the sentries. A man clad in bastard armour, boiled leather and half-rusted segmentata staggered out and winced at the daylight. He walked over to Atellus and Calidus and demanded their papers. He stared at the parchments hard, scrubbed his unshaven jaw. Even from his distance, Calidus could smell the sweet fug of acetum and stale sweat emanating from the guard. He handed the papers back without a word and waved them on.

"That man couldn't read," he overheard Atellus telling Brossicus as he approached his horse. "Some would consider literacy a useful skill for a customs guard to have."

The commander shrugged, spat into the snow and set his steed to a trot.

Inside the militarised zone approaching the Wall, Calidus felt the hum of civilisation hanging in the air. There were roadside shacks and shops, both timberbuilt and drystone, at first speckling the roadside sporadically and then becoming closer and closer together until whole strings of huts lined the road. The road hummed with the clack of traffic: carts and waggons full of sutlers and refugees with their meagre possessions bound tight in skins and blankets. Endless lines of hungry eyes and swollen bellies; children with bowed heads that seemed too large and heavy for their slender necks.

Mounted soldiers clopped past, nonchalant and stern-faced, handing goatskins back and forth across their mounts and caressing the hilts of the swords laid across their pommels. They nodded acknowledgements to Brossicus as he passed. Some asked for news from the city, which the commander imparted in few words. Their horses were ragged and angular, all bone and taut skin; the men themselves were little different. Their clothes were wound baggily around them, their armour a queer patchwork of leather, wool, and rusted hamata, the links half missing, helmets with full-face dryskin masks that looked exotic and evil.

Tumescent villages sprouted from the snow laden hills, peat smoke from chimneys curling into the air rich with clangs from smiths and laughter from inns. A dilapidated bath-house lurched awkwardly into the camber of the road, and as Calidus rode past a naked boy burst out, crazed with fear and slick with dark blood. He fell into the snow. A tangle of men spun out through the doors, and set upon him, twisting him over and dragging him back inside by the ankles whilst he wept and wailed and scraped for purchase at the snow.

They rode on, the dipping sun at their shoulders, and the silhouette of the Wall rising like an endless flat-topped mountain ahead of them.

"The Great Wall, the endless frontier of the empire," said Atellus. Calidus had not noticed him pull back alongside his own horse. "Now would be a good time to pray to your gods, if you have any."

CHAPTER 8

Aurelia woke into darkness, as she had every day recently. The windows had been boarded shut, the fat iron nails sealing the wooden planks tight against the walls. Her bedroom had never been plush and opulent – such things had never been to her taste – though compared to how it looked at the moment, it had been the epitome of luxury. Now it had been converted very efficiently into a serviceable gaol cell: all the furniture had been cleared out, and the rugs and wall-hangings removed. There was no mirrored glass, no chairs, no stools, no cushions, no blankets. Just a dull copper bowl for her ablutions. It had been emptied just once so far; the stench was unbearable. Yesterday, for the first time in a long time, she had offered up thanks to the gods that it was not summer.

Her husband had no stomach to kill her, at least not yet and not while he thought there were more uses to which he could put her. Her captivity and disgrace had to be kept a secret for the moment, so he could not just toss her into the city dungeons; his own disgrace would be unbearable. No, Aurelia had no doubt that she could count her remaining days on the fingers of two hands. It was only a matter of time before she met with an accident, and the illness she had been suffering from – as she had no doubt Crispus was giving his colleagues as the reason for her absence from society – finally claimed her. There would be no expense spared of course: tears and grieving from the professionals, commissioned threnodies backed by the throb of a cornu, and within a week or so Crispus would be openly bedding some slut from the Pinorum.

For the moment her main role was keeping his pets sweet, those Saxon beasts Quintus and Dexter: they had free use of her whenever they desired.

And that was often.

At first she had fought wildly, kicked out, snapped her teeth, spat and scratched like a cornered vixen. But she grew weary of fighting: all it did was cause her more pain, more beatings, gave them more sport, made them laugh more. So for the last few days she had just lain, eyes closed, stiff as a board whilst they grunted and pounded on top of her, behind her. She would not moan, would not cry. She squeezed her eyelids tight to keep the tears sealed in. She would allow them no satisfaction. They could take her flesh, but not her spirit. It was a small victory, but all she had.

Aurelia opened her eyes. Her left was still sore and swollen half-shut from yesterday's beating. Thin slats of greyish daylight streaked through the sides of the boarded-up windows. She could hear the rumble of the waking city outside.

Aurelia rolled out of her bed; the bronze-fitted timber bedframe had been left in the room, but her silk and down covers had been replaced by a coarse blanket of sacking stuffed with damp straw from her husband's stables. It smelled faintly of urine, and it made her itch. She woke each morning with red welts across her arms and legs. But without it she would have frozen. The nights were as cold as they had ever been.

She dressed in her shift, and put stockings on her legs. The dull light leaking into the room spread a little more, the noise from outside getting louder. She knew it was nearly the hour at which they would allow her to break her fast. She sat cross-legged on the rough wooden floor and waited in front of the door.

At first Crispus had allowed her no food. For the first two days. Only sips of soiled water, thick with phlegm from the Saxons. They laughed as they handed it to her, and she gulped greedily at it through parched, cracked lips. She was delirious with hunger. She heard sounds, voices of men in the cell with her. The emperor, praising her beauty, her guile, her cunning. Atellus, her eastern relief, her exotic deliverer – and she would have spat now at the thought, had she the saliva to spare

– grasping her arm fiercely, his eyes tight with withheld pain. He called her a whore, he slapped her. Her father, long dead Aurelius claiming he was proud of her, oh so proud, as proud as he would be of any son.

She had wept a lot at first, but the tears soon dried and she realised there was nothing left to expel. It only left her more dehydrated, more desperate with thirst.

Then Crispus had made his visits, with the questions, and the curl of his full lips. His smell sickened her: the stench of lavender powder, and oils, his fingers laced with sharp-scented unguents. His clothes mocked her, his fine soft shirts of sea silk and his velvet tunic seeming to pulsate in her drab world, almost unreal in their vibrancy. All she knew was the grey walls enclosing her, the sombre daylight through the cracks in the boarded-up windows, the dark wood of the flooring. There was no colour in her life: it existed only in its absence as though all joy and light had been leeched from her world.

He had come and interrogated her with a contemptuous complacency. He had given her an infusion of poppymilk to drink to take the pain from her flesh and loosen her tongue, but she had only slept and woken to the emptiness. In the days that followed, she had drunk the papaver often. It gave her pleasant waking dreams, and took the pain away from her encounters with the Saxon animals. But the last couple of days she had stopped, instead spitting the juice into her chamber pot.

She had made mistakes, she knew that. Otherwise Crispus would not have known. *Could* not have known. She had underestimated him, and she of all people knew how dangerous a man was her husband.

Aurelia shifted herself slightly on the wooden floor, and emptied her mind of thought and pain. She spoke with her father, her mother Camilla and the genius of the city, to ask for advice and help, to discuss options and suggestions. She occasionally heard from the spirits of her ancestors, long lines stretching back into forgotten ages and lands, from foreign shores where the earth was hot and bare and women and men alike died young; back further still, beyond, to when all people were fat and happy and peaceful. She saw faces sometimes – sometimes distant resemblances to her, ofttimes nothing alike – sometimes friendly, sometimes hostile, but always helpful.

Aurelia concentrated on her father, and sent the other images and voices back, swiping them aside in turn until they diminished, all except the proud Aurelius, and the great growling throbbing city that surrounded her, enveloped her, her father's city, the eternal city: Rome. *Her* city. She basked in the presence of her father, the rasp of his stubble, the scent of the sweat on his hair, the honeyed wine on his breath, the stiff tendons along the backs of his hands, the fall of the drape of his red-bordered ceremonial toga, and the sweet aching blue of his sad sad eyes.

She concentrated and breathed the image in and hugged her dead father and took courage and warmth from his embrace, and soon he was gone and she was alone and cold and aching in her dismal cell.

After a while, she was roused by the sound of footsteps outside her room and she knew, finally, it was time.

Aurelia felt her fists clenching reflexively. Her jaw was tight. Her heart thumped painfully in her throat. She felt the prickle of sweat on her brow.

The clack of the key thrust into the keyhole, the squeal of the metal turning against the wards of the lock.

The door opened from its jamb with a dull thud and she squinted as the torchlight from the corridor flared through, silhouetting the broad figure in the doorway. The door was pushed shut, and her world became grey again. There was the heavy tread of boots on the floor, and soon she could smell the man above her; rancid breath, stale sweat and a dark and heavy menace.

He put the wooden bowl of slops on the floor by the end of the bed. Aurelia's stomach growled and she was overcome by faintness, but she squeezed her nails into her palms and the flood of pain washed the sensation away. She rose softly to her feet.

"Where is my water?" she asked, her voice hoarse. Her voice felt odd and foreign in the room. Maybe she hadn't heard it for a while. Only screams and howls. Then the safety of silence.

"You broke the jug, remember, you dumb slut?" he growled. "No water for two days."

She felt a savage jolt of fear in the pit of her stomach. She made a move towards the slops. Quintus grabbed her head with one hand and pushed her back onto the floor.

"After," grunted Quintus. His mouth was an ugly purple gash across his face.

"I... I'm glad it's you, Quintus," she said, softly.

He seemed confused.

She walked slowly up to the Saxon. He stood two hands taller than Aurelia, and almost twice as wide. It had felt as though he were ripping her in two when he first entered her that day in her husband's interrogation chamber. She had bled for days afterwards. It still hurt to piss.

She put her head against his chest and her hand up to his cheek. Up close he reeked of garlic and mulsum. She had to stifle a retch. She had to do this. It was her only way of fighting; it was all she had.

"I can make you very happy, Quintus," she said, her voice catching slightly on the words. "It doesn't just have to be one-sided."

He coughed, then spat against the wall. "What you after, bitch?"

She lolled and made herself unsteady on her feet as she pushed away from him.

"Just a little more papaver," she said. "Just a little more each day. It helps."

Quintus grabbed her long hair in one meaty fist and twisted her head down. She whimpered and let out a howl.

"You are lucky that your husband gives you what he does, whore." He spat into her face. The phlegm was thick and warm against her eye. "You'll need more than that juice to forget about me." He used his free hand to undo the buckle of the strap holding his breeches.

"Please," she said, her voice strained with pain. She almost thought she could hear strands of her hair popping free from her scalp. "There are things I can do. Acts Crispus has trained me in. I have learnt much. I know you would understand, not Dexter. You are more intelligent than him. I thought he would not be able to...appreciate...my skills."

Aurelia felt the grip on her hair relax, slightly. She breathed with relief.

"Tell me more," said Quintus, his eyes narrow with suspicion.

"I don't need to tell you," she replied. "I can show you."

Aurelia rose to her full height and gently pulled Quintus's head down. She met his lips, cold and meaty, with a kiss, forcing her tongue through. She could taste the garlic and wine, and the lingering fug of his breath. She fought her gag reflex and felt his tongue in her mouth, fat and intrusive. She broke away, and fell backwards onto the awkward cloth of her bed. She beckoned him on, and he shuffled forward, his trousers coiled round his ankles, a lascivious smile twisting his lips.

Aurelia pulled him down onto the bed and kissed him again. She gestured for him to lie flat. She reached down with her small, cold hand and kneaded the man's thick penis. He let out a groan, and his eyelids softened, heavy with pleasure. She straddled him, sitting on his stomach.

"Can we come to an arrangement, Quintus?" she asked. "The papaver."

He grunted. It could have been an agreement, or a negation. It didn't really matter.

She deftly climbed on top of him then bent down to kiss him again, her eyes closed, her heart pulsing heavily in her breast, her stomach twisting and roiling. She slid a hand under the rolled blanket which served as her pillow and pulled out the crude shiv, its blade a jagged shard of broken pot wound tight round a wooden handle with twists of her own hair.

She pulled it out, and punched it hard and deep into Quintus's throat.

His eyes erupted, round and bulging, bursting pale from his dark face. She felt the huge muscles of his trunk tense between her thighs, but she threw her weight onto him, driving the blade deeper into his neck, heaving it back and forth cutting a ragged and ugly furrow in the flesh, feeling the resistance of tendons and the gristle of his windpipe. Aurelia wrenched the blade out of him, and thick spumes of blood coughed from the wound. He bucked like a wild horse, and she was flung off the bed, the shiv spinning out of her bloodslick hand and across the room. Aurelia fell hard onto the cold wooden floor, hitting her kneecap against the corner of the bed; she hissed with pain.

Quintus was making ugly choking sounds; his large hands were pressed to his throat, and his eyes blazed wildly and rolled back into his head as he kicked and bucked himself up from his prone position. He swept himself off the bed, blood jetting and spurting from between his large fingers. His trousers were still crunkled around his ankles and he tripped, falling forward and thudding heavily against the floor, an ugly crackling noise coming from his ruined throat.

Aurelia ignored the pain in her knee, and dived onto the man, digging her knees into his back, and grabbing his head, pulling it backwards, the blood surging across the floor, heavy fountains of gore, hot and desperate against her hands. She pulled and heaved backwards, clawing her fingers deep into his eyes, feeling the soft bulbs of them, squeezing digging pulling pulling pulling. Her muscles raged against her, aching and burning furiously, her head spinning.

A crack, like a breaking twig, and the huge man tensed again beneath her. She tried to let go of his head, but her fingers were stuck deep in his eye sockets. She wiggled them free, feeling her stomach pulsing wildly. She fell back off Quintus, his neck still pumping blood onto the floor, and vomited. It was mostly bile, hot and yellow and painful to expel. Beside her, the heels of the dead man drummed a morbid tattoo against the floor as his muscles twitched and released.

Aurelia scrubbed a hand across her mouth, then got to her feet, trembling with adrenaline and exertion. She felt clear-headed. Her hands and forearms were covered with Quintus's bright blood, warm and greasy. The room was filled with the coppery stench of it.

She knew she didn't have much time. But there was something she still had to do.

She walked across the room, and picked up her shiv. It had held well: the jagged pot sherd was from the water jug she had broken on purpose two days before. The handle of wood was a large splinter she had managed to work from the planks fastened against the windows. She had used the pot sherd to sever a few strands of her long hair, which she had twisted for strength and wound tight, over and over, looping and twisting until the blade was tight and immoveable at the end of the handle.

Aurelia walked over to the corpse of the Saxon, swallowed hard, and took the red-soaked blade to Quintus's genitals. She sawed and dug and hacked until his penis came off, a slab of shrivelled and pathetic meat, and she stuffed it into his mouth, using her fingers in his nostrils to lever open his jaw. She wouldn't be able to say a personal goodbye to Dexter, so she hoped this would suffice.

Aurelia moved to the door. Quintus hadn't locked it behind him. He never did; no doubt he never thought for a second that she would be able to get past him.

She put her ear to the door and listened. Nothing. She opened it slowly and looked out into the corridor. It was empty. She ran across to the next room, which was her old maid Lepida's quarters. She had disappeared the day before Crispus had sat her down in his study for that queasy conversation. No doubt Lepida would be found bloated and pale somewhere downstream of the city.

Aurelia tried the handle, leaving blood smeared across the wooden grip, and the door opened. She scanned the room quickly: empty.

She went inside and stripped naked, then rifled through her maid's wardrobe. There were some loose-fitting clothes, heavy winter garments, hanging from hooks within. She wound the undergarments round her, pulled on the thick stockings, and slid into some coarse winter breeches. Lepida had used them when she needed to purchase goods from the Rodam, disguising herself as a man to seem less vulnerable. The only women to be seen in the docklands were whores and cutpurses, and both were fair game to the me who lounged outside the taverns and spat and fought and collapsed on the muddy banks of the Isurius.

Aurelia pushed some smarter clothes aside and found a dark brown woollen tunic, which she shuffled into, and a deep black cloak which hung from a hook behind the door. The cloak had a smooth leather cowl which would be useful. She flung her old clothes under the bed, and went through Lepida's drawers and chests looking for a weapon of some kind.

114

Nothing.

Odds on, the old mare would have *something*, thought Aurelia. She wasn't foolish enough to go to the docks unarmed each week, surely?

Aurelia swept the bedclothes off and looked under the worn and stained pillows. Nothing. She emptied each chest she found, and looked under piles of clothing. There was a small row of bookshelves containing parchments flung haphazardly on top of each other: grocery receipts; recipes for medicinal decoctions; lewd stories written in spidery Greek script. She tumbled through them, but there was no trace of a weapon. Aurelia could feel the seconds raining down, tumbling away from her. Lost time, so much lost time.

She whimpered with frustration, then opened the door, checked the corridor and stepped out, shutting Lepida's door behind her. She pulled the cowl of her cloak over her head. If anyone saw her inside the compound, the facile disguise may buy her a few seconds, but nothing more.

She ran along the corridor of the east wing and past the steps leading down to the main atrium. She could hear conversation and laughter drift up to her from the lower stories. Crispus's personal guards would be down there, along with his innumerable associates and acquaintances: men from the gaming halls, soldiers, informers, spies. Boys from the high-end bath house on the via Constantina. Would they recognise her? It was too risky.

She carried on, crossing into the west wing of the house, and through to her nominal husband's quarters. She listened outside the door, then went inside. He would be at the principia at this time, waiting on the governor. But he frequently came back, to eat or fuck or pick up books and letters from his chamber. She had to be quick.

The first room was his study – a large space with bookshelves and a huge writing desk by the balcony doors. A dark wooden pedestal held an ancient water clock, which trickled softly in the silence. She walked inside and over to his desk. The surface was full of receipts, dictated letters from the governor, clumsily-written petitions from the patriarchs of the wealthy families of surrounding villages and towns, and correspondence from the other provinces.

Aurelia tore open his desk drawers, and found what she was after in the compartment nearest the ground: her letters. They were piled fat in the top of the drawer. She had to presume he hadn't been able to decode them yet – as far as she knew, the cipher was one known to only three people in the empire at the moment: herself, her agent, and the emperor himself. Possibly the beneficiarius, too. She would need to see exactly how much Atellus knew, and how much ignorance was feigned.

She scooped up the letters and tucked them into an inside pocket in the lining of her cloak. She slammed the drawers shut, and rose.

That was when she noticed him.

The servant was frozen by the door leading to the inner chamber of Crispus's bedroom. He was carrying a bundle of clothes in his arms, and another coil of sheets was flung across his shoulder. She could only see dark caverns where his eyes were, but she could feel his gaze on her, deliberating. Moving slowly, maintaining eye contact, she backed away from the desk, and towards the door leading out into the corridor.

Footsteps outside, voices.

Her heart leapt into her throat; cold sweat sheened her brow.

Three raps at the door, short and hard.

She darted into the corner, beside the door. She would have given anything for a weapon, for the chance to die in combat, on her feet, rather than be hurled torn and violated into a filthy cell again. Her eyes darted to the balcony and the window. There was always another way.

The servant stood staring at Aurelia for a few seconds, as she pressed her back to the wall, her breast rising and falling rapidly with the tension; the stillness was shattered by another triplet of knocks. The servant walked over to the door, fumbling the sheets into the crook of his arm as he moved. He grasped the handle with his free hand and pulled the door inward, opening it wide so it bathed Aurelia in its shadow.

"Where is the ab epistulis?" asked a voice, deep and rich.

"Where is that dastardly fuck, Crispus?" said another voice, high-pitched and breathless with incipient laughter. "We need his input on something. Very urgent!" More laughter.

"The ab epistulis is with the governor, at the moment, dominae" the servant said, calmly and clearly, inclining his head slightly. "Shall I send a runner with a message?"

High pitched laughter. The men sounded drunk.

"No, that won't be necessary," said the deep voice. "Come on." The footsteps and the laughter receded down the corridor. The servant looked over at Aurelia, meeting her gaze with a look that was half doleful and half encouraging. A brief smile touched his eyes and the corners of his mouth, then he walked out through into the corridor and closed the door softly behind him.

Aurelia heard the door click to and let loose a ragged breath.

117

She moved to the door, listened for a slow count of ten, then opened it and walked out and headed west towards the servant's staircase. She sped down the steps, her blood humming loudly in her ears, and emerged into the culina in a haze of steam and sweat and anguished shouts. Most of the noise came from a pair of cooks arguing violently over a heavy cauldron in the centre of the room; it hung down from a horizontal pole across two supports which straddled a blazing pit fire. She tiptoed past their backs, beneath the racks of jugs and beakers, past the copper ladles and basins and hanging knives which jutted like dragons' teeth from the metal racks suspended from the ceiling.

The culina was a hot stinking arena of hissing steam; the heat and damp seemed to soak deep into her lungs along with a lingering smell of herbs and spices and the powerful stench of muria. Half a pig was stretched out on a huge wooden board on a central table. It was surrounded by mounds of lentils, bricks of cheese, and whole loaves, fresh from the baking oven at the far end of the culina.

The people starve, she thought, whilst Crispus and his bitches feast like the emperors of old.

She crouched down and inched over to the table; obscured by a fug of steam, she reached up and snuck a heel of brown bread and wedge of hard cheese into her cloak. She eyed the knives desperately, but they were too close to the squabbling cooks, and the noise of getting one down was sure to alert them.

She slid through an open door at the far end of the culina and arrived in the servants' courtyard. The daylight and blast of cold air sent a splitting pain through her head. It was desperately cold, especially in contrast to the suffocating heat of the culina.

The ground was covered with slick ice and powdered over with fresh snow. The air was clear now, but the sky overhead was a sheer brittle grey which hinted at snowfall to come. Aurelia wrapped the cloak tightly around her, and turned round, into the jaws of a snarling beast.

She screamed and staggered backwards, slipping in the snow and falling heavily on her rump. The bread fell from inside her cloak and rolled across the cobbles of the yard.

The monster was a wolfhound, the size of a small donkey, lashed tight to an iron stake with a hemp rope wrapped snugly around its throat.

She scrabbled to her feet as the hound jumped and pawed and snapped at her, its body convulsing and twisting backwards as it reached the limit of its tether. Its fierce eyes burnt an angry yellow, and its ribs were all but sharp planks jutting angularly through the thin skin of the beast's flanks. It was covered with a mottled, wiry dark grey fur which faded away in patches to reveal red welts and bare flesh beneath. Aurelia stood frozen in terror and relief before she shook herself and moved backwards, tearing her eyes from the those of the creature before her. She snatched up her heel of bread from the ground and ran across the courtyard. She could see the heavy door set into the outer wall that led onto the ginnel running out to the via principalis.

Aurelia could feel her feet growing weary underneath her; her footfalls felt wild and desperate. The door wavered in front of her like a sweet apparition promising freedom: it was escape, it was *life*. She reached it, hitting it hard with the palms of her hands, falling into it, panting into the wood. Behind her, the barking of the hound still ripped through the crisp air. She waited for the shouts and calls and the crump of running footsteps across the yard, but there was none. Aurelia fumbled with the handle.

It was locked.

"We don't use that door."

Aurelia stifled a scream and whipped round. It was Iorvus, one of her husband's bodyguards. He was dressed in a tight leather tunic covered with bright scrubbed lorica hamata that clinked as he moved. A heavy spatha hung from his belt. He was not overly tall, but heavily built. He had long hair tied back from his forehead and thick sandy moustaches drooping from his upper lip, in the ancient Gaulish fashion. His hand was gripped tight around the hilt of his sword, the tension making his knuckles white as the pale snow.

Her legs failed her first; she simply couldn't feel them. She was mildly aware of the ground rushing up to meet her, and then the air dissolved in a strange buzzing. She could hear a long high laughter, drunken laughter and she could see her husband curling his lip at her as she hung and you will give me a name cara yes you will tell me the name I don't enjoy this no I don't you will give me a name and Atellus stood by her father and barked and barked until the blackness swallowed everything even thought.

CHAPTER 9

"Titus Faenius Magnus Atellus, beneficiarius imperatoris Valentinian, I give you welcome to Aesica."

The praefectus, sitting astride his black warhorse, inclined his head solemnly and struck his forearm across his chest.

"I give thanks, Aulus Ambrosius Germanus Apullius, praefectus castrorum Aesicae, for welcoming me to your fort."

Atellus returned the gesture from his own mount and watched the commander of Aesica. The praefectus looked back at him with hard blue eyes set like steel sherds in a lined expressionless face. Atellus had never met Apullius before, nor heard about him. He looked to be a solid career soldier, bred from local stock. This is as far as he would climb in the military, and he had done well to get here. The benficiarius knew that inside, beneath the cold and courteous facade of formality, Apullius must be gnashing his teeth with frustration at the presence of Valentinian's pet snooping around in his jurisdiction.

Apullius barked some commands to the men around him, and they broke apart to their duties.

The travellers had ridden through the sprawling vicus that seeped outwards from the garrison fort like a leak of humanity: a ramshackle agglomeration of houses, yards, smallholdings, shops and taverns that sagged out either side of the metalled road leading to the Wall. The Wall itself, the great vallum Aelium, loomed tall and imposing behind; the vicus rarely fell from its shadow, except at midday. It was a grey-soaked cliff, daubed with limewash and pitted with age. It was like a stretched serpent, rolling back behind the town, shivering with tension, ready to wrap itself around the dwellings and squeeze them to tinder if the whim so took it.

The Vallum Aelium was the god of the north, and all worshipped him. The deity was in their thoughts, in their eyes, absorbing their light, monopolising their view; it was their saviour from the ferocious tribes from the beyond. All the communities along the Wall – the garrison forts, the milecastles, the walled towns and sickly organic shanties that pooled out beneath its stones – all were brothers of the Wall. They shared common bonds: the same fears, the same woes, the same lives. They were more entangled with each other, and with the Wall, than they were with Rome.

Atellus had looked about him as they rode in through the vicus. Aesica was a spattlecocked mess of streets, scratched out of the tussocky landscape, like blade marks on a drill shield. The buildings were mostly timber, but there was some ostensible status divide. The tavern was stone-built, as was the high-end brothel, the bath-house and some of the larger central houses ringing it.

Brossicus and their escort had led them through the main via. Children, whores, beggars and tinkers lined the street, calling, singing, jostling, fighting. They were ragged and thin, burnt by sun and cold and wind, their rag-wrapped feet damp with snow. The sounds of workshops clanked and rumbled through the air. The via terminated at the south gate of the fort, dwellings clinging like barnacles along its length, entwining themselves in the safety offered by the route to the infantry garrison. The shanties ended abruptly some two hundred feet short of the fort, where the scrub was burnt back and the ground dipped down to the huge encircling scoop of the ditch.

Apullius rode out to meet them at the huge south gate, giving greeting to Brossicus. The Decanus peeled his contubernium away after they had dismounted, and the legionaries led their beasts past the double gatehouse and deep into the fort without a word of farewell to Atellus or Calidus.

The praefectus turned to face Calidus, the gateway a gaping maw behind him.

"Lucius Clodius Bassianus Calidus," said Apullius, "nephew of our most honoured praetor, this is a great honour. We will endeavour to look after your needs until we can arrange for an honour guard to escort you to Petriana."

"Thank you, praefectus," replied Calidus, inclining his head slightly. "The honour is mine. I have heard much about the heroic deeds of the warriors of Aesica."

Apullius laughed, but the noise was brittle and humourless. He turned back to Atellus. "I hear your journey was not without incident, beneficiarius?"

"We were attacked by a slingsman," replied Atellus. "One of our group was injured, most likely killed. His horse bolted with the body."

"A frequent occurrence," said Apullius emotionlessly. "Our messenger has already left today, but I will be sure to send one on a fresh horse at first light. It is not safe to travel by night. The missing man was a hireling of the governor, I believe?"

Atellus nodded. "He was."

The fatigue washed over him. He looked up, raising his face to a sky the colour of ash, and almost as thick. The air seemed to writhe around in front of his aching eyes, snaking through the crenels of the fort, sweeping down, as if sucked into the cold snowy ground, where it lingered and seeped through his tunic and breeches. Snowslush pooled underfoot. Fat snowflakes formed in the air and drifted heavily past his nose. He could hear singing and shouting from the vicus at their backs. Up on the battlements, fresh torches flickered into life. From inside the fort, the barracks, kitchens and drill-yards, came the dull and comforting crackle of soldiery. The smells of horseshit, stale sweat, leather and pigfat.

"Come with me," said Apullius, "I will show you to your quarters. You can bathe and get warm. I would be honoured to have you dine with me tonight."

The praefectus gestured for them to follow him, and he walked inside the fort, swallowed by one half of the double archway of the south gate. Atellus and Calidus followed, the fresh snow scrunching lightly under their boots. The metalled road shone hard and bright through wheel-trenches in the packed snow, the stone smoothed beneath centuries of hooves, feet and wheels. The great masonry of the gatehouse soared like a sheer cliff over their heads, voices from above trailing down like snowflakes from the timber palisade. The stone was limewashed, a dull grey smudged with soot-stains like thunderclouds, and the tar-slathered timber palisade above it glistened in the dying sunlight.

As they passed through the gateway, flames lit the interior of the fort, huge crackling lanterns atop timber boulevards stretching across the via principalis. To their right were the endless stone shacks of the barracks, long and low and on their left were the raised timber barns of the horrea.

They walked on in silence and tiredness, the throb of the fort pressing against them from all sides. Soldiers were drilling in the exercise yards around them, fighting with clacking lathes, volleys of breathy curses misting into the evening sky. The stench of the latrines hit them like cudgels, weighty pockets of foulness. There had not been rain enough recently to scour the filth and effluvium from the sewers, Atellus noted. Although it was still eminently preferable to the latrines of the eastern deserts in the middle of a drought. He suppressed a retch at the memory.

The principia loomed ahead of them, the main timber-built gate rising up from the solid stone foundations. Beyond the headquarters, Atellus could make out the long rows of factories. He could smell the piss-drenched leathery musk of the tanners and cobblers, and the heat and smoke of the blacksmith; the forge was burning whitehot in the distance, and he could hear the rap and clink of hammer on anvil. He knew that further back there would be butchers, reeking of the spicy warm smell of blood and hewn flesh; the carpentry warehouses, with the pleasant fuzzy whiff of sawdust and the ancient primal odour of damp woodshavings. Beyond that would be more barracks, end on end, and the stables, with their reek of warm wet horseflesh.

The two guards by the principia gates swiped a salute to Apullius as he walked past, and eyed the strangers warily: hard eyes, distrustful, stared out from sunken faces hatched by beard stubble. Atellus noted the lack of uniform: so far he had seen no two limitanei dressed alike, each one instead bearing a mad scrabble of cloth, leather and metal.

They walked inside the paved courtyard, facing the central building of the principia, containing the commander's house and ancillary buildings. Ranged along their left were a series of offices for the camp bureaucrats: the ab epistulis and his team of scribes, the tribunus militum and his team of corniculari. To their right, the courtyard was flanked by rows of workshops for the master smiths and craftsmen who controlled the finances and productions of their teams outside.

A gaggle of soldiers sat on the steps leading up to the commander's house, passing a wineskin back and forth. One wore only a thick wolfksin draped across his shoulders, his furred naked chest glowing palely in the moonlight. Laughter clicked across the paving stones. The snow was dusted fine and fresh across the roofs.

The men coughed a greeting to the praefectus as he passed, and one held out the wineskin for him. Apullius snatched it from the man's hand, then tilted it up and poured a thin stream of wine into his mouth as his men laughed and clapped. He handed back the skin and carried on walking up the steps, Atellus and Calidus following behind. The eyes of the limitanei were dark pebbles in the night, but the easterner could feel them on him, studying, calculating. He wondered how much the men knew about why he was there.

They entered the domus praefecti. It was warm – almost stifling – compared to the crispness of outside. The hypocaust heated the stone flags beneath their leather, iron-studded caligae. Atellus could feel the heat in the soles of his feet, brash and intrusive. Unfamiliar.

Apullius waited until they had entered, then shut the timber door behind them. The inside was sparse, but large.

"Welcome to my quarters," he said. "Simple, as befits an officer on the limes, but sufficient. I cannot offer you the hospitality you may have been accustomed to in the urbs, but I will do whatever I can."

"It is more than adequate, praefectus," said Atellus, formally.

Apullius nodded. "Beneficiarius, your quarters are along this corridor and through the open door at the end." He nodded towards the narrow walkway to Atellus's left. "You, Bassianus, are to be sequestered in the room next to mine," he smiled. "If you will walk with me, I will show you the way. Beneficiarius, shall I have someone show you to your own quarters?"

"I believe I can find my own way, thank you, praefectus."

Apullius nodded. "We will dine at conticuum. I will have someone meet you at your rooms when the meal is ready." He nodded then walked away to his right and up a set of angular stairs overlaid with a plush crimson carpet. Calidus followed behind him, his head bowed.

Atellus set off down the corridor. It was small and narrower than the way Apullius and Calidus had gone; a minor annex. The warmth of the hypocaust seemed to fade the further along he went, the heat leached from the grey stone by the cold outside. There were doors set in either side, though he could hear no noise from within. The walls were hung with faded maps painted on leather, and sunbleached banners that smelled faintly of damp and mould.

He reached the end of the corridor and walked through the open door. His quarters were small. There was a thick window set deep into the wall at the far side, and a broad fire-pit in the wall to his left; next to it, an iron-strapped trunk reflected the crumbling of ashes glowing contentedly in the grate.

Atellus looked over to his bed: it was a stretch of bundled, lumpen blankets on a buckled copper frame. Sad damp tassels hung from the corners. On the near-side of it were a desk of thick oak and a three-legged stool. The walls were adorned with sagging tapestries: the eagle standard a dull brown on a pale pinkish red; the glory of Hadrian, a faded pastoral scene of some balmy verdant climate. A triptych painting on a wood hanging depicted the conquering of the tribes, the building of the Wall, and the maiesta of Rome. Behind the hangings was bare cold stone, moist to the touch. A second small chamber beyond the main room contained a large copper laver surrounded by uneven earthenware jugs. There was the faintest murmur of warmth beneath the stone underfoot. Obviously the flames of the hypocaust were too anaemic to reach to the very extremities of the praefectus's house.

The quarters were musty, old, damp. Obviously they did not have that regular a turnover of guests here at Aesica to warrant the rooms being kept fresh.

Atellus noted that his belongings had preceded him: they were stacked carefully by the bed and atop the small table by its side. He wanted to bathe, to sluice the road from his scalp and steam the cold from his bones. He opened the door to the corridor to summon a servant. There was a soldier standing outside, staring outwards down the length of the passage. As the door opened he turned his head slightly towards Atellus.

"Sir?"

"Hot water for a bath," said Atellus.

He watched as the soldier nodded curtly and walked away down the corridor to fetch a servant. Under watch already, thought Atellus. Apullius did not waste any time. He shrugged and rolled his neck, stretching the sore taut muscles of his upper back, and walked back into his room to wait for his bath to be filled.

A train of tired, pale-faced servants arrived with basins of steaming hot water which they emptied into the copper laver. They were ragged and skinny boys and girls, barely into double figures, their eyes large and hungry, their hair angry and unkempt. The last arrived with a board containing a jug of oil and a strigil, and thick cotton towels flung over his slender arm. Atellus took the implements and gestured for the boy to leave; he was not interested in anything more exerting than a soak.

After the boy had left, Atellus stripped and sank into the water. The heat was exquisite. The aching muscles of his neck relaxed and sent a trill of pleasure through him. His body was covered in scuffs, scratches, bruises and the pale tracery of scars.

He soaked himself thoroughly then used the oil to build a soft gel on his dark skin which he scraped off with the sharp edge of the hot strigil. He carried on, lost in in the mesmeric movements, sweeping the strigil in long strips that rasped pleasantly against his skin, until he had stropped away the filth and cold of the last few days. When he had finished soaking, he towelled himself off and changed into fresh clothes brought from Eboracum.

Atellus sat at his desk and pulled out the letters given to him by Crispus: the reports from the agent in rebus. He sat looking through them. They were written in the common cipher, a simple enough code for any military man: the first letter was substituted for the one immediately preceding it in the alphabet, the second letter with the one immediately after, continuing to alternate. It was the most basic cipher to prevent them being intercepted by civilians. There were dozens of different ciphers, most of which Atellus had learnt himself from Valentinian when they had been promoted together under Julian. He had forgotten more ciphers than he would probably ever learn again.

The reports themselves were short and simple, written in a functional staccato. The agent had asked questions about the children who had gone missing, but found few answers. The soldiers were largely ignorant and had not heard anything. Others ascribed the disappearances to Cernunnos, hunting for fresh meat to tide him over until spring. The land was hungry, they said, and Cernunnos was hungry. If there were no beasts to hunt, then man must suffice, they reasoned. According to the agent, that had been a common response. Most limitanei were nonchalant about the issue; only the citizens of the vicus were afraid. They either refused to speak of it or hissed warnings – or threats – at him.

The agent had been diligent in contacting the parents of the missing: the fathers were never around, either dead or serving on some foreign front. Three of the mothers had disappeared and no-one could say where; they had simply 'gone'. Another two were simple and could speak no sense, but stared and sang and cawed at the clouds and the Wall. Two more were dead, of sickness, plague. Another two refused to talk to him, but just turned and walked away. He had been warned away by their friends, and remaining sons: young striplings, with glowing wild eyes dancing above toothless mouths, armed with rusted metal shivs, whittled castoffs filched from the smithies.

Atellus flicked through the parchments: dead-ends, rants about Cernunnos, flat-eyed stares from hostile limitanei.

The final missive was slightly different. A child had been snatched the night before it had been penned. There was fear abroad in the vicus, and the cold sweat of desperation, and the ink on the vellum was rich with the stench of both. The mother had sought out the agent, sobbing and wailing. He had spoken to her before, he recalled: she had been the friend of another who had warned him to mind his own affairs.

She spake of Cernunnos, wrote the agent. *Before, only the military talked of the Horned god. She was guilty, she said, and deserved the sword. She begged me to find her girl before she was cast into the flame. Before she went over. She was mad and bitter with tears. Much of her ranting made no sense; I had to beat some calm into her. She laughed and begged for more and tore herself. She spake of tainted gold. I gathered that she had sold her daughter. I asked her, to whom? She answered only, to the gods. To the Horned One. I filled her with wine and left her sleeping in my hut. I sought out Densligneus and he told me where to be this evening. I returned to the whore, but she was dead, foam and clots on her lips. I buried her in the snow, with but little ceremony: may the beneficent Sol forgive me but one more corpse is of no interest in these times. I will have more for my report on the morrow.*

That was the final letter.

Atellus rolled up the missives and tucked them inside a pocket within his foxfur cloak.

Densligneus.

The children were disappearing. Whether for meat, for trade, for rape, for joy, he did not know. He needed to find out why, and why it had led to the disappearance of the agent in rebus. He needed to find who had reported this to Valentinian, and why the emperor thought it so important to send him in person.

He needed to find this Densligneus and speak with him.

Atellus felt for his cloak again, his fingers drifting across the inside, near the hem, seeking a piece of stitching more prominent than the others, two unciae from the edge. He slipped his little finger inside the stitching and squeezed out the tightly rolled parchment, half the length and girth of his finger.

He held it in front of his eyes for a minute before unrolling it, recalling the day it had been delivered.

The late Autumn evening in Treves was ripe with the passing tendrils of summer; the last gentle caress of the sun's warmth lay across the dampening land, and the air was heavy with the scent of plums and plump vines. Atellus, merely a retired soldier, languishing in anonymity on the estates gifted him by the emperor, had been waiting by the river Mosella as the sun exhaled wearily behind the silhouettes of the spires and domes of the city.

He had been expecting a man, but instead it had been *her*; eyes the colour of ripe olives flashed out from beneath the wrappings of coarse linen around her face. Atellus recognised her instantly, even before he saw those eyes. He recognised the gait, the narrowness of the shoulders, and the defiant tilt of the chin. Their hands touched on the balustrade of the pons Augustae, their first contact in years, flesh on flesh, his first feeling of warmth since his half-death, and sitting in his cold chamber on the Wall, Atellus recalled the warm delicious shiver that had fizzed through his spine at her touch.

No, he had not been expecting her.

She had transmitted the message from Valentinian, her words curt and cool. He had been a fool for hoping otherwise: it had been many years since they had lain together, and any bond they may have formed had been long torn by time and distance.

The emperor's instructions were to proceed to Britannia, to return to the Wall. A vital mission, she had told him, of great personal import to Valentinian himself. But to Atellus, the words were as cold as the voice which delivered them:

131

the mission itself no more than a cushioned exile, the bitter taste of banishment sweetened by the honey of the promotion. He was to be beneficiarius imperatoris, a role created for him, a token of the emperor's trust and esteem. But Atellus could see through Valentinian's actions, and he told her as much: a chance for the emperor to rid himself of an old, troublesome friend. Even worse: a troublesome *pagan* friend. He was bad for the emperor's image, his respectability. Having Atellus in Treves was embarrassing. Valentinian practised Christianity, and surrounded himself with those who did likewise; Christians and yet more Christians filled his court. Valentinian barely tolerated the presence of the old gods in his staff anymore.

Perhaps, Atellus told her, there was nothing to investigate in the north, on the Wall; perhaps Valentinian just needed him to be gone.

All he had wanted then was to stay in Treves, in the old house. To wake up and look out over the sweet summer orchards in his grounds where he could walk with Petronia and Faenia again, where he could feel the warm wind on his cheeks and the soft sun-yellowed grass under his bare feet.

Her eyes betrayed nothing as she passed on the emperor's instructions, that Autumn day on the bridge. The sunset sent bloodred fins rippling along the Mosella as they looked out over the parapet each bathing in the other's silence. She had handed him his orders, in a tightly bound scroll, thick with the emperor's wax seal. Then she had handed him a second scroll, one wrapped tight into a delicate tube like the bone of small bird. Her fingers brushed his as she placed it in his hand, and she brushed her nose against his cheek as she whispered softly in his ear.

"Atellus," she had said. "I know why you want to stay here; I understand. But the man you seek?" She shook her head slowly. "I do not have a name for you. I know nothing of it."

His fingers had tightened against the stone balustrade, and he hung his head, his neck heavy, his unseeing gaze mesmerised by the purple undulations of the water below. "I believe you," he had replied, his voice cold. "But someone knows. Someone here."

She had squeezed his hand, her skin soft and warm against his own, and then she had left, gliding across the cobbles as innocently as she had arrived.

Atellus stood looking out at the river for a while longer until the sun melted into the skyline of the great city and the shadows stretched and swelled across the water. He gazed down at the thin tube of vellum in his hand then broke the neat seal with his thumbnail. It was not the seal of the emperor of Rome, but it was the seal of Valentinian: soldier, comrade, friend; *his* friend. Valentinian. He had read the brief note standing there over the silken smooth current of the Mosella, his eyes flicking across the cipher, his brain decoding it as he read. He read it again now, in his damp, frowzy quarters in the freezing north, his joyless cell set deep into the huge stones of the great Wall.

Amicus, it read. *My dear Atellus. Jovian's papers have been found. I have reason for sending you to the North. Trust in me, old friend, and trust in my actions. But trust no-one there. Our borders are riddled with treachery. There is more to this affair than pederasts and starving brigands.*

Find the agent and you will find your answers. And maybe mine too.

Believe me: I do this for you, amicus.

He rolled the scroll up tight, and replaced it in the half-stitched seam of his cloak. His fingers felt fat and uncoordinated. He fumbled and dropped the note three times before finding the socket.

I do this for you, amicus.

Atellus was hot. Burning. He felt the intensity of his whole life up to that point as a squeezing, clenching pressure within his breast, wrapped as tight as the coils of a ballista in tension.

He pulled his spatha from its sheath with a whicking rasp. It gleamed by the light of the oil lamps on the desk. He put the cold cold steel against his hot brow. The heat of the deserts was in him, blackening the edges of his vellum-thin soul, charring his virtus more with each day. He laid the sharp edge of the Damascus steel on the top of his forearm letting the weight of the blade nip slightly at his flesh. He tightened his grip on the leather-wrapped ivory of the hilt, and drew it slowly, caressingly backwards. The fine blade bit blissfully into the flesh of his arm. Succulent red blood burst forth, slowly at first then pooling and leaking across the contours of his muscle.

Atellus sighed, his eyes misting with relief and release. He felt a cool hand at the nape of his neck, soft fingers light in the fine curls of his hair.

"Julia," he murmured. "I am coming, my love."

He rose giddily, lightheaded, and used his spatha to cut the cotton towel into strips. He wound one around the gash, tying it in place and used another to wipe clean the blade of his sword, assiduously dabbing at each speck of blood before resheathing the blade and strapping it to the belt at his waist. He threw his fox-fur cloak over his back and opened the door.

The soldier was standing outside; he eyed Atellus warily, as a strange animal.

"I'm going for a walk," said Atellus, shutting the door behind him.

"Orders are to escort you, sir," said the soldier in a bored tone. "The vicus is dangerous."

"I will go alone."

"But—"

Atellus wheeled round and stared hard into the man's eyes. The soldier's cloak was a deep red cloth which was so dark with ingrained dirt it looked almost black. Beneath the cloak he wore a tunic of knotted flax, and on his head was the cupola of an old Pannonian helmet, tilted slightly back towards the crown. The steady eyes beneath the fringe of short light hair were a keen blue. He was young, maybe twenty winters.

"I am the beneficiarius imperatoris, soldier," said Atellus. "I don't know if you've been told that, so I will presume your insolence is down to ignorance rather than sheer impertinence. I act for the emperor Valentinian in thought and in deed, and you treat me as you would treat the emperor himself face to face. If I so much as cough, your balls will be bagged and you will carry them round your neck for the rest of your sickly life. Do you understand me, pedes?"

The soldier swallowed hard and seemed to be pressing himself back into the wall behind him.

"I walk, and I walk alone, soldier," continued Atellus, easing his tone and the pressure of his stare. "When I have left, you may tell the praefectus that I have gone and may be unavailable to dine with him this evening."

It was time to start flexing his muscles as beneficiarius, and stop pretending he was on a diplomatic mission. The sooner he could get immersed in this shitty task, the sooner he could get back to Treves. To Julia Faenia and Julia Petronia.

"Yes, sir," said the soldier, quietly, averting his eyes. He thumped a chest salute as Atellus walked away down the corridor.

***

135

Calidus shut the door behind him and looked around his room. He released a breath he did not realise he had been holding, and collapsed onto his bed. The goose-down mattress was soft, and low to the ground.

There was something about Apullius that made him wary. The man was hard and immoveable, like an impassive golem chipped from the Wall itself. But it was the way he looked at him, those sly glances when he thought Calidus wasn't watching, or the insinuation he put into his carefully chosen words. There was something raw and visceral and predatory about the man. Calidus fancied the praefectus looked at him the way a viper looked at a dormouse. The man's features were hard and heavy, his mouth solid and angular, his beard short and brittle. Everything about him spoke of dominion, of superiority, or aggression. Calidus supposed he could learn a lot from the commander of Aesica, yet he could barely wait until he was escorted west to Petriana.

Calidus sighed and cast another glance around him. His quarters were cramped and cold. At least, they were compared to the smallest of his rooms in Eboracum. Calidus felt a ripple of longing pass through him like nausea; for his uncle, his room, and most of all for the freedom of the smooth rainslick tiles of his rooftops. He missed Marina, with her soft hands and softer thighs. He felt as though his life had become a grim tale of cold and hunger and hardship and threat. He had always sought adventure, but this seemed different somehow. Bleaker, less heroic. More *serious*.

He rose and went to the second of his anterooms. Apullius had assured him that his were the very best chambers in the fort, second only to the commander's own. As befits such a visiting dignitary, Apullius had said, with that narrowing of his eyes, and the slight thinning of his lips.

Calidus shivered.

He pulled off his caligae and woollen stockings and luxuriated in the feel of the warm tiles beneath his toes. His own stench rose up to meet him, and he felt a quiver of disgust pass through him, followed by shame. He could use the commander's own bath-house, Appullius had assured him; had insisted, even.

Calidus had looked round the five rooms of his quarters, but there was no personal bathing room. There was a bedroom; a bare study with only a cabinet full of bottles of perfume and unguents; a half-filled library with shelves sagging under the weight of plump books, pages bloated with damp; and an antechamber filled by a lumpen and dusty triclinium. The triclinium was positioned next to two tall, frost-scratched doors leading out to a narrow balcony which overlooked the courtyard.

He got to his feet and walked across to the balcony windows and peered out through the thick glass: the night beyond was black. He could hear the swell and push of the wind against the wooden doors, see the froth of weak pale snow spitting against the panes. Further out he could see the flickering of the torches lining the ramparts of the principia compound, like stars sitting low and even in the sky, and, further beyond, the beacons burning atop the fort walls. The sound of howls and shouts drifted up from outside: Laughter, muffled through the glass. Through the billowing rags of cloud in the sky above, he could make out the beaming face of the plump winter moon, hanging bright and sweet.

Find out what you can...Cultivate some loquacity, Calidus.

He needed to get out and speak with the beneficiarius again. Find out more. Atellus had known his father, too. Watched him die. Stood aside, no doubt, as he squirmed in agony. He had always heard tales of the cowardice of easterners, how their men broke ranks in battle, and would rather lie with boys then fight with real men. He felt his fists clenching tight down by his sides.

A name, nephew, rang his uncle's voice in his head, *that I would give half of Eboracum for....*

137

He needed to stick close to the beneficiarius, to find out whatever he could. And if that kept him away from the praefectus and his thick lips, his greasy dark eyes, and his half-lidded insinuations about using his personal bath-house, then so much the better.

Calidus reluctantly strapped his cold, wet caligae onto his feet, swung open the door to his apartment, and walked out into the corridor.

CHAPTER 10

Atellus walked through the south gate of Aesica with a nod to the shivering soldiers who flanked him as he passed beneath the towering masonry. He had taken stock of the fort as he passed through, walking a brisk circumference of the grounds after leaving his room. He estimated that the garrison was roughly seventy percent under-strength. Half of the barrack-blocks were empty: a quick look inside the long narrow buildings told him they were used for gaming, whoring and fighting. Only the principal barracks by the south gate seemed to be used to house the soldiers. One of the horrea was completely empty of grain; at least half of the workshops lined up along the northern wall were derelict and used as dosshouses by drunken soldiers or pens for scrawny pigs and goats. The circumference walls of the fort looked solid from a distance, but up close they were crumbling, and weather-worn.

The soldiers themselves seemed half-feral and desperate. He had already observed that the limitanei wore no regulation uniform – he had expected as much before he had arrived – but these men were kitted in wild agglomerations of leathers, rags, skins, and rusted metal trinkets. Anything they could scrounge or find on the road that looked like it might dull a slingshot or arrow, or turn a blunted blade, had been put to use covering some body part.

Atellus had walked out to the west gate and met with the soldier guarding the massive timber doorway; he was gazing out over the ranged series of defensive ditches and banks beyond, though he twitched and half-turned at the sound of footsteps behind him. He was missing his left arm and as a weapon held a modified sithe in his right fist, the snath cradled against his knobbly shoulder. He was draped in a coarse wolf-skin, the fur worn off by age and weather. His head was bound thick with strips of dark leather that gave off a reek of piss. He wore what looked like a long necklace of miniature plough blades, dangling heavily from his shoulders to cover his chest and stomach. They were inscribed with Brythonic spells, and Greek curses, the edges of the letters red with rust. The bottom half of a discoloured toga, complete with the purple stripes of the praetexta, lolled like an ill tongue from under his makeshift armour. Atellus had asked him where he had obtained it. The old man – who looked gnarled and lumpen as an aged quercus – spat into the snow and squinted westward. He didn't answer.

Atellus shook his head at the memory and approached the south gate leading out into the vicus. The two limitanei guarding the entrance shut the postern after him as he left the fort. He trod unhurriedly along the frozen road of the militarised zone leading to the civilian dwellings. The night was broad and the clouds distant and high. Atellus's breath ghosted out in front of him as he walked towards the glowing torches of the village up ahead. Behind him the Wall glowered malignantly like a curse made stone, a vast encompassing curtain drawn across civilisation. He idly wondered what difference there would be between the men on the other side, and those guarding Rome's frontier. In Hadrian's time, perhaps there had been. But now? He couldn't be entirely sure.

Atellus knew he was being followed even before he heard the subtle scrape of nail-studded boots against the metalled surface of the road. He carried on walking, letting the darkness envelop him. The road was lined with flaming torches at twenty pace intervals. His shadow danced and skittered across the ground as the light flared and dipped with the wind.

Atellus eased his hand down to loosen his spatha in its scabbard and rubbed at the soft cicatrix along his throat. He silenced his thoughts and concentrated on his hearing: there was only one set of footfalls.

Atellus spun round, his shadow thrusting long in front of him.

"Beneficiarius," said a voice. It was the boy's.

140

"Scaeva," said Atellus. He could see the boy wince in the harsh torchlight. "Take your luck back to the fort. I have no need of it tonight."

He turned back to face the vicus without waiting for a response and carried on walking. Calidus jogged up to walk beside him. He was tall for his age, of a height with the easterner.

"I thought I would take a look around the town," said the boy.

"Did you get permission from Apullius?" replied Atellus, flatly.

"No," he answered, looking down. "Did you?"

Atellus smiled. "I don't need his permission."

"Neither do I," he returned. "I am nephew to the governor."

"I think, Scaeva," said Atellus, "with your luck, you may soon find out exactly what weight that carries up here."

"What does that mean?" said Calidus, frowning. Atellus said nothing, but carried on walking at a brisk pace. "I have reasons for being here, too, you know."

"I know your reasons," said Atellus. The lights of the vicus were close now, and they could hear sounds of angry conversation, laughter, the occasional scream. Underneath was a silent trickle of noise from the animals; the desultory lowing of thin, tired cattle; the occasional caw from a cockerel. "I don't want you around me, boy. Go back to the fort. Lock yourself in your room. Wait until you can get to Petriana. That is the best advice you will get from me, or anyone, for some while."

"I want to find out what happened to the children," said Calidus, ignoring him. "The ones that dis—"

"Look," said Atellus, rounding on the boy, grabbing the edge of his expensive cloak in his fist. He looked down into Calidus's open face, the boy shrinking under the force of his temper. "Amove te, little pube," he said. "This is not a game. This is not a chance for you to earn stripes from uncle Brocchus. Go back and hide in your room until you can get to Fullofaudes, because one man in three here would leap at the chance of buggering you inside out, a pretty young name like you. The other two would sell you to the brigands for ransom as soon as look at you."

He let go of the youth, and carried on walking.

"Your mad uncle should never have let you up here in the first place," he called over his shoulder. "Obviously he cares as little for your luck as everyone else does." He spat on the ground to avert the evil.

Atellus felt the contact against his back, forcing him forward and down and the next he knew his face was on the floor, grazed hard against the cold stone of the road. The boy's weight was on his back and he had one hand wrapped in Atellus's hair whilst his other gripped a dagger tight against his throat. He could hear the panting of his own breath and see it rising up in front of his eyes, bright with moonlight against the darkness. He couldn't see the blade at his jugular, but the edge felt sharp and unused.

"Tace simia!" the boy hissed, his mouth close up to Atellus's ear, his breath warm on his skin. "My uncle warned me about you, about the unlucky desert pig, the emperor's burden. You talk to me of foul luck?" Calidus spat to his right, out into the darkness. "You were an ill omen to your family, and to the emperor, and uncle says you are already half dead, and Valentinian sent you up here so someone else could finish the job."

Calidus pulled on Atellus's hair forcing his head back, jolting a grunt from his lips. "You say that my uncle means nothing up here?" he snarled. "Well being a beneficiarius means even less; it is a death warrant. If you are not bad luck, then I've never seen a man who is."

Atellus tried to laugh but his throat was stretched taut and it came out as a wheeze. "Maybe you are right." He strained to get the words out, and he felt the boys grip slacken a little. "Maybe we have more in common than I thought." His left arm was trapped under his body, tingling. His right was flat on the ground, level with his clavicle. "Maybe you could just give me a bit more air?"

Calidus's grip loosened a little bit. It was all Atellus needed. He brought his right arm across under his throat to grip the boy's wrist, turning it backwards and keeping it rigid, forcing the blade away from his throat. At the same time, he used his left hand and his core muscles to heave himself up. He had the weight advantage over Calidus, as well as surprise. The youth clamped onto Atellus's back as the older man rose to one knee and kicked himself backwards, down against the road, slamming the boy to the stone with him on top. Atellus's right arm still held the boy's attacking wrist; he squeezed it hard, crushing the nerves and tendons through the carpus and the boy howled with pain, his fingers springing outwards, releasing his weapon. The dagger clanged heavily off the stones.

Atellus had the boy trapped beneath his weight. He raised his left elbow and drove it twice into the youth's stomach. Calidus coughed and gasped. Atellus raised his head and brought the back of his skull down hard, the blow taking Calidus squarely in the jaw. The boy relaxed suddenly, his body flattening out limply against the metalled road.

The easterner got to his feet, and rubbed the side of his jaw which had struck the ground when the boy had pounced on him.

The little shit was fast; and vicious.

He looked down at the figure sprawled on the floor, pale and young. He would die out here if he left him. Or worse, depending who found him first.

He sighed, then bent down and picked up the boy's dagger. The hilt was ivory, inlaid with sapphires and garnets and edged with gold leaf. The seal of the governor of Britannia Secunda was etched into the base of the blade, just above the handle. Atellus tucked the weapon into his breeches, then scooped the boy up and tossed him over his shoulder, and walked away towards the vicus.

**

Calidus coughed and spluttered, and blinked his eyes.

He felt like he was choking, drowning. His head throbbed; it was as if someone was levering up the top of his skull with the flat of a spatha. He tried opening his eyes, but the burst of bright light sent a flare of pain rushing through his brain and down his spine.

"Drink," a voice said.

Something was being held to his lips. A hand had him by the scruff of his neck. The liquid smelled sweet and foul. He instinctively edged away from it.

"Drink," said the voice again. A woman's voice, rough and low. He let his lips part, and the viscous liquid slid across his tongue, around his gums. It took a second before he registered the burning. He coughed again as he swallowed it. Laughter. Someone thumped him on the back. His eyes opened fully, and he felt the torchlight burn through to the back of his skull.

"Goodun there, boy," grinned a gummy lady sitting next to Atellus. The easterner grinned at him and took a swig from the mug in his hand.

Calidus looked around him, groggily. He was in a tavern, slouched in a low wooden-backed stool. The floor was covered in straw and chalk, and mottled with old dark stains. The light came from two torches set into iron brackets in the walls. Two adjacent tables were full of silent men, drinking seriously, intently, as though it were their job, their solemn duty. The room itself was a small space; it looked more of a shack, with great timbers stretching across the roof, and discoloured thatch billowing and sagging like dismal yellow clouds overhead. The walls seemed half made of twigs and tangled treetrunks built into the structure. Cold air sliced in gusts through gaps in the timbers.

"Where are we?" he asked Atellus. His head felt like it was crumbling from the inside. He rubbed his jaw; it felt tender.

The lady sitting next to Atellus answered. "Yerrat the edge o the world, yungun." She laughed. She looked old, older than she probably was. Thin and pale, she wore a man's rough tunic across her body, but her arms were bare. Her hair was a burning red in colour. It was long and twisted into thick plaits that fell across her shoulder and down between her ample breasts. She had a small crooked nose, broken in more than one direction. What teeth she had left were black.

"The best tavern in the vicus, apparently," said Atellus drily. "Though I haven't had much chance to verify that."

"Tek ma word ferrit, darkun." She rose to her full height, which was not much, and laid a hand on Atellus's shoulder. "Ah'll leave you an yer pussy in quiet?"

The easterner nodded. "More of this," he said raising his mug.

"Me too," coughed Calidus.

Atellus raised a dark eyebrow at the boy and nodded his approval.

"What happened?" Calidus squeezed at the base of his skull with his fingers. Everything seemed to hurt.

"You attacked me, on the road," said Atellus. "I taught you a lesson."

"A lesson?" He rubbed his jaw and winced at the jolt of pain.

"Don't fuck with a desert pig." Atellus hid his smile behind his mug as he slurped the last of his wine.

Calidus shifted in his chair and felt down at his waist for his dagger.

"Where's my knife?" he asked, suddenly panicked.

"Calm down," said the beneficiarius. "I have it."

"Give it back," said Calidus, sullenly. The blade had been a gift from his uncle when he came of age. He missed its weight against his trousers; he wanted to caress the smooth handle, run his thumb across the edge of the steel. He felt vulnerable without it.

"Shut up," said Atellus. He leaned in closer to Calidus. "That fool's blade would pay the wages of every limitanei in the garrison's for half a year; a wage they haven't seen for over three summers. And the steel is so soft it would barely break the skin. You pull that out around here and it would be gone in the wink of an eye. And you along with it, most likely." He sat back in his seat and accepted the two drinks that the bare-armed lady brought over. He paid with a single coin. "Better for you if you'd left it back in your uncle's villa."

Calidus reached out for his wine, and Atellus handed the mug over to him. "It's mine, though," he said defensively.

"Your lucky weapon, Scaeva?" asked the easterner with an arched eyebrow.

Calidus stared at him. "Fuck you."

Atellus laughed. "I'll keep it safe. For a while."

Calidus frowned and drank down his wine, coughing half of it back out. He looked around him as he scrubbed a hand across his lips: the men ranged along the squat tables to his left were deep in conversation; they looked filthy and angry, but with the desperate slouch and sunken shoulders of tired, hungry, weary men. Looking closer he noticed some agitation towards the far end of the table. A woman, with pale straw coloured hair and milk white skin, was weeping. Her eyes were red, her pale flesh mottled with the soft pink of emotion. One of the men had her by the wrist and was shaking her, like a wolf at the neck of a newborn lamb. She shook her head from side to side, and her lips moved, but Calidus couldn't make out what she was saying.

"Drink up, Scaeva, if you have the stomach," said Atellus, tipping his head back, the mug to his lips. He lowered it, scrubbed the back of his hand across his mouth, and slapped the mug on the table. "Seems you're getting a taste for that acetum, and you're treating next."

Calidus frowned at him, then tipped the firewater into his mouth, and swallowed it, willing himself not to cough, staring at the easterner's dark eyes.

"You've been here before?" said Calidus, when he was sure it was safe to speak without choking.

"Here?" said Atellus, motioning with his head to their surroundings. "The Wall, yes. Not here. Not Aesica."

"My uncle said you helped to defeat the tribes on the other side," Calidus continued, in between sips of acetum. "That you fought close to my father?"

"Your uncle says a lot of things, Scaeva."

147

"Did you?" Calidus met the other man's eyes directly, and refused to look away. Atellus returned the gaze coolly, his face placid and devoid of emotion, his eyes dark and unfathomable.

"I fought with your father, yes," said Atellus after a while. "I fought with many men. More dead now, than not. They were bad times."

"And these aren't?"

Atellus smiled. He gestured to the red-haired woman who disappeared into an alcove at the far side of the room. She emerged with another two drinks which she brought over and handed to the two strangers. Atellus nodded towards Calidus, who pulled a follis from his coin pouch and handed it over. She bowed to him, kissed his cheek and went over to sit with the ragged, dark-faced men.

"What was he like?" asked Calidus, looking into the murky liquid in his cup. "My father?"

"Paterculus was a bright man; a good leader," said Atellus. "He was courageous, fierce. A good fighter. Perhaps rash; he led from the front, instead of the rear."

"Some would call that brave," said Calidus, looking up from his cup. His eyes were tight with emotion.

"Some would," nodded Atellus, leaving the rest unspoken. "There was certainly no faulting your father's bravery.

"We were at Vercovicium," he continued, "waiting for reinforcements from Procolita. There was a settlement half a mile away, just south of the old fort of Aurelium, which the enemy had plundered. They were raping and burning their way south." Atellus took a large swallow of his drink and relaxed a little into his hard chair. "Lupicinus had been sent by the emperor Julian to lead the combined forces of

Britannia, but they were too dispersed; discipline was too lax, motivation too slight. Your father was a commander at Vercovicium, and he was one of the first to arrive and see what Lupicinus was trying to do: to form a moving barrier, a string across the country, to absorb the incursions, defeat them in small battles, on terrain of our choosing, and drive them back up through the Wall."

Calidus took a sip of his drink. The firepit behind him burned and crackled sending pleasant gusts of warmth across his back. He watched Atellus carefully; the beneficiarius's eyes glowed inwardly with a strange fire, a tiredness that seemed to weep from his very pores. The beneficiarius loosened the scarf around his neck.

"We arrived by boat at Arbeia," he said, "with a small group of good numeri: Frisii from Germania. We marched westwards for days along the Wall, gathering the men from the eastern forts. But most were dead. The few that weren't had deserted. Villages burnt black, women and children mutilated and flung atop great hungry fires. The whole country smelled of death. The air was thick with carrion. It rained, cold and relentless."

Atellus took another gulp from the cup in his hand.

"We marched and saw only the traces where the enemy had broken through. They gave no quarter to the people they encountered. There were no survivors; none that we found. I have seen massacres – many, far too many – and this was one of the worst." Atellus shook his head slowly. "The mud, the wet, the cold, the dead. It was lucky for us we did not encounter them, as we would surely have perished. The reality was far worse than the accounts which had reached Julian, otherwise he would have sent more than a single under-strength numerus. But news travels too slowly, sometimes." He squeezed his eyes shut, battling the memories. "Lupicinus was grim, but determined. He was an old soldier; he thought he would die in Britannia.

149

"Eventually," he continued, "anxious, and weary of the march, we reached Vercovicium. It was the first hope we had encountered, the first suggestion of life, of safety. They received us with hostility and distrust, but at least they let us enter. Your father did; that was where I met him," he nodded to Calidus, "commanding the garrison. He was brimming with cold fury, Paterculus. He wanted to chase and destroy. But we didn't yet have the numbers. We waited, each day knowing that more villages were being sacked. There was a lot of anger in the air. Much of it directed at your uncle.

"Lupicinus and I rode two horses to death galloping to Eboracum for help, darting through holes in the enemy's ranks. We met with Brocchus, and carried the pleas of your father. Your uncle was a just and powerful leader; different from the man he is today. But he was scared of depleting the city's guard. There were harsh words. We left with barely a third of the share of the legio we had been expecting. Brocchus was wary. He had his own agenda; he couldn't see that if we failed to stop the enemy before they reached Eboracum, that his forces would be no good. The people had no stomach for a siege; they were hungry, scared."

"I remember bits of it," said Calidus. "Mater was scared. I recall not being allowed my favourite strawberries for dessert, and I got upset. My brothers were old enough that they went out into the city. They came back with news. I remember them saying the river was on fire, and my mother wept. I didn't know what they meant, at the time. But it has been in my dreams many times since."

"Further upstream from Eboracum," said Atellus, nodding, his voice low in the room, "they used barges to cross the river. Maybe they still do. The enemy cut the barges from their tethers and set them alight so we could not follow them without diverting to the bridge by Isurium Brigantum. The barges were swept downstream, probably into the city docks. More vessels may have caught fire. Perhaps that is what your brother saw."

Calidus nodded. "I remember mater crying a lot. I remember being hungry. I used to escape from my room, onto the roofs, and sit up there, in the rain, watching the people fighting in the streets, and seeing the smoke curling up from the horizons. I felt safe up there. And powerful."

Calidus's eyes glistened with the memories. Simpler times, or so it had seemed. For him, anyway. A wave of laughter broke across the table behind him, reminding him of where he was. The flickering lights were shrinking in their brackets; the shadows seemed to close in around the shoulders of the beneficiarius.

"I rode back to Vercovicium with the lion's share of the troops," continued Atellus, "whilst Lupicinus peeled off with a smaller force to gather reinforcements from the western forts. My men and I met scattered groups along the way, still laying into the dead, and burning the cottages. It was hard, desperate fighting, out of formation. Mud and filth and blood. The ground was bleeding that day. Men begged and wept as we rode over them, but all were slaughtered.

"Once we arrived back at Vercovicium, we found that the reinforcements from Procolita were there. With them, and the troops from Eboracum, we were strong enough to think about hunting down the enemy. We split into five roving cohortes spreading out from Vercovicium: four to cover the length of the Wall, and a fifth to head south to harry the flanks of the enemy marching on Eboracum, to pick up the straggling warbands and lighten the burden on Brocchus's legion. I led this fifth cohors and your father, a praefectus, served under me. Reluctantly. He did not trust Treves; not people from the city, nor Julian himself." Atellus smiled. "A true Briton.

"Our scouts found a small group of the enemy ahead of us, a warband of a couple of hundred. We cut around them to approach them from the south, hoping that if they broke, they would head north, away from the villages and farms. We attacked, surprising the warband, and managed to push the enemy north, back up to the Wall."

Atellus took a deep draught from his mug, and looked glassily up to the thatch above them.

"We followed them up," he said. "They were a smaller body than us, and could move faster. When we reached the southern militarised zone of the Wall before Vercovicium, we realised something was wrong." He spoke quietly. "The fort had been sacked."

"How?" asked Calidus. "What happened?"

"Half the limitanei posted to defend the fort had deserted; joined forces with the enemy, or settled themselves into brigand bands. The start of the huge companies you see raping the country now.

"The fort was crawling with foes; the enemy we had pushed north joined with them and they turned back against us, swelled with even more forces arriving from the east, flushed out and fleeing from the attacks of our fellow cohortes. We were caught by surprise, and by treachery: our own scouts had deserted before we were able to avoid a pitched battle. We stood fast and fought but there was no time for formation, for tactics. We were outnumbered three to one. We waded through blood and limbs, sweating through the cold and pissing with fear. They broke against our shield wall, and drove long spears up through the bellies of our horses. The flank broke after heavy losses. Desperate men, scared. They fled and were cut down."

"As the cowards deserved," sneered Calidus from over the rim of his drink.

Atellus looked over at him with an even gaze. "Cowards maybe," he said. "But you do not have the right to pass judgement until your own courage has been tested in a similar situation." Calidus lowered his eyes and shrugged moodily. Atellus took another drink from his mug and swirled the fierce liquid around the inside of his mouth. He swallowed it, closing his eyes to relish the burn as it hit his belly.

"My shield bristled with arrows," he continued, "until it was too heavy to hold with one arm. Weighted darts were hurled down from the battlements of the Wall, falling like deadly rain amongst us. The air crackled with the thunderstorm of screams: the agony of the wounded. We hid under the dead and whistling arrows punched into the flesh of the dead and dying alike, with an ugly dull sucking sound. You will come to associate it with battle, as any soldier will. My ears rang with a tumult of screams and prayers.

"Many of the soldiers were boys," said Atellus. Calidus felt the weight of his stern dark eyes on his own. "Your age. They went down trying to stuff their guts back into their torn bellies, crying for their mothers, shitting themselves with fear. The fortunate had their faces cloven in two, so their pain was brief. Your father went with his men. Paterculus fought well, but his group was outnumbered; we all were. Each man did all he could to stay alive, hacking back blades coming from two, three directions at once, stumbling in the mudslicks, slipping on the hot spilt blood, grappling hand to hand with the enemy who may have been his comrade only days before. It was hard to tell one side from the other; we wrapped red cloth torn from the dead men's clothing around our upper arms to distinguish friend from foe in the clamour of battle.

"It was dark when Lupicinus came from the west with reinforcements. We managed to drive the animals back up into their holes. A few held on to Vercovicium for weeks after, but eventually Lupicinus gave the order to burn them out. We assaulted the fort directly and lost as many men again as we had in the battle. We took them eventually, fearless half-mad men scaling the walls with ladders and managing to open the main gate from the inside to let us in. But from eight centuries, we had maybe one left. There was no celebrating. Just the dirge for the dead as we buried them in long pits along the base of the Wall."

153

Calidus was quiet. He could feel something burning, deep inside his chest, between his ribs and his belly. It could be the firewater, he thought. But maybe it was pride. Longing. Loss. He could feel moisture budding in the corners of his eyes.

Atellus was looking at him, his dark face expressionless. Calidus gazed down into his mug, hiding his emotion with another long sip. His head still ached, and his jaw too, but it was fuzzy and distant, as though the pain was someone else's, or the memory of a pain that no longer existed.

"What happened after?" he asked. His voice sounded thick, his tongue fatter than usual against his palate.

"After the animals had been driven back," said Atellus, "the resettlement began along the Wall. Some came back. But not all. Poor harvests make people lose faith in their leaders. A man with an empty belly is a dangerous, reckless man. You will learn that soon, Scaeva, if you haven't already. The whole province will."

Calidus looked at him.

"Some men and women emerged from the wildernesses and returned to their homes. They rebuilt; carried on where they had left off. It is the way of things. I have seen it so often. There were few young children though; most could not move fast enough to escape. They slowed down their families. Oftimes, they were left behind to die. Or were killed by their fathers or brothers. Children are rare along the Wall. It has always been so, along all limes."

"Even more so, now?" asked Calidus.

"So it would seem," replied the beneficiarius with a grim smile.

A loud noise over his shoulder made Calidus turn to face the other patrons. The pale-faced woman with the teary eyes was shouting at one of the men. He wore a wild, thick beard which climbed up to just below his eyes and hid his features. His face was down in his cup and he seemed to be determinedly ignoring the woman at his shoulder. Calidus couldn't understand the language. The words, in their twisted tongue, felt angry, the tone a bludgeon to his ears. The woman screeched and clawed her cheeks in desperation, then got to her feet, knocking her stool back onto the floor with a crack. She strode around the seated men, and across the room. Flames from the fire licked out at her legs as she passed. The man bellowed something at her as she left, his eyes burning wildly above the dark thatch of his facial hair.

Calidus watched, detached, as she fell to her knees in front of where Atellus sat, and gripped the sleeve of the easterner's tunic. Liquid sloshed from the side of his cup and onto her arm.

"Please, dominus," she said thickly, the words uncommon with her and heavily accented. "Please. You are from the urbs; you can help us!"

Atellus looked down at the woman. Her eyes were a pale blue, the flesh of her cheeks mottled red from the tears. Her clothes were rigid with grease and sweat and she reeked of pinguedo, her fingers daubed with fat and glistening in the torchlight.

"I beg, please. My daughter. You must find my puella, my corcula."

Atellus shook her from his sleeve, and took a sip of his drink. "What has happened to your daughter?"

The woman bowed her head, fresh sobs driving themselves up from her chest. She shook with emotion as she spoke, her eyes glowing with fresh tears.

"They took her," she said, unsteadily. "The Horned One took her, days ago. But she is alive. She is here, somewhere, in the vicus, she must be. They took her. Please."

155

"Tell me more," asked Atellus, calmly. He dragged over another stool from an adjacent table and set it down next to the woman. He tried to guide her up into it, but she faced the ground at his feet. "Who is the Horned One?" he asked.

"They came to my house in the night," she said, weeping into the floor, "and they offered me gold."

"Who did?" he pressed, his face tight, his eyes intense. "Gather yourself. Sit. Be calm and tell me all."

"I do not know, dominus," she gasped, her eyes squeezed shut. "They were men, in thick cloaks. Soldiers, I—"

The blow took her in the side of the face and drove her down hard to the straw-covered floor. Blood sprayed from her nose.

Calidus jerked backwards, nearly knocking his chair over. Laughter drifted up from another table.

The bearded man towered over the woman, who lay mumbling and twitching on the floor. He twisted a braid of her pale hair around his fist, and yanked her roughly to her knees. Her eyes swam and danced unseeing across the room; the lower part of her face was stained bright red with the blood raining from a ruptured nostril. Her attacker spat out some words to her in their native tongue, then looked intently at Atellus; Calidus he ignored, for which the boy was thankful: the man was huge and heavily-built, knotted muscles tight from endless hard toil. He only had a single eye, the other covered by a pale scar that ran from his scalp to his jawline ploughing a pale rut through his thick dark beard. The rest of his skin was dark and weathered, with deep creases fanning out from his eyes, his nose, his brow.

"Heed her not," he said slowly to Atellus. "The woman is ill."

He turned round, still clutching her hair, and dragged her across the floor towards the table where he and his comrades sat. Her feet scratched at the floor as she slid across, tangles of damp straw bunching under her rough woollen skirts. He let go of her hair and her head cracked down beneath his bench. He straddled his bench emotionlessly and continued supping.

Atellus rose to his feet, his eyes fixed on the bearded man. "That woman is in my protection," he said. His voice was steady and clear. A small man at the edge of the far table laughed, a thick treacly sound that dissolved into a hacking cough.

The bearded man answered without looking up. "This nonna yer concern, nigger. Go home while you have chance."

Atellus stepped forward, his right hand resting casually on the pommel of his sheathed spatha. "I need to speak with that woman. Anyone interfering or hindering will be charged with treason and executed."

The bearded man scrubbed a hand across his chops and looked across. He shouted something in Brythonic, and the table across the room laughed. The woman moaned and twisted beneath the man's bench.

"If yer so eager for an execution, nigger," he spat, nodding slowly to himself, "happen yill find one tonight."

He rose, and pulled a rusted dagger from his belt. The other men stood also, wild and ragged shades, like dark-dressed demons stained with mud and soot. They shouted and cawed into the beams overhead. The red-haired woman disappeared into her alcove.

Calidus sprang to his feet, but his legs felt rubbery and he nearly collapsed back into his own chair. He had no weapon, but he tensed his arms, clenched his fists together. His father had been a brave man, and had died wrapt in courage. If this is what it meant to be his father's son, he would do the same.

Atellus drew his spatha; it slid from the oiled leather scabbard with a rasp. His eyes were hard, dark and bright like polished stone. Calidus fancied he could see the trace of a smile tugging at the corner of the easterner's mouth.

"Citizens, sheathe your weapons."

The voice came from behind them and Calidus turned to look at who had made the demand. There were five limitanei behind them, stalking into the room from the narrow door leading to the side street from the vicus. They were dressed wildly, like savages spattered with tokens of Rome, but their blades were long and stained with use and their eyes were hard.

The bearded man stood his ground for a while, then tucked his dagger away into his belt. He spat noisily onto the ground, not taking his eyes from the soldiers. He shouted some Brythonic at them, and gestured. The soldier in command replied in the same tongue before turning to Atellus.

"I have orders to escort you to the principia," he said. "The praefectus requests that you do us the honour of accompanying us back to the fort."

It was not a request, but Atellus ignored the tone of the command. "The praefectus is generous," he said meeting the eyes of the soldier. "I would be glad of the extra swords." He turned to look at the bearded man and his accomplices, and the half-conscious woman sprawled at their legs. "These northern nights are wild and rife with bandits."

The soldier stood aside to give them free exit to the street. Calidus saw Atellus run his thumb hard along the blade of his sword, and flick the fresh blood down onto the straw before turning away from the men in the tavern. He sheathed his spatha and nodded at Calidus to follow him. He walked out, past the soldiers and into the dark and frozen evening. Calidus followed, and the soldiers peeled themselves out of the tavern behind him.

CHAPTER 11

Atellus reached across the table for a fig. They were clustered in a bronze bowl, brown and fat and juicy. They looked incongruous in this freezing country. To him, they sang of sun, of bright clear bluegreen seas, and warm zephyrs sweeping across the parched land.

"We have those imported from Ionia," said Apullius. He sat at the head of his breakfast table, dressed in a long velvet gown a shade of purple that Atellus reckoned was calculated to be just the right side of treasonous. There was a large metal cross fixed on brackets to the wall behind him, a symbol of the crucified god of the Christians. The crucified god of the Empire, he reminded himself.

"Very expensive," continued the praefectus, reaching for a jug of chilled buttermilk. "But worth it, don't you think? Just because we live at the end of the earth doesn't mean we have to live like beasts."

Atellus grunted noncommittally and thought back to the previous night. The commander of Aesica had not spoken to them personally when the 'honour escort' had delivered them wordlessly to the gate of the principia. Instead he had left a message that they were to break their fast with him, and that they would be summoned at prima.

Atellus had walked back to his quarters leaving the boy to tread reluctantly away in the opposite direction. He had hoped to sleep well, it being his first night under tile and stone, and on soft surface: the warmth and the security should have been conducive to an adequately restful state, even without the burden of the exhaustion that felt draped across his shoulders like a pallium. Yet he had woken each hour, his brow burning, his eyes scanning the blackness for moving shapes.

When dawn sent grey fingers probing through the darkness, he had risen to pray to the unconquered sun, before relaxing into a troubled sleep for a short time.

He was awoken by a loud rapping at the door. He had let her in, a woman, bent and silent, who must have seen sixty hard winters at least; she brought warm water, and wine, and set them down wordlessly on the table, her eyes sunken into the floor.

Atellus dressed in a fine cotton shirt with linen trousers. He had left his boots in the corridor the previous night, and when he pulled them on found they had been cleaned of mud, the leather polished so they shone in the daylight. The old famulus had led him down the corridor, through the main atrium, up the broad staircase and into a large adjoining room at the top. The table was already laid, and Apullius and Calidus sat opposite each other, the boy's posture rigid.

Atellus chewed on the fig; it exploded in his mouth, tasting of sunlight and yellowgreen grass. It wasn't as fresh as the ones he remembered, but then he had never tasted one which had travelled so far. He shuddered to think of the cost of importing such produce in from the empire, when Britannia starved and rioted beneath the very wheels of the cart which bore them north.

He looked around the table: Red and green grapes, black olives, greyish-yellow corn cobs, three brown and moist roast Guinea fowl, at least four types of hard cheese, knobs of black bread, butter, slices of a smoked meat that looked like pork, muria, and a bowl of sliced axungia. There were nuts and a selection of chilled vinum sitting in hammered gold buckets of crushed ice.

Atellus's stomach growled loudly.

"I was under the impression, praefectus," he said, "that there was a famine on the land. Looking at your table, maybe I am mistaken."

Apullius was gnawing at a Guinea fowl wing, the juice running down his chin. He reached for a goblet of vinum and rinsed his mouth with the cool wine, swallowing the flesh and dabbing his lips with a towel before speaking.

"There have indeed been bad harvests. The people have been starving for many days. This," he waved a hand over the heaving table, "is merely a gesture, to honour the dignity of our guests. Would you have me, beneficiarius, welcome the emperor's own emissary to my lodgings with a bowl of saltfish gruel and a mug of warm water? Some would construe that as an insult, a slight against the honour of Valentinian."

Atellus smiled. "I appreciate the gesture, praefectus, but I am not the emperor. A bowl of gruel will suffice. The vinum, on the other hand, I could well get accustomed to."

Apullius laughed, and raised his goblet. "I see you have fine taste then! But I would expect no less from a man so close to our emperor."

"So," said Atellus, letting the smile fade from his lips, "what can the rest of the soldiers expect for their meals?"

Apullius stopped laughing abruptly, and put down the bread he had in his fist. "Very little, to be frank, beneficiarius. Very little. There is famine, certainly in the north, and it gets worse with each passing week." He looked across the broad table at Atellus, his hard eyes stern, set deep within his heavy skull. "There are rumours of disease in the vicus. It has not yet entered the fort, but that can only be a matter of time.

"There is never enough grain," he continued, shaking his head, "and what beasts we have left are ill and slat-ribbed. Two thirds of what little produce we manage to import is lost to pirates and brigands. The situation is grave." Apullius leaned his solid frame across the table and met Atellus's eyes. "Eat and be thankful, is the advice I give my men. For tomorrow it may be gone."

The praefectus settled back into his chair and popped the dark bread into his mouth, chewing it intently, his eyes still resting upon the beneficiarius.

"I think, praefectus," said Atellus, "tomorrow has already arrived for most of your men."

Apullius took a drink of his wine, eyeing Atellus over the rim of the goblet, but remained silent. Calidus coughed and reached over for a piece of meat.

"I also noticed," said Atellus, "that the citizens speak of Cernunnos. Of the old gods. I saw shrines to Belatucadros when I passed through the vicus."

"That is true," replied the commander. "My predecessor tried to destroy them, in line with Constantine's orders, but there was riot and defection. We let the men keep their fancies. Life is very different up here, beneficiarius. If you are here to pry and poke into the men's beliefs, you will find much at odds with however it is done in Treves, or Rome." He waved a large hand, as if dismissing the subject. "Men die every day here: they collapse from want of food, freeze to death in the snows, watch their families burn when the bastards break through and decide to remind us they are still there. These people will cling to whatever eases their rough passage from this life to the next." He looked intently at Atellus across the length of the table. "I will be honest with you, beneficiarius: I will not be the man to stop them. I need functioning limitanei, not men with a grudge against their commander."

"I understand, praefectus," replied Atellus. "I am not here to force Christianity upon your men. I am sure others have plans for that."

"Indeed," nodded Apullius wearily. "I know that you cleave to the old gods as much as some of my men, beneficiarius."

163

Atellus plucked a grape from the bunch in front of him. It was small and dry. "I worship," he smiled. "That will change when the sun ceases to rise at dawn."

"As it happens," said Apullius, rolling a fig across the back of his hand, "I follow the faith of the emperor. By choice."

"That must put you in an awkward position."

"Not really," mused the praefectus. "I am a pragmatist. Living here, every day a battle, one has to be." He popped the fig into his mouth, and rolled his large eyes in satisfaction.

"Are your men sound?" asked Atellus.

"I trust them with my life, beneficiarius. As every commander must."

There was a short silence filled only by the sounds of chewing and clink of goblets and knives.

"I fought under Lupicinus," said Atellus, after swallowing a tough piece of bread, "against the incursions of seven winters ago. I did not know of Aesica, but many other forts lost many men. To the northmen; to the brigands; to the hills."

Apullius nodded. "I was not praefectus at the time, nor based here. I know Aesica lost some of her force. But the numbers have been steadily dwindling for much longer than seven winters. The cohort is Asturian, originally. Though any southern blood has long since been bred out. You may see the occasional pair of dark eyes, the olive-coloured skin. But I would say ninety out of every hundred men here are drawn from local stock, recruited from the sheep herders and farmers of the hills."

"Are they Roman?"

164

"They are Brython, beneficiarius. But their loyalty is to me."

"And not to Rome?"

"My loyalty is to Rome," said Apullius. "Theirs is to me."

Atellus sat back in his chair and reached out for some pork fat. He chewed it thoughtfully, feeling the rich flavour melt on his tongue before speaking again. "Only a foolish emperor would fail to see that as dangerous."

The praefectus shrugged. "I would wager my command that the same is true of every commander on the Wall."

"Fullofaudes?"

"Especially so."

"How much contact do you have with the dux?"

"Beacons each evening," said Apullius. "A rider once a week. I visit him personally twice a year. He will come to visit here on occasion. Every winter, usually."

"A good leader?" Atellus asked, swilling the last of his wine round his cheeks, feeling the tickle of the acid, the pangs of flavour prickling across his gums. It really was excellent wine.

"He is capable," said Apullius, after thinking for a while. "He has not yet been tested. Aurelius, the previous dux Britanniorum, was capable until he died. But the dux takes his orders from the legatus at Eboracum, who takes his from the Governor. The dux is a political pawn, rather than a true soldier."

"So you have little faith in him?"

"I have enough. The rest I have in myself, and my men."

"I appreciate your candour, praefectus," said Atellus with a nod.

"I have nothing to conceal, beneficiarius," replied Apullius. "Neither from you, nor Valentinian."

Calidus coughed. His dish was piled high with meat, cheese and grapes.

"Apologies, young sir," said Apullius turning to the youth. "Do not take this cynical talk of old soldiers to heart. You will learn much from the dux, and he will train you well, in soldiery and politics. For anyone continuing along that twisted and treacherous path, he will be a boon mentor, I can assure you of that."

"Might I ask, praefectus," said Calidus, after clearing his throat, "when you think it likely that I will be able to leave for Petriana?"

Apullius smiled, dabbing at his large lips with the edge of a warm towel. "My messenger is due to leave in three days and you will accompany him. Along with an appropriate honour guard of course. It would not do for my next message to the governor to be one informing him of the death of his nephew." He bared his teeth in what Calidus presumed was a smile, before turning back to Atellus. "But, beneficiarius, you have many questions, though none concerning the purpose of your...visit."

Atellus nodded. "What can you tell me of that?" he asked. "I have been briefed in Eboracum, but would like to hear the facts from you, if you would oblige me."

Apullius threw a meaningful glance at Calidus who was chewing on a piece of strong cheese; his confusion over the taste was painted across his face.

"The boy is safe," said Atellus. "He knows as much as I."

"Does he, indeed?" said Apullius. "Then allow me to continue. You are here to investigate our missing agent in rebus, of course."

Atellus loosened the scarf around his neck. He felt Apullius's eyes on it. "Indeed. And your missing young, praefectus."

"Of course," he smiled ingratiatingly and lowered his eyes to his place where a mauled leg of fowl sat swimming in grease and fig juice. He picked at it half-heartedly. "Any way I can help your investigations. The fort and its resources are entirely at your service, beneficiarius."

"Thank you," said Atellus inclining his head slightly.

"As for the agent," said Apullius, "I know he sent regular reports to the Governor. I know he was operating on the principle of testing the loyalty and steadfastness of our men. All the men, along the Wall. I believe I have no reason to fear his despatches."

"And when did you last see the agent?"

"Six days ago," said Apullius, "personally, though there are others who had more recent contact. I did not speak with him directly of course. It would not have been...appropriate for me to formally acknowledge his existence."

Atellus nodded.

"However," continued the praefectus, "I had two of my men keep an eye on him. Tertius is a centurion of my principal century. He last saw the agent in the milecastle to the west. 'Culuslupi', the men call it, if you will pardon their crudeness."

"What was he doing there?"

167

Apullius shrugged. "I believe he sometimes visited the men with buckets of ale and stories from the south. He was ostensibly here as a sutler and merchant. They grew used to him. He was good at his job, by all accounts." The commander's lips curled, whether in a sneer or smile, Atellus couldn't tell.

"How many men are stationed at the milecastles?"

"Woefully few," Apullius sighed, "and decreasing each year. Between here and Vindolanda to the east there are six milecastles; Suagrius, the praefectus at Vindolanda, is responsible for manning five of them. We have six men on the nearest fort, rotating shifts every half-moon. There are three milecastles heading west to Magnis, and we man two of them. Culuslupi is the nearest. I have six men on it at any time."

"And this Tertius," asked Atellus, "was the last to see him?"

"He bade him farewell as he left Culuslupi," answered Apullius. "The agent never arrived here. I have had men search the road between, but there has been no sign. The logical conclusion, as far as I can see, is that he either died by the will of God and was buried by snow, or dragged off by animals. Or," he said, reaching out for the last of the shrivelled grapes, "he was found by brigands." Apullius shrugged. "Of course, I understand why the issue is so sensitive. Any missing agent is enough to raise the hackles of the governor. But men disappear daily from the limes; it is part of life on the frontier."

"Then," said Atellus, settling back in his chair, "you believe his disappearance is not connected with that of the children?"

Apullius took a swallow of vinum, then dabbed at his lips. "Beneficiarius," he said, leaning forward across the table to look deep into Atellus's eyes, "I do not believe in the disappearance of any children. My main concern would be exactly why the emperor has an interest in such wild tales and hearsay. Who here, which troublemaker, has the ear of Valentinian and fills it with shit like this?" He slapped a large fist down on the table; the dishes leapt and rattled, and Calidus flinched.

"When we are under-strength and starving," continued Apullius, his faced mottled with red, his voice loud and stern, "when our men have not been paid for two winters, when the savages to the north plot and form alliances and scheme against us. Why has this crut about the whelps managed to stir the emperor's interest in our distant plight?"

"It is not for me," said Atellus calmly, "or you, praefectus, to question the emperor's motives."

"Of course," said Apullius, his cheeks glowing red with checked emotion. "Of course. But I genuinely believe that there is no great conspiratio here. Tykes go missing regularly. They run away, they are beaten to death by angry fathers, they are killed and buried in the snow by mothers who cannot afford to feed them and cannot bear to see them starve. There are families in that vicus who would think nothing of selling their whelps, or cooking them for food. I will not waste time chasing shadows and rumours. Not when a storm brews around us."

Atellus sipped thoughtfully at his wine. "Do you dismiss the possibility of brigands stealing the young? Or raids from the north?"

Apullius laughed, a rich treacly sound that seemed at odds with his heavy features. "Beneficiarius, those wild curs would never dare approach the Wall. Not to snatch children from the very bosoms of their family. They would be seen and cut down before they got close." He poured himself another beaker of wine and tossed a mouthful back with a snap of his wrist.

"By force, maybe not," said Atellus. "But by stealth? I know the northerners worship in the old ways, with blood offerings. Would they not take Roman flesh over their own kin?"

169

"If you knew the northmen as I do," said Apullius, "you would know that they would sooner burn their own diseased oxen than sacrifice a Roman chittle to their primitive gods. And there is no way for them to get within a hundred paces of the Wall without being seen." The praefectus stretched his arms around him, palms upward. "These are the greatest defences in the empire. Those dumb pigs to the north have only to look at the shadow cast by our walls and they shit themselves all the way back to their dunghills and hay heaps."

"When I was last at the Wall," said Atellus, "I noticed other commanders had more respect for their enemies than you seem to show, praefectus."

"Indeed," said Apullius, his eyes hard and tense. "And look what happened to them. Their blood still decorates the walls of their forts. But not here, beneficiarius, not in Aesica."

Atellus tore off a hunk of hard bread, and dipped it into a shallow dish of oil; the oil glowed gold by the light of the lantern hanging above the table. Apullius bent down to his own food; his neck was red, his eyes lightly swimming with wine. They ate in silence for a while; only the wind outside and the soft murmur of servant's boots along the corridor outside could be heard.

"There was a lady in the tavern last night," said Atellus, chewing thoughtfully on a sodden crust of oiled bread, "who begged me to find her child. Cernunnos had taken her, she said."

Apullius spat another mirthless laugh across the table. "Cernunnos, indeed. So the old gods are roving our vicus, snatching whelps." He picked up a greasy thigh bone from his dish and gnawed thoughtfully at the gristle before setting it down again. "She was clearly raving, beneficiarius. I am sure you can see that. The moon is full, the bellies are empty. The streets of that vicus are awash with pain and madness and I cannot afford to pay heed to it. If we want an end to the problems, let the emperor send troops to rout the brigands, let him send a fleet to sink the pirates who steal our grain. Instead, he sends you, beneficiarius, to chase shadows and bolster the fantasies of mad bitches."

Apullius coughed and lowered his eyes. The praefectus's large fists were gripping the table edge, Atellus noted, and the colour had risen from his neck to his jawline. When he looked up again, his eyes were soft and calm.

"Apologies, beneficiarius," said Apullius. "You have a job, as do I. As I said, I offer you the freedom of the fort. I ask only that you allow yourself to be accompanied when visiting the vicus, as it can be dangerous for strangers. I am sure you discovered this yesterday evening. If you can wait until the morrow, I will arrange for an escort to take you to Culuslupi, and you can speak to the men there."

"Thank you," said Atellus, inclining his head slightly. "Does the name Densligneus mean anything to you?"

"Densligneus?" The praefectus sucked his lip in and mused over the word, tasting it. "It means nothing. Should it?"

Atellus picked up a piece of hard cheese and crumbled it between his thumb and forefinger. "I am not yet sure, praefectus."

"Well, please forgive me, comrades," said Apullius. "I must prepare myself for parade." He turned to Calidus, a smile thickening his mouth. "Whilst the beneficiarius carries out his investigations, I would be more than happy to show you, young Lucius, the ins and outs of military life."

***

Calidus walked through the corridor, back towards his own chamber. His belly was full of rich food, and the sensation of having been able to eat until he was unable to stomach any more was a satisfying and comforting one. Every so often his guts let out a gurgle of disapproval at having to cope with such quantities so early in the morning. He dispatched another sonorous belch and noted the taste of creamy buttermilk on his breath.

Calidus winced again at the memory of his encounter with the praefectus just prior to breakfast. Calidus has been loitering outside his own room, waiting for a servant to escort him to the dining area. He had felt someone catch his arm, their grasp subtle but firm. He had spun round, indignant, fists clenched, and looked into the broad face of Apullius himself. The praefectus had pulled him close to his own body before backing Calidus up against the corridor wall; he was dwarfed by the height and breadth of the larger man. He had caught the sour pinch of Apullius's underarm sweat, and the sweet floral odour of his breath, his tongue lacquered with honeyed wine.

Apullius had been loquacious, rolling out questions about Eboracum, about his uncle, about his own ambitions. His hand had tensed around the youth's upper arm, his large fingers kneading almost playfully as he spoke.

Calidus has answered bluntly and guardedly, but the commander had continued regardless. Apullius was digging for information, Calidus knew that much, but he made certain he gave away as little as possible. He had learned from being around his uncle that even the most seemingly trivial nugget of information could be priceless to the right person.

In terms of his skills at ferreting for information, Apullius was blunt and nowhere near as subtle or insidious as other officers back in Eboracum that Calidus had had the misfortune to be left alone with. The camp commander was coarse and unsophisticated, at times as brutal and oppressive as the Wall itself. He was an overhand blow from a spatha, compared to the whicks and dashes of a poisoned needle employed by the more jaded career politicians in the city, the men and women steeped and seasoned for long sultry years in the intrigues and treacheries of provincial powerplay.

So he deflected and parried with ease as the praefectus threw the lumpen questions at him. Eventually they had walked almost to the main gate of the courtyard of the praefectus's quarters, and Apullius had turned him into the cold nook of a corner by the heavy wooden door, and laid a musclethick hand upon Calidus's shoulder. He lifted the youth's chin up with the calloused thumb and forefinger of his other hand, so he could stare into his eyes. The commander's were blue and severe, the edges creased, but not through laughter, or the happy crinkled smiles that had furrowed his uncle's skin; these were the fine scars etched from years of staring hard into dim misty horizons; of squinting into bleak blood-sodden sunrises; of scouring the bodies of living and dead alike upon frost-scratched and honourless battlefields.

"I know what you think, Lucius," Apullius had said, the corner of his mouth edged in a wry smile. "That I am after information about your uncle, about the state of affairs in Eboracum." He shook his head with a curl of his lips. "Brocchus is an old friend; Eboracum is a venerable uncle. I care nothing for politics. Just news."

Calidus was aware of the great pressure on his shoulder, the man's weight forcing down on him, rooting him to the spot, and the fingers chucking his chin were rigid, holding his face tight and firm.

"Just news, Lucius," Apullius repeated. "I am hungry for tales of the world behind the Wall. There would be no betrayal involved, no secrets that need be leaked, no confidences broken. Just idle sutler tattle. There are not many who can be entrusted to impart such to the praefectus, without weaving their own sullied woof into the warp."

The commander moved his face closer to Calidus's. "But I trust *you*, Lucius. I do trust you: noble birth, responsibility. *Breeding*."

Apullius moved his face away from the youth's and looked around him. "And this place, Lucius," he said, with an air of weariness. "There are dangerous men here.

173

Wild men. Because that is what we want: Killers. *Ferae*. To protect the borders, the boundaries. Of *your* soft and civilised world." He looked strangely at Calidus, his eyes shining, the hard flesh on the pad of his thumb stroking the fur of the youth's chin. "To protect the young, the soft, coddled in their cities, sleeping; unaware of the fury and death beyond the white stone walls."

The commander fell silent for a moment. There was the sound of the grim wind sucking and dashing through the courtyard outside, and the rail and yell of soldiers sparring beyond.

Suddenly Apullius clapped Calidus's back, jolting him forward. "And you, young Lucius," he said, his stern eyes throbbing with a lupine glow in the shaded nook, "you like fighting, yes? You want to see combat, feel the bite of blade on flesh?"

Calidus nodded.

"Of course you do, of course. I will arrange for some training for you from my best men. Good men. Fine training before we see you safely off to the dux."

Apullius looked hard into Calidus's eyes, before nodding and turning away. He walked past him and tore open the door leading to the courtyard. Icy air and soft spits of sleet thrashed inside in a flurry, and then the praefectus was gone, and Calidus was left with the gooseflesh on his arms and the faint odour of honeyed wine in his nose.

Calidus let loose another belch as he thought back to the encounter and shivered again; there was something about Apullius man that made his flesh feel greasy, made him long for the sharp edge of a strigil to strop his skin clean. He needed to stay with the beneficiarius, keep close to the easterner: to find out what his uncle wanted to know, of course, but also for his own safety. Atellus was the only man he had met so far who didn't see him as a catamite or a child. And he knew that the easterner had been tasked with looking after him; his only way of remaining intact seemed to be by staying with the beneficiarius.

He had seen Atellus soften slightly, seen talk ooze through the frosted edges of his facade like sap from a winter tree. He could get through to him and get more from him, but first he needed to stay with him. And if that meant heading to Culuslupi with him, so be it.

Calidus arrived at his own corridor, opposite Apullius's own stately chambers. The cold seemed to settle into the walls around him, despite the soft throb of heat from the hypocaust beneath his boots. A stale and coughing servant bustled past him with armfuls of dishes from the breakfast feast. If they were anything like their servants in Eboracum, they would all be feasting on the leftovers in the basement, hoarding them for days, parcelling them out evenly between themselves and smuggling them away to friends and families or humping them into the vicus to barter for drink or tools or sex.

He stopped outside his own door. It was slightly ajar.

A sweet lick of cold air dashed through the gap between the door and the wall. Calidus placed his palm flat on the old firm oak. The doors did not shut tight here; they were warped from the alternating heat of the hypocaust and the constant cold of the northern climate.

He pushed the door open.

He couldn't say why, but he felt uncomfortable: a deep and almost painful tightness in the pit of his belly. He could feel the fine hairs on the back of his neck prickling like the antennae of small *insecta*.

He walked inside and into the first room, his bedchamber.

Something was wrong.

He could feel it: an extra warmth, the soft pressure of a foreign respiration in the air. He looked around and his hand instinctively went to the dagger tucked into his breeches.

His room was just as he left it.

No; not quite.

His bedding – left dishevelled after he had kicked his way out the blankets earlier – had been pulled taut over his large bed; his pillows had been plumped, and a small oil lamp on the table to his left had been lit. The light from it spread softly through the morning dimness, a subtle glow that reminded Calidus how tired he was.

"Hello?" he called. Perhaps the servant was still in here, arranging his bathing room.

No response.

Something still bothered him though; something barely perceptible, but a tangible feeling that seemed to tickle at the very extremities of his awareness.

Calidus walked uneasily through to the antechamber, where a table with light snacks of olives and hard cheese of a soft brown colour had been set up on battered tin plates. He could hear the wind outside surging against the old stonework, pushing its slender fingers into cracks in the mortar, heaving against the building. It sounded cold and angry.

It was the smell that registered, eventually: a vinegary tang like posca, fat heavy particles crowding the stagnant air.

This was not the smell of servants; there was something brutal, and threatening about the odour. A voice in his head was yelling at him to get out, to run; to run fast to safety.

A cold shiver ran up his forearms.

As Calidus turned back towards his bedroom, the blow hit him hard on the side of his head, and he was on the floor before he realised he had fallen.

Darkness throbbed at the corners of his eyes, and a queer buzzing shook through his jaw and into his ears. He was conscious of a grunt and a laugh above him, behind him, and then the room disappeared into a treacly black void and all thought went with it.

CHAPTER 12

She was aware of the smell at first.

It was a thick and heady scent, like a soiled rag pressed tight against her face; the smell of the latrines, the thick rich reek of beasts of the earth.

Aurelia thought she would suffocate. She coughed and sat upright and the room exploded into a muddy focus as her eyes twitched opened; she had not realised they had been shut.

She was sitting on a straw-covered pallet, low to the ground. The room was dim and warm. A fire burned slowly beside her head, peat smoke curling up towards a vent in the thatched roof. She could hear the grunt and snuffle of animals pawing through the hay beside her. Pale daylight and cold gusts of air blew in through a half-open door at the far end of the room.

She tried to remember what had happened. She recalled sick vivid dreams laced with sweat and pain: back in her husband's basement. Although, she had never truly thought of the man as her husband, and now she had even less cause to do so. In her dreams she was hanging in Crispus's basement, hanging, bleeding and tired, delirious with thirst. Quintus and Dexter were there.

Quintus is dead.

The thought was foreign, like the voice of another entering her head from outside, yet she knew it to be true. Aurelia felt afresh the hot spurts of the man's blood as she tore through his throat with her fingers. It had felt good. Like the old days, when she had been young and vigorous.

She remembered escaping. Or at least trying to. She recalled the snowy courtyard, the hound.

Then nothing.

Aurelia looked around again, her eyes adjusting to the gloom. It was a dwelling; a very poor dwelling. Almost a byre. She was not bound, nor could she sense any injury. The door was open. She didn't know where she was, but she had the feeling that she had not been unconscious for long. If anything, she felt refreshed.

She could hear a voice outside – deep male tones – and then the door was kicked fully open and painful white light raged inside, illuminating the room. The man clattered the flimsy door shut behind him, and looked over at her. He wore long shaggy hair and a fierce matted beard in the native fashion.

"You awake, then," he said, looking away from her. He set a faggot of wood down beside the fire, then walked over to a cot at the far end of the room; Aurelia had not noticed it before. A woman lay supine on it, draped casually in rags, which parted to reveal a swollen stomach lined with angry veins; her belly looked ready to burst. The man bent down to stroke her head, and held a wooden cup to her lips. The pregnant lady drank in silence.

"You need be gone," he said, putting the cup down and walking over to her. "Better fer you, better fer me."

"Who...are you?" asked Aurelia. "And what...why am I here?"

The man walked across the room to her, stepping over a thin and wheezing goose, and brushing past a lame piglet. The latter squeaked and shuffled off. The stench of filth rose again, fresh and hot.

The man bent down to her and Aurelia shuffled backwards, but there was nothing menacing in his approach or physiognomy. He was older than she, and looked tired. He studied her silently, squinting in the dim light. Aurelia felt uncomfortable, but she met his gaze, unblinking. After what felt like a long while, he lowered his eyes and spoke.

"Found you," he said, kneeling beside her pallet. "In the palace grounds. Scared, you was. And I can see why, the things I've heard." He shook his head. "You were lookin to getout. I helped. Ye fell sick, dizzy." He shrugged. "I slinged yer oer me scap and brought yis here. Home."

Home, he had said. He was not smiling; he actually lived in this sty.

Aurelia was not shocked, though. She had lived in worse, in the line of duty. But those days were old, and she had grown soft and distant, become fond of opulence, of ease, of comfort. Many things had changed since she had been married to that wretch.

And many things would change now, she recognised.

"My thanks," she said. "I probably owe you my life."

The man shrugged again, then reached over to where a hammered tin cup hung suspended from a twig above the smoke of the peat fire. He pulled the cup down and handed it to her.

"Drink," he said. "For strength."

The broth smelled like leaf mulch. It was hard to tell in the gloom, but it seemed to be a viscous brown liquid. Aurelia put it tentatively to her lips. It was warm and sweet. She took a sip. The taste was not as bad as she had feared.

"Is…is she alright?" She looked over to the pregnant girl in the corner. She seemed to be sleeping. The soft susurrus of her breath floated through the room. Her belly rose like an ancient tumulus in the dark, ready to split.

"She will be," he said quietly. "Arter she purges."

Aurelia nodded. The child would be lucky to survive a day in these conditions. But there was little she could do to help. She was without home herself, or food, or position. She was most likely being hunted now. She had to get out of the city.

"Where are we?" she asked.

"Calles," he answered.

That was good; the slum district crammed up beneath the western city wall would be the last area Crispus would be looking for her. Unless he had learned more than she gave him credit for; in which case it would probably be one of the first.

Either way it was only a matter of time before his men caught up with her, and she would sooner eat herself alive than be taken by his ghouls one more time. Not after what she had done to Quintus. There were no more bridges to burn.

"I cannot repay you, I am sorry," she said, fixing her keen azure eyes on his. "I have nothing. Less than nothing. But maybe in winters to come, if the gods are kind to me, I can show my gratitude. What is your name?"

"Decius," he replied. "And I wan no reward. I am a tonsor by trade. I labour out at your palace, atimes. For your husband." He nodded at her. "Seen an 'eard doins I narn wish to think much on." He shook his shaggy head.

"Decius," said Aurelia. She set the empty tin cup down beside her and reached out to grasp his wrist. He drew away from her touch, his eyes creasing, but she would not let him back away. His flesh was leathery and thick. Warm. She could feel the thump of his pulse under her slender fingers. "Decius, thank you. I am in your debt. And now I need to get away. Out of Eboracum. North. Do you know anyone who could help me?"

He looked hard at her. The creases around his eyes gleamed palely through the dirt encrusted on his face. He pulled his arm free of her gripe, then got up and stoked the peat fire, pushing some more fuel onto it. He walked over to the pregnant woman. Aurelia could not tell if it was a wife or a daughter. The goose hissed at his heels as he passed, but he barely noticed it. She could see now how thin he was, his worn leather tunic sagging from the angles of his joints. He walked in a desperate agonising shuffle that seemed to bear the agony of his existence within each step, as though the effort of unfurling himself into the space around him was almost too great. He sat down beside the woman and gripped her hand, though he said nothing.

Aurelia lay back, suddenly tired. Her clothes itched. Her feet were colder than they had ever felt before. Her forehead was clammy. The fire purred beside her head, her nose filled with the reeking animal shit. Outside a man was screaming, high and wild like a toddler.

After a while, Decius walked back over and stood above her.

"I know some men could help," he said. "The way out be hard. The north e'en harder; south'd be better'r you."

Aurelia shook her head. "I must go north. I have friends there."

Decius nodded heavily. "I know some men."

"If your friends could help," said Aurelia, "I would be able to repay them once I got to the Wall."

She would have long enough to think exactly how she could do that, but it seemed more pressing at the moment to get out of the city, even riding on promises she could not keep. She could feel every passing moment as a ponderous weight on her shoulders, pressing her down to her doom. She could almost feel the kicks shivering through the shack door as Crispus's hounds forced entry and surged upon them all.

"They inna my friends," said Decius, shaking his head slowly. "Their type don't have *friends*."

***

It was colder outside than Aurelia had dared imagine. A haze of snow hung in the air like a strip of low cloud. Decius had given her a swatch of sacking to wrap around her face as a disguise. It also helped to keep the bite of the cold off her nose and lips. Unfortunately, it stank like pig shit.

They walked through the lanes of the Calles. The passages were narrow, barely drover's tracks, and the timber houses were built endlessly tall and crooked all around them, looking as if they would collapse with one strong gust of wind. The ground underfoot was frozen mud – in summer rains the tracks would be turned to stinking swamps, impassable to cart or beast. Now the huddled poor limped and fidgeted their way through the cold hours, gathered round steaming braziers or open fires on the corners and in the stone shells of fallen buildings.

Like many of the city's poorer districts, Aurelia recalled, the Calles had once been a wealthy area, a region close to what used to be the grand temple of Serapis, filled with tall houses, inns and brothels on every corner, with rows of opulent shops inbetween. After the sacking by the Allectine supporters and the plague that followed, the wealthy had never returned. Instead the area was shunned, seen as cursed by the gods, and it gradually crumbled and fell into the long grass and swamps of the wet months. And then the poor had moved in, forced out of other districts by rising rents.

Decius walked hurriedly through the uneven streets, turning off down narrow ginnels that Aurelia doubted she would even have noticed had she been alone. Her guide's feet seemed to pick out the troughs and ridges of the ground beneath them, while Aurelia tripped and slipped and twisted her ankles as her boots snagged on the irregular surface; it took all her energy and concentration just to keep from hobbling herself.

The sky overhead was a dolorous grey and the fine sherds of snow seemed to hang in the air, pricking her hands and forehead as she followed. Beyond the crammed and jostling timbers of the city around her she could hear the sounds of distant markets, of loud bartering and shouting, of yelled curses and entreaties. Tears and screams, and desperate moans, hung like an incessant pall around the Calles.

Decius stopped suddenly by a dwelling at the end of a lane where the path terminated abruptly in a tumbled mass of masonry. There were gaping slots in the large stones where timber beams had long since been hauled out and used for fuel. The sounds of the city at their backs seemed oddly muted and distant.

"Let me talk, and dun dispute what I say," said Decius, his voice low. He spoke slowly, his words measured and filtered before emerging from his mouth. "Need to put ye in context for em. Yar a woman travelling north to find trade. Forget all'a who you weres. Unnerstand?"

Aurelia nodded tensely.

The dwelling was a squat hovel with bulbous walls of wattle and daub and a tangled roof of thatch and wintergrass. There was no door, only a coarse and sootblack muleskin drawn across the threshold. Decius shouted inside, and waited.

A long, hacking, splintering cough erupted from inside, and Aurelia could hear sounds of shuffling movement. Long moments later, a crippled man swung the blanket aside and peered suspiciously out at them. He recognised Decius, and clapped a gnarled hand on his wrist, the other returning the gesture, but he looked at Aurelia – wrapped fat in her maid's clothes – with tight, beady eyes and licked his blistered lips.

"Wossis you gotta gift fer me, Decius?" he said in a throaty rasp of a voice. Aurelia could barely understand the man's accent.

"I ask a favour, Gildas," he said, turning his chin towards Aurelia. "The woman be a friend. She's need passage north. When yer bearns next rovin up?"

"North, eh," said Gildas. He had not lifted his filmy eyes from Aurelia for a second and she felt the heat and menace in his watery gaze. "Not now, not ferra bit. It will cost too, and not in beard-trims, Decius. Not in shearings, nay!" The old man spat out a laugh which dissipated into a coughing fit.

"I can pay handsomely once we reach the Wall," said Aurelia, her voice strong and firm, ringing in the cold air.

The old man looked at her, and chewed at his lip with a toothless mouth. "It speaks, it speaks," he mumbled to himself, "and such a fine voice." He looked up at Decius. "Where did you find it, hm, Decius?"

"She is a friend, Gildas," he replied firmly, "and we treat her wi' respect."

"Yes," said Gildas, shaking his head. "Rodius!" He raised his voice and shouted inside the hovel, over his shoulder, then collapsed into a coughing fit. It faded and he hacked up a gobbet and spat it onto the icy ground.

A younger man emerged into the daylight, bearded, long haired and well-built, with half-lidded eyes and firm square lips. He wore a leather smock that was streaked with grease and old blood. He smelled of death and wax. He looked first at Aurelia, then at Decius.

"What have you brought us, Decius?" his voice was low and soft.

"Goods for the north, Rod," answered Gildas, before the other man could speak, taking his eyes from Aurelia once more and looking up towards his son. "More goods for the north."

"I would like to leave today, if possible," said Aurelia. "I can pay."

Rodius looked at her, measuring her with those half-lidded eyes. "I am sure you can."

He had an oiled cloth in his large hands, and he used it to wipe his paws. "We leave in two days, when our goods are ready for transport. No sooner."

Aurelia felt panic fizzing up inside her, scalding her belly. "Please," she implored, "I need to go sooner, I need—"

"You *need*?" said Rodius, tossing the rag across his shoulder and fixing her with a keen stare. "These are times for need; it is all around you." He twisted his heavy lips into a smile. "We move bitches north for one purpose only: fresh quim for the animals on the Wall."

Aurelia felt the air between them filling up with the silence.

"She has people up north," said Decius, eventually. "She be a friend of Martella's." He took a step closer to Rodius. "This would be a favour for me, Rodius."

The two men looked at each other. "I thought you knew better than asking favours of me, tonsor," said Rodius. Then he laughed again, a curt whip of humourless noise from his throat. "Has Martella dropped yet?"

Decius shook his head.

"So you don't even know if the bastard is yours," grinned Rodius. He scrubbed a hand across the front of his smock making a rasping noise, keen in the cold air. "From what I hear she was fucking every sailor that came into port. The little runt will be black as a Numidian, for all we know." He smiled at the older man. "But you are a better man than me, Decius, to wait anyway. Half of Eboracum bets against you, but you are too stubborn to change your pips."

Decius lowered his head and exhaled, his breath pluming out into the cold air.

Rodius looked at Aurelia. "How are you called, woman?"

"Crassa," she answered. An alias she had used before in Britannia, and one always ready on her tongue.

"Well, Crassa, as a favour to our bastard-loving tonsor," he said, nodding at Decius, "we will take you. You will pay a siliqus for the transport and another for the food and shelter. And ten folles extra for the danger of slowing us down. If you do not pay, or cannot pay, then we will keep you until you do. One way or another. Do you understand?"

She nodded. The price was excessive, almost ludicrous, but she had no heft to barter, and Rodius knew it.

"It is of no moment to me," said Rodius, nodding, "whether you want to sit on some barbarian prick, or marry a louse-ridden catamite of a soldier boy. We travel to Vercovicium. You can make your way wherever you want from there, alone. I will speak with Vassu and Cuno. We may be ready to travel in the morning, but I make no promises. Be here at dawn."

Aurelia grimaced slightly. She had wanted to leave immediately, but had known that was unlikely. But, she reminded herself, first light was still better than two days hence.

"Thank you," she said.

Rodius turned to go back into the dwelling, then stopped. "And Crassa, I will ask no more questions, and you are to ask none of us. Be silent, be useful. The journey is dangerous. If you slow us down or cause trouble, we will kill you and leave you for the crows. Do not doubt me on this."

Rodius turned his back on her and disappeared into the hut.

CHAPTER 13

Atellus walked to the edge of the sand-strewn courtyard. The sand was old, frozen to the ground like an evil grit. The limitanei's boots were scuffed, their breeches scratched and torn from dropping to the ground when sparring. Some trained with wooden swords, others with metal. The crisp air was heavy with the clacks of wood on wood and the bright ring of clashing steel. Fine spits of snow were pushed and snatched across the air by eddies of cold wind.

"How often do they drill?" asked Atellus to his guide. The soldier – one of the oldest soldiers he had seen here, a gruff unshaven optio by the name of Bron – answered as they walked.

"Twice each day, dawn and dusk."

The sparring ground was a large clearing stretched out behind the third row of barracks, nestled in the corner of the fort. Upturned masonry, which had fallen from the outer ramparts, was used as seating for those watching the fights, or waiting their turn. Atellus saw chits of parchment change hands, alongside coins and scratched slates. Soldiers would bet on anything, he recalled. He had been the same himself; a soldier would bet on his own death on the eve of battle.

A huge storm of noise and energy washed over the courtyard, from fighters and audience alike. There were around fifty men sparring in pairs, and another thirty or so cheering and shouting abuse from the edges. The watchers turned to look as he and Bron walked past. Some spat on the ground not taking their eyes from Atellus, others hailed the optio, who returned the greeting with a nod or a grimace.

Atellus looked out at the fighting men. They were wild and angry, their blows lacking finesse or instruction. They looked as if they were fighting to stay warm.

"Form the men up," he said to Bron.

The optio paused for a second before bellowing a command that Atellus did not understand. The combatants slowed down, and stood panting, rags of breath frothing into the air around them. A few carried on hacking away at each other until Bron shouted again, and they sawed to a halt, squinting through their sweat into the flailing snow.

"Is discipline always this slack, optio?" said Atellus. He had nothing personally against Bron, though he had a feeling that the optio didn't like him. Atellus was a stranger, and unwelcome. But Atellus didn't want to give the man an easy time; he needed to push him, and push his men, and squeeze them until something approaching the truth came out. Looking out at their dark sour faces, he didn't think that would take too much effort.

Bron looked out across the ranks. "These men train to survive," he replied. "Not to dance into pretty lines for the emperor."

"The men," said Atellus, "would do well to remember that it is the emperor who pays them." He knew that this was an incendiary and ignorant comment, and he galled at the thought of it passing his lips, but needed to goad the men.

Bron snorted, a sound like ripping cloth, and spat onto the sand-scabbed ground. "These men haven't seen so much as a nummus for many months, beneficiarius. The emperor's, or anyone else's. Perhaps you can include that in your report."

"They swap bets on honour then?" said Atellus, smiling and gesturing at the men.

Bron looked at him, and shrugged. "It has been a while since you have been on the limes, beneficiarius?" said the optio, but did not wait for a response. "These

190

men bet grain, rations. Duties, armour, favours. Anything that gives them the motivation to heave their torn muscles into another day's cold."

Bron stared at Atellus a while longer, waiting for a response, then walked out towards the men who had formed into rows of ten, seven deep. They stood waiting, scowling, laughing. Atellus could see the optio weaving in between the ranks, barking commands in Brythonic. The men smiled, a few laughed.

Atellus stood, the fine snow whipping around his ankles and curling inside his cloak. He walked along the front of the first rank and eyed them up and down, each man in turn. Sullen faces and suspicious light-coloured eyes peered out at him. The men were a shambles: thin, ragged, not one in standard-issue uniform. Even for limitanei, they were wild; half native. They were dressed in a gallimaufry of boiled leather, sacking, and lorica hamata. The occasional man boasted some half rusted lorica segmentata, but most were dressed in the rusted chainmail, which hung and sprouted like strange growths from behind stained tunics and ragged cloaks. A handful of the soldiers had helmets, which they carried in the crooks of their arms: full face covers, or ridge helmets with pronounced seams. Some wore carved masks of wood which trailed in front of their breasts on pieces of flax hung round their necks. Others had painted scowls and grimaces daubed in woad. Their weapons were a motley assemblage of rustic scythes and daggers, or the flotsam acquired from old battles. There were very few regulation spathas and fewer shields of any size a man could take cover behind.

Atellus stopped pacing and turned to face them. He could hear them mumbling, snatches of conversation and half-stifled laughter. Their contempt hissed out like steam off horseshit.

"As a fighting unit," said Atellus, pitching his voice low but loud, "you are a fucking disgrace." He spoke clearly and his words carried in the air; he could see the men at the back straining to hear. "I have spoken with your optio, about your

191

discipline, about your craven and bestial fighting style. You are more barbarian than Roman."

"Fuck you, nigger."

The call came from somewhere near the back. Atellus pretended not to have heard.

"Silence!" roared Bron from behind him.

Atellus stood in silence and regarded the men. The sound of the wind gusting across the courtyard was all that could be heard, punctuated by deep crackly coughs from within the ranks.

"Thank you," continued Atellus, "for illustrating my point so...emphatically."

Sixty, maybe seventy men here, he counted. A standard depleted-century for a frontline garrison. The last real command he had held, in Ctesiphon, under Julian, was six thousand heavily armed and expertly drilled comitatenses. But a lot had changed since then. Much had collapsed.

Including himself.

Atellus walked up to the soldiers and stopped by a bearded man at the end of the second rank. He stared rigidly ahead with his one good eye; the other was stitched shut with fat grey sutures. His face was a mass of dark red fur beneath which hung a necklace of yellowed human teeth. He reeked of mulsum. Atellus was aware of the optio hovering at his shoulder.

"You," said Atellus to the one eyed man. "Name?"

"Pisso."

"Pisso, *Sir*. When were you last paid?"

Pisso looked uncomfortable. "Don recall, Sir."

"Are you fed well?"

"Better'n some," said Pisso. "Sir."

Atellus moved down the row and stopped in front of a short, clean-shaven man. His skin was darker than most, as were his eyes. His hair was shaved on two sides, leaving a strange fin of hair along the centre of his head. He was chewing something as Atellus approached.

"Name?" said Atellus.

"Senicianus, Sir."

"When were you last paid, Senicianus?"

The soldier looked up and smiled insolently at Atellus. His mouth was rows of large, abnormally white teeth. "I do this for the fun. *Sir.*"

Atellus stared at him for a long while. Senicianus chewed and stared back. He spat a wodge of brown gum on the ground by the beneficiarius's boot.

"I'm glad to see such devotion to the emperor, soldier," replied Atellus. "What gods do you worship?"

"The christus, sir," said Senicianus without missing a beat. "I am a devoted Christian, as the emperor in his wisdom has decreed." He had a smile like crushed glass, and his eyes burned with hate and distrust.

"A Christian?"

"Indeed. *Sir.*"

Atellus moved along, feeling Senicianus's stare burning through his back as he walked. He stopped at a large, broad-shouldered giant of a man; Atellus's eyes were barely level with his jaw. He wore a large breast-plate of beaten steel which was strapped across his wide shoulders; it comprised multiple segments with holes punched into the edges through which ran threads of rabbit tendon pulled taut and holding them together. The armour was stained purple with rust and blood. A heavy brown cloak swept from his neck down to just above the back of his knees; it would have been trailing on the ground on a normal-sized man.

"Name?" said Atellus. He could hear murmuring and jostling further down the ranks. The thin flecks of snow were becoming softer, fatter flakes. The icy wind sent them smudging into the cheeks of the giant where they stuck and melted.

"Bucaddus, sir." His voice was an ominous rumble, almost too low to hear properly. His Latin was heavily accented.

"Are you a Christian, Bucaddus?"

"Yes, sir." His eyes stared straight across, unblinking, directly over Atellus's head.

"How do you explain the shrine to Belatucadros I saw by the barracks?"

"It is an old shrine, sir, for the old gods."

"Do you know anyone who worships Belatucadros, soldier?"

He shook his head. "No, sir."

"How about Cernunnos?"

"No, sir."

"Do you know anything about children missing from the vicus?"

194

"No, sir."

"Do you know there was an agent in rebus based here at Aesica?"

"No, sir."

Atellus paused for a second. He could hear the wind wailing through the gap between the barracks and the fort wall. At the far side of the fort, the Wall itself towered high, its wood-tipped ramparts blocking the pale sun and sending shadows leaking onto the roof of the praefectus's house.

"If the shrine to Belatucadros is no longer in use," said Atellus, raising his voice to be heard above the wind, "perhaps we should destroy it. What do you think about that, soldier?"

"As you say, sir." Bucaddos continued staring straight over Atellus's head, towards the South Gate.

"Good. So you will help me by removing the first stones, Bucaddus?" said Atellus, his voice carrying on the wind and across the assembled men. "I will have a hammer brought from the stores. You can begin today. This is a great honour, soldier, to serve the emperor in such a way."

Atellus could feel the big man's uncertainty radiating out from him. He saw his eyes lash down over his shoulder, towards the optio, looking for guidance.

"The shrine to Cernunnos," said Atellus, raising his voice. The muttering among the ranks grew louder. "By the roadside leading to the vicus. A large shrine. Well maintained. I presume that is old too? Disused? Is there a man here who would balk at dismantling it on my orders?" He looked around, but no-one spoke. "What about the turf altar at the far end of the barracks," he said, sweeping an arm in the direction of the long low building. "Who will volunteer to heave the first sod? You, Bucaddos?" He slapped his hand against the large man's shoulder. Even through the

195

limitanei's shirt, he could feel the muscles vibrate with discomfort under his palm. Atellus grinned a cool vulpine smile that felt as cold to his heart as the wind did to his flesh. "Would you take all the glory for yourself, and not share it out amongst your commilitiones?

"We can use the bricks to build a church," continued Atellus. "A good Christian temple, right here in the fort, so I can tell the emperor how very devoted are the fighting men of Aesica to the religion of the empire."

Atellus walked along the ranks, feeling his back and neck needled by the eyes of the men. "Is there any man here who would dare refuse such an order?"

The wind sang off the cold brick of the fort wall. The limitanei stationed up on the ramparts were looking down at the assembled gathering.

"The emperor's edicts are slow travelling so far north," said Atellus. "But perhaps this will be mitigated by the zeal with which they are upheld once the word has been spread?"

He looked around, challenging them with his eyes. "As you know, warriors of Aesica…in a time of famine…of disease…of blood…it is clear that the old gods are no longer wandering the hills and plains of the north. They have gone…they have abandoned you. They have made way for the one true God. Do you not agree, warriors of Aesica?" Atellus turned round to face the men, his eyes searching out the ones he had spoken to. "Do you agree Bucaddos? You, Senicianus? You, Pisso? Good Christians all."

There was silence, broken by a long sharp cough like snapping twigs. Someone spat noisily. There was the sound of leather creaking, lorica clankling dully as men shifted position. From near the back came the sliding rasp of a stone drawn slowly across a blade.

Atellus turned to Bron. The optio was looking at him with open contempt.

"The barbarians to the north however," said the beneficiarius, "the undisciplined rabble, those undeveloped vermin, let us leave the stale old gods to them. Let them worship at the shrine of Cernunnos, let them spill blood on the altar of the Great Hunter. Let them in their ignorance, and their ignobility, propitiate these shades with the blood of animals. The flesh of virgins. The burnt offerings of their young and innocent." He lowered his voice as he walked closer to the soldiers. "Not for the warriors of Aesica, citizens of Rome, such feeble and bestial practices. No."

Someone called out from the back ranks of the soldiers, but Atellus could not make out the words; then another call, guttural and aggressive.

Atellus heard a clash of metal and a growl. Someone shouted from amidst the ranks, and a ripple of motion ran through the soldiers, along with a grunt of exertion. A man staggered out, was pushed, knocked and kicked, vomited from out of the pack, and fell to his knees on the frost scarred ground.

Atellus stared at the man, his fingers itching to grab at the handle of his spatha, but he resisted the instinctive urge.

The man's hands were pressed to his throat, a hot brook of blood pulsing out from between his leather strapped fingers. His eyes, split wide and white with surprise, looked out from a pale skull. He tried to get to his feet but fell back onto his knees, then collapsed forward and lay prone, stretched out and shaking on the ground. Blood pumped idly from the narrow gash in his neck. It steamed into a puddle on the ground, melting a hole for itself in the gathering snowfall.

Bron jogged over to him, and hauled the man onto his back. From within the ranks of limitanei, someone called out, in anger or pain. A few shouts and curses followed, turning into howls and spits of rage, then two men fell out of formation and collapsed on top of each other onto the ground, the dominant one twisting and forcing punches into the other man's face, his wrapped fists angry with fresh blood.

Atellus loosed his cloak and hurried over to where the optio was tending the badly wounded man. He draped his thick cloak over the casualty then called out to the soldier nearest to him.

"Your head strap," he demanded. "Quick, for fuck's sake!"

The man unwound the strips from his bald head and handed them to the easterner. Atellus took them and wrapped them round the hole in the man's throat, which was belching syrupy blood onto Atellus's arm. He bound them as tight as he dared for a neck wound, then stood up. The two brawling men shouted and cursed and flailed in the background.

"Someone pull those two apart," he shouted into the ranks, before turning to Bron. "Optio," he said, "where is your medicus?"

Bron nodded and called out to two of the soldiers. The men ran over from the crowd. A number had gathered round the fight, screaming abuse and encouragement, but none made any move to intervene. Chits and meat changed hands. Charms were rubbed, weapons fingered excitedly.

"Get him to Uricalus," said Bron to the two limitanei who ran up to his side. "Fast."

The soldiers nodded. One grabbed the injured man under the arms, and the other heaved his legs up, and they scuttled off towards the ring of workshops by the praefectus's house, a trail of dark red blood spattering the snow in their wake.

Atellus turned towards the fight; it needed to be stopped before it became a full-blown riot. Bron was already there, the optio hauling spectators onto the floor with inhuman strength. The beneficiarius waded over, and shouldered his way through to the fight, men scowling at him as he passed. He felt arms wrapping around his elbows, but he shook them off.

The combatants were flailing on the ground, tugging at each other's faces and necks and throwing desperate ungainly blows. The snow was mushed and dirty where they scuffled. Atellus walked up and grabbed the uppermost man by his hair with both hands and heaved him up and over onto the snow where he fell face-down. He grunted in pain, then leapt to his feet, eyes red with rage and exertion. His long hair was rope thick with grease and blood. His face was scratched and his nose twisted and swollen.

Atellus had turned to the man on the floor: he was motionless, his face a mask of raw meat, bloody bubbles erupting from his smashed nose. Something – a subtle sensation that he would not be able to verbalise, if challenged – made Atellus turn round in time to see the long-haired soldier launching himself towards him. The beneficiarius raised his left arm to block the impact, but the force and momentum of the attack knocked him to the ground.

The watching soldiers erupted in a roar. Dagger and spatha hilts were drummed against armour and those who had shields thumped them against the frozen ground in a sinister tattoo.

Atellus could feel the weight of his assailant on his chest, squeezing the breath from his lungs and the cold roughness of the ground against his skull. There was a grunt from above him, a sense of mass and muscle shifting, and the world exploded into a thick white shock of pain as his opponent's blow struck his face.

Atellus was aware of the weight lifting from his chest, and he dragged in a hoarse breath of fresh cold air that made his back teeth ache. He opened his eyes, felt for the blood at the back of his head where his skull had been slammed down into the ground. He held his hand in front of his face, and it shimmered surreally, his fingers daubed with a bright red ichor.

The noise in his ears — a faint whine and the muffled thump of his own heartbeat — resolved itself into the cheers and shouts of the soldiers standing around him. Some were silent, staring grimly at him, others yelling and whooping. He could see the large form of his attacker standing over him, victorious. Atellus backed away, scuffing his breeches along the ground. His hands were sticky with blood, and numb with cold. He felt nauseous and fought the urge to vomit, biting down and forcing his cramping stomach to relax.

The men were shouting in Brythonic. Their faces dripped with tight-cut hate.

"Finish him!" someone yelled in Greek. "Cut his black cock off, Qunavo! Fuck him!"

A whiplash of panic sliced across the nape of Atellus's neck, shooting through his spine and into his stomach.

He thought about drawing his spatha.

Atellus looked up at Qunavo. The man's shoulders were rising and falling with his heavy breathing. The man whose face Qunavo had beaten to a paste had been dragged off into the crowd. Perhaps by friends, perhaps by enemies. It was no longer Atellus's problem.

He pushed himself to his feet; the world, bathed in its crazed milky-cold sunlight, lurched and tilted violently. Atellus almost fell, but he squeezed his eyes shut, twice, three times, and tried to steady his vision.

"Qunavo," he said, his voice sounding thin and distant. "You inbred native shit." He smiled. "I thought I recognised the name. I was speaking to your mother last night in the brothel, lamenting her worthless toad of a son. She was a crap fuck."

Qunavo grimaced and spat onto the ground. He was a large, heavyset man, with long ropes of braided dirty yellow hair. There was a faded dark tattoo along one

200

cheek and a scar beneath his nose which pulled his top lip upwards, so his mouth was twisted into a perpetual snarl. His eyes seemed impossibly large, the pale green irises visible all the way round. He wore no amour, just a faded red tunic, tied tight with a belt around his waist. His arms were wound round with leather strapping as far as his ham-like fists. He rolled his neck and walked towards Atellus.

"I'll fuck your corpse, nigger," said Qunavo, his voice deep and certain. He reached down with a heavy arm and pulled a long flat-bladed dagger from his boot, wiping the metal along the front of his tunic. "And send your balls back to your children. Be careful who you fuck with up here. This is not Rome."

Atellus felt them behind him, his wife and his daughter; Julia Faenia and Julia Petronia, their faces tight with fear and tension, their eyes wide. He was all that stood between them and this animal in front of him. Atellus sensed a welcome heat rising into his chest at the thought of what Qunavo would do to his wife and daughter if he allowed him to win.

Atellus's fingers flexed, itching, desperate to pull the spatha from its scabbard, feel its reassuring weight in his hand, an extension of his arm.

Qunavo ran at him, the deadly blade held out in front of him, like a squat spiculum. He was a muscular man and his momentum sent him barrelling fast towards Atellus who sidestepped, whipcrack fast, and threw his fist towards the man's neck as he passed. It connected with a solid thud that sent a shockwave all the way up to his shoulder.

The soldiers gathered round, baying and cawing excitedly. Qunavo grunted with frustration. He turned round, rubbing the back of his neck.

"Enough!" A shout cracked through the air. "Soldier, stand down!"

The call came from just behind Atellus; the voice was Bron's.

Qunavo paid no attention to the optio, but swiped his dagger across at Atellus, slicing at his breast. Atellus leapt back, and the blade whistled through the air.

"Your optio gave you an order, Qunavo," said Atellus, his eyes sparking, mocking. His opponent snorted like a poleaxed hog, then spat on the ground; before the sputum had left his lips Qunavo leapt forward. It was a quick and explosive movement that took Atellus by surprise. He ducked to the side, but not quite fast enough. The dagger was raised high as Qunavo crashed down onto him. The two men fell heavily to the ground, and Atellus instinctively whipped his head to the left, and felt the air tremble as the soldier drove the knife hard into the frozen ground. There was a whine of metal as the blade snapped off.

Atellus pounded his fist hard into the snarling chops hovering above him, dripping sweat onto his face. He couldn't draw his arm back far enough to get any power into it, but he made up for it with speed: three, four, five strikes in quick succession. Atellus felt the sharp click of the man's nose breaking against his knuckles, and the warm spatter of blood onto his face. He brought his knee up hard into the man's groin. The flesh was jangly and unprotected, and Qunavo grunted in pain and surprise.

Atellus could feel the strength drain from his opponent's muscles, and he heaved himself up forcing Qunavo off him and onto his back. Atellus scrambled to his feet fast, and aimed a kick squarely at his opponent's face: Qunavo's neck snapped back under the impact and fragments of wine-stained teeth clicked across the courtyard.

The crowd fell silent.

Atellus looked down at Qunavo. The man was twitching on the ground, his hands cupping his smashed mouth, gums leaking bright red froth onto the ground.

The beneficiarius drew his spatha with a crisp click of metal against toughened leather. A reflected spray of cold sunlight shone from the blade.

Atellus felt himself surrounded by silence, but for the wind dragging its weight of snow through the fort, and the half-heard tears of his wife and child behind him.

He rested the spatha against Qunavo's neck, the blade biting into the angle of the jaw.

This man would have had no compunction killing me, Atellus thought. None.

When was the last time he had killed a man? He had to think. There was a time when he could have responded immediately, reflexively: yesterday, three eves ago, last moon.

But now it could be counted in seasons.

Someone in the crowd behind him grunted a comment, pitched low and ugly. Another took it up. The limitanei wanted blood. Atellus wasn't sure it mattered whose blood it was.

He withdrew the sword from Qunavo's jugular, and stood up. He placed the edge of the blade across the back of his left hand, let the weight of the Damascus steel nip into the flesh, then drew it slightly down and away.

Atellus tensed with the familiar sweet trilling gasp of pain, which became a cold ache. It took two beats of his heart before a fine perfect red line squeezed itself from the cut, swelling unevenly as it met the cold air. He clenched his fist, tightening the flesh and squeezing more blood out until it ran across his fingers. Atellus wiped the edge of his spatha on the side of his tunic until the blade was clean, then sheathed it and started to turn around to face the crowd.

He felt a hand fall on his shoulder.

Atellus gripped the fingers hard in a lock and spun round, pulling and twisting the arm as he went. He had a kick ready for the man, and managed to hold it just long enough to recognise the face of the optio.

He held the grip for a moment longer, Bron's arm twisted painfully, bone and ligaments scrunching against each other, before letting go.

The optio shook his arm free, an unreadable expression on his bearded face, and walked past Atellus and over to where Qunavo lay dazed on the ground. Bron hauled him up by the cords of his hair and dumped him forward onto his knees. The three of them were in front of the once-baying mob of soldiers. Now there was only the mumble of tense conversation, the shuffle of wooden betting tokens and parchments.

Atellus looked down and noticed white flecks against his boots. At first he thought it was snowflakes before realising they were bits of tooth embedded in the leather. He shook them loose and they disappeared into the snow.

"This man," roared Bron, addressing the crowd around them, "pedes Quintus Constantinius Qunavo, disobeyed a direct order."

There was complete silence now, except the weary sough of the wind as it scoured the courtyard and sent a dusting of snow and ice across the stone. Men coughed and shrugged and looked on tensely. Qunavo was staring groggily out at them.

Bron drew his spatha. It hissed its way from his sheath, a long, finely-made and immaculately clean blade. It was well looked after. The hilt was polished mahogany, Atellus could see, wrapped round with leather, and studded with bronze rivets. The optio laid it against the neck of the kneeling man in front of him.

"He disobeyed an order," repeated Bron. "All here were witness. Is there a man here who will defend his actions?"

Men studied their boots, cleared their throats. None spoke out.

"This is the penalty for insubordination," said Bron. He lifted the spatha. Atellus could see Qunavo had his eyes closed, his distorted lips moving silently in rapid entreaty to his gods. Fresh blood pulsed from his shattered nose, and more hung in strings from the corner of his mouth.

Bron brought the spatha down fast, a fine, precise movement, and Qunavo howled with pain and fell back, his severed ear spinning off his broad shoulder into the snow.

The injured man screamed and clapped his hands to his wound.

"Barracks," ordered Bron, addressing the men. *"Now."*

The soldiers filed away from the others, casting dark looks at Qunavo and Atellus. Some spat at the beneficiarius as they walked past.

Bron strode over to where the soldier's ear lay in a pool of meltsnow. He picked it up and flung it at Qunavo. It hit his chest and fell to the ground next to him.

"That's yours, pedes," he said. "Do with it as you see fit. Now haul your arse over to Uricalus."

Qunavo, his face contorted with pain, bent down and scrabbled in the snow with shaking fingers, and picked up his ear. He held it gingerly between the thumb and forefinger of one hand, the other clamped to the bleeding wound where his ear used to be, and shuffled off in the direction of the medicus.

Bron walked over to Atellus and looked up at him. The easterner was taller, but the optio was broader and heavier.

"Listen to me," said Bron, quietly, from behind clenched teeth. "I don't care who you speak for or why you're here. But you're fucking with my men. And no-one fucks with my men but me."

Atellus felt a movement by his thigh. He looked down and could see the spatha gripped tight in the optio's fist, angled up, the tip jutting up towards Atellus's crotch. He could feel it pressing against the thick material of his breeches.

"My advice to you, easterner, is get the fuck out of here. Say you've done whatever you're doing and fuck off. Before you lose the choice."

Bron withdrew the spatha and turned away, sheathing it as he strode off towards the barracks. The beneficiarius watched the optio walk off, his boots peeling layers from the ground, leaving dark punctuations in the snow. Atellus stood shivering as the wind raged and snowspit flapped in streaks and the sun withered and wept behind the trunks of the heavy clouds.

CHAPTER 14

Calidus could hear a voice.

It seemed to be high above him, though he felt a strange dampness in his ear that seemed to intensify with each word. There was a needlesharp whining noise which gradually melded with the voice until the latter swelled in volume. The darkness was gone like a gauze drawn from his eyes, and he was aware that he was lying on the floor, looking up at the figure of a man standing above him.

"...tyke, and take it all. Y'know."

The voice was familiar; it brought memories of cold, fear, piss.

Trentius. The soldier from the detachment which escorted them from Eboracum to the Wall.

Calidus raised his head. He realised he must have blacked out, though not for long. It didn't feel as though much had changed since he'd collapsed.

"Needs summa that tight arse," said Trentius, wrestling with his belt, "fore sumunner bastid splits it wide open." He laughed and bared his cracked and yellowed teeth.

"Wait," said Calidus, his tongue feeling large and fat in his mouth. He sat upright and put a hand to his head to stop the room spinning. "Please."

"Oh ahve waited, tyke," said the soldier. He was all lean stringy muscle and pale wipes of scarflesh along his wiry hairless arms. "Said ad getyer, dinna? Sumeer *warmer*. Where's yer pet nigger to save yis now?"

Calidus felt fear quiver through his belly. He looked up at Trentius. The same angry, hungry eyes; the same scarred cheek and stump of a nose; the dirty red hair, like a hovel-fire, and a shitspray of freckles.

Calidus heaved himself to his feet, unsteadily, and backed away from the soldier. Trentius smiled: he was savouring the fear, the anticipation. Calidus had heard stories in his childhood, of how the forest wolves could smell a man's fear from leagues distant, and it would drive them wild with bloodlust. Looking up at Trentius, he fancied he could see the same lupine characteristics in his twitchings.

The soldier wrapped the wide leather of his belt tight around the knuckles of his right hand. It creaked ominously in the chamber. Outside was the sound of a smith clanking away on his anvil, and beneath that the ghostly whisper of the wind ranging through the fort.

Calidus felt his muscles clenching, all across his body. He shuffled backwards slowly, until his calves thudded against the copper frame of his bed. His head throbbed dully but it was a distant pain, like the memory of an old wound, a wan shadow.

Trentius seemed to move in slow motion. Calidus could feel his own thoughts clunking through his head with a painful slowness: half-formed ideas, sharp ripples of panic, suggestions of movement, but his body was tense and still. He could feel his eyes flickering rapidly. Trentius was blocking his route to the door leading out into the corridor. The only other escape was through the heavy wooden slats covering the window set into the wall which looked out onto the courtyard. But there was no way he could get through that before he was dragged back into the room by his legs....

"Gonna githa fight, tyke?" said Trentius advancing towards the bed. He shook his head slowly, savouring the look in the youth's eyes. "Just makit hurt more. But am game."

Game, he'd said. Just a game. Like when he was scrapping with his gang back in the ginnels and wastegrounds of Eboracum: trading sweat and punches, diving around, rolling through filth and scrambling over collapsed masonry, tiptoeing along half rotten beams, and aiming hefty kicks at exposed shins.

Just a game.

Calidus acted before his eyes or body had a chance to betray his intentions. He almost surprised himself as he dived backwards over the bed. He caught the end of the frame with his ankle which sent a thrill of pain down through his foot, but he hit the floor and rolled across the ground towards the door leading to the study room. Trentius grunted and darted round the bed after him, but Calidus was already on his feet and through into the antechamber, the pain in his ankle dissipating with each step.

The boy fell against the far wall, by the side of a cabinet covered with trays full of lotions, unguents, powders and make-ups, and spun round to meet his pursuer. Trentius was walking slowly, taking his time, filling the space between Calidus and the only exit. He kicked himself out of his breeches so he stood naked from the waist down.

In an armwhip movement, Calidus seized up one of the trays of bottles and hurled it at Trentius. The soldier batted it away with a sweep of his taut arm, and the assemblage smashed against the far wall, glasses and ceramics shattering noisily, showering the room with fragments of pot and glass and globules of oil.

"Ah, tyke," hissed Trentius, "yis just mekkin it worse for theesen."

He was getting closer; in a few heartbeats, the soldier would be within a leap of him, covering all escape. Calidus didn't think much of his chances in a straight hand-to-hand brawl. He needed to be fast, decisive. There was still a chance to slip past, if he could rely on his smaller size and superior speed. He was young and fast, the soldier was older, and half-pissed on strong acetum.

Calidus feinted to the right, then sprang to the left, exploding into the wall, ducking himself tight as he went.

At first he thought the feint had worked; he saw Trentius lurch to his left to where he first thought the boy was headed, but the old soldier quickly heaved his mass back to the right to correct his momentum. Calidus was aware that he wasn't going to make it: the space was too small and there was no gap that the soldier wouldn't be able to cover. Beyond was the chamber itself and the door to the corridor, unopposed. Even as he moved, he could see it, tantalisingly real in front of him as he felt the iron straps of Trentius's fingers wrapping around the flesh of his neck.

Calidus made a noise – a howl, a whimper, something bestial escaping from his throat – and he felt himself being pulled backwards into the study.

But then the grip slackened. Calidus heard a curse in some ugly tongue, and the fingers relaxed. Trentius, barefooted, slipped, his foot swiping along the spilt oil on the ground. He lost his balance for a second and grabbed for purchase against the wall.

It was all the opportunity Calidus needed. He felt the grip slacken as the soldier went off balance. Squirming hard, he broke the contact with Trentius's fingers, and powered himself up through the antechamber, into the main bedroom, launching himself at the door. He thumped hard into it, forcing it deeper into its jamb.

Calidus heard the shout from behind him, the slap and grunt of the wiry man heaving himself onto his feet again, driving himself out of the room and towards him.

Calidus grabbed the handle and pulled.

The door was stuck fast.

He desperately clenched the wooden handle in both sweat-slick hands, tugging and wrenching. The door bowed inwards slightly, but the edges were wedged tight into the stone frame.

Calidus heard a whimpering noise and realised it was coming from within his own throat. He didn't dare look over his shoulder. Time had slowed to a pace that matched the slow push of the north wind. A bead of his sweat dropped from his forehead; he saw it plummet to the floor like a bloated raindrop.

It was instinct that made him duck.

Trentius's elbow slammed hard into the door; Calidus felt it shake beneath his shoulder from the impact. He turned to face Trentius, the soldier's large body and skinny pale legs seeming ludicrous in front of him. A queer laugh burst from between Calidus's teeth, and without thinking

just a game legs scratched from nettle bites back in Eboracum sweet spring days of rose scent and stolen wine and mouths sore from laughter just a game

he drove his fist into Trentius's stomach, putting his shoulder into it, lunging forward and feeling himself laugh maniacally as his knuckles sank into the flesh, heard the hollow grunt of the man above him, felt his mass toppling backwards, a scrabble of legs and arms and the smell of sour wine and stale sweat.

Calidus went down with him and heard the man's head crack against the floorboards.

He immediately pushed himself up using his fists against Trentius's chest. He could see the man's eyes swimming as he lay on the floor. The boy was overcome

211

with a vile, sickly rage, a sheet of anger and energy that consumed him, forcing its way into his muscles. He grabbed Trentius's greasy knotted red hair, and ripped his head up from the ground, slamming it back down again, feeling the sickly hollow thud again and again as bone made contact with the thick wooden planks. Calidus heaved the man's head up again with his fists, and felt a ripping through his fingers; he looked at his hands to see great strands of Trentius's fiery hair erupting between his knuckles. The limitanei was unconscious beneath him, a swelling pool of blood trickling from a deep gash in his scalp.

Calidus froze in horror. He could feel the man's forced breaths expanding his ribs against his thighs where he was sitting astride him. He pushed himself up, slowly, warily, his eyes never leaving the lids of the man beneath him, as if he would awake and stab out with his iron grip. But there was no movement.

Calidus put his hands on the floor and pushed himself to his knees, then onto his feet. Trentius was breathing still, but his breaths were ragged and choked, as though the air was snagging in his throat. Calidus realised he still had clumps of the man's hair in his fingers. He threw them down onto the soldier, and turned towards the door. His arms were shaking with the adrenalin and exertion. The room itself seemed more vivid, more real. The faint light seeping from under the door was so bright as to be painful.

He gripped the handle and heaved inwards. The door flexed but remained wedged. He tried again, and again. Behind him, Trentius grunted, and stirred.

The sweat pooled in the small of his back felt cold and painful to Calidus. He took a breath to calm himself and quiet the relentless thump of his heart. He pulled at the door again, trying to force all his muscles into the task, gripping and heaving back on the handle, but his hands slid off and he fell backwards, tripping over the splayed legs of Trentius and crumpling to the ground with a jolt.

"Shit."

Calidus looked around. Trentius's head was moving slowly from side to side, as though he was having nightmares. His naked legs with their insectoid bristles and his wilted penis looked pathetic and obscene.

Calidus shuffled to his feet and looked around the room. He was thinking about trying the window, the beacon of safety cowering behind the thick wooden slats of the hoardings placed across it. Then his eyes caught the gleam on the writing desk by the head of the bed.

His dagger.

He slid it off the desk, its ivory hilt cool in his hot palm, the tip of the heavy blade pointing towards the ground.

What was it Atellus had said?

... the steel is so soft it would barely break the skin...

Calidus walked over to the door and looked up at where the wood was jammed tight against the stone. He gripped the dagger firmly and forced the blade into the slender gap between the wood and the wall. He worked it deeper, wriggling it up and down until the top third of the blade had disappeared.

He settled his fingers around the hilt. The ivory was now warm and slick with fresh sweat.

A noise, from behind him.

Calidus felt a stab of fear through his guts.

He looked around: Trentius was raising his head from the nimbus of blood that surrounded his skull on the floor. His eyes were groggy and bloodshot as he tried to focus. His legs jerked as he tested the muscles.

Calidus turned back to the door. He felt his muscles turning to rubber, a fizz of tension bubbling down his spine. He forced himself to concentrate. There was only the dagger, and the tough old weathered wood of the door; nothing else could be allowed to distract him. He squeezed the hilt tight, and wrenched it to the side, the force shivering through the metal.

The sounds of Trentius stirring behind him burst through his bubble of concentration. Calidus forced every fibre of his muscles to work, threw the weight of his shoulder and upper back against the blade, towards the wall. He heard himself groaning, saw a trail of spittle dangle from his mouth. His vision was darkening, white spots dancing at the edges of his vision.

There was a crack, then a pop, like a knot of wood exploding in a hot flame and the resistance against the knife disappeared. Calidus flew forwards into the wall. His chin hit the stone with a crack, but most of the contact was absorbed by his shoulder striking the wall at the same time. He grunted and heard a ringing clatter of metal hitting the floor. He looked down towards the dagger in his gripe: the hilt was still clamped tight in his fist but the blade had snapped off.

Calidus turned sideways to let the door swing inwards in a gentle motion. It struck Trentius's foot. The man was sitting upright on his naked arse, a blood-soaked hand clamped to the back of his bleeding skull. He looked death and pain and confusion at Calidus, who lingered a second, meeting the soldier's rageful glare, before bolting through the open door and out into the corridor. He thundered fast away from his room, the motion whipping the flames of the bracketed torches into a spitting fury, as he fled the echo of his own footfalls through the dark complex.

CHAPTER 15

The valetudinarium was a long low building constructed of huge single timbers from split tree trunks. The outside was daubed with tar and covered with overlapping sheets of thick leather. A lingering stench of rosmarinus seemed to ooze from the very wood.

The inside of the building was dark and solemn and the biting wind could be felt through a thousand chinks in the woodwork. The cold seemed to rise up from the ground outside, past the thick stilts and through the raised floor, to spread out across the cots of the invalids like an icy miasma.

Men coughed and groaned within the walls. Some wept. Others mumbled incoherently under their breaths. The mephitic smell of sickness overlaid with naphtha and faeces was so ripe and pungent Atellus felt he had to wade through it like some deep bog.

The building was dark, even in daytime: there were no windows and daylight entered only through the gaps in the timber walls. At nightfall a row of dim oil lamps suspended from the rafters gave the only light; they daubed grim shadows across the floor and walls.

The medicus, Uricalus, was busy tending to himself with a bald and dirty goatskin of acetum. He was a small dark-skinned man, from Greek or Roman stock, with tight curly hair plastered close to his domed head. His eyes were large and sad, and the flesh around his cheeks and jaw was pouchy and sallow. Only his nose held any colour, a deep red from cracked veins and the relentless inhalation of pungent fumes.

Uricalus had waved Atellus down towards the far end of the valetudinarium. His words were slurred and disinterested.

"He won't shee another d-dawn," he had said, squeezing a fresh blast of wine into his throat. "The g-godsh will meet him h-h-half way, they will." He scrubbed the back of his hand across his mouth. "T-try not to b-*breathe* on them, man."

Breathing was the one thing Atellus wished he could stop himself from doing in this place. He had seen many such valetudinaria before; he had woken up in such places, in sweltering tents where your own sweat drips back on you from the leather, and sudden squalls blasted the desert sand into exposed wounds. Or where chizzums and breekers fluttered and whined their way in and feasted on the suppurating flesh of men too broken to wave them away. He had seen such places, drenched in the sweet metallic stench of blood, and the nauseating smell of shit; been woken into half dreams by men dying, or wailing or fighting imaginary foes. Had witnessed the madness and rages born of henbane tinctures and the sweltering heats of the Dog star: five men to pin down the patient, a sixth to lay firm blows across his chin until he faded.

Better to be hacked dead on the field than be dragged halfway and cast into the miseries of the valetudinarium.

Atellus shivered as he walked slowly along the length of the room, conscious of the rapping noise of his iron-studded boots on the wooden planks. He tugged at the scarf around his neck; the flesh throbbed in the cold weather and it ached when it was too hot.

And when a storm was fermenting in the heavens. And when he was afraid.

Most of the time, in fact.

The beneficiarius could see the shapeless mass of the soldier he sought on the last bunk on the left. The patient opposite him was a young limitanei sitting upright in his bed, staring straight ahead with a thick, treacly gaze. It unsettled Atellus. He noticed a trail of saliva dangling from the corner of the man's mouth.

Some man, he thought. The lad was a mere stripling, barely old enough to shave his chin. Perhaps the same age as Atellus himself when he had first joined up.

He batted the thought away angrily and turned towards the man opposite. There was a strong smell of thymus and rosemarinus near the foot of his bed.

The soldier's name was Silvius, the medicus had told him. Silvius was lying flat on his back, perfectly still. Beyond the thymus, there was a rotten sweet smell hanging around him. No doubt he had soiled himself. A sheen of sweat clung to his exposed skin. A goatskin blanket was crumpled atop him. There was no sign of Atellus's fine woollen cloak that he had laid across the man out on the courtyard; no doubt that was one of the perks of the job for Uricalus.

Silvius's neck was wrapped thickly round with linen bandages. His eyes were open and he stared up towards the timber roof which creaked and moaned under the ebb and sway of the wind. His face was worn and blanched, his greying hair thin and plastered to his furrowed forehead. The soldier's nose was fat and red and twisted at an angle, as if it had been broken many time.

"Silvius?"

The man's eyes flickered towards Atellus as he stood over him. The beneficiarius pulled over an upturned crate, and sat on it.

"Can you talk?" he asked.

Silvius swallowed slowly and painfully, then licked his dry lips.

"Water," said the wounded man.

His voice was a feeble croak. Atellus looked around him. He saw a bottle by the bunkside. He pulled the stopper out and sniffed it. Odourless. He took a sip: water. He proffered the bottle to the lips of Silvius, who dabbed eagerly at the moisture as it trickled from the spout. He squeezed his eyes shut to indicate that he had had his fill.

"You know who I am?" asked Atellus.

Silvius kept his eyes shut for a while before answering. "The black devil from the east, sent to test us." He replied. "I know." His lips curled into a grin.

"Apparently so," said Atellus, replacing the container of water on the table. "I am here to find out where the chittles from the vicus have gone. And why. And what happened to the agent in rebus who was embedded here in Aesica. You know that, don't you Silvius? You all do."

Silvius kept silent.

"Who attacked you, Silvius?" asked Atellus, quietly. "Who stabbed you in the neck? Which one of your friends has killed you?" He leaned a little closer and spoke clearly, each syllable weighted with truth. "Because you're going to die, Silvius, you know that, too."

"I'm not afraid of death, easterner."

"Nor was I," replied Atellus. "Before I died."

Silvius looked up at him. "What lies do you spin now, nigger?"

Atellus loosened the scarf around his throat, and unfurled it. It was damp and cold. He reached up and plucked one of the lanterns from the wall, lifting it from its hook, and holding it at his breast. His face was contorted into a fierce chiaroscuro: light like the flames of Orcus licking up against his charred flesh, brilliant eyes like volcanic rock smouldering in their deep caverns. And the flesh of the neck, the pale puckered cicatrix wrapped round the girth of the throat. Silvius's eyes bulged as if the shades of the netherworld had come grappling up from between the floorboards to seize his ankles and drag him down to the endless caverns of pain. His body tensed visibly.

"What is this?" he stammered.

"I looked down at my limp body," said Atellus, "swinging from the noose cast over the walls of Constantinople. The life throttled out of me, my face purple, blood in my eyes. And I looked down from the side of death and saw the life beneath me, saw my pathetic existence, my shell, struggling at the end of the rope like a lame dog tethered to a cord. And I had the choice of going, or returning to this husk." Atellus jabbed a thumb into his chest.

"And I returned," he continued, "for the love of my family; for them I returned, heaving myself up, back into this shitty life. And then I was scared, I was scared of not making it back, of this huge black and infinite doom behind me that was larger than all the mountains on the earth, deeper than all the oceans and with a voice that was all the thunders of all the skies at once. And it was terrifying, Silvius, *it was terrifying.*

"And I knew the voice was Death, and that I wanted no part of it. I ran, and ran, and ran back to this filthy, stale, bleached joke which we call life. And I made it, and I am thankful for that."

Silvius looked on in terror, fresh bulbs of sweat breaking out upon his cheeks and brow. Atellus replaced the lantern and rewound the scarf around his neck.

"What happened?" asked the soldier, his voice hoarse and cracked.

"I lived," said Atellus. "The cowardly swine Jovian ordered my death. I was one of Julian's most trusted generals: I fought by his side, I watched him die, the wound in his guts from the Lakhmid spear festering in the desert heat. We worshipped, Julian and I, the unconquered sun." Atellus fell silent for a moment and touched his first two fingers to his forehead. The sounds of the valetudinarium seemed to swell in the absence of his voice: howls; incoherent mumblings; a lad at the far end sobbing and calling for his mater.

"When Jovian stumbled like a buffoon onto the imperial throne," continued Atellus, "he was a raving Christian. He held on to me as long as he needed me, to see his armies safe out of the east. I cautioned him against suing for peace, against selling out our cities and forts to save his own pale, flabby arse. But he heeded me not. And when we arrived at court, he purged anyone who had served with Julian, accusing them of paganism, of sacrifice, of bestiality and treason. Even the Christians. Good, capable men. Jovian was the antithesis of Julian. Julian had judged the man by his deeds, not by the gods he worshipped. He surrounded himself with honest, capable men, Christian, Mithraist, cultist alike. All were slain at Jovian's command.

"I was gathered at dawn," said Atellus, his voice pitched low, just above the groans of the mad and dying, and the shrinking and settling of the timbers around them. "They dragged me from my bed and hauled me to the ramparts of the city walls. The sun rose like milky blood on the horizon. It was hot already, the city bragging and laughing beneath me, full of sweet life. They strapped the rope around the stanchion, and threw the noose over my head. I was not scared. I looked around, and all along the length of the city walls were Jovian's supposed apostates, his devils to be purged; men and boys alike fighting, crying, laughing. Others were unconscious, and hurled insensate to their deaths, tumbling from the walls, their necks cracking, their bodies thumping against the stone.

"The walls dipped and rose on the city's hills, the far side shimmering in the heat, but as far as I could see were men thronging the ramparts. The sun twinkled off the Saturnine gate and the smooth white domes of the temples; I remember squinting as I looked out, remember filling my nose with the fresh scent of the dew evaporating from the acanthus leaves in the morning sun. Fruits and spices from the markets below: sour cherries, apricots, fennel and musk.

"I didn't recognise the man who kicked me," he continued. "One of a thousand mean-faced grunts following orders. My hands were bound behind my back. But I had worked the leather strap loose. The sun and the fear made my hands slick with sweat. I was able to ease one hand free. So when I felt the soldier's foot in the small of my back, I leapt off and brought both arms up, gripping the rope hard, so it would break my fall. The pain was excruciating: I dislocated my left shoulder. But it didn't break my neck. Instead I hung by the throat, using my right hand to relieve the pressure while my left supported my weight from the rope. My muscles were in white hot agony. I could hear laughing above. Some wanted to finish me with an arrow. But instead they watched as I hung, and the strength ran out of my arm."

Atellus took the water bottle from the table, removed the stopper and took a swig.

"Have you ever had that, Silvius?" said Atellus, setting the bottle back down. "Where your own strength, the hard tension in your fibres, was all that stood between you and death? And your muscles scream and scream but you carry on, to preserve yourself, to survive. The mind is strong, you see, and the spirit is fierce, but flesh will fail. And there is nothing else to be done. So my neck took my weight and the noose tightened around my throat."

Atellus's hand went to his wound, his fingers moving almost unconsciously across the scarf. "And so I hung by the neck in the heat, feeling my lungs exploding under the pressure, wheezing and sucking the last of the warm, stale air as if it were cool sweet water. The Golden Horn twinkled beneath me like the jewels of the gods."

"And you died?" said the wounded soldier, his voice a rasp.

"I died," nodded Atellus. "The hand of Dis was at my shoulder, and the eternal night stretched away in front of me."

"And...how are you here?" asked Silvius. "How is it you stand before me now?

"I was cut down," replied Atellus. "How long after I first swung, I cannot say. It seems I had friends yet. Possibly friends of Julian. I was cut down, the rope severed at the stanchion, and a cart of hay mulch underneath to break my fall. I was carried away and tended for long days and nights by people who were no friends of Jovian. I believe now that those who cared for me were working on the orders of Valentinian. Others were not so fortunate. The city walls were black with carrion birds feasting on the rotting corpses. The stench rose in the heat and befouled the entire city and the roads in and out for days. A powerful gesture by a new, cowardly, emperor.

"So, Silvius," said Atellus, lowering his eyes to the dark floor beneath him, "that is why I fear death now more than I once did. And why you have good reason to fear it, too. I escaped once, but I know that one day Dis will fix his dread eyes on me again and pursue me. And I will not escape. We all will be devoured eventually. Prepare yourself, pedes, and do not be flippant or indifferent. For your battle will be fierce. And now you have my tale, and I want one in return."

The soldier closed his eyes. Atellus could see them throbbing and twitching beneath the lids. After a while he opened them again, and his gaze was distant. A thin bloom of blood, like a dark and sombre rose, was swelling through the linen bandages around his neck.

"You didn't die, easterner, on those city walls. Only one has the power to have risen from the dead, and that is my lord the Christus, the son of the only true God." Silvius squinted in pain with the effort of talking. "I have been a Christian for many years. And I do not shirk from spreading the good news to all I see. Even in these Godless wastes here. I have lived a good Christian, and I will die as such. My death will not be like your heathen dreams of the desert, easterner. I will soon be in my heaven, with my Father, and I welcome it with open arms."

Atellus lifted the bottle of water from the table and poured some onto the soldier's lips. He dabbed his tongue around the moisture.

"You must be keen to die, easterner," said Silvius, "despite your claims. You come here and address these men so. Not even the emperor at your side will stop them gutting you like a plump glis the first chance they get." He started laughing, but the pain made him wince and he fell back onto his pillow, exhausted.

"I know these men," said Atellus. "I know they aren't Christians. I know that they will give me nothing if they are calm, and conscious. I need to push them, stretch their limits, and see what leaks from the seams."

"You are wrong, easterner," said Silvius weakly. "There are some Christians. We worship together. But we are few. And the others barely tolerate us. They have blamed us for the famine, for the crop blight, for the endless winters and the disease. We anger Cernunnos, they say, with our 'wretched' dedication to our Father."

"Cernunnos is the god of the north," said Atellus. "Of the Britons."

"It is the false god of Aesica, and other forts. The god of the Wall. But there are others. It is the god of the tribes to the north also."

"And do they make sacrifice to Cernunnos?"

"We all make sacrifice to our gods, easterner, in different ways."

"Animals?" probed Atellus, lowering his voice. "Humans?"

"They have barbaric practices for a barbarian god," answered Silvius. "But I do not worship with the others."

"What of the vicus? The civilians?"

"They worship Cernunnos. By choice or coercion or simple-mindedness, I do not know. There are Christians few enough among them. The truth is slow to travel so far north."

"Where do they worship?"

"I do not know. I have no interest in their ways."

There was silence for a while, but for the groans of the sick and the creaking of frosted timbers. Silvius closed his eyes and lay still. Atellus sat and thought in the sad flickering light of the lantern strung from the wall.

"Who stabbed you, Silvius?" he asked.

The soldier opened his eyes slowly, heavily. It took him a while to see the beneficiarius; his gaze wandered and slipped in and out of focus.

"No good will come from me telling you," he said, hoarsely, his words slow and ponderous. "He will be judged by a greater authority than you. As must we all."

"Tell me *why* did he do it, then?"

Silvius looked pained and gaunt. He could be no more than forty, but he looked like a Methuselah.

"Why, easterner?" he replied, his eyes seeking and finding Atellus's face in the gloom. "Because I am a Christian. Because I have spoken out before, and would have done so again. These men are all God's children. But they are doomed as surely as you, or I. It is my duty to make them recognise the true faith. But they have no ears to hear."

Silvius closed his eyes again, and Atellus rose from his seat to leave. The crate creaked beneath him, and Silvius's eyes burst open, a desperate, oily fear in them. His hand reached out for the other man's. Atellus took it and clasped it.

"I know nothing about these children you seek, easterner," he said, his voice low and intense. "But they are gone. Sold, butchered, burnt. But the emperor's agent...he they tore limb from limb in Culuslupi. Sang and danced and bathed in wine, they did. I know because my comilitione, Lossio, was part of the group that did it. He boasted of plucking out the man's eyes like grapes off a vine."

Silvius laughed and broke back upon the bunk, wracked with pain. The bandages around his neck were sodden red with fresh blood, and he lay coughing and choking as Atellus walked out into the cold night air.

CHAPTER 16

Aurelia – or Crassa, as she was now called and had to keep reminding herself – shivered and pulled the blanket tighter around her shoulders. The iron-strapped wheels of the waggon seemed to search out every rut and pit in the road.

She looked across to her fellow cargo but there was nothing but desolation, pain and unshed tears in their young faces. There were twelve of them in total, wrapped in itchy furs and sacking at the back of the open waggon. Rodius sat up at the front, holding the leather reins of the two horses; sitting next to him was his brother Vassu and a large heavily-built man who Aurelia thought was called Cunovendus.

Vassu was lean and tight, and might have been good looking had it not been for a continuous look of abject hate on his face. It twisted his mouth and wrinkled his brow and made him look like a sour, sulking child. His actions mimicked his visage too, she noticed, as he manhandled the girls onto the waggon and belted a few across the mouth for whimpering too loudly.

Cunovendus was the driver, surly and laconic. He was tall and broad, and his body was roped with thick old muscle overlaid with more recent pouches of fat. He spoke very quietly and moved purposefully – there was no wasted energy. He showed no interest in Crassa or the other girls, and exchanged few words with the brothers sitting beside him. Instead he focused himself on beating the horses with a knotted rope and chivvying them on faster and faster.

For Aurelia, they could not go fast enough, though her bruised body was beginning to disagree with her. The waggon was strewn with hay, but it had long since gone soft and thinned out beneath the jolting weight of so many bodies. And she didn't need the acidic smell to tell her that more than one of the girls had already pissed freely where she sat.

The cargo – as the brothers referred to them all – comprised twelve girls and herself. They were freshly blooded orphans plucked from the streets, or the daughters of poor parents who could no longer afford another mouth to feed. The brothers were transporting them north to the Wall to be sold into prostitution at any vicus which needed them. The traders got a substantial amount of gold, free use of the girls, and enough provisions to last them a return journey. She knew the commanders of the garrisons would pay well to have fresh girls brought up. Anything to distract the limitanei from their empty bellies and thoughts of rebellion.

Aurelia guessed that the girls had barely seen twelve winters, but they had all aged well beyond their years. They looked like women, young mothers, rather than children themselves. Their lives will have been hard and they were about to get even harder.

But Aurelia felt powerless; such events happened everywhere, she reminded herself, all over the province, all over the empire. She was fortunate enough to have been born into a wealthy family, and so avoided the deprivations of the poor. Or she thought she had: what else had she been to Crispus but a worthless piece of meat? She was a whore, but her price had been higher, in every aspect.

She watched the smallest of the girls, Luci, as they bounced along the road together. The snow had started to fall again, and with it the air had seemed to harden until the sky pressed down upon them like cold steel. Luci was sitting next to her, wrapped so tight in rags and skins that she looked like an elderly scullion. Only the bright fierce young eyes peered out from beneath a sandy fringe of hair. Eyes as blue as the Ister in spring.

Aurelia reached out a hand to put it on the girl's knee, a gesture implying tenderness and support, but Luci shifted away and her eyes flashed an angry challenge.

Hard, thought Aurelia. Hard girls born into hard times.

Unlike her. Aurelia had let herself get soft, and barely an hour passed when she didn't curse herself for it. Instead of being wrapped up like a satchel of meat on a whore-waggon bound for death or servitude in the north, she could have been pulling strings, spinning webs back in the villa and the principia. She would never let her guard down again.

The previous night had passed in a delirium of anxiety and impatience. She slept on the pallet in Decius's hut, while the pregnant woman snored throatily in her cot. Decius wrapped a sheepskin around himself on the floor and woke every couple of hours to add more wood to the painfully small fire.

Decius had taken her to meet Rodius at dawn, outside the father's shack in the Calles. Rodius had walked her inside without a greeting and hurled a bunch of rags at her, told her to dress. He had turned away as she did so, and she watched as he took the clothes she had been wearing and cast them onto the firepit in the centre of the shack; he picked up a long stick, blackened at the end and stirred the clothes into the flames until they were burning angrily.

Not for the first time, Aurelia wondered just how much he knew about who 'Crassa' really was, and just how valuable she could be. She didn't feel comfortable thinking about it for too long; at the moment, this vile man was her only hope of fleeing the city and making it to the Wall safely.

After she had finished dressing, Rodius had introduced her to his brother. Vassu, simply scowled at her and spat, and the third man, Cunovendus, had merely looked at her in that expressionless and somewhat vacant way of his. Rodius had told her to get into the back of the waggon and stay quiet.

Over the next two hours they had driven achingly slowly around to two other locations along narrow lanes and through frozen swamps in the city to get to the blasted districts where they picked up the rest of the cargo: these shivering, teary and beaten girls, with all hope or joy driven from their eyes and the cold from the ground seeping up through the soles of their small feet and into their very hearts.

Aurelia had been concerned about the girls, but she was still too terrified at the thought of getting through the checkpoints by the city gates to pay much attention to their plight. The sun was a bare swelling of light nuzzling the underside of the sky when they trundled up to the West Gate and the checkpoint. Before they approached, Rodius had stopped and told them to be quiet and meek. Vassu belted a sobbing girl, and thrust her head down into the stinking soiled hay at the back of the cart. The sour-faced brother had come round to her, a fierce knot in his brows and told her to keep her eyes down.

"Don't meet my eyes, whore," he had snapped, "or I'll bite them out and shove them up your cunt." His breath had reeked of allium and sour milk. He leaned in close to her, and grabbed her wrist painfully tight. "Just cos you're older don't mean you're any better'n these bints. An old whore's a cheap whore." He spat again, his eyes blazing deep into her own, then he nodded as if satisfied and walked back round to jump onto the front of the waggon.

Old.

That was the first time she had ever been called *old*. It stung more than the rest of the sentiment; certainly more than being called a whore.

Aurelia lowered her eyes, and tried to make herself as small and unobtrusive as possible. She could hear her heart yammering in her chest as the soldiers stopped them at the gates. There was the clink of metal, and creak of leather, and the flickering dawn sparks of sallow lanternlight.

The guards were huddled tight inside the thick brick of the gatehouse, padded down with skins and blankets. Rodius improved their mood with cheese and bread and a goatskin of strong wine. The men passed it around and laughed, the spout tinkling liquid through their cracked lips and frost-numbed jaws. Aurelia couldn't understand what was said, but she kept her head down, and when the waggon lurched into motion again, and she heard the angry squawk of the gates being wheeled open, the thrill of relief almost made her forget about the cold.

The rest of the journey so far had been a misery of ice, discomfort, subtle aches and endless gloom. Even as the watery sun punched through the horizon and sent sheets of clear light across the sky, the weather was bitterly cold.

The track was soft with snow, and the wheels sometimes slid on hidden patches of ice below, sending the waggon skewing suddenly to one side. The girls tumbled about in the back, knocking elbows and heads against the wooden boards. They kept their heads down to shelter from the relentless bite of the wind, but Aurelia could still make out the drifting cackle of Vassu's laughter, and the stench of garlic wafting past overhead.

They did not stop for ablutions, nor for food. Instead, stale and half frozen crumbs of bread and tough smoked meat were passed over by Rodius. Aurelia did not dare think what beast the meat had come from; it was dark and salty. She placed a piece behind her teeth and sucked hungrily at it, her gums itching with delight. A goatskin of melted snow was passed back to quench their thirst. The girls clung to it with red fingers, the water painfully cold in their throats and hitting their empty bellies like molten lead.

For Aurelia, the world became a thumping mire of noise and cold filled with the clatter of hooves on frozen ground, and the crump of the waggon wheels biting deep troughs through the snow. The land rolled out behind her in a rocking, shaking motion that left her nauseous. The pristine snow-swept hills tumbled back towards the horizon, punctuated only by dark bare trees, branches heavy with snowfall, and drifting threads of smoke from hamlets and farmsteads.

Twice they slid off the road and into deep snowdrifts in the fossus. Vassu came around throwing his fists at any and all, beating the girls out onto the road to help dig them out. They used raw burning hands to scoop the snow out from around the huge heavy wheels, while Vassu and Rodius heaved from behind and Cunovendus flogged the flesh from the horses; the animals strained and whickered and flicked steaming sweat into the slush by the roadside.

The sun hung light and soft in the centre of the sky, then slowly descended, drawing down the barren blueblack darkness of twilight in its wake. The snowfall stopped and started and stopped again, until the world was a violet ocean of hillocks and tumuli in the gloaming.

They slid off the road a third time, the slick sawing motion of the cart immediately sending three of the girls over the side. Aurelia felt a thump and a bounce and heard a wet scream, and then the world was falling onto its side. She clung on to the far side of the waggon as it tipped onto its side but the force was too great and her grip was torn away from the planking. She felt herself tumbling, something hard glancing off her ankle, and then she struck the soft blanket of cold snow.

Aurelia pushed herself up. The snow was starting to burn against her exposed skin. Her ankle howled where she had caught it against the wheel of the waggon as she had been thrown out. She looked over and could see that one of the horses was crumpled into the snow, the great slats of its ribs ballooning out as its lungs filled and emptied desperately. The horse which hadn't collapsed was tethered to the upturned waggon, its halter tearing at its flesh. It whinnied and skipped and bucked wildly, thumping its hind legs against the driver's platform. The air was filled with sobs and moans from the girls.

Rodius and Cunovendus clambered over the waggon-boards to get to the horses. Rodius tried to calm down the frightened beast with strokes and soft words; he pulled down on its halter and slid his palm along its nose. Cunovendus bent down to the collapsed horse panting wildly in the snow. It was swinging its legs, trying to get to its feet. He released its reins and tried to heave it up, but it kept falling backwards sending plumes of powdery snow into the still air.

Aurelia looked over and grabbed a girl to her feet. She recognised Livia, a dark-haired child with bright blue eyes like ice chips. She had said something before about being a sutler's daughter, though she couldn't be sure. She moved on and found Turia rubbing her elbow, her young face scarred by the permafrown she wore, a mask of suspicion staring out at all she encountered.

Luci was lying in the snow not far from one of the waggon's rear upturned wheels; it spun lazily from the momentum, a faint squeaking and whishing in the air as she approached.

At first, Aurelia thought that the girl had been struck in the mouth when she hit the ground. Her lips were smeared with fresh blood and she looked dazed, but there was a long low groan coming from deep inside her chest.

"Luci?" Aurelia asked, as she knelt down next to her. "Are you okay? Can you get up?"

Luci's damp eyes flickered towards her, registering her presence, but she didn't answer. Aurelia grabbed the girl's hand, lying in the snow like a pale bird fallen from its nest. She tried to help her to her feet, but the girl shrieked, a piercing noise that echoed through the trees that surrounded the roadside. The last of the daylight was fading around them.

"Shut that whelp up, or I'll pull her fuckin tongue out!" shouted Vassu. He had come round, and was yanking the girls up by the crooks of their arms, or their hair, whichever was more prominent as he stalked past. Rodius and Cunovendus had come round and were pushing the waggon over, righting it. Luci coughed and sent a mist of blood out through her lips. It speckled the snow, standing out with a terrible glow against the grey dusk.

"She's injured," said Aurelia, looking up at the men with a fierce light in her eyes. She looked vulpine crouched in the snow in a pool of fresh moonlight. "Help her."

"I'll fuckin injure her, and you too, bitch!" snarled Vassu. The other two men continued heaving at the upturned waggon, Rodius hissing between clenched teeth, his face red with the strain. Cunovendus, as ever, seemed utterly unaffected. There was a creaking and splintering sound and the top wheel of the waggon, spinning through the air, tipped over, and the mass of wood, leather and metal crashed back onto the road spraying clumps of matted hay into the air.

Aurelia turned back to Luci. The girl's face was as white as the snow around them. She looked down at Luci's bodice, the bound layers of old reeking leather. She peeled back the swaddled clothing and exposed the soft swells of early womanhood hidden underneath like whispered secrets.

Luci's abdomen was crushed. The once pale flesh was a deep scarlet; a rubble of cracked bones jutted out at angles from the skin.

Aurelia stared for a heartbeat longer, then gently re-covered the child with her rags. She clutched Luci's hand tightly, but she wasn't sure if the child was conscious. Her eyes were closed, though her head moved from side to side in the crisp powder of the snow.

Rodius walked over, the snow crunching beneath him. He looked down at Luci.

"How bad?" he asked. His brow was knotted, whether with concern for the girl, or concern for his gold, Aurelia couldn't tell. She shook her head as an answer. Rodius clenched his fists, then walked over to the other two men. The other girls were scooping hay from the snow and bundling it back into the waggon. It was their warmth, their only comfort. A few cast uneasy glances over to where Luci lay.

"One horse and one whelp," she heard Vassu shouting at Cunovendus. "Fucking idiot. This comes out of your pay, you limp prick."

They made camp, walking out into the trees and leaving the waggon half off the road. They went far enough so they would not be a target for any brigands who found the cart. Their tracks could betray them still, but Rodius was willing to take the risk; the sky threatened at least one fresh snowfall before too long which would cover them up.

Vassu whipped at deadwood with a hatchet to make kindling for the fires, whilst Cunovendus used a large woodsman's axe to slice down boughs of fir trees. He swung away at the branches with long overhand strokes which thwacked into the wood, the noise echoing through the copse. The branches fell down into a makeshift shelter which they would sleep inside. It would provide some refuge from the wind, and also obscure them from any brigands who happened to pass through in the night.

When he had finished assembling the shelters, Cunovendus went back to fetch the healthy horse from the waggon. Aurelia and a girl named Prisca had fashioned a sled from three boughs which Rodius had instructed Cunovendus to break down for them. They placed Luci on the intertwined branches, Aurelia muffling the girl's screams as they moved her, and lashed the support onto the back of the horse's saddle. Rodius had told them to lead the beast behind the rest so that the

234

trailing gurney would obliterate their footprints, just in case brigands arrived before the snow did.

At the camp, Rodius handed out skins for blankets, two for each girl, and one for the men, then busied himself constructing a large sheltered fire inside a tree bole to hide the light. The roots of the upturned tree reflected the heat back against them. Cunovendus fed the horse dried barley and chaff from a sack they had brought with them.

Rodius and Cunovendus went back to the crippled horse and severed its jugular, the warm blood pumping hot geysers into the snow. They cut haunches of meat from the emaciated body and hauled them back to camp to roast over the fire. They cooked as much as they could, then salted it and wrapped it in snow and fresh hay for the journey. They ate heartily, tucking into the hot fresh meat. The girls seemed half feral as they gnawed into the hunks of hot flesh, juices flooding from their mouths and soaking into their vests.

They slept fitfully, packed together for warmth and listening to the sinister sounds of the wide open night; the pad of beasts prowling across the forest floor and the occasional squeaking crump of snow falling from over-laden branches.

Aurelia rose often to check on Luci, who gasped and sweated through the cold, but she was dead long before the fire was.

Vassu kicked them awake, the few of them that were still sleeping in the icy greyblack hours before dawn. Aurelia unwrapped herself from the skins. Her bones felt as though they were made of ice, a deep intense coldness that penetrated to the very core of her being. Even her thoughts were crusted with permafrost, as though she had lost the very memory of warmth. Her flesh burned and ached with the cold, and her toes and fingers were starting to go numb.

They left Luci's body by the embers of the fire.

Aurelia knew that the beasts would have her before the rest of them had even reached the road, but there was little she could do about it. She steeled herself and forced her gaze northwards, towards the Wall.

CHAPTER 17

Atellus pushed open the door to his quarters, and stood as it wailed inwards on its rusted hinges. He still had the smell of the valetudinarium under his nose, clinging to his upper lip: stale sweat, faeces, rotting flesh, lacquered over with the sickly tinge of rosemarinus. Even the musty damp smell of his chamber was preferable to that.

He stepped inside. The first thing he saw was the boy lying across his bed. His eyes darted instinctively left and right, searching for threats from the side. Anything unexpected sent the blood pumping and the adrenalin surging.

"Scaeva," he said, addressing the youth. "Get off my bed."

Calidus had been dozing, but at the sound of the beneficiarius's voice, he leapt up and off the bed, standing to the side.

"Sorry," he said, blinking and looking around. "I have to say, beneficiarius, your chamber is much meaner than mine."

Atellus walked inside and through to the copper basin on the table beside his bed. There was a jug of water by it. He poured the water into the basin with a drumming, tinkling sound. The water was still half frozen.

"I imagine," he replied, rolling up his sleeves, "that is because you are a more welcome guest than I."

He bent down and splashed the icy water into his face, sucking in air and puffing it out. The water was so cold it was painful, like dousing his cheeks with naphtha, but he scrubbed hard at his skin.

"You look terrible," said Calidus. "There is a bath house if you want to properly freshen up."

Atellus raised his head from the bowl and grabbed a cloth from the table next to him. He dabbed away at his face. He felt better, cleaner for the rinse. He wasn't sure whether it was the stench of the valetudinarium, the grazes from his fight with Qunavo, or the memory of hanging from the walls of Constantinople. Whatever it was, he had felt a burning heat just under his skin. The ice water had helped, but the burn was still there, subtle but persistent.

"Why are you in my room, Scaeva?" said Atellus.

Calidus lowered his eyes. "I wanted to talk about my father, perhaps."

Atellus poured some water over a gash in his forearm. He hadn't even recalled receiving it.

"Some other time, maybe," he said. "I need to work this evening."

"Maybe I can come with you?" said Calidus.

Atellus dried his wound with the cloth, and rolled his sleeves down. "No."

"I can be useful to you, we—"

"I said no, boy," said Atellus wearily. "Your place is here. I do not have time to shepherd you around. I have a job to do. You would be a liability. The vicus is dangerous, as you have seen."

"This damned fort is dangerous," snapped Calidus. "My own *chamber* is dangerous." He pulled something from a side pocket of his tunic and held it out to Atellus. "You were right... it was not much use in a fight."

The easterner took it. It was the jewel-encrusted, ivory hilt from the boy's ornamental blade. He turned it over in his palm, then handed it back.

"What happened?"

Calidus shrugged. "A soldier. He was waiting for me in my room."

"You stabbed him?" asked Atellus.

"No. But I beat him," said Calidus, a strange grin on his mouth. "I pounded his head on the ground. He was bleeding. There was a lot of blood." He felt good spilling it out to the older man, cleaner somehow. As though keeping the experience buried inside his breast was letting it fester and gain a queer power over him, a shamed feeling. "I left him there, and came here. Maybe he's dead," he shrugged.

Atellus looked at the boy. "Are you harmed?"

Calidus shook his head.

"Your uncle sent you up here," said Atellus, turning away and opening a deep chest at the side of his bed-frame. "Brocchus, despite his qualities, is an old fool, detached from reality. He's a nice man, but he is a bad governor." Atellus took out a new cloak, dark brown and weathered looking. "He sent you up here, a lad of your age, to train. To the limes of the empire, the wilderness. To live amongst men who would consider a wolf-pack more civilised than they. It is a matter of time before your arse gets opened up; you might as well get it over with. At least Apullius would protect you from the others, and keep you in some fancy clothes." Atellus stood upright and looked the youth in the eye. "I'd just pick your bed, Scaeva, and roll over for him."

Atellus could see the youth was grinding his teeth, his fists clenching. "That is what you would do, Easterner?" he said, his voice trembling with anger and shame. "Is that how you got to be Valentinian's catamite?"

239

Atellus laughed and shook his head. "Maybe you'll save your arse after all, Scaeva. Maybe so." He threw the cloak around his shoulders. There was no hasp, only a faded leather thong, which he pulled tight and wrapped into a knot so the cloak settled snugly on his shoulders and around his chest.

"You were meant to look after me, Atellus," said Calidus, his eyes flashing an accusation. He walked out across the room to come between the beneficiarius and the doorway. "You promised my uncle, whatever you may think of him, that you would see me safe. And I'm not out of your influence yet."

Atellus paused for a second, then reached down to check his scabbard. He eased his spatha loose, baring an inch or so of steel, then slotted it back in.

"Have you got a cloak?"

Calidus nodded.

"A rough one, like this?"

The boy shook his head.

Atellus sat down at the desk against the rough stone wall opposite his bed. He pulled out a piece of parchment from the top drawer, then picked up the old fine metal stylus and uncapped a small vial of ink on the side. Apullius had sent them up earlier at his request.

"You have until I finish writing this letter to get one, then I'm leaving. We're going to the vicus. We will not be seen or followed. If you let me down, I'll cut your balls off myself and hand them to Apullius."

"Where can I get a cloak from?" said Calidus.

"That's not my problem."

The boy pondered for a heartbeat, then darted out through the door and into the corridors of the villa.

By the time Calidus returned, Atellus had finished two letters. The first, his official report to the emperor, he would hand to Apullius, and ask him to send it with a rider to his contact in Eboracum. The contact, officially, was Governor Brocchus. If the praefectus had any sense, he would open the missive, glean what he could from the contents – written in a common military cipher – and forward the letter, possibly after redacting it or even replacing the letter with another. Atellus expected him to do that; it wouldn't really matter, because the second letter was his actual report to Valentinian, written in a complex grid substitution cipher known to only a handful of people. This letter contained the absolute truth of his findings and suppositions to date, and he wouldn't entrust it to Apullius's men. Instead he needed to find someone who could take it to his genuine first tier contact in Eboracum.

Presuming Aurelia had recovered from whatever beating her husband had inflicted on her this time.

Atellus folded the letter until it was a square about half the size of his palm, then slipped it into the pocket in his sleeve. The other letter he sealed with a drop of wax and an imprint from the pommel of his spatha. It was large and formal, and he left it on his table ready to give to Apullius in the morning.

"You found a cloak then, Scaeva," said Atellus, pushing himself up from his desk and turning to face the boy as he clattered in through the creaking door. "Where from?"

"I bought it from a servant in the basement."

Atellus looked at the cloak. Rough and itchy, with a loose weave and the stench of old cheese.

241

"It's good. How much did you pay?"

Calidus shuffled his feet and looked away from Atellus. "I gave the man the remains of my dagger."

The beneficiarius laughed, a sharp noise in the small chamber. "Then you will have given the man more money than he will ever have seen in his life."

"He was happy with the deal."

"If it means that much to you, Scaeva," said Atellus, "then you are welcome to come. But you do as I say, without argument and without hindrance. Understood?"

Calidus nodded solemnly.

"Do you have a weapon?"

"No," he said. "The dagger was all I had."

"Good," nodded Atellus. "I'm your weapon. Stay close to me, don't say anything or do anything unless I tell you to. And we should be alright."

Atellus blew out the lamp on his desk and walked out of the room, Calidus following close behind.

CHAPTER 18

The waggon was where they had left it, lurching slightly to the side where one of its wheels was trapped in a deep drift. It looked untouched, a fresh coat of white snow dappling its wood. There were no remnants of the horse's carcass, just fresh unbroken snow surrounding the wooden bones of the shafts. Cunovendus went round and hitched their remaining horse to the front, re-tethering the harness lines so the beast was lined up in the centre of the waggon.

Vassu punched and kicked the girls into action, forcing them down onto their knees to scoop away the snow from around the buried wheel, before swapping places with Cunovendus. Aurelia took it upon herself to organise the girls into two gangs, working six at a time, changing over when the diggers got too tired or too cold to continue. Most of the time away from the wheel was spent rubbing raw, stinging hands against clothes, and tucking them deep into armpits or groins. Rodius and Cunovendus pushed and heaved from the back of the cart, while Vassu hauled himself up into the driver's bench and used the knotted rope to thrash the horse into motion.

The girls dug hard, clawing and scooping the snow with their small hands as the daylight broke across the horizon like spilt milk. Rodius and Cunovendus heaved and sweated and slid on the compacted snow. Vassu threw his whip like a maul, the air around him filled with oaths and threats.

Aurelia was part of the digging team as they felt the wheel move, the great mass of wood and metal above them inching forward and upwards.

"Move back!" she shouted, pulling the girls closest to her away from the wheel.

Prisca, at the far side, was too slow.

The wheel was heaved up and over her hand by the vigorous straining of the horse. The sound of splintering bone was lost in the crunch of the snow and the shrieks of the girls leaping backwards.

Prisca started screaming, her arm twisted at an angle as she tried in vain to pull free. Aurelia rushed to the back of the cart and pushed with the men. The cart gave a bump and rolled up out of the fossus and onto the compacted frozen mud of the road. Aurelia, Rodius and Cunovendus fell forwards, face down into the snow as the waggon moved on, the horse heaving it onwards and the wheels clicking against the hard surface.

Vassu sawed at the reins and yanked backwards to stop the horse accelerating further. He drew it to a stop where it stood stamping, tossing its head and jetting plumes of wet breath from its nostrils.

Aurelia pushed herself up, and looked around. The world seemed surreally white, as if the sun had crested the horizon and gone straight to its apex without crossing the intervening space. There was a creaking silence all around split only by the screams of Prisca who was clutching her smashed hand to her bosom and rolling in the snow in agony. Vassu leapt from the waggon, and advanced on the injured girl. He pulled her up by her neck and slapped her hard across the cheek.

"Shutit, you stupid fuckin bint! You'll bring half the robbers and buggers in the north on us!"

Prisca bent to one side and vomited wetly into the snow.

Aurelia walked over to Vassu. "Let go of her," she said, firmly, meeting the sallow man's eyes.

Vassu switched his gaze to her, Prisca hanging limp from his gripe, whimpering. For the first time, his expression was not one of black anger and distaste, but an entirely new expression: confusion. He dropped Prisca into a weeping bundle in the snow, and marched on Aurelia.

She could feel her heart thumping heavily in her breast. The cold no longer seemed so consuming. Her blood seemed thicker, warmer. Vassu stood in front of her, an uncia or so taller and barely a span from her face.

"She is injured," said Aurelia, surprised at the steadiness of her own voice. "Hitting her won't help, but only slow—"

The blow caught her by surprise. She was on the floor without realising how she'd got there, a fat ripple of pain pulsing out from her cheek and spreading through her jaw, her neck, her scalp.

"You dare speak like that to me, you filthy bitch?!" shouted Vassu, his cries louder than Prisca's screams had been. "A filthy diseased old whore talks to me like that??"

Aurelia saw him draw his foot back as if to kick her, but he was stopped by Rodius, who clapped a hand on his brother's shoulder.

"Enough," he said quietly. "We need to be off."

Vassu transferred his furious gaze to his brother, then back to Aurelia who was picking herself up off the floor, and gingerly feeling the soreness along her cheekbone. She could see Vassu's knuckles were cut.

"Speak to me again, whore," he said through clenched, blackened teeth, "and I'll fuckin throw you under the wheels meself." He shrugged Rodius's hand from his shoulder, and marched off to the front of the waggon.

Aurelia went over to where Prisca lay, and gathered the girl up, feeling her swollen hand. It was bleeding heavily and the bones were like mulch inside. She could hear them crunch like grit across a pebble each time Prisca moved.

While the other girls were climbing awkwardly on benumbed feet into the back of the waggon, Aurelia grabbed a fistful of Prisca's hair and told her to bite down hard on it. She looked at her with wide tearful eyes, but did as she was instructed. They seemed impossibly bright and green in the sunlight bouncing up from the snow.

Aurelia gathered a handful of ice and rubbed it into Prisca's wounds, while tears streamed from the girl's eyes and the muscles bulged out of her clenching jaws as she bit down hard on her gag. When she had finished, Aurelia removed some of the leather strapping from around her own head, and wound it tightly round Prisca's maimed hand. The girl hissed and bit back a scream.

"Get on the fuckin waggon!" shouted Vassu from up on the driver's plank.

"Sssh," said Aurelia to Prisca in a low, soothing tone. "Nearly done. You will feel better. When we next stop I will gather some Mandragora and Salix to ease the pain."

Prisca looked at her dubiously, but said nothing. Aurelia finished wrapping the girl's hand then gently led her to the back of the wagon, helping her up into the damp hay. None of the other girls on the back extended a hand in aid, or even looked at Prisca as she scrabbled awkwardly aboard using her good hand. Aurelia followed her up, and perched herself in the back. The hay was cold and damp, and frozen hard so the ends of the strands pricked through her clothes.

They travelled hard through the day, the cold and the discomfort blending into a sullen grey fog of misery which seemed to drape across them all like a dark blanket. They saw no-one except a group of six riders: a detachment of soldiers riding north who galloped past without looking in their direction, metal clinking loudly and hooves a grim thunder on the road. They passed dead bodies, some on the road, fresh and barely blue, others bloodied remnants of persons, mauled and torn by the beasts and bandits of the land.

Prisca lay back in a corner, weeping silently into the hay. Aurelia had to undo the bandages twice to allow the blood to flow free, and ease the pain from the swelling. Her mangled hand was now a dark ominous purple, and half the size of her head. The other girls kept their distance, and looked out on cold land through colder eyes. Aurelia was the only one who gave her any obvious attention.

She clambered up over the hay lining and addressed the men sitting at the front. Each was wrapped in a thick bundle of furs, so they were only dark shapeless masses in a spitstorm of tiny sharp snowflakes. She had to squeeze her eyes shut, and the oncoming wind snatched her breath away before she could speak. She tugged at the man in the middle, Rodius. It took a while before he acknowledged. He turned round slowly, his face hidden deep within the cowl of a coarse cloak.

"What is it, Crassa?" he asked, his voice muffled.

"The girl," she replied, shouting to be heard over the wind. "She needs a medicus, or at least some help. Let us stop for a while, and I could prepare a poultice."

He looked at her intently, then over at the girls slumped in their rags and skins, covered over with hay blankets, like animals being taken to market.

"How sick is she?"

"Very."

"Could it spread?"

247

Aurelia thought. If she lied and said yes, there was a chance that they would let her tend the wound. But there was also the chance that they would throw the girl off the cart and leave her to die in the cold. She couldn't have that on her conscience.

"No," she answered.

"It is dangerous to stop," he answered. "Especially in daylight."

"You will get scant money for the girl," she persisted, "when her hand is the size of a melon and she is half dead with fever. Care for your profit, if you care not for Prisca."

Aurelia spat the name out as a curse, hoping to humanise the girl a little in the trader's eyes. She turned back and scrabbled down into the groove she had worked into the hay by the jostling motion of the waggon. She looked back and saw the thick shapes of the men huddled together, talking. Voices were raised but she could not make out the words.

Eventually the waggon slowed down. The flailing wind eased and the sound of wheels and hooves grew softer. Aurelia could hear Vassu gnashing and grumbling as Rodius leapt out of the front of the waggon as it slowed to a stop. She watched him walk round to the back.

"Vassu, feed the horse," he shouted as he walked. "Cuno, fetch meat for the cargo."

He appeared in front of Aurelia.

"Down, Crassa," he said. "Fix the girl and we're off. You have as long as it takes for the animal to feed."

"Thank you," she said, meeting his eyes. Rodius looked away and walked off.

248

Aurelia stood up in the waggon. The slender wheel tracks in the snow sheered off before her like long ropes trailing out into a white sea. The land around them was hilly and bleak. There were large swathes of forest on the surrounding hills but no sign of life: no trails of smoke, no scent of farmland in the clear air. The clouds overhead were dark and silent.

Aurelia stroked Prisca's hot damp brow. "I will be back soon," she whispered. "Be strong." She jumped down into the snow and looked around her. She was desperately trying to recall her old tutor telling her about the healing plants, Mandragora and Salix, and instructions for their preparation.

"I need a small fire," she said to Rodius. "Enough to melt a cup of snow."

He started to object, but she walked off, taking quick strides towards the trees that clustered and thronged the borders of the road. It was a small concession to civilisation, this thin ribbon winding fragilely through the crumpled and overgrown landscape. Nature was never far from encroaching completely and reclaiming this tenuous umbilical cord linking the north to the nourishment from the southern cities. She wondered how many more generations would travel along it, as they were, in sunnier or bleaker moods.

Lost in thought and weariness, she collapsed waist-deep into a snowdrift that had built up around the fossus. She fought her way out of it and burst through into shallower snowfall, where the ground had been protected by a thick canopy of overhead branches.

Aurelia walked deeper into the forest, a sense of calm and almost warmth descending on her, settling into her tense scalp. She could feel the subtle respiration of the trees, could sense the enveloping blanket of their branches and the crisp foliage underfoot. Deadwood crackled beneath her boots, and birds flapped and cawed as they erupted from their nests. She could hear, dimly now, the grimy baritone of Vassu barking threats over by the waggon. It sounded thin and distant, like a noise from the waking world scratching at the boundary of a dream. She had crossed the limes, was beyond Rome and within nature, that endless, ceaseless empire that would always prevail.

Aurelia looked around for the distinctive purple and white peduncles of the Mandragora root. They usually grew at the base of trees, if she remembered rightly, in damp and dark nooks and crevices. She fixed her eyes to the ground, her vision baffled by the bustle of colour and shape underfoot, the twigs and soil, plants and fungi, animal spoors and bones, stones and pits and skittering crawling insects.

There was something bothering her as she looked; something tickling the back of her skull, but she shrugged it off and concentrated on the task.

Aurelia was skimming the knobbled bark of an old Ulmus when her eye was snagged by the distinctive green oblongs of the Mandragora leaves, peeking out from beneath a large root the size of a man's thigh, which slithered out of the ground. She walked over to it, shuffling and crackling through the frost-glazed undergrowth, and knelt down. The hard ground bit into her knees, as she pulled the leaves closer towards her, examining the peduncles.

A noise.

Aurelia got up quickly, her heart thumping. She could not say why, but she was scared. A palpable fear had descended onto her skin, and the nape of her neck prickled in the dead air.

Apart from the settling of the forest life around her, there was no sound. Even the wind was stifled so deep inside the throng of trees. She was about to bend back down to the plant, when she heard something again. She couldn't say what it was, or even whether the sound was real, or just a sensation in her head. A dull, hollow sound, like wood on wood.

Aurelia was tired and tense. She looked around the forest, the thick foliage surrounding her seeming suddenly hostile. Her first thought was of a wolf pack; starving beasts driven to attack men by the fearful winter and intense starvation. She felt needles of fresh sweat along her spine, despite the cold. The forest pittered and dripped around her, far-off twigs snapping, snow melting, birds shifting their slight weight on boughs.

A curl of wind stirred the high branches overhead, and the trunks shook and creaked.

A scream.

Aurelia whipped her head around towards the road. There seemed to be a volley of sounds now, dreary and faded like a shadow from the winter sun, but definite and real. More screams, and shouts from the men. She gathered up the folds of her heavy woollen peasant stola, and ran back through the forest, scrunching her way through the undergrowth.

She was about halfway back, the urgency boiling the blood in her veins, when she stopped in her tracks. The drumbeat of her heart was tight in her chest and the exertion has made her warm and itchy inside her thick clothes. There could be no mistaking the sounds of combat and slaughter; the chime of metal and howls of pain and fear; screams and pleas for mercy and help; howls for mothers who had long since abandoned them.

Aurelia started towards the road, slower, more cautious. She headed south a bit, to where there was an opening of trees, and lay down on the cold hard ground, peering over the knuckle of an old root.

The first thing she saw was the bulky form of Cunovendus slumped against the side of the cart. His face was streaked with dark blood, and an arrow shaft jutted

251

from his bullish neck. His torso bristled with fletchings, their weight dragging his body down towards the roadside.

There were four men standing in the middle of the road, wrapped tight in dark brown linen scarves and bearing a motley assemblage of armour: iron plates hung down the chest of one; another wore a lorica hamata vest that was too large for him and dangled down to his knees; another wore the skin of a she-wolf draped across his neck, his face daubed black with stale clotted blood. The warriors looked bestial, like jackals rearing up on their hind legs.

Aurelia saw Rodius on his knees, weeping in pain. His left arm ended at the wrist in a raw and jagged stump. His other hand clutched at the wound, desperately trying to stifle the flow of blood which inked the snow bright red around him. One of the brigands held the blade of a large woodsman's axe at his neck.

Vassu was lying face down in the road. She saw one of the brigands walk over and kick him casually in the chest, then reach down and drag him up by the hair. The man was bare-chested, and wore his long hair tied and knotted above his head, so it resembled a large, shaggy hat. His skin was streaked with blood and dirt, and crusted blue woad in the manner of the northern tribes. He bound Vassu's wrists and ankles, then tossed him over his shoulder like a deerkill. He walked over to the waggon, and deposited him over the back of the horse, which whinnied and shivered, then stood still.

The battle was over, if a battle it had been.

The four men were talking in deep voices, and laughing. She noticed the girls corralled against the side of the waggon. Two more of the brigands were naked from the waist down, thrusting vigorously into Matidia and Livia, who were lying in a heap of spilt hay in the road. The girls were sobbing, the rapists laughing and throttling them with hard large hands, choking the life from their young throats, their plunging arses as pale as the snow around them as they battered their way inside the girls again and again.

Another of the brigands walked over and hauled one of the men off, and took his turn at Matidia, mounting her like a wild dog. The one who had been interrupted laughed, wiped his cock on his hands, and pulled up his breeches. He walked over to the girls huddled against the waggon, and tossed them onto the back of the vehicle, groping each one in turn, laughing as they screamed.

Aurelia saw one try to run – Vesta, she thought it could have been – and the man who was guarding Rodius laid his axe in the snow, the haft propped against his thigh. He nocked an arrow and drew the bowstring up to his cheek in a smooth, practised motion. He loosed it, and the heavy tip split Vesta's head like a ripe apple, lifting her off her feet and dumping her face-down in the snow. The body kicked spasmodically, and was still.

Aurelia felt a sensation of warmth in her hand and looked down. She was unaware that she had been clenching her fingers; they were rolled so tight into her palm that her nails had drawn blood.

It may be a blessing from the gods, she told herself. *Better this than the life of a Wall whore.*

A tall man, with a head shaved bare and wrapped round with leather straps in the military fashion, seemed to be the leader. He wore a thick layer of chain-link armour around his chest, and vambraces of hide and wood on his arms. He carried a large two-handed spatha, of the type used by the cavalry in years past; Aurelia recognised it from paintings in the emperor's palace in Treves. The spatha was a dirty grey colour, mottled with rust, but it still looked fearsome. He raised his weapon in one hand and jabbed it at Rodius, saying something.

Rodius got to his feet in great agony, and fell down again. The man standing over him with the axe laughed and kicked him between the legs. Rodius lay still, the stump at the end of his wrist pumping bright vibrant blood into the white snow. The swordsman moved on and hauled the two rapists from their victims. One finished himself hurriedly as he rose, spattering thin liquid onto Livia, who lay prone and shivering; both girls were naked and blue.

The swordsman walked over to Livia, his knee-length fur boots cracking in the soft snow. He gathered her up, wrapped her loosely in her torn rags, and pushed her towards the waggon. The other girl, Matidia, didn't move. The swordsman jabbed her with the edge of his toe, then gave her a kick. He bent down to examine her, then stood up and walked over to the waggon, hauling himself up to the driving platform where two of the others sat. The remaining four brigands jumped into the back, amidst the girls, laughing and whooping. The girls cowered and shrank as far back into the waggon as they could go.

The swordsman cracked the knotted rope onto the back of the horse, and the waggon inched away, slipping slightly on the compacted snow. The body of Cunovendus slid down onto the soft ground as the waggon moved away gaining speed and momentum. Soon, it had creaked and thumped its way out of sight and all Aurelia could hear was the caw of the northbirds in the branches overhead and the whine of the cold wind through the treetops.

CHAPTER 19

There had been no guard posted outside Atellus's quarters, but he knew that the front door to the building would be heavily manned, as would be the gates of the fort itself.

They went first to Calidus's chambers, and looked inside. There was a stale and sticky pool of blood in the centre of the room, but of Trentius himself there was no sign.

"He must have left," said Calidus, then realised he was whispering. The thought of Trentius, with his ugly stringy arms and vile twisted face, pumped fear into his stomach. He felt ashamed at being afraid.

"Maybe," said Atellus, looking quickly around the quarters. "Or maybe a servant scooped him up and took him to the valetudinarium."

They walked back on themselves, and Atellus turned down a flight of narrow stairs leading off the main atrium. The walls were misted with a sheen of moisture, and the air was muggy and thick. Calidus could feel the warmth of the hypocaust through the walls around them. They reached the bottom of the steps; to their right was the crackle and clatter of the kitchen. Two tired looking servants hurried past them carrying bundles of material, but they assiduously avoided their eyes.

They went through the kitchen which was filled with noise and the smell of hot water and strong cheese. Calidus saw Atellus speak with an old man bent over a pot, a coin changed hands and the man pointed to the far end of the kitchen, grabbing obsequiously at Atellus's sleeve and inclining his wrinkled head.

They walked through clouds of steam and scent, past bustling cooks and scullions. At the far end was an almost vertical wooden staircase alongside a ramp, leading to a hatch set into the kitchen roof. The old man pointed up at it, and caressed the nummus in his palm, bowing and nodding at Atellus. They climbed the stairs, and pushed open the hatch. A rush of icy air spun into the kitchen and sent the steam billowing like pale stormclouds around them. Atellus looked around and heaved himself out, then reached down to pull Calidus up after him. The transition from heat to intense cold was so strong that Calidus felt his flesh stinging, as if he was being pinched all over.

They were at the back of the praefectus's house, within the encircling wall. Calidus could see a short courtyard with stables, and a small smithy. From somewhere came the scent of baking bread, and it made his stomach gurgle loudly. He had not eaten since breaking his fast in the morning.

"Be quiet and follow me," said Atellus, moving away to the wall and along the inner length of the boundary towards the stables. There was a small postern beside the main gate for the horses. Atellus unlatched it and walked out, into the open space of the fort. There were ranges of factories opposite, a bakery from which the smell was emanating, a fletchery, a tannery, and a cluster of smithies lined up in a row with the furnaces glowing warmly through the dark air.

Atellus strode out, no longer keeping to the wall, but making himself as prominent as possible. Calidus followed on his heels, looking around him at the limitanei shouting and laughing as they milled around. There was a sullen group leaning against the pillars of the granary, drinking steadily from a clay pot; another group were tucked up tossing bone tesserae against the wall of the smithy. Others were wrestling each other, or taking turns aiming body-blows while others jeered and called and swapped chits and coins.

A few of the soldiers looked up at them as they passed, two figures in filthy brown cloaks pacing through the icy evening, but they paid them no heed. Calidus looked up to the ramparts and saw the bundled silhouettes of the sentries, but their attention was directed outwards.

They went onto the via principalis and headed for the south gate. The entrance was wide open, as soldiers and traders passed in and out of the yawning double arches. The crushed and bleary-eyed faces that drifted past like woodchips on a stream were so familiar that the guards weren't even bothering to check them as they passed.

Atellus approached the limitanei guarding the egress gate; the whitewashed masonry shone a dull white in the moonlight. The sentry looked drunk, Calidus thought as he gazed up at him. He was short and wide, but he seemed to sway with the wind as if he was standing on the deck of a boat. His face was wrapped tight with cloth, so only his half-lidded blue eyes looked out. He carried a rusted and notched spiculum which he was holding onto like a weary pilgrim, the shaft in the crease of his armpit. He wore no armour, just strappings of leather, which had mottoes etched into them in crude Latin and scratched pictures of phalluses and buttocks.

Atellus walked up to the guard confidently, and spoke low into his swaddled ear. Calidus saw the man nodding at the easterner, felt his wine-slick eyes wander over them both. He tried to pull the cloak further across his shoulders to hide within its folds. The other guard shouted obscenities and boorish greetings to some of the soldiers and sutlers who came past.

Eventually Atellus turned to Calidus and jerked his head towards the gate. They both walked under the huge maw of the gatehouse, felt the echo of conversation around them, and then they erupted into the biting wind of the outside world. Unprotected by the massive walls of the fort, the weather seemed harsher and more belligerent out here; Calidus noted grimly that his toes had already gone numb. There was the merest hint of fresh snow in the air, and the road was a slick surface of slush, melted under wheel, hoof and foot.

"That was easy," said Calidus as they walked out, the wind snatching the words from his lips.

"Everything is easy with gold," said Atellus drily.

"So he won't report us leaving?"

"He said he won't, Scaeva," replied Atellus. "But he will. All I've done is buy us time. Hopefully enough to get lost in the vicus. But maybe not. Lift your feet, boy."

They hurried down the road, dodging through the traders and beggars and the lost and ragged drunks scratching at the roadsides. The night was thick and wild, the torches on timbers along the roadside framing a fragile tunnel of Romanitas through which they walked while death and the unknown pressed against the darkness beyond.

Calidus could see the cluster of lights and smoke from the vicus up ahead. The last time he had been on this road with this man, they had fought. Atellus had struck him unconscious, then carried him to a tavern on the edge of the habitation.

The north entrance of the vicus was framed by a small timber gateway, though the doors had long since tumbled free of their hinges and been used for firewood. Instead the gatemouth yawned open, and the usual assemblage of rag-swaddled whores and beggar-children sat on stones and sifted through frozen masonry blocks for wood or food. They stared up at the travellers with tired, desperate eyes.

A child wandered up to Calidus, his long sandy hair streaked tight against the boy's scalp from long hours in the snow. His small fingers were edged with the ominous soot of nigrum and his face was a gaunt mask of greyish blue. He wore a man's boots that were large enough to reach his knees and his body was bound tight with sacking. His round, white eyes seemed abnormally large in the gloom.

The child dived over and clung firm to Calidus's leg as he walked past, then looked up at him, imploring, desperate, dying. Calidus stopped in the road, unsure what to do. He glanced over at Atellus. The beneficiarius moved across and struck the child with the back of his fist, and the beggar fell back with a whimper into the puddles of meltsnow.

"Don't meet their eyes," he hissed at Calidus, grabbing the youth by the arm as he stumbled over the splayed legs of a drunken woman lying in the road. She looked young, not much older than Calidus himself, but her face was covered with boils, and her eyes rolled madly back in her skull. "You look at them and they'll follow you to the everdark for a crumb of bread, or a flake of your golden shit. You understand?"

Calidus nodded.

"Keep your head down."

Atellus let go of his arm, and the two carried on walking purposefully through the vicus, past the rickety wooden shacks by the roadside, cramped family dwellings, flimsy roundhouses of woven twigs draped with hides and stuffed with thatch or clods of clay. Others barely had walls, just rooves of wooden planks and timber supports. The dwellings stretched back as far as they could see in the torchlight, squat homes with sodden mires of trails between. Some inhabitants had laid down slabs of wood and split logs to make pathways through the half-frozen mulch.

Every so often there was a turf or timber shrine by the roadside, occupying its own niche clear of people and buildings. They were built to varying proportions, and with varying degrees of craftsmanship; some were quite elaborate with ornate carvings and finely smoothed altars, whilst others were rude piles of turf and pebble with inscribed wooden tablets stacked in front.

Wrapped in their cloaks, no-one paid much attention to the two strangers: just another pair of damned wanderers trying to survive another cruel and cold night.

Towards the centre of the vicus, the buildings became more solid, some with stone foundations. There were more people on the street, warming themselves by huge communal fires, drinking and cursing, shouting at the whores outside the bath-house. The bath-house itself was large and prominent, the focal point of the vicus, and many of the roads and trackways circled and sloped down to it. It was for the more well-heeled travellers passing along the Wall, or limitanei on leave. Its walls were stone, and had once been decorated a bold and lustrous turquoise, but the paint had long been weathered away and was peeling in huge chips like treebark. There was a hint of figures sketched on the walls, but now the lanterns illuminated crude graffiti: phalluses, curses and slights in Latin and some indecipherable languages of the north. Women leaned outside, drinking, laughing and calling, teasing the workers and soldiers who passed through.

They passed a large tavern, with stone foundations and thick wooden walls; Calidus recognised it as the one Atellus had carried him to and roused him with draughts of a strong, hot elixir. There were three other taverns in Aesica, strung out across the centre, each with its own factions of clientele. Some fought outside, or vomited wetly into the snowdamp streets.

A large shrine to Huiteris loomed to the right of the furthest tavern. It had a foundation of bricks robbed from older buildings, and a finely carved wooden plinth upon which were blackened bones and a carved ivory triune figure, along with stylised woodcuts of a boar and a serpent. Atellus looked at the assemblage as they passed.

"Human?" asked Calidus, eyeing the bones, his voice pitched low. Three boys, probably younger than Calidus but looking like middle-aged men, staggered past, their shoulders slumped under the weight of bundles of fresh firewood from the forest. An older man walked behind them, with a sour-stern face, and carrying a large pitted axe. He eyed Calidus as he passed, staring deep into the cowl of his cloak.

Atellus shook his head, after they had passed. "Animal." He answered. "Pig, perhaps."

"Do these people sacrifice beasts to their gods?" Calidus asked, looking after the two who had passed them.

Atellus did not answer.

They walked further, past a string of huts that smelled sharp and coppery and were daubed with crusted blood: impromptu abbatoirs, long out of use. There was barely enough meat to keep one such hut in labour. From somewhere off to their left came the clang and clink of a metal-smith at work, whilst outside a ramshackle shop-front up ahead a tired-looking fletcher slouched over his knees, paring wood; he looked up and squinted at them through the torchlight as they passed. A drunken boy wheeled past in front of them and fell onto his face. A lumpen whore, lying on rags and bloated with child sang comforts to herself, the breath of her words steaming out into the cold air like sad ghosts.

Atellus and Calidus continued along the main track and entered a slightly wealthier area, indicated by the finer houses on both sides with stone foundations and tight angular timbers stretching up two storeys. Some had stone frontages, others small outhouses. There had been an attempt at a metalled road, though it had long fallen into disrepair.

Atellus led them both past one of the houses, and through a lane, other dwellings craning over from either side. There was the sound of laughter and the smell of woodsmoke in the thin air. They passed an argument in one dwelling, and a couple fucking loudly in the next, the grunts and moans sounding through the translucent glass of a window.

They walked more slowly now, the muddied tracks giving way to frozen grass underfoot, the buildings becoming smaller and further apart. They could see the glow of fires from the main road through the vicus, and the huge greyish bulk of the Wall towering at their shoulders, the sentries like gods looking down at them. Calidus felt very exposed.

"Where are we going?" he asked, pulling his cloak further around him, trying to squeeze himself deeper inside it. The cold air was sawing at his flesh, cutting through to the bone with an iciness that numbed his fingers.

Atellus remained silent and walked on. The wind gathered force and whipped at the edges of their cloaks, snapping them back and forth and driving damp spitules of fresh snow inside. Calidus could make out a dark form standing out from the blackness beyond, a looming presence. Atellus bade him stop with a hand on his chest.

"I saw this when we first rode in, Scaeva," he said.

Calidus squinted through the darkness. Perhaps a hundred paces away was a dark line delineating the copse of trees at the southern edge of the vicus. Directly in front of him – and the reason Atellus had gestured for him to stop – were the remnants of a single quercus oak, a huge splintered trunk jutting into the sky like a giant jagged tooth; it was twice the size of Atellus as he stood beneath it. Nailed to the tree hung the splayed form of an adult heifer, the body pale and surreal, the throat slit and the foot of the tree sticky with half frozen blood.

"Shit," said Calidus.

He walked up to the base of the tree, the dead beast frozen tight against the bark above him. There was an assemblage of votive gifts gathered in a crook between the roots which erupted from the surface: crude woodcarvings, inscribed metals, and coins of long-dead emperors from lands that no longer existed, ptolemaics and rusted denarii. Up close, Calidus could see that the tree had been struck by lightning some time ago; the wood was charred black, and heavily weathered. Raising his eyes to the carcass above him, he could see some words or symbols had been carved into the flesh of the animal, but the moonlight wasn't strong enough for him to discern them clearly. Something about the grisly sight disturbed him deeply, a primal fear of some deep ancient sorcery beyond the ken of his young years which penetrated directly to the depths of his ageless soul.

He shivered violently and turned away. "Someone really wanted that cow up there," he said, quietly. Atellus was behind him, kneeling down and sorting through the offerings.

"Yes," agreed Atellus. "All that good meat wasted. That could feed half the vicus for a night. Instead, the crows get it."

"What is it for?" said Calidus, still looking up at the carcass. For some reason he found it difficult to tear his eyes from the spectacle.

"A shrine to Cernunnos," answered Atellus. "I've seen others before. This is quite basic. But they're usually away from the vicus, somewhere to function as a liminal point between civilisation and nature; man and beast."

"The horned god," whispered Calidus. "I thought they were forbidden. The old gods, I mean. In Eboracum, there are only Christians, now."

263

Atellus spat a laugh. "Are you so gullible, Scaeva? Don't believe everything your uncle tells you. There may be no large formal shrines to the old gods, but that does not mean they are not worshipped. In cellars, in the backrooms of taverns, in gardens, in forests. In *secret*. The old gods don't just get up and walk away forever because the emperor tells them they no longer exist."

"And what of you?" asked Calidus. "Do you still worship the old gods?"

"I follow my beliefs, boy," came the reply. "I do not change them for the whims of another. They are a part of me. I could sooner change my right hand."

Calidus laughed, a strange boyish sound in the darkness that pressed around them.

"What is so funny, Scaeva?"

"I just think," said Calidus, the white of his teeth showing in the dark, "that such *resolve* is the reason you are now freezing up here in the north, as far away from Treves as the emperor could banish you."

Atellus smiled, and nodded. "No doubt."

He continued sifting through the votive deposits, turning them over in his brown hands. A gust of wind lifted the cowl from his head, and sent his neck scarf trailing out behind him in the night.

Calidus shivered again. "What are you looking for?"

Atellus studiously ignored him, and carried on inspecting the objects: an inscribed bone checker; a collection of slate curse-tablets with pictures and garbled Latin scratched waveringly into the surface of the stone; a beaten copper dish; a collection of black cockerel feathers; a necklace of mixed canine and human teeth.

264

The stiffened corpse of the heifer creaked overhead as the wind pushed against the broken trunk.

"Atellus." The whisper came from the boy, strained.

"What?"

"People."

He looked around. The layer of snow across the field glowed softly like an upturned cloud; the gaudy sprinkle of stars gleamed overhead. A crackle of distant noise rose up from the vicus.

Then he detected something else: conversation. He waited, ears straining, and the voices became clearer and closer.

Atellus got to his feet and wordlessly grabbed the boy's elbow. Calidus followed him as he led him behind the great shattered trunk of the oak. "Don't move," hissed Atellus. "Don't speak, don't breathe."

They crouched there behind the massive bulk of the quercus, wrapped tight in their cloaks, the snow melting under their boots, soaking their feet with icy water. The frozen wind sliced past their noses.

The seconds fell heavily on their shoulders as they waited, the voices getting more distinct. Calidus could make out three men: two spoke in low rumbles, and a third had a higher voice that could be heard above the gusts of wind. He waited uncomfortably, the tension vibrating through his arms and legs, and icy sweat pooling in the small of his back. Beside him he could sense the soft rise and fall of Atellus's breathing.

"...else would they fucking go?" said a deep voice. Its owner sounded large and surly.

"Bumming in the fuckin trees, I dunno."

Calidus could hear the rasp of the snow being crushed beneath heavy footsteps.

"Wait," said the man with the higher voice. "Look."

The footsteps stopped.

"Prints."

"Could be a wolf," said one of the men, slowly. He sounded uncertain, wary.

"Wearing boots, you arse?" came the reply. "They were here. Parus, get the others."

Calidus heard the snick of blades being drawn, and then the crunch of rapid footfalls through the snow. He almost shouted out as he felt a hand on his shoulder. Atellus was looking at him intensely. He could see the bright white nimbuses of the other man's eyes in the darkness. The remaining two men were walking around; Calidus could hear the snow squeaking as they moved. He continued looking at Atellus. The easterner moved a hand down to his boot, slowly, his dark flesh blending with the night around them. He grabbed something and waited. A gust of wind rolled through the copse of trees to the south, soughing through the bare branches. Atellus pulled something free from his boot, and handed it to Calidus. It was a dagger: short-bladed but heavy and sharp. The boy wrapped his fingers around the hilt. The weight was reassuring, comforting. It was still warm from Atellus's boot. He looked across to the easterner.

The beneficiarius was holding up five fingers. He dropped them one at a time: four, three.

Two.

Calidus tensed, his heart whomping through his ribcage.

One.

Calidus didn't wait to see if Atellus would get up: he was already on his feet and around the trunk himself, his eyes searching desperately for the owners of the voices, the snow seeming unnaturally bright, the flares of torches from the vicus like a wild and desperate congregation of suns.

"Greetings," said Atellus. "I am beneficiarius imperatoris, Titus Faenius Magnus Atellus. Whom do I address?"

The man in front of him at first leapt back with surprise, a flicker of shock flaring through his eyes. He was not young, perhaps of an age with Atellus, but his hair was long and tied back from his forehead with a leather thong. The shock was quickly replaced by a look of determination, a fixed and impenetrable stare.

Calidus looked to the man in front of him, a huge bear wrapped tight in fur hides. His head was entirely shaven, but a long plaited beard trailed from his chin down to his chest. He eyed the boy with derision, and a calm confidence.

"Beneficiarius," said the long-haired man. He had the higher voice of the two, and it was steady and confident. "Perhaps you will do the honour of accompanying us to our lodgings? I fear this night is cold and dangerous. There are wild beasts prowling the perimeter of the vicus. Bandits. *Shades*." He had a long spatha gripped in his fist, the blade pointing down towards the ground.

"Who sent you?" asked Atellus. "You were searching for us. Why?"

Calidus watched the bald man spit into the snow. Over his shoulder he could see the flickering of more torches, getting closer. Three, four, five of them.

"Atellus," he said, but the easterner had already noticed them.

267

"Who sent us, nigger?" said the long-haired man, a laugh on his lips. "Cernunnos sent us, and He is displeased with your presence here." The blade of his spatha rose from the ground until it was pointing accusatorily at Atellus. "Befouling us with your foreign gods and your stupid *fucking* questions."

Atellus unsheathed his spatha with a smooth, whiplike motion; it flashed as it caught the moonlight. Calidus heard a roar and turned in time to see a long wooden cudgel crashing down towards his head. It seemed to be in slow motion, the bulk of the man like a bull charging towards him, the strong scent of acetum seeping from his pores, the filthy sweaty stench of the addled hides that he wore and slept in year round. Calidus noted the iron studs in the end of the weapon, and the timid moon hanging over the shoulder of the big man, peeking out like a scared child, shining off his smooth scalp.

Calidus spun round and dodged the blow, an instinctive reaction, and his momentum carried him to his knees in the snow to his left. The big man waded past him under the force of his own blow. Calidus had the dagger up and into the back of the man before he even had time to realise what he was doing. It passed through the layer of hide and he felt it bite into the flesh and gristle of the man, deep, the resistance straining his muscles, the impact shivering up his arm.

The big man sighed, the sound seeming amplified. Somewhere to his left he heard the clash of steel on steel, and the grunts of exertion. There was another noise, from across his shoulder, and Calidus suddenly buckled under a massive impact in his side like a hefty kick.

He found himself lying in the snow, his thoughts groggy and jumbled. He shook his head and tried to get to his feet, and a searing pain flooded through his entire torso, an evil sawing, burning agony that scorched his thoughts and sent him falling back to the snow. He could hear shouts all around, and saw through the moonlight the shaft of the arrow jutting from his cloak. It seemed unreal; his cloak was pinned tight around him, but there was no blood, and no pain as long as he stayed still. He turned his eyes upwards and saw men standing above, looking down at him. One – a short, small-featured man with hollow, mirthless eyes – was gazing down at him with disinterest; another was hauling to his feet the giant figure of the bald-headed man who had collapsed in the snow to his left. He looked around and saw Atellus go down beneath three men. The world seemed to move slowly and heavily as if in a dream, the language of the men above him was mumbled and indistinct, and Calidus could feel the motion and tilt of the earth beneath him before everything disappeared into a thick blackness darker than the darkest night.

CHAPTER 20

Aurelia could see the smoke trails from large fires up ahead, rising neatly above the line of trees until they were scattered by the wind higher up. The light was beginning to leave the sky, the damp sun collapsing into a cloud bank beyond the horizon.

She stopped against a fallen tree to take the weight from her feet. She had walked far over the course of the last day, through hard terrain, with a constant fear like an ache in her womb. After the brigands had left, she had waited and waited until she was certain they were gone. She had crept out and walked slowly across to the fallen men. The air was still and quiet, and stank of fear and blood. The snow was mottled bright red.

Aurelia had gone first to Matidia, lying still and blue. Her eyes were closed and her face looked peaceful and pure; she looked at the bundled rags lying to her side, the girl's sole belongings in this world. She picked them up and spread them over Matidia's body before walking off, up the road towards Vesta.

She could see that the girl was dead before she got close enough to touch her. The heavy barbed arrowhead, entering from behind, had ruined the girls face.

Aurelia walked back towards Cunovendus, the giant man slumped in an ungainly heap where he been leaning against the waggon. Arrows jutted from his chest and arms. Another protruded from his neck. His mouth was smeared with a trail of blood and vomit. Soft flakes of snow fell on his open eyes. She heaved him onto his back, looking nervously up at the road in case the brigands had returned, or if more were on the way, drawn to the sound of pillage like wolves to a blooded calf. She patted down his tunic, and the folds of his cloak. He had a small amount of silver sewn into the hem of his tunic, and a supply of cooked horsemeat in his cloak. She took these and moved away from the body.

Rodius lay face down in the snow. She was conscious of his back rising and falling slowly. The snow was melted around him. A raven, glittering a deathly blueblack against the snow, hopped along the edge of the road and cawed.

Aurelia stood above the man for a second then knelt down beside him. His pale face was turned to the side, and his hot breath was steaming out, melting the snow in front of his face. His tongue dabbed at the soothing water. She grabbed his shoulders and mauled him over. He gave a short guttural scream of pain, and lay back, panting.

"Crassa," he said, his blue lips squeezing into a pained smile. "Or whoever you are."

His face was almost as white as the snow in which he lay. She looked down at his arm; his hand had been hacked roughly off in a mess of sinew, splintered bone and torn tunic. Rodius had managed to staunch the flow of blood by tucking the stump of his wrist into his armpit.

"Be calm," she said, then got to her feet and hurried over to Cunovendus. She tried to drag the cloak from his body, but it was stuck firmly in place by the arrows that bristled from both sides of his body. Instead she unwound the leather strapping from the man's forearms and rushed back over to Rodius. She grabbed a handful of Rodius's cloak, and told him to open his mouth.

"Bite on this," she said. "Do not scream." Rodius did so. She rubbed the leather in the snow to cleanse it, then wrapped it in a tourniquet around the man's stump, pulling it as tight as she could. Rodius tensed and grunted, teeth clamping hard on his bundled cloak, tears squeezing from his eyes. The pump of blood from the wound slowed to little more than a trickle.

Rodius spat the cloak from his mouth.

"Leave me," he said, his voice a croak. "I will die here." His head fell down to his chest.

"If you want," shrugged Aurelia. "I have done what I can."

He used his remaining hand to rummage around inside his cloak. He produced some meat, and a small flask of strong mulsum, his fingers shaking wildly as he proffered them to her.

"Take these," he said.

Aurelia looked at him, and he returned her gaze, his eyes blue and bloodshot with pain and stress.

"There is a village," he said, "maybe half a day's walk from here. Follow the road as far as the abandoned checkpoint, then head east. You can get there before nightfall. They may help you. They may not. Mention my name."

"Will your name make them help me," asked Aurelia, smiling bitterly, "or kill me?"

Rodius shook his head and looked as if he was about to speak, but his chin dropped to his chest again.

"I am going to the Wall," said Aurelia quietly. "How far is it?"

Rodius started laughing, then regretted it. "Far," he said, shaking his head. "You will die long before you reach it, Crassa."

"Maybe," she replied. "But I aim to try." She gathered her clothes around her, and stood looking off towards the north, where the road was a mere indent underneath the snow. The trees were blanketed thickly, the air white and opaque.

"If you are serious, Crassa," said Rodius, "then maybe I can repay your kindness." He tried to push himself up to his knees, but the loss of his hand seemed to unbalance the man, and he had difficulty adjusting to the loss of weight. His long hair hung heavily from his scalp, stained with sweat and blood, crusted with frost. His face was sallow and drawn, dark sacks hanging from the pale orbs of his eyes. He shook and trembled.

Aurelia watched him as he dug something from his pocket; it was remnants of horsemeat. "Take this." He offered it to her with a quivering, blood smeared hand.

"You could help me by guiding me north," she said. "If you are man enough to try."

He laughed, and this time there was a background of tears to the noise that he coughed from his throat. "I do not have time enough in this world to help you, Crassa."

Aurelia turned to look at the fire they had started for her earlier, before she had left to gather the mandragorum. It was smouldering, the ashes glowing a deep orange. She nodded towards it. "Maybe your courage can buy you time enough."

Rodius looked towards the embers and swallowed. She could see the bulbs of sweat hanging from his brow, see his parched tongue as it flitted between his blue lips. Perhaps the deed would kill him. Perhaps not. It didn't really matter. At least he would not be alive for when the wolves or the bears came and started feasting.

Aurelia helped pull Rodius up to his feet, and he staggered lopsidedly, weary from the shock and blood-loss. He padded unevenly over to the fire, like a drunkard. It was set into a ring of stones just the other side of the fossus. The snow was melted around in a circle beyond it. The air above shimmered as the heat rose. He got to his knees, and stayed looking deep into the red ashes for a long time, as though beseeching them for clemency.

Aurelia kept a wary eye on the road. The air was still and noiseless, and there was no sign of human life for miles around. If any riders were approaching, she would hear them long before they happened upon her.

She looked again upon Rodius: he was bowed down, his forehead touching the cool snow, his lips moving in silent prayer. She did not know which gods he spoke to, or which ancestors he asked for help. She did not turn away as he gathered folds of the cloak deep into his mouth, and drove the stump of his wrist into the firepit. There was a hissing noise, followed by a pitiful and nauseating groan of pain that came straight from the man's chest, bursting forth through his lungs like the wails of all the spirits of the dead passing through his tormented flesh.

Rodius tumbled backwards into the snow, and was silent.

Aurelia walked over. The air reeked of roast pigflesh. She heaped snow onto the man's cauterised wound, and pulled the bundled cloak from his mouth. She looked around at the stones around the firepit. They were all smooth, but one had been sheared in two from the heat, and the edges were fine and sharp.

She went over to the body of Cunovendus and painstakingly used the edge of the sharp stone to hack at his cloak around the arrow shafts to release their pressure. The sun felt high in the sky when she had finished. She dragged the cloak around her shoulders, revelling in the warmth and protection. She knew that the bit of extra cloth would mean the difference between life and death if she had to spend one more night in the open.

Aurelia walked back over to Rodius as he was stirring. She paused and thought for a moment, then hacked at the edge of her cloak with the edge of the sharp stone. When she had sliced the hem open, she ripped off a strip of the cloak, rubbed it clean in the snow then bound it round Rodius's wound as a makeshift bandage. She crushed some ice in the fold of her cloak, and dripped the water onto his lips. His tongue lapped gratefully at the moisture. His eyes opened, and she saw the ghost of a smile touch the edge of his lips.

"Crassa," he said, then closed his eyes again.

When he woke again, he stayed conscious. He moved his arm, unwrapped the bandages and inspected it; the singed, blackened flesh was still ripe with the smell of burned meat.

"How is it?" asked Aurelia.

"The pain is beyond anything–," he began, then shook his head, finishing in a whisper. "Anything." He wound the cloth around his stump tenderly, the corners of his eyes creased with agony.

"Can you travel?" asked Aurelia.

He nodded slowly, and dragged himself to his feet. "If I don't, I die."

"Are you hungry?"

He shook his head, and started walking north along the road. Aurelia waited for a while then pulled the large cloak, pockmarked with holes, further around her and set off after him.

***

Now, half a day later, sitting against the fallen tree at dusk, watching the distant smoke rise, she could hear the laboured breathing of Rodius as he approached. He had directed her east, off the main north road in the hope of finding shelter for the evening. He was certain that they would not survive a night, even with a fire.

Aurelia had to agree. The cold had bitten down hard as the sun fell into the stark angular slashes of the distant hills warping the horizon. The snow had picked up intermittently, for which she was thankful: just enough fell to obscure their tracks from anyone who might be following.

Rodius shambled up and put his good arm on the tree trunk, panting. When his breath returned, he spoke.

"My cousin's village," he said, jerking his chin towards the line of smoke.

"How is your arm?" asked Aurelia.

"The pain in my arm," said Rodius, a weary smile creeping across his face, "is now matched by the pain in my feet from keeping pace with you, Crassima." He gathered snow in the corner of his cloak and squeezed it into his mouth. Aurelia did the same, though she was not thirsty; she knew it was essential to keep moving, lest her muscles seize up. She was more troubled by the endless gnawing pain in her stomach. The hunger was so intense it stalked along beside her like a constant companion, an enemy at her side taunting and tormenting her every step. Even the pain in her heels and blisters on her toes, the slow creeping exhaustion in her every muscle, could not compete with the incessant bleating of her stomach. They were rationing what little horse-meat remained. Rodius had tried to show her how to catch a crow earlier, by sneaking up on it and pouncing, but the bird flew away before she had even got close.

"How far is it?" she asked Rodius, rubbing her hands against her clothes to restore their warmth after handling the snow. "Will we make it before dark?"

Rodius stopped drinking and looked over towards the forest that separated them from the habitation. "Yes, if we move well."

"Then let us move," she replied, and pushed herself off the trunk. Her muscles howled in protest, but she drove them on with images of fresh roasted meat, thick hot stew and ladles of hot spiced wine.

They trekked through the perpetual night of the forest, sending beasts and birds scuttling out ahead of them. Rodius looked nervously around for sight of wolves or bears, but no creatures approached them. Aurelia thought she saw a huge boar with tusks the size of her arms blustering through the undergrowth at one point, but it was gone almost as soon as she had seen it.

They waded through the trees, a strange warmth seeming to exist beneath the thick canopy of the branches overhead. When they finally emerged into a violet half-world – the sun a cracked leaking ember spilt across the low clouds – she realised there was a problem.

"The smoke," she said. "There's too much."

Rodius nodded, clutching the edges of his stump with his good hand as he did so. The flesh was itching, he had said before, enough to craze him, and his face was twisted into a constant grimace. "That is not chimney smoke. And it is not fresh." His chin sank down to his chest. "This bodes ill, Crassa."

They carried on walking in silence, each lost in their own despondency, and entered the village shortly before darkness plunged across the land.

The village was utterly destroyed.

Some houses were still burning, lazy flames crackling and smoking as they chewed through the timber buildings, but most were mere charred and blackened shells. Bodies of the slain littered the road, men and older boys. The women and children may have been taken for rape and sale, or eventually food. Aurelia walked past one infant, its head split open upon the stones of the village tavern, its young bright blood speckling the snow around it. In the centre of the village was a pyre of burnt bodies, a tangle of blackened limbs that looked unusually small. There was an overhanging stench of seared flesh that disturbingly made Aurelia's stomach rumble in hunger, even as she fought back a retch.

"The bodies shrink when they burn," said Rodius in a distant voice. "The fire consumes the *genius* and so the body is but a feeble shell without it."

"What of your cousin?" asked Aurelia, weary, turning away from the smouldering corpses.

Rodius shook his head. "I know where he used to live."

Aurelia followed Rodius as he wended a path through the broken and bloodied streets. She could feel the warmth of the fires on her back and the cold of the meltsnow seeping up through her boots. Rodius's kinsman's house had been a proud timber construction on the eastern side of the village, but was now no more than a pile of collapsed rubble and scorched timber. Rodius wanted to search through the ruins, but Aurelia pulled him back.

"We need to look to ourselves now," she said. Rodius resisted briefly then nodded. He tore his eyes away from the ruined mass of charred wood and brick, and turned away.

They went to look for any carts or mules that may have survived, but there was nothing. As the wind picked up and sent fresh sparks raining down from burning thatch, they found a hut that had collapsed in on itself, the stone foundation blocks dry and still warm from the fires. There was room enough inside for them both to sit; they tested the fallen beams and found them sturdy. Rodius went to fetch fire from the flames which were still devouring some of the houses outside, while Aurelia strung up a doorway of plundered branches to keep the wind from sweeping in on them.

Rodius returned with a cluster of flaming tindersticks and built a sturdy small fire, then went out again and came back with a small skin of sour wine, and half a burnt loaf of tough bread. Crassa watched as he pulled something metallic from within the folds of his cloak and extended it towards her.

"A blade," she said looking at the proffered dagger.

"I found it by the pyre," said Rodius. "Take it."

Crassa shook her head. "You keep it," she said. "I feel it will be more use in your hands than mine."

Rodius pondered for a while, staring hard at the woman next to him, then returned the dagger to the folds of his cloak and busied himself tearing off chunks of the hard bread with his incisors. Aurelia feasted as though it were the emperor's own banquet, gnawing at the bread and trickling sweet wine over her teeth. They slept wrapt in their cloaks and huddled close to each other by the smouldering embers of their fire.

Aurelia woke just before first light, her toes and feet aching with cold and her head throbbing. She went and gathered snow and stuffed it into the empty wineskin, then swilled some icy water down with a small crust of leftover bread. She shook Rodius awake with difficulty. His eyes were bleary, but his flesh was less pale, and his lips were tinged with pinkish colour.

They set out again on foot, their muscles stiff and screaming in protest, but they drove each footfall into the snow through force of will, and watched as the sun poured cold citrus light into the world, illuminating the ruined village behind them and sending long shadows stretching out ahead of them.

Rodius navigated, taking them north through deep virgin snow and small copses of gnarled trees, so that they would meet the north road at an angle. They drove through, feeling the faintest brush of kindness on their skin from the sun; the radiant blueness of the sky hung overhead like a still, distant ocean. The abatement of the drilling cold lifted their spirits a little as they walked and chewed on tough rinds of stale smoked horsemeat.

"And why is it, Crassa," began Rodius as they slid easily down a snowy slope towards a copse of thick bare trees, "that you are so keen to reach the Wall?"

"I have business there," she answered. The pale light was hurting her eyes and making her head ache again.

"I see," replied Rodius, wryly. "Our change in circumstances has not loosened your tongue any."

Aurelia shook her head. "Business more noble than yours, slave-peddler."

"Noble?" laughed Rodius. "I wouldn't wipe my arse on nobility, Crassa. I am a peddler, true. A trader. In goods or people, it makes no difference."

"In children?"

"And what life do you think they would have prowling the streets of Eboracum like bare rats?" he replied. "How long would their miserable lives last, Crassa? At least we give them life. Not a pleasant life, but life nonetheless."

"And who is to say they would prefer that life to death?" Aurelia said. "I know which I would choose."

Rodius looked over to her. "And what gives you the right to make that decision for them?" He shrugged broadly, his handless wrist looking angry against the whiteness of the snow behind it. "I am a trader. Wine, barley, women. I am not like my brother; I do not relish their discomfort. But these are difficult days, and each man must do what he can to survive and find his own bread. And each woman, of course." He nodded over to her, with a smile.

"And what of your swine of a brother?" asked Aurelia, looking sideways at him. "You saw what happened to him?"

"I did not," said Rodius. "They took us unawares. Cuno was dead before we even realised they were loosing arrows." He grimaced at the memory. "They were upon me before I had time to draw my blade."

"Vassu was not dead," said Aurelia, "when they took him."

"He is alive?" Rodius stopped in his tracks for a second, looking at Aurelia as she nodded an affirmation. He shook his head and plunged forwards into the snow with renewed vigour, catching up to Aurelia within a few long strides. "Then he will soon wish he were not," he replied. "His fate is his own, and he has trod his own path to it."

They walked in silence for a while, loosening their cloaks against the infant heat of the winter sun. "I know your name is not Crassa," he said. "I know you are associated with the principia somehow, and that there will be men who would pay a fortune for your return."

Aurelia looked at him as they panted and strode on through the snow. "Then," she said, "you already know too much."

"I knew this before I agreed to take you," he said. "Believe me, I thought about the alternative. Had I told Vassu, or father, they would have called me mad and beaten me to the floor to claim you as a prize."

Aurelia shook her head. "Then why didn't you?" she asked. "Are you more *noble* than they?" She laughed upwards into the crisp air, a sweet ripple of sound through the clear daylight.

Rodius was silent for a while. "I like to be sure of my facts before doing anything rash. You were brought to me by Decius; a man I respect. I realised it made no difference: I could deliver you to the Wall and then hand you over, if I wanted."

"You are an animal," said Aurelia, firmly, shaking her head. "I should have left you to die on the road."

"But you didn't," he said quietly. "And I promise you, Crassa, you will not regret it."

"I already do," she said, quietly. "I don't expect you to care a whit for the empire, for Rome, for Valentinian. For civilisation, even. But my business at the Wall is to stop treachery."

"One leader is much the same as another," said Rodius. "It wouldn't really matter that much whether we have Rome collecting our taxes, or warriors from the north, or from across the seas." He stopped for breath, and turned to face Aurelia. "When was the last time you looked around you, Crassa. Further than the opulent gardens of your villa, or whatever comfort you were used to. Rome doesn't seem to be helping most of her people."

Aurelia had stopped also and placed her hands on her knees, breathing heavily. "How do you know it wouldn't be worse without Rome?" she demanded, once she had breath to speak.

"How do you know it would be?" he returned. "The politicians are corrupt: they seize the grain for themselves, they cease the pay for their troops, let their poor die in famine while they gorge on roast pig and imported figs. Whatever you may have seen in Eboracum, Crassa, is nothing compared to the rest of Britannia. Believe me, the further north you go, the more the mood sours. I would be wary of what news or messages you carry to the Wall, for the wrong words can lead you to your grave faster than any brigand's sword."

She stared at him for a while, whilst the sun lapped against thin wisps of clouds overhead and the chuttle of birdsong bounced through the air. "I am well aware of that, slaver. Well aware." She lowered her gaze and looked onwards. "We need to make good time." She gestured for him to take the front. "Lead the way."

They walked on in silence, the barren land seeming to leach the light from the hanging sun until it faded and the sky became the colour of woodsmoke. A slicing wind spilled from the surrounding hillsides and needles of fine snow swung to and fro in the air.

It was near dark when Aurelia saw the smoke. A thin line, bent like a sickle by the eddying wind. She pointed it out to Rodius, who was struggling, head down, his face creased with pain and exertion. His wrist had been throbbing again. She knew when he was in pain, as he stopped trying to talk to her.

"A village?" she asked as he squinted at the horizon. The origin of the fire was maybe two folds of the land away, from the bottom of what looked like a deep tree-lined gully.

Rodius shook his head. "A camp." He stood and thought for a long while, until Aurelia was unsure whether he was sleeping on his feet. "Brigands maybe; soldiers perhaps. But more likely brigands."

"Or refugees," said Aurelia. "They may share their fire and food. We could get closer and see."

He shook his head. "It is too dangerous. If it is brigands, they may have scouts posted nearby. They may already have seen us."

"Then there is nothing to lose," replied Aurelia. "We need shelter for the night, and we will walk nowhere tomorrow without some kind of sustenance."

"I am sorry," said Rodius shaking his head. He had intended to take them north and west to rejoin the road, but either his direction, or his knowledge of the route of the north road had been askew. He had expected to cross it hours ago, but as yet the land was still pristine and untouched in all directions as far as they could see.

"Come," said Aurelia, walking onwards. Rodius willed his feet to continue after her as she plunged down the slope. Soon she was lost under the curve of the hillside.

"Fool woman," he muttered under his breath, and spat, the warm phlegm gouging a deep trench in the snow. His feet were numb with cold, and all his muscles ached and screamed as he forced them into action. Each breath was like fire in his lungs, and the pain at the end of his wrist was such that he wanted to dash it against the trunk of each tree they passed.

He had barely slept overnight. He had been kept awake by the cold, but also by the constant noises from outside: wild beasts scouring the doomed village, and phantom horse-hoofs upon the tracks that made the sweat spring out upon his brow despite the temperature. There was also the smell, the sinking, clinging stench of roasted flesh that hung around the wood and brick of the ransacked dwellings. He had thought of his cousin, and his death, and the days they had spent as children hunting coney across the yellowgreen fells; fond days of hacking their way through forest tracks overgrown as thick as thatch to set snares for badgers, and skinning them for their pelts; presenting the hides to mater, and the kiss he had got for his trouble. He remembered the summers that stretched as far as the south sea, and the warm ripe smell of the foliage around the village, the trees sweating happily in the warmth and the ancient caves and carvings they had found beneath the waterfalls up in the wilds beyond the Old Invictus farm.

But most of all, he thought of his left hand.

Rodius lay there and felt his fingers tingling and throbbing, itching; the hairs on the back of his hand standing taut. Except he no longer had any fingers, any hand. Still, he fancied he could move them, could feel the tug and stretch of the muscles, the infinitesimal weight of the earthpull as he lifted each digit in turn and rotated his non-existent hand palm upwards, flexed the elbow, and brought it up in front of his face. Except, when he opened his eyes, there was nothing in front of him: just a mocking space, and the ugly rump of his wrist bound in the dirty sweating makeshift bandage.

Each time he would try it, sure that the sensations were real, and that his disfigurement had been a vile starvation dream, exacerbated by an acetum binge.

But each time, the hand he hoped to see in front of him was not there.

Rodius dragged his tired body down the slope after Aurelia, gritting his teeth and slitting his eyes against the snow which was blowing inside his cowl; each whip of wind seemed to drive the moisture directly around his clothing and seek out the chinks of exposed flesh where it would cause most discomfort.

He caught up with her near the bottom of the slope. There was a wide river cutting through the landscape there, the banks a tumble of stone and moss and stunted bare bushes fat with snow. The river itself was frozen, many unciae deep; a sweet bluewhite crystalline track wending through the whiteness.

"The river," said Rodius.

"You know where we are?" asked Aurelia.

"I do," he nodded. "It is called the *Tes* by the Britons, as far back as memory recalls."

Aurelia clambered down the embankment, her soft boots slipping on the icy rocks. Rodius came down after her with more difficulty, his unbalanced body and the lack of handholds sending him falling more than once, splitting flesh on sharp rocks, the cold whistling into the wounds like tiny arrowheads.

The air was still. A group of corvids exploded from a nearby copse with a crackle of wings. Aurelia wanted to set off across the river, but Rodius grabbed her arm and shook his head, laying a finger across his lips.

They hunched down behind a large boulder and waited. The cold crept into their joints. Rodius could feel her tension as a vibrating aura. Their breaths wisped in front of them as they knelt together in the snow. The frozen river before them sparkled in the daylight.

Apart from the occasional rustle of wildlife, there was absolute stillness and silence.

After what felt like a very long time, Rodius nodded to her, and they both emerged and set foot onto the frozen surface of the river.

To Rodius the crossing seemed to take half a day; they were exposed, visible from miles around and from almost any point ahead of them. There was no cover and no way of hiding. They held onto each other and shuffled across the ice, listening as the wind scoured its surface with small pebbles from the rocky embankments. He had to stop himself trying to sprint the final few paces, but he held firmly onto Aurelia and quashed the urge.

They arrived at the other side, and scrambled up the small icy stone bank, taking it in turns to clamber up to the next firm footing, then reaching down to help the other up. They fought their way up to where the ground levelled out, the snowy edge of a bank of trees, the roots large and intertwined, and glazed with a rime of ice. Aurelia looked around and noticed an opening through the copse, like an oval doorway. She turned to point it out to Rodius, but his attention was fixed on the ground not far from the riverbank.

She followed his gaze and saw what he was looking at: a dark smudge of brown standing out starkly against the white snow.

Rodius walked over to it, slowly, his eyes first scouring the forest around them for movement, and then the ground for tracks. Aurelia followed carefully in his footsteps. He bent down to reach the object that had caught his gaze, almost falling due to his poor balance, and reached out, sweeping the flakes of fresh snowfall from it.

She could see that it was the cheap sacking that she was wearing underneath the cloak she had taken from Cunovendus. It was streaked and smeared with crusted blood which had soaked into the clothing, making it heavy and dark. The folds were frozen and stiff.

"The girls," she said, in a whisper.

"Look." Rodius jerked his chin away from the clothes, towards the start of the trees. There was a single pink stain visible against the snow. Aurelia walked forward, her feet crunching through the snow. As she got closer, she could see it had dimensions, legs, like an upturned spider.

A hand.

She heard a noise then realised it was her own sharp intake of breath.

A girl's hand, the flesh soft, the bones small. At the wrist it terminated in a dull darkish tear. She looked around, but there was no trace of the rest of the body.

The smoke from the campfire they had seen earlier rose up above the trees to their right, thick and white. She could smell the scent of the burning twigs, carried on the heft of the wind, and fancied she could hear the snicker of flames gnawing at the wood.

CHAPTER 21

Atellus was aware only of the darkness.

It was thick and heavy, like a coarse blanket, and it reeked; it seemed to clog his nose and squeeze inside his mouth filling the gaps between his teeth. The darkness choked its way down his throat, and into his lungs until he felt as if his heart was about to explode under the pressure; a burning heat seemed to rise up from inside his belly and cover his head in a sheen of sweat.

Head?

He had a head. A body. Hands; arms.

He was aware of them suddenly, inside the darkness, because he was aware of the pain. A savage, gnawing, grating sensation through his bones that made him gasp and grind his teeth together until they squeaked.

There was a voice too, above him, a slushy drawl.

Singing: soft, low singing.

Atellus tried to force himself to waken fully, for his eyelids to spring open, and sweet consciousness to come flooding in, illuminating the dark. He was somewhere between sleep and wakefulness, a bleary limbo that pressed ponderously on his eyes and filled him with a humming fear.

The voice was getting slightly louder.

Atellus tried to force himself up. He felt as though all his muscles were straining against invisible bonds; as if he needed to tear himself up, a savage ripping of consciousness that was almost painful in its brutality, like a scraping across the surface of his brain.

The world outside smudged into view, and he felt his lungs suck in a sharp inspiration.

The room was dim, but radiant compared to the netherworld he had woken into. His eyes juddered across his environs, taking in the details: he was lying in a bunk, propped up at an angle on a rough bundle of sacking. Lanterns burning low hung from the walls. The strong odour of sweat and faeces and rosemarinus filled his nostrils.

He was in the valetudinarium. The singing had stopped.

"Good...morning," slurred a voice from above him.

Atellus looked up and blinked into the heavy face of Uricalus. The medicus's large red nose hung like a spectre in front of him, and his round sad eyes were glossy from wine.

The beneficiarius tried to speak but his mouth was dry. Uricalus seemed to realise this and unstoppered a jug, tilting it to Atellus's lips. He sucked in a draught, and spat it out again.

"Acetum," he spluttered, scrubbing his mouth with the back of his hand. He was aware of a dull pain shooting through his arm.

"Off corsh," said Uricalus, smiling giddily. The medicus tipped the bottle to his own lips and drank deeply. "Nuthing but the finesht for the beneficiariush." He winked at Atellus, took another swig, then stoppered the bottle and set it down.

"Do you have no water?" said Atellus. He could still feel the sour fizz of the wine on his gums.

"Water?" said Uricalus. "No...no, not at the moment, man."

"This is meant to be a fucking valetudinarium, not a tavern."

Uricalus laughed. "Ah, yesh, yesh...although I would prefer the latter, of coursh, I would!" He smiled glumly to himself.

Atellus felt a pain run up through his ribs. He looked down to see his torso was wrapped tight with half clean strips of bandage.

He had been bested, out by the shrine to the Horned God.

He had fought hard against the one, but then three more had surged forth, appearing like demons from the milky cauldron of the night, and they had driven him down. He had heard a yell from the boy Scaeva and then he had fought desperately but he was knocked to the ground by something; the night and the cold had disappeared in a storm of kicks and stamps and punches.

"You will live, beneficiariush," said Uricalus. "A little longer, at leasht." He laughed, a brittle noise like a twig cracking slowly. He held his thumb and forefinger an uncia apart. "A little, little longer."

Atellus tried to sit up in his bunk. His ribs howled in pain, but he pushed through it, the discomfort vivifying him, burning away the stupor. "I'm glad your prognosis is so positive, medicus."

Uricalus shrugged. The moans of the injured drifted over from further down the barrack-like valetudinarium.

"What of the boy?" said Atellus. "Calidus?"

The medicus made a smacking sound with his lips, and ran a small hand across his short curly hair. "The boy did not fare ash well ash you, that'sh true, hm."

"Is he alive?"

The medicus nodded briskly, then unstoppered the jug of acetum and took another sip.

"Yesh, yesh, he ish alive," he said. "His shide was piershed by an arrow. I've removed the barb, of corsh, and the shaft." He flapped his small hands. "But the boy has losht much blood. But he ish young. Who can shay? It'sh a matter for the godsh, not a mortal such ash I."

"Who brought us in?"

The medicus looked confused for a second. "Why, the boysh of corsh, our noble warriorsh!" He laughed again, his face reddening, until the laughter deteriorated into a hacking cough. "Shaid you were shet upon by localsh...rough typesh. Itsh lucky they found you when they did."

Atellus nodded slowly. "You are the only medicus here?"

"I once had an asishtant," He said. "He died."

"And you are able to treat all the wounded?" asked Atellus. "Single-handed."

Uricalus laughed again, then pounded a fist on his chest to stop himself. "Oh, oh yesh, I manage. Two of three die before I get round to them. The resht ushally die within a few daysh. I have no equipment, you shee. No shpatulae. No drillsh. No opium, of coursh. Even herba apollinarish ish shcarce."

Atellus thought for a second, using his mind to probe the pain in his flank. "Have you asked Apullius to requisition some for you?"

"Ha!" Uricalus sat down heavily on the edge of Atellus's bunk, crushing his leg. The beneficiarius grunted, and Uricalus shuffled aside a little. "Apulliush! Yesh...I

291

have ashked. Of corsh. I ashk each week, Cernunnosh my witnesh, but I get nothing. There'sh no gold for shuch luxuriesh. And of what little doesh get shent from Eboracum, the brigandsh take their shixty pershent. Ash alwaysh." He nodded to himself then ran a hand across his greasy dark hair, and reached out for his jug of wine. He tilted it up, but found it empty and slapped it down on the floor by the bunk. "And they are the onesh friendly to us. If the brigandsh from the easht catch the waggons...."

He shrugged and left the sentence hanging.

"I don't know how much longer the Wall can shtand this," said Uricalus, his voice a weary rasp across the timber around them. "The deathsh from famine, from attacksh by our own people, wild with anger, with hunger. Raidsh from the north, from inshide." He laid a bony finger across his large red nose, his dark saggy eyes glistening with eagerness. "There ish even talk of raidsh from the garrishons to the easht and wesht. Then there are the desherters...."

"How bad is it?" asked Atellus through gritted teeth, shifting his weight on the bunk. His side was aching as thought he had been kicked by a horse. "The desertions?"

Uricalus smiled grimly. The torchlight pooled on the raised surfaces of his face making him look like an ancestor's death-mask. "I don't know what Apulliush tells you...but theresh maybe two or three every new moon. And they take thingsh with them: food, equipment, suppliesh. Not even accounting for what the officersh shkim off the top for themshelves." He shook his head wearily.

"What of Fullofaudes?" said Atellus. "Why not send word?"

The medicus coughed out a contemptuous laugh. "Why don't *you* shend meshage to the dux, beneficiarius? Me, I would rather lasht at leasht a few yearsh more." He got up off the bunk. The timber squeaked sadly in the gloom. From somewhere down the far end of the valetudinarium came the sound of noisy vomiting. "Living here ish hell," said Uricalus. "But at leasht it ish *life*. If you will excushe me, beneficiariush, I need to get more wine."

"Where is the boy?" asked Atellus as Uricalus shuffled away towards his small office at the far end of the valetudinarium. The medicus jerked a thumb over his shoulder without looking back.

Atellus raised himself further up and carefully eased his legs over so he was sitting on the bunk. His head swam and black motes sparked across his eyes. His ribs ached fiercely, as did his sword hand. He looked around for his spatha but could not see it anywhere. He cursed vigorously into the dark. He was answered by a long drawn out laugh that trickled out into heavy sobs and moans.

Atellus pushed himself to his feet and stood up slowly. His flanks howled with pain, but he squeezed his eyes shut and fought away the waves of agony that rippled through him. He waited to gain his balance and strength; the pain seeped away somewhat, leaving only a memory of its former potency. He tested his weight and walked a few steps, gritting his teeth against the pain, shaking his head to dispel the dizziness.

Confident he would not collapse, he set off walking down the corridor, scanning the bunks for the figure of Calidus. There were tossing, weeping soldiers, some naked and bleeding, others sweating and thrashing despite the cold. Others looked at him with slick shiny eyes, their lips trembling. Some tried to speak, mumbled at him through splintered lips, stretched out arms for water. He walked past, and saw Calidus lying down on a bunk in the corner. He was covered with a thin drape. His face was pale, his dirty blonde curls stuck to his forehead with sweat. His eyes were open, and his lips cracked into a smile.

"Atellus," he said in a hoarse whisper.

The beneficiarius smiled. "How are you?"

Calidus shook his head. "I have been better." He drew the drape back so the pale flesh of his stomach was exposed. His lower abdomen was covered in angry purple bruising, some of it beginning to turn a dark yellow. At the centre of the bruising, towards the side, was puckered wound like a small mouth. It was stitched closed with thick dark twine. The flesh around it was bright red and swollen. "I've been...much better," he winced.

"A fine scar you will have there, Scaeva," said Atellus. "Worthy of a man."

"I tried to fight," said the boy, lowering his eyes, "but I did not see this. I was on the ground before...." He trailed off, his cheeks damp.

Atellus sat down carefully on the edge of the bunk and laid a hand on the boy's shoulder. "You fought bravely. I saw you. You took your man down. We were outnumbered. There was nothing more we could do."

Calidus sniffed, and nodded slowly. "I hate it here. Boys are dying, rotting around me. Or mad, gibbering at me. The pain is too much."

"It will fade," said Atellus. "I will ask the medicus to get you something for the pain. To help you sleep. You will be healed before you know it." He squeezed Calidus's shoulder and got up. "I will make sure you are safe and cared for here. Apullius should be able to arrange to have you cared for in the principia, so at least you will have to endure no longer in this toilet."

Atellus walked away down the corridor, through the moans of the sick and dying, past the sprawled meat of the dead. The nails on the soles of his boots thumped against the timber floor. He strode down towards the medicus's office. He felt stronger with each step, his muscles less stiff, the pain in his ribs subsiding a little. The office was a small shack entered through a splintered and decrepit wooden door, the slats of which rose neither as high as the ceiling or as low as the floor. He pushed his way through to the inner sanctum. There was a small table, behind which sat a scuffed and warped wooden chair and a tripedal fire brazier with a few embers smouldering weakly in it. Behind these was a row of mouldy parchments hanging from hooks set into the far wall.

Uricalus was sitting back in his chair, sipping at a skin of wine perched on his chest. He looked up disinterestedly when Atellus walked in, then returned to suckling at the spout. Atellus shut the half-door behind him, then stood there and waited. After a while, Uricalus stopped drinking and looked up at him.

"A meshsenger came," he said, "from the praefectush. Wanted to shee you." He paused to belch. "I told him you were ashleep."

"Where is my sword?"

In here Atellus could hear the wind straining against the wooden beams. Two lanterns set in wooden brackets in the wall shook with the creaking timbers. He was reminded of the hold of the trader's ship that had brought him across the sea to Britannia. There was something suffocating about it, making him feel queasy.

"Your shord?" said the medicus, squinting and shaking his head. "I never shaw it."

Atellus walked up to the table where the swarthy medicus sat – a pile of dark skin, drooping belly and sharp bones – and slammed his fists onto the surface. Uricalus snapped backwards and toppled from his chair into a heap by the brazier. His eyes were skinned wide, dark coals ringed by the yellow of his scleras.

"My spatha, medicus." Atellus spoke firmly and clearly, though he did not raise his voice. His fists were hard against the weak timber of the table. He could feel it scraping his flesh where the veneer had splintered beneath the force.

Uricalus's mouth worked two or three times before words came out. His hand seemed to snake across the floor of its own volition, searching for the dropped wineskin.

"I...I...do not know...I never shaw it," he spluttered. "They brought you in...."

"They?"

"The sholdiers...the patrol. They usually take what they want as shalvage...they figure mosht will be dead shoon anyway...."

Atellus nodded, and removed his fists from the table. He walked around it to where the medicus sat on the floor, his left hand stroking the wineskin like a cringing hound. He tried to edge away as Atellus approached, but the easterner crouched down to put his face on a level with the older man's.

"Look after the boy," he said, staring hard into Uricalus's eyes, unblinking. "Get him water, bandages, whatever he needs. Don't let the animals near him, or I'll pull your eyes out and shove them up your arse. Do you understand?"

The medicus looked terrified. He nodded slowly.

"How soon can we transfer him to the principia?" asked Atellus. "I want him out of here before he becomes worse than he was when he was brought in."

"I... I will need orders from Apulliush," said the medicus.

"You have order from me."

"The boy shouldn't be moved...jusht yet. A day or two, maybe, and we will arrange for him to leave."

"Good." Atellus stood up to his full height and extended his hand down to the medicus. Uricalus looked at it apprehensively, then gripped hold of it. Atellus heaved the man up, and patted him on the side of his arm. "And don't let him die," he said, "or you do."

Uricalus started trembling. Atellus reached out and grabbed the wineskin that was clenched tightly in the older man's gripe.

"I'd stay away from this," said the easterner, "for a while. At least until the boy is fit and healthy again."

Atellus lifted the wineskin up at arm's length and squeezed a thin golden trickle of liquid into his mouth. He scrubbed his hand across his mouth and sighed.

"Remember what I have said, Uricalus." He rubbed his eyes and walked out, into the main hall and through the door into the courtyard beyond.

CHAPTER 22

Rodius realised that after so many hours lying down, even the snow became comfortable.

At first the cold and wet were unpleasant, and the incessant wind raking his back was painful. But after long hours in the same position, judging time by the slow arc of the pale moon and counting the pulses of pain through his wrist, he was coming to appreciate the softness of the ground.

His eyelids had flickered and sank a few times now; he was sure he'd caught himself before Crassa noticed, but he didn't know if he could fight sleep for much longer. The weariness clung to him like a wet shirt, and he wasn't sure whether he'd wake up again if he fell into the darkness here, at this time.

They were waiting, laid flat behind a tumble of rock at the knap of a short hillock, just outside the copse of trees where the brigands were camped.

Watching.

Watching.

Still.

At first, he had been nervous, the adrenaline keeping him alert as he scoured the trees for lookouts and strained his ears for the crunch of snow from a scout's footsteps. But that was long past, and his body was tired and weak. He could use a drink: a nice thick beer, to fill his stomach and put a warmth in his bones. He could almost taste the brew in his gullet now. He licked his cracked lips realising he'd almost fallen asleep again at the thought of a mug of ale in his paw.

He shook his head to freshen his senses and looked across at Crassa. She must have felt his gaze, as she turned her head slowly and returned his look with a tense smile.

She was a fine-looking woman, Rodius thought, and not for the first time. But he'd had no appetite recently. Not since Sedebelia had died. He still felt a crushing feeling around his throat when he thought of her, even though it had been many seasons past. Crassa was a strong woman, but she hated him, and everything he stood for. Sedebelia had always understood him; she had understood everything. She was a good mare and had needed little discipline, unlike some of the other milchsows his friends had taken up with. The way she had nursed him through the nigrum in that first houseless winter, and taken up her blade to slice a haunch off the debt-collector when he came calling….

"Rodius."

The voice was pitched low, but there was urgency in the tone. He opened his eyes – though he had not been aware of closing them – and saw Crassa in front of him. The sky was dark now, an angry black, rather than the milky violet of dusk.

"Wake up," said Crassa.

"I was just listening," said Rodius. "Intently."

"Of course," she replied, turning away from him.

Was that a smile on her mouth? Rodius looked down the slope towards the clearing in the midst of the trees. He could see the welcome glow of the fire, and see the entrails of smoke scattered across the moon. There had been no scouts, and no lookouts. If there had, they would both have been dead, or worse, long since.

"Are you still sick of being alive then, Crassa?" he asked, with a despondent smile.

"Are you not yet sick of being a coward?" she countered, her blue eyes steady and calm.

Rodius shook his head. He looked off towards the brigands' camp. If they were caught, they would be tortured and killed. They would rape Crassa until her mind snapped, then burn her eyes out.

He lifted his stump of a wrist to her, and grinned. "Why not let them finish what they started."

They both emerged from the tumbled limestone crowning the hillock, and skulked slowly down through the snow towards the copse of trees. The gleaming moon was obscured by thick ribbons of cloud trailing across the sky and the snow underfoot seemed to pulse with a pale grey light.

Rodius felt the cold, but his heart was beating so fast it seemed as though he was generating an internal heat that would keep him warm through the bleakest storm. He was certain that every footfall, every click and scrunch of snow under his boot, was amplified like a yell through the quiet night. He expected a raised voice, the clatter of arms: a quick and brutal death.

And would he try to save Crassa? he asked himself. Did he owe her? What right had she to save him, to snatch him away from the warm embrace of death and condemn him to life as a handless freak? A weakling, a poor and destroyed beast left to hunger and freeze on the shell of the earth. It would have been more merciful of her to let him die out on the road, as his warmth seeped into the snow and the numbness of rest overtook him.

Would he defend her? In whose name was he even here? Chasing the ghosts of lost whelps through the night.

Lost in bleak thoughts, Rodius just managed to check his momentum before he walked face-first into a tree. The copse loomed up like an army of shades in front of him. Beyond was silence except the odd crackle of birds through the branches, and the occasional muffled crump of snowfall from the canopy overhead.

And there was his brother, of course.

Although it would be better for them both if Vassu were dead. He wanted to get close enough to the camp to show Crassa that her whelps were out of reach, and then leave before he caught any sign of his brother. Though, he conceded, the chances of Vassu still being alive still were slim beyond plausibility.

He could see the dark form of Crassa to his right, slipping from tree to tree. She was a strong woman that one. He smiled; she also had much bigger balls than he.

Rodius pushed himself away from the trunk and moved out, feeling naked and exposed. The inside of the copse was dark beyond belief, and curiously warm, the air thick and heavy compared to the open. There was less snow on the ground; his eyes ached from the effort of trying to discern twigs before he stepped on them. The glow of the guttering campfire was visible through a split of light between the trees.

He could see Crassa drop down to her belly. He did the same and crawled slowly over to her. Crawling was difficult with only one hand; he kept forgetting and alternately putting his weight on his stump, only to collapse and have to bite back oaths from the pain. The sharp branches and stones underneath jabbed through his clothes. He was sweating when he reached her, and sucking in deep breaths underneath his cloak to muffle the sound of his strain.

When he caught his breath, he saw Crassa pointing. He squinted away through the darkness and waited for his eyes to adjust to the gloom. At first he saw nothing; then his peripheral vision detected a slight movement between the trees maybe fifty paces ahead of them. He watched it for a while, studying the silhouette, but there was no more activity. He felt Crassa's breath on his ear as she moved closer to him to speak.

"A guard?" she whispered.

Rodius shook his head slightly. "Hound."

He put his chin down on the cold ground. He could feel the blood and tension humming through his body. Crassa placed a hand on his shoulder, then he was aware of her rising to a crouch and moving off, slowly. He watched the still form of the dog for a while to see whether it stirred, then followed her.

She travelled light and fast in a sweep around the periphery of the camp. Through gaps in the trees as they passed, Rodius could see the timber buildings in the clearing: it looked to be a fair-sized settlement. He guessed at twenty to thirty solid dwellings, with maybe the same number of shabbier constructions made from branches and old hides. It had probably been here for a few moons at least.

They kept moving round, skirting the edge of the camp. The glowing fire grew more distant. Rodius caught up with her and put his mouth to her ear.

"This is madness, Crassa!" he hissed. "Even if we could get inside without being seen, we have no idea where the chits are. Even *if* they're here, we do not know if they're *alive*. But we *are*. While we stand here and hold back, we have our breath!"

"You really are over-fond of life, whoremonger," she said, her voice thick with contempt.

"And you do not respect it enough," he replied, sinking his head.

"I respect it enough to preserve it whenever I can," she said. "Even for those who are not so deserving."

He rubbed a hand across his chin. The stubble rasped under his fingers. "And what of your noble business? Your great haste to reach the Wall? Where are *your* priorities, then, Crassa?"

Her eyes flared in anger at him. At first he thought she was going to strike him across the face, and he felt the muscles in arms tensing in anticipation. Then she looked away and slumped down against a tree, the folds of her oversized cloak swallowing her up into a deeper darkness.

He watched her for a while, the mists of her breath pluming out from under the cowl. He knelt down beside her.

"I need to try," she said, after a long silence. She sounded breathless, tense. "They deserve that much at least. No one else will try for them. What chance have they ever had?"

"There are too many lost in this world for you to care about them all," whispered Rodius. "And why be selective? Why care for one and not another?"

Crassa looked up at Rodius, her eyes bright. She opened her mouth to speak, but closed it suddenly, her teeth clicking.

Footsteps.

Rodius pressed himself and Crassa deep into the shade of the tree trunk. He could see the whites of her eyes reflecting what little light there was, could feel the warmth of her body underneath him, the strained rise and fall of her chest.

There was a trickling sound, which rose in intensity.

Rodius shifted his position slightly to get a better look. Carefully he inched his face out beyond the cover of the tree.

He could see the tall silhouette of a man standing in the dark of the trees. He was humming softly to himself whilst he pissed. The noise was now a crashing flow, a river in spate crackling through the quiet. He saw the long matted hair of the man; he was facing away from them.

Rodius acted without thinking. On some primal level he knew that any pause or deliberation would see the opportunity pass. He was on his feet before he was even aware of it, walking gingerly through the forest floor, hearing his footsteps but aware that louder too was the sound of the micturant and the bass rumble of his humming. He moved in a calm remembrance of the way he and his cousin used to stalk deer in those long sweet summers years past.

The distance between them was closing rapidly. He listened to the flow of urine peter out, saw the man shift his weight between his feet.

Now.

Rodius felt for the hilt of his dagger. The blade was tucked into the loop of his makeshift belt. He had fashioned it from bark-stripped hazel branches. He had eaten so little lately he could hear his empty belly goading him each time his breeches slackened enough for him to need to twist the cord even tighter around his waist. He silently slid the dagger out and felt its comforting weight in his hand.

He turned to his victim, aware of the breath of wind on his cheek and the coolness of the iron hilt in his palm.

The man was taller than Rodius, by half a head at least. His back was broad and square, the slope of his shoulders betraying slabs of hard muscle underneath.

Rodius felt unbalanced by the loss of his hand; he needed the surprise, the viciousness.

He could smell the man: the stench of the warm sweat from between his legs and the sour reek of his steaming urine.

Rodius brought the dagger up in a long sweep from behind, stopping it precisely as the point pricked the flesh of the man's throat, and rammed his mouth to the man's ear.

"Speak and you die," he grunted.

Rodius had never felt the lack of his other hand as badly as at this moment. He needed to reach around, cover the man's mouth, drag him backwards, unbalance him, take him to the floor. Instead he felt feeble, vulnerable. He had to be fast, not give the animal time to think.

He kicked down hard at the back of the man's locked knee, and the brigand's leg shivered, his weight causing him to half fall to one side. Rodius used the blade of the dagger to guide him down and forwards, like controlling a horse with the pressure of the thighs, pressing the metal tip into the man's jaw.

"To your knees," he hissed. The man did as he was told. Rodius could smell the wine seeping from the man's pores. He was probably so drunk he would fall asleep with the dagger at his thrapple. "Fall forward, face down."

He did so, slowly.

"Do as you're told and you may live," whispered Crassa.

Rodius looked up at her; he could feel the big man's muscles quivering beneath him with anger and suppressed tension. She was standing in front of them, looking calmly at their captive. The brigand raised his eyes, the muscles in his back flexing as he tried to lift his neck; if he had the courage to try and test Rodius's control, they would both be fucked.

Crassa knelt down by the man's large head and looked down at him. His eyes were dark and bloodshot. In the scant light, his features were a mass of crags and shadows, his hair a thick bestial mane. His breath reeked of stale meat, sweet wine, and rotting teeth.

"The girls you took from the waggon on the north road," she said. "Where are they?" Her voice was clear, low and calm. But there was a deadly menace beneath the surface that was communicated by tone, and the angry flash of her eyes.

Rodius felt the man stare up at her, even as his dagger pressed hard into his throat. He felt warm blood trickle over his knuckles. The brigand spoke low, his mouth barely moving for fear of puncturing his jaw on the point of the blade.

"No...girls."

Crassa spoke again, shaking her head. "We know they are here. Tell us where they are kept and you will live. There are limitanei surrounding the camp. You will all die." She stared hard at him, willing him to speak.

"No...girls."

Rodius could see a trail of drool running from his lips to the ground.

The only warning he had of the attack was the ripple of tension along the top of the big man's back, and then Rodius was off balance, the edge of the blade away from the man's throat. Rodius dropped it, and threw his arm and the weight of his body across the brigand's mouth.

He muffled the shout just in time, the sleeve of his arm wedged tight into the other man's jaw.

All Rodius's weight was on the brigand's face; the man's hands scrabbled for purchase in the folds of Rodius's cloak. Then he felt a dull hard blow to his head and the world spun and fizzed in a shower of pain. Rodius heaved his face away from the flailing arms, and pressed his weight down into the man's nose and mouth.

A surge of pain exploded through his arm, shivering and thrashing its way up into his shoulder and neck. Rodius fought back a scream of pain; the bastard had bitten his arm, powerful jaws and large square teeth gnawing away through his sleeve.

Rodius felt his strength going, his balance toppling; he was slowly being forced away from the man's face and onto the ground. His legs scratched at the snow-dusted dirt as he tried to spread his weight and dig his boot heels in.

It was no good; he was moving. Rodius could feel his grip on the man's face slipping. In a breath's time he would be able to bellow out and bring death on them both, presuming he didn't destroy them himself first. He could feel the sweat dripping from his forehead, his muscles howling out for mercy, his stump throbbing and burning worse than it ever had.

Rodius felt a jolt underneath him. A noise, like a gurgling coming from the man's throat. The pressure of the jaws on his arm eased, the great heaving ocean of muscle grew tense and rigid. The fight seeped away from beneath him and the man became still and placid.

Tentatively, he slackened his smothering hold on the brigand, letting his muscles relax. They were aflame with the exertion, and unflexing them made them hurt more. He was panting hard, his breath like steam in front of his eyes. He was aware of a warm wetness spreading up from his side. At first he thought he had wet himself in the panic of the struggle, and hot shame crept across the nape of his neck. He caught a movement behind him, from the corner of his eye, then felt a hand on his back.

Crassa.

He eased backwards, sliding off the brigand, who was trembling faintly beneath him. His eyes were open and staring. The hilt of Rodius's dagger jutted from the side of the man's throat; thick bubbles of fresh blood seeped from the wound. He looked down and saw he was covered in the man's gore.

He moved aside as Crassa knelt by the big man's face, and gathered the drapes of her cloak into thick bunches, pushing them over his face and nose. She pressed down, careful to keep the man's blood away from her body. Rodius watched as the sweat sheened on her forehead, her eyes fixed with concentration. The gurgling beneath the cloak was faint and muffled. After a long while, the big man's feet drummed desperately against the floor. Rodius hurried over and lay across them, clamping them down.

They waited in silence. There was only the faint shiver of the dying man beneath them both, and the smooth twoot of an owl overhead.

Then all was still.

Rodius got up slowly, wearily, and withdrew his blade from the brigand's throat. It was wedged tight, stuck between the jawbone and the spine. He put his foot on the man's chest for leverage and heaved with his arm, inching it from side to side. Eventually it squeaked out, followed by a fountain of dark blood that shone black in the moonlight. He wiped it on the sole of his boots, and tucked it inside the loop of his makeshift belt. He watched as Crassa uncovered the man's face with her cloak and stood up. She betrayed no emotion.

"Where did he come from?" she whispered to him. The air was quiet.

"I didn't see," said Rodius, shaking his head. He pointed towards a shack on the outer edge of the encampment, a squat shabby construction that looked flat and small silhouetted against the snow. "If I lived there, this is probably where I'd piss."

They both moved over slowly, ears tingling with the strain of listening out through the ghostly night. The shack approached, and as they broke through the cover of the trees, the camp swelled into view before them, opening up like a winter sunset across the land. Timber huts and tents stretched out, encircling a large open space in the centre where the remains of the fire glistened a sombre red.

At the far end of the camp a silhouette appeared, a stumbling figure staggering out into the deep snow. Rodius pressed himself and Crassa against the side of the shack, drenching them both in shadow. They waited, barely daring to breathe in case the plumes of their breath betrayed them, until they could hear the footsteps of the man returning to his tent.

Rodius inched around the frail timber wall of the dwelling. He tried to peer through the gaps in the wood panels, but the inside was a deep dead blackness. The entrance was a thin hide hung across a tiny doorway; Rodius wondered how that big man – if it indeed was his dwelling – could fit inside. He got to his knees and pulled aside a corner of the hide. He could see nothing inside, but there was no sound either. Without thinking, he shuffled his way in and stood, hunched, inside.

The shack stank of stale sweat and spilt wine and semen.

There was the faint sigh of breath in the thick air; he could feel someone else in there. He willed his eyes to adjust to the darkness, but he couldn't discern anything recognisable. He gently eased the dagger from his belt, felt the cool handle in his palm, the faint stickiness of residue left over from the dead man lying outside for the wolves.

Rodius took a step forward. His shin struck something hard. He could feel the warmth of another body nearby, sense the minute disturbance of the air, the soft thrum of a beating heart.

"Girl," he said, softly, low. "I am here to help."

He took a chance. It may be one of Crassa's chits, or it may be a brigand bitch.

There was a stifled sob. He went down to his knees; the darkness was less opaque now and he could make out a cot by his feet, and a shapeless mass swaddled inside it. He tucked his dagger back into his belt and reached out his hand to the creature.

"Girl," he said, softer.

He felt a small hand grip his through the dark.

"Be quiet," he whispered, "and stay close with me."

He turned back towards where the darkness was less intense than the surroundings, towards the thin belt of dimness that signalled the entrance. He let go of the girl, and felt with his hand outstretched and grabbed the hide, pulling it back, and driving himself under the low beam of the lintel.

Rodius looked around as he scrabbled up through the disturbed snow, his knees damp. There was no sign of activity.

And no sign of Crassa.

He turned round, and grabbed the girl by the loose drapes of her clothing, hauling her up and out into the night air. He could see her breath illuminated by the pale moon overhead. He couldn't have said which one she was; he'd never paid much attention, and they all began to blend together after so many trips.

He looked into her large eyes. They stared straight ahead, through him. It was bitterly cold and she was dressed only in a rough shift. She didn't shiver, but he saw her lip trembling and the faint insect noise of her teeth clicking together.

"Where are the others?" he asked, gently. He tried to keep the urgency and fear from his voice. "Do you know where they are?"

There was no answer. The chit barely blinked at him.

"Be quiet and wait here."

He guided her gently into the deeper shadows against the side of the shack, and turned round. He thought he heard a sound. Where the fuck was Crassa?

Rodius listened. Nothing. No sound, no movement. He moved round to the other side of the shack.

And saw his brother.

Vassu was standing back by the corner of the dwelling. He had a wiry arm wrapped tight around Crassa's neck, hugging her to his chest. She was red-faced, and her feet were slightly off the ground. Vassu looked taut and drawn, haggard. His face was covered in scratches and welts, his cheeks sunken, his dark eyes bloodshot. His chest was heaving with the exertion, and the muscles in his bare forearms stood out like iron cords.

"You want the bitch back, then cut me free," he spat, his voice low but his words weighted with hate and desperation.

"Vassu," said Rodius, his voice a whisper. "Frater, it is me. Rodius."

311

There was a noise coming from his brother's throat, a crackle and a hiss intertwined. Rodius thought it was a laugh.

"My brother is dead," he said. "Are you his shade?" He made the hissing noise again in his throat. It terminated with him spitting onto the snow.

Rodius moved closer to his brother, the scant starlight playing across his features.

"It is me Vassu," he said, as clear and audible as he dared. "I am no shade."

Vassu stared in silence for a while, his wide white eyes flitting across the other man's body, taking him in. He licked his lips soundlessly. His arm relaxed and Crassa fell to the ground. She moved backwards, weakly, rubbing at her neck.

"Rodius?" said Vassu in a creaky tone that sounded at the edge of hysteria. "Frater? Your hand, Rod? By Dis, where is your hand?" He hissed again in the back of his throat. He made a desperate clawing motion towards his brother, then sank slowly to his knees, shivering. "Free me, frater. Quick."

Rodius noticed for the first time that his brother was bound by a thick noose around his neck, but his arms and legs were untethered. Vassu held up his hands, and Rodius could see that the fingers were jutting out at irregular angles. "They snapped my fingers like twigs, Rod, and left me here to starve and fight their hounds away from my flesh." His eyes were wild and damp. "Please, frater, cut me loose."

Rodius stood staring at the pitiful form of his brother. He was a liability to them; he always had been: a hot-blooded, mean, confrontational man. Even their father had detested him.

Rodius walked closer to his brother, and studied him: the lean face, the short dark hair, the once bright eyes and smooth fleshy cheeks had now imploded with pain, hunger and torment.

"The choice is not mine, frater," he said, looking into Vassu's eyes.

"Then whose, Rod?" he said. "Whose fuckin choice is it? The bint's?" He hissed in his throat again, his eyes the moist black pebbles that Rodius remembered from his youth.

Rodius stepped back and used his good arm to help Crassa up from where she was sitting on the ground, clutching at her throat. Her eyes were red.

"He wants to be freed, Crassa," he said to her. "It is your choice."

"You talk to the dumb whore as though it is an equal, frater," said Vassu, quietly. "You always were the weak link. Your lost hand; me, here, dying in my own filth. Who stopped the waggon?"

Vassu moved closer to his brother and lowered his voice, which trembled with suppressed rage. "Who was soft and dumb as the whores we carried, eh, Rod?" He continued, spitting on the snow. "You free me now, or I wake the whole fucking camp. You'll be buggered to death before sunrise, you and your fucking pet!" He spat again.

Crassa held out her hand for Rodius's dagger. He pulled it from his belt and proffered it, hilt first. She took it and walked over to the bound man, not taking her eyes from Vassu's.

"Rodius," she said, "I will need tension on the rope."

He walked round behind his brother, wordlessly, listening to the night around them for indications of any other sentries or late stirrers. The rope was wrapped tight around a deep stake in the ground, much the same as one might use to secure a huntsman's hound.

"Lie down," she said to Vassu.

313

He stared at her in open disgust. "Any tricks, sly witch," said Vassu, "and I will make sure they rip your cunt out of your throat. I will watch, and die happy." He spat again, at her feet.

Aurelia said nothing as Vassu lowered himself to his knees, then lay on his belly. Rodius gripped the cord tight with his hand, bracing himself with his feet against the side of the shack; the tension held the rope taut and stiff.

She held the dagger up, starlight sparking from the blade, and brought it down against the side of the noose of rope wrapt around Vassu's neck and began sawing at the thick plies. When the tether was half-severed, she slipped the blade over and held it tight against the man's neck, the point digging deep into his skin until a bulb of red blossomed at the end and glittered like a tiny jewel in the moonlight. Vassu gulped and strained beneath Aurelia, but she lay atop him in the cold, and made soothing noises into his ear.

"I could drive this into your jaw, worm" she whispered, stroking his hair with her free hand as though comforting a cat, "before you had time to scream. Your life is mine. If I choose to release you, it is because I pity you, and because you may be of use. Do not underestimate me, ever again, because I will not gift you your life so lightly next time."

Aurelia drew the sharp blade in a tight, pressured arc across Vassu's throat, supporting the weight enough so the tip barely broke the skin. She drove the bloodied edge of the blade into the half-cut rope, then worked it up and down, sawing at the threads until a tug from Rodius sent it popping free.

Crassa got to her feet and handed the knife back to Rodius. She turned to face Vassu who still lay on his belly, rubbing his scratched neck.

"For your freedom," she said, fixing him with a level gaze. "Where are the girls, the others? How many are alive?"

Vassu used his elbows to push himself up onto his knees, then bucked himself upright. He didn't acknowledge Crassa, or look in her direction.

"What next, fratercul?" he addressed Rodius, mockingly.

"Answer her," said Rodius, nodding at Aurelia.

"The whelps are all dead," he said, still addressing Rodius. "We need to leave."

Rodius went around to the other side of the shack, and grasped the girl's hand, bringing her over to them. She seemed to wilt in fear when she saw Vassu's silhouette in the darkness.

Aurelia looked at her. "What is your name, filia?"

The girl looked ahead of her without answering. Aurelia grabbed her small cold hand and gave it a squeeze.

"Where are they?" Rodius asked Vassu again, the girl standing as a silent accusation between them.

Vassu spat. "Some are dead. The others taken as chattel." He trod closer to his brother, rotating his neck, feeling his freedom. "Do you want to fight the entire village, fratercul? You and your tame whore?" He spat again.

Aurelia was about to speak, when a thundercrack of sound rose into the night. It was the barking of a hound. Fierce, defiant, angry, the noise shattered the night silence. Other hounds took up the call from deep within the woods around them.

Rodius swore under his breath, then grabbed Crassa by the shoulder and hurried back, away from the open spread of the encircling camp and into the soothing darkness of the trees. He ran, hoping that Crassa and the girl were behind him, trusting that they would have followed him. His wrist stump throbbed and tingled as he ran. Even over the sinister crunch of his own footsteps he could hear the camp stirring behind him, the noises echoing through the trees; cold grunted shouts of enquiry and words flung loud and coarse into the hollow night.

Rodius moved as fast as he dared, skipping over roots, smacking through low branches and creepers, plunging deeper and deeper into the woods. Up ahead he fixed half an eye on the tantalising chinks of moonlight through the far side of the forest. He felt rather than saw Vassu catch up and run level with him, his crippled hands tucked into his armpits, his shoulders swaying as he ran.

Rodius slowed a little and looked behind him: he could see the silhouettes of Crassa and the girl following close behind. They needed to break free of the forest and head north and west, put a safe distance between themselves and the brigands. Then they could find the north road and keep it at their sides a half mile distant. Make for the Wall.

He wondered whether the body had been found yet. If not, if it lay undiscovered until daybreak, then they had a chance of survival.

The barking rang out from beyond the woods. Hopefully the hounds would stir frequently in the night, woken by wolves or bears; their handlers would investigate and find nothing amiss and then silence the mutts with a sharp blow to the muzzle. The beasts would whimper and tuck their tails between their scraggy legs then slump in the woodpile and sulk into a shivering sleep.

Hopefully.

Rodius waited for Crassa and the girl then pushed them in front of him, before scanning the woods behind. Satisfied they were clear, he picked up his own pace and ran after the others. He did not think they had long left before first light shimmered across the horizon. There would be no following their tracks by dark. But come daylight, they would find the dead man, see their tracks, and begin pursuit.

They shambled through the thick trees as a ragged group, stumbling over roots and splitting lips on unseen branches, while the fear of pursuit made them loath to slow down or stop. The hounds were still yelping, and Rodius was thankful for the noise masking the sounds of twigs snapping and snow scrunching under their feet.

Rodius was at the rear; the open land beyond the forest surged into view like an oncoming wave.

But there was something else, something silhouetted against the moonlit night sky.

A huge shape, black and wild except for the shards of its white teeth, bounding along towards him, leaping branches, accelerating.

A shiver of fear and shock ran through his gullet. It was an ugly primal fear shivering through his bones, turning his bowels to water.

Hound.

One of the beasts had been loosed from the encampment and had tracked them here. If his handlers came following fast enough, they would all be slain.

Rodius barely had time to think before the hound was upon him. It whipped across, lunging at his leg, shouldering him with its flank. The creature was the size of a small donkey, all lean muscle and tight anger; Rodius felt the touch of bristly, wiry hair against his clothes before he was jolted off balance and into the side of a tree. He rebounded hard, collapsing to the ground.

Rodius's looked up into a dark thatch of grabbing branches crisscrossing his vision. He kicked out instinctively and felt heavy contact followed by a whine; he lifted his head and saw the hound scurrying away a few paces, its fangs bared, its tail curled tight down against its crotch. It started growling: a deep crackling phlegmy sound that came from its lungs rather than its throat.

Rodius shuffled backwards, balancing himself on his good arm. His back hit something solid; the trunk of the tree that he had fallen into. Facing him, the hound crouched low, snarling, a coiled slab of energy and hunger.

Rodius drew the dagger from his belt. The blade felt pitifully weak and small compared to the wolfish monster in front of him. He saw that Crassa and the girl had slowed and were approaching him, unsure. He distractedly waved them away with his stump, without lowering his weapon or taking his eyes from the creature in front of him.

He knew the dagger wasn't enough. If the animal pounced, he would need to have it at the right angle for it to penetrate the flesh: the beast would have to fall vertically upon the blade in order for its own weight to drive it through to the heart. But the chance of that was slim. It was more likely that the knife would be wrenched from his hand pinning his arm against him, rendering it useless; the animal's teeth would tear through his neck, and he would have to silently endure the awful pain and suffocation, the stench of the dead meat from the animal's maw and the bristly tickle of the fur on his skin as the creature ripped off his face and jerked him back and forth like a toy....

There was a whistle, high and long and pure in the night air.

Rodius watched as the beast cocked its mangy ears, and tilted its large head, the snarl frozen on its chops.

The whistle sounded again, shrill and clear through the trees. The hound bounded around and ran through the darkness of the forest, back towards the camp.

Rodius let go of a breath he hadn't realised he'd been holding, then wiped cool sweat from his forehead with the back of his hand. He held his dagger rigidly in front of him, as if the beast were only backing off before a full frontal assault. Crassa walked over and stood above him, reaching down. He slowly and jerkily replaced the dagger behind his belt, and grasped her hand; she tugged him up, onto his feet, and they both ran for the woodbreak and the pale syrup of dawn threatening the horizon.

Rodius looked behind as they ran, expecting the hound to emerge angry and desperate from the woods, but all was silent except for his own heart beating loudly in his chest and the rasp of his breath in his throat.

CHAPTER 23

"Beneficiarius."

"Praefectus."

"Please," said Apullius, rising from the high-backed chair within his office, "sit down."

"Thank you." Atellus pulled out the small seat opposite the commander's broad desk and lowered himself into it. His ribs ached from the brief walk through the cold, across the courtyard to the principia. Dawn was just beginning to break, and there was a softness settling into the air that laid over the crushed-glass cold of the night air. The courtyard had been busy with the smell of baking loaves – the coarse and airy ones that the baker would produce, pushing the scant grain as far as it would go – and the hiss of quenching iron from the blacksmith's forge. A few soldiers were milling about in groups, waiting for parade, and the warmth of the coming sun.

Atellus looked around him as he sat. Like everything else he had seen in Aesica, the commander's office was a picture of faded grandeur. He imagined little had been changed since construction, excepting the superficial touches added by the generations of officers who had sat in charge of Aesica: furnishings, tapestries, paintings, statues, all jostling for position as signs of wealth and triumph. The room was an explosion of faded pictures and hangings looking down on carved chairs in different styles – Atellus recognised Danubian craftsmanship on a table, and Numidian signifiers on the chair set against it – desks hauled in from different parts of the empire, yet none more recently than half a century ago. There were rugs and shelves of manuscripts, parchments, wood- and leather-bound books, all caked thickly with dust. Everything was a show of opulence and comfort, but outdated and with an air of disuse.

Apullius sat directly in front of an empty fire grate. The remnants of his breakfast were on the desk in front of him; crumbs of fresh warm bread, ribbons of sliced salted meat, and bowls of fig stones. Atellus's stomach gurgled uncomfortably; it was a while since his last meal.

"How goes your recuperation?" asked the praefectus.

"My wounds are minor," said Atellus, waving it away. "But the boy took a bolt to the stomach."

Apullius nodded gravely. "I have been informed. I visited him in the valetudinarium, but he was asleep. Uricalus advised me not to wake him. We must hope he pulls through."

"It would not bode well for the governor's nephew to be killed on your watch, praefectus."

Apullius smiled; a vulpine grin. "I was given to understand the 'watch' was yours, beneficiarius?" He relaxed back into his big chair and folded his large hands across his hard stomach. "I assure you the boy will be well cared for. The medicus says he will be fit to move in a day or so, and then I have insisted on him sharing my quarters, to assist with the recuperation." He smiled again, a thoroughly unpleasant stretching of the lips. "Can I tempt you with some Iberian figs? Or some fresh Caledonian ham, perhaps?"

Atellus nodded, and reached across for the commander's leftovers. His ribs flamed and cracked as he bent forward, the sweat coating his brow, but he kept his eyes level and his face smooth.

"It is very fortunate," said Apullius as he watched Atellus eat, "that we had a patrol in the vicus. If they had not turned up to find you under attack...." He rubbed a hand across his jaw, his large steel-blue eyes mesmerising across the table. "Well...who knows how much worse it could have been? I am sure the boy will recover, and you seem in rude health already, beneficiarius."

"And what of our assailants?" asked Atellus.

Apullius's lips pursed. "They managed to elude my men, unfortunately. I do not think they were brigands. Possibly local robbers from the vicus who saw you as easy targets."

"My blade," said Atellus, chewing on the firm flesh of a pale green fig. "Was it collected?"

Apullius stared back at him, his face expressionless. "No, I regret that it was not. Most likely the men who besieged you took it. To sell, or to own. It may well turn up. Do you value it highly?"

"It was Damascene steel."

The praefectus nodded slowly, recognising the value of such an item. "Then I am not optimistic of its recovery. It may be traded south, or north, presuming it will not simply be melted down." The first bar of pale greenish sunlight flared through the high window at the far side of the praefectus's office. It fell on Apullius's shoulder like a naphtha flare. "I will instruct our armourer to furnish you with something befitting your rank, beneficiarius." The praefectus stood up and stretched his thick neck from left to right. "If you are feeling up to it, I shall instruct an honour guard to escort you to Culuslupi this morning. It is a short hike."

"I would appreciate that, praefectus."

"Excellent," said Apullius. "Then if you can be ready by tertia at the south gate, I will make the arrangements."

**

Atellus looked up into the gloaming. They were marching at a tough pace and his wounds from the previous day were mewling through his coarse clothes. He needed a decent sleep, a full meal, a chance to recuperate. But he couldn't show any weakness. Especially not now.

"Is the pace too fast, beneficiarius?" asked the optio. Marius was leading his escort – his honour guard – of four limitanei. Apullius had been apologetic, saying he could spare no more from the border. "We can slow it a little," continued Marius, without the hint of a smile on his face. "We will still reach the sentry fort not long past dark."

The optio was a lean, tall man, with thick ropes of dark hair that coiled around his neck. He had large, slightly tilted eyes that made Atellus think of the powerful big cats from Numidia that used to be slain at the games at Treves before a big celebration.

"No, optio," said Atellus, forcing his voice to be loud and strong. "I am just enjoying the scenery."

Marius let a small grin seep across his face before turning away. Atellus ignored it and threw a look across the rest of the men. He recognised two of the detachment: one face he couldn't place, but the other was all too familiar to him.

Qunavo, he realised, was accompanying him to Culuslupi.

The large man with his perma-snarl was there, studiously ignoring Atellus, keeping his large pale green eyes to the ground. His thick yellow hair was wound round with dirty bandages, covering the wound where his ear used to be.

323

Atellus could not imagine why he had been sent along on this detachment. Unless it was pure infelicitas; perhaps Marius did not know about their earlier violent encounter.

The limitanei were a ragged crew, the only nod to standard Roman military dress being the occasional spill of lorica hamata down across someone's belly, or a scarred and chipped oval shield slung across one's back, the paint faded and scratched. The rest of their equipment was an assemblage of whatever garments would keep them warm, and any armour or weaponry they had stolen from the battlefield, or won in bets from the older veterans. Qunavo wore only a tunic under his cloak, girt with a large thick belt, and leather strapping wrapped tight along his arms and legs.

Atellus watched them as they marched alongside. A couple met his gaze and spat, then laughed with their comrades, or exchanged words in guttural Brythonic mingled with bastardised Latin. Atellus couldn't make out a word of it. At one point, after they first stopped for food, he had asked if they were there to protect him from Cernunnos.

It was a tall, muscular soldier who answered, with a dark lipless face fuzzed with dirty stubble. He spoke without looking at Atellus, or slowing his pace. "It is better not to jest about the gods, foreigner." He punctuated his warning by spitting onto the ground.

"You address me by rank, *pedes*," Atellus had replied, coldly.

The man turned to face him, then walked up to him until their faces were unciae apart. Atellus could feel the soldier's breath on his cheeks and smell his odour seeping through his armour.

"It is better not to jest about the gods, beneficiarius," said the limitanei. He carried on staring at Atellus a while longer before turning his face to one side and spitting onto the snow. They continued their repast as they marched.

The Stanegate was broad and well paved. There were parts where stones had been robbed away, possibly by the limitanei themselves to repair the forts after attacks. Weather and time were often fiercer enemies than the tribes to the north. They had set off later than planned with the sun beginning its slow arc towards the horizon. Atellus had visited the armourer first, a scrubby, hairy-faced old drunk known only as Map, who eyed him suspiciously as he talked, and then disappeared into his workshop without a word. Atellus had stood waiting, and the armourer had come out once more, and looked intently at him, studying his height, his build, the length of his forearm, his shanks, his upper leg. Then he had disappeared again without speaking. When he returned, he carried a heavy spatha with him, which he gripped by the blade and handed over, hilt first.

"Whet it against a stone each day," he said. His voice was a mumble from underneath his thick moustaches. "I have cleaned it, treated it. Bound the hilt with leather." Map stopped to belch. "It is old, but good enough. It should last a few combats. It's the best we have, at the moment."

Atellus had taken the blade and half-heartedly run through a few drills on the practice ground. It felt different, cold: *alienus*. There seemed to be no communication between himself and the weapon. His previous spatha was an extension of his own arm; this new one felt more like a burden, an encumbrance.

Atellus whiled away the remaining hours talking with Calidus in the valetudinarium, recounting his days in the east, and the Germanic battles of his youth. The boy looked thin and weak, but more alert than he had been before. He seemed jittery, scared. Uricalus had been looking after him, albeit in a gruff and resentful manner, and the boy always had a full jug of cool water at his side. The medicus sweated and shivered through his lack of wine as he tended the youth, changing his bandages, cleaning the wound with warm water and nettle sap.

"I don't feel safe here," said Calidus, his voice low. Even in daylight, the valetudinarium was dark and cramped. There were no windows, and although Atellus could hear the wind soughing across the timber, he couldn't feel a stir of it inside. The air was heavy and dead.

"You are as safe here as anywhere," said Atellus. "Your uncle will ensure that."

Calidus looked at him for a while. "There are worse things than death."

Atellus nodded. "Uricalus will look after you. It is in his own interest. And a man like that is only ever interested in himself."

He had left the boy in the valetudinarium and set off to meet Apullius by the Southgate. The praefectus had introduced him to Marius, and the optio had gathered his men and ordered the group to strike due south, to meet the Stanegate so they could make good time.

"The west road is in a bad condition," Marius had explained as they walked. The other soldiers marched with faces down, hurling curt conversation to each other which often exploded into ripples of laughter. There was a short man amongst them that Atellus recognised, but he could not place. His eyes were half-lidded, bored, and his features seemed squashed together, his cheeks too wide. When he caught Atellus looking at him, he stared back for a second before sliding his gaze away and studying the road at his feet as though the secrets of the gods were engraved there. "The next two sentry forts are abandoned," continued Marius, "and the road seldom used. The stones helped in sealing the westgate, which was the fort's main weak point in years past."

326

Atellus had noticed that the west gateway of Aesica had been bricked up. "When did that happen?" he asked.

Marius shrugged. "Before my days, beneficiarius."

"Are there no stories of the old days passed down amongst the Britons, optio?"

Marius looked across at him. Another member of the contubernium, tasked with carrying the camp equipment, clanked and rattled beside them, the accoutrements hanging upon the rigid planks of his shoulder pack.

"No," said Marius. "If it was before my first breath, beneficiarius, then it holds no interest for me. It may be a single day before, or a thousand years, it is neverborn to me. I carry only my own reality."

Atellus looked around them: the bare trees, the grey snow, the harsh dark lines of the hillsides, and the screaming bulk of the Wall. "Your own reality must be very comforting to you, optio."

Marius inclined his head slightly but said nothing.

Atellus could guess what had happened to the Westgate without Marius's input. The garrisons of the Wall had been thinned by troops loyal to Constantius following him to the continent in support of his claim as Augustus. The numbers were never recovered, and the excess sentry forts fell into disrepair. Possibly they were used as bases by brigands or insurgents from the north. The forts became a liability, staging points for counter attacks from the tribes. So the roads were torn up and the brick used to seal the vulnerable parts of the forts. Which, for Aesica, was the Westgate. Culuslupi was the nearest habitable fort while the rest were an uncomfortable no man's land, where the Wall itself could be friend or foe.

Vercovicium to the east was large enough to sustain its own western flank sentry forts, hence Aesica's eastern flank was relatively secure.

They walked on through the cold and the flurries of creeping snow. There were fresh flecks of sleet in the air, and the afternoon seemed to thicken around them, the whiteness becoming complete, until only the ridge and slope of the land ahead betrayed where the road lay.

Atellus noticed the debris of a wrecked checkpoint, a squat stone building gutted by fire, blackened and empty inside. The carcass of a dead animal lay inside, and the stench of decay rose even beyond the frozen flesh. Further on were the splintered remains of an upturned waggon; the snow settled heavily on the broken wheels and struts pawing the sky. The collapsed shells of a timber-built hamlet disappeared to their left, emerging from the hillocks and folds of the land, before being reclaimed again.

"Are any of the villages up here still inhabited?" he asked Marius.

Marius shook his head. "Not for many years. In my youth, I recall there were patrols each day along the roads. But even then I remember no villages. None that lasted more than a few moons, anyway. Now, no-one would be insane enough to try and live this far north unless they were tight to a garrison. If the famine and the cold didn't kill them, it would be the northmen, or the stoats."

"Stoats?"

"The brigands," replied the optio. "They are vicious and merciless and unafraid; they are pests. They are crepuscular too, like stoats; they thrive at twilight and before dawn. They are alike in many ways."

They marched through the afternoon without stopping. As the sun sank into the hills, a tall soldier with a scar crossing his lips came over to Atellus and handed

328

him a few crumbs of bread, meat and cheese, and a swig from a communal flask of wine. He accepted them wordlessly and ate as they walked. There were no others on the road, no human tracks within sight. It was as if the land was deserted and swept away under a pale sheet of ice and hunger.

Just as dusk was threatening, Marius ordered them off the stanegate road. They squeezed through a small snicket sunk into the cleft of two hillsides. It was overgrown and threaded with dead trees bearing a canopy of heavy snow; powdery flakes fluttered down as the breeze stretched the branches.

Atellus pushed through the opening after Marius, following the rest of the limitanei. The hill slopes loomed tall on either side, though the air was warmer here, unstirred by the wind. They walked north for a mile or two, the steep slopes at their flanks shrinking and softening and diminishing into rolling hillocks of bare snow, scarred grass and tangled gorse bushes. Eventually they opened out onto a track cut through the wilderness; it was frozen mud overlaid with snow and ice, but it made the progress much easier than hacking and stomping their way through the untamed growth around them.

"It is an old drover's track," said Marius, after Atellus queried him. "One of many in the area. All limitanei must be familiar with them, for crossing between the Wall and the Stanegate. It is wise to know the access points and speed is always an advantage when moving around this territory."

Glowering up ahead was the monstrous stretch of the Wall, frowning along the horizon, laid across the land like a sinister belt of darkness. To the west, and framed by the red agonies of the dying sun, Atellus could make out the broken form of one of the unused mileforts, the tumbled masonry sawing into the sky like jagged teeth. Small trees and bushes webbed out from between the stones.

Reclaimed, he thought. As it all eventually must be, in ten winters or ten thousand.

Marius led them west, towards the fleeing sun, along what looked like a goat track, a narrow walkway that went between thickets of shoulder-height spine-grass. The snow dusted off upon his cloak and his jacket, so Atellus emerged soaking wet and twice as heavy as when he had entered. The wind screeched past overhead carrying more sleet in its arms, scattering it loosely on the men.

"It is not much further," said Marius.

They walked until the darkness had wrapt itself tight across the land, and only the sad dripping light of the stars brushed the hillsides. Even the soldiers were quiet, except for the sad clucking of the mess tins on the backpack of the carrier.

Marius stopped suddenly and raised a clenched fist, the moonlight glowing off his knuckles. He drove his elbow downwards, and the limitanei sank to a deep crouch on the ground. Atellus followed their lead. The optio crouched and raised the flat of his hand to his men, circling it round so all could see, then moved stealthily ahead for a while. The men waited in silence until he returned.

"There is a fire up ahead," he said, his voice a tight whisper, the whites of his eyes gleaming. "It is small."

He addressed two of the limitanei by name, and told them to sweep round to the right; the remaining two, including Qunavo, he told to move in from the left.

"Beneficiarius, we shall take the centre."

Atellus nodded, and loosed his spatha in its scabbard, muffling it with his free hand. It felt brittle, ungainly and coarse to the touch; a stranger rather than an old friend.

"*Quickly,*" ordered Marius, addressing his men, "and *quietly.* Decimus," he whispered to the carrier, "silence those pots, or I'll silence you."

The commands were obeyed without dissent, despite the soldiers' apparent lack of discipline. They obviously followed their own codes and systems, ones that had kept them alive for years on the harshest of frontiers; their own ways which left no time for paying lip-service to the superficiality of the parade-ground.

Marius and Atellus moved forward quietly. The sounds of the evening seemed to be amplified: the sough of wind through the tall grass; the rustle of nocturnal creatures stirring beneath their feet; the flap of owl-wings heavy in the night; the terse breathing of the two men.

Atellus could see the fire now, a small glow up ahead, probably burning in a shallow pit. He couldn't hear any voices. There was no trace of their comrades sent to flank the camp; it was as if they never had existed, whicked away by Cernunnos, their screams dumb in the night. He tried to send out his mind, searching for the imperceptible clues in the air that his normal senses might overlook. His instinct for danger, his intuition, was silent.

He saw Marius gesturing at him to stay where he was, saw the optio loosening his spatha in its sheath and inching it out, slowly so as not to give off the telltale rasp of steel on leather. Marius moved forward, and Atellus followed him instinctively; he was no longer used to obeying commands.

Marius pounced towards the fire, but there was no-one sitting there. Atellus came up to his side and secured his blind spots, eyes fiercely scanning the tall grass, the dips of the land, his heart pounding, muscles tingling with suppressed energy.

The two flanking parties walked nonchalantly out of the grass towards them.

"Nothing," said the tall man who had warned Atellus earlier. He thought his name was Bellicus. "The stoats have scurried off."

331

Marius nodded, but he didn't sheathe his blade. The fire was burning low, with tight small flames; smokeless fuel from dried kindling. It was set into a round pit about a foot deep, up against the trunk of a large tree. There were blankets and sheets around the fire, and the debris of a hasty meal. The remains of a small moorfowl lay spatchcocked on a twig to one side.

Atellus walked over and examined the camp.

"The food is still warm," he said, addressing the optio. "Whoever was here cannot be long gone. There are provisions here for two. Refugees from a village, maybe?"

"There are no villages near here," growled Marius. He bent down to the fire, up to the limit of the melted snow and walked in a large circle around the perimeter. "Tracks of one, heading that way. They are small: a bint, or a child." He pointed south. "Bellicus, Vannus – follow them, and be fast."

The soldiers nodded and cantered away, swallowed up by the pressing darkness.

Marius extinguished the fire – "That'll be a beacon for any stoats in the area" – and gathered up the blankets, distributing them amongst the remaining men.

Bellicus and Vannus returned before long, a young woman pinned between them, struggling. She was not long out of childhood, but her face was hard and etched with lines of hard living. Her eyes were a brilliant flashing blue that lit up her face like jewelled torches. Her hair was long and black, tied in a band over one shoulder. She was dressed in a thin and ragged fox-skin jacket and thick riding breeches that were worn through at the knees.

The two soldiers laughed and threw her to the ground beside the firepit. She stayed down and looked up at them, with a gaze of mingled fear and disgust.

"Is it armed?" asked Marius.

"Not any more," laughed Bellicus. He tossed a short dagger over to the optio, who caught it overhand and studied it before tucking it into his belt.

"What's your name?" he asked, walking over to the woman and looking down at her.

She spat at Marius's feet and remained silent. He looked down at his boot for a second then snapped off a hard kick to the woman's face. She fell to the side with a grunt. Marius walked up and wiped the toe of his boot on her clothes. He bent down, twisted a handful of her hair in his fist and pulled her up to her knees.

"What is your name?" he said again, calmly.

"Barita," she said through swollen lips. Her nose was bleeding.

Marius let go of her hair and she crumpled to the ground. "A slave name," he said, sneering. The other soldiers were laughing and snorting.

Atellus walked over to the woman. "Barita," he said. "We are not here to hurt you." There was lingering laughter from Vannus. "You are no threat to us, we know that." He paused for a second to allow her to absorb this. "Tell me what you are doing here. Tell me who you are with."

The sleet that peppered the air was getting thicker, becoming snow. A fierce wind was stirring high up. Atellus could not feel it yet but he saw the way the branches of the distant trees were whipping back and forth. The boughs directly overhead were moving also; thick clumps of snow fell onto his back and spattered the ground.

"There is no-one else, easterner," said Decimus, seeing Atellus scouting the landscape. "There was but one set of tracks leading away from the fire; perhaps they do not teach about such things in the palaces and brothels of the east." He moved round to face Atellus. "Whoever owned the bint is gone."

The soldiers laughed. Marius, Atellus and Barita remained silent. When the laughter trickled away, Vannus walked up to the woman and hauled her to her feet. He groped around roughly for her breast, and she fought and squirmed as he laughed. Bellicus walked up and helped pin her arms to her side; his comrade belted her round the face with the back of his gloved fist; the leather made a cracking noise against her cheek. She sagged in Bellicus's arms and he dumped her to the ground, semi-conscious, and gave his comrade some space. Vannus started ripping the clothes from her body, exposing the pale flesh.

Decimus jeered and shouted; Qunavo laughed and watched.

"Optio, order your men back!" said Atellus. "This savagery is not part of Rome. Leave it to the northmen."

Marius looked evenly at Atellus. "Victori spolia, beneficiarius. Savagery is relative. Life on the border is savage; and here a man needs to be savage to survive." He smiled, showing large, straight, white teeth. "Just a little."

Atellus walked closer to Marius, shouting to be heard above the wind. "We are not at war, optio, and this is not a request. It is an order."

The two men stared at each other as the wind scooped great handfuls of snow from the fat dark clouds and hurled them across the land. The grass sighed and wept as the gusts swept through it.

"*Please, no!*"

Atellus turned as the woman begged. Vannus had her up against the trunk of the tree, his breeches down around his ankles and his pale arse ludicrous in the cold snowy air.   A dark shape dropped from the tree like a large branch, right on top of Vannus, knocking him down to the ground and away from Barita. The shape moved, and rolled so that Vannus was atop it, but facing upwards and flapping like a dying fish. In the darkness beneath the tree it was hard to discern what was happening. Decimus yelled in fear, and Atellus heard the word 'Cernunnos' tumble from terrified lips.

Vannus was thrashing and kicking, a strange sickening gurgling noise coming from his neck. Atellus could not see the trapper wire wrapped around the soldier's throat, but he saw the trail of red sparkle in the moonlight as the wire was yanked deeper into Vannus's skin, severing the flesh, the windpipe, the arteries. Blood bloomed and swelled and ran down the soldier's neck and onto his clothes. His legs flailed and drummed against the ground.

"Run, Flavia! Flee!" The shout came from the assailant: a desperate strong voice rising high above the wind and beseeching the shrinking moon. The girl gathered herself and ran, and Atellus was aware of Qunavo and Decimus chasing after her.

Atellus rushed forward, drawing his spatha, and held the point to the attacker's eye. Marius had come up alongside him, his blade drawn. The attacker was still heaving at the wire which had bitten deep into Vannus's throat; the soldier twitched and bled on top of him.

"Stop!" commanded Atellus, "or I will drive this through your skull."

The man looked at him, and released his grip from the snare. Atellus glanced down at Vannus, but he could see as soon as he got closer that the man was as good as dead: released from the attacker's gripe, the wire was still embedded deep in Vannus's neck. A bit longer and he would have been decapitated. His body was shaking and his naked legs twitching; his eyes were rolled up into his skull, and blood gushed from his nose and mouth, as well as the gouge in his throat.

The assailant pushed Vannus's bulk off him, and he slithered out from underneath it, two spathas directed squarely at him. Atellus levelled his blade at the man's breast, ready to drive it in at the slightest sudden movement, but he seemed placid and resigned. Marius kept the point of his blade at the man's jaw and patted him down for weapons. Bellicus knelt down beside the body of Vannus and checked for life.

Marius sheathed his blade, trusting Atellus to cover him, and moved up beside the man; half a head taller, he looked down at him. Without warning, he rammed his fist into the other man's face; there was a crunch of sinew as the nose exploded under his knuckles, and he fell hard to the ground in a spray of blood.

Marius spat at him as lay there, his hands pressed to his smashed nose, blood seeping through his fingers. "Your death will be long and agonising, scumfuck."

The snowstorm was whipping around them now, their words snatched away by the wind and replaced by facefuls of ice-spray fresh from the heavens. The air was a mixture of treacly darkness and flowing white flecks. The cold was creeping up into them, even the bones of the fire providing no warmth.

There was a scream that rose above the sound of the wind. The man tried to get to his feet but was kicked back down by Marius.

"Down, dog," he said. "When they've finished fucking her up the arse, you'll be next."

"I want him," said Bellicus, his dark lipless face a mask of pain. "I want to finish him. Slowly."

Marius put his hand on Bellicus's shoulder. "You will, *pedes*."

"I will kill the fucker once for each year we have been contuberniae."

336

The captive looked up at the limitanei and spat a thick wodge of blood onto the ground. Atellus met the man's eyes and caught sparks of hate and desperation.

Qunavo and Decimus returned, with the woman slung over Qunavo's shoulder, Decimus holding his spatha across her neck.

"Decimus," shouted Marius. "Pass them the rope. Bellicus, bind them both, tight. We need to reach the fort or we will all die out here."

Atellus looked at the man named Decimus, the cluttered features and wide jaw, the insolence of his eyes, and was again struck by the familiarity of the face. It annoyed him that he could not place it, though an uneasy feeling in the pit of his belly told him that it had not been a happy meeting.

Atellus looked again, and something about the way he held his blade to the girl's throat annoyed. Or rather, the blade itself.

Bellicus was busy tying the prisoners' hands behind their backs, twisting their wrists up at a painful angle. Their feet were shackled to each other's, so they walked in a shuffling gait through the thick grass and calf-deep snowfall. With nothing to stem the bleeding from his wound before it congealed and clotted inside his swollen nose, the front of the killer's tunic was drenched in a red.

Marius led them all across the tussocky moorland, Atellus bringing up the rear. The Wall was a great animal at their shoulder as they walked bent into the thrashing wind. The wild snow piled up on their backs and their shoulders, inside their tunics, on the roundels of their shields and in the crescents of their chain armour.

"A nice blade you have there, pedes," said Atellus to the back of Decimus's head. He had to shout to be heard above the storm. He saw the man's shoulders hunch in response.

"A gift from my father," said Decimus, into the wind.

"Damascene steel, is it not?" asked Atellus.

Again the shoulders hunched, this time in a deep shrug. "I know not. It does its job."

Decimus picked up his pace, widening the gap between himself and Atellus. He carried on walking, bent into the rising fury of the storm, squinting for a desperate glimpse of the shelter they all sought. Eventually made out the shape of the sentry fort, Culuslupi, emerging through the blackness, high and tall and square; a bastion of shelter. There were no torches blazing through the thick windows, no silhouettes of sentries on the ramparts; no shout of challenge or welcome.

Just the howl of the storm within the endless darkness.

CHAPTER 24

"You called yourself Barita," said Marius. "He," he gestured towards the man, "called you Flavia. *I*," – he jabbed his thumb into his chest – "I call you *liar*. You lie to an optio of the army of Rome, an officer of the emperor."

Inside Culuslupi, Qunavo and Decimus sat sprawled in front of the huge open hearth in the centre of the room. There had been tinder and kindling stacked up next to it, and a pyramid of wood already in the firepit. The heat stretched a soft warm glow across the cold walls and the sparse pale smoke drifted languidly to a vent into the upper floors.

The woman shook her head. "Barita is...*was*...my slave name. My birth-name is Flavia."

Marius walked over to the wall with his hands clasped behind his back, before turning on his heel and striding over to the captives. "An escaped slave," he said.

Flavia remained silent.

"Answer me," said Marius, his voice quiet and authoritative in the enclosed space. "And speak truthfully, for each silence, each falsehood will be carved out of his flesh." He pointed to the man who sat beside her. "What is the nature of your relationship?"

She darted quick, nervous glances to her fellow. He nodded.

"We are...lovers."

"You are a slave *whore*," spat Marius, baring his teeth.

Atellus looked at the captives. Flavia and her lover were each sitting on plain wooden chairs pushed back against the far wall; their ankles were tied to the legs of the chair and their wrists were bound behind the backrests. Bellicus was walking round with a taper, lighting the torches set into metal brackets on the walls. The sentry fort was small and basic: the south door they had entered through led directly into the main hall. The ceiling was high and made of old timber with a circular hole cut as a vent for the hearth which took up most of the middle of the room. There was a great square mess table close to the west wall beside which was a short door leading to the larder. In the corner of the east wall was a spiral staircase leading up to the second floor, which contained the sleeping quarters, armoury and access to the Wall rampart. In the north wall was a very narrow corridor which led to a small metal-strapped door which opened out into the land to the north of the Wall.

Atellus noted that there was no sign of any guards here, though there was chilled food in the larder and places had been set at the table, complete with half-drunk goblets of wine. Bellicus had picked one up, sniffed it, swilled it twice round the cup and then downed it. Finding it to his taste, he moved on to the next.

"How many soldiers should be here?" he asked Marius once they were inside. "These were built to house half a century."

"There is usually a garrison of eight here," replied Marius. "A contubernium from Aesica on a rotating basis each half moon."

"Then where are they?"

Marius shrugged. "On patrol, perhaps?"

"All of them?"

Marius was silent.

Atellus looked at the optio, but said nothing. There was something very wrong here, and he knew that the optio was either hiding things, or outright lying to him. He got up from where he sat by the stairwell that led to the upper floors, and walked over to the captives.

"Flavia," he said, addressing the girl. "My name is Titus Faenius Magnus Atellus. I am beneficiarius imperatoris, and I act on behalf of Valentinian. I have the power of life over you both." There were sniggers from the men around the room. The noise echoed off the wood and stone. "Answer me truthfully and I will see you both come to no harm. Where are you from?"

Flavia seemed unsure and lowered her eyes to the floor. Atellus stood waiting.

"Hibernia," she answered, eventually.

"And you are a slave?"

"No," she said forcefully.

"You were, though," said Atellus.

"I was," she agreed.

"You escaped?"

She nodded. "I was born a slave," she said, her voice defiant. "I will not die one." She smiled, though to Atellus it looked more like a grimace; he noticed that all but two of her teeth were missing. She had difficulty meeting his eyes as she spoke; most slaves were encouraged not to, and it was a habit they rarely broke once freed.

"I had a good master, at first," she explained. Her accent was thick and Atellus had to strain to make out what she was saying. "My mother gifted me that much when she sold me. When he died I was auctioned off with the rest of his estate. I was passed around the villa owners like any other chattel. When one tired of raping me, he would pass me over to his brother, his uncle, his friend. That was my life for many years.

"When I got older and less pretty," she said, grimacing at the floor, "they just beat me. I would have been dead by now if I hadn't fled."

Marius, until now listening in silence to Flavia's speech, grunted indignantly. "Does the slave choose to leave the master? Does the blade choose not to leave the sheath?"

The soldiers laughed. Atellus ignored the optio's words. He turned to Flavia's lover. He was broad and muscular even when tied to the chair, but his neck and shoulders were slightly hunched. His face was a red mess of dark congealed blood from his shattered nose. He was breathing hard through his mouth, and every so often coughed and wheezed.

"What is your name?"

"Manius Maurus Barbarus." His voice was deep, and he spoke Latin well, though with an accent.

Atellus looked closely at the man before speaking. "You were born in Germania. You are an ex-soldier, and were charged with cowardice. You were convicted and condemned to labour in the mines, which you have done for some years. In Hibernia, I imagine," he concluded, looking over at Flavia.

Barbarus looked up at him with fierce eyes which shone brightly out of the blood-spattered visage. "You are almost right," he nodded. "I was born in Raetia, but I was a limitanei on the Rhenus for many years. How do you know this?"

342

"Your accent I placed as Alamannic; you have the convict's mark inked on your neck; the back of your hand is branded for cowardice. You squint in the light and your back is hunched, so I presumed you worked in the confines of the narrow shafts of the tin and gold mines. Most such mines are in Hibernia; as was Flavia, with whom you have an acquaintance."

There was a slow clap from behind, leather gloves thwacking against each other.

"Very good, beneficiarius," said Marius. "An excellent demonstration of investigatory technique. If you don't mind, I would like to conduct the interrogation from here, as these criminals are within the jurisdiction of Aesica. And I believe you have other matters to attend to."

Atellus turned round to look at Marius: tall, supremely confident and certain. The authority of the beneficiarius was obviously outside the ambit of his world view.

"And what would those matters be, optio?"

"Our agent in rebus?" he replied. "This is where he was last seen alive."

***

Atellus knew that he would not be able to endure long up here on the rampart. The narrow walkway was slippery with ice, and the chest-high wall provided scant protection from the raging storm. The air was a blitz of snow and ice particles, with wind so strong that it was a struggle to face it; he could hear it thundering as the gusts buffeted the nooks and corners of the Wall.

He had used his shoulder to force the trapdoor at the top of the stairs; the weight of snow piled on top of it had almost made it impossible to open. He'd heaved himself up into the maw of the storm and scanned the platform. There was no-one there, nor sign that there recently had been.

He steeled himself and trudged over to the parapet, bent against the wind, and ducked down between the crenellations to study the dark infinity beyond. The sad stained limewash of the Wall glowed beneath him like a sheer cliff face. The land beyond was bare, stripped of scrub and trees, just a pale undulating blanket barely visible through the snowstorm.

Far away there was a dark line of distant trees and foliage. Atellus scanned the ground for as long as he could bear, but he saw no signs of movement. He turned round and hurried back towards the trapdoor, folding himself down into it and pulling it shut overhead. It crashed to with a thud, and the full violence of the storm was instantly muted; there remained only the wail of the wind against the stone, and the creak of the old timber. Louder still were voices from downstairs, laughter and curses. Marius's stentorian voice rang through the brickwork with only grunts and mumbles in response.

Atellus climbed down into the second storey sleeping quarters. There were bunks for twenty men, in two rows of ten along the walls. A second room where there had once been more bunks instead bore traces of where the wooden frames had been ripped out to make room for gaming tables and storage space for weapons. A third room was a small latrine.

Something was disturbing Atellus, but it took him a while to place it.

The smell.

Or rather, the lack of it: there was no odour of stale sweat; no cast-off clothing, or washbasins rimed with rings of dirt and sweat. And despite the absence of water, there was no idle waste in the latrines. Although Aesica itself was still served by a half crumbled aqueduct, there was no connection to the outlying sentry forts. Even in winter, the place should have been reeking. Instead, there was something sanitary about the fort, as though it had seen no habitation for a while. But there were no signs of violence either; no spilt blood staining the floor timbers, no disarrayed furniture. No sign of hurry or anger or fighting. Just the thump of the wind outside and the soft crackle of the fire from the ground floor.

And the screams.

The first shriek hadn't registered with Atellus, but the second tingled against his ears like the cold eating through the walls. There were shouts and curses, followed by laughter.

Atellus walked hurriedly over to the staircase winding down to the ground floor, and thudded down the steps, the noises growing deafening as he descended.

He kicked open the frail wooden plank which served as a door at the base of the staircase, and walked through into the main hall. He saw the great hulk of Bellicus wrestling Flavia from the chair she was bound to; she kicked and howled, but the soldier barely noticed the blows. Barbarus, still tied to his chair, was straining against his bonds, the seat squealing and wailing with tension as his muscles pulsed and writhed, but each time he opened his mouth to spit or yell, he was answered by a heavy back-handed blow to the face by Decimus. Qunavo stood, laughing, whilst Marius watched them all from a seated position, his heavy spatha laid across his lap, the hilt of the short gladius jutting from the scabbard at his hip. He drank wine and smiled.

"What is this?" demanded Atellus as he entered. The door to the staircase slammed shut behind him and rattled awkwardly. The wind boomed outside, like mighty waves against a ship's hull.

"Ah, beneficiarius," said Marius, raising his voice to be heard above the moans of the slave girl. Bellicus had ripped the dress from her hips and was forcing her legs apart and shuffling his cock out of his breeches. "Any rotting cadavers? Blood-soaked clothes? Signed and sealed testaments of guilt?" He laughed at his own wit, and swilled the wine around his jug. "Or was there just the cold, cold wind, and the black night grinning down on you?"

Atellus ignored him. "Pedes," he said, addressing Bellicus, "stop your assault or answer charges." There was an ugly and potent tension in the room, as if with a single thundercrack or windgust the balance of power in the room would shift. Bellicus carried on raping the slave girl as she moaned and screamed beneath him. Barbarus twisted and raged against his bonds while Decimus held him back, twisting his face so he was forced to watch the assault. Thick sweat ran from his brow and mingled with the blood from his nose, so he looked like a painted shade gathered and hauled from Pluto to spit his seal on the display.

"Fuck you!" bellowed Barbarus, sucking air through broken teeth and bloodied gums. "Fuck you all! I will kill you, I will destroy you, I will—"

He was silenced by a blow from Qunavo who had moved over to lap up the captive's misery from closer range. "Boring," he grinned. "Sing a different song, scum. She's ripe, that bitch of yours, ain't she?" His filthy blonde tassels swung as he tilted back his head and laughed. "She'll be wide as the south gate of Stanwix by the time we've finished with her!"

Barbarus lunged forward in his chair, his eyes red with rage, but Decimus stopped him with a wiry arm round his neck. "No, no," he said in his clipped, hollow accent. His eyes were half-lidded as he spoke, as if he was disinterested, though the grin on his chops betrayed his glee. "You stay here. You got the best stool in the theatre right there."

Flavia wailed on, her breath cracking into small sobs.

Atellus walked over to Decimus. "Your sword, man," he demanded, his voice raised to echo off the walls. "Where did you say you got it?" He held out his hand. "Let me see it."

346

Decimus looked up at Atellus, his half-shut eyes seeming to glitter with some malignant amusement. He drew himself up to his full height, which put his forehead barely level with Atellus's nose. In the background Bellicus grunted and thrashed his way into Flavia, who was breathing in tight pained gasps. Decimus slid his blade from his scabbard, holding it up between himself and the beneficiarius, twisting the weapon so it glinted in the torchlight, admiring it ostentatiously. He pursed his lips and nodded in satisfaction.

"A fine blade, indeed, easterner," he said. "A gift from my father, I said. Or did I find it? I struggle to recall."

Atellus took a step towards him. "Or," he said, his voice low and firm, "perhaps you bought it from a black marketeer in the vicus. Yesterday perhaps, or this morning?"

"Ah!" Decimus laughed and shook his head. "Perhaps that was it, perhaps it was." Marius laughed in the background, and Barbarus wept noisily into his own chest. "Or even," continued Decimus, taking another step towards Atellus, "I took it from some black bitch who was squealing and bleeding into the snow? Some nigger whore who does not know when he is not wanted."

Atellus swallowed.

With a sudden movement Decimus brought the flat of the blade down onto Atellus's outstretched palm. He screamed with pain and whipped his hand away, staggering backwards. The room erupted with laughter as Marius and Qunavo showed their appreciation.

Atellus looked up at them with eyes reddened with pain. "It was not townsfolk who set upon us." It was not a question, but Marius answered.

"It was not, beneficiarius," he said, his words still tinged with laughter. "And were it not for the fact that Apullius is getting soft in his years, you and the little catamitus scab that clings to your tail would not still be alive today."

Atellus wiped the sweat from his brown with his strong hand, and involuntarily took another step backwards. The fog began to clear. Qunavo's presence here was not mere infelicitas. It was all part of the plan.

Julia Petronia, Julia Faenia. I will be strong.   , all powerful unconquered sun, shine your light into this dark hole at the edge of the world.

Atellus caught himself taking another step backwards and instead forced his protesting muscles to move towards his enemies. He walked forward and drew his spatha with a fierce click of leather, holding the cumbersome blade outstretched towards Decimus.

Without taking his eyes from the man in front of him, he raised his voice and addressed the rapist behind Decimus.

"Bellicus pedes, stop instantly on the orders of the emperor." His voice was steady. He did not shout.

Bellicus was buried deep inside the slave girl, and he showed no signs of stopping, or even of having heard.

"Beneficiarius." The unctuous voice was that of Marius. "I really don't think he *wants* to stop."

Atellus half-turned towards the optio before realising his mistake: he no longer had sight of Qunavo. He had time to curse himself inwardly and spin around before there was a crack of intense searing pain across his scalp, and his eyes were veiled by a blackness that rang and swelled until his head and the world outside it seemed to collapse under the pressure.

348

He came to with his face against the cold floor, the howls of Barbarus echoing through the rafters and bouncing off the stone around them. There was an agony of tight heat burning through his skull. He reached up a hand to touch his head and the movement made him vomit onto the floor. He could hear laughter and muted voices around him through the ringing and surging in his ears. The wailing of Barbarus was draped over all like a shroud of misery.

Atellus expected his hands to be damp with blood; he thought Qunavo must have tried to take his skull off with a blow of his blade, but there was no blood, only a crippling agony that made him want to weep to the pit of his stomach.

After a seeming eternity, Atellus pushed himself up from the floor. The room spun wildly. He was aware of Qunavo standing above him, holding his gladius in his meaty fist. It felt as though a whole moon had passed over and dragged him through the other side of its shade, but it had been a mere handful of breaths.

The fucker had flat-bladed him across the back of the head.

Atellus was dimly aware of his own spatha on the floor where it had fallen from his grasp a mere arm's length from him. He made as if to go for it, but Qunavo gave a laugh and kicked it across the floor towards Bellicus, who had finished with Flavia and was towering over her tugging squirts of hot piss onto her face as she wept. He scooped the blade up off the floor, and hefted it feeling its weight. Barbarus wept and spat in his chair through a curtain of blood and snot.

Atellus sank back to the floor in resignation and pain, and felt a boot to the face as he did so. It connected with his chin, and he felt his jaw snap back, his head connecting with the stone floor.

More laughter above him, in coruscating circles like vultures overhead in the parched desert wastes...the tug of the rope rough against his flesh...the nausea and dizziness as he looked over the edge of the walls....

He snapped to as he felt hands grappling him up, his arms forced tight behind his back so his shoulders erupted in flaming agony. He must have let out a shout, as Decimus laughed. He could smell the man's breath above him, the odour of his stale clothes and the metallic tang of blood rising from his tunic.

"Stay down, you fucking black pig," spat Decimus. "Move again and I split your fuckin head in two."

"Come now," laughed Marius, "this is the beneficiarius imperatoris! Let us show him the respect he deserves."

Decimus grunted, and moved away in confusion as the optio rose from his chair and walked slowly towards the prone figure of the easterner. He walked past Flavia who was shuffling on the floor in a pool of blood and urine, her face a torn mess of tears, shame and pain. Marius looked down at her with disgust.

"Kill the whore," he said to Bellicus. "We are running out of time."

Flavia screeched in terror at his words, and scrabbled backwards away from the big limitanei. Barbarus roared, a wordless yell of pain and anger and desperation that sent a shiver passing through even the cold stone. Outside, the wind renewed its attack against the walls as if in response to the primal noise, an echo of savagery and loss.

Qunavo grabbed Barbarus by the head and hurled him down to the floor, still bound to the chair. His head cracked smartly off the stone flags, and his legs thrashed and kicked futilely.

"A blade," yelled Bellicus, looking around the room. Decimus tossed him the spatha which had once belonged to Atellus, and Bellicus snatched it from the air with one huge paw.

Atellus tried to rise whilst Decimus was still far enough away to prevent him; he was on his knees and staggering forward to where Bellicus raised his own spatha above the cringing ex-slave. Light from the rush torches spun from the dull blade. A noise left Atellus's throat, whether of anger or threat or exertion he wasn't sure, but he propelled himself forward off-balance and collapsed short of the big soldier, his ears ringing with Flavia's screams. Bellicus's first blow with the edge of his blade struck her head, but did not silence her; the second and third sliced away the screams along with what remained of Flavia's face.

Atellus did not pass out, but time seemed to alternately coagulate and then shift anxiously like the wings of a locust. He was hauled to his feet and felt his hands being bound with a rough leather thong that bit angrily into the flesh of his wrists. He felt the warmth of blood where the skin broke, and the small heat was like a friendly torch to him. He shook his head, willing the pain to dissipate. He was forced down into a chair opposite Marius.

Atellus looked to his left, and saw the semi-conscious form of Barbarus, head lolling onto his chest, bound in the same fashion, slumped into his chair. Above him was Bellicus, tipping a beaker of wine into his throat. Beyond him were Decimus and Qunavo; the former was masturbating furiously over the corpse of Flavia, her head all but detached from her shoulders by the blows of the spatha which had once been sheathed in Atellus's own scabbard. Qunavo was standing to his right, a strange smile twisting his toothless mouth.

"You may suppose," said Marius, calmly sipping from his goblet, "that any pretence is over."

CHAPTER 25

Calidus woke suddenly.

The world was a hazy darkness, which gradually resolved itself into the greyish shades of the valetudinarium. He had come to loathe the confines of the long narrow room, its timbers tolling the endless howls of the injured, its walls and floors reeking with the incessant stench of decay and fear and filth. It had been his life, this ward, enwrapping his existence so completely that he almost had difficulty remembering a time before it had existed; before its coarse wooden walls that creaked and sucked with the pulse of the wind, before the flickering twitch of the guttering lanterns had leeched all the colour and exuberance from his world.

But now, at least, he was cool. The last evening was the first where he had been able to rest completely without the world seeming to be on fire within his head, without the heat of his own flesh repulsing him, burning his nostrils. Last night was the first he hadn't woken time and time again with the blanket wrapped around him and the sheets of his rough cot drenched with his own sweat.

The pain in his side was duller than it had been, but it never left him entirely; it was certainly more manageable after the wine which the medicus insisted on slopping down his throat thrice a day. At first the pain seemed enough to drive him cowering and crying into the furnace of his own head; a constant gnawing, slicing hurt that ripped and writhed through his abdomen and spread in waves of agony through the rest of his body, thick insidious ripples of pain spreading through his bones, his muscles. As the days – and the endless hot, wearisome nights – had passed, the pain had dulled, and the fire in his head had sunk to smouldering embers. Now, the remnant of the pain was a constant throb in his side that was more of a memory of the pain that had gone before than a pain in its own right. Only when he moved and tried to get to his feet was the sensation more disagreeable.

And this last night had been a cool sleep of pleasant dreams: dreams of childhood, exploring the abandoned buildings of Eboracum, scrapping with his friends, building dams across the weaker tributaries of the Isurium. Pathetic boyish dreams of fresh summer mornings of dew and promise, clear weather, and balmy afternoons that ran for miles towards the swellings of the horizon.

And now he was awake and staring upwards at the coarse soot-stained roof of the valetudinarium. His stomach tingled with the excitement at being moved out of this vile den of the sick; the medicus had told him as much earlier. Even the prospect of dodging the over-interest of the praefectus was appealing compared to spending more hours in this pit of death and pain.

Calidus idly wondered what had woken him. Certainly not daylight; the world outside was dark and still. He could feel the night thick outside.

He listened to the sound of the wind beyond the walls, heaving and thrusting against the frail timbers of the building. He could feel the slices of cold air as they darted in through gaps in the wood and lashed through the claggy, damp sickness of the interior. He could hear the mumblings of the dreamers around him, the heavy, congested snores of the sleeping, the mumblings of those too scared or tired or pained to be allowed the respite of slumber. Further away, down at the far end of the building were the howls of the damned, those blighted in the head, or tormented by demons. Even now, with his hears having become accustomed to them, such sounds made Calidus's fresh crawl.

His ears detected a soft and subtle movement; a door being opened and gently pulled to.

Was it Uricalus?

The old medicus had treated him well, if sourly at first, his temper improving as he managed to take more slugs of the wine he offered his patients. Sometimes he stopped and sat with Calidus, felt his brow, poured fresh clean water for him, changed his linen. Occasionally he spoke of his days on the battlefields of the east, but only when he was well into his cups. He seemed twitchy, always looking over his shoulder, his eyes darting like a cornered vole's.

Sometimes the medicus was awake in the evening, laughing or arguing with himself, staggering through the valetudinarium and sweeping the shelves and caskets for dregs of stashed wine.

Was it Uricalus?

Calidus shifted his head slightly on the rolled blanket that served as his pillow. It was rough and scratched his neck, caught in his hair, but it was more than many of the other men had. Some primal instinct forced him to keep still; Calidus could not say why, but he had an unpleasant sensation rippling through his muscles.

Something was wrong.

Footsteps now, and a hushed voice; there were people at the far end of the valetudinarium, two blocks away from him, maybe forty cots between them. The lick of cold air around his toes betrayed the gusts of chill air that had come in from the opening of the door. Outsiders, then.

Not long after he had been dragged into the valetudinarium – when he could barely distinguish reality from amongst the fragments of pain- and fever-dreams – there had been an incident overnight. Three soldiers had broken in to the valetudinarium in the hour before dawn. They were looking for an old comrade, a gambling friend who had welshed on a bet. They stabbed him through both eyes, and the neck, muffling his screams with his own blanket. Others saw, but said nothing. Calidus heard, and saw the men leave, stealing away into the night. When morning came and the medicus discovered the body, he scooped up the remains with barely a word. When the Praefectus's men arrived to find out what had happened, no-one had seen a thing, not even those still spattered with the victim's blood. That night, if never any other before or since, every sick man in the building had slept the sleep of the dead. The murder was ascribed to a 'visitation', and the body was burned beyond the Wall the following afternoon.

If you had enemies, Calidus realised, the valetudinarium was a very vulnerable place to be. He felt the buds of sweat on his forehead, despite the cold air.

The soft footfalls on the timber floor were getting closer. A stifled laugh coughed into the air. How many voices? He thought he could make out two. No, three. There was a deeper voice, less distinct, that only sounded as a chesty bass rumble.

Calidus could feel the wound in his side tingling. Adrenalin surged through his body; every part of his brain told him he was in danger, yet he had no reason to suspect so.

As the sound of the footfalls swelled, the noise of the whispers grew in clarity. Calidus strained hard to make out words.

"–is he?"

"–fuck shud ah know wayr?"

"–nise that skinny ponce from a mile off."

"–take–"

Calidus tensed beneath his blanket. He didn't want to move his head, or any part of himself to draw their attention in his direction. His muscles were cramping and tensing uncomfortably, frozen into position. He racked his brains for a plan, an escape, a weapon of some kind. There was nothing.

He had never expected this, not really; had never been well enough to consider it.

Trentius.

He knew it, as surely as he could feel the wound singing in his side.

Calidus's face was slick with sweat. He could hear the sound of snoring rising and cresting like breaking waves further along the valetudinarium.

If he waited for them to pass, he could get up and walk out of the valetudinarium and make his way towards Apullius's quarters. Or he could run into Uricalus's office and wake the drunkard. How much support would he get? How safe could he be?

And then there was the question of his strength: he was weak, and he didn't know how much pressure he could put on his body. Could he run? Would the movement tear his wound open?

He didn't know. But he knew what would happen if Trentius found him here, and it didn't bear thinking about. Better to die bleeding in the snow than be at the mercy of that foul animal.

The men were walking closer, pausing every so often to peer at the slumbering forms. In incremental movements, Calidus tried to inch the blanket up and over his head, to squirm his face deeper inside. He hoped that if he could obscure his face, the men may move on before reaching the end of the valetudinarium and doubling back on themselves for a more detailed inspection. There were many invalids here, and it was dark; the intruders couldn't check them all in much detail.

Further down the hall, a man wept noisily. The sound sent tight fizzing shivers up and down Calidus's arms.

"—sick an' fuckin broke!"

Soft noises: now they were closer, Calidus could hear the ominous scratch of their nail studs on the floor timbers.

Closer, closer.

Closer.

They were level with him, his whole body sensed their presence. The blanket was up over his face. Only his hair was showing, but his hair was dirtier and more tangled since Trentius had last seen him. He could hear them breathing above him, smell the warm odour of their presence.

They passed.

He felt his muscles relax, tension released like water spilt from a jug. He thought about making his move, readying himself for lifting the blanket, and heading out towards the door. He pictured the distance in his mind: twenty, maybe thirty—

Calidus screamed.

Something had grabbed his ankle.

A cold, tight gripe. His eyes sprung open, his head jerking upwards and the blanket falling from his face, in time to see a meaty fist forcing itself over his mouth. He felt himself being wrenched away, dragged off the cot, and he landed heavily on the floor with a thump, a rage of pain bursting out from the wound in his side.

Trentius stood over him, smiling, one hand wrapt round his ankle; his face was dark and swollen and broken and as ugly as a murder. A second figure hung back, behind Trentius, and another figure loomed over Calidus's face, peering down, the sole of his boot pressing painfully on his bare shoulder. Except for Trentius, he did not recognise them. Soldiers, of course, with tight scarred faces and hollow eyes.

"Tyke," said Trentius, softly, and it was a vile whisper of anticipation and joy. Far behind his dark, narrow eyes, a sinister fire flickered into life.

Calidus lashed out with his free foot, hard and desperate; the movement sent an undulation of agony through his abdomen, and he let out a gasp, but he felt the blow connect with something soft, and he heard a faint grunt of pain from Trentius in response.

The contact jarred Calidus back a little and the pressure of the boot on his shoulder slacked. He used the opportunity to snake his arm out and punch upwards into the groin of the man standing directly over him. He felt his sharp knuckles make contact with something soft and pendulous and the man collapsed backwards, wheezing.

Trentius's gripe on his ankle had slackened. Calidus ignored the pain in his side, seizing his chance and scrabbled backwards along the rough timber planks of the floor, splinters peppering his calves and palms as he moved. The man who had been stood above him was doubled up alongside the cot of a sleeping invalid. He was aware of the movement from Trentius and his comrade a handful of paces in front of him.

Calidus managed to lurch up onto his feet, almost falling backwards with the effort. His legs were unsteady but his muscles held firm, the adrenalin giving him the strength he didn't think he had. He turned and ran without thinking, his bare feet slapping the floor, the dark forms of the sleeping patients rolling past him on either side. There was a faint light coming from Uricalus's cell at the far end of the corridor, and although Calidus could barely see anything in the dim light, he knew the exit was just to the right of this. He could hear the sound of pursuit behind him; the sick and ill were waking around them, shouting, grunting, weeping. All attempts at stealth were gone and Calidus knew he was running for his life.

He skidded hard into the main door, and ripped it open. The night was cold and dark, the air illuminated by a faint spill of light from the low moon. Calidus pounded out and leapt down the steps onto the hard gravel of the courtyard, his bare feet singing with the pain and cold. There was a dusting of snow on the ground and his bare limbs screamed from the cold, threatening to drown even the murmur of pain from his side. He ran hard across the courtyard, through the dim silence of the pre-dawn, hearing the sounds of pursuit behind him. He could see his own breath pluming in front of him as he ran through it, arms and legs pumping, muscles on fire. He could see the squat long shape of the barrack blocks up ahead. There were no shouts behind him, only the grunts of exertion and the clatter of nail studs on the frozen ground.

Calidus reached the side of the barrack block, and leapt up onto the wall, his arms stretched high, his flank a pool of hot pain. His fingers gripped the edge of the roof tiles, and his bare feet found purchase on the wall. He kicked and pushed and forced himself upwards. He could hear his pursuers beneath him; so close he fancied he could feel their breath on his calves.

There was the slightest brush of fingers against his foot and he kicked down wildly in disgust and panic; he felt some contact, and kicked against the stone wall of the barracks, his toes and soles bleeding and torn and cold, boosting himself up, grappling his chest onto the outer lip of the curved roof tiles which faint dangerously loose beneath him. A loose, relaxed part of his mind mused that perhaps it was only the ice keeping them stable. He scattered the thoughts from his head and heaved and pushed and worked through the pain that seemed to explode all over his body until his feet were up and kicking wildly in the air. His chest was fully onto the roof now and he reached out and grabbed further along the roof, further along the snowy, icy tiles and his fingertips grasped a curved upturned rim and he heaved and rolled and tensed all his muscles and boosted himself further up onto the middle of the roof where he lay for a second, recovering, wondering whether his heart was going to burst through his chest or his head explode from the pain and exertion.

"We gotchas tyke," spat a familiar voice. "You gon live up there forever, ye fuckin piece o quim, ye shit!"

Giddy, breathless laughter. The men were drunk, angry. Calidus felt his stomach rise and fall wildly against the roof tiles. He could feel the heat of life leaving his body with each breath. His side felt wet and painful.

He gathered his will and agonisingly pushed himself up to his feet, so he was standing on the roof of the barrack block, and looked in all directions. A stinging pain sliced into his neck, and a stone bounced off and thudded dully onto the roof tiles. There was more laughter from below as another missile clattered off the tiles by his feet.

Calidus kept low and walked across the roof, all the way along the length of the barracks. There was a gap of maybe two paces between the end of his barrack block and the next one. He sucked in a lungful of cold, purifying air and leapt. He landed with a clatter on the roof of the next block. He could hear the voices of men waking beneath, wondering at the noise. Catching his breath, he got to his feet, steadied himself and ran along the length of the roof. At the end of the block, there was a gap of another two paces, and then the sheer wall of the fort; unbroken stone stretching up to the timber rampart and the sentry walk above.

Calidus looked down; he could no longer see Trentius and his allies, but he could hear them panting and squabbling beneath him.

He knew he needed to be decisive. He could see only two ends for himself if he refused to move on from here, and neither was pleasant: death of exposure on this frozen rooftop, or caught by Trentius and his animals below.

He looked over to the fort wall again. The bricks were large and old, the mortar in between loose and weathered. He could see a few holds for his hands and feet.

Could he try it?

Calidus shivered. The pain in his side swelled and pulsed like a writhing beast. His feet and hands were numb. He needed to act fast, if he was going to act at all.

He hadn't come to Aesica to die like this; he had his honour, his familia, his uncle's words, his mission. What would Atellus do in this situation? He grimaced at the thought; he couldn't imagine the beneficiarius ever being in such a compromising situation; surely he would have stood his ground and fought all three and died as man, rather than fleeing like a hare, like a *child*.

Calidus spat in disgust and steeled himself. He walked over to the edge of the roof; his numb toes hung over the edge of the tiles. He looked across to the wall, feeling sweat on his forehead, despite the cold. Inside he felt as if he were burning. He imagined he was back in Eboracum, on a cool spring evening with a warm, soft, smooth-skinned girl waiting for him above. He squinted through the dull moonlight, saw the holds where his fingers were to grip, imagined the impact of his body against the wall and the sting of his fingers as they clutched for purchase.

Voices rose up from below, and he jumped.

The air was refreshing, almost soft and tender for a second, before dizziness stole across him with the wind whipping through his hair and into his eyes. The contact as he hit the wall knocked the cold wind from his lungs with a gasp. His foot had managed to secure a ledge on the sharp edge of a long brick, though the impact jarred his ankle; his left hand had grabbed the corner of a viewhole cut into the turret of the internal staircase.

Calidus felt himself falling backwards, but tensed his core muscles and pressed himself close to the rough reassuring bulk of the wall. His side was screaming with pain, but he swaddled the agony into a tight bundle and flung it into a dark corner of his mind. He was aware of the sensations, but they were distant, as far off as to be someone else's. He looked up, and began scaling the wall, searching out finger-holds and toe-holds at full stretch. The wind was bitter and painful against his flesh.

Below him he could hear the voices of Trentius and his men; they sounded confused. Maybe they had not seen him leap through the darkness and onto the wall. Perhaps it would be the last thing they would have expected; maybe they were waiting for him, circling the barracks, leaping to get a view. Maybe they would try to climb up, and find him gone. He needed to keep moving, and not think about the ground, which was peeling away beneath him; the drop now would surely be lethal. If he was lucky.

He carried on climbing, losing himself in the motions, the exactness of his grips and the agonising squeeze of his tired muscles. He looked up, the wind whipping his hair into his eyes and mouth. The wooden rampart was just above him: it formed a slight overhang, but there were plenty of grips amongst the timber. He reached it and swung himself round, pulling himself up, feeling alive and potent, the night wind scorching his bare flesh, the blood pounding and thrashing through his veins as his muscles squirmed beneath his icy skin.

Calidus pulled up onto a cross beam, then pressed his body tight to the rampart and swung himself over. He was on the walkway now. He sucked a breath in as he saw the dark figure of a sentry to his left. Deep into the shadows, Calidus crouched, waiting, watching, though the dying moon was barely spilling enough light to see by. There was no movement. Slowly, the rhythmic sound of snoring drifted across on the wind: the guard was asleep.

Calidus walked away from the sentry, hunched slightly to minimise his silhouette, and looked down over the ramparts. The land over the Wall beneath him was dark and sinister. There was no refuge for him on that side, only death. He scurried along the rampart until he reached a part of the fort which overlooked the road leading towards the vicus.

There was no other way down.

He heaved himself over the rampart, careful not to look down, and felt with his ice-like feet for jutting timbers and struts onto which he could balance himself. He lowered himself down and crouched on the timber. The horizon was ablush with the first light of dawn, a solemn reddish haze across the distant hills. The wind was biting and fierce out here, exposed as he was to the full force of nature. His arms and legs shivered uncontrollably. He was dimly aware of a trail of blood from the torn wound in his side. He felt tired, and unbelievably hungry. Black spots jittered in front of his eyes. He pinched his skin tightly, the pain waking him up, sharpening his vision.

Calidus lowered himself slowly and felt for chips and nicks in the sheer wall. The masonry was more weathered this side, and there were more ledges and chinks in which his toes and fingers could get purchase. He eased himself down, one hold at a time, always maintaining three points of contact with the wall despite his eagerness to reach the safety of the earth. He could see the lamplights of the two sentries ensconced in the main double gate, but as long as he was quiet, and kept away from the road, he should be fine.

He dropped the last seven feet, and rolled as he landed, scratching himself in the thick gorse that grew up at the base of the wall. He crouched in the thickets for a handful of breaths, listening, rubbing his wounds, but there was no noise except the distant twoot of an owl, and the dull lowing of weary beasts from within the vicus.

Calidus could feel the agonies of the cold now, and the pain of his side burst through into his head with renewed vigour. He looked down and could see that he was bleeding. Not heavily, but steadily. He put his finger to the wound and luxuriated in the warmth of the blood. He tried to get to his feet and almost fell; the second time he steeled himself and managed to stay upright.

He hadn't thought of what to do once he had escaped Trentius. There was nowhere else to go but the vicus, and the only place he could remember that seemed warm and familiar was the tavern he had been to with Atellus when they had first ventured out of the fort. The dwellings were a short distance away, but to Calidus it seemed a trek of many miles. He kept low, moving slowly, out of the fresh dawnlight, and away from the faint metalled swell of the road. The going was tough and painful, but he found a furrow in the undergrowth which made the journey less arduous. Twice he had to cower and keep still as laughing soldiers staggered back towards the fort along the road from a long night of whoring, drinking and fighting.

Calidus staggered through the weather-warped gate-posts and into the vicus. The streets were quiet but he thought he could remember where the tavern was. His limbs were heavy and he no longer felt the stinging cold in his feet and fingers, just a heavy blanket of weariness. He felt he could drop to the ground and sleep until summer. The wound in his side throbbed and ached and he could feel each scratch and abrasion on his flesh from the escape. He could almost hear the lids of his eyes sliding shut, defying his will, his body refusing to suffer any longer. He just needed to walk a few more steps, towards the doorway, to gather enough strength to rap upon the door and then he could be warm and safe and –

Calidus collapsed into the ditch by the side of the road and lay unmoving, as still and silent as the first powder of morning snow which settled gently on his bare arms.

CHAPTER 26

Atellus tried to respond but found his mouth too dry. He could barely part his swollen lips and his breaths came raggedly through his damaged nose. The optio made a gesture and Atellus found his mouth tugged open by thick fingers, and oily wine sliding over his tongue. He coughed and hacked until his chest burned.

"You are here," continued the optio, "because I have been instructed to remove you permanently from the Wall. You are seen as a disruptive influence. You are to be killed," he said clinically, "and your corpse cast over to the other side."

"Fuck you," spat Atellus.

"Oh no, no, beneficiarius. No." Marius raised a slender finger, then took another sup of his wine. "This can be as painful, or as simple, as you choose to make it. We are each the master of our own choices, as I am sure you know. One of the few things we can be sure to be master of. And you have chosen this path, this path which has led precisely here, by your own words and actions."

"My path was chosen before I arrived, you corrupt merda."

The optio shook his head. "Other paths were available to you, and their presence well signposted. This situation," he gestured lazily at their surroundings, "is all your own doing. It would have been preferable for us to send you back to Treves with a few simple answers to a few pointless questions. That course has been well pointed out since you arrived here. By Apullius, if by no others. I am sure Brocchus would have also given you steer on that issue."

Atellus shook his head. "All of fucking Aesica is corrupt."

"I think you will find that word has little meaning outside of Treves, beneficiarius," said Marius lounging back in his chair, his wine held up to his nose. "If indeed," he continued, raising his eyebrows, "it has any meaning *within* that city. You are certainly the highest rank I have ever killed. Almost like killing the emperor himself." He seemed lost for a second in his reverie, his gaze twinkling inward before focusing back on Atellus. "This is indeed a special occasion for me. I need to savour it more completely."

Atellus spat a wodge of blood onto the ground.

"The emperor will send men after me," said Atellus. "Hordes. He wants answers. You have no idea what you are instigating here, optio."

Marius shook his head. "By all accounts, beneficiarius, the emperor wants rid of you as much as we do. There will be no difficult questions. There will be no body. And if there is, for some wild reason, some form of follow-up, then this situation is simply outside the jurisdiction of Aesica. The questions will be asked of Magnis instead. The Wall is the most dangerous place in the empire, and few bother asking questions of what transpires up here. This is the end of the last chapter of the book. Ilicet."

Bellicus laughed, then helped himself to more wine from the flagon that was on the table next to Marius. He raised it towards Atellus in a mocking salute, then downed it, rivulets trickling down through his ragged fiery beard.

"The agent?" said Atellus, thickly. "You did the same to him, I presume."

Marius shrugged. "I have never heard of the agent. If he existed at all, he is long dead. This fort has been abandoned since I was a mere bairn, as they say here."

"You're in out of your depth, Marius. You have no idea what you're doing."

Marius laughed, an unctuous treacly sound. "On the contrary, beneficiarius, I know precisely what I'm doing. I have been born into this life. I have been groomed for it. I know what it takes to acquire true power. And this is one of those moments which defines a man. A moment which sets out his determination, his philosophy."

"And which makes you a liability to Apullius," countered Atellus. "And to Brocchus."

"Brocchus knows nothing," said Marius, scornfully. "And Apullius is more mine than I can ever be his."

Atellus tried for a gambit. "Crispus is a dangerous man."

Marius's smile faltered, if only for a second. "Now that," he said, gesturing at Atellus with the rim of his goblet, "is true. But he is not dangerous enough, beneficiarius." The smile returned with a brilliance that seemed to hurt Atellus's eyes. "Nowhere *near* dangerous enough." He took another sip of his wine and savoured the taste in his mouth.

***

Atellus had stopped counting the blows long since. The pain had become meaningless. He was dimly aware of laughter from above, but his ears were both swollen and there was a constant ringing and surging inside his skull that seemed to obliterate every external noise.

Laughter, or crying? He couldn't be sure.

He tried to open his eyes. One was gummed shut with blood, and massively swollen. The other was relatively unscathed, though his vision swam when he tried to focus on anything, and he felt queasy. It wasn't long since he had vomited, so his stomach was empty, otherwise he would be heaving again.

367

He was going to die here. He had almost resigned himself to it; and embracing it, he found a calm and tranquillity, underlaid with a beautiful excitement.

But there was something hard and cold in the pit of his belly which kept him from wallowing in his fate. There was the voice of Julia, and the eyes of Petronia. The thought of them twisted his guts, made his lungs burn afresh and his veins fill with angry blood. He thought of the slave-girl, Flavia, and how she had been abused and desecrated.

What if that had been *his* wife? *His* daughter?

"Once more, beneficiarius," came the voice. It sounded distant, fuzzy, surreal. "Your instructions from the emperor. Bellicus can keep going all night until his knuckles are as raw as your face. And then we simply let Qunavo take over."

More laughter. Atellus raised his head with some effort, and tried to focus. Marius was sitting opposite him, just out of reach; Bellicus was towering over him. Atellus could discern the large soldier's reek even through his swollen, clotted nose.

He spat noisily towards the optio. "Fuck you."

He was aware of Bellicus drawing back his fist, and then the world exploded in pain and a bright white light that seemed to scorch its way through his head and behind his eyeballs. He felt dizzy and was aware of a falling sensation, and within a second his head connected dully with the ground. He was still tied tight to the chair, but unable to move.

"Pick him up, you fucking ape!" The optio's voice was brittle and sharp; the words hurt as they scythed their way into Atellus's ears. "I want him to talk, not die. Not yet."

"Dominus," grunted Bellicus in assent. Atellus felt the soldier's large rough hands on his shoulders, and was aware of being lifted up. A distant part of his brain noticed the flax around his wrists was slightly looser; there was more give. One of the rear struts of the chair had cracked, and loosened the bindings.

Bellicus lifted him upright in the chair. The soldier stank of sweat, meat, blood and sex. The soldier spat thickly into Atellus's good eye.

"I'm going to cut your balls off, nigger, and watch you eat them."

There was no aggression in the soldier' voice; it was a statement of fact, of anticipation.

Atellus blinked to squeeze the phlegm from his eye. There was a noise to his left. He looked over and saw Barbarus taking blows to the face. Decimus had hauled him up out of his chair and was standing behind him twisting the man's arms behind his back while Qunavo laid into the convict's face with slow, heavy, deliberate strikes. The sound of the impacts cracked through the hall, and mingled with the guttural laughter of Decimus.

Atellus spat on the floor again, his phlegm thick with blood. The room swam in front of him. He felt as if the ground was shivering with the sucking of the wind outside. Perhaps this was the thinning of the barrier between this world and the next, he thought. Maybe he was in some liminal state where nothing was quite real. It was seductive, enticing.

He shook his head, feeling the pain sharpen his senses and drew in a ragged breath, his ribs and shoulders stinging with the movement.

"You owe me your life, Qunavo," Atellus spat, projecting his voice outwards with all the strength and authority he could gather. "Where is your honour? Do you Britunculi have any concept of it?"

He gained Qunavo's attention long enough for the soldier's eyes to flicker in his direction as he was midway through unwrapping his next punch. Barbarus sensed the opportunity, and ducked his head to one side. Qunavo's punch carried on through the space where the convict's head had been and squarely into Decimus's face. The latter fell backwards, blood bubbling from his shattered nose, and Barbarus dropped to his knees.

Decimus recovered, one hand to his pouring nose, and launched himself at Qunavo, his face a torn mask of fury. The two men went down and hit the ground hard, rolling heavily across the stone floor.

Atellus reacted without thinking. He wrenched his shoulders hard forward, snapping the strut of the chair to which he was bound and freeing his arms. The momentum carried him on, towards the optio lounging on his chair, his gaze distracted by the scuffle between the two limitanei. Atellus propelled himself forward faster, lowering his head like a ram and driving it full into the optio's chest, overbalancing him in his chair. The two men thumped to the ground, the optio gasping beneath Atellus's weight.

The beneficiarius was first to gain his feet, digging his knee into Marius's stomach as he rose, and twisting backwards so his still bound hands could scrabble for the hilt of the optio's sword. Bellicus, distracted by the tussle between his comrades, was slow to react. He eventually reacted to the optio's snarls and groans and turned to the beneficiarius, dashing towards him. Atellus's fingers grabbed the ivory hilt of the optio's spatha, and he jerked his body and shoulders upwards, tearing the blade free of its scabbard and twisting himself at the same time so that the blade was held upwards, angled towards Bellicus. Unable to stop in time, the large soldier's momentum drove him onto the point of the sword, the spatha biting deep through his flesh and into his bowels.

Atellus was driven forward by the weight of the contact, and the spatha was nearly wrenched from his awkward backhanded grip. He clutched it fast, the sweat beading his bruised face, and tore himself forward, away from the big man, tugging and twisting at the spatha. It slid out jaggedly from Bellicus's guts, opening a large exit wound, and Atellus felt the hot blood spray onto his forearms. He dug his feet against the ground and leapt aside from the wounded soldier and his flailing desperate momentum. Bellicus staggered awkwardly, disbelief and shock painted across his broad face, and collapsed onto Marius who was struggling to get up from where he was bent over his fallen chair.

Atellus turned, his back to the far wall, chest heaving, blood inching from freshly torn wounds on his face and scalp. He snatched a look to his left: Barbarus seemed mesmerised by the corpse of Flavia, which lay crumpled and defaced on the floor.

"*Barbarus!*" he shouted, his voice a whipcrack in the hall. "To me! Rally, man, *rally!*"

The convict turned his head, his eyes glassy, but some deep, primal part of him responded to the commanding tone. He ran over, his arms bound behind his back.

"Quick," said Atellus, turning and flipping the spatha in his hands so the blade was facing upwards. "Cut your bonds."

Barbarus turned and stretched his wrists apart as far as the knot would let him. He sawed the flax against the blade, wincing as the steel missed and bit into his flesh. Qunavo and Decimus were gradually tiring of each other's blows and coming to realise that something was amiss. Marius was pushing the bulk of Bellicus off his legs and getting to his feet, shouting oaths and obscenities towards his men as he did so.

"Faster!" said Atellus. Barbarus sawed away, sweat streaming from his brow, his breathing hard and laboured, his face a mess of blood and bruises. With a click, the flax parted and the convict tore his wrists apart.

"Take the blade," said Atellus.

"Your bonds," said Barbarus, taking the spatha.

Atellus turned, but there was no time. Marius was approaching, and the other two limitanei were close behind. He limped to the far corner, towards the coarse wooden planks of the dining table, and leapt onto it, almost misjudging it, hampered as he was by his bindings. The wood was sturdy and solid, for which Atellus was grateful. He fought to his feet, standing tall in the room, his head swimming and his vision darkening. His entire body burned and ached. He tensed and flexed his wrists, feeling the cords give slightly, but his hands were still bound fast.

Atellus scanned the room quickly and saw Barbarus fending off Qunavo and Marius, waving the spatha like an anguished man, sucking up strength into his beaten crippled limbs from the agony of Flavia's fate, and the all-consuming hate that burned inside him. The third limitanei, Decimus, was running for him.

"Cmon, nigger," spat Decimus, his mottled and decrepit gladius in his fist. "I'll make it quick," he lied.

The limtanei approached the table on which he stood, and swung the gladius, but the blade was too short and Atellus danced backwards easily. He waited for the momentum of the swing to carry Decimus to full stretch, then he leapt forward and aimed a solid kick at the soldier's face, with the iron studs of his boot.

Decimus fell backwards with a howl, his already broken nose smashed again and streaming fresh torrents of blood.

Atellus felt a mix of sweat and blood running down his forearms. He wriggled his wrists together, changing the angle, squeezing his fingers together, willing his bones to contract. He rubbed the flax against the back of his breeches. He could feel his hands slipping through the loop, infinitesimally slowly; he could feel each grain of material passing each nerve on his skin. He growled and spat and swore and bled.

Decimus returned, wiping blood from his face with forearm. His gladius was out and angled towards Atellus who danced back towards the wall, keeping the length of the table between himself and the soldier. Decimus did not speak now, but made strange gurgling noises in his throat. Atellus could hear the breath wheeze and fart through his shattered nose. The limitanei swung at Atellus's legs, and he leapt into the air, landing awkwardly on an ankle. Decimus capitalised and swung the gladius in an overhead stroke. Atellus fell backwards, and the blow gouged the flesh of his shin. He screamed with pain, and the noise brought a smile to Decimus's broad, blood-stained mouth.

Atellus was dimly aware of Barbarus being driven back by a volley of sword blows from Qunavo and the optio. Marius had taken Bellicus's sword from him as he lay dying, and was using it with skill and precision. Barbarus would not be able to hold out much longer.

Atellus gave his wrists another tug, and squeezed them together, and his right hand sprang free. He barely had time to feel the triumph before he saw Decimus approaching the edge of the table and drawing the gladius back for another blow.

Atellus got to his feet with effort, blood from his injured shin making the table slick, and leapt upwards, the gladius sweeping the air where his ankles had been. When he landed he bounced straight away, over Decimus's extended arm and onto the man himself, feet first. His boots crashed down into the soldier's neck, driving him to the ground. Atellus fell off awkwardly, and rolled across the stone floor, allowing his shoulder and his momentum to take the impact. He rose fast, and heard the metallic clank of the Decimus's gladius hitting the stones. His opponent was on his knees, dazed, and clutching at his throat.

Atellus darted up, freeing his left hand as he rose, and snatched out for the gladius. It was heavy and its weight dragged at his arm as he hefted it blade first from the floor, just as Decimus's hand snatched at the space where the hilt had been. Atellus hefted it into the air, flipping it over so he could catch it by the hilt, and ran the length of the hall towards where Barbarus was driven into a corner by the relentless blows from Marius and Qunavo.

Atellus struck a full-handed slice aimed at the optio's neck, but Marius must have sensed his presence, or read it in Barbarus's eyes, and he slid to the side at the last moment, leaving Atellus's blow to nip at the flesh of his neck and drag through the cloth of his cloak.

"To me!" yelled Atellus, as he aimed a return blow at Qunavo, who was ready and parried it with his own spatha. The room rang with the angry squeal of metal on metal.

Barbarus ducked forward to the left of the Qunavo, hacking his blade along the man's ribs as he went, and Atellus and Barbarus backed themselves towards the narrow doorway set into the north wall of the fort. Decimus had rushed to join the other two soldiers, armed with a leg from the chair which he had ripped apart.

Bellicus lay untended on the ground throughout the battle, gasping and bleeding. His blood-soaked hands clutched at his belly to hold back the dark purple coils of his guts which slithered around his fingers.

Atellus pushed Barbarus into the passageway leading to the heavy oak door, and backed in himself. The confined space meant that their assailants would have no advantage of numbers. They could fight only one at a time, and with limited room for making blows: Atellus's gladius, a short thrusting weapon by nature, was an advantage.

Marius stood in front of them, watching his captives back away. He rubbed at the bruise on his neck where Atellus's blow had landed, turned by the thick material of his cloak.

"Back away, beneficiarius," he sneered, his once tight dark curls hanging loosely in front of his eyes. "Go through that door and you are as good as dead."

"It seems preferable," mumbled Atellus through thick lips, keeping his dark eyes fixed to the three men in front of him, "to staying here to enjoy more of your hospitality."

The optio threw back his head and laughed; a strange, foreign sound echoing through the fort, reverberating from the cold stones, answered only by the moans and sobs of Bellicus. Atellus could feel the cold wind from outside racing in like knife nicks from under the door behind him.

"Oh," said Marius, "we had so many more courtesies to extend to you both. But I suppose we will have to leave that for our friends to the north. They will finish what we have started here, benficiarius, have no doubt about it."

Barbarus had backed into the door, and he fumbled behind him for the latch. The door opened inwards and was bound by heavy iron straps. He raised these with a clunk and a slap of metal on wood, then reached up to remove the bolt by the top of the door, and knelt down to upheave the bottom one. The wind flew at the door dashing it open against the convict. The cold air swept down the narrow corridor and set the torches flickering in the main hall.

Marius took a step towards the men, and Atellus levelled the gladius at him. His chest was heaving, his eyes swollen and smudged with sweat and blood, his clothes torn and filthy with the same. The icy wind was welcome to his dazed and weary flesh: it gave him energy and woke his senses. He leaned back to speak to Barbarus, not taking his eyes from the men in front of him.

"Run north, head for the tree-line," he said. "There will be covered pits for the first twenty paces, so tread carefully; there will be scattered caltrops too. Find shelter, or we will die before the night does. I will find you, if I can. If not, may the great Sol welcome us both by daybreak." He spat onto the ground.

The convict shook his head tersely, and weighed the sword in his fist. "We cut our way out." His voice was hoarse and tight.

Atellus shook his head. "We are in no strength for a fight. Not when we are outnumbered." He reached behind him with his free hand, and clasped the convict on the shoulder. "Go."

Barbarus hesitated and Atellus spoke again. "You have no stomach for life without your woman...you wish to die surrounded by the bleeding bodies of her tormentors." Atellus turned briefly to shoot a look into the convict's eyes; it was met with a tight nod. "But you will die in vain today," he continued. "Escape and live and we will avenge her properly, Barbarus."

Barbarus steeled himself, then nodded and staggered through and into the face of the storm. Atellus moved backwards, followed by Marius who inched forward, a distance of six or seven paces separating the two men.

"Flee, imperatoris cinaedus," sneered Marius. "*Ignavus!* Let the wolves and the savages fight over your bones."

Atellus grabbed behind him for the door which flapped and creaked under the force of the wind. He found the edge and pulled it open behind him, feeling the biting cold of the wind against his back.

"There will be a reckoning, optio," said Atellus, his voice as low and cutting as the wind that growled along the passageway. "You will find that your own reality will soon become much less comforting."

376

Atellus backed out through the door, slamming it shut after him. He turned and ran through a cold so thick it was like a hand pushing against him. The darkness was massive and terrifying around him, dwarfing even the towering Wall at his back. He could see the huge berms of the defensive ramparts either side of him, the staked ditches yawning out in a blackness that even the night shied away from.

Atellus pounded through the snow, the ground thick and wet beneath his boots, the air lapping at his wounds. The land in front shimmered an ethereal grey, the snow rising in undulations across the denuded swell of the hills. He could hear the shouts of pursuit behind him. Up ahead were the footprints of Barbarus, fast filling up with fresh snow. His breath whipped out in front of his eyes.

He needed to be aware of hidden ditches. He knew from fighting at the Wall in years past that the hidden defences usually dappled the first hundred paces beyond the Wall. Perhaps there weren't any here; perhaps the ground was frozen enough that they wouldn't give under his weight. He had no choice but to run, and run faster and faster. If he slowed, his pursuers would cut him down. He would need to trust to the fates and take what was awaiting him.

Atellus could feel the vast emptiness around him, and the looming expanse of the Wall gradually receding behind him, diminishing while somehow becoming bigger, longer, more encompassing until it became the very horizon and there was nothing that could escape its endless embrace. Ahead there was only the bleak snow and the endless dark of the night. He heard calls to his left and behind him, shouts. He tried to will his legs to move faster, but his weariness was seeping into every cell of his body, his limbs feeling heavy and sodden, his head swollen and stuffed with down. Even the thoughts that flickered in the hollow of his head seemed to hurt him.

He could hear the forced breath and pounding footfalls of someone behind him, closing in on him. The storm was surging and pressing harder, the wind seeming to fling him back towards his pursuers, the snow stuffing his nostrils and his eyes, freezing his teeth and his gums clogging his lungs with each desperate breath he drew. He strained and clenched his soul, trying to squeeze more heat from his muscles, more energy from his lungs and his flapping heart....

...and then the pain.

Huge spires of agony ripping up through every muscle in his body.

Atellus hit the powdery snow before he even realised he was falling; he felt as if his body were being devoured by flames. His muscles were cramped tight, and his brain was awash with searing white heat. He felt nothing but pain, saw nothing but pain, and writhed spasmodically in the snow, moaning beneath the laughter of the wind.

"Cripplers, those caltrops," said a voice above him, speaking above the wind. Atellus felt, rather than saw, the man crouch down next to him. "I've heard men cry like bairns with those spikes inside their heel."

Atellus opened his eyes, not realising he had been squeezing them shut. Qunavo knelt beside him, his thick bleeding face whipped by his own ragged hair in the wind. There was a dumb scar where his ear had been.

"You'll see, nigger, about Britons. About *honour*." The soldier held his sword out towards Atellus's throat. Far off came the call of voices, snatched off at wild angles by the wind.

He looked up into Qunavo's pale green eyes, unwavering above him, his sword inching towards the easterner's ear.

"Left me a pretty scar for my trouble, right? A tale for the wenches." His face split into a bitter smile. "Aches like you couldn't believe, nigger, in this weather. Or maybe you can believe, now, hm?"

378

Atellus felt the weight of the cold blade resting heavily against his hot flesh.

In a sleek movement, Qunavo whipped his sword down and into the snow beside Atellus's head. He reached down and took the beneficiarius's boot, lifting it up, half dragging the man towards him. He looked at the caltrop embedded deep in the leather. It had pierced between studs, straight through and into the flesh. Qunavo took a grip on the two spikes that remained outside, lying flush against the sole of the boot.

He gripped his fist, tensed hard and pulled. Slowly, the spike of iron inched out from the flesh. Atellus gnashed and bit down on his cloak, choking back screams, tears squirming from his eyes.

Qunavo removed the bolt with a grunt and jerk, spraying dark blood onto the pristine snow. The storm whipped around them, their surroundings obscured by the flurries. Atellus could barely tell which way the Wall lay.

The limitanei held the caltrop up and turned it round in his large fingers, before flinging it out into the night.

"You have a slow count of thirty," he said, gathering his sword from the snow and getting to his feet. "Then I will follow. And if I catch you again, you will die by my hand. You tell me I know nothing of honour!" He spat down at Atellus.

The big man hefted his sword, then squatted on his haunches, the wind sending his long matted hair lashing away from his face like demonic serpents. His eyes were steady on the easterner.

Atellus slowly got to his knees. The pain had lessened to a constant dull throb that radiated from the base of his foot and seemed to climb his spine all the way up to the nape of his neck. He tested his weight and found that he could stand adequately if he shifted the burden to his right foot. He stood looking at Qunavo for a second longer, and the soldier met his gaze levelly. Atellus turned and limped off in the direction of his gaze, into the full force of the wind.

He bit back the tears of pain, each step feeling like heavy dull blows to his back and kidneys, and moved slowly, testing the ground with each foot. He became conscious of the time trickling away, and he sped up, until he was cantering in a shambolic gait, away, deeper into the night and the wild fury of the storm, until all was a milky white around him and the cold was a crushing vice across his chest. The tug at his legs told him he was heading upslope. The noise of voices and calls disappeared away from him – in which direction he couldn't tell – and soon there was only the scream of the wind and the thump of his own heart in his chest.

Atellus dropped to his knees, his wild breath squeezed from his tight lungs. He wanted to lie, to drop down, to sleep and sleep and sleep. But he knew that if he fell here, he would die where he lay. If not from his pursuers, then from the ravaging storm, the cold, the scouring wind. He needed to carry on.

He heaved himself to his feet again, feeling the pain from the caltrop wound, and staggered on, up the hill, fighting his own weight as well as the buffeting wind which threatened to push him back down towards the Wall. He looked away, behind him, trying to penetrate the veil of snow that whipped and spat in every direction. Far off he could see a flickering light, high up towards where he thought the clouds must be. It was answered by another, further along, and then another, further still and barely visible. The flames swelled and dimmed in the night sky, then repeated their action before the night was once more reclaimed by the darkness.

Beacons, Atellus realised. The chase is off and they are sending word to Aesica. By morning, if Apullius wanted, they could have a unit of horse searching for them, or half a company, if he wanted. Or no-one at all.

Which would probably be just as effective, he thought grimly.

He carried on, forcing himself away from the danger and beyond, cresting a slight hill, before stumbling again, falling hard and rolling down the slope, accelerating with each tumble, the snow filling his clothes, filling his mouth, suffocating him. He crashed through thickets of sparse foliage and struck something solid at the bottom with a thud that winded him. He roused himself, slowly, and found himself amidst a cluster of tumbled masonry and timber. Slithering on his belly, he used the last reserves of his strength, and dragged himself into a crook of the bricks which offered some shelter from the raging storm. He tried to dig himself into the snow, and wrapped himself in his cloak.

Atellus needed heat and warmth, but it was too risky, and he was too exhausted. He lay back and felt his head climbing, as though his spirit were clambering from his body. He could see Faenia and Petronia sitting opposite, looking at him with their warm eyes, his wife's warm so warm body, her soft soft skin. He felt comfortable just looking at her. He could look at her all night, and stay awake through the cold, and wait for the scant glow of the sun as it cracked through the stormclouds. He could wait all night, here with his wife, with his beloved daughter. A family, together again.

He felt warm already.

CHAPTER 27

"Until the sun touches the tip of that tree," said Rodius, pointing with his remaining hand towards a tall fir which stood out from the rest. "No longer."

Aurelia collapsed onto the cloak which the slaver had draped across the snow.

The day had been tiring for them all. Rodius had set a demanding pace, and fear had driven the others to match it. Whenever one had fallen into the snow, or refused to get up after the short break, Rodius had reminded them of the threat at their heels.

"They will track us for days," he had said after Vassu complained at being kicked to his feet. "You wait for them if you want, but don't hold me back." And his brother had frowned and muttered curses under his breath and risen and set off with the others, dragging a little behind. He kept his own company, Aurelia had noticed, and wept silently over his mangled hands. He paid no mind to his brother's missing hand. Aurelia herself, he studiously ignored, with an almost comical determination.

The girl still refused to speak, and there was nothing more than a flicker of the eyelids that Aurelia could prise from her. Vassu simply sneered and spat into the snow.

"The whelp is cracked in the head," he hissed at his brother. "She's good for nothing but wolf fodder. And the chit slows us down."

"She whines less than you," said Rodius, breaking off a crust from a heel of bread with one hand and passing it over to Aurelia to give to the girl. She smiled as she handed it over, and watched the girl place it in her mouth, chewing slowly. At least the girl ate. She walked too, and did so until her legs gave way and she lay in the snow. Then Rodius carried her for a mile or two, and Aurelia supported her when he put her down. Then she walked unaided again. In this way they were able to cover handfuls of miles before dark.

The girl was strong, Aurelia knew, and she had spirit. The words would come, in time.

Until then, Aurelia spoke to her and soothed her as if she were her own child. This girl was their one triumph, their token snatched from the bear's maw, the only child she could save. She was a testament to her own efforts, and a reminder of her own failure.

One girl alive, of twelve. And for how much longer? Sometimes she failed to convince herself that they were not merely stalling the inevitable.

She looked to the horizon. The dripping ochre sun was a hair's breadth from the treeline. Her legs throbbed and ached; her eyes stung from the snow glare. The bark and whine of a hound shattered the crisp air. She thought she could hear voices too. They were behind, far behind, but not far enough. The last snowfall would have obliterated their tracks, and made them harder to find; their pursuers would have to spread out and cover a larger area. They were getting further from their camp. With luck they were sight-hunters and not scent-hunters. She hoped they would give up, soon.

"How much further?" she asked Rodius.

"To the road?"

"To the Wall."

The slaver frowned into the cold sky. His hair had fallen across his shoulders, and his face was mottled pink with the cold. "A day, perhaps. Maybe more."

Vassu grunted.

"Something to say, frater?" said Rodius, getting to his feet and scrubbing the powdery snow from his breeches.

Vassu shook his head and spat. "What is our plan, then?" he sighed.

"We should strike the north road before dawn," answered Rodius. "Then we travel by night and sleep by day. It'll be warmer, so we shouldn't need fires."

"And we just stumble off-track and into the wilderness to be food for the bears. If the brigands don't catch us first, of course. If not these," he jerked his chin back towards the rolling hills they had escaped over, "then any others. It doesn't really matter much. We are dead men in any case."

"As dead as if we had left you chained like a beast outside their camp?" replied Rodius. "You were keen to come with us then, brother." Rodius spat and reached down to the girl. She weighed very little and seemed to float up as he pulled her to her feet. "If you have a better idea, we would all like to hear it."

"You know my idea," he snarled, unfolding himself from the ground.

Aurelia knew his idea also. He had expounded on it in great detail earlier in the day. They were to head south, back to Eboracum where they would sell the bitches and try to salvage what little dignity they could from their disastrous venture. He knew a money lender who would loan them enough for a new waggon and a beast to pull it.

"You do that," Rodius had answered. "We are heading north."

"North!" said Vassu. "Fucking north! What is fucking north? Stop being led by your cock and use your brain. This shrivelled up slut isn't worth the trouble."

"I owe her my life," said Rodius, simply. "As do you."

Vassu had spat and said no more on the matter, though his muttering did not relent.

They walked hard as the sun collapsed and the thick solid clouds massed overhead. The winds grew more savage and biting, and the drifts became deeper and the land wilder. They each staggered wrapt in their layers, bunched up together for warmth, and bent into the sobbing wind.

Rodius pulled them up suddenly, and gestured for them to wait while he disappeared into the night. The moon was barely visible through the clouds, and each of them was lost in their own morose thoughts. The land was craggy and wild here; great sheets of stone loomed around them, as though entire hills had been split in two by some giant axe-stroke. A few gnarled and naked trees danced and wept into the wind.

"Crassa," said Rodius, appearing from the side.

The slaver beckoned for Aurelia to follow him. They were standing on the edge of a sheer cliff, with a drop of maybe twenty paces straight down. At first Aurelia thought it was a frozen river far below. But as her eyes adjusted to the gloom, she saw that it was the arrow straight path of a road.

"The north road," she said.

She felt Rodius nodding beside her. The road itself was thick with fresh snow, but the swell of the camber was visible, as were the fossae at either side. The trees on either side had been cut back, and the line stretched out into the distance, as far as the pale moonlight would let her see.

"We rest here," said Rodius. "There is some shelter down the angle of the slope, away from the road. It will serve us for a few hours."

Aurelia nodded. Danger lay at both ends of the road for her. Only the high gods themselves could know how this would end.

They shivered and slept through the cold daylight, and walked through the night, the moon and the stars their beacons as they marched. There was silence but for the howling of distant wolfpacks and the song of the wind through the trees. They ate little and infrequently. The girl collapsed often from hunger and exhaustion and had to be carried. Vassu tripped into a deep snowdrift and was hauled out by his brother. Aurelia lost count of the amount of times she thought her body would simply refuse to rise after a rest, and she thought she would just lie in the snow and sleep and sleep. But Rodius always pulled her gently to her feet and sent her moving; she gritted her teeth and squeezed her fingers into her palms and willed her desperate, weary legs to move forward once more, north, towards the Wall.

***

Aurelia shielded her eyes from the wet sun that was collapsing into the distant hills. The silhouette of the Wall was visible rolling out across the horizon. Closer by, she could make out the thin reeds of chimney smoke that came from the vicus. Further along, the crumbled ruins of the aqueduct that had once provided water for the villagers and limitanei rose up beyond the swell of the land. Now the stone had been pulled apart for building materials to repair breaches in the Wall, or provide masonry for the houses of the wealthier civilians.

"Aesica," said Rodius coming up to stand beside her.

Aurelia nodded, squeezing the hand of the girl beside her. She had still been unable to prise a word from the child's mouth. Instead, Aurelia had taken to calling her Galla; the girl showed no sign of whether she approved of this or not, but any name was better than none.

Their journey north had been arduous, but uneventful. They travelled the north road by dark, and in silence. In the daylight hours they slept, and trailed the route of the road half a mile inwards of the road itself, to avoid ambushes or soldiers. The weather was grim and bitter, and the cold was perpetual. Sometimes Aurelia felt she could never be warm again, as though her very bones were filled with hard ice that would never melt. She wrapped herself and Galla in their blanket and pressed close for warmth, but the air was still painful, and it was difficult to snatch more than a few minutes' sleep at a time.

They were all weary, exhausted and hungry. Rodius and Vassu barely spoke except to exchange curses; the brothers walked apart from each other, each wrapt in their own dark thoughts. Occasionally Aurelia could hear Vassu mumbling to himself, long rumbling diatribes against everyone. Especially her. Once she walked off to find twigs for a fire, and caught Vassu weeping silently to himself, face pressed into the smooth bark of a sorbus tree. He had turned and seen her, his face broken, his eyes wet and sad. He seemed more frail and human than she had ever witnessed, and the weight of bitterness and hatred that lingered on his brow seemed to have melted as the snow under the sun. But the change was gone with the next gust of wind, and he was ranting and howling at her about sneaking up on him, the prying bitch that she was. So she had turned her back without wearying herself to respond, and sought the kindling in a different part of the woods.

They waded through snowdrifts as deep as their armpits, and walked into the bleeding sunsets which set crimson fire sweeping across the hillsnow. They marched with their bellies empty, the taste of tough days-old hare-flesh still salting their gums, and their hearts pounding at the faintest sound that split the still air. Only Galla seemed indifferent and unperturbed by their conditions. She walked when Aurelia walked, and rested when she did; took her meals and shut her eyes in perfect

387

unison with the older woman. The wind and the cold seemed not to touch her, nor the fear and uncertainty crease her young brow.

Rodius called the girl 'hollow'; Vassu of course found much worse names to use. Aurelia just treated her as if she were a normal, lively girl. She took comfort from her presence, almost as if the girl was a validation of her own existence, her own reality. Trudging through the cold and the endless frozen wastes, past scenes of desolation or destruction, Aurelia began to doubt her own senses, her own concepts of time and place.

"Aesica," spat Vassu. "Fuckin civilisation at last. Such as it is up here in the shitlands. Now we can sell the two bitches and get back on track."

Aurelia ignored him, as did his brother. Rodius scratched at his stump of a wrist, absentmindedly.

"Do you have friends in the vicus?" he asked her.

She nodded. "I did. And I have no reason to suppose they are no longer my allies."

Vassu barked a laugh. "Yes, so you can get your whore's gold and give us our share, right?" He laughed again and spat onto the snow. As usual, his mangled fingers were tucked into his armpits. Whether for warmth, or to ease the pain, Aurelia could not say and Vassu had not volunteered any information since joining them.

"We can reach the vicus by dark," said Rodius. "If we make haste."

They slid down from the hilltop which they had scrambled up to get their bearings, and moved down towards the north road. They passed more and more traffic, heading both in and out of the village: blank-faced refugees with only the tattered clothes on their backs, soot-black faces scarred by tear-tracks. There were soldiers, mainly afoot but sometimes on weak, thin horses. No-one spared a look for the group of four. They were a regular sight so close to an urbs, and each beholder was enwrapt in their own woes and sufferings; none had the emotional currency to spare for those of others.

So close to the Wall, the road was mainly clear of the deep snow; only the faintest smudges of fresh fall were visible above the metalled surface that lead to the south gate of the vicus. They reached the first scattered farmsteads of the periphery just as the last song of the sun was throttled silent by the towering bulk of the Wall.

They walked through and beyond the cracked and splintered wooden palisade that crept around the south of the vicus. There were no soldiers on the gates, just a man curled into the corner with a blueblack face who may have been dead or may have been drunk. Torchlight flickered at random intervals along the mud-churned streets which spun off from the main north road as tracks of knee-deep sludge. The air rang with the shouts and calls of the vicus life, and the reassuring smell of chimney smoke curled into the clouds overhead.

Aurelia brought them to a stop in the middle of the main road. She stood in silence whilst the thronging villagers parted around her: they were carrying wares back to sheds, fetching tinder and kindling for the long evening ahead, using crude sticks to drive forth emaciated milchecows which they had been unable to sell. Ragged children swept in and out, playing, begging, or just staring with dumb eyes and bruised jaws.

"Wait for me here," she said to Rodius, after a while. "I won't be long." She gripped Galla's small hand, and the pressure made the girl walk with her.

Vassu shot out an arm across the girl's neck, stopping her from following. His useless fingers were like red twisted stalks quivering in the air.

"Heel, bitches," he snarled. "You piss off and then we never see you again, right?" He used the wrist of his other arm to wipe fresh snowflakes from his eyes then blew his nose noisily into the snow at his feet, a mixture of blood and snot. "I'm not as stupid as he is." He jerked his chin towards his brother.

"I give you my word," said Aurelia calmly, "that we will be back."

Rodius clapped his large hand on his brother's shoulder, and looked him directly in the eye. "Pax, Vassu. Let them be."

Vassu stared at Rodius for a while, then raised his arm, so it was no longer barring Galla's path. The girl shuffled over towards Aurelia. The two brothers watched as Aurelia led the girl through the lane, deep with half-frozen filth, leading up into a cluster of timber and thatch dwellings. They struggled through the sucking, stinking mud and turned a corner so they were out of sight.

Rodius leaned against the side of an old half-scorched building that looked like it may once have been a smith's workshop. The inside reeked of excrement, and the floor was covered with old, damp straw. Vassu followed him and lounged next to him. The two brothers looked out at the dark sky and the darker clouds pushing down on them from overhead. There were spits of snow dancing through the air which they both knew would get heavier over the coming hours.

"This is what we have come to, brother," said Vassu, his eyes fixed on the mud their feet were buried in. "A pathetic situation. A pair of cripples."

Rodius shook his head slowly, wearily. "At least we are alive."

Vassu half snorted, and shook his head, but he did not speak. His face was tilted down, his nose sloping to the wet ground, his lank hair plastered to his sallow face. Rodius was pale and his eyes were frosted. The sagging empty sleeve of his tunic drooped out across the end of his stump. The fingers of his remaining hand flexed and shivered in the dark crisp air.

"We can get back, though, brother," said Vassu. "Get some gold from this whore. And even if she has fucked off with the whelp, Scotius owes us. He should be up here this time of year. We could get enough for a waggon, take some grain back to the city, then buy more whores with–"

"No, Vassu." Rodius's tone was final. "No more. Not for me."

Vassu shook his head slowly. "You want to starve then, brother? You want father to starve, to die before our eyes? You remember hunting for rats by the riverside? Chewing the old leather to still the belly pains? You remember that? Drinking warm meltwater, and–"

"Yes, I remember," said Rodius, interrupting him. "I remember. But...not this. I am changed." He lifted the ruined end of his arm and gestured with it towards his brother. "I am a different man now."

"You are a *weak* man now," said Vassu, turning away.

"Maybe."

"The soldiers here pay half a year's gold for faceless bitches for the savages to send to their gods. You tell me another way of earning such sums."

Rodius shook his head. "Enough. I want no part in it, brother. You do as you must. Dealing in whores is one thing. Selling whelps for butchery is something else."

"Yes," spat Vassu, with a crooked smile. "Their suffering is shorter."

Rodius was about to reply, but was distracted by a shout from further down the street. They looked over in time to see one short, dark-skinned man strike a tall man from behind with a thick nail-studded cudgel. The taller man fell forward into the snow with a grunt. There was a scream and shout from his companions, and the mess descended into a brawl, blood and sweat dissipating the snow around them as they fought and bit and kicked on the road. Others gathered round and jeered or shouted taunts; still others shouted bets to onlookers. A couple of limitanei approaching down the road stood still, looked down towards the brawl, then turned round and casually walked back the way they had come.

"A clever man could make money here," said Vassu, rubbing his broken fingers into his armpits.

"A sick man could make money here," replied his brother. "A sly man, without morals."

"You once were those things, Rod," snapped Vassu. "Don't try and wipe out your history so fast. You haven't changed. Only the dream has." He turned away and spat into the mud at his feet. "You'll wake, brother. Soon."

Crassa and the girl appeared from round the corner, melting out of the dark and the mud like pale-faced shades. They seemed unconcerned by the sounds of the brawl further down the road. The shouts and screams punctuated by the clack of wood on wood rang through the night, lifted high on the wind. The snowflakes grew fatter and softer and tumbled to the ground more slowly.

"My friend is not at home," said Crassa, addressing herself to Rodius. "I could not get any gold."

"Ha!" shouted Vassu, but Rodius silenced him with his arm across his brother's chest.

"Enough, frater," he said, then turned to Crassa. "There is a man, Scotius, who owes us gold. We will find him and take what we need to give us lodging and food for a few days."

Crassa inclined her head slightly. The mute girl looked up at Rodius with wide, white eyes that gleamed through the darkness. Vassu kept quiet, but Rodius could hear him chuntering and mumbling into his chest.

The foursome set off onto the road, slipping in the mud and the packed snow underfoot. Vassu led them at a rapid pace through the winding roads and twisted ginnels until they arrived at a broad opening which looked up at a row of larger dwellings; these were grander and set back from the scattered slums they had passed through.

Scotius lived in a relatively large timber-built house towards the fort side, where most protection was afforded, both from the elements and the bandits. It had foundations of stone, and thick smoke billowed up from a chimney stack, centralised in the local fashion.

Rodius told the women to wait for them down a thin alleyway towards the rear of the house. Aurelia and the girl settled themselves on an upturned wheelless waggon, and drew their cloaks around each other. Aurelia produced some salted squirrel meat for the girl to eat. Galla ate without taste or interest, but Aurelia made sure she chewed and swallowed each bite.

The two brothers went round to the front of the house, and Aurelia could hear their loud raps on the wooden door. There was muffled conversation, then the door was shut and there was only the sighing wind and the hum of activity and traffic through the vicus and into the fort. Aurelia smoothed the girl's hair over her ears and tried to rub some warmth into her soft pale cheeks.

"We will not be here long, Galla," she said. "Do not fret. We can soon leave this miserable land far, far behind."

A spiral of good-natured laughter fizzed out into the air from inside the cottage, and there was the slamming of a door. Rodius and Vassu appeared from round the corner, the latter draping his arm lightly across his brother's shoulders.

"We have the gold," said Rodius to Crassa as they approached. "And a recommendation for an inn."

"Though we intend to steer well clear of anywhere that sick fat fuck would choose to rest his head," laughed Vassu. "And his cock."

"He was happy to pay what he owed?" asked Aurelia, getting up from the skeleton of the waggon, and arching an eyebrow at Rodius.

"Not exactly," he answered. "But after Vassu took the kneecap off his paid strongarm with a single kick, he wasn't in a position to refuse us."

"And a bit more besides," laughed Vassu. "For goodwill of course."

"Which you could translate as," said Rodius, "'take the money and get as far away from me as possible.'"

"Did you see his face when he saw your hand?!" laughed Vassu, clapping his brother on the back.

"My *lack* of hand you mean?" snorted Rodius.

"It does make you look tougher, brother," said Vassu. "Like you have less to lose!" He laughed again, and Rodius briefly joined in.

It seemed to Aurelia the first time she had seen Rodius smile since she had first met him, except for the bitter grin he wore as armour. The two men seemed as brothers for the first time, and even Vassu's face was cleansed by the good humour.

Rodius led them out through the flailing snow and along the main road through the vicus, stopping at a tavern which spilled light and noise out into the dark. A handful of men were sitting or lying in the snow outside the door. Some smiled lasciviously at Aurelia and the girl as they walked through. Vassu took them through the crowd and over to a pale thin lady with an eruption of bright red hair.

"Good evening, Muconia," said Vassu, with an elaborate attempt at a bow. "How's my favourite clap-addled whore on the Wall?"

Muconia squinted at him as he approached, and then her angular face cracked into a broad, toothless smile.

"Vassu!" she exclaimed, cocking her head to one side. Her fiery hair, twisted into thick plaits, fell across her shoulder. "Thought tha'd be long dropped ba now."

"Nearly," he answered, with a grin, "but not quite. We seek a room—"

"Two rooms," said Aurelia, firmly. Muconia narrowed her eyes and looked her and the girl up and down. The laughter and raised voices, almost like shouted threats, coalesced in the air around them. The stench of spilt acetum and honey-beer was thick in the air, a sickly sweet tang that made Aurelia's eyes itch.

"Two rooms, if you have them," said Vassu, turning to sneer at the women. "Your very fuckin cheapest."

Muconia moved closer to him. "An how'd thee be payn fa these rooms? Wi the droblets from ya silver tongue?" She burst out into a thundercrack of laughter, as did the topers and women leaning nearby. Aurelia could feel their eyes on her. She stared back defiantly until each man and whore in turn dropped their gaze.

Vassu did not reply, but merely dipped his twisted fingers into the pocket of his cloak and pulled out a gold coin between his knuckles. He placed it in Muconia's palm. Rodius came up behind and addressed the innkeep.

"Show us to the rooms, please, Muconia. We are tired."

Muconia took in his missing hand, dirt-smudged face and the bitter red tint of his eyes. She jerked her chin for them to follow her, then took them round to a narrow staircase set into the wall behind a thick oaken countertop. She led them up a narrow staircase to the topmost storey of the tavern and along a narrow corridor lit by dim torches set in iron brackets. Icy gusts licked and spun through the corridor and sent the paltry torch flames guttering.

They were led to two rooms, one at the end of the corridor, and the other door set into the south wall next to it. Muconia nodded at them, then looked at the nummae in her hand.

"Commer dun for vittles whenever."

She walked back off down the corridor, shaking her head, the fiery plaits dancing in the dim light.

CHAPTER 28

Calidus woke just before dawn.

He knew it was approaching daybreak as the building was quiet, and the only sounds he could hear were the incessant thump of the wind against the timbers of his room, and the dim rumble of snoring from the room next to his.

He was aware that he was dry, and warm, and that the torn wound in his side had been cleaned and bandaged. He dimly remembered being fed some thick, foul-tasting broth that settled across his teeth and gums like oil and lay burning heavily in his guts.

But he felt better, stronger. He thought he was safe, for a while, though he could not remember how, or why, or even who he was supposed to be safe from. Occasionally he bethought himself back at his uncle's villa in Eboracum, the daffodil-yellow flare of daylight only minutes from cracking its way through the windows of his chamber and signalling all the youthful promise and joy of another unbroken day.

But a part of him knew that was fantasy; his reality now was pain, dirt and cold. And fear.

He lay back and slept, slept well and dreamt deeply and when he next woke, she was in the room with him. She sat at the end of his bunk, and gnawed at a piece of what looked like leather, twisting it into the side of her mouth and working it with her few remaining teeth, much as a hound would work a bone.

"Arite ther, yungun," she said. She was strangely ageless, though her face was ravaged and pale. Her hair was a cascade of fiery red, plaited so it fell down between her breasts. Calidus thought he knew her from somewhere, though he couldn't say where.

"Good morning," he replied.

The red-haired woman stopped gnawing at her meat, and looked at him carefully. She reached out a hand and put it against his brow.

"Yer better today, yungun."

"I feel better, "he replied. "Warmer. What happened? Who do I need to thank?"

"Na thanks." The woman waved it away with a flick of her arm. "You, yungun, don member me, do yis?"

He squinted at her, and shook his head slowly. "You...are familiar, I... I do remember you," he added quickly. "I am sure we've met, but.... I can't remember." He dropped his eyes to his coverlet.

"Yer frend brung yis in. Dark un, from the east. Ya left with a bad ed from the drunk."

Calidus nodded as the recollection clicked into place. "I remember. Atellus."

The woman nodded. "I owes him. Saved me. Saved many. Eers back, when the beasts from th' north poured through. Derk, derk days," she mused. "Will see em agin."

"Have you seen Atellus?" he asked, hope giving him enthusiasm. "Is he here?"

"I anna seen him since he were here wi you."

398

"Where...where was I?" said Calidus, trying to expel the swelling disappointment. "Did you—"

"Snorin cold in thoutside," she said. "All tummled in the snay. Bit later, you wunna be talking nae, yungun."

"I...I'm sorry, but I have no coin to pay for—"

The woman waved him away with the flick of her forearm. "Nairmind that. Stay. Stay til yer fit, an not before."

She got up to her feet and resumed chewing at her dried meat. "Ahll send Sennus up wi sum grub. Rest, yungun."

She walked out of his room, closing the door carefully behind her. Sennus arrived some time later, a tall broad man with an utterly inexpressive face punctuated by a huge raw-looking wound along his neck and lower jaw. He slapped a wooden bowl of slop onto the table at the foot of the bed and left without a word.

Calidus rose from the bed and drank down the contents of the bowl with a ferocious hunger. It tasted foul, still, and the consistency made his teeth itch, but it seemed nourishing, and the warmth in his belly made him feel like his strength was returning.

He went to sit down after finishing the potion, but the sound of voices made him move towards the door. There was a female voice, which spoke softly; he couldn't discern the words. Then a male voice, angry and aggressive.

He pushed the door to his room slightly ajar and peered out into the dim corridor.

The male voice was getting louder. As Calidus peeked out, the door at the end of the corridor burst open, swinging inwards, and an olive-skinned man of medium height and build stormed out, whipping the door shut behind him with a crash. Calidus ducked back away from his own door and heard the angry, heavy tread stomp past his door, and then the rhythmic thump of footsteps descending the wooden staircase.

He waited for a slow count of five breaths, then cracked his door open again. The door at the end of the corridor was slightly ajar, having slammed back from when the departing man had clattered it shut. He could hear another man's voice, pitched low, and a woman's voice which was high enough for him to discern certain words which piqued his curiosity: Eboracum…. the emperor…the beneficiarius….

Calidus quickly shook himself into his dry clothes which were layered across the foot of the bed, then opened his door and crept out into the corridor. He waited, listening for a while, and when he was sure that there was no sign of any immediate movement from either inside the room or on the steps behind him, he trod stealthily along the length of the corridor, towards the far room. The voices gained volume as he moved closer. Beneath him he could hear the dim rumble of laughter from the drinkers gathered in the tavern hall.

He stood beside the door, his heart seeming to beat too loudly, his breath fizzing from his lungs.

"–emperor do that?" said the soft male voice. "It doesn't make sense."

"There are skeins so tangled that even the emperor cannot know the extent," replied the female voice. Calidus tried to peer in through the crack between the wooden planks of the door and the rickety jamb, but all he could see was a portion of dimly lit timber wall, and the edge of what looked like a table. "But I apologise for being dishonest with you, Rodius."

There was a silence that stretched across the room and out into the corridor. Calidus edged away from the door when the man spoke again:

"If you trust me now, tell me all. From the beginning."

Calidus pressed himself closer and listened. Nothing existed for him but the door and the voices coming from the other side of it; he strained to hear every word, each dropped syllable, until he could see every gesture hinted at by the intonation as if the speakers were reciting in front of his eyes. He continued to listen, oblivious even to the footsteps thumping up the staircase behind him.

The blow to his buttocks drove Calidus forward through the door, sending it smashing open, and pitching him tumbling into the room where he fell sprawling over the bed.

The occupants leapt up, and the man was armed within the flick of an eyelid, Calidus feeling the cold blade of a sword pressing down against the nape of his neck.

"Stay down," said the man, his voice like the flecks of snow scraping the windowpane.

Calidus didn't move.

"Found him outside," said Vassu, entering the room and slamming the door shut behind him. "Little shit had an ear to the door." He spat onto the timber floorboards.

"Pick him up," said Crassa to Vassu. "And don't spit on the floor in our room. Do what you like in your own."

Vassu grumbled into his chest, but he walked through and hauled Calidus to his feet, spinning him roughly and frisking him with the flats of his palms. Satisfied that he carried no weapon, he forced him down onto the floor, and slapped him twice around the face with the backs of his knuckles.

"Who are you?" asked the woman.

401

Calidus looked around the room before settling his eyes on the woman opposite. There was a large, broad-shouldered man towering above him with a short blade in one hand, and his other ending in an ugly stump just above the wrist. The man who had earlier stormed out of the room was standing to his right, chewing something and wearing a face painted with fury and bile. His dark, narrow eyes were screwed tightly beneath dark curled hair. There was a girl, a few years shy of his own age, who sat on the bed and stared blankly and peaceably at him. And there was the woman sitting on a low stool opposite him. As he was slouched on the floor, she seemed to loom over him, though she was small and slender. He had the vague idea that he had seen her somewhere before.

"Lucius Clodius Bassianus Calidus," he said, working some saliva into his dry mouth. He had thought about giving a false name, but decided that his best chance of safety this far north would be to emphasise his connections with Apullius, the praefectus of the camp. His arse still ached from where the sallow man had kicked him, and he had fallen awkwardly on his elbow which throbbed angrily.

The woman's eyes tensed visibly at the sound of his name. "Why were you eavesdropping?"

Calidus looked around him uncertainly. "I...I heard you mention the name of a f... of someone I know."

"A friend?" smiled the woman, picking up on his error.

Calidus looked down noncommittally. "The beneficiarius imperatoris."

"And what is the beneficiarius to you?"

Calidus's mouth worked, but his brain couldn't function fast enough. Surely the wrong answer here would see him killed. As though picking up on his dilemma, the woman spoke again.

"Your only hope of surviving this night is to tell the truth," she said placidly. There was something about her delivery that told Calidus she was not bluffing. "And I will know if you are lying. Speak."

Calidus swallowed. "He...is my guardian. Was. Until I reach Stanwix."

"And where is he now?" asked the woman, her eyes visibly softening but her voice if anything even more tense.

"I don't know."

The woman sighed. "You are nephew of Brocchus, praetor of Britannia Secunda?"

Calidus nodded; a small part of him was proud that his name had been recognised so far north.

Vassu whistled. "We could ransom this little ferret for a lifetime's worth of gold."

"There will be no ransom," said the woman tersely, then turned to Calidus and softened her voice. "What did you overhear? Be honest, and I may be able to help you. If you lie...I will leave you to Vassu." She nodded towards the dark-haired man with the twisted face, who grinned in recognition.

The woman stood up from her stool and her presence and force seemed to dominate the room; of a sudden, her bearing and carriage were noble, as though she had unfurled her regality into the room by rising to her feet. She offered her hand to Calidus, and he reached out and took it. It was clear to him who was in charge of this group, and where the authority lay.

She gently guided Calidus to his feet then led him over to the bed, where he sat beside the vacant girl who – it seemed to him – was somehow both there and not there at the same time.

"I heard," said Calidus, "that you work for the emperor. That there is a plot for rebellion. Here in the north."

"You work for the emperor?" said Vassu, the words catching in his throat.

The lady nodded. "Vassu," she said, her words spoken in a tone which was used to giving orders. "Fetch some wine from downstairs; good wine. And some meats, if Muconia has such."

Vassu looked a moment at the woman who spoke to him, and then he departed wordlessly. The one-handed man relaxed and re-sheathed his old sword, and lowered himself into a high-backed chair at the foot of the bed. The woman seemed to be lost in thought. There was only the crackle of wood in the small fire at the heel of the room, and the spit and scratch of the snow against the window glass.

Vassu returned shortly with a large stone flask of wine and two plates of cold meats.

"Cost a fair fuckin haul too," he grumbled, setting the wine and food on the table which sat between the two beds. "Who's payin for this luxury, hm?"

"Sit down," said the woman. She walked up and poured out a spill of wine into a beaten copper goblet which was also on the table. She took a sip from this and handed it to Calidus. He took a sip and passed it on to the one-handed man. The wine was sweet, but not overly so. It reminded Calidus of some of the vinum from his uncle's cellars, the kind that flowed freely over those languid and heavy formal repasts of so long ago.

"This is Rodius, and this Vassu," she said to Calidus gesturing at each of the men in turn. "They know me as Crassa, but that is not my name." She moved over to check that there was no-one outside in the corridor before continuing. "I am Aurelia Augusta. I was the wife of Mettius Marius Crispus, ab epistulis to the praetor of Britannia secunda."

Calidus recognised her now; he had seen her at just such formal dinners with his uncle. Crispus was the slick and authoritative eminence in which his uncle seemed to have a little too much faith; the man always made Calidus feel uncomfortable, though whether that was his knowledge and air of superiority, or something more sinister, he couldn't be sure.

But the ab epistulis's wife had changed from when he had last seen her; she seemed to have aged a decade in those intervening months. Maybe he had aged too, Calidus reminded himself, as she had no sooner recognised he than the other way round. Her face was sterner, harder somehow, yet no less regal then he remembered. Her eyes seemed brighter and wilder, and her hair darker and heavier. She looked thinner too, gaunter, and the set of her shoulders and crease of her brow betrayed the presence of a heavy burden of weariness.

"What I am about to say," continued Aurelia, "will put your lives in danger; it makes us bound together in a manner stronger than any physical tether. It also puts my future and safety in the hands of each of you. By telling you this, I show that I trust you.

"If anyone wishes to leave," she continued, "they may do so now, and seek their destiny. If you stay, we stay together. Until you die, or until I give you freedom to leave."

"You are the whore Crassa to me," snarled Vassu. "What makes you think you can order *me*? A stretched-out bint like you?" He spat wildly onto the floor, the phlegm coloured dark red by the wine. "You think you can tell me what I can and can't do? I could snap your fucking neck like a chicken's!"

Calidus noticed the one called Vassu was practically red with anger, his face sour and contorted, spittle dancing from his lips with each word. He gave off a sinister hum of energy and malevolence which Calidus had rarely seen before.

Aurelia looked calmly at Vassu as he stood trembling, his bent fingers quivering by his sides. She walked over to him softly, so she was looking up to him, her head barely reaching the bridge of his nose. Yet somehow, noticed Calidus, some trick of the light or other effect made it look as though Aurelia were looking *down* at Vassu. She seemed larger, somehow, as though her genius had leapt from her breast and was towering over the stained face of the man.

"Listen to me, Vassu," said Aurelia, softly. "Your life is mine. If it wasn't for me, you would be dying with a rope round your neck whilst the brigands cut hunks of meat from you every time they needed food." Vassu winced at the recollection. "There were times on the road when I stood over you as you slept and considered plunging your brother's sword into your neck. I thought it would be simpler for me. Simpler for us. I wasn't sure whether you could be trusted."

Vassu swallowed heavily, the ball of his throat bobbing beneath the dark, days-old stubble.

"I wondered whether you were worth sparing," Aurelia continued. Her voice was pitched low, and quiet, yet each person in the room could hear each syllable she uttered as though she were declaiming it from a grand hall. "Whether the foulness and hate and bitterness were a shroud beneath which were the bones of a decent man. A man of honour. A man who could *fight*. I gave you the benefit of my doubt, Vassu, and I spared you."

Aurelia moved away from Vassu then, and held her hand out for the cup of wine, which Rodius was holding. He topped it up from the jug and handed it over. Aurelia took a sip and looked over to Vassu again, who was unable to meet her eyes. He looked wilted, and his eyes were no longer tight with anger, but open and pained.

"I have destroyed many greater, tougher, men than you, Vassu," she continued. "Sometimes with my own hands; sometimes through agents. But for your sake, and ours, stop your endless threats and your foul jibes. I am bored of them. Scurry off with your tail tucked against your manhood, if you will, and carry on your whore-mongering elsewhere.

"But if you speak of this," she continued, "or of me, to anyone, know that you will not live to see the next summer." She laughed, an unpleasant, cold noise that sent a ripple of fear up Calidus's spine, and took another sip from the copper goblet, speaking to the room: "Perhaps none of us will anyway."

Calidus looked at Vassu expectantly; the sallow man's mouth worked, as if he were trying to respond, and he stood in the room, seeming unusually exposed and ungainly. After a pause, he sat down on the short stool, and turned his eyes to the floor.

"I served at court under Julian," said Aurelia, as if there had been no interruption, "and stayed on for Jovian. By the time Valentinian came to power, I was well respected within the palace. I was made an agent in rebus under Valentinian, and was soon his most loyal confidante. He entrusted me with many roles, across the years. My most onerous, was being installed in proximity to the governor of Britannia Secunda, and having to marry a vile weasel of a man named Mettius Marius Crispus.

"It was imperative to Valentinian that I gained the trust of the province's inner circle, as fast as possible and I realised that marrying the ab epistulis was the quickest and most convenient means of doing it. Once there, I had access to the regional network of agents."

Aurelia lowered her voice, took another sip of wine, then passed the goblet over to Vassu. He looked up at her with a quiet, becalmed gaze, and took a deep draught. He handed it over to his brother, who did the same before the drink landed with Calidus. There was a small amount of wine left, and he offered it to the girl who sat on the bed. She stared ahead without acknowledging him, and Aurelia guided the cup from his proffered hand towards his own mouth. He drank and finished the wine.

"There has long been mixed information coming from Britannia," she continued. "It has always been a volatile area. All the limes are sensitive points. There is often talk of rebellion in the north."

Rodius seemed to nod, as if in recognition, but Calidus shook his head. "My patruus cannot–"

"Brocchus has never been implicated," said Aurelia, with a lopsided smile. "Except, perhaps, by wilful ignorance." She laid a hand on Calidus's shoulder. "You need not worry that helping me will be detrimental to your uncle.

"My husband is an ambitious man," Aurelia continued. "He was ostensibly the point of contact for the agents and informers on the Wall. In actuality, he wasn't. He was fed enough sterile information to make him believe that he was, but knowledge in the hands of a man like Crispus will always be a threat to the emperor. Instead, all reports came to me, unbeknownst to the ab epistulis. I scanned them and wrote reports for Valentinian. But one day, by ill chance, Crispus intercepted a message."

Aurelia moved over to the tray of salted meat, and plucked a piece up. She tossed it casually into her mouth and chewed, then washed it back with a fresh cup of wine which she again handed round the assembly. She moved over to the door to check again that there was no-one listening outside, and then resumed, her voice even lower than before.

"I had a few trusted men – and women – who could carry messages between the Wall and Eboracum. One of these was travelling as part of a merchant caravan when they were attacked by brigands. My contact managed to survive but was badly wounded. When he reached the city, he was raving about his message and needing to speak urgently to me. The notion of delivering his intelligence had probably kept the man alive throughout the rest of the journey. He died soon afterwards. But not before Crispus's men had reported back to him. The body was searched, and the message found."

Aurelia seemed to take a huge breath, her eyes clouding over with the effort of the telling. Her voice remained steady and soft.

"He asked me about the note, and when I refused to betray my source, he had me imprisoned, and tortured. I am ashamed to admit," and here her voice cracked a little, "that under the agonies of the treatment, I gave him the name of my contact in Aesica, from whom the message originated. He drugged me and kept me prisoner in his quarters, where I suffered constant abuse at the hands of his men. I have no doubt he would have killed me, once he had squeezed all the information he needed from me. He is a very ambitious man. And very, very dangerous.

"I escaped and fled, under disguise from Eboracum, with help from you, of course." Here she nodded at Rodius and Vassu. "Foremost in my mind was the need to get to Aesica, by any means possible, and warn my contact that he was known to the ab epistulis. There could be few worse men in the empire to be in possession of such a secret."

"The information he gave you," said Rodius, "was to do with insurrection. Rebellion. Is that correct?"

Aurelia nodded. "It was. And the danger is complete, as I see it. If Crispus manages to interrogate the agent, he will find out about the planned rebellion. Knowing Crispus, he will do whatever it takes to benefit himself with this knowledge;

it is my belief that he will commandeer a force of the legate at Eboracum and march north with the intention of quashing the rebellion. He would naturally assume that this would put him in the emperor's favour, and with a legion at his back, he could quite reasonably assume praetorship of Britannia secunda. There would be little Brocchus could do to stop him."

Calidus gasped at this, and felt his fingers clenching into fists.

"And would that be so terrible?" asked Vassu, without looking up.

"I am sorry you have to hear this, Calidus," she said, turning to him with a gentle look in her eyes, "but if he succeeded, Vassu, then no, it would not be so terrible for Britannia. At least, not at first. Strong leadership is severely lacking here, and Crispus can certainly mimic some of the superficial qualities of a leader. But," she said, shaking her head, "he will not succeed. All he will do is force the hand of the rebels, and make them act earlier than our reports suggest. Crispus has no concept of the size and organisation of this incursion. This has been planned for years. They would crush Crispus, and his legion. Our only hope, for Britannia to remain unfragmented is to stall, and hinder the final push of the rebels. This will give Valentinian time to free up a force of comitatenses from the Attacotti defence in Gaul so that they can match the force and crush the incursion.

"Anything else," she concluded, "will end badly for Britannia. I am quite sure of it."

"What of Atellus?" asked Calidus. "He is beneficiarius imperatoris. Does he know nothing of this? I thought he was sent here on a mission to find some missing children."

Vassu laughed and covered it with a grumble.

"Yes," said Aurelia, looking up at Calidus with her crisp blue eyes. "Yes Atellus is here to investigate the missing and the dead. The emperor sent him here to do just that. The missing ones – and it is not just children that the beneficiarius seeks – are linked with the rebellion. I do not doubt for a second that Titus Faenius Magnus Atellus is aware of that by now. Valentinian sent him here for two reasons: firstly, as a decoy to conjure up the illusion that the emperor was interested in matters no deeper than the death of a few youngsters, to deflect any attention from my own operations. And secondly for a reason that is known only to Atellus and the emperor himself. And Atellus himself," she added mysteriously, "may not know fully know, yet."

Aurelia seemed to shake herself, and then her keen eyes flashed and sparked with energy once more as she turned to Calidus.

"Where did you last see Atellus?" she asked.

"In the fort," said Calidus. "I was in the valetudinarium. He came to tell me he was leaving to visit the milefort to the west. I had to escape from the fort not long after that. I do not know if he has returned."

"He may not return," said Aurelia, sadly. "And you are injured, and talk of escape. What is your story, Lucius Clodius?"

Calidus related all that had happened to him since arriving at Aesica, finishing with how the landlady of the tavern had dragged him in from the snow and certain death, and fed and warmed him back to health.

"She's a whore to her tailbone, Muconia," nodded Vassu. "But she's soft inside."

"What now?" asked Rodius, reaching for dried meat from the plate that was being handed round. "What do *we* do here?"

411

Aurelia looked up at him, and Rodius almost flinched under the force of her gaze. "We become shades. Unseen, unnoticed. We blend in to the vicus. Keep away from soldiers, from merchants. I will try to find my contact, Densligneus. We will see if we can find trace of the beneficiarius, if possible. Beyond us in this room, and Atellus, we must presume that everyone else is an agent of Crispus's, or else involved in the rebellion."

"I have seen no sign of rebellion," said Calidus. "Just filthy, hungry, desperate people. And half-mad limitanei."

Vassu sneered. "What would you know, boy? You've been north for a handful of days."

"For many moons there has been a different mood on the Wall," agreed Rodius slowly, pensively. He looked at Calidus. "Hungry, desperate people are exactly the type to rebel. They have nothing to lose, and everything to gain."

"You say rebellion," spoke Calidus, addressing Aurelia, "and a big one. How many people are we talking?"

She looked at him squarely. "Everything north of the Wall."

Vassu coughed, and blew his nose into his hand.

"Every man and child who can hold a weapon will descend unopposed as far as Eboracum. We need to ensure the emperor's forces are mobilised before that happens." She looked at each of them in turn. "The future of Britannia hangs by a hair."

"Fuck Britannia," coughed Vassu, looking up at Aurelia. "I fight for myself, and my things. Not the emperor and all his gold and whores and slaves."

"Fight for whatever is important to you," dismissed Aurelia, dropping her level gaze on Vassu. "But fight you will, when the time comes."

CHAPTER 29

The air was full of roars; of pain, of anger, of desperation, of exertion. And the sky rang with the clash of metal: on metal, on wood, on flesh. A wild, haunting swelling surge of pain, like all the thunder in the world, was coalescing and flailing around Atellus's skull.

It was the noise of battle.

He was there, in the midst of the carnage, his face and arms sticky with blood, his hair plastered to his scalp with blood and sweat. Overhead hissed with the ominous whistle of arrows, and the screaming bellow of onagers in action. He could hear the sinister whine and thump of ballistae from the battlements towering like sheer cliffs overhead.

There was shade where they fought, and for that he was thankful.

But still, Atellus knew that something was missing.

He stood amongst the chaos, amidst the dead and maimed and mutilated, his ankles deep in pools of blood and viscera beneath him. He could see Petronia and Faenia above, on the battlements, reaching over. Their visages were masks of hate as they poured scorching naphtha onto his upturned face.

He screamed and howled at the heat of the burning; his hands, his lips, his eyes.

But the pain was cold and the sound of his own screams and the roar of the battle was only the howl and chant of the winter wind.

Atellus fought to open his eyes, which were frosted shut.

He focused his vision and looked around, seeing only dark cringing trees and the endless ocean of snow.

But then there were hands grasping him and slapping his face. And he felt himself being hauled up, up, and onto the back of a beast, which a small part of him thought was one of the war-elephants of the eastern wastes, even as another voice in his head told him it was a merely a horse. He was unable to resist even if he had known what it was he was fighting against.

Atellus was aware of the rhythmic thump of hooves and the swaying jolt of the landscape unfurling itself around him, the cold clapping his cheeks as he bounced through the air.

He heard a voice, but the words it spoke made no sense to him, and soon the whiteness grew so intense it became a blackness which swallowed him.

***

When he woke again, it was dry and warm, and dark. He could hear a fire crackling contentedly nearby, and he could smell the sharp odour of red meat and spices. He sensed that he was lying on his side, and opened his eyes.

He could see a large man sitting cross-legged on a reed mat next to a fire which he was prodding vigorously with the edge of a sheer, narrow sword. The man looked over to Atellus, sensing that he was conscious.

"You mind if I play, chap?" he asked, and without waiting for an answer, the man picked up a darkwood lyre from where it leaned against the wall beside him, and he strummed a chord. Not satisfied, he squinted and fiddled with the tuning pegs until the sheepgut strings resonated in harmony.

The stranger sung a long bass threnody, his voice low and mingling with the rush of the wind outside. For the first time Atellus noticed Barbarus, his comrade's hands and feet bound, lying on his side. His eyes were open and wild and he sobbed heavily, the breaths seeming to be torn painfully from his lungs.

The lyrist stopped his lament, his large fingers tumbling across the strings of the instrument before coming to a stop. He cleared his throat and put the lyre back against the wall beside him.

"A good one that, chaps, eh?" he spoke. "Yes." He resumed prodding the fire with his sword.

Atellus tried to move and found that his hands were not bound like Barbarus's were. He slowly shuffled himself up into a sitting position and gingerly looked around him whilst he waited for the dizziness to abate. He appeared to be in some sort of rude shelter which looked like a cave. There were indications of homeliness: a fire-pit, a short table of stout wood, some reed mats, a large wooden chest, and piles of blankets and furs. There were also niches carved into the walls inside which were stored jars and herbs, and cuts of salted and smoked meat. Atellus saw iron brackets set into the walls, inside which burned short torches which gave off a queer odour. To his right, the far inner ends of the cave were too dark to discern anything. To his left, Atellus could hear the storm raging outside: there were huge folds of leather hanging down across what he presumed to be the cave entrance, which were weighted at the bottom with trussed stones. The leathers crumpled and thumped under the violence of the elements.

The singer was squatting but his dimensions betrayed his height. He was older than Atellus, with a round, slightly jowly weathered face, crossed with creases and folds of leathery flesh and old puckered scars. There were faded red tattoos across his forehead and left cheek, and on the backs of his hands. His short hair was a bright white colour, and looked brittle, as though stiffened with dye. His clothing was a mass of layered leather and furs, in the manner of the tribes – winter ranging clothing – though he spoke perfect Latin. He scratched under his clothes frequently.

"Who are you?" asked Atellus, finding his voice. His limbs felt deathly cold, and his toes and fingers ached, but he could detect a delicate warmth slowly creeping through his body. His face stung from the cuts and bruises and his eyes felt too big for their sockets. The wound from the caltrop was a dull throb running up from the sole of his foot and into his crotch. He thought that the cold was keeping off the worst of the pain.

"Who am I?" was the reply. "Who are any of us, easterner? Well," he laughed, still staring into the fire, "you are Titus Faenius Magnus Atellus, beneficiarius imperatoris. He," he jerked his skull back at the weeping and moaning figure of Barbarus, "appears to be an escaped convict scum." The figure spat into the fire, which hissed back in response. "And I? Who am I?"

He turned to look at Atellus for the first time. One of his eyes was half shut, the lid pulled down by an old scar, and the iris underneath was a cloudy white.

"I am Marcus Constantius Drustanus."

"You are Roman?" asked Atellus.

"I am, Roman," came the answer, followed by a short low laugh. "As Roman as you, indeed. As Roman as the backs of the emperor's bollocks."

"How do you know who I am?" Atellus rubbed feeling back into his arms, and the backs of his legs.

"Know? *Ha!* We all know about you, beneficiarius."

"You are a soldier?"

"I am Arcanus," replied Drustanus.

Atellus knew of the Arcanae: tough and merciless men, hardy inhabitants of the north, in the pay of Rome, who ranged back and forth beyond the limes and passed intelligence back to their paymasters.

"Who do you report to?" asked Atellus. "Who pays you?"

Drustanus looked at him for a while, and pulled his blade out of the fire. The end glowed red in the dim cave.

"Those are two, separate questions, beneficiarius," came the reply. "I report to Fullofaudes. My pay comes from an agreed collection agent."

"You are a long way east," said Atellus.

"We Arcanae are always a long way from everywhere," he said, then emitted his low laugh that seemed to rumble in unison with the storm outside.

"It seems I owe you my life, Drustanus," said Atellus. "And you have my sincere thanks."

"That you do, beneficiarius," he replied. "And him." He jerked a thumb over towards Barbarus.

"I request that you release him," said Atellus. "He is bereaved and has been treated coarsely. I can vouch for his intentions."

Drustanus eyed Atellus warily. "You have both taken a battering, by the looks of it."

The Arcanus then got up and shuffled across to where the convict lay on the floor, weeping into his chest. Drustanus loosed Barbarus's bonds, but the convict lay insensate, lost in his own grief. Drustanus sat down again by the fire, and began prodding the flames with his sword. There was silence in the cave, broken only by the call of the storm outside, and the crackle of the fire within.

After a while, Drustanus laid down his sword and took the pot from where it hung from a cross branch placed between two crotch sticks either side of the flame. He looked into it, then crumbled a few dried herbs inside. He added some red powder poured from an earthenware pot, and spooned the concoction into three separate bowls. He handed one over to Atellus, and placed the other beside Barbarus.

Atellus took the proffered bowl, and eyed it warily. Drustanus saw this, and deliberately slurped up a mouthful of the broth.

"If I wanted you dead, beneficiarius," he said, "you would never have woken." Then he laughed and tipped more stew into his mouth. It trickled down his mouth and over his chin onto his chest. "But if you do not want it, then I will gladly have it."

Atellus tasted the soup: it was rich and salty and hot. Small hunks of meat bobbed up to the surface, possibly rabbit. He took another swallow and soon he was tipping it into his mouth as Drustanus had done. It seemed to send warmth radiating out from his belly and into his extremities.

"Barbarus," said Atellus, looking across at the convict. "Eat. For strength."

Barbarus ignored him. The sobs had stopped now, and there was only a glazed emptiness in the man's eyes.

"Is he touched?" asked Drustanus, frowning at the man, but addressing Atellus. "He seemed more lucid earlier."

"His watched his woman murdered by limitanei," said Atellus.

Drustanus frowned and pursed his lips. "I should hand him in to the nearest garrison," he finally said, wiping the inside of the bowl with his large fingers and licking them noisily.

"Which is where?" asked Atellus. "Where are we?"

"Indeed, we are around five leagues north of the Wall. The nearest fort would be Aesica. There used to be a skeleton garrison on the milefort at Culuslupi, but not for some years."

"No more talk of handing this man in," said Atellus, meeting the Arcanus's eye and shaking his head gently. "He fought beside me, against my assailants. He is more friend to me now than any man north of Eboracum. Do you understand?"

Drustanus returned Atellus's level look. "Absolutely, benficiarius. If you vouch for the man, then I trust him as I would the emperor himself." He smiled.

"My thanks," sighed Atellus. "You will be rewarded for your efforts." He put his bowl down on the ground. "What do you know, Drustanus?"

"Know? Too much, I'd say." He laughed.

"About me," pressed Atellus.

"I found the convict on patrol," he nodded towards Barbarus. "I was on my way here to escape the storm when I chanced upon him. He was dead-tired and desperate and raving about meeting someone. I did a few short circles, and found you in the shelter. I would have moved on without a second thought had I not caught glance of your cloak from beneath the snow. Fortuna obviously smiles on you, easterner."

Atellus rubbed the caltrop wound on his foot. "Clearly."

Drustanus put his bowl down, and stood, hunched slightly because of the cave's low roof. He scratched angrily under his clothes. "Damned lice. You'd hope the cold would kill the buggers. But no." He scratched again. "I need to check on Drufax, then we can talk at length. Please, treat my cave as if it were your home." He sketched a half-mocking bow.

"Drufax?" said Atellus with a raised eyebrow.

"My horse," replied Drustanus. He walked over to the leather flaps at the cave mouth, and removed two of the stones with which they were weighted down. The wind pummelled the skins back and forth as it grew louder, and the icy air and spits of snow howled their way into the cave. Atellus shivered.

Drustanus left the cave and the sound of the elements was again muted.

"Don't trust him."

Atellus turned to Barbarus, who was now sitting upright, and licking the soup from the bowl. His eyes were red and swollen with tears. He looked like a ragged-haired skeleton upon which hung the threads of desperately soiled clothes. Atellus could see that the tips of his fingers were dark with nigrum.

"What?"

"Don't trust him," spat Barbarus. "He is Arcanus, the scum." His words finished in a fit of coughing.

Atellus looked at Barbarus questioningly before speaking. "I have heard mixed reports of the wanderers," he said, "from when I was last here. There have always been those who thought they were too similar to the northern tribes. But that is part of their role. They need to be discreet when roving."

Barbarus spat. "Traitors, all," he sneered. "How did he know about us?" He jerked his head in the direction of the cave mouth. "What are the chances of him stumbling upon us both? In such a storm, and such an area? He will hand us over to the animals as soon as he can."

The convict fell silent and busied himself with his broth, interrupted only by coughing and the occasional wheeze from deep within his chest. Atellus removed his boot carefully and inspected his caltrop wound. He limped out to the door and fetched some crushed snow which he placed in his empty food bowl. He rinsed out the dregs of his meal, then refilled the bowl and used it to wash his wound.

Drustanus returned, signalled by the swelling rage of the storm from outside. He replaced the stones on the entrance drapes and stomped inside. His clothes were plastered with snow and his flesh was red and chapped.

"It is fresh out there, ha! By Jove, it is evil weather." He shrugged out of his thick cloak, and laid it beside the cooking fire, then piled more logs on the flames. The light and heat dulled briefly before exploding with a new vitality as they devoured the fresh fuel. "I think we have a few more hours before it passes. Then it shall be fine."

"Do you have any embrocation for wounds?" asked Atellus.

Drustanus came over and looked at his foot, squinting in the dim light. He moved into the corner of the cave and from a niche in the wall produced a small glass vial containing a fine powder.

"This will help," he said. He tipped some of the powder into Atellus's bowl and added a little snow until it formed a paste. "Put it on the wound."

Atellus did as he was told. It stung on contact, but then a warm feeling spread through his foot and up his leg. Drustanus produced some cloth from another niche and rinsed it in water which he warmed over the fire. Once it was dry, he wrapped it around Atellus's wound, and tied it off.

"Thank you," said Atellus. The Arcanus mumbled an acknowledgement, then went into a dark corner and pulled out a delicate thin bone pipe, with a carved wooden stapple and bowl. He settled himself cross-legged on one of the reed mats, then broke up a fine dried leaf and thumbed it into the bowl. He lit it with a taper from the fire and puffed contentedly on it a few times until the bowl glowed a warm red. He offered it to Barbarus.

"Coltsfoot," explained Drustanus. "Good for the chest. Especially in this weather, of course."

Barbarus took the pipe and inhaled deeply, coughing. After a few breaths, his lungs seemed calmer. He offered it on to Atellus, who waved it away.

"It helps with sleep too," said Drustanus. "Sometimes it can be hard to clear the mind before laying down."

Atellus nodded. "Maybe I will try some."

Drustanus smiled and handed the pipe over. Atellus took a few breaths, and coughed them out again.

"Slowly," said the Arcanus. "Be gentle. Sip the smoke. Breathe it deep into the lungs."

Atellus's second attempt was more successful. He handed the pipe back, and leant against the cool wall of the cave.

"Quite a place, isn't it?" said Drustanus, gesturing around him. "Maybe our ancestors weren't so foolish after all. The temperature is the same in the heights of summer or depths of winter. A little fire like this can soon warm the whole cave. And practically invisible from the outside, unless you knew what you were looking for."

"It's functional," nodded Atellus.

"I suppose you are used to the quilted chambers and smooth concubines of the imperial palace, eh, beneficiarius?" He laughed and spat out a thick plume of smoke.

"What do you know of the garrison at Aesica?" said Atellus, ignoring the jibe.

"Aesica?" said Drustanus, his laugh stopping abruptly. "I don't often have call to go to Aesica. They are quite insular. Many of the forts are, in these rough days. They are hungry men, a little odd."

"They sacrifice to the old gods," said Atellus.

"I have heard stories," nodded Drustanus.

"Children."

Drustanus paused in his smoking, and looked into the thick blue smoke curling up from the bowl. The wisps seemed ethereal in the strange firelight, and the shapes writhed in the subtle draughts from outside.

"I have heard strange stories of the men of Aesica," said the Arcanus after a while. "Many of us have. From the other forts, from the villages to the north. They are isolated, secluded. Threatened from south and north; even from the west, in days not long past. They are distant from Fullofaudes' eye. But they are no worse than some other forts along the Wall. The limes are dangerous. Add to that the starvation and the pestilence, the poverty.... You have desperate men. Very desperate," he repeated, nodding to himself.

"Desperate men make Valentinian nervous," said Atellus.

"As well they should," replied Drustanus.

"What does Fullofaudes make of it?"

"Ha! What can the dux do?" Drustanus took another mouthful of smoke, and leisurely exhaled, sending it writhing up towards the roof of the cave. "Fullofaudes has his hands full of raids and brigands and remilitarising after Constantius ripped the innards out of the garrisons. He gets emissaries from Aesica, and the other central forts. They give him the news he wants to hear. Fullofaudes is a good leader," he finished, after exhaling another mouthful of Coltsfoot. "But he is only one man."

"I believe," said Atellus, "that the limitanei of Aesica have killed an agent in rebus working for the emperor. They tried to kill me, which is why you found me in the condition you did."

His words were answered by the wind buffeting the cave mouth.

"These are serious allegations, beneficiarius," said Drustanus, after a solemn sip from his pipe. "But I do not doubt that you speak the truth. I am not surprised," he finished.

Atellus inclined his head slightly.

"I can escort you to Stanwix," said Drustanus after a pause filled by the crackling fire and sough of the wind outside. "You can report directly to Fullofaudes, if you like?"

The beneficiarius shook his head. "I need to return to Aesica. I have a charge there whose safety I need to guarantee. And I need more details about what is going on there."

"They will butcher you, easterner," said Barbarus from the midst of his silence. Drustanus looked at him through a pall of pipe-smoke before turning back to Atellus.

"The convict is right," said the Arcanus. "They will finish what they started. Surely the risk is too great?"

"I will go in disguise," replied Atellus. "A merchant, a refugee, whichever. There is more I need to uncover. My work there is not yet done."

Barbarus shook his head slowly.

"Then," said Drustanus, "I will escort you on horse as far as Aesica. The limitanei would be looking for two men on foot, not a man accompanied by a ranger. And with that limp, you would be lucky to cover ten miles a day before you collapsed."

Atellus considered the suggestion before speaking. Drustanus smoked and Barbarus looked at the pulse of life in his wrists.

"Thank you," said Atellus. "I accept your offer."

Drustanus nodded as though the matter were sealed. "And what of him?"

Atellus looked over at Barbarus. "I could use an ally, if you are interested?"

The convict looked up. His eyes were thick and glazed with grief; the dim light of the cave seemed to suit his sensitive vision, as he was no longer squinting. "I must return to...to Flavia. To... say farewell." He lowered his gaze, and his head. "Justa facere. She must be allowed to rest."

Atellus nodded. "Then you must go."

426

"Culuslupi is twelve miles southeast of here," said Drustanus. "Travel by darkness and you should reach it unopposed."

Barbarus nodded.

"Half a mile east of the milefort there is a discoloured piece of masonry in the bottom of the Wall. Scrape at the ground beneath this and you will find it is hollow. There is a narrow tunnel where, with effort, a man could pass through to the other side."

Barbarus nodded his thanks, his face still lowered to the ground.

***

They slept well, in the warmth and under skins provided by the Arcanus. The fire provided sufficient heat, and Drustanus woke twice in the night to replenish the logs and keep the cave at a comfortable temperature. Atellus and Barbarus, destroyed by weariness, slept through the night and beyond daybreak. When they woke, there was no sign of the Arcanus, but a low fire was still burning in the cave. The sound of the storm pummelling the land was gone, and there was a fine light spilling through the gaps in the drapes at the cave-mouth.

Atellus went to look outside. The weather was sharp and crisp and still. The land was muffled with a heavy cloak of bright white snow which seemed to glow in the sunrise.

"What is your story?" asked Atellus after he returned and sat opposite Barbarus.

"My story?" said Barbarus, in his deep voice. He coughed angrily, deep wracking wheezes tugged from the bottom of his lungs. When it subsided, he continued. "A tale of woe and grief, easterner. I would not bore you with the details."

"We have nothing else to do, for the moment."

"We should leave before he returns," said Barbarus. "With *friends*."

"You still do not trust him?"

Barbarus shook his head. "I have heard and seen too much of the Arcanae to last me many lifetimes."

Atellus sighed and unwrapped the bandages from around his foot, then bent down to inspect his wound. It seemed better, and did not throb as much. His face felt covered with welts and cuts, though there was no looking-glass or water in which he could see his reflection. Judging from Barbarus's mess of blood and scabs and swellings, he imagined he looked not too dissimilar.

"I fought here, before," said Barbarus. "On the Wall."

"You were a limitanei?"

"I was," he replied. "Stationed in Germania, on the limes of the Rhenus. I was transferred to Britannia after a brawl. A bad one; the other man never woke from his injuries. From here I fought countless times against the northerners."

"Were you there under Lupicinus for the incursion?"

Barbarus nodded. "I saw many die, so many good men. We were at Onnum when our scouts reported a horde approaching. Half our number had fled, the rest were riddled with disease, or maimed. We would be outnumbered four to one, at least. They had the momentum." His eyes, squinting once more as the natural light seeped into the cave, seemed dull and introverted.

"We were ranged along the Wall," he continued, "laughing and weeping from fear, drinking. Not a man there was sober. Wives and children were long gone. Men

428

disappeared like shades in the night, flitting off never to be seen again. When the enemy came, they had broken through at Vercovicium, but we never got any message until they were upon us, behind us.

"The destruction was total. I saw them driving through the hindmost. No quarter given. We would have been the same." He shrugged, and shook his head wearily. "I fled. I sheathed my sword and ran from my friends, with the sound of their slaughter behind me, chasing me. Their screams have been echoing through my chest ever since, coward that I am."

Atellus shook his head. "You were caught and convicted for desertion then?"

Barbarus nodded. "After the tribes had been driven back, and the breaches in the Wall fixed, there were detachments sent out to search for deserters. Many were killed, as brigands. I headed for Londinium on foot. The journey was evil and hard, but I deserved it. I was turned in by a family I laboured for on the banks of the Tamesis – I made no secret of my past, and think I willed to be found. I did not fight. It was a relief to be taken. I thanked my betrayers before I was dragged away."

"I had a command during the battle," said Atellus, unable to keep the contempt from his voice. "I would have had you executed on the spot and strung up as a warning, your guts hanging for the carrion."

Barbarus nodded sadly, unable to meet the other's eyes. "And I would have agreed with you. I despised myself: a coward. A dog. I abandoned my comrades, my friends." He lifted up a large hand and flexed it in front of his narrowed eyes, coughing as he did so. "I was sentenced to be executed, but it was commuted by the governor. Britannia had lost too many with Constantius; we could not afford to slaughter our own, he had proclaimed. I remember it being read out to me; bits stuck in my head. I was numb. I didn't feel anything at the time. It was the same to me whether I lived or died."

"You were sent to the mines?" said Atellus. "That is worse than death, some would say."

"And they are right," said Barbarus, the stress evident in his voice. "I was branded and tattooed as a coward and deserter and sent to Dumnonia where daily I laboured until I dropped. Sometimes I felt as though I were pushing myself to see whether I could make myself die. But my body would not give in. Instead I woke after scant hours sleep and plunged down into the caverns of the netherworld once more, getting closer to Pluto each day, until I could feel the warmth of his breath on my eyeballs.

"Day nor night existed," continued the convict, "nor feelings. I worked hard and grew strong. The foremen realised I was good. They fed me more so I could last longer and mine more tin. I saw comrades drop around me, dying of starvation, of illness, of bloodlung and rockfalls. There was no point in forming friendships, even had I been inclined. The same face was rarely with me for more than a few shifts.

"Then I was transferred to the deep mines of Hibernia." Barbarus rubbed the wounds on his face with his hand. His hair was long and lank and greasy from sweat and blood and dirt. "I volunteered for the hardest jobs. I wanted to crush myself, to end the pain, to torture myself for my cowardice. I was determined never to be scared, never to flinch from danger. Never to give men cause to call me a coward. Never again to have reason to loathe my own company.

"After winters and summers," he spoke, "I was trusted and made a foreman. I sometimes had to report to the estate owners on the edge of the mines. That was how I met Flavia. Or Barita, as she was then called: a slave girl. Her master Pusonius was a worthless worm of a man, who abused her and crushed her daily. She brought me bread and meat which she stole from the kitchens. She risked so much for me."

Barbarus collapsed into silent tears. Only the shine in his eyes and the rapid heaving of his huge, emaciated chest betrayed the torment inside. He finished with a hacking coughing fit which dissolved into wheezing breaths drawn in as though through a thick gauze.

"I knew that I needed her," said Barbarus, when he recovered his breath. "To survive. And she needed me. I escaped that night and broke into the villa of the landowner, that rat Pusonius. I took her with me and we fled by night, hiding in the mountains, hunting hare and rustling sheep. We decided to flee to Arbeia, and work passage by boat to Gaul. We travelled slightly away from the Wall, but matching its course; to follow it was safer than going by other roads, yet we needed to keep far enough away so we weren't seen by the limitanei. We got as far as you saw.

"And now," he said quietly, his voice barely a whisper dulled by the unrelenting rock of the cave, "she is dead. And I am not. Justa facere."

"Justa facere," agreed Atellus. "But then what, Barbarus? I could use your help, in Aesica. Prove to me you are no longer a coward. Maybe you can avenge Flavia's death?"

Barbarus looked up at him, a spark of life deep within his dull eyes. "Maybe."

There was a whipping noise, and the drapes at the mouth of the cave flew inward, and Drustanus stormed inside.

"You are awake at last," he said. He was shrouded by cold air and brought the wet and wind of the outside world into the womb-like cave. Atellus shivered.

"We need to leave," snapped the Arcanus. "Drufax was attacked last night, by wolves. He fought them off but he has been lamed. I had to crush his skull with a boulder. "

He swept into the inner cave and extinguished the fire, before rummaging in one of the far corners.

"At least there's plenty of fresh meat to keep us going," he grinned, bitterly, pulling out a long clean spatha and collection of leather pouches and knapsacks. "I saw mounted men patrolling the Wall," continued the Drustanus, tossing some clothes and skins to the two men. "Probably looking for you. It's only a matter of time before they try here. Some of them know about this place. We need to move."

CHAPTER 30

The air was fresh and bitterly cold on Atellus's face. For the first two miles, adrenalin had kept him warm and eager. Then the pain in his foot began to increase, and his pace slowed. The snowdrifts were so deep in places that they fell in chest-deep and had to be hauled out by the others.

Barbarus was accompanying them south, now they had no steed. The land to the north of the Wall was much the same as the land to the south, but it felt different to Atellus somehow. Wilder, more desperate. They had already passed three flayed corpses, frozen into ghoulish contortions, hanging from the lower branches of the bare twisted trees around them.

"Brigands, maybe," said Drustanus. "The Attacotti are strong here and do not tolerate lawlessness. Or Romans." He finished with a rich peal of laughter. "They could be months old. Or as fresh as this morning. In these temperatures, it's hard to tell."

The Wall was an eternal dark horizon at their shoulder. To Atellus, it stretched into infinity on both sides, broken only by the undulation of the land, or a distant pocket of fog.

"You see this?" asked Drustanus at one point as they stopped for breath and water. He jabbed his thumb at a small bone which hung from his neck by a narrow thong of leather.

Atellus nodded.

"The finger bone of my father, Serano," said Drustanus. "A great man. He comes with me wherever I go. He is with me, always." He hefted his blade. "Taught me everything I know about this."

"Was he a military man?" asked Atellus.

The Arcanus laughed. "Of sorts, beneficiarius, but not one you'd recognise, I daresay." He twisted the thong between his thick fingers. "My father was a freedman down in Londinium. He moved north to fight on the Wall, where he took wife. I was captured by the northerners before I became a man. Whether they wanted me for ransom, or propagation, I was never sure. But I managed to escape during a raid by a Roman scouting party. They nearly killed me for a savage, but I managed to convince them to take me back to the Wall. My father and mother were long dead, slaughtered in one of the many counter-raids, and I joined the military."

"The best choice for an orphan boy," said Atellus.

The Arcanus nodded. "Indeed. My father had trained me well, and the barracks at Vercovicium finished it off. I fought well and hard for many years. But a merda of a praefectus arrived from Gaul. He was an evil and sadistic man, half mad. We were beaten and starved, or condemned to death by being sent on impossible details north of the Wall; I watched friends die, if they couldn't transfer south in time. I deserted and went to the Colledig tribe of Attacotti north of Banna. I fought hard and after we were decimated by a battle with the limitanei, I became Warlord of the remnants. We lasted and thrived for years, the group grew, but I was not satisfied. I heard that the old praefectus was dead, lynched by his own troops, so I defected back to Rome and offered my services as an agent."

Drustanus laughed at this point, a hearty rich rumble that seemed to bounce across the snow around them. The sun glittered in the whiteness all around and there was the sound of birds wheeling across the crisp, deep sky.

434

"They tortured me," said the Arcanus, after he had finished laughing. "I did not know why I expected otherwise. For moons they locked me in cells and beat me, starved me, ripped my flesh. When they were satisfied I was genuine, I was sent to Fullofaudes. He told me of the Arcanae, and of my duties, should I accept them. I did, and have not regretted my choice in five winters."

"You change your mind a lot, Arcanus," said Atellus, coldly. "Perhaps you need to decide who your master is."

Drustanus laughed. "Why, *I* am my only master, beneficiarius!" He spread his hands. "This lifestyle suits me. I am happy enough here, if any man can be granted happiness."

"And what of the brethren you left behind, Arcanus?" asked Barbarus with venom. "The men on both sides you turned against."

Drustanus turned to look at the convict with a flat gaze. "We enter this world alone, *reus*, and we leave it alone. Anything else is just a temporary delusion."

***

As afternoon rose, and they marched across the brae of yet another endless white hill, Atellus became aware of an uneasy sensation prickling his back. He turned and scanned the ranged trees bristling up from the frozen land, but there was no sign of movement. Overhead, birds wheeled and cawed. Far off in the distance, to the south, were strings of smoke rising tall and straight into the air.

"You feel them too, hm?" said Drustanus, moving up beside Atellus.

The beneficiarius nodded.

"We've been followed for the last two miles or so. Probably just scouts, but it's hard to tell. These people can hide in a fold in the ground you wouldn't even know was there."

They carried on walking, the pace slow, trudging through the deep snow, and keeping low at the banks of the hills and beyond the wild scraggles of foliage and dead trees which marked the end of the defensive area north of the Wall. Here the land was less wild, the snow less deep, and Drustanus seemed to know all the sheep tracks and shortcuts that wove in and out of the trees stippling the wilderness.

Atellus never lost the feeling that they were under surveillance. He kept hearing sounds coming from around him, from the sullen grey shoulders of the wintry trees to his left, and from behind the rockfall on the narrow track behind him. Upon the northern horizon was a wild flurry of evergreen trees, which could hold an entire army unnoticed. He wondered how much of it was just his imagination.

They stopped and ate a rude meal of smoked horseflesh washed back with crushed snow. The drink was so cold it stung their teeth and made their throats ache.

"Why are we squatting on our arses," said Barbarus, "when we are being followed by a band of men who would flay us alive and nail us to the trees?"

Drustanus looked across at the convict. "If they want to catch us, they will. Don't matter whether we run from here to Aesica, or slither on our bellies. They'll show themselves when they're good and ready." His eyes scanned their surroundings. "But they're there."

They finished the repast and carried on, Atellus dragging his aching limbs and screaming foot into the painful rhythms of movement again. There was no wind, the air was still, and the only sounds were the fusp of their own breathing and the occasional crack of Barbarus's cough.

The sun was dripping towards the horizon, pushing the shadow of the Wall across the tumbled land. The Wall itself looked dead and ancient, like the rotting timbers of some long beached ship. There was the faint odour of smoke in the sharp air, and the scent of tree sap.

Atellus noticed a figure up ahead, a tall silhouette facing the dying sun. He pointed him out to the others.

"Yes," said Barbarus. "Do as I say. Do not speak. Do not move, and we may survive. Keep your eyes down."

They walked on, slowly, towards the unmoving figure. "And what is to stop you handing us over, Arcanus?" asked Barbarus, his voice pitched low.

"Nothing," was the reply. "Nothing at all. But if they kill you, then there is a good chance they will kill us all. I'd rather not die today."

Atellus felt the watery squeeze of fear in his belly. He was in bad condition; he had a limp, and countless wounds from his beating. His gladius was old and cumbersome.

As they came nearer, Atellus could make out the details of the figure standing ahead of them: he was a tall man, with long, dark hair that fell in plaits down his broad back. He wore leather trousers, scarred with blood and filth, and a thick wolf-skin draped around his shoulders. At first Atellus thought he was bare-chested, the fading sun striking sparks from his pale flesh, but as he got closer he could see that his belly was bare whilst his chest was covered with lorica segmentata; old armour, but burnished and well cared for. The visible skin of his face and arms and stomach was covered in tattoos, intricate loops and whorls in vibrant blues and dark reds. He leant on a long metal-tipped spear, and an ornate spatha hung heavily from his hip. There was a wrap of cloth and skins upon his head, spun round with

437

chain armour, which tumbled over his hair and down the back of his neck. He was bearded, the hair matted into strange frozen waves with frost and woad.

As they approached, Drustanus brought them to a stop twenty paces from the stranger, and called out in Brythonic.

The stranger answered in return. Atellus knew fragments of the language from his time in Britannia, but the dialect and speed of conversation passed over his head.

Drustanus responded with his palms held up and outward, then turned to his companions. "Wait here," he said. "Don't move, don't speak. Don't even fart."

The Arcanus walked over towards the stranger, crunching a path through the pristine snow. He was half a head shorter than the other man. Atellus listened for the tone, but all he could hear were the lyrical undulating qualities of the Brythonic tongue. He looked around him; there was the edge of a verdant forest to their left, which rolled outwards as far as they could see. Far off to the south was the thick line of the Wall shining in the gloaming; he could see the distant glow of fires, smudged against the dusk – beacons along the Wall. The sky was cloudless and the first needles of the distant stars pierced the grey firmament.

After some time, Drustanus returned to them, his face red and dark as the sky above them.

"He is a spokesman for a small warband of Attacotti camped in the trees," said Drustanus. He spoke low and clipped. "They have been tracking us for most of the afternoon, as we knew. They identified you both as Roman, and wanted you as gifts for my safe passage. They know me as a mercenary who gives them intelligence about...your kind."

"What did you say?" asked Atellus.

438

"I said no, that you were sworn men whom I am taking east to spy at the request of Gadeon of the Scoti."

"Did he believe you?"

"Maybe," he sighed. "But I will need to barter the cost of our passage."

"We have nothing," said Barbarus.

"I know."

"Did you tell him that."

"I did."

"And his response?"

Drustanus looked down at the broken snow by his feet, his broad red face darker than usual, the deepening twilight around them seeming to emanate from his mood. He wearily unsheathed his long cavalry spatha and hefted its weight in his hand.

"At least," he said, "we can die with honour. What man could ask for more?"

"What's the bad news?" grinned Atellus, the delicious fizz of adrenalin shaking through his body already.

"The bad news," smiled Drustanus, "is that death won't be all that far off."

Barbarus spun his weapon in his hands, then bent down in the snow and smoothed the blade against the crisp coldness.

Drustanus busied himself with laying down his excess baggage, tightening the belt around his stout midriff, running his thick fingers across the lower blade of his spatha.

Atellus looked up towards the last flames of the dying sun; it was a bad omen. The night was swallowing up the earth from behind them, a trundling pall of death rippling across the land. Soon it would engulf them all. Each day is killed by night, but the returns with the next dawn. Life is an incessant struggle in perfect balance.

Atellus tested his injured foot; he needed to remember to take his weight on his left leg, otherwise he could find himself collapsing at the worst possible time. Death was a certainty, but at least he could take a handful with him.

The tribesman was standing, unmoving, watching them. Gradually he relaxed and hefted his long heavy spear onto his shoulder, and marched up the slight acclivity towards the treeline. He gave a long ululation as he walked, which was answered by another from the forest to the north. A body of men seeped out from the darkness between the trees and descended down the incline; they spilled across the snow like a trickle of blood across pale flesh.

Atellus counted maybe a hundred warriors in total, dressed in skins or wound round with thin cloth and torn cloaks. They bore cracked and rusted spits of armour, tokens from long lost battles, and strange swatches of clothes, ancient and new, some fashioned from beasts, others pilfered from corpses of Roman and kinsman alike. Not a few had missing arms or hands. Others hefted long oval shields above their heads, or long square shields of heavy leather-wrapped wood such as were used by the ancestral legionaries of decades past. The crowd surged down towards them like a deadly and unstoppable wave of fury and death. Not fast – they were not running, but stalking, calm and immoveable, unconcerned, while bellowing taunts and laughing and spitting.

Barbarus leaned in towards Atellus. "I will not disgrace you, or myself, beneficiarius," he said. "Our reprieve was brief. But I am not afraid to die here."

Atellus clasped his forearm. "Die with honour."

"Honestum mori," the convict nodded, and scrubbed the hair from his eyes, which no longer squinted in the dimming light.

"This should be fun, fratres," said Drustanus, rolling his neck and slapping his chest; his hands were trembling from the adrenalin. "I haven't seen odds like this since Thermopylae."

Atellus felt nauseous. Far out, beyond the encroaching horde, just in front of the dim maw of the forest, he could see two figures gazing down at him: Faenia and Petronia. He wiped a hand across his breast and mumbled a prayer to. He could not protect them from this. But he was not expected to; they were not behind him; he was not repulsing the horde from their delicate flesh. Instead they were far back, beyond. He was diverting the threat, to allow them to escape; the victory had already been won. He felt the release of a huge tension in his shoulders. There was something pure about this death: not tied to a chair at the mercy of a twisted optio, but sword clutched in hand, in the midst of battle.

The Attacotti clan came closer, a slow inexorable tread that seemed to last forever. The world seemed to shake under the heavy tread of their massed boots.

Barbarus bowed his head, knuckled his broken nose, and mumbled words to his gods and to Flavia; Drustanus gazed at the field with an open and relaxed look, his eyes slack, his sword-hand quivering; Atellus looked up to the star-stippled sky and saw the endless ages in the infinity above. He looked down again, bringing his gaze and his mind back to the mortal realm, which seemed so small and insignificant beneath such an ethereal tapestry overhead. He could see the faces of his enemy, faces of brothers and fathers and sons, faces of friends, comrades, much as he had fought with. They were relaxed, and smiling, some laughed, some spat, some wavered as if intoxicated. All were dressed in the same abysmal patchwork of random scraps and flotsam of armour. Beards frosted with rime; knuckles white with tension; noses red with cold.

The three men levelled their swords and stood facing their opponents.

The warband stopped thirty paces away, staring at the trio. The leader was in front of them, addressing the front ranks in their own tongue. His voice rose and fell. He turned to face the three men, and raised his voice, addressing Drustanus.

Drustanus called back, his voice ringing through the still night. Atellus could feel the heat and mist of breath from the horde, feel the pulse of the blood in their collective veins and the earth itself seemed to rise and fall with their breath.

"What did he say?"

"He gave me another chance to give you up, and they would set me free."

"You should have taken it," said Atellus, his breath pluming out in front of him. "Better two die than all three of us."

Drustanus shrugged. "What is one man in this world?"

"It depends who that man is," countered Atellus. "You have chosen your fate and I salute you for it."

"Some say no man chooses his own fate."

Atellus nodded. "Let us end this."

Drustanus shouted some words out to the mob, who laughed and jeered in retort. The ones who were armed slapped their blades against their armour or shields or bucklers, and those who had no weapons merely made thrusting gestures. Some in the front pulled their cocks from their baggy breeches and waved them at the men, their purple tongues lolling from their mouths.

The leader raised his long spear above his head. Atellus realised it was a customised spiculum: he could see the tapered shaft and the finely worked iron barbs. He wondered why he was noticing these things when he was mere unciae from death, and let a laugh escape his lips.

Drustanus turned to him with a queer smile. "Nervous, beneficiarius?"

"Always, Arcanus," he replied. "My whole damned life."

Drustanus laughed, and the sound merged with the roar of the charging men as the leader jabbed his spiculum towards them.

CHAPTER 31

Rodius awkwardly wrapped the ragged cloak around himself and shuffled away through the mud towards the cluster of timber shacks that lined the side of the track. His face was buried deep in the cowl of the hood; the material stank of pig piss and ancient ingrained sweat. He thrust his nose out a bit to suck in a lungful of fresh cold air.

What was taking her so long, he wondered? Aurelia had been gone for the time it took him to shuffle three whole circuits of the vicus. Each time he came back to their meeting point, she was nowhere to be found. Maybe they shouldn't have split up. Her face would be recognised no matter how many rags and flea-pocked skins she swaddled round herself. There was no hiding the haughty dignity in her eyes.

Their intelligence-gathering missions had not gone well so far. They had each taken it in turn to venture out into the vicus, and pick up what details they could. In the bars, the brothels, the ramshackle bath-house. Just leaning on a cracked and weathered piece of masonry and eavesdropping on the passersby.

They had learnt little they didn't already know. People were hungry, and tired. Disease was spreading, as was fear: of brigands, of the gods. More specifically, of Cernunnos. Cernunnos roving at night, wild and angry, stealing child, man and beast alike. There was poverty and drink and death at every turn, and the emperor was spoken of only in brutal terms.

Rodius and Vassu had talked with the limitanei, at the gates and in patrols along the north road. They had subtly asked about the beneficiarius, but all those queried either denied knowledge of any such visitor, or spat and walked away without responding. Even approaching soldiers in their jars at the tavern, there was no talk of the easterner. One man Rodius had spoken and diced with, a large broad-faced barbarian with a missing ear, had seemed to bristle at the mention of Atellus, but he kept his mouth closed and would do nothing but frown and spit and demand more wine.

"We must presume he is dead," said Aurelia to Calidus. "If he appears, he appears. But there is nothing we can do to aid him, at this time."

Aurelia had focused most of her efforts on finding her agent in rebus, the one she called Densligneus. She had never seen him, but had only a contact address in the vicus. Each time they had tried so far, there was no-one present. They had tried to make discreet enquiries, with the help of Muconia, but these had come to nothing.

Rodius moved on through the snow-covered street. There had been a deep and bitter storm which came lashing across the vicus overnight, snow falling so thick it could not be seen through, and the whole world was consumed by the thrashing blizzard. They had sheltered up in the tavern and waited for the storm to abate, sipping at bowls of warm broth and drinking back beaker upon beaker of sweet spiced wine. The next morning, they had ventured out into a white wilderness; the air as still as a frozen pond. There were adults and children frozen dead in barns and in the wings of tumbledown dwellings, and slat-ribbed beasts besides. The snow was pristine: neither drab, desperate horses, nor trade waggons could make passage through the buried roads, until the limitanei were sent out to clear the route around the vicus and south as far as the old stanegate. Gradually, the vicus shook and shivered and raised itself back into a semblance of weary life, and the citizens thronged the streets and begged and bartered and vomited along the road, and the poor were swept into the frozen mud of the crisscrossing side-streets.

Rodius and Aurelia had come out so she could ask for alms around some of the older dwellings to the east of the vicus, with a view to questioning the

445

inhabitants. Her method was to only ask a few innocuous questions of each person; nothing that would attract suspicion, yet when the answers from a few were combined, they provided a fairly comprehensive set of intelligence. Doing this on the west side of the vicus, they had been able to gather that no grain had arrived in the vicus for the last moon, and that Cernunnos was their only salvation. They learned that the beneficiarius had arrived at the fort some time ago (as they already knew from Calidus) and had been seen in the vicus since, but that he hadn't been sighted in a few days. News travelled extremely fast around the vicus, being a small and isolated outpost: any events were sucked up with eagerness by the inhabitants, and spread like wildfire.

However, the information they received depended largely on who they asked. Some thought that Cernunnos was prowling the frozen nights and snatching children from their beds to devour their flesh, so hungry was he, driven from his starving forests. Others thought that the rich landowners were sacrificing the children to appease Cernunnos, who had blighted the land. Still others maintained that the praetor was refusing to send grain north and the Wall was being abandoned as a lost cause.

Desperate people in desperate times. But they kept on existing, even as their wives and children and friends died around them.

Rodius sighed loudly, his breath pluming out in front of him. He did another circuit of the vicus, shuffling forward, head bent, eyes scouring the snow for scraps of food, or the darting movement of a rat. He stopped outside the brothel and squatted untidily by a snowdrift. His rags made him inconspicuous; none of the richer inhabitants of the vicus deigned to even look at him as they stumbled from tavern to brothel and back. What else was there for the wealthy to do, but wait out this damnable winter in as much luxury as possible, and try and avoid the poor and the dying as far as possible? Rodius sneered at their backs as they and their hired strongarms walked past, their noses ostentatiously thrust into the air.

He waited around, watching the punters file in and out, the odd one stopping to spit at him, fewer still offering him a coin, which he accepted with mumbled thanks. There was idle talk about the winter, about grain, about large bands of brigands massing in the forest to the south, about the tribes to the north becoming restless. Rodius came to the conclusion that those who had anything of import to say kept it for inside the baths, and did not debate on the street, and certainly not in this bitter weather.

He slithered to his feet and walked along the road, huge drifts of snow clambering up the sides of the brick buildings on either side. The main road leading to the fort had been largely cleared, yet the manifold side roads – scurrying off on all sides like tributaries of a river – were thick with snow, though by now compacted and dirtied by the hundreds of footsteps.

Rodius tucked his hand deeper into his cloak and walked away through the side-street, picking his steps carefully, planting his weight firmly before moving on. He lost himself in the twists and turns of the haphazard village, past the huts and stalls and thick hide tents of the poorest inhabitants, children weeping and shivering beneath blankets and sackcloth, or scrabbling after rats as they whipped between dwellings.

The inhabitants eyed him with suspicion and dislike, or else their eyes slid off him as one of their own, just another one of the beaten: another fellow waiting to die, sharing their blackened fingers and toes and noses and their sunken cheeks and hacking coughs.

Rodius made a quick left, then a sharp right along a narrow passage where the snow was barely trodden and seeped upwards onto the thatched roofs of the surrounding slum, and where the path stank of shit and disease. He quickly walked through and came out onto a broader track where a couple of two-storey houses with stone foundations signalled the start of one of the wealthier districts of the vicus. These backed onto expanses of pasture-land frozen hard and untouched by man or beast for many winters. Rodius carried on walking, the shouts and calls and squabbles of daily life rising around him. Eventually he stopped at the corner of a narrow, abandoned shack which was open to the elements. A few old rags covered a body inside; whether sleeping or dead, he could not say, nor did he have any interest in finding out.

Rodius stood waiting for Aurelia, as the sun seemed to shrink in the sky and the cold rose up from the icy earth. He shrugged himself deeper into his cloak, and exhaled warm air out through his nostrils. His stomach growled at him from under his layers.

Even Vassu had been helping out, in his own way, Rodius acknowledged. With bad grace, and mumbled curses, true enough, but at least he was playing a part. It had been he who had managed to get the information from a drunken limitanei that the beneficiarius had passed through the vicus some days ago. Before that there was a complicit wall of denials from the military. Not that it helped them at all; but there were times when even he doubted the veracity of the tales which Aurelia had spun. But doubt had become a decidedly uncomfortable feeling in Rodius's belly, even though he had lived most of his life with it. Now, he felt much more at home with giving the woman the benefit of his trust. There was something in her eyes and her demeanour that rang true. Even Vassu had not openly contradicted or insulted her since she had taken them into her confidence and formed their little band.

But there was only so far that the gold they had twisted from Scotius would stretch; after that they would be homeless and starving alongside the worst dying wretches that he passed in the frozen gutters, the shit and meltsnow pooling under their seeping warmth.

His father was dying in rags in Eboracum, but his brother was here, and *alive*, a survivor in a blasted land, like himself.

Rodius lifted his hand and wiped the half-frozen mucus from the end of his nose. There was a short, half-limping figure swathed in coarse cuts of cloth and a patchwork cloak opposite. He recognised the clothing, if not the gait, of Aurelia. He waited patiently until she came over, then she walked past him and turned into the narrow alley behind the rundown building. After a quick wait, he followed her. It was thick with hardened snow, and he had to climb through to reach beyond where Aurelia stood.

"Anything?" he asked.

She looked up to him, her eyes cool like frozen lakes, and shook her head. Rodius let a sigh escape from between his clenched teeth.

"Me neither," he said, shaking his head.

"I think," said Aurelia, "we need a closer look at the agent's dwelling."

"Inside?"

Aurelia nodded, and scratched at her skin beneath the coarse clothing. "We are reaching the limit of what we can achieve here, on the surface at least."

Rodius nodded. "There are only so many times we can tread the same cold path. And our money will only go so far- there is but little left as it is."

Aurelia looked up at Rodius. "I will stay. As long as it takes. I need to. You may return to Eboracum."

Rodius shook his head. "I stay with you."

"No, Rodius," said Aurelia. "I would ask you to take Galla to safety and look after her."

"I can do that here."

"There is no life here for a girl," she replied. "Nor for anyone, for that matter. And I have messages that I trust you to deliver. You can be more use to me in the city than you could possibly be up here."

Rodius shook his head wearily, but stayed silent. Aurelia hid her face deeper inside her cowl and walked out of the ginnel and into the main street. Rodius waited for ten slow breaths before following.

The agent's dwelling was the long timber-shack which trailed out from the path, at the crest of a shallow slope which followed the contour of the land through a scrub-like sward laid thick with snow. The front entrance was a solid oak door, and the only concession to windows or natural light was a single carved round hole in the far end of the building, which was boarded over from the inside. Rodius walked round to the front entrance, which was perpendicular to the main road, along which a few inhabitants of the vicus struggled through the frozen snow, hacking and puffing. Rodius scanned them warily but their eyes were fixed to the ground, and their red faces did not waver as they passed.

Rodius met Aurelia by the door. She knocked again, a light but complex staccato rhythm which Rodius could not have emulated without a few tries. They stood listening; there was only the curious cawing of crows overhead, and the sleek susurration of the wind along the gaps between the timber houses.

Aurelia repeated the knock.

Nothing.

"Can you open this?" she asked Rodius.

He looked at the door, pushed against it with his hand, testing its weight and the firmness of the hinges. There was a large keyhole set into the left side of the door. Rodius bent down to look through, but the inside was black.

He stood up again. "Maybe," he said. "Could be noisy though."

"I'll watch for soldiers." Aurelia walked out onto the path, a mix of compacted snow, ice and slushy mud. She looked up and down, then turned to Rodius and gave a terse nod.

Rodius stepped back from the door then launched a hefty kick at the lock. The sound cracked through the still air and the door and its frame shimmered, but the wood stood. He backed up, his leg still trembling through the force of the impact, and looked at Aurelia. She nodded again, and he aimed a second strike at the door.

There was a grinding, splintering sound, and the wood buckled either side of the lock. The crack of the breaking timber seemed to echo around the quiet edge of the vicus.

Rodius fell against the door and nudged it with his shoulder, feeling its stability. The lock was an iron construction held fast into the timber jamb set deep into the wall. He aimed another kick squarely at it, and there was a brittle snapping noise and the door juddered inwards with a howl of shearing wood.

Aurelia waited for a while before tramping back up the path, her feet following the divots of their own earlier footprints. Rodius waited for her on the threshold, spatha drawn. He noticed the glint of metal on the ground: the heavy iron door key. It was locked from the inside.

Whoever lived here was still inside.

Rodius kicked the key away; it jingled across the floorplanks and disappeared into the darkness at the far edges of the building.

Aurelia arrived and they walked inside together, shutting the ruin of the door behind them. The interior was dark: the only light came from the cracks between timbers and from under the doorway, slivers of brilliance like sword-blades stretching across the room.

"Prop it open," said Rodius. Aurelia tucked a wedge of broken planking underneath the door. Rodius walked through towards the single circular window at the far end, and opened the slats which had been drawn across it. Cold air whipped inside.

There was a single bare bed, atop which were piled tangled blankets. A large desk was set against the wall beside the door, and trunks and cabinets were scattered about the floor. There were agricultural tools stacked against the far wall, and some fixed by struts across the low ceiling. Beyond the main room, which ran the entire length of the structure, were two other chambers, which were accessed by pushing through tanned goat hides hanging down from the ceiling.

Rodius took in the entirety of the room with a sweeping glance. It was basic, if solid and large. The dwelling of a man who worked the land, though it looked unlived in. "Have a look in those trunks. I'll go through to the back."

He walked across, footsteps rapping along the timber floor. The skins hanging down were heavy and damp. He swept one aside. The interior was so black that even the light from the open door wouldn't penetrate it. A sweet, musty smell filled his nostrils; he closed the drape.

Rodius walked back, and looked around the room. He found an old oil lamp on the desktop, weighting down a sheaf of hand-scrawled papers. He gave them a cursory glance – they seemed to be accounts from the land – and looked around for a flint and steel. He found a striking stone close by, and lit the lamp after a few attempts. There were two more oil lamps in the room; he lit both and handed one to Aurelia, putting the other back on the desk, away from the open door.

He returned to the darkened chamber, pulled the drape aside and extended the lamp into the room. The space was long and narrow, the floor covered with damp hay. There was the carcass of a goat folded up in one corner. A few flies fizzed and swarmed as he moved inside. Rodius wished he had another hand to clamp his nostrils shut and stop him gagging; the odour was of old, stale shit and rotted goat-flesh. He shone the light round, then walked back out, coughing.

"Something's died in there," he said to Aurelia, "but not your agent. It's a pen for the beasts. Or, it *was.*"

Rodius moved round to the next room separated by a similar drape of hides. He pushed it aside gingerly, and stepped in. It was a short room, with a single cot on the floor, a range of hides overlaid onto a straw base. There was a simple table, on which was a crude ceramic mug. There was a low stool and a timber trunk, which was open and empty.

Rodius looked back towards the cot. A single pale hand could be seen protruding from underneath the stacked hides.

He put the lamp on the squat table, and knelt down next to the bed.

It was a large, man's hand. Not a peon or a labourer's rough paw, but a soft hand with slender fingers ending in manicured nails. The skin was a dull white, tinged with blue.

Rodius reached out for the hides, and heaved them back with a tug. They uncovered the body of a man, fully dressed. He was dead, the top side of his skull caved in and a great frozen pool of blood and brain matter congealed under his scalp, soaked up by the hay. His eyes were half lidded, as though looking out with a querulous disinterest, his jaw slightly ajar, and the edge of his purple tongue visible between neat rows of white teeth.

He called for Aurelia, and she came in. Her face betrayed no shock or distaste at the sight; just a cool appraisal of the situation.

"Is this your agent?" asked Rodius.

She did not speak, but knelt down beside the corpse, and prised open his jaw, with some effort.

"Fetch me the lamp," she said, and Rodius handed it over. She looked inside his mouth, then scanned his face. She was silent for a long time.

"This isn't the agent."

"Are you sure?"

She nodded. "As sure as I can be. He has no wooden tooth, in his upper left jaw. His hair is the wrong colour, though that can be changed by dyes. His eyes are a different colour. And this man is maybe half the age of the agent I am looking for."

Rodius was silent a while. "Then who is this?"

Aurelia remained silent for a while before turning to Rodius again. "How long do you think he's been here?"

Rodius frowned. "The cold makes it difficult to tell. The snow would preserve the body. I couldn't say."

Aurelia stood up. "I need to go back and look through the papers."

"Is there anything relevant?"

She shook her head. "Not yet. He left in a hurry by the looks of it, but not enough of –"

Aurelia froze, her eyes wide.

"What—"

She silenced Rodius with a glare and a squint.

He listened. At first there was only the distant hum of activity in the vicus, and the sough of the wind across the worn timbers.

Then there was the unmistakable crunch of approaching footfalls in the snow.

Rodius gestured for Aurelia to stay where she was, then got to his feet and moved out to the main room, edging his way round so as to keep out of sight through the open door. He inched over to the edge of the doorframe, and peered out, down through the glare of the daylight.

The edge of the vicus opened panoramically in front of him: the crisp white slope leading up to the dwelling; the blocky slums of the timber-built village; the taller two-storied dwellings closer to the road; beyond, the huge bulwark of the fort; and encircling everything, stretching, uncoiling itself across the earth, from one end of the land to the other, was the massive bulk of the Wall, the eternal end, the limes.

And halfway up the track leading down through the snow-swathed scrub were three men, treading intently, purposefully up towards the house they were in.

Rodius cursed under his breath, then dived back over to where Aurelia stood waiting, in the room with the dead man.

"Three men, on their way up," he said.

"Limitanei?"

He shook his head. "Too well dressed," he said. "Maybe comitatenses."

"There's no other way out." It was not a question, but Rodius shook his head anyway.

Aurelia blinked for a second, a dark shadow of despair passing across the sky blue of her eyes. In a second it was gone as though it had never existed.

"I'll shutter the window," she said, decisively. "You get the door."

Rodius nodded and sprang outwards, into the main room of the dwelling. The door was still wedged open by the piece of timber which Aurelia had used for that purpose. He grabbed it and wrestled it out, the wood squeaking against the timber of the door, but he kept the door open, not wanting to betray their presence just yet. Behind him he could hear the slats of the window being closed by Aurelia.

"Is the lock damaged?" Aurelia whispered from the other side of the building.

"Yes," he replied. "But the door opens inwards, and the timber is solid – we can barricade it."

She nodded; their eyes met.

"We need to get the door shut," said Rodius, "and the trunk in front of it before they have time to put their shoulder to it. They're halfway up. We need to be fast. Are you ready?"

She nodded tersely.

Rodius slammed the door shut, then pounced across to the other side of the trunk and heaved it over with his one hand until it was in front of the door. "Help me with the bed."

They could hear the shouts of surprise and activity outside, the cracking of the snow becoming harder and more regular as their pace quickened and the soldiers threw themselves up the incline towards the building.

Rodius hefted the bed frame up with his one hand, and heaved it clumsily up onto its side where it collapsed into the centre of the room. Aurelia was ready for it and dragged it over. Rodius was at the other side within a breath, and the two manhandled and mauled the heavy timber bedstead up onto its end and propped it at an angle against the door.

There was a thump from the other side of the timber, and the bed shifted slightly.

"Open the door," was the command from outside, "for soldiers of the comitatenses."

Rodius's eyes scoured the room until they fell on the table. He darted over and, curling his arm around the heavy table leg, dragged it over, the oil lamp falling to the floor with a thud and extinguishing the flame. With Aurelia's help, they angled the table against the door as an extra bastion, and stood at each side, chests heaving in the dim light.

There was another thump against the door; a pause, then another, harder blow. The barricade still stood solid.

"Open the door!" The shout was muffled as it passed through the timber. The Latin was perfect, the voice accentless.

"On whose authority?" demanded Aurelia.

There was a silence from outside, followed by a sharp laugh.

"On the authority of Flavius Clodius Bassianus Brocchus," came the reply, a different voice from the previous. "Praetor of Britannia Secunda."

"Aurelia Crispi," said the first voice, its tone stentorian and authoritative. There was another snort of laughter from another of the party outside. "We have come to humbly request your presence at the principia in Eboracum. There are concerns for your safety."

"I am sure there are," she spat witheringly, raising her voice so all outside could hear. "Whores of Crispus."

Laughter.

"Do not be scared, Aurelia" said the voice. "You will be safer in your husband's loving embrace, than out here with these savages."

"Who is it that speaks with such insolence?" shouted Aurelia, her anger audible in her words.

"Catugnavus, of the praetor's personal guard."

"I remember you, Catugnavus," replied Aurelia coldly. "I thought you had more brains and courage than to scurry around after the worm Crispus."

There were sounds of chuckling outside which were quickly stifled.

"Do you really want to die out here with that one-handed whore-monger?" shouted Catugnavus. "Returning you to the ab epistulis is but the meagrest part of my work here. Finding you has already occupied enough of my time."

There was a smash at the boards blocking the window: the crack sounded like thunder in the room. Sherds of wood fell like hail and sunlight streamed through, cutting through the dimness.

Rodius sprung over towards the window in time to see an arm flung over. He struck it hard with the edge of his spatha, the blow biting deep into the flesh of the forearm. He heard a crack as the bone splintered, and a shrill scream, and the arm fell back like a dead viper.

There was more howling and commotion from outside.

"Anyone tries to enter, and I will cut the fucker down!" screamed Rodius, bellowing. His heart thumped in his chest and the adrenalin pounded through his veins. He felt hot and angry and exhilarated.

There were worse outcomes, he thought, than a noble death here protecting the lady.

Rodius stared up at the window, expecting another attempt. There were more thumps at the front door and the barricade trembled slightly. Outside, the howling had turned into a low sobbing surrounded by the spit and hiss of intense voices.

"Aurelia," shouted Catugnavus, "come out now and we will spare you hurt. The barbarian will die, of course."

"Who is this cunnus?" asked Rodius.

"Catugnavus was a centurion with the legion at Eboracum," answered Aurelia. "He was involved in a scandal with a noblewoman, and demoted. The praetor found and employed him as sub-head of his own guard, on a huge salary. I see now that that was obviously at the behest of Crispus."

"Leave, if you want," said Rodius, looking down at her.

She returned his gaze steadily. "I would rather die here. If they take me alive, I would soon enough be praying for death."

Rodius nodded in agreement.

"I give you to a count of three, Aurelia Crispi," shouted Catugnavus in haughty tones. "After which we will cease discourse and consider the matter terminated. Do you understand?"

Aurelia did not answer but instead looked over at the window. Rodius reached up and pulled down one of the rudimentary and rusted sithes fixed laterally to the roof beams. He held it out to Aurelia.

"Cover the window," he said. "Anything that appears, cut it. Don't think, just swing up and over."

She nodded and moved over to the circular window, standing in a red-gold shaft of late afternoon sunlight. Rodius braced himself against the barricaded door. The air was bitterly cold and still, but his weatherworn face was slick with sweat.

"One." The voice from outside rang through the silence within the dwelling.

Rodius braced himself.

"Two."

Aurelia shared a look with Rodius, taking her eyes from the window for a second; Rodius noticed her knuckles shone bright white around the snaith of the sithe.

"Three."

Rodius exhaled a breath he hadn't realised he had been holding, and waited.

Waited.

The contact never came. Aurelia was straining, her muscles tiring under the stress of holding the long sithe straight. Rodius was pressing himself awkwardly against the upright table, forcing his bulk against the door.

He could hear voices outside and the sounds of activity; the flurry of footsteps were punctuated by odd knocks and clunks against the solid timbers of the dwelling. They could hear the breathing of the men outside, and muffled snatches of conversation; the occasional laugh or curse.

Aurelia let the sithe drop, and rested her aching arms; Rodius backed away from the barricade, muscles screaming. There was the faintest essence in the air, something familiar and sharp and unpleasant.

"What are they doing?" whispered Aurelia.

Rodius paused, uncertain. Then the noises and the smell clicked into place, and he sheathed his blade and rubbed his hand across his damp brow.

"I know what I would do," he said, shaking his head softly.

The sound of more cracks and thumps against the sides of the building echoed through the timbers; they came from the sides, then the back. There was a clack and clatter of something – many things – landing on the roof, and rolling.

Aurelia heard a distant sounding crackle first, before the first tendrils of smoke crept in between the gaps in the timbers.

"Fire," said Aurelia, her face blanching.

Rodius nodded grimly.

CHAPTER 32

Atellus stood frozen and watched.

The Attacotti host descended on them with a roar, over a hundred heavy men, meat and hair and clothing and arms rushing into the declivity with a fearsome momentum. He felt the ground quivering beneath his feet, and the air rushed and tingled against his face.

Maybe he could take one with him, as he died. Great sol, he implored, let him at least take one with him into the next life.

Atellus tensed against the impact, his spatha rigid in his gripe as he chose a target from the mass of bodies hurtling towards him, when he became conscious of another sound, from behind. Barbarus was shouting something, but the voice seemed as distant as the stars in the ether or the shades of the dead.

He felt a stiff arm across his breast from behind, and huge force pressing him down, pulling him backwards, until he felt his balance shifting, and he knew he was going to fall. Gradually the approaching horde fell away from his vision, and the trees and the stars seemed to blur and merge and with a thump he was on his back in the cold snow.

As he lay stunned, there was a vibrating, coruscating crack from behind him, or rather a series of cracks whipping and snapping through the air with a violence and aggression that he felt in his spleen. Looking up, as he was, the stars were obscured by incalculable spits of darkness, like ferocious rain streaming horizontally across the sky.

Arrows!

Atellus kept down until he heard the violent thumps of the bolts driving home, burying themselves deep in flesh and wood and snow. There were metallic shrieks as some struck off sword and armour, and the hum of men straining for sanctuary flared and erupted into the desperate howls of the injured.

Atellus raised his head and looked over his shoulder, back over Barbarus who had pulled him down for his safety, beyond into the dark and wild wastes of the grey land.

He saw figures on horses, riding fast, hooves cracking a staccato drumbeat from the frozen ground. Behind them were soldiers, the silhouettes of men aiming lean, deadly, composite bows into the sky. Through the gloaming, he saw them loose before he heard the snap of the bow-strings being released, then heard the eerie whistle as the missiles ripped overhead once more.

Once the arrows were past, Atellus scrambled to his feet amid a chorus of screams from the ranks of the war-band. There was an ominous chant in the air, which was coming from the troops behind him. It was deep, intimidating, triumphant; he did not recognise the words, but they seemed to be in the Brythonic tongue.

"Who the *fuck* are they?" he screamed at Barbarus, helping the convict to his feet. His only response was a shrug. Drustanus was next to them.

"Our fuckin saviours, is all," said the Arcanus.

The horses thundered past the massed ranks of the warriors and the riders hacked and swung heavy spathas down on the backs of the rearmost men, some of whom had already fled for the safety of the trees. The warband was consumed by shouting, roared commands, yells of pain, bestial grunts of anger and courage.

The infantry rushed up behind the horse, a throbbing mass of figures in a vague formation which loosened and scattered as they approached the enemy. The Attacotti warriors held and formed themselves into a semblance of a shield-wall, those lucky enough to have them squeezing their way through to the front and locking themselves arm to arm, faces as pale as the snow, streaked with dirt and crumpled with tension.

Atellus, Barbarus and Drustanus stood frozen, caught between the two opposing groups. The forward charge of the newcomers swept over them, like a tide streaming either side, collapsing onto the Attacotti shield-wall with screams and shouts of rage and fear. The surge seemed to continue endlessly, men draped with spits of lorica hamata, and leather caps, some carrying the oval shield of the limitanei, others with rude square bucklers and nail-studded clubs; Atellus struggled to tell the two armies apart.

He stood and turned to watch the men flow around him until the congestion backed up, and men at the rear pounded round to take on the flanks.

The air was filled with the grim and angry noise of metal on metal and the screams of the injured. There was a fuggy stench of sweat, and the sharp metallic tang of blood, with an undercurrent of shit from those whose bowels had been voided, either in fear or death.

The three men found themselves in the rear ranks of the host; Atellus guessed at maybe seventy of them, along with ten horse, so their apparent saviours were still outnumbered roughly two to one.

"Come on!" he said, grabbing the other two. "We know whose side we're on; at least these fuckers didn't kill us on the way over!"

Atellus led them round to the right flank, to fight alongside the opponents of the Attacotti. Here the combat was most furious, and the living were scrabbling over the bodies of the dead and maimed to reach over the brim of the enemy shield-wall.

Atellus squeezed past and caved in the face of an Attacotti with an overhand blow of his spatha; the man had just been about to drive a rusty-barbed spear through the ribs of the soldier to Atellus's left. The dead man fell backwards, and was grappled clear by his comrades and a new warrior fell into his place, swinging wildly with a small agricultural hatchet. Atellus parried the blow with his gladius, the blade ringing out and the contact shivering through his arm. The snow at his feet was melting and becoming an icy slush which filled his boots and mercifully numbed his caltrop wound. He was vaguely aware of Drustanus to his right, and then Barbarus, hacking and driving with his spatha beside him, and before the hatchet had a chance for another swing, the man was clutching at his arm which spouted thick sprays of dark blood. Drustanus sawed his own spatha back and forth into the mess, hoping for contact, but for him there was only the wrist-spraining judder of metal against wood.

Atellus found himself forced forward from behind, torrents of sweat dripping from his brow and stinging his eyes. Pushed by the surging of the men behind and around him, he found himself face to face with another Attacotti, a large square-faced warrior with long braids of fiery red hair and clear grey eyes. He seemed calm in the heat of battle and he held a large pike, the butt propped firmly against the ground, the shaft set against the edge of the man's square legionary shield, the blade aimed at Atellus's breast. Atellus felt himself being driven towards the pike-blade; his sword-arm was trapped by the man to his right, and his feet struck a body on the ground.

The man to his left suddenly seemed to dive across the pike-man in front of Atellus; a blow from a maul had caved in his face and shattered his jaw, sending him collapsing beyond the front rank. He collapsed directly onto the pike of the Attacotti warrior, and the spearhead buried itself awkwardly in his chest. The pike was carried down towards the ground under the weight of the unfortunate soldier, who screamed for his mother in Brythonic and bled heavily onto Atellus's legs. His sword-arm freed, Atellus hefted up the gladius and drove it squarely into the face of the pike-wielding Attacotti, who was struggling to free his weapon of the dying soldier and had let his shield angle to the ground. The gladius clipped the top of the man's shield, and dug its way into the warrior's scalp, which seemed to lift his fiery hair off in a fountain of blood. He screamed and released the tension on his shield, and the attackers drove forward, their weight and momentum carrying them through the gap, trampling the pikeman into the bloody snow beneath their surging feet.

Atellus regained his balance and scrambled over a wall of the dead and dying; some writhed in pain, others were still, but all were shedding blood into the pale snow. The ground around the battle was a dirty slush, slippery with gore and filth, and the air was positively humid with sweat. The stench was unbearable. Atellus stood atop one of the dead, chest heaving, and looked around for his companions.

There was no sign of Barbarus; Drustanus was ahead of him and to the right, part of the attacking force that had driven forward into the breach.

Atellus leapt down and hobbled across the snow, smeared black with guts and shit, and pushed forward, next to Drustanus, who saw him but had no time for acknowledgement, engaged in parrying an overhand blow from a rusted gladius. Atellus punched his own sword directly underneath the opponent's outstretched arm, and there was the crump of resistance as his blade slid up into the man's armpit. Atellus wrenched the blade back out as the man fell away, jerking it to and fro to release it as it caught in bone and sinew, and proceeded to lay about him, left and right, flinging sweat from his drenched hair and feeling his heart tearing through his chest. He felt a blow land on his shoulder, but it was flat-bladed, the contact unclean; the Attacotti's strike had been deflected by the rim of the man's own shield. Atellus turned to face his assailant, mouthing a silent thanks to, then kicked out at the centre of his opponent's shield. The unexpected strike drove the soldier back slightly; he was a short man with dark hair shaved at the sides and with a crest running down the middle. Atellus watched his opponent as a long axe-blow came from the side and lifted the top half of his face off. The body fell into a heap, the shield collapsing on top of the twitching remains, and the attackers forced forward, trampling the man into the blooded snow.

Atellus turned to his right in time to parry a blow from a warrior who had just freed his sword from the guts of his opponent; the injured man was bent over clutching the steel as it was withdrawn, reluctant to see it leave, as though it was holding his life in. The beneficiarius stepped back to give himself space for combat, and his opponent swiped instead for Drustanus who managed to duck under the blow; the attacker followed it up with an overhead blow which would have cloven the Arcanus's skull in twain, but Atellus dived forward and hacked at the warrior's knees which were visible from behind the edge of the shield. It was an ugly, ragged blow, but the blade bit into flesh and sinew and struck bone and the man crumpled vertically down, screaming, his sword tumbling ineffectually from his gripe. Atellus's blade was wedged tight into the injured man's flesh, snags in the blade caught tight and deep in the bone, and the weight of the man falling snatched the weapon from Atellus's sweat-slick hands.

Atellus got to his feet, his eyes scraping the ground in all directions looking for a weapon. Drustanus appeared at his elbow and tossed a blood-smeared spatha over to him. Atellus caught it overhand and nodded his thanks.

The Attacotti shield-wall had collapsed now, and the battle consisted of ragged single-combats spread out in a harried circle. The great hooves of the cavalry galloped back and forth, harrying the flanks and rear of the warband, and rear archers picked out individual targets with precision; the whip of bowstrings and fizz of arrows filled the air around them, audible over the clash of arms and screams of the dying.

Atellus strode over in a surreal bubble of calm as small pitched battles erupted everywhere around him, until he saw one of his comrades go down under the axe of a large Attacotti with a completely bald head and long winding tattoos covering his scalp. The axeman saw Atellus approaching and spat blood onto the snow. He rocked his axe-blade loose from the corpse's neck, and approached Atellus. His first swing was long and unexpected, aimed at midriff level; Atellus was only just able to leap back in time, slipping on the compacted slush and blood, and going down hard to one knee, which winded him. The second attack was an overhand blow aimed for his head. Atellus rolled to his side, and the axe buried itself deep in the snow and mud.

The Attacotti strained to pull it free and Atellus used the opportunity to scramble to his feet and slash at the man's back, but the axe was wrenched free in time and the strike parried by the thick ash haft. The Attacotti held his weapon well; he was comfortable with it, and aware of its advantages, strong enough to make the most of its weight and momentum. He held it like a long staff, across his breast, parrying Atellus's thrusts, until the warrior saw that he was slightly off balance, then he sprang into life winding the axe over his head and swinging it low and deep; the range of the weapon was fearsome, and the speed with which it uncoiled was dizzying.

Sweat stung Atellus's eyes, the stench of death filled his nostrils and the sounds of battle assaulted his ears and seemed to ring inside his skull. His opponent was howling and roaring bestially at him, nonsensical words and curses and chants to his gods or whatever else was spilling from his tattooed mouth. The axeman leapt towards Atellus, hands tight around the helve, unfolding the swing as he did so. The beneficiarius dropped to one knee, low, underneath the arc of the swing, and drove his spatha upwards into his opponent's belly. The momentum of his opponent drove the blade deep into his body until the metal erupted from the other side, Atellus's fists wrapt round the hilt pressing against the man's stomach. The weight and uncontrolled momentum of his opponent pushed Atellus down into the slushy ground, and he felt the Attacotti's stench envelop him, the musk of his odour, his life, mingled with the sweet bilious scent of the fresh blood.

Atellus heaved him off with some effort and tugged the sword from the body; the Attacotti groaning with each jerk and tug. Atellus looked around and saw he had space to wipe his blade on the vanquished man's tunic, which he bent down to do. The bald warrior was still alive and shuddering with agony, his face turning as blue as the ink on his scalp even as his life reddened the snow around him.

His large brown eyes stared at Atellus; they were moist with pain and loss and his look was one of confusion, incomprehension. His lips moved, but the words were too soft to catch. His head fell back, and his chest rose and fell rapidly as his heart pumped his blood into the thirsty land.

The sounds of battle were diminishing around Atellus; there were but a few skirmishers finishing their fights in the centre of the combat, but the main force of the Attacotti had broken and fled for the forest at the top of the slope. The horse charged after them as far as the treeline, slashing down, opening men's skulls and backs alike, slaughtering all who were within reach, but they did not pursue them into the woods.

Atellus stood and rested his hands on his knees. The battle heat rose shimmering above the melting snow, like a mirage in the desert. There were jeers and shouts and howls from the dying and mutilated. A handful of soldiers went round checking the dead and dispatching the living; they seemed to enjoy their job, laughing and singing as they did so. Indeed, why wouldn't they, thought Atellus? They were alive, for another day at least. He had acted the same way himself, countless times before.

He saw Drustanus limping towards him and they clapped shoulders. Atellus nodded questioningly at his leg.

"A lucky blow by some fucker with a maul," he said, shrugging it off. "I'll live."

Atellus nodded. "You see Barbarus?"

Drustanus spat. "He acquitted himself well, pains me to say it," he hissed as he transferred his weight onto his good leg. "Saw him dive over the shield wall and lay into the fuckers like a one-man wolfpack." He shook his head. "If he's still alive, he'll be up at the front, probly ripping the survivors' throats out with his teeth!" He barked a brittle laugh.

Atellus stood, feeling the cool air in his lungs, the fresh wind plucking the sweat from his face. He looked around the battlefield, clusters of celebrating men, others too weary to stand but lying and basking in the snow. Maybe half the number of the Attacotti band were strewn across the field, mainly clumps of them at the edge of the shield-wall, like driftwood left at high-water after the recession of the tide. There were perhaps forty dead from their allies, though it was hard to tell as they looked barely different from the men they were fighting. Up at the treeline, the horses wheeled and whinnied as the last of the horde were chased off. Some of the men were bending down, sawing at the bodies of the slain; collecting scalps of red and blonde hair which they passed over to their commanders on horseback; these officers fastened the grisly ornaments to the saddles of their mounts so they swung in the breeze alongside other, older and more withered, trophies.

The soldiers who walked past, laughing, or crying, or stumbling, were dressed in leathers and skins and rags and the potpourri of armour and weaponry he had seen at Aesica. Some wore necklaces of human teeth, or shrunken ears; others chewed leaves which they had pulled from pouches made from dried and stitched flesh: testicles, cheeks, other cuts.

Atellus saw a figure speaking with one of the cavalry, and was happy to recognise the broad long-haired silhouette of Barbarus, just visible in the twilight. The convict walked down, slowly towards Atellus and Drustanus. After a while, the horseman wheeled his mount and trotted down after him, reining up next to the two men.

The horse was smaller than others Atellus had seen but well-fed and cared for. It wore an elaborate halter and bridle with dried scalps hanging from the breast-girth and reins. It was a pale dun colour, and well controlled by the rider's knees.

The horseman sat rigid in his four-horned saddle, looking down at them. He wore a light mail shirt, a metal face-mask helmet and furs. A patchy cloak ran down his back and onto the horse's rump. His forearms were bare and the pale flesh covered in thick dark hairs, hatched with old scars. The rider removed the face-plate of his helmet, and Atellus could see his fierce, calculating eyes weighing them up. A long cavalry spatha hung from the front nearside saddle horn; it was streaked bright with fresh blood.

He spoke in Brythonic, his voice deep, and Drustanus answered. As the horseman spoke his eyes moved over each of them in turn. Barbarus joined the group and gave Atellus a grim nod. His face was slashed with blood and his clothes were sodden. The horse danced nervously at his arrival; the rider steadied his whickering steed with his heels.

"Ave, beneficiarius imperatoris," he said in rough Latin, addressing Atellus. "I am Solinus, optio of the garrison at Procolita."

"My thanks to you, optio," said Atellus. "We owe our lives to your timing."

"We have been tracking that band since morning," he replied. "We needed to make a move before dark. The conditions were not favourable."

"We are glad you did."

The air was full of the soft low moans of those without the lungs to breathe deeply, and the screams and shrieks of those in mortal pain. There was both the bass and treble of agony, an endless threnody of pain and death rising and falling on the whims of the wind. The sound of the limitanei's celebrations could be heard around them, sharper, jubilant, more vital; flagons of acetum were passed around as the men went through the dead and dying and either helped them or finished them.

The flowing hair from the fresh bloodied scalps trailed out from Solinus's steed. "We can give you escort with us to Procolita," said the optio.

Atellus shook his head. "Thank you, but we make for Aesica."

"You will not reach it before night."

"We intend to travel by night," said Drustanus.

"Do you know well the men of Aesica, optio?" asked Atellus.

Solinus looked up at the stars needling the velvet sky overhead. "I know well no man, beneficiarius, except myself," he replied. "I would stay clear of Aesica. They look to their own interests. We all have to, on the Wall. They will have no time for the emperor, for rank, for strangers. They have time only for survival." He looked down hard at Atellus. "As do we all."

Solinus raised his open palm in a farewell salute, then wheeled his horse round, and rode away; the hooves of his mount thumped the snow, spitting up powder which twinkled in the moonlight. He shouted in Brythonic, some hoarse commands to the other riders, who in turn shouted at the men, riding around and bellowing down at them. Within a matter of moments, the men were formed up and moving out, heading westwards towards the setting sun. Their shadows stretched long behind them, lapping across the carnage like ghosts of the dead.

"We should move on," said Drustanus, wincing as he tested his weight on his injured leg. "The northerners will be back before too long to reclaim their own."

472

The three men ate some food which they found on the corpses of the slain, slaked their thirst with water from the meltsnow, and did their best to patch their wounds. Drustanus's ankle was strapped up and the bleeding had stopped, and he refused Atellus's offer of a shoulder. They set off eastwards, the howling of the wolves cutting through the forest around them, as the night deepened and the sick moon grinned down upon them.

After a lengthy march, Barbarus halted them. "I shall take my leave here," he said. "I can see the milefort."

"Yes," said Drustanus, frowning. "There is Culuslupi." The Arcanus pointed off south towards where the wall's faded whitewash which glowed spectrally in the moonlight. "Remember what I said about getting through. Fortuna."

Barbarus nodded. Atellus gripped his wrist and clapped his shoulder. "Fortuna."

"Thankyou," said the convict, and he melted away into the night. For a while his silhouette was visible like a shade over the glowing snow, until that too was swallowed up by the darkness.

The other two pressed on westwards through the night; the travel was slow, the terrain rough and the snow deep, and each step was an effort. The cold settled on their shoulders like an enemy, chewing at their exposed flesh like a blunt-toothed beast.

They marched until they were ready to drop, and the lights of Aesica were a pale red smudge against the underside of the dark clouds; every so often Atellus saw the flare of a communications beacon from further along the Wall, which sprayed light over the masonry and the wooden ramparts and sent shadows dancing across the ghostly land, before it burned itself out and all was dark again.

Drustanus angled them off north towards a copse of trees visible in the moonlight. They reached them and made camp within the roots of an overturned fir, gathering deadwood and stacking it interwoven against the splayed roots. Drustanus managed to start a small fire, shielded by stones, and they slept fitfully by its light.

They woke with the dawn, and walked on, cutting a large circle around a temporary encampment of some kind. Drustanus thought it could be brigands, or possibly an advance detachment from Aesica. Neither he nor Atellus wanted to get close enough to find out.

As the anaemic sun dragged itself up into the sky, they approached Aesica, angling east then south so they could approach the fort from the front and not risk being shot by nervous limitanei on the ramparts. They stopped at the base of an acclivity which would lead them into a direct sight-line of the gate-house opening out onto the flat expanse of the Wall.

"How will we get through?" asked Atellus. "The guards will be watching out for me. They will know me by sight."

Drustanus nodded. "I have given this some thought. Do you trust me?" he asked.

"Yes," said Atellus. "I have no reason not to. You saved my life in the snows and fought beside me."

Drustanus nodded tersely. "I need to bind you," he said, producing a rope of flax from his cloak pocket. "To get through the gates, it will look less unusual if you are my prisoner. I have brought others back in similar manners, to claim a bounty from the praefectus. I will get you past the sentries. Once we are into the fort, you will keep your head down. I will lead you away, towards the south gate, and into the vicus. It will be dark, and my face is well known there. No-one will ask any questions."

Atellus turned round and held his hands out behind his back. Drustanus tied the flax carefully around his already bruised and cut wrists, and loosened the knot slightly.

"That okay?"

Atellus nodded.

"Keep your face covered at all times," said the Arcanus. He unwound some thin, stained leather bands from his forearms and handed them to Atellus. "Pull your cowl further over, and wrap these straps around your face and nose."

They carried on walking, lifting their knees high out of the drifts of snow and sinking deep into the next with a crunch. Drustanus led them around the defensive areas, weaving paths through the invisible pits and caltrops, navigating a safe path to the main north gate.

"What is the plan?" asked Atellus, keeping his voice low.

"I shout for entry," he replied, "and explain to the gate-guard that you are a brigand caught poaching. They'll let us in and send us through the fort to present you to the praefectus. I will take you around as if to the principia, then swing past the barrack block and out through the south gate."

"And no-one will question this?"

"No," he replied. "They don't give a damn. And if anyone did get too curious, I have some gold to increase my persuasive powers." He laughed.

The gatehouse loomed large and square ahead of them, the Wall stretching out either side like huge bestial wings; Atellus felt as though he were being led into the maw of some great and malignant animal.

A voice called out a question from upon the battlements. Atellus felt his flesh crawling under the imagined weight of the points of dozens of arrows trained at his chest. The fort towered above him as a mountain of flat sheer stone peering down with its eyes of ballistrariae. The Wall was the god of the north, and the god was displeased to see him again.

Drustanus bellowed out a string of Brythonic, followed up with Latin. "Open the door," he shouted. "Arcanus with captive!"

A small door opened, a sliver of light in the great façade of the north gate which grew into the form of a man, a commander of the guard. He stepped out, hand on his spatha hilt, and stared at the two men.

"That you, Drustanus?"

"Aye it's me, Tam, you old sod," said the Arcanus. "Let me in for wine and food, it's fucking freezing here." He laughed, easily.

The soldier named Tam stepped back and jerked his head towards the small opening in the gate.

"What's that you got?" he asked, sniffing and spitting onto the snow.

"More meat for Apullius," he replied. "And more gold for me."

"And more vinum for me at the tavern this evening, eh, friend Arcanus?"

"Don't push it, Tam," he laughed, "but we'll see."

Drustanus prodded Atellus forward through the gateway hatch. They were in a narrow brick-lined corridor, which led out to the main armoury of the fort. A row of long barrack-blocks was ranged to the left, and the huge grounds of the principia were directly ahead. To the right were workshops and stables, though both seemed empty.

Atellus walked forward, the limitanei casting a disinterested glance at him as he passed. He kept his eyes to the ground, fixed on the shuffling gait of his own feet. He was aware of a hand at his back, steering him forward.

Soldiers were sparring in the yard; others throwing dice against the walls of the barrack-blocks or drinking in clutches, spitting and coughing into the snow. A tall man came up to them, and looked directly at Atellus, who averted his gaze immediately. He was a large soldier, with a long half-healed scar across the bridge of his nose and. His dark hair, peppered with white, was cut short in the old way. His clothing was more refined than the other soldiers: he had a long shirt of lorica hamata which hung down to his bare knees. His cloak was a deep red and he wore a well-fitted helmet. The soldier addressed himself to Drustanus.

"What have you here, Arcanus?"

Drustanus laughed. "Greetings, Maglorius! And how are you?"

"What is it?" the tall soldier repeated, his voice deep and quiet, his tone authoritative and spare.

"What is it, indeed?" said Drustanus. "Only your missing emperor's bitch, Maglorius, that is all. Alive, as promised."

Atellus whipped round, straight into the fist of Drustanus. He fell to the ground, landing awkwardly on his bound arms.

Colour seemed to leach from the world; the bright pale pink dawn sky, the slick infinity grey of the walls, the blood-red of the soldier's cloak. A buzzing filled Atellus's head. He spat blood up at the Arcanus, and shook his head, trying to meet his eye.

"You'll find the other at Culuslupi," continued Drustanus, rubbing his knuckles. "Trying to bury his whore. He could not be persuaded to join us."

"The praefectus is not so interested in that one," said Maglorius. "He will not live long. Let him run free with the other rats, until the storm comes to wash them all into the same sewer."

Atellus rolled over onto his front, then got to his feet via his knees. He looked at Drustanus, who returned the gaze flatly.

"I will remember this, Arcanus," said Atellus, quietly. His dark eyes bored deep into the other man's skull.

"I hope it keeps you company in your final hours, nigger," said Drustanus. He laughed and slapped Maglorius on the shoulder.

"Come on then, centurion," he said. "The gold, if you please."

Maglorius pulled a heavy pouch from under his cloak and counted out a handful of solidus coins which he dropped into Drustanus's outstretched hand.

"Now," said the centurion after resealing the pouch and replacing it within his cloak, "I will wait for you to give it all back to me through the taverns and brothels."

Drustanus smiled. "Oh, your wish is my command, centurion." He sketched a mocking bow to Maglorius, and with a last smile at Atellus, walked off through the fort, towards the south gate and the comforts of the vicus.

CHAPTER 33

Clouds of thick black smoke were rolling in through the gaps between the timbers and underneath the door. It smelt oily and sweet. The interior of the dwelling was already getting murkier and the air thicker.

"Keep low," said Rodius. "Cover your face with your sleeve."

Aurelia did as she was told. There was laughter outside, but it sounded tinny and distant. She could hear a sinister crackle as the swelling flames took hold against the stacked kindling, and beneath that the sinister susurration as the fire ate into the thick timber of the building itself.

"Come out, or burn," shouted Catugnavus. "I don't care which." More laughter.

Rodius and Aurelia were both coughing now, retching as the top half of the air in the dwelling turned a dreamy, billowy grey. They could feel the heat from outside pressing in on them as a wave of pressure.

"What are our options?" asked Aurelia between coughs.

"Die in here," said Rodius, "or die out there."

Aurelia frowned as the fire crackled. It sounded as if the whole structure were under attack from outside, an ominous throb and smack and a juddering and shifting of the timbers as they expanded in the heat, hissing and popping. Water trickled in from above as the heat melted the snow lying on the roof.

"The window?" said Aurelia, looking hopefully up at the sliver of crisp violet sky outside. She could see the black smoke rolling and curling upwards past the circular aperture.

Rodius shook his head. "They'll be waiting for us."

The heat was becoming unbearable; they huddled in the centre of the large room, greasy smoke unfurling itself over their heads, pawing its way along the ceiling like some great dark wave. The metal implements hanging from the beams were beginning to glow from the heat.

Rodius told Aurelia to get low to the ground, and he rushed back in to the dead man's room. The floor was wet with melted snow, and steam was hissing from the outside. Some of the damp hay was folding and twisting as the first sparks of flame landed onto them. There was a sweet smell which rode over the guttural oily stench of the naphtha smoke.

Rodius ducked over to the corpse, keeping low and sucking in large lungfuls of clean air from just above the ground. He grabbed the stiffened body with his hand, and hauled it up and over, kicking the sheets up and swatting the hay away from the floor.

There was something bothering him, something tickling the back of his mind.

His thoughts were disturbed by a cry from the main room followed by a splintering crash; the whole building juddered and shook angrily. Heat and smoke whipped up into Rodius's face, and the sound of the flames gnawing through the tough brittle wood intensified. He rushed through saw one of the crossbeams settling from where it had collapsed, the huge trunk slammed into the ground showering flaming debris from the roof onto the floor. He saw Aurelia on the floor in the centre of the room, flanked by the savage fiery timbers, rolling back and forth to extinguish patches of flame on her clothes. Rodius rushed over, and used his own cloak to pat away the flames until they faltered and died. Coughing wildly, as though his very stomach was trying to exit through his mouth, Rodius scooped up Aurelia and tucked her under his arm. Feeling the heat sear his face and chest, he moved around the burning timbers and tried to regain his bearings.

The ceiling was now a wild massacre limned by angry red flames and backed by the thick black smoke. The pulsing, pressing heat was like an assailant in the room with them; sparks and singed flecks of burnt timber fell from the sky like phosphorescent snow.

Rodius carried Aurelia through the stifling, choking atmosphere and into the other empty room with the animal carcass. He laid her gently on the steaming hay.

"Thank you," she said, swiping embers from her clothing. He nodded in response, then set about kicking at the deep patches of hay on the floor, getting to his knees and ripping up a great handful of it and flinging it over his head. The chatter and moan of the fire was less loud here, the rear of the building catching slower than the front, where the incendiaries had been focused.

"What are you doing?" asked Aurelia, her voice barely audible above the surge and crackle of flames from outside. She sounded calm and resigned.

There was a roar and a crunch as some more structural beams collapsed from the main room, taking down the drapes of hides covering their room; the full fury of the inferno kicked and wailed beyond in the tumbled, red-black remains of the dwelling. The heat pushed them back and set the straw at their feet aflame.

"Somewhere!" spat Rodius, sweat streaming from his body. His face was dark-red and damned and the edges of his long hair were singed. Aurelia shuffled over to the centre of the room, driven back by the heat, and pressed down to the floor by the thick black smoke. She coughed and hacked and spots danced in front of her eyes as she looked up at Rodius, like a Colossus in a fever dream, a raging Polyphemus with his head in dark volcanic clouds which glowed a ruddy scarlet.

Rodius kicked and heaved and bucked, as much to keep his stifled, scorched body away from any point of heat for too long, although there seemed discernment and purpose in his motions. His foot struck something in the far corner – Aurelia felt the drum of the contact through her ear which was pressed to the mercifully cool boards beneath her – and Rodius fell down as if struck from above.

He rose, his shaggy besmirched head ascending into the dark clouds, moving to Aurelia as if in slow motion, his chest heaving and thrumming with explosive coughs. In his hand was a huge square of wood: dark, cool wood, which fell back against the far side of the wall. Aurelia looked up and saw the ceiling overhead, a beautiful and mesmerising vision of the heavens: the layers of undulating dark cloud took on the faces and postures of her fears, and she could see the ethereal beauty of the heavens: a panoply of bright red and yellow stars, lines intersecting and flickering amidst a sound of thunder like the laughter of the gods in her ears.

The next she knew, she was flying, or felt weightless, and there was an irresistible force on her arm, and then she was cool – blessedly gloriously cool – and the coolness only served to make the very memory of the heat unbearable. She opened her eyes and seemed to be staring up from the bottom of some dark pit, and the light and heat from above was ferocious.

Rodius ducked down low after bundling Aurelia through the aperture in the ground, and climbed down the narrow ladder, feeling the cool ground swallowing him up and the searing pain in his flesh easing and soothing; he slammed the trapdoor shut above him and darkness consumed everything. There was a splintering crash and the earth around them shook as the rest of the dwelling came down atop the hatch, sealing them in there as surely as if it were their own tomb.

The ground was still hot, and flickers of evil light danced into the gloom from above. The feasting of the flames was a muted roar from overhead.

"Where are we?" asked Aurelia. "If we are dead, I am most disappointed."

"There was a trapdoor," said Rodius inbetween wracking coughs. He spoke, but Aurelia could only make out the occasional angles of his form illuminated in the threads of light from overhead. "I don't know where it leads. If it leads anywhere. But we need to move away from the fire."

Rodius was standing hunched in a short alcove, which seemed to be the breadth of a man's height, and an unknown length. The walls were shored with timber, and the air was cool and musty. A few unciae in front of his face, the darkness was absolute and the pressing weight of the entire earth seemed to loom above them like an ocean.

"Can you move?" he asked.

Aurelia nodded, then realising he wouldn't be able to see, answered. "Yes."

Rodius moved forward gingerly, his arms held out in front of him. The fingers of his remaining hand felt wood, and he traced them down and around until they met no resistance. Using his hand as a wand, he traced out the edges of an aperture spreading out from the ground at his feet which was just large enough to accommodate a man in a shuffling position, on hands and knees. He knelt down and moved forward.

"Follow me," he said to Aurelia. "We need to crawl."

They slithered on, the air growing cooler and staler as they moved away from the fire as the countless tonnes of earth over their heads felt like a silent, insistent pressure. Rodius felt a constant itch in the small of his back, before realising it was the awareness of the crushing death over their heads. Sweat trickled from his brow. The air grew thicker and warmer.

"How did you know this was here?" panted Aurelia through the absolute blackness.

"I should have realised it sooner," said Rodius over his shoulder. "Your agent's house was locked from the inside. The window was shuttered."

"Yes."

"But he wasn't in there," said Rodius. "Just the body of an unknown man. So your agent must have got out. Maybe he knew his place was under observation; someone in that line of work would have contingency plans. I wasn't expecting this, but I was hoping for it."

"Just in time," said Aurelia. "So where does it go?"

"I don't know," said Rodius. "Far enough for the exit to not be observed from the building, I presume. Beyond that...I'm not sure. I was worried it may just be a pit, for hiding until it was safe to emerge. And we'd find your man down there."

"But not so far," said Aurelia with a wheeze of relief.

They crawled on through the thick air and the ominous dead silence around them, until a change in the air quality made Rodius stop. Aurelia crawled into the back of him with a noise of surprise.

The passage seemed to end suddenly.

Rodius balanced himself by wedging a shoulder against the ceiling, then put his hand out and felt in front of him. There was only cracked and splintered timber. He moved his hand down to the level of his chest and met the same obstruction.

"Fuck," he said.

"What?"

He felt lower down, a panic rising up from within him, visions of being trapped there and suffocating, or dying slowly of thirst in the darkness with the weight of all the world atop him….

He waved his arms frantically and found an opening, level with his thighs. There was maybe enough room for a man crawling on his stomach to squeeze through. But there would be no turning back, no turning at all.

He swallowed hard.

"It gets narrower," Rodius said, keeping his voice level. It sounded strange to his ears, in the confined space.

"Much?"

"Yes."

Rodius got onto his stomach and slithered forward, pushing himself awkwardly into the black unknown. It felt hot, and tight. Once his body was all the way in, a terrible crushing fear rose up from his scrotum and passed up his spine and into his throat. He had to fight back the anxiety, the desire to scream and thrash and try and scuff himself backwards; he stopped, and felt cold sweat ooze from his scalp and trickle into his eyes.

He knew there was nothing behind him but fire and suffocation and a slow choking death. He carried on, tense.

"Are you ok?"

The voice came from outside his own bleak thoughts; he had almost forgotten that Aurelia was with him.

"Yes," he said. "You?"

"I've been in less pleasant situations," she replied. "But not many."

Rodius carried on, squirming forward. His ultimate terror was finding the earth solid in front of him, that the tunnel was unfinished, half-made, and they would die in a dark underworld of cramp and fear.

Something heavy ran across his shoulder brushing his ear; he could feel its legs on his back. A shiver ran through him. Seconds later there was a moan of disgust from Aurelia. He pressed on, using his elbows and knees to move him along in the confined space, but it was slow going, especially with only one hand, and he kept collapsing to his side against where the earth was shored up by frail and creaking timber planks. Dirt was in his mouth, his eyes, clogging his nose. Each breath was a laboured gasp, and he could hear Aurelia having the same problems.

There was another change in the air quality; the space seemed bigger, and fresher. He tried to test the height of the tunnel with his head and found he could lift it fully. He tentatively got to his knees and realised he could stand hunched. Far along in the direction he was facing was the merest glint of light, a slight dimness that stood out from the endless black that seemed to stretch into infinity and make his eyes and brain ache.

For a second his heart leapt with hope.

"I think we're at the end," he said to Aurelia as she bumped into his calves. He helped her up; she could stand to her full height. They walked for a short while, arms outstretched, and the dimness swelled until there was the hint of luminescence around them. Rodius could make out that the sides of the tunnel were now made of rough, hewn stone. They seemed to be in some sort of basement or foundation. As they approached the far side, small beams of agonising light shone down through small gaps in a timber door set into the low ceiling. There was a narrow wooden ladder beneath it, fixed to the wall.

Rodius climbed a few steps up and pushed on the trapdoor with his shoulder. It gave easily; he applied a little more pressure, lifting it slightly so he could peer out. Clear white moonlight poured through and pulsed painfully at the back of his eyes. He squeezed them shut to let them adjust, then propped the trapdoor open slightly. He could see weeds and parts of a broken fence-post. To his left was masonry: the wall of a dwelling. There was no-one around. He listened intently for a while, but there was only the squawking of the birds in the sky and the soft buzz of activity from the vicus which sounded sufficiently distant. He could smell smoke in the air, and the memory brought him out in a cold sweat.

Rodius was anxious for fresh air and space and let his desperation quash his caution: he heaved open the trapdoor so he could clamber out. The wood was heavy and the top was covered with clods of earth and bristleweed so it blended in with the land around. He pulled himself into the crisp cold air and sucked in huge lungfuls: it tasted as fine to him as any wine. He bent down and helped Aurelia out, then closed the trapdoor behind them and carefully replaced the camouflage so it remained hidden.

They were standing behind a large derelict farmhouse. The building was a mere shell of blackened stone and singed beams; most of the timbers were collapsed in on themselves. The smell of old death and decay hung in the still air. The masonry was slowly being robbed for other dwellings, though it was obviously sufficiently distant from the centre of the vicus to have kept a remnant here for this long. The outbuildings were also burned and the timber and stone mostly robbed; the fence-posts surrounding the property were either broken or missing. The growth of the plants and weeds around them betrayed a dereliction of a few years at least.

Rodius and Aurelia walked into the ruins of the building. There were bones in a corner, though Rodius could not tell if they were those of man or beast, fresh or ancient. A small fire had been made there quite recently, tucked behind one of the fallen beams. The sky was open to them overhead.

"What now?" he asked.

"We need to tell the others," said Aurelia.

Rodius nodded.

They walked on across the bare snowy fields, away from the gutted farm-dwelling, the trees like eerie sentinels on their flanks, and the smoke and heat of the vicus shimmering up ahead. The Wall itself stretched terse and rigid across the horizon, long and tall, the ramparts seeming to scrape the sky which hung low and thin and pale, like steam above a monstrous serpent.

They covered their red-burnt and soot-stained faces with the cowls of their hoods and trudged on through the snow.

CHAPTER 34

Calidus was sick of it. He was sick of the cold; sick of the itchy rags he had to don each day; sick of the looks the soldiers gave him – along with the merchants and the wealthy men of the vicus – when he could have bought all of them with one fifth of his monthly stipend from his uncle.

Most of all, he was sick of the whinging, sullen, sour-faced man at his side.

Vassu rarely spoke out loud. But when he did, it was a moan, or a curse, or just a throaty expectoration which always landed somewhere all too near to Calidus's boot.

They had been walking through the vicus in endless circles, both together and alone. Galla trailed behind Calidus as she always did, a mute shade at his heels, and no amount of pleading could induce her to go along with Vassu; nor he to take her.

There had been no sight of Atellus, nor contact with any who had known him. There was no news of anything worthwhile in the vicus except the usual lamentations over the lack of food, and the preponderance of brigands on the roads and in the surrounding forests. There were others half-mad who passed them, weeping about Cernunnos stealing their babes, or beggars convinced the emperor was thieving their grain, or that there was a huge horde of savages waiting to sweep through the Wall and send them all to oblivion.

They walked back on themselves, their pace slow and despondent and their footfalls laboured. Only Vassu had any bounce to him, and that was no doubt because he had been ferreting information from the bath-house. He looked warm and relaxed for a change, the pinch at his eyes and the shallow furrows at his brow less defined. There were times when he looked almost pleasant, and then as soon as

Vassu realised anyone was looking in his direction, he would scowl at them and dribble a string of oaths from the corner of his mouth. Something about the man was seedy and wrong, and Calidus wouldn't have trusted him as far as he could kick him.

They walked through the sludge and snow of the vicus, past the ribbons of smoke from the dwellings and the clang of the smiths and the chattering chaos of the abattoir. The air stank of blood and cold and dung and smoke. There was still the thick black cloud which hung like a ghostly pall over the south east of the vicus; there had been a ferocious fire at one of the old farmhouses earlier in the day. A crowd had gathered – Calidus, Galla and Vassu among them – and had stood watching the flames. Some for the warmth, others to see who was dead. But no man made any attempt to go and help out.

"They'll be long dead," said one, "black as yon smoke."

No-one seemed to know who resided there, or care very much. The best they could get was some intimation that it was a smith of some kind, or a herdsman, but no-one was certain. When the flames died and the smoke became thicker and more pungent, the crowd dispersed.

"Another wasted day," spat Vassu from behind him. Calidus ignored him. They headed through the narrow lanes where the going was awkward, and merged with the main metalled road through the vicus. Here the snow had been cleared and the crowds were thicker and walked with more purpose.

"I bet your uncle could use a good trader, eh boy?" said Vassu.

"Don't call me *boy*," replied Calidus sharply. This had been another of Vassu's familiar themes: trying to acquire a position for himself in Eboracum. Calidus tugged at Galla's hand, and she picked up her pace a little. He was aware he was striding too fast, but he wanted to get back to the warmth of the tavern and a bowl of hot broth with the sumptuous steam warming his cheeks. "My uncle has higher standards than you seem to think, Vassu."

Vassu grumbled in response and kicked at a large rat that scurried across his path. "I remember when there used to be actual cats and hounds in this dump," he said. "Instead of just these rodents of their size."

"Where are they now?" asked Calidus absently.

"Where, boy?" he laughed, a sound like ice cracking. "In people's bellies. Or their latrines more like. Floating on a river of effluence down to Eboracum."

The laughter came to a stop as he walked into the back of Calidus.

"What the fuck—"

"Look," said Calidus, pointing at the tavern. They had turned the corner of the main road and onto the subsidiary upon which the building loomed. There were limitanei lounging outside the building, looked bored and dangerous: two men either side of the main door.

"Shit," said Vassu, simply. "Looks as if they're on duty. Not that you can always tell with these weasels."

"Trouble?" asked Calidus.

"Stay here with the bint," he replied. "They could recognise you."

Vassu walked off towards the tavern door with the confidence of the innocent, or the drunk. The soldiers let him pass with only a stare and he walked inside the barn-like hall. He saw a few topers scattered around, with the odd recumbent figure stretched along the length of a bench, snoring gutturally. The large pit-fire in the centre of the room was smouldering. Lined up along the bar, talking with Muconia, were three serious-looking soldiers in immaculate uniform.

Vassu took this in, trying to catch Muconia's eye, but she was deep in conversation with the soldiers. He moved around to the stairs leading up to the chambers and flexed his fingers, testing them. Once the swelling had gone down, he found that he could use his digits much as before, though they were horribly misshapen and their strength greatly reduced. He would get used to them though; well enough to wield a weapon anyway. Death was never far off from a man who could not defend himself ably. One of the first things he had done with Scotius's gold was to haggle with an old toe-rag in the bar to purchase a simple but well-made long-bladed dagger to keep at his hip; he used his fingers to absent-mindedly caress its leather-wrapped hilt. Swords were expensive and hard to come by, even in a military town, but this would do for the time.

His fingers ached as he withdrew them and pushed them deep into the folds of his tunic. At least the constant pain had gone; now they only ached like a bad tooth when the weather was cold. Which, Vassu conceded, was all the time. He offered up a quick prayer, to whichever gods were listening, for Spring to come quickly.

Vassu walked up the stairs with a lighter tread than usual and appeared on the first floor landing. He could hear sounds of disturbance ahead of him, and turned the corner just in time to see five soldiers kicking through the door at the far end. With a crack and splinter of wood, the flimsy door burst inward after the second kick and five armed men streamed in. Vassu stood frozen to the spot, listening to the shouts and curses, the sounds of metal clashing against metal and furniture tumbling and collapsing. The timbers thundered under Vassu's feet as he stood shivering, unsure what to do.

There was a howl of pain emanating from the room, and then desperate language tripping from someone's throat.

Vassu stood still.

An injured limitanei fell through the door, collapsing into the landing, and bleeding darkly from a large wound in his neck. His companions either side of the door stooped down to help him up, and one desperately tore his own shirt and wrapped the cloth around his comrade's wound. The injured man gurgled and wheezed as the breath whistled through the gash in his neck.

Vassu felt himself taking a step forward. His deformed fingers were hovering around the hilt of the long-bladed dagger, which hung concealed beneath the layers of his cloak.

There was a sudden commotion in the doorway in front of him and a cluster of men struggled out, his brother Rodius clasped between them, his arms twisted awkwardly behind his back, and his face blistered and covered with fresh blood. He looked semi-conscious. The limitanei dragged him through the corridor and past Vassu, down the stairs. Next, Aurelia was carried out, half-tucked under the arms of a large soldier with a dirty red beard. She looked abused, her face swollen and dark, and her eyes glassy, but she was able to look at him and stare at him with recognition. There was nothing but hate and loss in her clear blue gaze, and Vassu found himself shaking his head, subtly, slowly, hoping she could comprehend his meaning.

She was dragged past him and down the stairs, the laughing soldiers following, some limping, some bleeding, some helping the injured man. They pushed past him as though he were a piece of awkward furniture, and clumped down the stairs and into the main hall of the tavern.

Vassu felt a pain in his hand, and looked down to see he was gripping the hilt of his spatha tightly through the material of his cloak. His knuckles were bluewhite, the bones and twisted ligaments of his fingers howling with pain.

He forced himself to slacken his grips, and walked down the steps feeling lightheaded, as though he were watching himself descend the staircase from above, looking down at the mop of his own greasy dark hair and the jut of his aquiline nose. He reached the bottom and saw his brother on the floor, the limitanei taking it in turns to kick him in the ribs. The floor around his face was wet with the blood he spat out.

Vassu emerged from the stairwell unobserved, his penury obvious, his clothes drab and dark enough that he sank into the very fabric of the room around him, fitting in as a piece of ugly furniture, or another dead-drunkard clogging the floor space. He heard Muconia talking to the well-dressed soldiers: they were sat at a table in the corner, their tankards full, their plates piled with rare and expensive cuts of meat.

"–half a job."

"No," said Muconia, her face stern, her hair seeming to sizzle in the dim light, like the dying embers of the fire in the centre of the hall. "I never promised that."

"It was the boy and the bitch we wanted," said one of them, his voice plummy and supercilious. "One-hand is of no interest."

"The boy will be back at some point," said Muconia sullenly. "If your clumsy hounds haven't scared him away for good."

"Let's hope for your sake, whore, that he is." The soldier tipped the last of his drink into his mouth and stood up, pushing back his chair from the table. He jerked his head towards the door, and the other two seated soldiers stood up and walked with him.

"Bring them both," he called out to the limitanei who were assaulting Rodius and leering over Aurelia. "Keep him alive until I say otherwise."

The soldiers left the building dragging their captives with them. Vassu stood there, unseen, as Muconia reached over and helped herself to the unfinished wine. He stared at her as she drank, the sticky liquid running down her chin. Then he moved silently towards the door, away from the smells of beer and peat smoke and the delicious soporific warmth, and broke out into the cold bleak pale light of the winter.

CHAPTER 35

Maglorius led Atellus at sword-point through the fort and round towards the principia. The wind buffeted his flesh as he walked, and the cold penetrated to his very core, but he felt a strange numbness inside.

He was greeted by the familiar grey-green stone of the fort, with its peeled whitewash and its scribbled graffiti. The air around him was permeated by the surly insolence of the limitanei, the stench of sweat and shit and rusted metal, and the fusty odour of damp, decaying wood. Looming up ahead, seemingly out of place amongst such squalor and deprivation, was the relative grandeur of the principia and its grounds.

His hands were still bound behind his back with the flax that the traitor Drustanus had tied, but Maglorius had pulled it tighter so it bit into his skin. Atellus cursed himself for not trusting Barbarus's instincts about the Arcanus, then, after a quick oath of vengeance, cast it from his mind. He needed to focus on escaping the situation he was in, rather than lamenting wrong choices. He looked up to the sky and saw it matching his mood: darkening with clouds and hung low with threat. He grimaced at the thought of another storm brewing beyond the horizon.

They walked around the principia, Maglorius nodding to the guards as they passed, and along the rows of barracks which stood long and silent and empty. Other than the clang of the smithy's hammer reverberating around the fort, Aesica was strangely silent. The optio prodded him forward towards a short door set into the fort's west wall.

"Knock three times," said the centurion "With your foot.". Atellus did as instructed. He could feel the blade of the spatha jutting into the flesh just below his armpit. A solid driven thrust by the centurion and he would be dead almost before he would have time to feel the wound.

The door was unlatched from the inside, and a dark-faced, red-eyed soldier looked at them both, then nodded at Maglorius. They folded themselves inside and into a narrow antechamber with a single desk and ledger. Beyond this were rows of dark, damp pit cells. The stench made Atellus's eyes sting. There were two more limitanei inside, unshaven and looking as if they did nothing but drink and dice in the gloom. Two of them shuffled round and grabbed him by either arm.

"Where you want it?" said one of them to Maglorius. The centurion shrugged and turned.

"Keep him fresh till I get back."

One of the men gave a laugh and Maglorius opened the door leading into the courtyard. Pale light drenched the inside for a moment, and then was gone.

The two limitanei dragged Atellus along the corridor before opening a cell door at the far end and flinging him inside. There was a drop of a few feet, and Atellus landed heavily on his side, cracking a couple of ribs. The soldiers laughed as he cried out in pain, and then slammed the door shut above him.

He managed to wriggle himself into a sitting position with his back against the far wall. There was nothing but absolute darkness on all sides, so that his eyes conjured lights and shapes in front of him as he sat, spots and threads of luminescence spiderwebbing across his vision.

He was alone in the cell: he couldn't feel the warmth or the soft respiration of another presence, but he could detect the cluck and skitter of creatures on the floor around him. The ground was damp, and water seemed to pool in the corner. There was a vile stench of stale faeces, blood and fear.

He lay back for a while, resting his head against the wall behind him. He was dimly aware of succumbing to a thick, desperate sleep, when he was snapped awake by the sound of footsteps overhead. He waited as they approached and the door was thrown open once more with a clang that seemed to explode into his ears.

Atellus watched as a flame appeared up above which flickered and sent pools of light sweeping across his cell. He heard voices and saw the silhouette of a tall, broad soldier stepping down to join him. The soldier carried the torch, though the glare stung Atellus's eyes and he could not discern the face beyond the flame.

"Get me a seat down here," said the voice, calling up to the guards. It was strong and commanding, but it did not sound like Maglorius. There was a bustle of activity above and Atellus saw a wooden stool passed down to the soldier, who thumped it on the ground and sat astride it.

"Beneficiarius," said the visitor. "I must say your lodgings are looking rather glum." There was no trace of humour in the voice; it spoke the words as a pronouncement, and there was no concern inflected in the crisp authoritarian tongue. The soldier laid the torch on the ground at his feet, and his face appeared in a harsh chiaroscuro.

"Apullius," said Atellus, spitting out the word. "What an honour."

"You flatter me, beneficiarius," he replied, and Atellus could hear the smile twisting his thick lips. "Kind words from one so powerful."

"Power is relative."

"Indeed," laughed Apullius. "I daresay the lowest of the rats in the corner of this cell have more power than you at this time. More power over their own destiny."

"Your power is based on treachery," said Atellus, "corruption, betrayal."

498

"All power is, beneficiarius," came the reply. "All power is. If not, it is just an illusion, a mere dream. All of Rome's power is built on such tenets. Would you disparage me for following in the footsteps of our esteemed emperor?" He laughed softly. "The Arcanae have served me well. Drustanus has earned his gold."

"I'm glad you are so quick to trust."

"Trust?" queried Apullius. "Why should I not? As long as his interests are intertwined with my own, we are perfect commilitiones."

"You trust him to fight for Rome?" asked Atellus.

"Oh, I never said that, beneficiarius. Drustanus will fight for gold. Like most of the Arcanae. Mercenaries, to a man."

Atellus laughed bitterly. "And when the gold runs out?"

"I trust him to do what is best for himself," said Apullius. "And his people."

"His people?"

"Drustanus is loyal to his blood," said Apullius. "Like most men here on the limes. It is a fealty which transcends boundaries, languages, tribal enmities. Whether he has fought from this side of the Wall, or for the Attacotti, or the Scoti on the other, he has always fought those who are enemies of his blood, and joined with those who are brothers to him. The division is not always as simple as *Roman* and *barbarian*."

The praefectus remained silent for a while. When he spoke again, his voice was lower, less declamatory. "Men such as Drustanus, such as I, have more loyalty, more maiesta than you whores of the emperor could ever comprehend. You serve blindly, and follow orders willingly, regardless of the outcome. Even if your own people, your own *blood*, suffer because of it."

499

Atellus looked up at his persecutor; his face seemed to be carved from some fierce limestone, the angles pronounced in the harsh light. It swam above the darkness like a portent, an omen in the blackness around him. Every fibre of Atellus's being ached and every part of his body hummed with a ferocious sadness emanating from the pit of his stomach.

"I know what happened to your family, Titus Faenius Magnus Atellus," said Apullius softly. "The whim of a mistrustful emperor sends you home to find them butchered where they lay. The sumptuous blankets and drapes paid for by your service to the emperor were sticky with their blood. The servants fled to leave them to their opulent coffins."

Atellus was shaking his head, a huge burning coal flaming in his belly, rising up into his chest, engulfing his lungs as it passed, forcing itself into his throat choking him with its heat, and up into his skull. He could not think, could not be, for existing itself was the most intense pain he had ever experienced. The memories he had fought back, pushed down, for so long, rose again like some foul miasma.

"Jovian killed your beautiful wife, your innocent daughter," continued Apullius. "He killed you, Atellus, on the walls of Constantinople, but somehow the gods preserved you. And yet you return to the lap of the emperor, like a beaten cur awaiting the final mercy. The empire that destroyed you and your family. Why trust one emperor and not another?" The praefectus gave a short laugh and slapped his thigh, shaking his head. "If Rome killed my love, sullied my blood, I would dedicate my life to killing Rome. But not you, easterner. You are a different kind of...man."

Atellus felt that he could not breathe; his chest was tight, as though crushed in the gripe of some huge fist.

Julia Faenia. Julia Petronia.

The truth he had never been able to face; the memories he had killed as surely as his wife and daughter.

His life. His hope. His everything.

"So tell me, *Atellus*," said Apullius leaning forward to him, their faces within unciae of each other. "Why do you work for the emperor? Tell me *why*. Because I simply cannot understand, barbarian that I am."

Atellus was silent, his eyes glazed with inner pain, sweat glistening on his brow in the candlelight. He shook his head weakly, and a strange noise clicked from the back of his throat.

The praefectus shook his own head and sat back. "Your emperor will soon be finished. Rome itself cannot last. How much influence do you think Valentinian has here? In Aesica? On the Wall? In Britannia, even?" Apullius's words were inflected with contempt.

"People die of starvation and disease," he continued. "The limitanei – good men, all, some with families – have not been paid for countless moons. Beyond the Wall, the meanest of the tribes enjoy more freedom and food than these poor animals get, starving and freezing each night playing at being the eyes of your emperor. What does Valentinian do about that?"

Apullius stood up and disappeared from the range of the torch flame; he was a grey and hidden shade sliding through life, Atellus half-catching glimpses of him as he passed, like clouds scudding past a dying moon.

"Here, on the Wall," said the praefectus, "life is different. I can't expect you to understand that. A soldier, you may have been. But life is very different in Rome, in Treves, in the great desert cities of the east. What would you know about my men, about their families, their wants and needs? Here, Atellus, imperium means nothing.

Religion is *everything*. Here, life is short, and death is for eternity. These men would swap ten of your emperors for one whisper of Cernunnos. These men have stronger ties through their gods then the emperor can forge for them.

"The men wish to sacrifice to the old gods," continued Apullius, "and who am I to stop them? They believe their salvation is in the hands of Cernunnos." The praefectus gave a heavy shrug. "Maybe it is. The poor harvest, the fierce weather, the pestilence on the land. Has the emperor helped with this? No, he has not. But Cernunnos will."

Atellus could hear Apullius's footsteps as he paced slowly the length and breadth of the small cell. But his eyes were filled only with memories of his wife and daughter; their laughing faces, their fresh beauty, and the day he had walked in to see only the ugliness of their mangled, defiled bodies.

After being cut down from the walls of Constantinople, he had returned from the east in secret, posing as a trader, each mile of the many hundreds as painful to him as a blow to the stomach; he rode horses to death and purchased fresh ones until he arrived in Treves in the dead of the night and ran on foot to the gates of his villa. There were no lights burning, and no servants keeping watch. The gates were flung wide open.

He had let the hope form in his mind that Julia Faenia had taken Petronia away and fled to her family's estates in Narbonensis. He had gone inside the villa and seen the destruction caused by looters, the defilements, the breakages, the scorch marks, and the slatherings of blood smeared across walls and doors.

He had died once before, swinging from the walls of the great city, and now, such was the gods' hatred of him, he had died again.

His beautiful wife; his perfect daughter.

He could go back and join them, gather their mutilated, rotting bodies into his arms and smother himself on a blazing pyre and if decreed it they could spend eternity in each others' arms, a tripartite embrace.

Only vengeance kept him alive as a withered husk of his former self, an automaton that ate and slept and survived only for vengeance.

"I pity you, beneficiarius," said Apullius, breaking through the depths of Atellus's memories. "From what Crispus has told me, you are a broken man. A damned thing. A creature. I would have let you come here and tell Valentinian what you may.

"'Children are being sacrificed to Cernunnos', you would report; 'the crucified god, the Christos, has been rejected', you would say, 'as have Constantine's edicts'. But what of it, Atellus?" asked Apullius. "The same story can be told across the limes. An agent in rebus, even, killed."

Atellus could make out the silhouette of the praefectus wheeling round to face him.

"But...you would find no proof of that," said Apullius. "No. Nothing tangible. You would be recalled to Treves, and before Valentinian could take decisive action either way, the empire would be threatened from another angle, from a more tangible, more physical, foe.

"But, Crispus," continued Apullius, "he was very insistent that you be killed. Not just killed: maimed, tortured, mutilated, *then* killed. He said he asked for you to be sent up here. Why would the man hate you so much, Atellus? That is what I do not understand."

Atellus looked up wearily; lifting his head slightly felt like the greatest effort in the universe.

"I fucked his wife," said Atellus in a flat tone. "Many years ago."

The praefectus laughed. "Is that all? He is a petty man, Crispus. All the most powerful are, as I am sure you know. Perhaps you two lovers will get to say farewell before you are sent to the next world. She is currently being held up in my chambers until we have word from her loving husband." He finished with a mocking laugh.

Atellus looked up at the praefectus, uncomprehending. "But she is in Eboracum."

"She was in Eboracum," agreed Apullius. "But she fled up here. Why, I have no idea, but Crispus was most concerned that we retrieve her."

"The man is a pathetic snake," said Atellus in an emotionless tone.

"You believe that he poisoned Julian?" queried Apullius, his face creased in genuine interest.

"If anyone could poison such a great man," said Atellus, "it would be that worm." Apullius nodded, the light raking his cheekbones as his head moved up and down. "But your days are limited, Apullius," continued Atellus. "I have already sent word to the emperor. He will know that you sacrifice children to forbidden gods. He will know that the limitanei of Aesica are not to be trusted."

"Well done, beneficiarius," said Apullius slowly. "I see that Valentinian sent the right man after all. Eventually." He smiled, his large square teeth shining in the reflected torchlight. "Of course I read and vetted your missive to the emperor before releasing it. I presume you sent another, by more...covert...passage. But presuming your real message – if indeed you ever sent one – gets through Crispus's network of agents, I fear it will be too late by the time the emperor learns of events."

"What do you think will happen?" said Atellus. "That the emperor will recognise you as Caesar of the west and leave you in peace?" He couldn't resist spitting a laugh.

"With the size of the force at my back," nodded Apullius, "he will have little choice. All the northern tribes are united, with allies from across the oceans. The Attacotti, the Scoti, Saxons from Germania, the Suiones and the Geats. Any limitanei from along the Wall still loyal to Rome – if such exist – will have to choose between fighting and dying, or joining us. But I know what their choice will be. By the time Fullofaudes is aware of what is happening, our forces will already have out-flanked him."

"And then you march on Eboracum," whispered Atellus

"Indeed."

"And Londinium," Atellus continued. "Treves. Rome. Constantinople."

Apullius laughed deeply. "You think me so ambitious, beneficiarius? I am flattered. No, all we want is Britannia to ourselves. Our own army, our own grain. A chance to pay taxes to benefit ourselves, and the chance to worship our own gods, before they punish us again."

"All the tribes united?" queried Atellus, sceptically. "That is the delusion of a madman."

Apullius tutted. "Not at all. The Arcanae report that the tribes beyond the Wall are ready to join forces with us, under the auspices of the old gods, fighting together for freedom from the yoke of Rome. Gods more powerful than the petty emperors who have fought and squabbled over whores and gold for years without number."

"You forget," said Atellus, his voice deep and raw, "that most of the limitanei along the Wall are soldiers from the empire; they were not born here, they have no loyalty to the land, to the people of the north. Your people are as foreign to them as I."

"They have been here long enough," replied the praefectus, shaking his head in the dimness, "to consider this their Home, beneficiarius, I can assure you. I was one myself: my father's father came to Britannia from Raetia. This is my land now and these are my people. I think you will find that the others are the same – these are hard times, lives are short, and memories too. A man wants but a patch of land to call his own and enough freedom to provide for a family. Is that too much to ask?"

Atellus hung his head with a smile. "So much trust for one who openly talks of betrayal. Of treason."

"Trust is not an issue where the gods are involved."

"Which gods?" said Atellus.

"Does it matter?"

"It does to some, you will find."

Apullius rose from his stool, and gathered up the crumpled embers that were the remnants of the torch. The meagre flames danced and spat and the shadows chased each other across the grey slimy walls of the cell.

"You are to be guest of honour at the event tonight," said the praefectus. "Cernunnos is looking forward to meeting you."

CHAPTER 36

Rodius paced the cell visually again. He certainly did not have the strength or ability to do it physically: he was chained by the neck to a heavy lead weight, a circular disc the size of a large dish, and one of his legs was lame: judging from the intense agony, and the fact that he could put no weight on it, he reckoned the long-bone was snapped. He could not see out of one eye, but felt no pain there. He wasn't sure whether it was swollen shut, or whether his brain had been jolted and something inside had been severed. Had he been able to see a reflection of his own face, he would have gazed upon a mask of crusted blood and ominous swellings. He kept counting how many teeth he had left, probing the empty sockets with his tongue. Three. Earlier he had four, but one must have fallen out as he dozed.

In his head, the cell was maybe four paces by three. There wasn't light enough to see, but something beyond his available senses told him the dimensions were correct. There was no sound except the occasional bark of laughter from the guards above, or muted conversation from the other cells; he couldn't tell whether this latter was real, or merely echoes in his head. Surely the walls were too thick to allow the sound to pass through?

Rodius replayed the scene in his mind's eye, time and again, wondering whether there were any tells he should have picked up on, any indications of treachery, anything that he could have done which would have led to a different outcome for them both.

Aurelia and he had returned to the tavern and Muconia had let them in and sent them upstairs. She would send food and wine up after them, she had said. Had she sweated a little too much? Had her voice wavered a little? Were her eyes shiny with apprehension, with excitement?

He could pretend all these things, but it didn't make them true. He just didn't know.

They had walked upstairs to their room. Vassu, Galla and the boy were still out. He had taken off his cloak, glad to be rid of the weight and the stink of oily smoke with which it was suffused. Aurelia was sitting, examining her face in the side of a tankard, dabbing lotion on her burns. They had spoken slowly, both overcome with fatigue. He remembered collapsing onto the bed and closing his eyes. Was it then he had heard the footsteps and voices in the corridor? Or was he just imagining he had, tormenting himself?

He recalled opening his eyes a crack as Aurelia moved towards the door.

And then the door had exploded inwards and flung Aurelia back onto the floor. He had leapt up, confused, disorientated, his spatha already in his hand even though he could not recall having drawn it. One man came through, two, then another squeezing in behind him. He had curled his handless arm around Aurelia and flung her like a child against the far wall, putting his body between her and the intruders.

The first man he had cut down with a blow to the neck; he hit the floor writhing, and leaking blood, his neck broken, his windpipe severed. The second man struck Rodius on the wrist with some kind of iron maul and the pain had made him scream drop his spatha, but he had fallen to the ground, ducking another swipe, and grabbed it again. He saw that a fourth man had entered and darted over the bed to seize Aurelia by her wrist. She kicked and fought like a vixen in a snare, but the soldier yanked her towards his fist, dropping her with a single punch.

Rodius recalled shouting something wordless – his throat was sore from the smoke and the pain felt good – and launching into another mad and desperate attack. He deflected a handful of blows then struck out at a man's exposed arm, slicing the flesh and snapping the wrist like a dry twig. The attacker dropped his weapon and fell to the ground, screaming. Another man he slashed along the leg, but the third came along and struck him on the shoulder with a stunted swing from a long blade. It hurt now, though the bleeding had long since stopped; the blade had bitten shallowly because of the lack of power behind the blow and the muffling effect of his clothing. He jabbed back half-heartedly with his spatha but then there was an explosion of darkness and he remembered no more.

He woke up in this cell in more pain than he had ever felt before, and thought he had a companion who moaned incessantly, until he realised that the noises were coming from his own swollen throat.

He had been spoken to once, by a tall man who said he would die the following evening, but he could recall no more of the conversation, if indeed there had been more.

Rodius knew the time was approaching: he wondered how he would die, and whether the gods had seen that he had fought well and valiantly, and maybe that some of what he did could atone for the less proud moments of his life. He hoped for death by the sword, like a warrior. He hoped he would not suffer too much, and the end would be quick and final.

He would see his mother again, perhaps, in the eternal fields, and be seven again. Seven summers was when he had felt comfortable and happy; his belly had been full, his brother was pleasant, his parents worked and laughed, and his days were full of play and promise. It was always spring in his memories; there was no bitter winter, or sweaty summer, only a cool, pleasant childhood that stretched from birth to infinity.

He heard footsteps overhead, but they seemed to pass him by. Voices too. It was the voice of his father, teaching him how to skin a hare: the skin was to be pulled off like a glove, after the right incisions had been made.

Rodius laughed. His father had been a good huntsman and trapper, many years before. There was usually something for the pot.

He had tried looking for chinks of light which may have betrayed the presence of daylight outside; or above, or wherever it was. Yet there was nothing but the infernal dark. It pressed in on him like a hand over his mouth. He wanted to scream at times, to shatter the darkness to show the daylight beyond, like a drape snatched back to reveal a lamp.

Something ran over his leg at one point, and he was glad of the company. It had probably been a rat. He was hungry, but not hungry enough to eat it raw. He could talk to it, touch it, feel the rise and fall of its furry flanks, the moisture of its breath on his flesh, the warmth of the blood rippling through its tiny body.

They ate rats, back in the slums of the Calles. They were considered a delicacy; even though some said they were diseased, and caused nigrum. But Rodius knew nigrum was caused by the frost, not the rats, so he continued to catch them and enjoy them. His father enjoyed the tail, but Vassu was too squeamish to eat it, no matter how hungry he was. He had been a delicate youth, Vassu, many years back. A different person. Rodius had eaten the eyeballs once, but had been sick. They heard tell of neighbours who had eaten the flesh of their own dead child. Stories. Such stories in the starving city.

Rodius thought he could hear voices overhead now, and the sound of expectoration. He couldn't imagine getting that much moisture into his mouth; such a luxury, such a waste. He needed water.

He leaned over his shoulder, wincing at the pain in his shattered leg, and licked the wall. The moisture was ice cold, a balm on his tongue. He continued in different patches along the wall, then lay back, enjoying the sensation. Such slight hints of moisture had only made his thirst more potent.

Surely, he thought, death would be better than this living torment.

He shivered again. The cold was absolute, an angry blanket of pain that settled itself over him. At times he grew numb and forgot the cold, then he would wake to it again, as a man from a dream, and its pain and gripe would be twice as relentless. Each breath sent angry stinging cold air into his lungs; he could feel them filling up with it and expelling it, warmed through his nostrils. He tried to imagine fires, the memory of blankets and warmth, pictures of rampant flames in his head, but it was if he had never been warm. What was warmth to him? What use was it if it had ever existed but never was to again?

He would give all his memories for a tiny guttering flame.

There were definitely footsteps overhead now; they were coming closer. He could hear the sound of a key clacking and clunking its way into a hole, the screech of metal grating against metal, and then the explosion of noise as the door swung against the wall. The sound was terrifying, after such dead silence.

Rodius looked up. He could see the light of a flame above, but it hurt his eyes, even as cold and dismal as it was. His heart was fluttering weakly in his chest and his mouth was painfully dry, his tongue cleaving to his palate.

There was the silhouette of a figure above: a tall, broad shape. Rodius blinked and squinted, wondering whether there was anything really there or whether he was feverish, or dreaming. Or dying, even. The figure seemed to have tight curled horns on its head, extending outwards and upwards, like a beast, a goat standing firm on its hind legs.

The goat-creature turned, and Rodius saw a torch in its hand. In the painful glare of the flame, he could see more of the creature: it seemed to have a long shaggy pelt of curled knotted hair, indeed like a goat, or maybe a wolf. Its face was a grim and twisted mask of what looked like deformed flesh with ragged large eyes and a dark muzzle. The figure dropped into the cell and approached him, and he stared up at it with a mixture of curiosity and fear. It moved like a human, with long confident strides and an even gait.

It walked like a soldier.

Rodius looked up into the strange bestial face flanked by the endless loops of the horns, into the face of Cernunnos, and he saw the figure draw its arm back. It had something in its gripe, a long dark tube, and he saw it coming down towards him as if in slow motion.

Rodius had the energy and inclination to shut his eyes, but nothing more, and waited for the blow.

***

Calidus pressed his hand into the gap between the two stone blocks and hauled himself up again. He knew to keep three points of contact on the wall against which he was pressed, and he knew that looking down was bad.

But he looked down anyway.

The sheer flank of the Wall stretched away beneath him, the masonry smooth, the pitted bricks disappearing into darkness below. Somewhere down there was the hard frozen ground, invisible to his eyes. There were plenty of foot- and finger-holds in the chipped and weather-beaten Wall, especially from this side; unsurprisingly, the soldiers weren't so concerned about people climbing over to get to the north side of the Wall, so any disrepair was usually overlooked.

The night was cold and his fingers were tense and numb, but Calidus focused on testing their strength before heaving his body up to kick into the next foothold. Overhead, the night sky was daubed a sullen yellow by the fire beyond the Wall; he could hear voices and the crackle and snap of flames devouring wood.

Galla was beneath him, waiting for him, swaddled deep in the shadows at the base of the Wall. He'd wrapped her in his own cloak and told her to stand guard, to make a whistling, hooting noise if anyone came near, like the call of a toot-owl. He didn't know whether she understood or not, but it was all he could do to reassure her and make her feel involved somehow.

The alternative, of course, was sending her with Vassu, which was never an option for any of them. The sullen, swarthy man had made it clear what he was going to do, and how. So they split up for the evening, and would meet later by the bath-house. Even from this distance, Calidus could still hear the drinkers, throats soggy with wine, dancing and fighting outside the tavern, arguing in preposterously loud voices.

Calidus was nearly at the rampart now; it was a cruel overhang, difficult and treacherous, but nothing he hadn't dealt with before. Although, the cold and the ice set into some of the cracks in the masonry made it trickier than he had ever encountered before.

The Wall seemed curiously bare of sentries tonight, he had noticed. Perhaps it was something to do with the huge fire beyond.

Calidus's feet found sturdy holds, the cold from the masonry seeping up through the thin leather soles of his boots. He flexed and leapt, grasping the timber crossbar of the rampart's underhang with both his hands. He felt the impact shudder through his muscles, heard the slap as his hands made contact, and then came the sickening, dizzying sensation as his fingers slipped and the momentum of his jump carried him forward, away and into a sweet pendulous arc down to the frozen ground some forty feet below.

But he clenched and tensed and prayed to the myriad gods he had never believed in, and somehow his fingers caught, his cold flesh finding friction in the grain of the timber, and he steadied and stayed himself. He didn't wait to stop swinging, but used the momentum to throw his legs up and under the other crossbeam. He was secure, for the moment.

Calidus waited a while, to see whether the noise of his contact had alerted any limitanei up above, but there was nothing except the pop and rasp of the fire beyond, and the solemn bass rumble of distant, intertwined conversation.

He pulled himself up to a better position then reached up and over to grasp a slight protuberance of the side timber of the rampart. He got a hold he considered adequate, then loosed his legs' hold on the crossbeams and pulled himself up, his feet scrabbling for purchase on the side. He found it, and boosted himself up again, this time gripping the top of the rampart, his hands in the gaps between the blunted points of the vertical timbers. He waited for ten fast heartbeats, then heaved himself up and peered over the inner rampart onto the Wall's walkway.

There was no-one there.

He used his forearm muscles to pull himself up until his stomach was atop the points of the timbers, then kicked with his legs and sent himself clear of the stakes and onto the walkway itself.

Taking a minute to catch his breath, Calidus stood up and peered over the rampart and out into the northern beyond.

CHAPTER 37

Atellus was woken by the sound of the cell door opening with a bang. His dreams had been pleasant; he felt the vestiges of a smile on his face. He had been in their vineyards outside the villa just beyond Treves. He was walking with Faenia and Petronia, and telling them of his battles at Moguntiacum and Ctesiphon and the heroism of Julian. He had loved Julian, loved him as an elder brother, or as a son does his father. He would gladly have died for the man, and that was the level of loyalty felt by most of the troops who served under him. Rome would never see such a leader again, he knew.

Atellus had lifted his daughter onto his shoulders, in his dream, and she had laughed. The sun had been a pale orange in the sky, and the last of the summer warmth was still in the air. They would go back inside the villa, and they would eat a fine meal of roast snipe, turnip and apricots and he would tell Julia Petronia a story until she drifted into slumber, a tale about a magical ring that rendered the wearer invisible. And then he would go and make love to Faenia and he would feel as if love was the entire meaning of the existence of the world and everything in it. And the following day, he would return to Julian's armies and march east, the taste of triumph already on his lips and the light of certain victory blazing within his dark eyes.

And then the door had opened and woken him into his dark and grisly hell of existence.

Atellus woke up cold. He could see the light of a flame above, and the silhouette of the figure carrying it. The torch-bearer climbed down into the pit with him and Atellus watched as the flames gradually revealed the sharp contours of the face of the centurion who had first led him here.

"Beneficiarius," said Maglorius, pulling out a long dagger that glistened in the candlelight. "Your bonds."

Atellus looked up at the hard, lean features with the long pale scar bisecting the face. He shuffled round in his cell. His joints were stiff, his limbs aching. He proffered his scratched and swollen hands to the centurion.

Maglorius sawed into the bonds and they parted with a click. "Listen to me," he said as Atellus rubbed feeling back into his sore wrists. "You have friends in Aesica." Maglorius pulled a sealed letter from his pocket. "This is for you; read it at your leisure."

Atellus took the proffered letter, and looked at it as if he had never seen one before; he could not make out the seal in the dim light. He tucked it into a pocket in his cloak; bewildered, confused, disorientated. The centurion offered him his hand, and Atellus stared at it.

"What trick is this?" he croaked. Speaking was painful, he discovered.

"No tricks, beneficiarius," shrugged the centurion. "The choice is yours. Come with me if you want to live. Stay here if not."

Atellus wavered for a second, then grabbed the centurion's hand. Maglorius hauled him to his feet. Atellus wavered a second, the darkness spinning around him, but it settled and he rubbed his eyes with his cold-numbed fingers.

"Follow me," said Maglorius as he placed the torch on the walkway floor, level with his head. He heaved himself up out of the cell pit and through the door, then reached down to help Atellus up after him before bending down to retrieve the torch. They were in a narrow corridor lined on each side with similar pit-cells, and Atellus followed the demonic light as Maglorius moved down the walkway. He was aware of a dim noise, like a faint slapping, coming from up ahead; he looked out beyond the bauble of their torch's light and could see another flame, larger and more intense, casting out a thick smudge of pale yellow luminescence into the antechamber.

The flame came from a large lantern on the desk of the guardsmen. The two guards were bent over the desk, their throats sliced open and their fresh blood still pooling upon their desk and dribbling onto the floor with a soft patting noise.

"You?" said Atellus.

Ahead of him, he felt rather than saw the centurion nod. Atellus reached down and prised a spatha from the hand of one of the dead men. He tested the weight and the strength of the blade; the tang was solid in the hilt; the metal was notched but strong. A fair weapon.

Maglorius opened the door into the moonlit night; the air was fresh and vital and despite the cold it sent a thrill of vitality through Atellus. It was different from the dead, dank, stale cold of the cells: this coldness at least had *life*.

The fort was deserted; the stars glistened in a huge unfurled tapestry of darkness overhead.

"Where is everyone?" asked Atellus.

"Sacrificing to their gods," said the centurion with a curl of his mouth.

Atellus nodded. "Beyond the wall."

"Yes."

"Thank you," he said. "Why–"

"Not everyone in Aesica is corrupt, beneficiarius."

517

"You have my thanks," said Atellus again. "Do you know where they are keeping Aurelia? The woman taken by—"

"I know of whom you speak," said Maglorius. "She has left already. She was not the property of the praefectus, but a contingent from Eboracum. They rode out some time ago to bear her back."

Atellus swore inwardly. Aurelia, the woman to whom he owed his life. The woman who knew his work, knew his life, knew the emperor as he did himself. She had severed the rope from which he swung in Constantinople, had arranged for the cart to cushion his landing and carry him to safety and a second life.

He had never known whether to kiss her or curse her for it.

Atellus shook the thoughts away, like rags of cloud in a storm.

"Calidus, the boy," he said. "The praetor's nephew. What of him?"

"I know nothing of him," said Maglorius. "But if you have any sense, you will leave Aesica as soon as possible, and head south. Warn Brocchus of your findings if you can, but head south. I must leave now."

Maglorius strode away, across the fort and beyond the barrack-blocks. Atellus was left standing in the fresh crisp air, shivering; the shivers gave him pleasure. He patted the letter in his cloak pocket. Beyond the north wall of the fort, he could see the flickering light of a huge fire. He followed his curiosity and moved round the barrack-blocks to the other side of the principia, the stonework squat and dominant in the gloom like a monstrous creature on its haunches, about to pounce.

He followed the circumference of the internal wall, keeping to the shadows in case of any soldiers on patrol, but there was no sign of life within the fort. He reached the north wall, and moved around to the narrow corridor which he had been led through only a day before when Drustanus had betrayed him to Maglorius.

518

Atellus's head spun with questions, but he gritted his teeth and forced them down to be addressed later. He could not spare the time or energy on them now.

Atellus moved carefully though the corridor, the sounds from the other side of the huge barrier intensifying as he crept nearer to the doorway set into the huge gates. The main gates themselves were maybe twenty feet tall and made of half-trunks of trees strapped with uncia-thick leather cords and topped with iron. The iron itself was spattered with the accumulated maculations of centuries-old rust. Atellus wondered idly how long it had been since those huge gates had swung open to let out swathes of men, whole legions marching north in aggression and confidence to tame the barbarian hordes. The ghosts of ages past whistled through the wind across the splintered timber and were otherwise silent.

He tested the squat postern set into the curtain wall beside the main gate and found it open. He pushed it ajar and tentatively peered out; there was darkness pressing up against the Wall, and beyond was the glare of a huge fire, burning gaily into the night air as an inferno in the wilderness lands.

Atellus stepped out and walked forward, beyond, as close as he dared get. There was a huge assemblage of soldiers and civilians alike, hundreds of spectators gathered round the inferno which sent the light of midday scything through the darkness around them. People pressed upon people so that the crowds were ten to twelve thick in concentric rings around the pyre.

Atellus stalked closer, keeping to the track, the snow glistening on the undulations of the land around him. The ground was clear within many feet of the fire, the sere grass looking brittle and dry in the artificial brightness.

Next to the fire was a tall man clad in a long wolf-skin cloak, and wearing a mask of dried skin upon which were affixed large rams' horns. Beside him, held up by tall cloaked soldiers whose faces were daubed with red pigment, were two young girls of maybe ten summers apiece. Even from a distance, Atellus could see they looked terrified, their faces crumpled and stained with hard-shed tears. Standing beside them, his arms tied around his neck and looped back on themselves to produce a painful and uncomfortable-looking contortion, was a tall, long-haired man. Atellus noticed one of his hands was missing.

The man in the ram's horns was speaking out loud, his voice carrying across the assemblage.

Atellus recognised the voice.

It was the voice of Apullius.

"—harvest, and warmth of days long past. Great Cernunnos, we make these offerings in recognition of your glory and potency. Humbly we ask of you to return to your favour we wretched wanderers, and beseech you to consider us worthy of your presence in these dark times. We, your brothers in the north, hereby offer these tokens of our esteem. Hear us, Cernunnos magnus."

The Apullius-creature raised a long ram's horn to his mouth and blew a haunting, braying refrain. It echoed through the night, seeming to shiver through the very stars above the auditors' heads: a deep barritus, bewailing loss and fear and crumbled hope.

The blast was greeted by a wordless roar of encouragement from the assemblage and they raised their fists into the air; those with weapons pumped them up and down, or beat hafts and hilts against bucklers, shields, armour. The result was a terrifying cascade of aggressive noise rolling like midsummer thunder across the wintry downs. The horn note soared above the clamour, a constant throbbing treble to the bass chants and roars of the men.

The Apullius-creature made a signal to the men holding the prisoners, and the three were marched closer to the fire. Atellus could hear the girls screaming in fear, pleading for their maters and paters, tears streaming down their curdled faces. He was aware of his hand snatching for the spatha by his side, as if of its own volition, and before he knew it his muscles felt the tug of the weapon's comforting weight in his grasp.

The girls; of an age with his Petronia.

What could he do, he thought desperately, one man? It would be certain death.

Now is not your time.

The voice was not his, but seemed to penetrate straight to his skull, bypassing his ears. It was a feminine voice, soft yet strong, firm; he almost recognised it.

"We commend this flesh to you," bellowed the Apullius-creature, "mighty Cernunnos."

The fire surged and leapt as if in anticipation. Atellus could feel the draughts of warmth from where he was; the heat so close to the pyre must have been intolerable. The wood had been stacked carefully into a pyramidal structure, so the pyre would burn hot and long.

With a grunt and a heave, one of the soldiers with the tinctured face hurled the first child, squealing, into the flames. Atellus saw the figure enter the inferno, thrash and buck, kicking sparks and flaming kindling into the crowd, who backed away hastily. The screams continued for a short while before ending with a hiss.

The one-handed man was pushed towards the edge of the pyre. He walked slowly, and did not struggle, as though utterly accepting of his fate. Two of the soldiers grabbed him, one at each shoulder, and heaved him into the hungry flames. He seemed to go willingly, almost leaping away from his captors, as if attracted by the bright searing tongues of flame, as a moth to a candle. Atellus saw him fall languidly into the fire, before raising his single fist to the stars in defiance, a white and red flaming salamander, until he fell back into a dark twisted shape. The fire seemed to hiss and wheeze as it digested its victim, but then there was silence, broken only by the muted sobbing of the remaining sacrifice.

A part of Atellus recognised that the victims must have been doused with some form of accelerant in order for the flames to engulf them so quickly and completely. Naphtha, perhaps, and even as the word came to mind, his nose was filled with the rich sweet scent of it, and the memory of melting flesh.

The soldier carrying the remaining girl moved closer to the fire; she was pressed into his chest, and seemed to be squirming wildly, drumming her heels against his shins. He was leaning back, away from the wicked heat of the flames. He took a slight run-up and pitched the writhing creature forward. She fell awkwardly, legs splayed, into the pyre, dislodging some wood and sending the flames into an angry fit of red and black sparks. The girl screamed briefly, a shrill penetrating noise that seemed almost to drive Atellus to the very brink of his own sanity.

He wondered how his wife had screamed as she met her end. And Petronia, his daughter, his blood. How had she died? Had they had been violated by the assassins? Tormented?

Atellus was grinding his teeth so loudly that he could barely hear anything else. The assembled crowd around the pyre were silent, lost in a mute introspection of the horror and sanctity of what they had witnessed.

The Apullius-creature strode forward after a pause and raised his arms up to the stars.

"Cernunnos magnus, accept our sacrifice." He bowed his horned head. "The tribes will gather under you, to worship and adore you as did our fathers' fathers in days long past." He looked out at the crowd assembled around him; faces made bestial by the light of the purring, sated fire. "People of Aesica. People of the North. The tribes of our family, united as fratres, as are we, under Cernunnos, are travelling now from the north, from the east; from the south and from the west. This night we will become one people again, and reclaim the bounty of the land that is rightfully ours. No longer shall our babes starve at our breasts as the Romans grow fat on the milk of our land; no longer shall we see our sons and daughters waste and die before us, not while our land remains under our feet. No longer!"

Atellus was aware now of another sight beyond the brightness of the pyre: the horizon was lit with a fine line of light, almost as if dawn were breaking infinitesimally slowly, and hours early. Gradually, as he watched, the light resolved itself into hundreds upon hundreds of individual beacons, flickering like stars born from the land and rolling across the hills. The darkness was pushed back, defeated by the unfurling luminescence, and Atellus felt the ground beneath his boots trembling, quivering under the united weight of numberless footfalls.

It looked like an army on the march.

***

Calidus watched from his vantage point as Rodius and the two youngsters were murdered. Standing tall on the empty battlements, he could see the land for miles around, and had a perfect view of the assembled crowd. He wanted to do something, to call out, to shout for the gods to stop such slaughter, but his voice caught in his throat and he knew that there would be no point other than to call attention to himself and maybe add one other to the sacrificial tally.

He scanned around the scene, expecting to see Aurelia among the prisoners, but there was no sign of her. Perhaps, he thought numbly, she had already been cast into the pyre before he arrived.

The horned man was speaking again. From this distance, and even with his keen eyes, the illusion was such that when Calidus first saw him, his instinct was to cower and cringe behind the ramparts and shiver until the powers had passed; part of him thought that the gods were indeed walking the earth amongst the peoples of the north. But gradually he had calmed himself, quelled those primal fears instilled from boyhood tales, and carried on watching, seeing the fur-cloak and the crude mask of the horned one, and realised that the apparition was only their priest.

Calidus was shivering with the cold, and eager to return and tell Vassu of what he had seen; he was conscious too of Galla waiting below for him, freezing and scared. If Aurelia was gone, then the girl truly had no-one to care for her; who was he to fit into that role? The thought made him smile inwardly. Despite his protestations to Vassu, he was barely past boyhood himself. He needed to look to his own woes and carve out his own future in the land – he could not care for a mute girl-child about whom he knew nothing.

As he was thinking, and feeling the shivers running through his flesh like the first ripples of illness, he noticed the lights on the horizon: tens of them, becoming scores, becoming hundreds, until he could no longer estimate the numbers. They were strung across the length of the horizon like an infinitely fine necklace of glittering jewels, draped over the snow-smooth hills.

The sight sent a surge of fear into his belly, and he felt his heart begin to pound heavily in his chest.

He watched as the host approached, slowly and inexorably and with the inevitability of the tide seeping onto the shoreline. Some were mounted, many hundred, but the bulk of thousands were afoot and arranged in ragged legions.

To his right, east along the Wall, he saw the distant warning beacons flare up, their flames licking the toes of the stars staring down from the dark sky. There was no response from the fort at Aesica, and the relay died before it could pass westward.

The northern tribes were on the march and their numbers were more than he could possibly have imagined, despite what Aurelia had said. He realised it was all too late: they had failed.

Calidus watched in horror as a sole rider parted from the magnificent host, like a spark detaching itself from the flame of a roaring fire, and sped towards the pyre. The rider paused in front of the bestial priest, and Calidus could see there was talk between the men, before the rider galloped back towards his host. Those gathered around the fire began to move back towards the fort, slowly filtering away from the pyre under a cloud of talk and palpable excitement.

Calidus stood, frozen, as the great north gate set into the Wall began to swing inwards. The creaking of the ancient timber snapped him from his daze, and he quickly darted away, up along the rampart to begin the treacherous climb back down towards the vicus.

CHAPTER 38

Vassu looked out from under his cowl, and took another sip of his spiced acetum. The drink was good, and hot, but it only added to the raging fire in his belly. It was best that he do this job alone: the mistake had been his, and it had been costly.

The tavern was loud and full of merrymakers; some bedraggled soldiers lay along one of the tables, singing out of tune. A few other groups of civilians were engaged in deep talk, or arm-wrestling, shouting angrily at each other in jest, trading curses across the length of the room. There were weary farmers with frost-scratched faces; smiths with soot-stained paws and singed whiskers; whores young and old lost in their cups and doleful reminiscences.

And Muconia, leaning against the far wall. She had not seen Vassu, or had not recognised him if she had. And that was because he hadn't wanted her to.

All he needed, all he had been waiting for, was a chance to get her on her own.

And he knew his chance was coming.

Vassu watched her from underneath the knitted brows of his hung head: watched as she walked across the bar and down towards the cellar door where the wine was kept. She always had a few ex-soldiers who acted as her bodyguards, and they were usually more drunk than most of the punters. But recently she had barely scratched her arse without them flanking her and looking for trouble.

But now the taller of the two guards was talking to one of the whores at the table beside the fire; the other was half asleep on his fist, propped on the bar. Muconia pulled a long ring of keys from somewhere inside her capacious bosom, and unlocked the stout door leading down to the cellar. She opened it a crack and disappeared inside, closing it gently behind her.

Vassu eyed the guards carefully, then stood and walked across the room, trying to make his gait casual. He felt the sweat running down his spine, pooling in the small of his back like a stagnant bog. He realised he had half a cup of wine clutched in his left hand; he tipped it into his throat and set the empty cup gently on the edge of a table as he passed. He carried on walking, and gently levered open the cellar door a crack and folding himself inside. He closed the door after him, hearing the latch click shut and waited on the other side, at the top of the steps, for a slow count of ten, to see if either of Muconia's paid chimps were following, but there was nothing. He could hear the woman grunting at the bottom of the steps as she hefted amphorae around, working under the light of a dim oil lamp.

Vassu descended, no longer trying to be silent, and flipped back the cowl from over his face.

"Issat ye, dog?" called Muconia over her shoulder. "About fuckin time someone came to help. Durrun kna what ah pay thee dunces fowr." She did not look, but continued rolling one large amphora off another one until its base hit the ground with a dull thud.

Vassu walked up to stand beside her.

He drew his sword; it cleared the scabbard with an evil snicking noise. He tested his grip; his fingers were stronger these days, much stronger. He hoped they would be strong enough.

"Muconia," he said, and watched in satisfaction as she froze at the sound of his voice. He could almost feel a smile creeping onto his lips.

She turned round slowly and Vassu could see the muscles in her face twitching as she struggled to control her shock; she hid her fear with a large, wide smile showing her remaining blackened teeth.

"Vassu," she said, refining her accent. "Sneaking up on a lady. You know you're not allowed down here. But now you are, you may as well help, I spose."

"Why, Muconia?" He shook his head sadly. "I thought I could trust you. I told people – told my brother, my own blood – that you were worthy of our trust."

The redhead turned away, her hair twinkling in the lamplight. "I dunno what you on about, Vassu," she said in a quiet voice. "Now give us a ha–"

He gripped her red hair and twisted it round his fist, yanking her towards him, and pulling her exposed pale neck towards the point of his gladius.

"Scream and you die, bitch," he spat. "Just tell me why, and I may let you go."

"Vassu," she grimaced, "cmon, stop messin, eh lover? We can come to some–
"

He grabbed her tighter and pressed the point of the blade into the soft pale flesh of her throat; a small bulb of bright blood appeared from the broken skin.

"Talk."

"They...they said they'd kill me, Vassu, if I didn't give them the girl," she said, wincing with the pain of his grip, her eyes straining madly between his own and the blade at her throat. "They wanted the boy too, right, and I kept him out of it. I made sure you two was out when they came, but that was the best I could do. They said they'd burn down the place and everyone in it. They was serious men, Vass, hard men. Bad men."

"I know the type," he sneered. "How much gold did they give you, whore?"

"Gold, Vass, I don't–"

She stifled a groan as his gladius dug into her skin again. He saw the flesh was red raw and daubed with ugly smears of bright red blood. It looked impossibly bright, under the flickering lamplight, like strings of fine rubies. Muted sounds of merriment drifted down from upstairs. Someone was thumping noisily on the thick floorboards above their heads. Dust drifted down on them both.

"How much?" he asked, quietly.

She turned her eyes away from his. "More than I'd see in two winters, Vass. So much gold."

He shook his head. "You are lost, Muconia."

"What you gonna do, Vass?" she asked, weakly. "We go back a long way, you n me. We can share the gold, maybe move to–"

"Give me my brother's blood money?" he spat, his eyes wide and wet. "I suppose you would. And I imagine I wouldn't see the evening out, eh? Treacherous whore."

He looked into her large, sad green eyes, their lids quivering with tension, her beautiful red hair cascading down across his arm like a fiery waterfall. She shook her head slightly, seeing something in his eyes, and he drove the sword in, deep and hard. She didn't make a sound, but jerked roughly in his arms and became a weight; he cradled her tenderly as she descended to the ground. He laid her down flat and withdrew the blade with a wet sucking noise, and more bright ruby blood splashed onto his boots and the stone floor of the cellar. With the metal gone, the blood flowed freely, spouting from her neck in great angry pumps which turned the floor a deep crimson until the blood and her hair mingled into a bright red corona around the dying woman.

Vassu washed his blade with wine from the amphora she had been moving, then scrubbed it dry on his sleeve and sheathed it. He stood and watched Muconia until her chest stopped rising and falling, and a look of peace and relief melted over her hard face. Satisfied she was empty, he walked up the stairs and out through the cellar door, and through the tavern and no-one saw him leave just as no-one had seen him enter.

He walked out into the crisp dark night air, and walked along towards where he had agreed to meet Calidus and the girl; it was the designated meeting place which Aurelia had dictated, hidden enough to be safe, and central and raised enough to give a good vantage over the main roads in and out of the vicus.

They were waiting there, Calidus and Galla, when Vassu arrived, shivering beneath their cloaks in the lee of one of the old fallen-down merchants' houses on the east side of the vicus. Calidus saw him and leapt over, shrugging his blanket from his shoulders as he rose. He stood and faced Vassu, and the older man could tell from the youth's eyes that he brought no glad tidings.

"My brother..." said Vassu, his eyes red-rimmed and wild. "Did...did you see?"

Calidus nodded and turned his head down.

"Tell me." He had wanted to go himself, but there was no way he could climb the sheer walls with his twisted fingers and feeble grip.

Calidus told him all that he had seen, and Vassu listened without speaking. When the boy had finished, Vassu sat down on a tumbled piece of masonry and stared into the dark grass which had reclaimed the foundations of the building.

He was aware of the sucking and squelching noises of a horse approaching through the narrow muddied street. Calidus looked up, wary, but Vassu continued staring down at the ground. He had neither energy nor inclination for violence; instead he felt compelled to let fate take him where it would.

The horse approached, without haste. The rider was dressed as a soldier; he wore pristine clothes with a long crimson cloak tumbling down his back and onto the rump of his thin mount. His face was hard and firm and a large scar crossed his nose and cheeks.

Calidus looked up at the stranger, meeting his eyes with a defiant gaze. The soldier ignored him while he dismounted and soothed his steed with a gloved hand on its muzzle. He then looked from Vassu to Calidus.

"Lucius Clodius Bassianus Calidus?" he said, addressing the boy.

"Yes."

"My name is Maglorius," he said in a deep bass rumble. His words were hard and unhurried. "I was a centurion serving under Apullius. I am a friend of Atellus, and Aurelia."

Calidus gaped. "Where? Where are they? Are they alive?"

"They are both alive," he replied. "Though time is not their ally. Atellus is here in Aesica, but if he remains here much longer, he will be dead. Along with everyone else."

Calidus simply nodded.

"A horde of tribesmen from the north are entering the fort even now," continued the centurion. "They will massacre everyone in there and then they will descend on the vicus and put it to the flame. What they cannot eat, or fuck, they will kill. You should leave now, while you can still be of use."

Calidus felt his legs turning to water beneath him, the world seeming to dip and lurch as a cold wave passed over his breast.

"What do you mean, be of use?" stammered Calidus, when the dizziness had passed.

"Aurelia was taken from the fort not long ago," said Maglorius, "by a detachment of soldiers from the legate at Eboracum. They are taking her back to the city. If they succeed, she will die. I aim to prevent them getting there. Ride with me, or remain here, the choice is yours."

"Why should I trust you?"

Maglorius shrugged. "The choice is yours," he repeated.

"What of Atellus?" asked Calidus. "We cannot leave without him."

Maglorius shook his head. "He has matters to attend, and it will take more than me – or you – to draw him from them. He must follow his own path. You should look to your own."

Calidus turned to look at Vassu, who was regarding them both with his glum, dark eyes. Galla sat swaddled in her cloak nearby; only her small pale face was visible emerging from the wrapped and folded coarse cloth which enshrouded her. Her eyes were large and clear, and her pale, straw-coloured hair fell down around her cheeks. She looked placid and defiant at the same time.

"We will ride with you," said Calidus, turning back to Maglorius. "But we have no mounts."

Vassu cleared his throat and spoke. "I know where I can procure a couple of beasts," he said, his voice calm and steady.

From the direction of the fort came a ululating cry, and the clash of arms.

It had begun.

"I will meet you by the south gate," nodded Maglorius. "If I am not there by tertia vigilia then I would advise you to ride hard for the south."

***

Vassu walked alone through the dim streets of the vicus; there were few villagers out, except the dying and the starving and those raving with madness or fever. Even the beasts of the town seemed to have fled, as if their keen and subtle senses had picked up on the impending carnage. The fort of Aesica, looming over the vicus itself, was lit up with flares of flame, and its walls rang with howls and shouts. There was a curious heat and tension in the air, as if before a thunderstorm; a weight to the atmosphere that seemed to press down on him as he moved.

Vassu walked on and arrived at the house whose thick wooden door he and his brother had knocked on only a few days earlier; it seemed to Vassu months distant, the gulf between life and death, at least as far as Rodius was concerned. There were no lights lit in the building; it looked cold and drowsy. Vassu leapt up and hauled himself over the wall surrounding the grounds of the large property. Looking for the stables, he saw the low squat building over by the south wing of the villa. He ran over, tracing the beams of the moon overhead and feeling the biting brilliance of the clear stars on the nape of his neck.

Rodius was dead, and he, Vassu, was alive. What cruel trick of the gods was this, he cursed?

He walked up to the stables and found the doors locked. He kicked at the silent wooden slats: once, twice, and the sound thumped across the empty courtyard, but the door held fast.

Vassu walked back over to the villa and studied the outside of the building; there was no time for subtlety. He bent down and used the ends of his twisted fingers to lever up one of the stone flags that paved part of the courtyard path. He hefted it onto his shoulder, and hurled it through one of the ground floor windows. The pane of glass shattered with a brittle splashing noise which rang out through the clear night.

Vassu elbowed the loose shards away from the sill and heaved himself up and into the dwelling. He could hear sounds of hurried activity in the house: the stamp of feet and hoarse conversation of shocked, sleepy voices. Drawing his gladius, he waited in the darkness for a count of ten, until his eyes had adjusted to the dimness and he became aware of the moonlight pouring through the open window behind him. He found himself in the central hall looking up towards the main staircase. Walking over to the steps, he bounded up them two at a time, meeting a servant on the upper landing.

"Keep out of my way and I won't fuckin' slit you open!" he growled, and the servant fell back into the shadows. "Where's your master's room?"

The servant, a scrawny looking youth with a hatch of fuzz on his chin, cowered and cringed, his thin mouth working silently as his eyes bulged out at the intruder.

"Fuckin tell me!!" hissed Vassu, raising his weapon.

The servant pointed with a trembling finger towards the north wing. Vassu ran through, past more gaping, scurrying servants until he found the most extravagant looking doorway and began kicking his way inside; the door splintered and buckled under the second blow, but the lock still held.

Vassu felt, rather than heard, the movement behind him, and swung round with his gladius up just in time to parry a blow from one of the bodyguards. The contact shivered through his arm and made his damaged fingers ache around the hilt of the sword.

"Wait!" he shouted, stepping back and splaying his free hand upwards towards his assailant. He was a large dumb-looking labourer type with a shaved head and a dark brown cloth patch covering his right eye. "Wait! The whole fuckin' vicus is under attack; the northerners are here. They'll rape and burn every fucker that moves. You need to get the fuck out – everyone does. You really goin' to die for this greasy fuck who pays you a pittance and spits on your name?"

The man looked at him slowly, his long sword still up, his good eye narrowed in hostility. In the silence, the sounds of battle from out in the vicus filtered through the windows, and the man's ears twitched.

"Go an see for yer fuckin' self man," said Vassu, intently, willing the man to listen, "and flee while you still can."

He waited for the man's resolution to falter, and when his opponent backed away, lowering his sword, and spun on his heels, running for the exit, Vassu turned back to the chamber door, and levelled another kick at it. The door splayed open with a thump, and Vassu fund himself face to face with Scotius the merchant, in his nightclothes, a whore covering herself with the drapes of his bed. The man had fallen to his knees at the foot of his huge bed, his legs tangled in the rich sheets.

"Please," he spluttered, struggling to get to his feet, and failing. "Take what you want. But, please...." He broke off, as he recognised the intruder. "Vassu?" he said, his face curling into a grimace of distaste.

535

"Scotius, you fat cunt, no time for fuckin pleasantries," snarled Vassu. "I need your horses, two of them. The rest are yours, and you'll thank me for waking you so rudely in the middle of the fuckin' night." He ran over and hauled the merchant to his feet by his hair. "We need the key to the stables, and the main gate, understand? Your brain full of goosefat too, ya cunt??"

Scotius was shaking all over, but he moved out of the room and into the landing, towards the stairs. "What...what's happening? Where's my damn guards?"

"They've legged it, and you'll be doing the same if you want to live. Hurry up!!"

The merchant waddled down the stairs and pulled a ring of keys from inside a niche hidden behind a large bust of the emperor Constantine. The servants were up and rushing around the house in a chaos of activity, but none seemed to pay any attention to Vassu leading their master into the grounds at sword point.

They arrived at the stables, Scotius shivering violently in the cold night. The sky to the north-west seemed to be ablaze, washed with dirty reds and ominous glows, and the roar and clatter of battle could be heard in the air like a distant storm. From somewhere in the night came a horrific, thrilling scream; flames could be seen lighting up the narrow grimy streets of the vicus. The village was beginning to waken to the threat.

"Come on!" hissed Vassu. Scotius fumbled with the keys, and slapped the iron into the heavy lock. He twisted the key with a thump and the stable gate swung inwards under its own weight. Vassu stomped inside and selected two of the largest, strongest-looking horses, untethered them and led them to the wide doorway.

"The rest are for you," he said to the merchant with a laugh. There were maybe four other beasts in there. "See how beneficent I am?"

536

Vassu led the two horses across the grounds, crunching their way through the ice and frost, over to the front gate.

"Open it," said Vassu to Scotius.

The quivering merchant produced a large key and turned it in the lock. Vassu heaved himself onto the larger of the two horses, and kept a steady hand on the rein of the other. The merchant swung the big gate open with a creak. Vassu was not even levelling the gladius at him anymore; the man was operating on bewilderment and obedience.

"Now get the fuck out of here as fast as you can, if you want to stay alive," said Vassu, wheeling his horse and petting it to allay its fear of the lights and noise in the air. "Thanks for the beasts. I'll pay you back one day. My word," he laughed, and rode out at a canter.

The streets of the vicus were now gradually filling with people in various stages of dress and degrees of panic. Some ran to and fro, screaming, others simply looked curious. A small knot of unarmed soldiers ran up to Vassu to try and take his spare steed, grabbing at his legs as he passed, but he hacked down at them, catching one on the head and sending him crumpling to the ground, and the rest moved aside as he galloped past.

Before long he was at the south gate, along with a steady train of rolling waggons from those who had been able to organise their affairs in time, or who had known of this in advance. He rode out, looking frantically for the three, but could see nothing. He looked up at the sky: the non-pointer stars of ursa were at an acute angle. And was that a glimmer of dawn on the horizon to the east?

Was he late? Vassu wondered to himself, scanning his surroundings, the din of chaos and slaughter behind him ringing hard in his ears. Had they left without him? Had they been slaughtered by the gathering mobs?

He heard a hiss, and looked across into a patch of scrubland by the recently-torched cottage. At first he could make out only a clump of shadows, but they gradually resolved themselves into the shape of a figure holding a horse. He spurred his mount and rode over at a trot.

"Well done," said Calidus, emerging from a clump of tall furze bushes.

"We have lost too much time," said Maglorius, melting out of the surrounding shadows and mounting his steed. "We need to move south, rapidly."

Calidus took the reins of his horse from Vassu and leapt up onto it as though he were born on a saddle; he reached down to help Galla onto the beast and she clambered up awkwardly and clutched her frail arms around the youth's waist.

"Let's fly," said Calidus, a strange smile etched across his pale face.

The three riders kicked the flanks of their beasts, and thundered off onto the great road, the vicus burning and howling behind them.

CHAPTER 39

There had been two guards on duty at the entrance to the principia; one had been sleeping as Atellus approached, and the second was unconscious before he had time to raise the alarm. A quick blow to the side of the head sent him crumpling to the floor like a sling-downed bird. He had crept in through the side entrance which led into the servant's quarters. There had been a few of them milling about: heads down and swimming in the misery of their own lives and the enormity of their tasks; none queried him, and few even so much as gave him a second glance. Those that did may well have recognised him from before.

Atellus had looked for Calidus in what felt like every room in the sprawling, decrepit headquarters building, but there had been no sign of him. Even his own luggage brought from Eboracum had vanished; it was as if every trace of both of them had been scrupulously removed. He prowled out, fighting back the urge to shout the boy's name, to set his voice ringing off the silent stone corridors, to shatter the grim conspiracy of the principia.

He had made a blood pledge to the boy's uncle, to Brocchus; he had promised that he would look after him and see that no harm came to the lad until he was able to reach Fullofaudes in Stanwix.

But then he had also promised himself that he would avenge his wife and child.

He had made a promise to Julia Faenia and Julia Petronia that no harm would befall them whilst he was campaigning with Julian in the east.

So many broken promises.

Atellus rushed out of the room and into the next, again fighting the urge to shout the boy's name, a brutal urge born of frustration and desperation. Outside he could hear the sounds of combat, which had started up not long after the gates had been winched open and the barbarians welcomed with open arms.

What hope did they have, he thought, against such a force now that the gate had been opened? Even before Apullius would realise that their intent was not on forging a new brotherhood under him, it would be too late. There were good soldiers at Aesica, hard fighters; limitanei, the toughest of all the emperor's men. And the wildest. But they would not have a chance against the superior numbers of the northerners, against the surprise, the flanking. It would be chaos. A massacre.

Atellus heard a sudden whoosh of air from outside, and a few choking screams rattled off the brickwork. He ran to the nearest window and looked out; he could not see over the periphery wall of the principia, but there were tongues of flame leaping up from the direction of the granaries. The air was a tumult of shouts and howls overlaid with the incessant ring and clatter of metal on metal. A few of the limitanei had made it up onto the ramparts and were aiming arrows down at the attackers, but there were twenty northerners surging up the steps for every archer, and they were soon cut down and hurled from the battlements. It would not be long before they reached the principia and proceeded to loot and ransack their way through the building.

He was running out of time.

Atellus picked up his pace along the corridor, kicking open the doors and looking inside as he ran; he was sure he had been down here before, but he could not say for certain as they all blended into one. The apartments here were definitely more opulent than those of the previous corridor. He was met with screams and pleas from some of the occupied chambers, the inhabitants no doubt convinced the barbarian horde was already within their own walls.

Atellus pressed on, people rushing past him in either direction; not servants, but the terrified fleeing residents of the principia, the families of the ranking soldiers. There was terror and distraction in their eyes, and they stumbled and fell over each other with their prized possessions bundled awkwardly in their arms.

Atellus knew they would not make it out of the fort — never mind the vicus — before being slain: there was no better way of advertising your riches than by huddling them to your chest and waddling towards the exit as fast as you could shuffle. The marauders would be waiting for them and hack them down and claim their prizes. He had done it himself, in long-past days.

Atellus reached the final room at the end of the corridor and shoved the door open: it was empty, a huge chamber with a large squat bed covered with soft white duck-down sheets, and bordered on three sides by elaborately-carved planking, in the old fashion. A candle burned on the nightstand, and fresh clothes for the morning were folded over the back of a gilded chair. Atellus checked each of the sub-chambers and found them all empty.

He sat on the bed, leaned against the gold embossed fulcrum, and ran a hand through his dark hair.

The scar at his neck throbbed. The sounds of death and massacre pressed against the coloured glass window at the far side of the room. He could hear the thumps and screams coming from the distant corridors of the principia.

The enemy was inside, now.

Atellus could discern the sounds of pedestals and statues being toppled, and hangings ripped from walls and set ablaze. The corridors echoed with screams and the sounds of pleading.

Atellus calmly settled himself and drew from his pocket the letter which Maglorius had passed on to him. In the light of the chamber he could make out the seal. It was Valentinian's personal stamp, rather than that of the emperor; there would not be many who would recognise it, certainly not in Britannia. It was smudged and dirty with travel, but unbroken.

He snapped the wax with his thumb, and unfurled the slim parchment, wondering why this had been handed to him now. How had it reached the centurion, and what was his role in the emperor's tangled plans? Presumably the communication had been sent here to await his arrival at Aesica. It could have reached here months ago, or merely hours. He put the questions out of his head and focused on the letter itself.

It was a short missive, unsigned, but Atellus recognised the emperor's handwriting: Valentinian had written this himself, rather than dictating to his scribes.

Amicus, the letter began. *My dear Atellus, it grieves my heart to commit this information to paper. But I believe this has been handed to you at the right time, and is a confidence that cannot be shared in person. I told you before that Jovian's papers had been found. Amongst them were details of the order given for your execution. You know already that Crispus prepared the order for authorisation.*

Atellus's felt his eyes tighten and the muscles in his arms contract as he read on. Feeling the parchment fold and tear under his fingers, he forced himself to relax.

He did the same for your family's execution, Valentinian continued. *The assassin was the beneficiarius imperatoris under Jovian, a Burgundian by the name of Titus Sempronius Asellio Petrus. Petrus carried out other assassinations of political undesirables. When I took the purple, I was only aware of his position as beneficiarius. My ab epistulis demoted him and sent him off to the remote limes as an agent in rebus.*

He was posted to Aesica.

The missing agent you seek there is the man who killed your wife and child.

Amicus, do with this information what you will. But whatever your actions in this, I can assure you that there will be no repercussions from me.

V

Atellus felt numb. He dropped the letter onto the timber floorboards which shook with the violence of the massacre beyond the walls.

So the agent at Aesica was the man who slaughtered his family. Yet what was it Marius had said back in Culuslupi? That he had not heard of the agent and that if he had existed at all, he would be long dead.

So the agent was absent, or dead. Either way, Atellus had been denied his vengeance. He had been sent to Aesica to find what had become of the agens in rebus, as well as the children who had been disappearing from their beds. He knew now that the soldiers at Aesica were sacrificing the bairns to the old gods. There was no reason to think that the agent had not met the same fate as the girls and the one-handed man he had seen pushed into the hungry flames earlier.

He hung his head and let hard tears drop from his eyes. His chest shook, but he made not a sound and the fort beneath his feet wept blood for him.

Crispus: the viper.

He had always harboured suspicions about that rat's role in carrying out Jovian's orders concerning himself and his family. But he had spared the rat, on account of his marriage to Aurelia, and not wanting to compromise her position in controlling Valentinian's network in the north. But there was only so long he could go on denying himself. He had sated his urge for vengeance with the knowledge that the man who wielded the blade which severed his wife and child's connection to this world was still walking; kept himself strong with the certainty that one day he would find him. Now that man was almost certainly dead, and his vengeance could only be satisfied on Crispus.

He needed to stay alive long enough to get to Eboracum. He needed to leave this world with the relief of knowing that he had sent Crispus ahead of him.

Atellus stood up. There was chaos and blood and agony in the corridor outside. He could hear screams and howls of triumph and anger. His spatha was leaning against the soft edge of the bed. He reached down and picked it up, just as the door shivered under the force of a shoulder and a tall man thundered into the room under the momentum of his own charge.

Atellus reacted without thinking. Everything was very clear to him now. There was nothing more he could do for the boy, but he had a new goal in mind.

He swung the spatha up and across in a side-blow aimed at the intruder's face as he skidded past him. The metal connected with the man's face; there was a scrunching noise as the man fell, blood pouring from his scalp. The blade was buried deep in his skull, and the weight of his falling body dragged Atellus's arm down to the ground.

Another soldier erupted into the room with a scream of rage. Atellus stepped on the dying man's face and wrenched his sword out with a squeak of bone, just in time to block the overhanded blow of the spatha coming down towards his own head. The metal rang and sparked in the room, and the impact knocked Atellus back into the fulcrum of the bed, winding him.

Atellus recovered faster than the other man could regain his balance, and he thrust his spatha into the attacker's soft exposed belly. He jerked forward, over the blade, with a look of surprise in his green eyes. Atellus kicked him off the end of his spatha, his guts uncoiling themselves on top of him as he fell.

Atellus stood ready to meet the next attack, but there was none.

He looked down at his assailants. They were clad in skins and rusted armour. They looked little different from the limitanei; maybe they *were* limitanei.

He wiped his sword and sheathed it, then looked out into the corridor. Six more warriors, their faces daubed with blood and soot and twisted into mad rictuses of hate and frenzy, were pounding down the corridor. They saw Atellus and hooted in triumph and anticipation. He backed up and slammed the chamber door shut, then heaved and dragged the two dead bodies over to block it. One of the men groaned, leaving a trail of wet purple intestines behind him as he was moved. The floor was sodden thick with the men's blood.

Atellus knew he had little time. He darted across to the small window, even as he heard the thump of his pursuer's boots along the corridor. He used the pommel of his spatha to break the glass, knocking out the remaining jagged edges which rose up like bestial teeth from the wooden frame.

The door into the room cracked heavily as the weight of the men collapsed into it. The base of it remained solid, propped by the weight of the dead, but the top of the wood splintered and cracked away from the jamb.

Atellus levered himself up and shuffled out through the window, squeezing himself tightly through the space.

He wouldn't fit.

He tried to shrug his way out of his cloak and it ripped at the shoulder, snagged in a talon of glass. There was another attack at the door, and one of the

545

men collapsed through the shattered timbers of the door, stumbling over the bodies of his comrades. He looked around and made a launch for Atellus.

Atellus used the rip in his cloak to tear the material free; it fell from his shoulder awkwardly. He dived and wriggled, the broken glass and splintered wood of the window-frame biting into his flesh, snagging his hair, chafing his hands. The warrior in the room was almost upon him. With a flash of inspiration Atellus pulled his spatha from its cord and threw it down to the ground; he slipped out after it, a stray piece of glass tearing into the flesh of his forearm as he fell. He collapsed onto the stone flags of the courtyard with a thud, and rolled away to soak up the force of the impact. He turned and looked upwards and saw the face of his attacker above him, shouting in Brythonic and spitting down at him.

Atellus got to his feet, his bones still shivering with the impact of the landing, and cast around for his spatha; he found it some feet from where he had landed, the moonlight pooling in the blade's fuller. He snatched it up and looked around. The fort itself seemed to be on fire: the sky was everywhere daubed with an orange hue, the low clouds reflecting the glow of the flames which roared and crackled on every side. There were pitched battles scattered across the ground, though every Aesican he recognised seemed to be hopelessly outnumbered.

He ran across to the wall surrounding the principia and vaulted up it with his foot, leaping upwards to catch the top edge with his hands. He heaved himself onto the rim of the wall, squatting between the rusty iron arrow-heads which protruded from the concrete, and looked around him.

The granaries were burning fiercely, as were the barrack blocks and some of the workshops to the north. All around, men died and screamed and ran and pled for mercy in Latin or Brythonic; emaciated horses screeched and bolted from flaming stables. The invaders were mainly sweeping around beneath him to get to the rich pickings of the principia. Atellus dropped from the wall and into the main courtyard beyond the principia, then ran along the road leading to the south gate. Men fought and died in the streaming red glow of the endless flames which twisted and writhed around them in all directions. There was no smell but that of dark smoke which had choked the freshness from the sky and cauterised even the musk of spilt blood on the ground.

He could see the huge gates open at the far north side of the fort, and more northerners were streaming in as he looked, wave upon wave upon endless wave, stretching back into a bustling malignant darkness that blended into the blanket of the night. There was a string of limitanei bravely fighting their way back towards the principia, but they were hopelessly outnumbered, and soon to be flanked by the forces streaming in down their sides. Dead men, Atellus conceded.

He ran for the south gate and saw three warriors detach themselves from a large skirmish and rush over to him. He stood his ground just in front of the double gateway, and found a limitanei at his side, the man's sword unsheathed in the darkness and glittering red from the fires.

Three on two was better odds, thought Atellus grimly.

The three swept straight at them, with no tentative play or posturing. The limitanei to his right had a hefty oval shield, and the first attacker hit it full on with his axe, the wood shivering and cracking under the impact and forcing his comrade backwards; but the assailant left himself open to a counter-attack and took a stabbing blow to his groin from around the side of the shield. He collapsed to the ground drenched with his own screams. Atellus met the second of the enemy, parrying his first blow and sliding the warrior's blade off his own, then ducking so the momentum of the attack carried the attacker beyond and over him. Atellus leapt forwards and stabbed upwards with his spatha, meeting the frantic charge of the third man. His blade caught in the warrior's armour, and the man's momentum snagged Atellus's spatha from his hand, sending it spinning to the cold grit of the courtyard with a metallic shiver.

Atellus rolled on the ground, feeling light and agile without the bulk of his cloak and grabbed out for his weapon, snatching at the hilt and swinging the blade upwards in one smooth fluid motion, readying it for the next attack. He found himself back to back with his comrade who was frantically fighting off another attack, the sword-blows slamming into his shield with thunderous grunts which shattered his arm and drove him back into Atellus, howling out in pain. The beneficiarius parried another thrust from the warrior in front of him before rolling into a deadly counter-attack swipe which was blocked by his opponent's blade. Atellus cursed and jinked away from the warrior's retaliatory hack and dropped down to his knee, bringing the spatha blade up and across in a fierce sweeping gesture which nearly overbalanced him. He felt metal connect with flesh, the beautiful tug on his wrists signifying a wounding strike, and he heard the grunt of pain from the man above.

Atellus got to his feet as his opponent staggered backwards, bleeding; his comrade was about to be driven to the ground by the relentless sword-blows of his attacker who was head to foot a mishmash of armour: a chain mail vest hung across his torso and leather blacksmith's bracers stretched up his long, thickly muscled arms. On his head was a full-face helmet, of the type worn by the clibinarii in the east.

Atellus darted round the other side of his comrade's shield, timing it just after a blow and drove his spatha deep into the exposed throat of the attacker, his only weak spot. The force of the attack was like a violent punch, sending the man staggering backwards. Atellus heaved his blade out of the man's neck as he fell backwards, blood gouting over him as he retracted it. The warrior clutched at his wound and trembled, quivering as he stood, his hands pawing at his iron helmet, smearing it with the dark slime of his own blood. He collapsed and shook on the ground, the blood pooling around his grasping hands.

The two survivors stood beside each other, breathing hard. Atellus turned and looked into the face of his companion.

The face of Apullius.

Shorn of his priestly trappings as the bestial likeness of Cernunnos, the praefectus looked like any other grizzled veteran of the limes.

"You fight well, beneficiarius," said Apullius, a wry smile on his face. He stood and dropped the edge of his shield into the ground so it leant against his shoulder, then winced in pain as he grasped his broken arm.

"Had I known it was you," replied Atellus, "I would've killed you before they could."

Apullius shook his head, but remained silent.

"This is your dream," snarled Atellus. "This is where your trust takes you."

Apullius seemed dazed. He had a long gash across his forearm, his lorica was blackened and burned, and his eyes bulged pale and white from a face black with soot and crusted blood. His features seemed swollen in the crazy light of the sweeping fires.

"That dog Drustanus," said Apullius slowly, looking at the carnage that surrounded them. "The Arcanae." His face tightened as another bolt of pain shot through his smashed arm. "They have their own agenda."

"They are more northerner than Roman," said Atellus.

"So am I!" screamed the praefectus. "So are we all." He waved a hand to take in the fort around them, then gave a small humourless laugh. "Well, beneficiarius," he said. "That makes two of us betrayed by that slippery bastard. Drustanus assured me the northern tribes were ready to join forces with us, to unite. He brought offerings and emissaries. All false." He shook his head again, as if overcome by some internal pain that was greater than his ability to think. "It was not supposed to be like this. Not like this. My people are dying."

"You will all be dead before dawn," said Atellus emotionlessly. He watched the coming army sweeping forward, hacking their way through the ragged limitanei defence. "Shouldn't you be there, with your men?"

Apullius shook his head. "They are all dead. We all are walking corpses. I will guard this gate. I will die before I let one of those traitorous animals set foot outside this fort."

Atellus looked him in the eye. "Then you will not live long, praefectus."

"Honestum mori, beneficarius," said Apullius slamming his good forearm across his chest, his face a crumpled mask of despondency and pain. His eyes flickered and shone in the light of the silent moon overhead.

"I choose to *live* with honour," replied Atellus. He spat at the feet of the praefectus, before turning his back and running off through the south gate and along the metalled road towards the vicus.

The town was aflame. None of the northerners had made it this far yet, Atellus noted, so the chaos must be looters, or brigands from the forests around the north road, capitalising on the fear and confusion. He ran on, along the road which glistened under his feet, the frozen snow set dancing by the bright moonlight.

The blow caught Atellus on the shoulder, and he tumbled forwards under his own momentum, striking the road hard, splitting his lip.

"Hello again, nigger," said a familiar voice.

Atellus turned round, spitting blood onto the road, and looked up. He saw two dark figures standing over him. They led two horses by their reins; their hoofs clopped uneasily against the road, their eyes rolling at the noise and flame around them.

Atellus tried to get to his feet but met a spatha blade pressed tight into the side of his neck, just level with his scar: the rough shiny skin of the cicatrix, the pale death of his old life. He looked along the blade and into the smug face of Marius.

Atellus said nothing but spat a thick mouthful of blood onto the man's boots.

"Fuck you, black bitch," snarled Marius. "You shamed me once by escaping. It won't happen again."

"Have I interrupted you and your cunnus fleeing the battle with your tail between your legs then?" smiled Atellus.

Marius shook his head. "You ignorant fool," he said, his arrogant broad lips curling with distaste. "I would expect no better from your kind, eastern dog that you are."

Atellus could see the hate and contempt scarring that refined face. The optio's arm was trembling with suppressed rage.

"Say goodbye to whichever pig-gods you worship, filth."

Atellus looked down the length of the sword and into those dark patrician eyes; he could see those fine descendants of that blood stretching back all the way to the Republic, those legions of ancestors who had invested their everything to culminate in the agglomerated pride and maiesta of this lone optio, seed of their noble seed, who froze and scratched and starved amongst the animals of the northern limes in the very arse of the empire. Atellus felt a smile twitch across his bloody lips.

Marius snarled and pulled back his sword for the death stroke. Atellus closed his eyes and felt his smile broaden.

Suddenly the night seemed to come alive and leap at the optio. A blade flashed a burnished red in the bleeding night sky and the optio's sword-arm was severed at the elbow; it fell to the ground with a clang, the blade still gripped tight in the fist. The night-made-man turned and punched his blade into the stomach of the optio's companion, who grunted and slid backwards off the blade to fall heavily on his arse like a toddler who had not quite learned to walk.

Marius screamed and whipped his stump around, the blood spurting into the chill darkness around them.

"I will see you beg," came a voice from the night, "murdering scum."

Atellus looked up and saw Barbarus grabbing the optio by his head and forcing him down to his knees.

"I will see you beg for your life," said the convict, "for your dignitas. Do you recognise me, merda? Look into my eyes: *do you recognise me?!*"

Marius looked up, tears of pain pooling in his large dark eyes, and squeezed them shut immediately. He started blubbering and sobbing as he clutched the stump of his arm and bent down, prostrating himself before the man who had become his god, the master of his life.

"Beg, Roman," hissed Barbarus.

Marius shook his head slowly, his large eyes uncomprehending the twist of fate which could have changed his circumstances with such rapidity. Tears streamed down his cheeks, he shook on his knees in the road like a sick dog. Behind them, Marius's accomplice groaned and wept and quivered in the snow, clutching his torn stomach with desperate white hands.

Barbarus's face was twisted with a bestial rage, a look of such profound and malignant hatred that Atellus wondered why Marius did not die of terror on the spot. Instead the optio leaned forward, pressed his cheek to the quivering steel of the blade whose point was nestling into the gap between his clavicles and murmured incomprehensibly.

Barbarus looked down at the man, his face a sick rictus of anger and sadness. He grunted and fell on the hilt of the spatha, driving it down with all his strength between Marius's collar-bones. The optio jerked and gasped, his eyes popping wide open, and a quivering vowel died on his tongue even as his life exploded from his ruptured heart.

"It is better than you deserve, scum," said Barbarus quietly. He put his foot on the shoulder of the twitching body, and wrested his spatha loose from its breast. Marius's corpse slipped down onto the cold road and bled his fine patrician blood into the unfeeling snow.

Atellus got to his feet and approached the convict, slapping him on the shoulder. "I owe you my life, Barbarus," he said. "And I swear from this moment on that I will heed your advice whenever you choose to give it."

Barbarus looked confused for a second then stooped to wipe his blade on the dead man's cloak.

"The Arcanus?" he queried.

Atellus nodded. "I am leaving for Eboracum. Will you ride with me?"

"I will," said the convict, and the two men grasped and shook wrists, like their fathers of old.

They mounted the horses which Marius and his man had been riding, and set them at a trot heading south down the main north road, through the scattered and tumbled remnants of the vicus. The road was littered with corpses, and illuminated on both sides by flaming buildings. To the left and right the air was filled with the screams and wails of pleading citizens: begging for help, for transport, for death. Children ran in wild circles in the road and were trampled by horses and carriages fleeing the destruction. Desperate men grasped out from sewers and dragged the rich from their steeds and waggons, dashing their brains into the snow. Others hurled burning logs at the caravans as they passed, setting them aflame for no reason other than to have fellow companions in Pluto. People fought in the streets, brawled and bit and scratched and howled abuse. Women lay naked in the cold, waiting for the next animal to mount them, their minds having long since departed the broken husks of their bodies.

Atellus and Barbarus kicked their mounts into a canter and ploughed through the vicus, the death and destruction mounting on each side of them as they galloped, the hipposandaled hooves striking sparks from the metalled surface.

Atellus lay across the back of his steed as they thundered through the darkness and past the screaming and the dying, sending refugees scattering off the road ahead of them. He looked back and saw the mighty Wall, the great symbol of Rome, the impermeable barrier, its shadow cast up onto the clouds above it by the howling, dancing flames beneath. From where he sat, it looked as if the entire Wall itself were aflame, the great serpent protecting the limes was dying, the whole earth shaking and wailing in response to its death throes. The sky rained fire and the earth would open to swallow the just and unjust alike and the living would envy the dead.

CHAPTER 40

The pace Maglorius set was relentless, but the three always seemed to be half a day behind their Aurelia and her captors. They tracked them relentlessly over the hard miles, the snow freezing around them and the fires of the burned villages and farms marking their route south like ghoulish cairns. They struck camp at first light, eating rude meals of tough biscuit and smoked rat in their saddles, and riding until the sun peaked in the still air. As the others slept, Calidus hunted hare and mice with his sling, but had no luck; the winter was hard, and populations had thinned.

Twice they passed the remnants of brigand attacks; dead refugees spilt across the road like so many split twigs from the trees overhead. Children stared out at Calidus with wide glazed eyes, their young bodies mangled and stained with their own blood and that of their parents. He told Galla to shut her eyes at such times, though whether she did or not he could not tell; he knew only that she held on to him tight, her small cold arms wrapped around his waist as he spurred the horse on.

"Do we check for survivors?" Calidus had shouted ahead to the centurion.

"We have no time," he replied, "nor are we able to help any we find."

The fact galled Calidus, but he knew it was true. And they rode on along the endless grey road into the folds of whiteness ahead, the trees like upturned crowsfeet on either side, the broken bodies and burntblack waggons receding behind them.

At times it seemed as if the whole land was aflame around them; each bend in the road seemed to reveal a new twist of smoke stretching up to the cloudless sky, or the smell of burning lingering in the air. Still they rode and ate and slept wrapped in their cloaks in the lee of icy boulders or the rootpits of upturned trees, and huddled together for warmth by a meagre fire. Maglorius checked the signs of passage of the soldiers ahead, like spoors of some wild beast: the scattered remnants of fires, the stamp of hipposandaled hooves in the patches of snow spilling out from the fossae.

Often they saw or felt missiles fly past their heads as they rode; slingshots thwocking against the metalled surface with a sharp report, or slicing into the snow with a click of displaced air and a soft thump. There was nothing they could do but press themselves low against the warm pulsating bodies of their steeds and thunder on through the daylight.

Calidus thrice noticed the ends of a fine rope tied across trees at either sides of the road. He mentioned it to Maglorius at camp.

"Traps for riders," said the centurion, his blank impassive face giving nothing away. "The rope is twisted thin and strong, then dipped in lime. It is stretched taut across the roadway and the first rider that passes loses his head; and his horse to the brigands."

Calidus swallowed the meat which felt even tougher than before. More danger to worry about. He looked over at Galla, who was chewing in silence, her eyes fixed on his own. Was she listening? Could she even hear? He reached over and patted her hand, and she blinked.

"How do we avoid them?" he asked.

"We don't," said Maglorius. "We hope that someone else has already sprung them."

Vassu made a clicking noise in his throat. The man had been silent since receiving the news of his brother's death. Not even his customary grumbles and curses. He ignored them all, and fingered his spatha studiously. Calidus wasn't even sure what he was doing with them anymore, unless it was the secure passage – relative to travelling alone – to Eboracum. He broke his silence now as he spat into the snow and turned to Maglorius.

"What is your history, centurion?" he asked. "Why have you left your unit to help us?"

"I have no history," said Maglorius, chewing, disinterested. "Remaining at Aesica would be a fool's death."

They broke camp after what seemed like minutes of painfully cold half-sleep, and saddled their mounts, to leave. There were birds cawing above them, and Calidus noticed the powder kicked up by a group of rabbits whipping across a clear snowy field. The sun shone weakly above them.

They rode out and the frozen, ice entombed country unfurled itself at their sides. They passed huge caravans of refugees heading south, for the safety of the walls of the great city. The farms and hamlets and villages were emptying their populace onto the roads and tracks leading to Eboracum. Traders and deserters brought news of the north in exchange for food and lodging, and the news was always grim. They passed whole units of deserters, injured and dirty: ragged men like tramping barbarians too weary to speak or even raise their eyes in shameful salute.

As the sun collapsed into the snowy hills of the westerlands, the dusk spread like a bruise across the sky. The ripple of light on the horizon betrayed their approach to the city.

"It is too late," said Calidus. "Surely they have reached the city already"

"No talking," shouted Maglorius from over his shoulder. "Just ride."

All three men kicked at their sweating mounts and set them pounding along the congested road towards Eboracum.

"How far are we from the city?" asked Barbarus stretching his hands out to the fire.

Atellus finished chewing the last of the seeds the convict had foraged from the copse of trees where they were camped. They tasted acidic, but they stilled the painful cramps in his stomach.

"Another day's ride," he replied. "Is your arse sore yet?"

"It was a bloody pulp the day after we set off," the convict grimaced.

Atellus smiled. After he had finished telling his tale, Barbarus had reciprocated. When they had parted outside Culuslupi, Barbarus had made for the gap in the Wall which Drustanus has described. But there was no such passage. He had cursed and spat the Arcanus's name across the length of the Wall, but he had made his way to the milefort. After lying in wait to check that the fortlet was empty, he had scoured the surrounding areas. Barbarus thought there was a chance that the details Drustanus had given him may be correct, even if the location of the passage was misinformation. Two miles west of Culuslupi, he found the patch described by the Arcanus. But these milecastles were staffed by a detachment of limitanei from Vercovicium. He had hidden in the forests to the north until he discovered the sentries' routine, and then made his move under darkness. He reassured himself that the guards were stationed to prevent a full scale tribal attack, and were probably not looking out for individuals. Even then, his only worry was that his presence would break their boredom and so incline them to hunt him down.

Barbarus had managed to remove the loose masonry and dig his way under the passage, which was frozen and stuffed with snow. He had torn his fingers to rags scraping away at the hard earth, but the importance of his mission drove him on. He passed through the tunnel and covered up his route as best he could, then moved south away from the Wall and any patrols. He came across two burned out farms, their occupants freshly massacred. Further along the route was evidence of brigandage – children hanging from branches, their flesh plucked away by the birds and the beasts of the trees.

He nearly stumbled into a brigand camp, and laid low for half a day in a damp and frozen declivity while he waited for them to pass on. He eventually struck north and scouted his way to Culuslupi. The castle was deserted as he had expected. He tried to gain entrance, but the door was as solid and impenetrable as ever. He tried scaling the Wall, but the masonry was smooth and icy and he was not skilled enough at climbing. He racked and tore his hair and wept, before realising that it was unlikely Flavia was still inside the fort: the optio scum had probably ordered the castle cleaned and the corpse removed.

Barbarus sat and thought about what would have happened: the order to clean the hall; the necessity of removing the body from the castle; the desire to do it with as little effort as possible.

Any tracks would long since have been removed by the storm which followed their escape. He walked along, to the copse of trees to the south of the milefort, and found traces of dried blood against the bark of a tree. He followed the trail south and found more remains; a hand, which he buried in the earth as he passed. Her body had clearly been deposited away from the fort, and the remains picked up by some ravenous animal or beast-pack.

Barbarus had fallen to his knees and wept for a full day, letting the cold drape itself around his shoulders, pulling him down with its soft susurrations and promises of a warm quiet sleep, down to meet his Flavia.

He was woken by flares to the west which reminded him of Atellus's words and the desire to avenge his beloved. He trekked by night across the wilds towards Aesica where he had arrived in time to see the northerners seeping into the fort and the chaos which ensued. And then, by some obscene benevolence of the gods, his path had led him to the main road just as Atellus was at the mercy of his tormentor.

"I owe you my life," said Atellus.

Barbarus shook his head. "It is I who owe you, beneficiarius. You gave me the greatest gift possible, the only salve for the pain in my heart."

"Only by chance," replied Atellus.

"I do not believe in chance," said Barbarus looking up towards the heavens.

They rode south again, the threat of more snow in the tall dark clouds which rose like a ghostly mountain-range up ahead. There were more refugees on the road now, clustered together for safety and warmth, and the snow was packed solid under their tramping feet. There were more dead too, their blue bodies left where they lay in the road, the tears freezing on the cheeks of their kin as they shuffled south. Cold and hunger were the biggest killers, but there were constant reminders of other agents of death: the brutal remnants of brigand attacks, and evidence of maulings by wild beasts driven from the forests by hunger and desperation.

Atellus kicked his horse on, conscious of the weight of the barbarian menace at his tail and the urgency of his task ahead in Eboracum. He prayed to sol that Crispus would still be in the city by the time he arrived. The shades of his wife and daughter clung to his path and travelled with him; he could never see them, but only caught their movement from the corner of his eyes, or the slightest hint of their forms shimmering in the crispness of the horizon at dusk. They visited him as he slept, and he woke feeling more fatigued than when he had lain down.

After two days in the saddle, Atellus caught the first gleam of the early morning sun on the walls of Eboracum. A pall of dark smoke hung over the city, rising up to mingle with the angry clouds. A soft pelt of fresh snow lay on the ground. The refugees walked to the sides of the road, in the fossae, to make way for the constant stream of horses and traders' waggons which rumbled towards the city; too many had been trampled and crushed by those unwilling to be slowed by the throngs of people.

As they approached, Atellus could see the formation of a new town outside Eboracum; there was no room for the refugees within the city itself, so the settlements outside were expanding, seeking safety in proximity to the mighty walls. A bedraggled sprawl of tents and timber huts speckled the land around Eboracum, an endless stubble of the destitute and desperate. There were no roads between, only deep trenches of trampled mud and compacted snow.

The going was slow through the shanty as people begged for alms from anyone on horseback. Most traders had strongarms who beat the crowds back with cudgels, but Atellus and Barbarus walked their horses through, trying to ignore the pleas and the eyes.

"If we had some food, maybe–," begun Barbarus, reining his horse in next to Atellus.

The easterner shook his head. "They will be dead within a day or two," he said. "If the cold does not kill them, or the pestilences, then the enemy will destroy them utterly. They are easy pickings. If you had food, you would be wiser to keep it for yourself. You will need it soon enough."

Barbarus shook his head but said nothing.

The walls of the great city reared above them, high and seemingly impenetrable. The smell of woodsmoke filled their nostrils and the crackle of fires was audible from inside as they pulled up at the checkpoint. Two tired and grimy soldiers barred their path; they looked young and angry. Atellus could feel them eyeing him up – they obviously weren't sure what to make of them. Their clothes

561

were ragged and torn, but the fact that they led mounts indicated that they had money, or status. Or once had.

"Turn round," barked the soldier next to Atellus. "City's full."

Atellus looked around him. To their sides, numberless others were being told the same message; the entire north gate was a row of soldiers from the legate turning back the refugees, damming the flow and sending the wave to break amongst the rubble of the shanty town outside.

"You do not know whom you are addressing, pedes," said Atellus, gazing down at the soldier with hard black eyes. "I am beneficiarius imperatoris, and this man is my commilitione. We are expected by the praetor."

The soldier seemed uncertain; his eyes travelled over Atellus, and his steed. To his right there was a disturbance along the line; someone was trying to break through. There was the metallic clink of weapons being readied, followed by shouting and jostling. The other refugees behind Atellus pressed forward, causing a surge.

Atellus kept his eyes hard on the young soldier's beardless face. The noise from inside the city rose and throbbed like a thunderous waterfall, or a distant storm. There was something ominous and imposing about the noise; something larger and greater than anything conceivable.

The soldier blinked twice, three times, as if shivering the uncertainty from his eyes. "Go through," he said at last, jerking his head backwards.

Atellus and Barbarus rode slowly through the large gates, the crowd behind pushing and squabbling, the discord spreading from further down the line, the panic and desperation making beasts of the men and women.

The two comrades walked through the gatehouse and into the city, the grey sky hanging low over their heads, the multi-tiered buildings on either side like stanchions propping it up and keeping it from collapsing inwards.

The streets were thronged with people: peasants, artisans, traders, whores and soldiers all madding and swirling in a giant ocean of humanity. The people formed different tides and flowed along the causeways and streets, sometimes detaching to coalesce as knots which slowed the fluvial mass around them, and sometimes breaking off and disappearing into yet smaller alleys and ginnels.

There was a tension in the air that was palpable, like a smothering hand; the air was damp with fear and expectation. The ugly black trails of smoke from fires seeped up into the sky, and the smell on the air was of ash and death and blood.

Twice Atellus and Barbarus had to beat people away with the flats of their blades as they tried to throw themselves onto their mounts, or cut the reins from their grasp. The mood of the city was grim.

"Soldiers leaving, every day," they overheard one man bellowing. He was standing atop the skeleton of an old half-burned cart; it was tipped upside down beneath a canopy of overhanging masonry which looked as if it would collapse with the next breeze. "Deserting. They have lost hope. The city burns around us. Find succour in the one, true God. Make peace with Himself, and you–"

As they walked further into the city, they saw similar prophets at other corners, each with a band of onlookers who gaped upwards and nodded as the soft snow fell and gathered on their shoulders.

There was looting and robbing and brawling; Atellus watched as a small group of men overran a screaming woman and pounced on her, knives flashing in the dim half-light beneath the tall buildings. A space in the crowds opened up around them as people hurried away, not wishing to get caught up in the ugliness.

The few soldiers who were around seemed uninterested in civil order; they drank and fought amongst each other, or marched towards the principia with stern faces and hands quivering on the hilts of their swords.

"The city's already beaten," sneered Barbarus.

Atellus nodded. "It is always this way. The city will thin out of its normal inhabitants; some soldiers will desert depending on how bad morale is. Then the space gets clogged with refugees. Disease spreads, food becomes even scarcer. Depending on how hard the attackers hit," he continued, "or how long they can be bothered to press their siege, the city will fall. Brocchus's only hope is holding out until reinforcements can arrive from Valentinian. If he deigns to send them."

"Valentinian may let Britannia fall?" asked Barbarus with a raised eyebrow.

Atellus shrugged and pushed past a group of men fighting like wild hounds over a flagon of acetum. One was screeching like a woman, blood running down his face. Some were dancing even as they fought.

"I do not know what the emperor's priorities are," he said. "Not any longer."

They continued pushing their way through the streets. Occasionally they would pass a smoking or burning building, surrounded by screaming women and children. There were overturned waggons in the roads, their contents feverishly looted and the drivers left for dead by their spinning wheels. A sense of normalcy descended as they moved closer towards the centre, through the shanties and shacks of the poorer parts and towards the tall stone buildings and wider roads. There seemed to be less panic and confusion, with disciplined soldiers stationed in front of key buildings, and the large fora bustling with traders and merchants selling produce to the rich.

They kept pressing through the crowd, following a steady flow which led them across the via Constantina and towards the principia. The praetor's headquarters was surrounded by people milling around the walls. The building and its estates were ringed with soldiers from the legate. The mood of the people here, Atellus noted, was not ugly; just curious.

For the moment, at least.

He gestured for Barbarus to follow him and the two men pushed their way through to the side gate which led directly to the inner courtyard and the stables. There were less people round this side, but the gate was guarded by five legionaries.

Atellus saluted them as a superior as he rode up, and the men reluctantly returned the greeting with suspicion etched deep into their faces.

"I am Titus Faenius Magnus Atellus, beneficiarius imperatoris," he said, his voice rich and strong, "and I demand an audience with the praetor. This is my colleague, Manius Maurus Barbarus."

The soldier in charge was an optio: old, with a face was covered with iron-grey stubble. His solemn grey eyes regarded Atellus without giving away his emotions, in the way that veteran soldiers developed.

"Do you have identification papers, dominus?"

Atellus shook his head. "My name and description should be sufficient for the praetor. We will need our horses stabled while we wait."

The optio averted his gaze for a second before speaking. "Please wait here, beneficiarius."

He walked away, through the gate and into the courtyard. The other soldiers fingered their weapons and eyed the two men nervously. They were young, and their gaunt faces were pale, their eyes wet. They had probably not seen combat yet, thought Atellus. They would see it soon, though, and only the will of the gods would keep them alive to witness the end of it.

The optio returned, and saluted.

"Apologies, dominus, but the praetor has left instructions that he is to be disturbed by no-one today. Perhaps, if—"

"Do those orders come from the emperor himself, soldier," said Atellus, "or from the upper orifice of that snivelling wretch of an ab epistulis?" He leaned closer to the legionary, so he could feel the warmth of the man's breath on his face, and stared deep into his grey eyes. "I will see Brocchus today, or the whole city will feel the absence of the emperor's gaze. At such a *critical* time as this, that would be a woeful outcome of our little discussion, optio. Do you understand?"

The optio's gaze was steady and resolute. The two veterans looked at each other for a long time, the air grey around them, the soft dabs of snow falling in the air between them. The optio nodded tersely, then snapped round and growled out orders to the men.

"Open the gates," he barked. "Barrus, take the horses to the stables. Corax, escort the guests to the principia. Find Ruui."

Atellus nodded his validation to the optio. A thin, tall soldier, who looked as though he was barely old enough to shave, walked up, looking ungainly and awkward in his heavy armour, and took the reins of their mounts. Another legionary, of medium-size and wearing his uniform more confidently, came up and saluted. His face was pinched and swarthy, his nose extending outwards like a beak. Atellus could see how he had acquired the name of Corax.

"Follow me," he said in a nasal voice. "If you please, beneficiarius?"

Corax led them through into the courtyard. The ground was blanketed with fresh snow, interrupted only by the criss-crossing tracks of servants on errands hurrying to and from the principia to the ancillary buildings. The sky overhead was choked with dark smoke and clouds; there was a heady odour of burning in the air around them. The sounds of panic from the massed refugees could be heard in the distance, swelling and breaking against the outer walls of the city.

Corax pushed through a crowd of soldiers gathered around a small postern set into the inner wall of the principia; the men were passing around a flask of mulsum and trading insults. A couple spat at the ground as Corax walked past, and stared hard at Atellus and Barbarus, their lips curling, their eyes dark and contemptuous. The legionary paid no attention but heaved the door open and walked inside.

They entered a large dimly lit room, with the faint odour of roast meat tickling their nostrils. Atellus's stomach growled angrily; he could not remember the last time he had eaten properly. His clothes barely fit him, and his limbs seemed more angular than before, the narrow slats of his ribs visible through the dark vellum of his chest. It only troubled him insofar as it caused his strength to wane. He asked Sol to grant him sufficient resilience to see his duty through to the end.

Corax led them through the room; as his eyes adjusted to the light, Atellus saw that it was some kind of larder, or storage facility, probably a temporary house for the deliveries to the rear gate of the principia. Huge sacks of grain bulged out and lolled atop each other in one corner; in another were boxes of herbs and spices, stacks of amphorae of countless dimensions, oils and wines and perfumes. Atellus could not tell how long they had been there, nor whether they were full or empty. The room stank of myriad rich scents, some sharp and peppery, others blunt and earthy, and there was a dampness which hung like a miasma in the air.

They walked through the room, past endless wooden scaffolds containing sacks and crates and jugs and bottles which towered up to the ceiling overhead. There was a small door at the far end, open, with a handful of servants scurrying around gathering products under the direction of a stout bald foreman who spat and heckled as they laboured. The workers kept their heads down, but the foreman glanced at the newcomers as they passed, then reluctantly stepped out of the doorway so they could go through.

The passed into a small antechamber which reeked of garum and which itself opened out onto one of the main connecting corridors of the principia. Corax turned right and took them along this, the turquoise Sassanid carpet thick and plush beneath their boots, the walls covered in a lustrous wood panelling hung over with faded flags and standards from distant battlefields and intricately woven tapestries depicting military victories. They walked on, up one flight of broad polished marble stairs, and then along a wide statue-lined corridor, before they crested another shorter staircase.

Corax gestured for them to wait and rapped on a set of tall double-doors set into the wall to their right. They waited for a long while, the sounds of muted conversation and raised voices alternately drifting down the corridor from elsewhere in the building. A few servants scuttled past them in both directions, heads down to the ground; some legionaries marched past, tight and formal, their weapons and armour clinking belligerently as they walked.

The door was opened by a tall thin man, with tightly trimmed black hair. Atellus recognised him as the man who had met him when he first arrived in the principia what felt like months ago. He eyed Corax and the other two, his gaze seeming to linger a little longer on the easterner. His lip had a permanent curl, and his nose was sharp and wet.

"Yes?"

Corax saluted half-heartedly. "I have been instructed to introduce these two men to you, Ruui. They seek urgent audience with the praetor."

Ruui coughed, a dry arrogant sound. "Papers?"

Corax shook his head. "This is the beneficiarius imperatoris, and his assistant."

Ruui looked at them again in more detail. "You may leave, Corax," he said after a long pause.

The legionary saluted again, then strode hurriedly down the corridor in the direction they had come from.

"It is well for you, beneficiarius," said Ruui, "that I remember your face from our last meeting." The thin man walked forward and gestured them both into his office, still staring hard at Atellus. "I have keen eyes for a face."

Atellus nodded. "My thanks."

The two men walked into the office. It was a large square room, sparsely decorated with rows of shelves on which were piled papers, manuscripts, papyri and jars containing viscous fluids. There was a single large desk and cathedra, and three smaller stools, inlaid with ivory and gilt, on the other side of the desk. A large window looked out over a long private courtyard which was choked with thick snow and glowed blue with ice. A small fire flickered in a grate behind the desk.

"Sit, if you like," said Ruui. "I will speak with the praetor and see what I can do." He closed the doors behind him as he left.

Atellus drifted over to one of the stools and sat down, his limbs heavy with weariness, and let his throbbing head fall into his hands. His brow felt warm, the air from his nostrils hot on his upper lip. Barbarus walked across the room, looking around, his face expressionless, his eyes squinting in the bright lamplight.

"We should leave," said the ex-convict, after a while. His voice was low and grim.

"Leave?" sighed Atellus through his hands. "Why would we do that?"

"What if he is not fetching the praetor?" replied Barbarus. His face was dusted with dirt and shone with sweat and suspicion. "But armed men instead. Men of the same persuasion as that optio fuck from the Wall?"

Atellus raised his aching head from his hands, an improbably hard motion, and focused on the other man.

"Then we lose," he said. He pushed himself up to his feet, his muscles groaning. "We need to see Brocchus."

"Is it worth the risk?"

"Yes."

Barbarus walked around the desk and looked at the papers on it; he coughed desperately, raising his fist to his mouth to stifle the noise.

"There must be another way," he said.

Atellus forced his tired brain to think. If this was a trap, and Ruui worked for Crispus rather than Brocchus, then they were as good as dead, or worse. If the man was to be trusted, then they could have their audience with the governor, locate Crispus and finish things.

Finish. *Terminus.*

The word was beautiful and peaceful and even the mumbled thought of it, like the breeze from the flutter from a sparrow's wing, seemed to lull him into a calm and satisfied stupor.

But there was a tension whirring inside Atellus, a feeling as though a great insect were trapped inside his breast, its brittle wings vibrating against his ribs, flapping through his sinews.

He needed to trust Barbarus's intuition – the man had been right about Drustanus.

"Okay," said Atellus, nodding at his companion. "Lets go."

He moved towards the door, and yanked it open, Barbarus at his heels, and looked out into the corridor. A single servant-girl was scampering along carrying a huge silver platter of food. He stepped out, followed by Barbarus who closed the door softly behind them with a click.

"This way," said Atellus, turning to the right and striding briskly along the corridor. It dog-legged sharply to the left, and he stopped before swinging round, his heart thumping in his chest.

Something made him halt, an unease, a faint queasiness at the base of his skull that stayed his feet. He held out his arm to Barbarus and gestured for him to get back. He could hear the thump of feet from around the corner and the muted clunk of metal against metal.

Atellus moved back along the corridor, and grasped the handle of the first door set into the wall to his right.

Locked.

He moved down the corridor, trying the doors desperately while scanning around him for any niches or recesses into which they could dive. Barbarus sensed his purpose and urgency and did the same along the opposite wall.

He could hear voices, now, nearing them, and the rumble of many footsteps getting so close that they seemed to merge with the thump of his own heart in his chest.

He tried the next door.

Locked.

He moved down and felt a hand on his arm. He swung round, and found himself staring at Barbarus's face, intense squinting eyes glistening with urgency. His comrade jerked his head back, towards an open doorway.

Atellus dived after him and both men disappeared into the room, Atellus tensing his fist around the handle, fighting his adrenalin to stymy the shakes in his hand. He closed the door softly behind them.

The two men were enveloped in darkness, with only the faintest glimmer of pale light from behind the thick drapes overhanging what seemed to be a window at the far end of the chamber. Atellus put his ear close to the door; he could smell the scent of the worked wood, feel its warmth against his cheek. Muffled, he could hear the thud of numerous footsteps and the jangle of weaponry, then lower still, the hum of voices.

The noises stopped as the group reached the door of what Atellus presumed was Ruui's office. He dimly heard the click of the latch opening, and felt the shiver of the sound through the adjoining wall as the office door was pushed open. He could hear raised voices, sounds of urgency and motion. He moved away from the door, deeper into the darkness.

"Atellus!" Barbarus spoke in a tight whisper.

He turned round, waiting for his eyes to adjust to the darkness and for greyish shapes to form themselves from the blackness. He moved away towards the far wall and the dim glow of light that seeped from beyond. As he got closer, he could see the light was from a window, which was all but covered by thick heavy curtains. Barbarus put a gentle hand on his shoulder, and he felt the man's warm breath on his ear.

"It is only a matter of time before they look for us in here."

"Yes," said Atellus, nodding in the darkness. "What options do we have?"

In response, Barbarus pulled back part of the curtain, revealing a large frozen balcony which glistened blue in the moonlight.

Atellus nodded, then moved forward, the curtain sweeping back behind him, obscuring them both from the suffocating darkness of the chamber. He worked the catch on the lower window and pushed open the wooden frame, which swung out onto the balcony. Freezing cold air hit him like a slap to the face. He stepped out, and Barbarus followed, closing the window behind them.

The statue-tipped crenels of the south wall of the principia stretched away to either side; the windows and balconet doorways to their left and right were topped and framed by elaborate pediments and architraves. There was a swathe of private, walled gardens directly beneath them. Torch and lamplight from windows pricked through the darkness around them as the two men stood exposed in the night air, their hurried breath wisping in front of them.

"Where do we go?" said Barbarus, his teeth clicking.

"Up," replied Atellus. He angled his head back to look towards the principia roof which loomed stories above. "A bit, at least. You see that curved balcony over there, with the bronze pillars and the torches?" He pointed away off to their right and over their heads. Barbarus nodded. "I think that is the praetor's quarters. It would be a good place for us to start."

"Right," said the convict. "And how the fuck do we get there?"

Atellus looked at him flatly, without answering.

Barbarus swallowed. He stretched and leapt up onto the railing of the balcony, then across onto the ornate tracery work which framed the large window through which they had exited the room. Atellus heard the sound of the door being thrown open inside, and voices shouting. He followed Barbarus's lead and clambered up onto the railing of the balcony, then across onto the window. The stonework was thin and slippery beneath his boots and his feet felt thick and large and cumbersome. He reached up and grasped the fluted columns to the side of the window and scraped his way up, his fingers thrilling with cold and effort. He could see Barbarus above him, his feet slipping and scraping for purchase against the stonework.

Don't look down, Atellus told himself as a tongue of cold wind pressed against his cheek and into his thin clothes. *Don't look down.*

He moved up, reaching for a handhold, finding it easily amongst the elaborate carvings, then swung himself across to reach for the whorls of the carved bracket of the balcony across to his right. In the night air he could smell fires, and hear the endless chant of the town, a long oscillating vibration of wordless anxiety pitched just low enough to serve as a bass counterpoint to the keen melody of his own fear.

He followed Barbarus's movements, grasping for the same holds. Occasionally, as they moved incrementally across the broad and endless face of the principia, he would see the crumbling dust of the stone flurry down like a miniature snowstorm. Sometimes there were larger breakages, and he heard the swollen curses as the convict lost a hold. But he always recovered.

Atellus followed and the night laughed and taunted him, throwing the wind at his back, and spitting fine cold snow in his eyes. Beneath him, he felt the town pulse and throb with boil-like eruptions of fires. Somewhere, a shrill scream split the night and was silenced abruptly.

After a seemingly endless agony of sweat, screaming ligaments and frozen flesh, Atellus looked up, the sweat blurring his vision, and saw the narrow curved balcony of the praetor's office within grasping distance.

His concentration was swept aside by the thick waves of relief pulsing through his body; his fingers aimed to close around a handhold along the side of the fluted window column to his right. Instead they clenched around air, the tips scraping the cold marble.

Atellus felt himself falling, a strange light-headedness that seemed to come across him in slow motion. Panic spurred his feet as his body writhed and flexed to regain his balance, to fling him back against the safety of the wall. But instead, he fell, and the shout stuck in his throat like a stone. Atellus was conscious of the ground beneath him, sickeningly far below, a vague white quilt that looked serene and deadly.

And then there was a shock of pain around his wrist as the inevitable arc of his fall was arrested by Barbarus's hand grasping him.

The world seemed to speed up again and he reached up with his other hand, across to the balcony of the praetor's office, and grabbed hold of the ledge, the stone icy and rough beneath the pads of his fingertips.

He looked up. Barbarus was wrapped around a granite stanchion from the balcony, his free arm holding onto Atellus's wrist where he had caught him. His face was a rictus of pain and concentration as he heaved the beneficiarius upwards, towards the railing. Atellus felt the muscles in his forearms screaming as he tried to lever himself up with his scant grip on the balcony. He felt himself rising, the wind sailing around his dangling legs. He kicked up and got a foothold on the balcony, though he was almost horizontal in the air now, his back trembling and itching furiously as he imagined the drop beneath it and the frozen ground ready to snap his spine to shards with a deafening impact. Atellus could hear Barbarus grunting, could see the soft gasped mist of his breaths in the air, and the feathersoft brush of the moonlight on his forehead. Atellus squeezed and felt himself rising, and his whole torso seemed to pulsate towards the safety of the balcony. He loosened the grip of his free hand, and clutched for a more secure hold, above and across his shoulder: a grooved plinth. He made it, and jerked himself upwards, pressing his body against the beautiful cold stone of the balcony parapet.

Atellus paused for a moment, to let the pain in his muscles subside, then vaulted over onto the security of the balcony floor, before reaching back to clasp Barbarus's wrist, hauling him up.

Both safely on the balcony, Atellus clapped a hand on the other man's shoulder. "Thank you," he said.

Barbarus inclined his head solemnly, then turned towards the window leading in to the praetor's office. The curtains were almost fully closed, but in the seam of light visible down the middle Atellus could see the thin, gaunt form of Brocchus pacing back and forth across the room. At the far wall, standing relaxed but aware, were two of his legionary guards. Leaning against the far wall of the room, Atellus could make out the large form of the governor's personal bodyguard, his red beard glowing like cinders in the torchlight.

The two men stood together outside, the cold wind whicking the sweat from their brows, their breath hissing out into the darkness between them.

"Shall we knock and beg audience?" grinned Barbarus, coughing into his fist.

Atellus smiled. "I had something more direct in mind."

The beneficiarius stepped up to the balcony doors, and aimed a hard snapping kick towards the wood where the two doors met. The frame gave way with a crash and the doors exploded inwards, buffeted by the thick drapes of the curtains. Atellus and Barbarus dived through, ripping swords from their sheaths as they went forward.

The bodyguard reacted first, as Atellus thought he would, whilst the legionaries stood frozen against the back wall, trying to take in the situation. The man covered the distance between them in a heartbeat, the long double-edged sword in his hands sweeping down towards Barbarus in an angled slice. The convict parried the blow and fell backwards against the curtain even as Atellus followed it up with a slash at the bodyguard's arm. He felt the weight of the sword digging across flesh, and the man fell back with a howl and a spray of bright blood; his sword thumped down on the carpeted floor. Brocchus squirmed back against his desk, his face pale, his eyes wide and fearful.

"Flavius Clodius Bassianus Brocchus," said Atellus, eyeing the two legionaries against the wall who had only just drawn their weapons. "My apologies for the urgency of our entrance, and lack of protocol, but we request an immediate audience, in the name of Flavius Valentinianus Augustus."

Atellus stood panting, his dark eyes raking the praetor's blanched face. Barbarus regained his balance, squabbling his way through the thick curtains. The bodyguard clutched his wounded arm and eyed the intruders malignantly. The two legionaries at the door levelled their weapons at the strangers and swapped looks between them and the governor.

Atellus watched the recognition spill across Brocchus's face, and he relaxed visibly. "Beneficiarius imperatoris," he said, after clearing his throat. "I will of course grant you audience." He wiped a hand across his forehead, then spoke to his bodyguard. "Gargilianus, go and find the medicus, and have your wound treated." He turned to the legionaries. "Go and wait outside my door. See that I am disturbed by *no-one* until I command otherwise."

Brocchus moved round to the other side of his large heavy desk, as his men stumbled and edged their way from the office with uncertain glances at each other. Gargilianus left a spattered trail of bright blood behind him as he hunched his way through the door.

The praetor sat down behind his desk and gestured for Atellus and Barbarus to take seats opposite him. "Pray, sit down," said Brocchus. "And do sheathe your blades and close the drapes behind you. The chill will settle to my very bones."

CHAPTER 41

"This is it," said Maglorius, stopping them outside a huge pair of iron gates. The house beyond was large and flat and long. Lamps glittered through the distant windows.

Vassu coughed a curse and rubbed the wound on his neck again. His hand came away with fresh blood.

"Leave it be," said Calidus. "Or you'll fiddle your way through to the bone."

The boy was wounded himself, a graze across his nose and cheek and a deep gash along his left forearm which was bound with material from Maglorius's cloak; the centurion had sliced bits off to staunch the bleeding of their wounds. Only Galla was unscathed, though her cheeks seemed to glisten damply in the moonlight.

Had she been crying, wondered Calidus? And was that an improvement? He had lost count of the times he had wondered whether she was truly alive. She sometimes seemed more animal than girl. She followed and moved and swirled among them, though she never seemed to be really there; it was as if she were a shade. If it wasn't for Vassu's muttered comments, Calidus would have started to doubt whether the girl was real at all. He didn't even know whether he looked out for her simply because Aurelia had done so, and now she was no longer here he felt obliged to take up the burden; or whether there was something more primal about it, that he cared for her like a sister, because she was alone and vulnerable and he in a position of responsibility.

He placed pressure on his arm wound, and the warmth of his hand eased the throbbing a little. He looked up at the villa in urbs again. Aurelia was in there: either she was alive and they could retrieve her, or she was already dead and they could avenge her. Death seemed to lie in every direction, for them all. He was almost close enough to lose his fear of it.

They had a close brush riding through the riots, with the ugly crowds baying for blood and desperate to seek safety within the walls of Eboracum. The very fact that they rode horses made them a target. They had trampled over the long-dead and the dying even as they had ridden through the streets to escape the mobs.

If it wasn't Aurelia's abductors who killed him, thought Calidus, it would be the rioters, or the approaching hordes of savages from beyond the Wall.

He looked over at Maglorius; the centurion was standing tall and solid, only a slight tightness at the corners of his eyes betraying his wounds. His military clothes were covered with a rough, dun-coloured cloak which hung down to his knees. If it had not been for Maglorius, they would not even have made it into the city. They had been turned back at the gates, and caught in the fighting in the shanties outside. It was only when he revealed his rank, and his familiarity with the centurion in charge, that they were ushered through.

Their ride through the outer, lawless streets of the city had been hard and slow. Vassu had been pulled from his horse and slashed, his steed stolen before the others could even react. Whether the beast had been taken for meat or for freedom, it mattered little. The incident served only to blacken the scowl on Vassu's face as was pulled up to sit behind Maglorius. Calidus himself had been attacked and nearly dragged from his own mount, but the centurion had brought his spatha down on the assailant's head, splitting it in half and sending the man quivering to the floor. The other attackers had backed off then. But there had been many others and Maglorius had hacked a path for them through the throngs. Usually at the sight of a well-wielded spatha, most of the mob veered away to find easier targets, but others were more persistent, or desperate: some used long spicula, jabbing at their horses' soft underbellies. Maglorius's own mount took an injury this way, and left a trail of dark blood behind them in the night. Eventually they had pushed through the pockets of violence, past the burning townhouses and taverns, beyond the screams of the tormented, and into the safer parts of town which were still patrolled by disciplined soldiers, and private militias in the pay of the nobles and merchants.

Calidus looked around him, craning his neck up to the large houses. They were in mons Pinorum: a wealthier part of town, where the streets were quieter. The sounds of the rioting, the smell of burning and the glow of the angry fires were away towards the poorer peripheral districts to the north and west: The Rodam, Acula, the Calles.

Maglorius had instructed them to tie their horses up in an abandoned shed half a mile back.

"Maybe the girl should wait here?" suggested Vassu, addressing Calidus. He finished off testing the knot he had awkwardly tied with his mangled fingers.

It was a thought he had borne himself, Calidus conceded. He turned to Galla and saw the widening of her eyes.

"Galla," he said, his voice calm. "It will be dangerous, and difficult. You could stay and tend to the horses, and–"

The girl shook her head violently, and clung to Calidus's arm. He smoothed her light hair with the flat of his hand and looked at the others. Maglorius was checking the knots binding their horses; Vassu's lips were mumbling, his crooked fingers dry-washing each other, like some kind of rodent.

Galla had her face downturned and buried in Calidus's armpit. Her ribs rose and fell with dry sobs. She was definitely displaying more emotion than he had seen before, Calidus thought. It was just a shame that it was always negative.

"Okay, you come with us," he said, softly. "But you must look after yourself. Stay close to me."

Maglorius finished checking the knots lashing the horses to the timbers and examined the animals themselves. He ripped up a tunic and tied it in large bands around the wound on his horse's flank, whispering softly into the animal's ear as he did so. Then they set off on foot, and Calidus asked if the beast would die. The centurion had merely shrugged and remained silent until they reached the villa.

"How do we get in?" asked Calidus, looking through the gates. The villa was huge, as were the grounds. "There will be guards."

"Many," nodded Maglorius. Vassu wheezed something from between his teeth. "But getting in shouldn't be a problem. There is a servant's entrance to the rear which is not as well guarded."

"You've been here before?" asked Vassu, frowning.

Maglorius nodded. "A few times. It is the abode of the praetor's ab epistulis."

"Her husband," said Vassu quietly.

"Tantum in nomine," said Maglorius.

"We need to get in there," said Calidus, suddenly feeling the urgency of Aurelia's predicament.

Maglorius placed a finger across his lips, then led them all round the perimeter wall of the villa; it was brick-built and the height of two men, topped by rusted iron spearheads. As they walked through the slush and snow of the city, Calidus could hear the roar of panic to the north, and the sinister crackle of burning by the riverfront. The massive walls of the principia loomed ahead of them, the building lit up by countless lamps and torches. They reached a large gate to the rear of the building, which opened onto a broad alley leading out onto a further road perpendicular to the via principalis, the main road of the city which stretched all the way to the south gate. A short distance down from the large double gate, hidden in a fold in the curtain wall, was a postern. Maglorius told the others to keep tight in to the wall, then walked up to the postern door and knocked four times.

There was only the sough of the wind and the distant chatter of the city. From over in the principia were the sounds of soldiers drilling in the courtyard.

Maglorius knocked again, four times.

A voice called out. "Who is it?"

"Maglorius."

There was the slam of a bolt being drawn back, then another, and the door swung heavily inward. Calidus could see through the shadows as a lean wiry man leaned out, a torch in his scrawny gripe, and looked up at the centurion, squinting into his features.

"What the fuck you doin here, Maglorius?" The man's voice was mean and high-pitched, the tone sulky. "At this hour? Don't you know the city's fallin apart?"

"Stop werriting, Senilus," said the centurion, "and let me through."

Maglorius pushed the door open, and mauled the servant inside, beckoning to the others to follow as he did so. Calidus and Vassu pushed forward and through the postern in time to see Maglorius drive his fist into the throat of Senilus.

The old man staggered backwards, dropping his torch on the ground. He raised his hands to his throat even as he fell backwards onto his bony arse. A strange crackling noise was coming from between his lips. Maglorius half-knelt and drove the pommel of his spatha into the old man's temple. It connected with an ugly muted slap. He collapsed backwards with a jerking motion, and lay still. His torch fell from his hand and extinguished itself in the cold slush on the ground.

Calidus looked around; they were in the internal grounds of the courtyard, though protected from the main building by the corner of the guard's cell, a rude wooden shack in which the sentry passed his time. The inside of the cell was dark.

Maglorius strode round and hauled up Senilus by the armpits, gesturing for Calidus to take the legs. He did so, and he centurion directed them towards the guard cell. They passed inside. Calidus noted a small dirty cot, a rickety table and a rough stool. There was no room for anything else. A few mean vittles and a jug of mulsum sat on the table. It stank of old food and sweat and urine, and the cold seemed to rise up from between the wooden slats of the floor.

"You knew him?" asked Atellus. The dead man's legs twitched unpleasantly under his fingers.

"I did," said Maglorius. "But today is the end of his usefulness." He dropped the upper body into the corner of the cell. "For me at least."

Calidus laid the man's heels down on the ground slowly, almost reverentially. Senilus's face was pale, blooming to an angry purple around the temple where his skull had been cracked. His claw-like hands were frozen in their grip around his red and swollen throat. His lank hair was a dark grey, speckled with white and his lips and eyes were tight with a frozen pain.

"How did–", began Calidus, but Maglorius held up a broad palm to silence him. He stared straight ahead, listening intently, then went out of the guard house gesturing for Calidus to follow. They met up with Vassu and Galla just outside.

"Go round to the back of this hut," said Maglorius to them all. "Quickly."

They edged out of the cell, following the shadows into a narrow space between the curtain wall and the timber rearside of the sentry cell. Calidus could hear shouts and the whinnying of horses. The courtyard became brighter, the shadows more pronounced. From above, the freezing snow fell heavily and wearily onto their hair and shoulders.

Calidus was at the front of the huddle, crouched tight against the wall and swathed in shadows. He moved across slightly, inching the tip of his head out from behind the guard cell wall until he could see into the courtyard. There was a group of men lashing horses into place, tethering them to open-backed waggons. Servants dragged more waggons from within a long, low building that looked like a workshop, and grooms struggled with frightened steeds pulled from the stables at the far end of the villa.

"They're leaving," said Calidus in a whisper.

"Yes," said Maglorius. His deep voice, pitched lower than usual, seeming to rumble from out of the desolate ground itself. "Sooner than I expected. Crispus's luxuries, sent out in advance before the armies arrive. He will transfer his riches to one of his properties in the south. Londinium perhaps. It would not do for him to lose all his personal wealth."

"What of Aurelia?"

Calidus felt rather than saw the big man shrug. "If she is alive, she will be with Crispus," he said. "He will not leave until he is certain the armies will surround the city. It is quicker and easier for one man to escape on horseback than a household's worth of gold and fineries."

Vassu spat noiselessly into the snow.

Two heavily laden waggons creaked into motion, the wheels sliding in the slush and ice. The servants pushed them from behind, faces straining and mouths gushing mist into the night air. Slowly, the ponderous steeds gathered motion and hauled the waggons to a rolling pace across the courtyard. A couple of servants ran ahead, shouting for the sentry.

Calidus and Maglorius melted deeper into the shadows as they approached.

"Senilus! Gatesman!"

"Stupid old fuck is asleep."

"Then we'll pound the frozen shit out of his old arse!"

Laughter. Calidus could hear the iron studs of their boots on the icy ground, and the ragged gasp of their breathing.

"Wake up, you old cinaedus."

"You get the old shit, I'll check the gate."

One of the men rapped on the door of the guard cell with his knuckles.

Calidus felt the sweat pooling in the small of his back, despite the bitter cold. If the man opened the cell and found the body, the alarm would be raised. They would be hunted, cornered. He decided to get Maglorius to help him push Galla over the wall, if it came to that. At least the girl could escape. How long she would last would be another matter, but at least she could die on her own terms.

Another knock. "Senilus, we need the fuckin gates open, you old toad."

Calidus heard the door of the sentry hut swing open. His fingers ached, his hands were balled into fists so tightly. His calves screamed with the effort of squatting. He caught sight of Vassu's strained face, glum and determined. Maglorius was invisible to him, and Galla was only a ghostly figure behind him, though he could feel the delicate weight of her slim cold fingers on his arm.

"You lazy old—"

"Dorius!" shouted one of the men from the other side of the guard-cell. "Gate's open; the old fuck probly thought he could sneak off to one of his whores again."

There was a pause, then footsteps, heading out of the cell and towards the gate.

"No, he's sleeping in there. Flat fuckin out. Reeks of mulsum."

"No surprise there, then."

They heard the sound of the heavy gates being rolled open, the hinges howling, the wooden planks grunting as they scraped against the ground. The two waggons trundled out, their drivers shouting down to the other servants. A troop of guards followed on horseback. From the noise of the hooves and the voices, Calidus estimated about twenty of them.

Gradually it grew silent, and the sound of the heavy doors rolling back into place rumbled like a deep thunder through the still night.

Calidus inched backwards, his legs spasming with great bolts of pain, his breathing heavy and laboured, as the footsteps of the two servants came closer to the cell again, their voices a stern mumble on the breeze. Snow piled up alongside him; he shivered even as he felt as though his insides were aflame. Soon the words became audible.

"—next time. The gaffer'll flay the old fuck alive."

"Too right," came the reply. "Let's get in first and rip his pubes out."

The footsteps got closer then stopped abruptly.

"Nah, Dorius, fuckit," said one. "We needs get our stuff packed; and lock up the stables. The old sod'll get what he's owed. One way or another. Letim kip."

There was a grunt, then the footsteps tailed off across the length of the courtyard.

Maglorius got to his feet, melting from the shadows like a large cat. "Stay here."

He trod out into the open courtyard, finding a route from shadow to shadow, moving fast across the surface, his footsteps almost soundless through the deepening snow. The two servants were ahead of him, trudging slowly through the snow towards the stables. Overhead the clouds were thick and angry and the snowfall was getting heavier. A thin sliver of moonlight sliced down the side of the villa up ahead. Maglorius waited until the first of the men had entered the stable door; his fellow waited outside, clapping his hands together and tucking his fingers into his armpits. Within three bounds, Maglorius was upon him and his dagger was in the man's neck, severing his spinal column neatly, just below the base of the skull. His grunts of surprise muffled by Maglorious's other hand, he crumpled into the centurion's arms, who lowered him gently to the ground.

Maglorius waited for a second, then edged towards the stable door where the first man had entered. He could hear him humming tunelessly to himself as he wound tethers of rope around the wooden partitions and slapped stall gates shut.

"Come on, you lazy slut," he called over his shoulder. "I'm not doin this all by meself."

Maglorius walked in. The place stank of shit and rotting hay and damp. He sheathed his dagger, then eased his spatha from its scabbard. He walked nonchalantly towards the servant, who had his back towards him, busy coiling a length of rope around his forearm. When he was barely a pace away, Maglorius levelled the blade at the back of the man's head.

"Turn around slowly," he said, his deep voice resonating in the wide space, "and don't utter a sound." The man paused in his job, frozen for a second whilst his brain registered the unexpected. Eventually, he turned to face Maglorius, the loop of thick rope still around his forearm. He looked up into the centurion's face.

Maglorius looked him over; this was not a fighter, nor a man of strength. He was only mean and sullen and tired. The city was full of such men. The empire was.

"Where is your master?" he asked, keeping his voice low but hard.

The man's eyes were wide, frozen on the tip of Maglorius's sword which was an inch from his throat.

"Where is Crispus?" asked Maglorius, his voice quiet and steady.

The man's throat wobbled slightly as he tried to speak, but he seemed no more alive than Senilus.

"What is your name?" asked Maglorius. "Obey me and you will live, unlike your friend."

At this, the man's eyes rose again to meet the centurion's; they looked damp and disbelieving. He had short brown hair, cut into a ragged bowl atop his pale head. He bore untidy moustaches and the barest scrub of a beard. A chunk of his upper lip was missing. He stank of piss.

"Enestus," he stammered. "I am Enestus."

"Good, Enestus. Now where is your master? Tell me and you have nothing to fear."

The servant's eyes flicked towards the spatha again. His arm was trembling visibly.

"Remember, Enestus," said Maglorius, "few men are worth dying for. And that rat is not one of them."

Enestus swallowed. "He...he is dining. In...in his study."

Maglorius nodded. "If you are lying to me, Enestus, I will cut your cock off and beat you to death with it."

Enestus winced. "I'm not lying, I swear," his eyes dropped again. The man's breeches darkened with a swelling pool of urine.

"Where is the captive, the woman brought here earlier by the legionaries?"

Enestus swallowed. "They took her to the Master's chamber."

"Where is that?"

"The top floor, *dominus*...the only room on the top floor."

Maglorius nodded. The only sign of his intention was a slight tightening of the muscles around his eyes as he drove the spatha forward with a smooth, rigid motion, straight through the throat of Enestus. The blade slid in easily, punching the man back slightly and driving him into the side of the stall. Maglorius twisted the sword, then followed the weight of the man down to the ground. Enestus's eyes were wide with shock, and his hands trembled weakly in front of his breast. The centurion yanked free his sword; it withdrew with a sucking sound and the man's neck vomited thick pools of blood which looked black in the dim light of the oil lamp overhead.

Maglorius stooped to wipe his blade on the dying man's cloak. Enestus made a thin rattling noise as the life flooded out of him, his lips working soundlessly in shock. Then the centurion pulled the body deep into the shadows of one of the far stalls. He went back outside, checking to see if anyone was around before dragging the body of Dorius inside and laying it next to his companion. Then he left the stables, closing the door behind him, and ran back to the main gate, keeping to the shadows cast by the impassive moon.

The others were as he left them, squeezed together for warmth.

"Follow me," he said. "Keep low and quiet. Aurelia is in Crispus's chambers, on the top floor of the villa."

They followed Maglorius across the shadows of the courtyard, hugging the corners and deep angles of the walls until they reached the servants' entrance which led directly into the scullery. The door was shut, but Maglorius pushed it open.

"It's not locked," said Calidus with amazement.

"It never is," replied Maglorius. They entered into a gorgeous all-encompassing warmth which rinsed the aching cold from their flesh. They were in a long, low room which was thick with steam from the hot sinks and cauldrons. Servants emerged like pale weary shades from the endless fog, carrying dishes, clothes, or fuel for the hypocaust fires at the far end. The newcomers were lost in a humid fug as they walked along, but no-one challenged them, or even looked in their direction. Occasionally soldiers walked through, groping the occasional servant-girl or spitting oaths at one of the older women, but they spared not a glance for the others.

Maglorius pushed through as though he were familiar with the layout. To Calidus, after the initial joy of the warmth had faded, it was a hell of heat and noise and pipes and sweat. The water in the air seemed to settle on his lungs leaving him coughing heavily and feeling as though he were drowning. When Maglorius finally pushed open a door into a hot brick-built corridor devoid of ornament or decoration, he was so relieved he almost fell to the floor sucking in huge gasps of dry, cool air.

"They don't have a scullery in your uncle's palace, then?" asked Vassu mockingly.

Calidus looked up at the sallow man and nodded. "Yes," he said. "But I've never been there."

Vassu sneered in reply.

Maglorius led them down towards the end of the narrow corridor. They passed dozens of passages opening out on either side and Calidus could see yet more corridors stretching back into darkness, an endless tangle of dim, damp warrens. Servants' quarters, perhaps. He felt he could get lost down here and not find his way out for days. He looked across at Maglorious, searching for signs of discomfort or awkwardness in the man's features, but the centurion's face was expressionless.

A few servants scurried past, eyes down. At the far end of the corridor was a large double-door, made with thick oak panelling, which looked more opulent than the side doors they had passed along the way. Maglorius stopped in front of it and turned to them.

"If we are confronted," he said, looking at Calidus and Vassu, "let me speak. Keep your heads and eyes down, and you will not be noticed. If I give the word – and not until – draw your weapons and fight for your lives. Do you understand?"

Calidus nodded, and was aware of Vassu doing the same. He felt Galla squeezing his hand.

Maglorius opened the door and walked through, the others following behind. Calidus saw they had entered a lavishly-decorated corridor which was lined with statues and wall-hangings. The centurion strode through, towards a narrow spiral staircase on their left which spun up to the higher stories of the villa. As they turned towards it, a large swarthy man walked down the final steps and emerged into the hallway. He was heavily muscled and his face was covered with a scrubby beard, slashed through with old pale scars. His eyes were half-lidded and set deep inside his angular face. He was dressed in coarse clothing, though the sword at his waist was large and the scabbard ornate. He stopped in front of Maglorius for a second, his lids widening in surprise, his right hand hovering over the hilt of his sword.

"Dexter," said Maglorius. "Ave, fratrus."

The swarthy man's face brightened, though there was still a spark of suspicion deep within the caves of his eyes.

"Centurion Maglorius," said Dexter, his voice deep and slurred. "I didn't know you were visiting."

The two men reached forward and shook wrists. Calidus kept his face down, his cheeks burning. He recognised Crispus's bodyguard and knew that the familiarity could be reciprocated. He stared hard into the ground, counting the threads and wefts of the carpet beneath his boots.

"Neither did I," said Maglorius. "Until recently."

"I hear the savages are through the Wall," said Dexter, his voice like crushed glass.

"They are."

Dexter whistled, then grinned showing the deep red gaps between his rotten teeth. "Then we do not have long. You are just in time to help me have fun with my master's troublesome bitch."

"Excellent," said Maglorius, smiling.

CHAPTER 42

"I am asking for your *help*, beneficiarius!"

Brocchus stood in front of his elaborate solium, resting his fists on his desk and staring across at the two men standing opposite. Atellus stood rigid on the other side of the praetor's desk, staring darkly back at Brocchus. Barbarus seemed bored and lounged nonchalantly against the curve of a tall-backed cathedra, fingering the notches along the edge of his sword. The discussion had gone downhill since Atellus had confessed to returning from the Wall without Brocchus's nephew, knowing nothing of his whereabouts.

"I am aware of that, praetor," replied Atellus. "But my work here is finished."

"Your *work*," scoffed Brocchus, his voice rich with contempt. "You never had work here, beneficiarius. Your work was to leave the presence of the emperor and not risk tainting his noble religion with your embarrassing pagan practices. I am surprised you did not find more kinship on the Wall than in all of Treves."

"The Wall is rotten, Brocchus," said Atellus calmly, "and you have known it for some time."

"That is quite an accusation, beneficiarius," said the governor quietly. "I presume you have evidence to back up such claims?"

"Damn the evidence," snarled Atellus. "We will all die and your city will go up in flames. You know this as well as I. Stop thinking of your politics for once, Brocchus, and govern your province."

"That is why I ask for your help!" replied the praetor, his voice rising in pitch. His hair was less neatly coiffed than before, and the purple pouches under his eyes had grown. He looked thinner than previously, noticed Atellus, though the change was good for him. "I ask for your help, the aid of an experienced commander. My city is rioting...one of every two soldiers is deserting. There is a stream out of the south gate faster than I can dam, and all we have seething at the north gate are desperate wretches who are more bone and tears than muscle and spirit."

"What do you want me to do about this?" said Atellus calmly. "You should have looked to this problem years since. It is too late now." He shook his head wearily. "Where is your ab epistulis?"

"I presume he is in his villa at the moment," said Brocchus, his eyes narrowing at the change of direction.

"And where is that?"

"What," said Brocchus, slowly, "do you want with Crispus?"

"That is between me and him." Atellus moved closer to the desk that separated him from the praetor, and leaned over it, speaking in a soft and brutal undertone. "Ask no more questions about this."

Brocchus allowed a grim smile to play across his lips. "Who am I to question the emperor's concerns? Many men will suffer in the days to come."

"Sol grant it, they will," said Atellus from behind gritted teeth. "His villa – where is it?"

"I can have my men take you there, beneficiarius," said Brocchus, waving a loose palm to indicate his disinterest in the matter. "The streets are not safe at the moment, as I am sure you have experienced."

"More of your men, Brocchus?" laughed Atellus, straightening up from his position over the desk. "I am sick of them. I can trust no-one in the frozen wastes of your province."

"Help *me*, Atellus, help Rome, and I give you my word I will help you. Help the people. Help this city. Without some guidance, we will all perish."

"Oh no. Not all, praetor," said Atellus coldly. "I have seen the waggon-trains being prepared in the grounds. I know what happens in sieges."

Brocchus stared resolutely back at Atellus. "That is not me, beneficiarius, nor ever has been. My servants, my trusted few. I have made provisions for their safety. I will remain with Eboracum, with my city, my home, until the end. Whatever end that may be."

The two men stared at each other until Barbarus thought the space between the dark eyes and the blue eyes would catch alight and scorch them both to cinders.

"What of your generals?" said Atellus finally.

"I have some good men," said Brocchus. "But not enough. The men believe they are fighting a doomed battle."

"You must arm the citizens," said Atellus. "Give them a part to play; they have most to lose. Bring them to the walls, make them fight for their homes and their families. Swell the numbers of your ranks; put the soldiers in charge of the citizens."

"The troops will rally for you, Atellus," said the praetor. "You are the beneficiarius imperatoris. To them, it will be a like a visit from Valentinian himself. You can strengthen their resolve, remind them that they fight for Rome."

"They will fight for their families, Brocchus, and themselves. Not for Rome."

597

"Help them do that, then. They need a leader; someone inspirational."

"That should be your role, praetor," mocked Atellus.

Brocchus smiled gently. "I am a politician, not a warrior. A diplomat, not a fighter."

Atellus wiped a hand across his forehead. He looked sallow and drawn, tired and beaten.

"You owe me, Atellus," pressed Borcchus. "You gave me your word to look after my Calidus, my nephew. Now he is alone in the wilds, or dead. Do this last thing for me, as recompense."

Atellus winced visibly. "When I have concluded my business with your ab epistulis, praetor, I will do what I can to defend Eboracum. I may as well meet my darkness here as anywhere else."

***

Atellus did not know the name of the servant who was leading them. He was wending a circuitous route through the backstreets towards what he assured them was the villa of the ab epistulis. The man was short with a dirty blonde splash of hair. His face was sunken and twisted. He could have been any age between fifteen and forty.

"How much further?" said Atellus.

"Just round the next corner, dominus," came the reply.

Atellus looked to Barbarus at his side; the convict took his meaning and shook his head slightly. He did not know whether it was a trap either. Brocchus had seemed genuine. But then he had built his career around just that; all politicians did.

Atellus loosened his spatha in its scabbard and felt a sudden pang of loss for his blade of Damascene steel. His mind wandered back to the night at Aesica; was the man who his sword had passed on to now dead? Had it been taken by another, a northman perhaps? He idly hoped whoever the owner might be, it was someone who respected the weapon, the quality of its materials and craftsmanship.

The night was cold and snow was falling heavily around them; drifts were already accruing in the narrow lanes which the servant led them through. A few rats the size of tomcats darted across the alleyways in front of them, ploughing through the snowdrifts and sending white spray onto their boots as they passed.

Overhead hung low, heavy clouds, the undersides of which glowed a burnished orange reflecting the light of the fires which raged through the city as the people rioted. Old personal of professional grudges were settled; rival gangs used the impetus to destroy each other; pillagers took what they desired: women, clothes, food, gold. Atellus had lost count of the times he had seen the same. People made him sick, now; he cared little for them, for their welfare, for their survival. He cared little in the baking, sweat-drenched cities of the east, and he cared even less here amongst the freezing grey bricks of the north.

Somewhere, he knew, amidst the violence and the hate was a desperate core of people, families perhaps, willing to fight for their homes and their loved ones. Others, Atellus conceded, would simply cower and beseech their various gods for the storm to pass them by. They believed that if it wasn't the invaders that killed them, it would be the disease or the hunger or the cold. Or even their own neighbours. And, they would think, if not this time, then the next. What was the point in dragging themselves through this bitter and grim existence?

Atellus didn't know; he would be glad to be rid of it himself. And join Julia Faenia and Petronia in the land of the eternal sun.

The servant led them up to a small door set deep into a wall, and rapped at it three times. There was no response, so he tried again. After a third time yielded no result, he pushed the door, and it swung inwards.

They walked through into the deep snow of Crispus's courtyard.

"This is the villa of the ab epistulis?" asked Atellus.

"It is," replied the servant. "Dominus."

Barbarus coughed, then whistled. "It's almost bigger'n the fuckin principia."

The courtyard was devoid of tracks, the layered snow fresh and pristine. The servant led them through to another door in the villa itself. He pushed it open and shouted in. A domestic servant, a fat short woman, came bustling through. She looked panicked.

"Cunittus!" she almost yelped. "What are you doing here? I thought the gov–"

"Stop yatterin', woman," he snapped, and the domestic seemed to deflate under the force of his stare. "Take these here digny-taries to your master, fast as you can."

"I... I don't...that's not my–"

Cunittus launched a kick at the woman's fat belly, and she doubled over. "Just fuckin do it woman, I'm not waitin to die discussin niceties with the likes of you."

The woman's face turned red as sunset as she coughed and struggled for air. She nodded, and backed away to let them into the scullery.

"Take them straight to the ab epistulis," said Cunittus. "No questions, no waiting, no announcin. Orders straight from the praetor himself. You understan', woman?"

She nodded, her cheeks still purple and her eyes watering.

"And sort out that lazy cunt of a gatekeeper. Door's wide open, anyone can come in." He gave her a hideous leer. "And believe me, Ria, before too long, they will."

Cunittus sketched a half-mocking bow to Atellus and Barbarus, then turned round and walked solidly across the courtyard, retracing the dents of their own footsteps to the outer gate.

They followed Ria through the suffocating steam of the scullery and into a warren of corridors. She took them up a narrow staircase, and then another, the steps cold beneath their boots, the walls tall and narrow. Eventually they reached what Atellus presumed was the third floor of the villa. They were led out of the staircase and into a palatial corridor at the far end of which was a set of large double doors, painted purple and covered in gold tracery. Ria shuffled timidly along to the doors, where she knocked three times.

"Enter," said a voice.

The fat servant turned to Atellus and Barbarus and averted her gaze.

"Beggin your pardons, dominae, but you can enter now and I'll retire."

Atellus barely nodded and the fat woman sprinted off with a speed he would never have thought her capable of. He moved forward and pushed open the doors to Crispus's office. They swung inward heavily, on smoothly oiled hinges.

Crispus was sitting at the far end of the room, at a huge desk inlaid with a marble and mother-of-pearl finish which sparkled in the light of the oil lamps set into brackets on the walls. The ab epistulis was eating from a selection of silver platters, a long thin jug of chilled wine at his elbow, whilst scratching away with a quill at a piece of long, narrow vellum. He did not look up as they entered, nor acknowledge their presence.

Atellus and Barbarus moved forward, the latter closing the doors softly behind them. Their footsteps were muffled by the thick carpet underfoot. The only sounds were the sobbing of the wind at the windows, the scratch of Crispus's quill and the delicate trickle of water from a large clepsydra on a pedestal by the window.

At first Atellus had thought that the man was alone; on a closer inspection of the room, he found the man-slave, inconspicuous, blending into the very essence of the room around him, as much a part of the furniture as the desk his master leant over. He was naked, as he had been the last time Atellus had seen him, crouched on a sella curulis near the balcony windows behind Crispus. The slave's naked body was as taut and immobile as granite, his absent eyes mere puckered folds of skin. His face was bruised and cut with what looked like fresh wounds. His lyre lay at his feet, untouched.

The scratching stopped, and Crispus laid the quill down atop the vellum with his tapered, be-ringed fingers, and looked up.

The ab epistulis froze for a second, his immaculate composure solidified into a surreal portrait of the man in all his fusty, preened, bureaucratic glory. His fringe of oiled curls hung down to the level of his dark brown eyes, and the stench of perfume seemed to coagulate in Atellus's nose. The faint memory of a twisted smile still played across the man's full dark lips, slightly parted to expose his pristine, square teeth. Like a child's teeth, Atellus thought absently.

Crispus's eyes burned feverishly as he recognised the man in front of him. They moved rapidly, flitting across Barbarus – unfamiliar, but undoubtedly dangerous – and then over to the closed doors.

"Smells like a fuckin' brothel in here," grunted Barbarus, screwing up his eyes.

Atellus spat on the floor. "It must be the cunt behind the desk."

"B...beneficiarius, well met," said Crispus, running his fine fingers through his hair then down across the breast of his fine tunic. He looked at Barbarus with a sneer. "And your friend. I do not believe I have had the pleasure...?"

"Enough, Crispus," growled Atellus. "You know why I am here."

Puzzlement splashed across Crispus's slightly effeminate features. "I really don't, beneficiarius," he said. "Am I to presume that your mission to the Wall has been successful and you have the answers? I have heard that the savages are–"

"Satis!" roared Atellus, his voice quivering with rage, and Crispus visibly shook and his frame recoiled as if the impact had struck him in the breast. "I am here to kill you. To gut you like the filthy weasel you have always been. And it is not before time."

Crispus swallowed. "Very well," he said. He pushed himself back from his desk and raised his hands to show the two men that he was unarmed, then stood up and moved slowly over to the far corner of his desk. He inclined his head slightly. "If that is your desire, beneficiarius."

Atellus faintly heard the sound of a bell clanging somewhere outside, but the sound was lost within the tumult that raged inside his body. Images of his loves – his Julia Faenia, his Petronia – rose like dizzying bubbles from within him; the point between his navel and the base of his sternum seemed to burn with a white heat.

The man who killed his wife and child was dead, but the man – no, the animal – standing before him, was responsible for their deaths. More so than anyone left alive on the earth.

"You would slay an unarmed man?" said Crispus, looking directly at Atellus.

"Just as you would slaughter an unarmed woman and child," replied Atellus from between gritted teeth. "Although you didn't even have the courage to wield the blade yourself, of course. To see the faces of those you *murdered*." He spat on the thick carpet.

Crispus laughed, a ringing, musical sound. "Ah, so you have found out what you think is the truth. Very good. I suppose that beast on the Wall told you? The agent? I would be wary of anything you hear from those lips, benefic–"

Atellus shook his head. "I have not come to talk," he said, his voice tight and cold. He felt as though he were floating above his own body; he fancied he could look down and see the top of his own head, and Barbarus's. He had relinquished control of his own motions. Even his voice seemed to come from an infinite distance away, as though it was the late vibrations of his speech, the memory of his words in his mind, rather than the words themselves in his ears. "You are already dead to me."

Crispus backed away from his desk towards the balcony window as he saw Atellus moving towards him. The easterner had his spatha in his hand, its blade cruel and blue in the subtle light, though he did not recall unsheathing it.

Barbarus stood back, and watched the deafmute slave with a disgust painted broad across his large features. This was not his battle, and Atellus did not need him.

"Hear me out, Atellus," said Crispus, his normally clear ringing tones strained and broken. "You are after the wrong man."

Atellus moved forward, and Crispus edged backwards.

"You fucked my wife!" spat Crispus. "You soiled my property! I never thwarted you. I begged Jovian for leniency for your wife and child."

"Liar."

"There were other parties who implored against me," said Crispus, his words tumbling over themselves in his eagerness to expel them from his tongue. "Valentinian was one. There were others. Do not underestimate the deceit of that man, Atellus."

"Mendax," repeated Atellus advancing on the ab epistulis. He was within a couple of paces of the man now, his spatha raised level with Crispus's chest.

"You know better than any, Atellus," he said, stammering, ignoring the blade beneath his throat. "We both know, you and I, in our line of work, that no-one can be trusted implicitly."

"Do not compare yourself to me," snarled Atellus.

"We are not so different, you understand?" came the reply. "Would you send me to the grave not knowing for certain? The doubt hounding you to your death? Why deny yourself the truth about your family, Atellus?"

Atellus's head felt as though it were twice its size and stuffed with feathers. A thousand voices clamoured for attention inside it; images of the emperor, of Aurelia, of his wife and his child and their slaughtered bodies; their eyes beseeching, their hands imploring. Shame; loss; betrayal.

He felt his hand quivering as it held out the spatha. If there was even the slightest hint that the animal was not lying....

He looked into Crispus's dark black eyes; they were glistening. With madness; with triumph; Atellus could not tell.

The doors crashed open behind them and Atellus, sensing threat, instinctively wheeled round.

And felt the dagger blade enter between his ribs like a tight angry punch.

He staggered backwards, as Crispus yanked the knife out with a grunt of triumph. Atellus turned to the ab epistulis, even as the room filled with shouting and noise behind him. Crispus was grinning, and in his hand he clutched the blood-wet blade.

"*Atellus!*"

The beneficiarius recognised the shout as coming from the lungs of Barbarus, but the entire room seemed far, far away. He slashed with his spatha at Crispus and the man fell backwards, ducking away from the wild blade. Atellus let the momentum of the swipe turn him round to look for his friend.

Four men had kicked their way into the room; they were all armed, and Barbarus was defending himself desperately against two of them. He was pressed back into the far angle of the room. Two more men had peeled off to make for Atellus.

It was the last thing he saw before he felt the ground rise up to meet him, and the darkness swallowed everything.

CHAPTER 43

Maglorius, Calidus, Vassu and Galla followed Dexter up the narrow, winding staircase. The odour of the man tumbled backwards behind him down the stairs, and Calidus had to fight the urge to actually pinch his nostrils shut. We probably reek just as bad, he thought.

"Who're the others, centurion?" said Dexter over his shoulder as they climbed.

"New servants," said Maglorius, nonchalantly.

"The bitch too?"

"Yes," he replied. "I hope I can make some solidi if I can get it down to Londinium in one piece."

Dexter barked a laugh. "Ha! Fortuna, fratrus." He stopped on the stairs mid stride, and peered back towards Galla, who returned his gaze stolidly with her pale blue eyes. "Maybe after we finish with the bint upstairs, we could take turns this un, eh?" He elbowed Maglorius in the shoulder. "Break 'er in?"

Maglorius looked down at Galla, who was now gazing at her feet, then back up at Dexter. The centurion smiled. "Of course."

Dexter laughed appreciatively and resumed his ascent.

He led them up to a short door which opened out onto a long, broad corridor which was draped with tapestries and wall-hangings interspersed with statues and pedestals rising from the deep carpet. Dexter walked across to a single set of double doors, and pushed them open.

They walked inside to a large, bare room. The furnishings were opulent but unused, and there was a surreal, ghostly air about the room which Calidus noticed and which gave him a shiver. It was like a replica of a woman's chamber, rather than an actual one. Aurelia lay on the bed in the centre of the circular room; her eyes seemed half-lidded. Calidus's hands felt warm and wet; he looked down and saw that his fists were clenched and damp with perspiration. He wiped the sweat against his cloak.

Dexter strode across the room, lord of his domain, and laughed. He looked down at Aurelia and spat on her face. She did not move. Calidus noticed that her hands and legs were bound with rope, and shackled to the pillars of the bed.

"You remember Quintus, centurion?" said Dexter, not taking his eyes from the woman beneath him.

"Yes," said Maglorius. Calidus looked at the centurion and wondered, not for the first time, who the man was and why he had helped them thus far. Was he leading them here only to hand them over? What were his motives?

"This dirty quim killed him," continued Dexter. "Opened his throat. Cut his cock off and stuffed it in his mouth." He seemed to smile fondly as he spoke; whether of Aurelia or Quintus, Calidus was not certain.

Dexter stood up to his full height, then turned to face Maglorius.

"Send your chattels to the basement, Maglorius. You can collect them when you leave." He smiled, a broken toothless grin. "The wench can stay though."

Maglorius shook his head. "What's wrong with her?" he asked, squinting at Aurelia.

"She has only had wine," he replied. "To...*placate* her. That and a few punches." He laughed, a crackling, guttural sound that resonated throughout the eerie chamber. "Kicking like an angry mule when we got her here. She would've flung herself from the window if we'd let her."

"I'm glad you stopped her," said the centurion.

"I'll go first," said Dexter, removing his sheath.

"No," said Maglorius. "Keep your blade with you."

Dexter turned round to look at him in puzzlement. He saw Maglorius draw his spatha.

"Things do not always work out as we expect," said the centurion.

Dexter smiled uncertainly. "Tell me you are fooling, fratrus?"

Maglorius did not smile, or even blink. He gave a barely perceptible shake of his head and raised his blade.

"It is because we have fought side by side that I honour you to die with your weapon in your hand, in combat."

Dexter frowned and drew his blade. It was a long tapered spatha, of fine craftsmanship. Calidus idly wondered where he had got it from; it was no common soldier's blade.

"You seem very certain that I will die, Maglorius," said Dexter, his eyes narrowing. He shook his ragged brown hair out of his eyes, and turned sideways on to the centurion, shrinking the target available to his opponent. "Three against one is not fair."

"They will not interfere," said Maglorius. He tilted his head slightly so his words travelled over his shoulder; Calidus knew they were directed at him. "Free Aurelia and take her downstairs. If she cannot walk, carry her."

609

Calidus nodded and moved around past the back of Maglorius and towards where Aurelia lay on the bed. He used his own spatha to cut through the rope which bound her ankles to the bedposts. He felt Dexter's eyes on him, but there was no other movement. Vassu came round and cut Aurelia's hands loose. The hum of suppressed energy was palpable in the room, a live and deadly miasma they were all conscious of. It was like the warmth and density of the air just before a thunderstorm.

And then it broke.

Calidus was speaking into Aurelia's ear when the ring of metal on metal shattered the tension in the room. Dexter grunted and fell back against a small wooden table beside the bed, lifting his blade up in time to parry Maglorius's second blow. The sound exploded around Calidus as he helped Aurelia up off the bed; her face was pale and her brow was damp as if with fever.

"Help me," he said to Vassu. The other man aided him wordlessly and they supported Aurelia between their shoulders. Galla looked on worriedly, her small mouth and large eyes damp with concern and fear. There was definitely progress, thought Calidus absently. Of a kind.

Maglorius and Dexter launched into each other, their blades becoming long, looping, deadly extensions of their arms; the room cried and howled and sparked around them as their blows dug into wood and sent bottles and mirrors and statues shattering against walls.

"The whole fuckin' villa guard will be on us," spat Vassu.

"Maybe we should help him?" said Calidus

"You heard what he said," came the reply. "He doesn't want us. He can look after himself. It would dishonour him if we were to unbalance the fight."

Calidus nodded. "Okay. We need to get out."

They carried Aurelia towards the exit, their presence lost on the two fighters, and Vassu used his shoulder to heave open the double doors. They shuffled out into the corridor which was empty in both directions. Calidus let himself revel in the possibility that the rest of the villa was empty, and Crispus' guards had fled. He stopped their movement and leaned against a wall. From far downstairs came the sounds of servants scurrying around; incomprehensible orders were shouted, and met with brief responses. He cursed inwardly.

"Aurelia?" said Calidus.

She shook her head on his shoulder, but her eyes opened, and her feet seemed to tread along the carpet with more pressure than before.

"Aurelia?"

"Calidus?" she replied, her eyes blinking and then opening.

Vassu reached over and lifted her chin up. "Cmon, wake up. We're not safe yet. Need to get out of here. So we can die at the hands of the savages instead of your fuckin' husband." He barked a laugh.

"Watch...your tongue.... when you speak...of my *beloved*," said Aurelia, her lips curling into a smile.

Vassu grinned.

"Can you walk?" asked Calidus.

She shrugged her way off their shoulders and put her weight on her own feet.

"A bit giddy, but okay," she said.

"You're not hurt?"

She shook her head. "I've known worse." Her eyes focused on the waif at Calidus's side. *"Galla."*

The girl's eyes looked to hers, and there was warmth in them. She reached a hand out for the girl, who pondered it for a while, then grasped it with her own.

"We need to move," said Vassu looking to either side. The sound of Maglorius and Dexter destroying the room behind them filled the corridor. It was pure luck that it had attracted no-one yet.

"Where's that pig?" asked Aurelia. "Crispus's hound?"

"Dexter?" said Vassu. "Hopefully being spitted by Maglorius."

"Maglorius?" said Aurelia, her eyes widening in shock. "From...from Aesica?"

"Yes," said Calidus. "He helped us escape and brought us here."

Aurelia went strangely silent, the sounds of the combat from the room behind them enfolding them mesmerically, until Vassu shook her gently by the shoulder. "We need to go."

She nodded decisively. "Down the staircase...Crispus will be in his study."

"We need to escape, Aurelia," said Calidus. "Not–"

"You escape, then. And take the child," she replied. "I am going to kill Crispus, whether you are with me or not. The empire does not need the likes of him loose, and growing fat on the fallout from the north."

Vassu swore under his breath, but he said nothing. Instead he looked at Calidus. Galla was looking at him too, he realised.

"Then we go together," said Calidus without hesitation. "No more separations."

Aurelia guided them in the right direction; she knew every nook and cranny of her own villa, even down to the meanest cubby-holes and serving-hatches used by the servants and slaves. They went down three small flights of stairs and encountered no-one. When they came out into another major corridor, there was a cluster of servants shouting hoarsely at each other. Aurelia hurried past them without even looking.

"No-one will bother us," she said confidently. "Everyone will be desperate to secure their own safety."

"So it's just we who are insane," grunted Vassu.

"So it would seem," said Aurelia, calmly. "Crispus's study is at the end of this corridor."

They hurried across the plush crimson carpet and towards the doors at the end of the room. Calidus realised that he had his spatha in his hand; its weight was reassuring and terrifying at the same time. He looked across and saw that Vassu was armed also. As they got closer, they could hear the shouts and howls of combat coming from the open doors at the end and Calidus could make out the shape of a figure sprawled on the floor; it looked strangely like Atellus, Calidus noted, with the dark complexion and the broad shoulders. It must be his brain fooling him, he thought, until he heard Aurelia shouting beside him.

"*Atellus!*"

CHAPTER 44

Barbarus knew he was going to die.

He had felt the first few slashes of the blades as his attacker's weapons slid off his desperate parries and clumsy counters. The impacts shuddered through his screaming muscles, even as the blade tips bit home in his flesh. He had felt them, the jolt of the contact, the sweet sharp pain that was like a fiery light racing up and down his flesh and exploding in his skull. But then he was only aware of a numbness.

He had seen Atellus collapse and thought to himself that now was as good a time as any to die. He would see how many he could take with him. There was laughter somewhere in the room, a curious high laughter, and he had to check that it wasn't himself. He thought it was the ab epistulis.

The soldiers who had entered kept away from Atellus: the man was prone on the floor, and hence not a threat. Instead they had all surged towards Barbarus. They were not great fighters, barely competent, otherwise he would have been long dead. Instead, he backed into the corner of the room which was secured on one side by a tall bookcase. That meant they could only face him two at a time, though that was hard enough. They could rotate, fresh arms, fresh bodies, whilst he wilted and suffered and bled.

And he was losing. And that was when he heard the shout.

"Atellus!"

It was a woman's voice, and it didn't register at first. But he noticed that shortly after the shout, he was having to try less hard to defend himself, and he realised there was only one man fighting him. A tired, ill-trained soldier.

He looked across at the man's face. He was young, barely more than a boy with a long face and wisps of blonde hair sweeping out from under leather strapping wound around his scalp. His eyes were a bright green, tense with concentration and exertion.

Barbarus used all of his reserves to parry one more stroke and slide in under the man's deflected blade to lunge upwards with his spatha. It put him at full stretch, and he knew that if he missed, or even grazed his foe, he was open and vulnerable and as good as dead.

But it did not miss.

He felt the beautiful shiver of resistance run up his arm as his spatha sank deep into the belly of his assailant. His momentum carried him up and drove him down on top of the man as he fell, so they collapsed together.

He wrenched his blade from the man's torso: the metal gave a squelching gasp as it came out along with part of the boy's guts. He was howling and screaming for his mother, but the sound was sweet and beautiful to Barbarus's ears: the sound of victory, and his own survival.

He looked up and saw fighting. There was a woman standing over Atellus; guarding him perhaps. A lithe man, young, was fighting a ragged and desperate battle with his spatha, back to back with a sallow man, handsome but worn.

He did not know who they were, but he knew that they were on his side.

Barbarus got to his feet and launched himself at the back of one of the guards, swinging his spatha in an overhand blow which opened the man's neck and left his head hanging onto his torso by a bare flap of flesh. The body collapsed to the floor, jetting blood.

Two on two.

He walked over to Atellus, and saw a woman and a girl standing over him. They were lifting him to his knees, one dabbing at a deep wound in his side. He was being tended.

Barbarus looked out towards where the ab epistulis was shrinking back towards the windows which opened out onto the balcony. His face was pale and white. He saw Barbarus looking his way, and lurched backwards, stumbling over the feet of the naked slave who was cowering away, holding his muscular frame over his broken lyre.

"L-Look," stammered the ab espitulis to Barbarus as he stalked forwards. "I…I don't know you. I bear you no grudge, nor you I. I have wealth which can be yours. There are signed letters on my desk behind you. For gold, in Londinium. Take them and go."

Barbarus did not even look towards the desk.

Atellus had come to kill this worm; maybe even now, Atellus was dead.

"You do not even know me, man!" shouted Crispus vehemently as his attacker advanced.

As Barbarus stepped forward, his spatha raised at an angle, the fresh blood smearing the lustre of the blade, he became aware of an odd noise. A guttural growl, more bestial than human.

Crispus edged backwards, his heels striking the hard thigh of the muscled slave, that odd eyeless man who simpered and wept atop his lyre. He saw confusion and surprise melt across Crispus's face, before turning to annoyance, and anger. He saw Crispus kick down absently at the face of the unseeing man, and heard the wretch grunt with the contact.

Barbarus stopped advancing as he saw what was unfolding in front of him.

616

The naked slave, growling deep in his chest, had reared from his supine position, like some primal avatar erupting from the earth, a roused Neptune bursting forth from the ocean bed. He grabbed Crispus with both hands, lifted him up off the floor and slammed him down into the ground, howling in a strange, throaty ululation that made the hair on Barbarus's neck stand up. He saw the huge slave grasp one hand in the other to form a massive organic mace, and raise them over his head, bringing them crashing down into Crispus's shocked, spitting face. After the first blow, the pleading started, and by the third it had stopped, the ab epistulis's mouth shattered into a bloody ruin; his face was barely recognisable, a swollen mask of blood, his nose and lips smeared half across his once pristine visage. His fine clothes were soiled and torn, his delicate fingers – raised in a futile gesture to ward off the blows – were twisted and broken.

The slave pounded down, again and again, swinging his huge arms like a smith's hammer and laying into his master's face, his torso, his genitals. The sounds the blows made turned even Barbarus's stomach. Eventually, the slave seemed to tire, and the sobbing howl died in his throat.

The slave gathered up the twitching form of Crispus, heaving him over one broad, muscular shoulder. He slowly and calmly felt his way over to the window leading out onto the balcony. He kicked it open and a flurry of snow whipped into the room and swept around Barbarus's legs. The air was cool and welcome in a room which now smelled of sweat and blood and shit.

The slave walked out onto the frozen balcony, with his master over his shoulder, and leapt head first into the blackness of the night.

***

Calidus looked into his opponent's fierce brown eyes, and saw the merest hint of tension around the lids which betrayed the attack a moment before it arrived.

He brought his spatha up just in time to deflect his opponents' blow, and his blade was flipped backwards by the impact, nearly wrenched from his grasp. He jerked to one side and managed to avoid the follow-up kick directed at his groin. The man was sweating and shouting obscenities at him, but his mind had long since drifted away from such superficial threats.

He had lost Vassu some time ago; it could have been moments or days ago for all he knew: all sense of time had dissipated amidst this maelstrom of pain and danger. His muscles hummed with energy, his senses painfully keen. They had been fighting back to back. He presumed Vassu was still alive; the only reason he had for supposing this was that he himself was still alive. If Vassu's opponent had joined the fray, Calidus knew he would have been tripping over his own guts by now.

Vassu had been taking on two of the guards. Calidus had been aware enough to realise that Atellus was either dead or dying on the ground not far away, and the lone man who had been fighting off the guards on his own had despatched his own foe and helped out Vassu with one of his.

He dipped to one side suddenly, and swung his spatha outwards at stomach level where it clashed with the other man's blade in a clang of steel which dragged another explosion of curses from his opponent's lips. Calidus knew the man had difficulty reading him: his own style may be choppy and ugly, but apparently that meant he was unpredictable; indeed, his uncle had often said that about him. For a second his thoughts wavered over to Brocchus and whether or not he was safe, but Calidus dragged his concentration back by force of will. It was tiredness allowing his mind to wander, and he needed nothing but pure focus on the man in front of him in order to stay alive. His opponent may have been old, but he was a trained fighter, a veteran, and he was utterly dangerous.

His assailant was counter-attacking now, blow after strained blow, which Calidus was parrying by instinct; if he stopped to think what he was doing, the blade would surely have been buried in his neck. He felt himself stumbling over something behind him, but he managed to regain his balance and whip his spatha up and across his body to deflect the next attack.

Calidus's muscles felt like wet sand; his head was pounding violently and the sweat from his hands was slickening his grip on the leather-wrapped hilt of his blade. His opponent was winning and he knew it. His dark face, with its peppery short beard and brutal stub of a nose, was grinning triumphantly, even as he shouted obscenities about Calidus's mother.

The man's next blow took him by surprise; he looked as if he stumbled, causing his thrust to come forward openly and unexpectedly. The attack which Calidus expected from above came from further down, a wild lunge at his breast. He managed to drop his spatha in time to block it, but his wrist was twisted painfully, the blade fell from his hand and he collapsed to his knees with a yell. The momentum of his foe, and his lack of balance, sent him crashing into Calidus's shoulders, slamming him down to the ground.

Calidus looked up.

The ceiling seemed impossibly distant, higher than the farthest stars. The light of the room was dim, but glowing subtly and flaring up with a life of its own. He saw his enemy rising to his feet above him, his sword clutched in both his large fists. Calidus felt weary and strangely calm. He did not try to move, to roll away or to whip his hand out to each side for a weapon. There was no fight within him, only a dull acceptance, and a sense of peace and flickering excitement.

His opponent raised his blade up, both hands wrapped around the hilt which was level with his shoulder, tip pointing downwards at Calidus's throat, ready to drop it down. His insane, sweating face looked almost sublime to Calidus in that moment; he was Pluto come to claim him.

And then the top of his head snapped backwards and his face seemed to collapse inwards under the force of a sword blow.

The body fell slowly backwards.

Calidus blinked.

Maglorius stepped away from the falling body, his spatha blade still buried deep within what had been the face, now a disfigured mess of blood and bone. He wrenched his blade out with a rocking motion that squeaked and sent Calidus's stomach roiling. He heaved himself up with his abdominal muscles and promptly vomited onto the deep, soft carpet. It stank.

"Thank you," he said to the centurion, as he scrubbed the back of his hand across his mouth.

Maglorius nodded then walked away.

Calidus looked around. Vassu was standing, chest heaving, over the body of his opponent. Atellus was reclining on a lectus, surrounded by Aurelia, Galla, and the broad, hard-looking man who had been fighting when they entered. The floor was red with the blood of the dead and the injured.

He got unsteadily to his feet. The exhilaration was gone; he just felt incredibly tired. He walked slowly over to where the easterner lay on the lectus; his face was ashen, his lips bloodless. His eyes were shut.

"Atellus," he said. The sound seemed to come from afar, the voice not his own.

The beneficiarius opened his eyes. They seemed to gaze out at Calidus from the ends of impossibly long caverns.

"Scaeva," he said, and coughed out a laugh.

CHAPTER 45

Atellus tore his gaze away from the land beyond the battlements, and turned back to the optio standing rigidly beside him. The old soldier looked calm; old soldiers always did. They had met often with death, and it had lost its fear. They had few expectations of life, and no terror of the grave.

"We'll have a chance," said the optio. "As long as we have these walls."

"We have more than a chance," said Atellus, supressing a wince of pain as his wound griped again. It seemed to burn through to his very core and out the other side. Especially in this endless, ripping cold. "What is your name?"

"Comitus, sir."

"Well, Comitus, you've survived this long. You have my respect. Just keep doing what you've always done."

"Yes, sir."

The optio saluted and turned away to look down the battlements at his men ranged along the rampart of the city walls. They were a ragged and semi-professional lot, more farmers than soldiers, and the optio knew it. But each one of them was worth ten of the legionary-cowards who had fled the city. The southern gate was not likely to see the worst of the fighting, but fighting there would be, one way or another, and most of these men and boys would die.

Atellus carried on his patrol of the walls; they were old and decrepit in parts, but they would serve them well in need. He looked back at Comitus and his men. They manned a line of five ballistae facing south along the main roadway which ran to Lindum and then on to Durobrivae and eventually down to Londinium. The ballistae were old engines, in bad condition, but they had fired test shots earlier that day. The great twang and thump had sent stones crashing into the frost-stiffened trees to the south. They would serve a purpose.

Eboracum boiled and smoked beneath him. From here on the walls he could see the vast expanse of the almost endless towers and roofs of the city spreading out below. The eaves peered out from deep quilts of snow which shone in the moonlight. The stars overhead gazed down incuriously; they had seen it all before, many times, and would see it all again. There was still a large stream of deserters and civilians pouring from the south gate, trying their luck heading down towards Lindum. It would be for the best: they could not hope to withstand a siege with so many people to feed, and starvation would be their greatest foe. Every mouth and belly that left increased their chances.

He stopped on the north wall to speak with a young cavalry commander who was now supervising a six-man team operating two manuballistae: two for each machine and two to run errands or take over from exhaustion. The machines were relatively new and in good condition. The powerful metal struts were free from rust. They had an adequate supply of six-inch metal bolts to last them at least a few days. The soldiers were thin and grey-faced. They seemed not to care whether they lived or died at the moment.

Atellus spoke a few words from his own experience of sieges, and clapped them on the shoulders. They turned round, and drank from flasks of cold wine, and spat from the ramparts, or warmed their fingers by the bright pyres which burned every fifty paces for light and warmth and fuel. These men – the pride of the legion of Eboracum, at thirty-percent of its full strength – were dressed shabbily; they were hungry, harried and desperate. Their clothes were more regulation than the limitanei on the Wall, but they would have been beaten to death by the Legate officers in Treves if they had dared to come within half a mile of the emperor.

Atellus walked on, looking out into the darkness which rolled north with the wild land. The snow overhead was weakening, but on the horizon it looked to be blizzarding. Perhaps the weather would whittle the enemy's numbers down.

There was a hum of fear and tension rising up from the city below. Atellus recalled times, as a young soldier, when he had relished it; times, leading his men onwards under Julian, when he had marched on cities and felt the inhabitants' pain emanating from out of the sombre stone walls, the agony of trepidation and anticipation. He had lapped it up then. It was the taste of death, of imminent battle. It was what he had lived for, he and every other soldier. It was their reason for existing.

Young men are fools and know no better.

Atellus placed a hand on the bandages wrapped tight around his abdomen. The area where the knife had entered between his ribs was moist and hot. He would need his dressing replaced before too long. He had broken open the wound by climbing up the ladders to gain access to the walls. He had felt it go and clenched his teeth and kept climbing.

He recalled the hours before when he had first woken to find his wound being tended by Aurelia: Calidus and Barbarus had carried him from Crispus's villa and into the principia where Scaeva had taken them straight through to his uncle. A medicus had been summoned, and cleaned his wound with acetum, rubbing a decoction of willow leaves into it, before stitching it up and giving Atellus an infusion of silphium for his fever.

The wound still stung in the cold weather, and he felt as weak as an infant, but it no longer bled as profusely, nor did he have as much trouble breathing as he thought he would. The tip may have deflected off the rib and not allowed the blade to enter the lung as deeply as he had feared.

Atellus placed his pale brown hands on the white snow-dusted crenel of the rampart and peered over. The desperate shanty that had formed up around the city walls was practically vacant. Some residences had been dismantled and loaded onto the backs of those who headed south. Others remained, awaiting the fire and destruction of the approaching army. There were no lights down there, no hum of conversation. Anyone down there now would be dead before daybreak.

He looked out, trying to pierce the darkness of the stormclouds overlapping the night sky. He thought he could see winking fires to the north, like fallen stars. Burning hamlets, most likely.

They were approaching; he could almost hear their voices on the wind.

"Atellus."

He turned round to face Brocchus's nephew.

"Scaeva," he greeted him, and saluted. Soldier to soldier.

The boy returned the gesture and smiled.

Boy, thought Atellus? He was more man than boy now. Transformed. His hair longer, the beginnings of a scratchy real beard on his face instead of childish wisps of fur. His eyes looked deeper and harder, his gait more solid and grounded. Life was beginning to eat into him, as it must them all. Calidus was growing up.

"What news?" asked Atellus.

"Aurelia would like to speak with you."

Calidus led him down the solid stone steps by the east gate, where there was less violence and unrest than at the north. Most of the rioting had calmed down, and the feuds burnt themselves out as the inhabitants realised there was a much greater threat approaching. It was always the way with sieges.

"Did you find your girl?" Atellus asked as they walked.

Calidus shook his head. "Marina is gone," he said. "The house is derelict. How long, I have no idea."

"If they are wise they will be heading south."

"If," said Calidus, "they managed to leave at all."

Atellus nodded. He had not wanted to mention the possibility that the family had fallen foul of the rioters.

They followed the via Consularis through the wealthy Constantinus district and took a turn along a small lane that led north through a nameless poorer district, the streets clogged with snow, the tenement-like insulae giving way to timber-built houses; the dwellings were rickety and piled atop each other as if scattered by some careless titan's hand.

"Is your uncle busy?" asked Atellus. The governor had shed twenty years since Calidus turned up alive and well – he had found a new exuberance and pride in his nephew.

Calidus nodded. "I have rarely seen him so enthusiastic about his duties."

Atellus had to grudgingly admit that Brocchus was doing well. He had made himself visible to his people, inspecting the soldiers, giving speeches from the gates of the principia to massed crowds; organising the rationing and distribution of grain and fresh water.

Calidus led Atellus through to a long low timber building with stone foundations, like a wealthy noble's barn. Inside were numerous officers drinking mulsum and vinum, warming themselves by a large central hearth and talking in low voices. From what Atellus overheard, they spoke of past victories, old slaughters, heroic deeds and legendary drinking binges.

Calidus pushed past some of the clusters and through to a small room at the back which was closed off from the main hall by a thick drape of treated cow-hide. This led to an antechamber on the floor of which lay Barbarus, sleeping with his cloak as a pillow, outside a stout wooden door. An eyelid flicked open as they appeared, and rapidly shut again.

Calidus gave four raps with his knuckles in a strange rhythm, and a woman's voice answered.

"Come in."

Calidus opened the door and stepped inside, over the sleeping form of Barbarus. Atellus followed him into a small, cosy chamber. It was a square room with three stools ranged up against a high-burning fire. Metal cups were on the floor. Turning on a spit over the flame was the meat of a creature that looked like a cat, or a small dog. There were empty cots set against the far walls, in which various people slept depending on when their shifts finished. Aurelia and Maglorius sat in two of the chairs up against the fire-pit. The centurion was red-eyed from the smoke and turned the spit in small, slow circles. Aurelia sat back in her chair and sipped from a bronze cup.

Atellus walked over and sat down next to Aurelia. Maglorius wordlessly handed him a beaten bronze goblet filled with a hot, spiced liquid. He took a sip and felt the warmth melt through his frozen, tired muscles.

Calidus sank onto the ground next to the fire, and pulled some meat from a bowl laid beside Maglorius's heel. He bit into the honey-glazed, roasted meat, and gazed thoughtfully at his feet until Aurelia caught sight of him. She looked at him wordlessly until he felt uncomfortable and spoke to break the silence.

"It is funny," he said, gnawing away at a mouthful of gristly meat. "My uncle gave me the strictest command to return to him with details of the informant who leaked news to the emperor of the deeds on the Wall. Undermining him to Valentinian." He smiled. "He wanted to rip their guts from their bodies."

"And?" said Aurelia, with an arched eyebrow.

"It was you, of course."

She smiled, but said nothing.

"Not that it matters much, now, I suppose," said Calidus.

Aurelia shook her head. "The world moves too fast, now," she said. "I never used to think so. Perhaps I am getting old." She smiled, before changing the subject. "How is Galla coping?"

Calidus shrugged and swallowed a mouthful of meat. "I think she likes her rooms in the principia," he replied. "It is the only time I have seen her smile, at least."

"That is something," nodded Aurelia. "She may be recovering."

"I'm sure she spoke a word, yesterday," said Calidus, reaching out for a handful of dried beans.

"A word?" said Aurelia, arching an eyebrow.

"*Snow*," nodded Calidus. "I'm sure she said *snow*."

"I'm surprised she let you leave her side today," mused Aurelia.

Calidus grinned. "I told her I was going to speak with Vassu. She can't bear to be within sight of him."

Aurelia nodded.

"Perhaps," said Calidus, "if we can keep her away from Vassu, she might recover completely?"

"Perhaps," said Aurelia. "And speaking of the whoremonger do you know where he is?"

"Probably," Calidus replied, from around a mouthful of food, "by the docks. Drinking or whoring. I can't imagine him doing anything else."

Aurelia nodded thoughtfully.

"I have a task for him," she said. "Would you be kind enough to find him?"

Calidus continued chewing, staring at the dancing flames of the fire. He looked weary and worn. But he nodded. He threw down the bones into his dish with a click, and got to his feet.

"I will look," he said, "but I cannot guarantee I will find him." He walked across the room and pulled the door open. Atellus had a glimpse of Barbarus dozing in the ante-room beyond.

Aurelia nodded. "Be careful, Calidus."

"I will," he replied, tapping the sheathed spatha hanging from his hip. He slid out into the antechamber, returning Barbarus's smile as he stepped over him, and closed the door behind him.

Atellus sat eating and drinking in silence for a while, recovering from the bleakness of the city beyond these walls. Inside here everything seemed different; quiet, warm, almost pleasant. Aurelia had asked to speak to him, but neither party seemed willing to intrude their own requirements into the safe, warm dreams of the other.

Eventually, he broke the silence. "You do not have a task for Vassu," he said. It was not a question.

Aurelia shook her head. "I would rather the boy not be here for the time being."

"Better for him if he left the city altogether," said Atellus.

"I think he can make his own decisions now. He was vehement about staying. The blood of the praetor is not quite as craven as you seem to believe."

Atellus nodded, and took a drink of his wine. Maglorius remained silent.

"Has his body been recovered?" asked Atellus.

Aurelia shook her head. The deafmute slave had been found dead in the grounds of the villa, beneath the balcony but there had been no sign of Crispus's body, besides a few bloodstains across the snow.

"It is unlikely he survived," she said. "Perhaps some of his toads gathered the body up to see what they could plunder."

Atellus stared into the fire. "I will never know," he said, softly. There was silence again, and the wind could be heard pressing against the walls from outside, whispering and insinuating like the shades of the dead.

"How are the defences?" asked Aurelia.

Atellus shrugged. "Adequate. I'm not sure it will matter."

"You think they won't try to breach the walls?"

"They may," he shrugged. "But I don't think they have the training or inclination to build siege engines. They may try to use hooks or ladders to escalade the walls. But they will lose too many men; too much morale. They should move on to easier targets before long."

"They could undermine the walls," said Maglorius, his voice crackling above the fire.

"They could try," nodded Atellus. "Again, I am not sure they have the skill. We could dig countermines. I have some experience from campaigns in the East. But there are easier ways for them to take the city. They could cut off supply routes: even with the population halved, the city would not last more than a month before men will be eating horseflesh, or the soles of their own boots. It is not a great step from there to men eating their own comrades."

Aurelia shivered. "Have you seen such a thing?"

Atellus nodded, and took a drink of his wine. His dark eyes glittered in the light from the fire. "I have seen the aftermath. In Amida. Those who were alive seemed half mad; the living envied the dead."

The beneficiarius said nothing further, but drank in silence. After some mouthfuls, he placed his empty cup down beside his stool. "They will camp outside, and sing and jeer and feast. They will try to break morale. Then they will try to bribe the guards, the gatekeepers. They will encourage dissent and betrayal. Besides starvation, that is our greatest threat."

Maglorius nodded sombrely, and there was silence whilst the flames flickered and the knots of scavenged wood cracked and popped. Outside, the shouts and calls of the drinkers echoed through the wooden walls.

"They will not have the luxury of time," said Maglorius, his deep voice seeming to resonate with the very creaking timbers around them. "A force of comitatenses from the emperor could be here within the month."

"If he deems Britannia worth saving," said Aurelia, looking at Atellus. He returned her gaze levelly, before jerking his head in the direction of Maglorius and arching an eyebrow at Aurelia.

"He saved your life," she said gently. "And mine. We can speak freely before him."

"I cannot vouch for Valentinian's intentions towards Britannia," said Atellus slowly. "He sent me here. Whether curse or reward, I am not sure I know."

"He gave you hope," said Aurelia. "Kept you alive. You would have long been dead had Valentinian not given you this thread to clutch at."

"I lived for vengeance," said Atellus. "But I have been thwarted. The beast who murdered my family is long dead and gone, in the frozen wastes. The only other man I could avenge my family on has disappeared. Or is dead himself. Where is my hope now?" He raised a clenched fist and bounced it gently off his thigh. "You were always blind to his machinations, Aurelia. Do you think for a second he would have gifted me my chance for vengeance if the agent in rebus had not outlived his usefulness? Been too much of a liability to be allowed to live? He sent me there to tidy up his loose ends. Maybe the man was responsible for my family's deaths, maybe not."

"You were the best man for the task," said Aurelia. "You are a pagan. Who better to sniff out paganism in a distant province than a sun worshipper like you." Atellus looked over and saw that she was smiling, a subtle twist of the lips.

"Atellus," she said, laying a delicate hand on his shoulder. "The agent on the Wall is not dead. Titus Sempronius Asellio Petrus is his name, and I can assure you that he is as alive as you and I."

"They killed him," refuted Atellus, shaking his head.

"They killed *an* agent," said Aurelia. "A decoy. He lived in a farmhouse at the edge of the vicus. He was killed in his room and I have seen his body."

"I thought the agent was torn to pieces in culuslupi?"

"Rumours," replied Aurelia. "To draw you out there, perhaps, and make your disappearance less problematic for Apullius. I can assure you that the real agent in rebus was never discovered. Petrus lived in Aesica itself and fled when we did."

"He is alive," said Atellus quietly, his eyes smouldering within his dark sockets. "You are sure of this?"

"I am," she replied. "And I know he is here in Eboracum."

Atellus was silent for some time. The wind wailed outside, as the merriment in the room beyond grew more raucous. Maglorius sipped at his mulsum. Aurelia watched the flames throw shadows across the timber walls.

"You know him?" asked Atellus. "You know where he is?"

Aurelia nodded. "Both. Although I did not until today. He filled in more than a few gaps in my own knowledge of events."

633

Atellus gripped his cup in his hand, his knuckles white with tension. "He killed my family. My wife. My daughter. Murdered them in their sleep."

"The emperor Jovian killed your family, Atellus," said Aurelia softly. "He gave the order, and without that, nothing would have happened. The agent was merely a factotum." Her words seemed to make the flames dance in front of her eyes. "But I will not stand in the way of your vengeance.

"Valentinian sent you to the Wall," she continued, "to find out to what extent paganism was being practised and how much of a threat it was to his authority. The children disappearing were of no concern to him. It was what they represented that was much bigger."

"Why send me if he had two agents on the Wall?" asked Atellus. "What could I offer that they couldn't?"

"The first agent," said Aurelia, "was Petrus, who I knew only as Densligneus. He was deeply embedded on the Wall, and had been there for many years with only short excursions back to Treves to relay information deemed too sensitive to be committed to vellum. I had indications from my contacts that there were certain people becoming suspicious of our agent; they were jealous of his rise to seniority and so probed a little deeper than we had prepared for. A second agent – a junior, unskilled, and ignorant of Densligneus – was sent to find out what he could of operations at Aesica. We realised that the second agent would be uncovered, and thus deflect suspicions away from Densligneus."

"A sacrifice?"

"If you will," she said, quietly, nodding at the flames. "It worked. He was killed, as you discovered. Densligneus is still alive."

"Then why me?"

"Two reasons," she replied. "Firstly, to remove you from Treves: you were seen as a liability since your family were killed. The emperor was wary of you, and wary of how close you were to him. As a practicing pagan, you were undermining his Christianity, and his influence. His potens, his authority. It looked bad."

"I understand that," said Atellus quietly. "I would willingly have taken myself away from him, from Treves, had I been given sufficient time to grieve."

"Valentinian feared that space," said Aurelia. "He thought you may be mired in your tears, and take your own life. He acted to prevent that. And so he wasted no time." Aurelia reached across and touched Atellus's wrist. "It was wise of him to do so, Atellus,"

Atellus nodded.

"You were sent," continued Aurelia, "to find the original agent, Densligneus, and exact your vengeance. Valentinian had received as much information as he needed from the man. He knew months ago that the garrison at Aesica was corrupt, that they and the Arcanae were in collusion with the tribes beyond. He wanted you there, and he wanted the agent dead; he was beginning to fear that Densligneus was becoming too entrenched, that he was more of Aesica than of Treves, if you take my meaning. You were to be his judge, and his executioner. It was the tidiest way of doing it. Crispus eagerly seconded the emperor's proposal. He thought it would mean certain death for you. Sweet revenge for him, at last."

Atellus nodded. "The snake said he had requested my presence here. I suppose that was half true. But If Valentinian knew there would be an invasion, why has he not sent a force to defend the province?"

"He has priorities elsewhere," replied Aurelia. "The comitatenses are campaigning against the Alamanni. They are much closer to Treves than we. Britannia has never been at the top of any emperor's agenda. Not since the days of

Hadrian himself. Whether or not Valentinan will send a force now, I do not know; I have lost contact with him. Perhaps he is beginning to see me as a liability also. Indeed," she smirked, "I am telling you all this. Perhaps I *am* a liability." She smiled a soft and weary smile.

"So by killing Densligneus, by disposing of Petrus," Aurelia concluded, "you are fulfilling your destiny as Valentinian's tool."

"We are all tools of the emperor," said Atellus, his words caustic. "I have never thought otherwise. Only Julian was any different."

"And look what happened to him," said Aurelia. "A good emperor must be as hard as the mountains and as relentless as the ocean tide."

Atellus nodded and spat into the fire; the flames hissed angrily.

"Great sol knows I have lived and suffered," said Atellus, bowing his head solemnly to the ground. "If I am to die here it makes no difference to me. Treves is no more home for me than these frozen soils." He looked up at Aurelia. "Who is this agent?"

Aurelia met his eyes with her clear radiant blue ones, her face seeming ageless: fresh and youthful whilst also unfathomably old.

"You already know him, Atellus."

Maglorius looked across at the easterner; the centurion's face was large and angular in the harsh shadows, his features heavy and solemn. He opened his mouth and brought his teeth together with a thock. He ran his fingers across them. His front two lower teeth were made of a dark, almost black wood. He looked at Atellus calmly. There was no confrontation in his eyes; only a vague hint of expectation.

"You," said Atellus, "are the agent Titus Sempronius Asellio Petrus." He looked down at his hands and realised he had crushed the bronze flagon between his strong fingers. He seemed numb. Only the wound in his side was humming with a consistent ache. "You killed my Julia Faenia. My Petronia."

His eyes stung wildly as he spoke, and in response to Maglorius's nod.

"I did," said the centurion gravely, "and may the gods forgive me for it." He hung his head. "I do not expect you to."

"Leave us," said Atellus to Aurelia. She looked at him softly as he spoke, and her eyes contained a world of mysteries. But she rose from her chair, and glided over to the door like the smoke from the fire, and she was gone before Atellus even realised she had heard him.

Maglorius sat quietly, his large body hanging low, seeming to be sucked down towards the floorboards. The fire crackled and the light danced across the contours of his face.

Atellus got to his feet, and drew his spatha. The click of the blade leaving its scabbard made Maglorius blink, but he did not move. Atellus walked over to the centurion; to the agent in rebus; to Densligneus; to the murderer of his wife and his child. The movement of his own bones felt lumpen and heavy, titanic, and the room around him was surreal.

Maglorius turned in his chair to face Atellus, and looked up.

"I do not want to stop you," he said, his voice monotone, his eyes damp with emotion. "The choice is yours. And I would do the same. But I am a different man now. I used to carry out the emperor's orders mindlessly. I did whatever was asked of me. I have personally killed forty-three people for Jovian and Valentinian, acting on their direct orders. It was what I did. My life. Since being on the Wall, I have

637

realised that I was being played like a lyre by other men. I do it no longer. I am remorseful for the actions I have done. But if it were not I, then it would be someone else.

"I am truly sorry," he said, the tracks of hot tears running across his cheeks, "for what I did to your family, Atellus."

The beneficiarius raised his blade, tears in his own eyes; his chest seemed to be aflame, his lungs were boiling, as though he were sucking fire in through his nose, instead of air. He felt dizzy. He lifted his spatha up, gripping the hilt with both hands, and angled the blade downwards.

Maglorius opened up his chest, and tilted his head back, looking up at his executioner. His throat was wide open. Atellus felt the weight of his spatha condensed into the point of its blade, which he rested almost tenderly above the centurion's chest, just above where the clavicles met.

"Sol invictus me deducet et feceris me a tenebris," muttered Maglorius. He closed his eyes.

Atellus felt the weight of the pendulous sword in his hands. His muscles seemed to be made of water, barely able to suspend the blade. His face was hot. He could almost hear the voices of Julia Faenia and Julia Petronia, but he could not make out the words; only a low humming which could have been coming from the air around him, or even inside his head. It made thinking difficult.

Vengeance.

He had lived for this very moment, without even realising it at times. The culmination of his life's wishes for more moons than he could care to count.

Atellus looked down at Maglorius, saw the centurion's hard, battle-worn face, his skin darkened and coarsened by the weather and speckled with old scars. He was unafraid.

He tightened his grip on the leather-bound hilt; it felt damp and warm.

Atellus had lost count of the number of men he had killed, the number of lives he had shortened. When he had taken his first life, he had been devastated and swore to remember the face of every man slain by his own hand. But as the numbers mounted, the faces blurred and became less distinct, until it no longer seemed to matter, until each death was no more to him than squatting for a shit in the morning.

But this death was the most important. This was the only one he had truly *wanted*, had sought and prayed for.

The wind squeezed through the cracks in the timber and sent the flames whipping out of the fire-grate. Shadows danced and flashed across the small room.

Atellus could smell the spice from the jug of acetum, and the axungia from the greasy bones on Calidus's cold earthenware plate; could hear the soft rumble of Barbarus snoring on the other side of the door; could sense the stars needling through the snowclouds high overhead, and the moon frowning and melting the sky a cool grey.

He felt the words forming in his breast, and he fought them but they struggled into his mouth and onto his tongue.

"Did...they die easy?" he gasped, his lips tense. Maglorius opened his eyes, as grey as the surface of a frozen pond. "Answer me, shit."

The centurion swallowed, a motion which brought the point of Atellus's spatha against the skin of his throat.

"They did not even wake," he said, his voice barely audible. "It was...a seamless transition."

The tears were rolling down Atellus's cheeks. He tried to steady the blade, but the tip wavered erratically. His hands were shaking; his whole arms were.

Maglorius's eyes were closed again, and his breathing was even and deep.

Atellus squeezed the hilt of the spatha and prepared to throw his weight into it, to bring it straight down, through the throat, parting the skin and muscle and sinew and bursting through the heart. No bone to catch the blade or skew the aim. A clean death; a soldier's death.

It was more than he deserved.

***

Barbarus watched as Atellus opened the wooden door, and half-fell out into the ante-chamber.

He collapsed down into himself, his legs crumbling beneath him, and he wept. Deep long streams of unshed tears that shook his body until he thought his heart would come free of his chest; part of him hoped with all his being that it would. He wept until the wound in his flank wept blood alongside him, and the coarse grain of the planks beneath his face were as damp and warm as his own cheeks.

When he rose, the wind was like a bestial howl outside and the laughter from the main hall had died. Barbarus was sat beside him, sipping at a mug of wine. Atellus tentatively got to his feet, with a steadying hand from the other man, and walked out, through the hall and into the night air.

CHAPTER 46

The snow whipped into the faces of Atellus and Barbarus and gnawed at their exposed flesh.

The two men stood high on the ramparts, directly above the northern gate house. Beneath them on either side, stretched out along the lengths of the huge winding walls, were hordes of the city's defenders: professional soldiers, farmers pressed to defend their land, city-dwellers who barely knew hilt from blade, all clustered around artillery weapons and drinking in clutches around the huge burning pyres. There was a hum of anticipation and excitement. In the streets of the city, more fires burned brightly and there was a bustle of energy and motion seldom seen at such an hour.

The beneficiarius turned to the convict and spoke.

"I have not had time for this before, Barbarus," he said, "but I intend to do it now, before the battle begins."

He turned to face Barbarus and gripped the man's shoulder with his right hand. His left arm he laid parallel across his own breast; he motioned for the convict to do the same.

"Manius Maurus Barbarus," he said. "I, Titus Faenius Magnus Atellus, beneficiarius in the name of imperator Flavius Valentinianus Augustus, exonerate you of any crimes you have committed in the past. From this day, you are a free man, and you will die a free man, with your honour intact."

Barbarus gripped his comrade's right shoulder in response. He smiled faintly and met the eyes of the beneficiarius. Atellus looked older, wearier, but less crooked, somehow, less tortured.

"Perhaps we both will die as free men, Atellus."

The easterner nodded thoughtfully, and dropped his arms back down to the crenel in front of him. He looked out across the battlements along the darkness of the night-drenched lowlands his eyes pulled towards the twinkle of moonlit ice from the river Isurius far below. He could hear the secretive murmur of the wind moving across the land beneath him, and beyond that, the sounds of an army on the march; the faint rattle of metal on wood and the sinister thunder of the ground trembling under thousands of feet and hooves. Atellus could feel it through his muscles, so subtle it could have been the echo of his own heartbeat.

"They are coming," said Barbarus.

Made in the USA
Charleston, SC
03 March 2016